MARY WESLEY

THREE NOVELS

JUMPING THE QUEUE

THE CAMOMILE LAWN

HARNESSING PEACOCKS

MACMILLAN

LONDON

Jumping the Queue first published 1983 by Macmillan London Limited
The Camomile Lawn first published 1984 by Macmillan London Limited
Harnessing Peacocks first published 1985 by Macmillan London Limited

This omnibus edition first published 1992 by
Macmillan London Limited a division of
Pan Macmillan Publishers Limited
Cavaye Place London SW10 9PG
and Basingstoke

Associated companies throughout the world

ISBN 0 333 58591 7

1 3 5 7 9 8 6 4 2

A CIP catalogue record for this book is available from
the British Library

Phototypeset by Intype, London
Printed and bound in Great Britain by
Mackays of Chatham PLC, Chatham, Kent

CONTENTS

JUMPING THE QUEUE

ONE

All week Gus had been fussed by Matilda's unusual activity. He stomped round the house peering in through the French windows, craning his neck through open doors, eyes bright, head to one side, listening. She could hear his feet slapping on the brick path as he moved from the kitchen door to the window. Soon he would leap onto the garden table, look in, try to catch her eyes. He did this inelegant jump flapping his wings, hitting them against a chair as he strained for the table. His blue eyes met hers.

"Gus, I have to make this list, it's important."

The gander throttled gentle anxious noises in his throat, flapped his wings, raised his head, honked.

"Shut up." She tried to ignore him, concentrating on the list: *any trouble with the pump Peake's garage they know its vagaries. For ordinary electric work Emersons in the High Street, telephone in book in kitchen table drawer.*

Gus honked louder, slapping his feet on the wooden table.

"Shut up!" Matilda shouted without looking up. Butcher, baker, post office, garage, doctor, dentist. They won't want those. Vet – they won't need him, solicitor, bank, police. They would perhaps only need these. She checked the telephone numbers, put down her pen and went to the window.

"Oh Gus."

He nibbled her ear, making crooning noises as she stroked his cool neck sliding her hand from his head to his breast, feeling the depth of his feathers, their beauty and strength, parting them with her fingers until they touched the warm breastbone. Affected by her touch Gus excreted onto the table.

"What a way to show love." Matilda moved away to the kitchen. Guessing which way she was going the bird jumped off the table and half ran, half walked to the kitchen door where he stood peering in, knowing he was not allowed inside the house.

Matilda ran water into a bucket. The telephone rang. Gus honked.

"Hullo, hullo, I can't hear you."

"This is Piers."

"Yes, John, how are you?"

"Haven't you had your phone mended yet?"

"No."

"You should. It's months since that dog bit it, broke it."

"What?"

"I said it's months since—"

"He hated the bell, the noise hurt his ears, so he jumped at it, bit it."

"You should get it mended, it won't cost you anything."

"Oh." Matilda ran a finger over the sellotape holding the machine together.

"He's dead anyway."

"I can't hear you." She smiled at Gus in the doorway shifting from foot to foot.

"I said he's dead."

"I heard you. What do you want?"

"I want to know how you are."

"I'm all right, John."

"Piers."

"All right, Piers. It's awfully silly to change your name at your age."

"It's always been Piers."

"John to me. This call's costing you a lot. What do you want?"

"Are you coming to London?"

"Don't know."

"Do you good to have a change."

"I'm going to have one."

"Going somewhere nice?"

"I can't hear you."

"Get the phone mended."

"What?" She waved to Gus.

"Heard from the children?"

"Yes, no, fairly lately."

"Matilda."

"Yes?"

"Get the phone mended, it's dangerous, you might need it urgently."

"Mind own biz."

"What?"

"Goodbye, John."

"Piers."

"All right, Piers." She replaced the receiver, lifted the bucket out of the sink and sloshed water over the table stained by similar previous events. The wet wood steamed in the sun.

"Like some maize?" She stood looking down at Gus. "Come on then." Gus followed her while she fetched the maize. She threw a little on the grass. The gander ignored it.

"Gus, you must eat." She sat down and the bird climbed on to her lap. "Eat, you fool." She held the bowl. Gus ate a little, pushing the corn about with his beak while she stroked him, pressing her hand along his back then curving it round his breast. "You must keep up your strength for all those pretty ladies. You will like them, you know you will. You won't be lonely with them."

Gus got off her lap to stroll about cropping grass before coming back to stand behind her, leaning his neck over her shoulder, twisting it to peer up into her eyes.

Matilda sat looking down the valley, tired. trying to think whether there was anything left undone.

The house was scrubbed, polished, hoovered, the beds made up with the best linen. Silver, brass and copper shining. Stores in the cupboards and larder. Bills paid, desk tidy, list of the whereabouts of people and things they would need all written, every spider captured and put outside before its web was destroyed. All done. Only the picnic basket and bathing things to get now. And Gus.

"Such a betrayal. I can't help it, Gus. Geese can live to be thirty or more. I can't wait. You will be all right."

A Land-Rover drove up the lane, stopped by the gate. A man got out. Matilda stood. Gus honked angrily, the rims of his eyes showing red. Matilda shook hands while Gus hissed and threatened the man's ankles, his neck stretched out, head low.

"Good afternoon. He's a fine bird. I brought a sack."

"Oh yes, you said. You said that would be the best way. Would you like a drink?"

"No thank you, I'd better not. If I get this fellow loaded up I'll be on my way, then he'll have time to get to know his harem before dark."

"They won't hurt him?"

"No, no, no, a gander rules his geese. They haven't heard of women's lib."

"He rules me—" The man nodded, unsmiling, looking down at Gus.

"Your other gander?"

She glanced away. "A fox got him. I think I told you."

"Yes, of course you did."

"Gus, don't!" The man sidestepped as Gus pecked his calf. "I'm so sorry."

"That's all right. Thick trousers. I keep them all shut up at night now. He'll be safe."

"He's always slept in the scullery."

"Well yes, but he will get used to his shed, stable actually, stone floors, geese are messy birds. I hose them down, the stables."

"I slosh water over the scullery floor, it's got a drain in the middle, a sort of grating." What a stupid conversation. Couldn't he get on with it and go? "Shall we get him into the sack?"

"Okay. You pick him up as you know him, put him in. That's right. I'll tie this round his neck so that he can't hurt himself. Ouch! That was sharp."

"He's frightened."

"Yes, of course. There we are. I'll take him now, he'll be all right, don't worry. Soon he'll be with his harem. Six of them."

The man carried Gus to the Land-Rover, put him over the tailboard. Gus did not stop honking as the man drove away.

"Fucking harem. I must be mad." Matilda went indoors, poured herself a stiff whisky, switched on the radio for the weather report. High pressure continuing over the Atlantic, very hot, very dry.

The telephone began to peal again. Matilda went up to the instrument and pulled off a strip of cellophane, letting it ring until it tired. Now the picnic. She took a basket and put in butter, rolls, a slab of rather runny Brie, some peaches, a knife, a corkscrew, a bottle of Beaujolais.

"Right," she said out loud. "Right, I'm ready then." A final look round the house, appallingly clean, strange. She shut the windows and the front door, picked up the basket. A spider of vast size scurried in at the kitchen door across the floor and under the dresser. "You win." Matilda stepped out carrying the basket, locked the door, put the key under the bootscraper where only a fool would leave it for any fool to find. Into the garage, into the car, start it up, drive off. "If you exist keep an eye on Gus. See that he is all right. Please." Matilda prayed without faith as she drove fast down the lane which led to the main road. A god with

6

wings was a credible God but not in the guise of a man driving a Land-Rover. Matilda trod hard on the accelerator. The noise of the engine failed to drown the sound in her mind of betrayed honking.

In the empty house the telephone rang to an audience of one spider.

TWO

She switched on the car radio to drown the sound in her mind. I will not think of it. I will suppress it, forget it, bury it as I have done with other things all my life. Go away Gus, go away. She turned up the sound.

For many days now she had carried her transistor about the house and listened as she scrubbed, swept, hoovered, polished, dusted. As she worked she had heard Mozart, Beethoven, Bach and Brahms, pop and pop and pop, the news. Rumours of war, violence, here, there and everywhere, only it isn't war now, she had thought, it is Guerillas, often pronounced Gorillas, who bomb, shoot or kidnap, hijack planes and trains. An active lot these Guerillas/Gorillas, forever in the news, by no means unsympathetic, full of ideals and always on the hour every hour between quiz games or music, *Woman's Hour, Listen with Mother*, the news and weather imperceptibly changing as the days passed and she startled spiders, catching them in a tumbler, putting them out of doors before destroying their webs. The weather hot, continuing hot, traffic jams on the motorways, the French industrialist kidnapped from his home, the vanished bride on her honeymoon – perhaps she had realised her error, fled – and the Matricide. The police hunt for the Matricide and the Vanished Bride followed her upstairs and down as she dusted and swept, lifting the transistor from one piece of furniture to the next.

She had considered matricide. Why was killing your mother so special? Worse than killing your wife? Your child? Worse than being a Guerilla/Gorilla? He looked quite nice in the photo they showed on the box. Six foot two, they said, brown eyes, fair hair, large nose, speaks with an educated accent. One would hope so from a person who had weathered Winchester, Cambridge and the Sorbonne. One would hope so but just as able to kill his mother as the Guerillas were able to blow people up, shoot them down. A lot of Guerillas had also been to the Sorbonne or Harvard or Oxbridge.

Matilda had thought, as she put clean sheets on the beds, that anyone with any gumption was capable of anything if brave or annoyed enough. She, when she had a mother, had often longed to kill her to stop the incessant prying and interfering, the possessiveness. Poor Matricide she had thought vaguely, her mind turning to her own children. Did they? Would they? They would like to, she decided, noticing that there was now a talk on roses purring out of the radio. They would like to but they were not among the brave – possibly Claud. Yes, Claud—

He had, this Matricide, killed his mother with a tea-tray. Marvellous! A heavy silver tea-tray. How nice to be rich. Had he when a child toboganned down the stairs on a tea-tray? Perhaps people who went to these posh educational establishments didn't.

The spiders were a great worry. Old cottages were full of spiders of all sizes, some as large as a mouse when they scurried across the floor at night, others tiny, found in the mornings in the bath with wistful legs. Anyway, it being August and the Silly Season, the media babbled on about the Matricide every day, though it was true not quite so much latterly, rather favouring the Bride. He had not been seen since he left his mother's house after banging her on the head with the tray, not been seen so not been caught.

"Makes the police look silly," Matilda had said to Gus feeding him his midday mush. "Makes the police look idiotic, doesn't it?" Gus had made his throttling noises and Matilda had gone back to sweeping away her house's character. "Dirt of ages," she had hummed to a religious programme. "Dirt of ages made by me! Oh, how filthy I do be." Well, it was all clean and tidy now, Matilda thought, as she drove, and although it's latish, not sunset yet. Not quite yet, time enough for my picnic. I have tidied myself out of my house with the spiders. I betrayed Gus. Now I can have my picnic in peace, delicious Brie and Beaujolais unbothered by God in trousers. Petrol. It would be stupid to run out of petrol. She drew in at a garage and waited. No attendant came.

"It's self-service," a man called to her, easing himself into the driving seat of his car and adjusting the safety belt across his stomach.

"Oh hell!" Matilda felt shame. "Bloody hell!" She got out of the car flushing with hate.

"Excuse me, could you – I can never manage, would you fill her up for me, please?"

The man there to take cash, give change, watch that there was no hanky panky came slowly out of his glass box. He exuded contempt, the chauvinist swine.

"How many?"

"Fill her up, please." Matilda waited by the glass box watching the man jiggle with the petrol pump, push the nozzle roughly into the tank, stand idly as the liquid gurgled in. Sexy in a dreary way, she thought. Inside the glass box the man's radio was playing. "Here is the news." She listened to the weather, still fine and hot. The Prime Minister – the Common Market – the airport strike – the bomb alert – the hijack in Italy – the kidnapping in France – the five sightings of the Matricide seen in Los Angeles, Hong Kong, Bermondsey, Brighton and Kampala. High pressure over the Atlantic would continue for some days—

"Any news?" The man came back.

"Only the usual stuff. What do I owe you?"

The man named the price. Matilda paid exactly counting out the change, which seemed to irritate the man.

"Sorry. I thought it would help."

"Ah, you remind me of my mother, she's pernickety too."

Matilda felt insulted. There was something bourgeois about being pernickety.

"Do you want to murder her?"

"Sometimes." The man laughed. "Only sometimes." He was counting the money. "Guess he did away with himself. Here, you gave me 10p too much. Got remorse poor sod."

"Oh, sorry."

"Your loss not mine."

"Not quite as pernickety as you thought."

"No." The man grinned. "Did they say what ransom those French kidnappers are asking?"

"I didn't hear. I don't think it said. Why?"

"Good way to make a packet."

"Yes, I suppose so. Well, goodbye. Thank you." Matilda got back into her car, leaving the safety straps unused. They hung dusty and twisted. She was afraid of them, afraid of being tied down, tied in. She checked that her picnic basket and bag were safe – bathing suit, lipstick, comb, pills for hayfever, pills.

"The Pillage". Rather a bad pun but it had been funny in the context he had used it in. "Now then," Matilda muttered, starting the engine, "don't think of *him*, don't think of Stub and don't think of Prissy, think of anything else, Gus, no, not Gus. That fat man tying himself in so carefully. Did he feel loved and wanted? For crying out loud, how could he be wanted, so fat and ugly?" She drove fast but carefully, not wanting an accident. The radio was playing pop. She turned it off and began to sing:

> "Pop, pop, poppity pop
> They all pop in and
> They all pop out
> Pop is the name of the girl inside
> She sells the ginger pop you see!"

Why had her grandmother told her not to sing it? Was it vulgar or was there some hidden indecent Edwardian meaning? What silly things she remembered from childhood. She went on singing, "Pop, pop, poppity pop. Must pay attention here, not miss the turning" – which led by devious lanes to the cliffs from where she would walk to the beach.

"They all pop in and—" here was the turning, a lot of cars waiting to get out on to the main road, people hot and sunburned, tired after too long a day on the beach, on their way home to supper, tea or the pub.

As she swung the car into the lane she caught the eyes of a holiday dog hanging his head out of a car window.

> "They all pop out
> Pop is the name of the girl inside
> She sells the ginger *pop* you see!"

Matilda didn't want to think about dogs. Suddenly she realized why her grandmother did not like her to sing the ditty. Miss Renouff, blue eyes and shingled hair, had taught it to her. Grandpa had cast an appraising eye in that direction. All dead now of course. All popping over for that lot.

The lane twisting between tall banks led to the cliffs. She parked the car in the cliff car park, took out her picnic basket, swung her bag over her shoulder, locked the car.

All round her families with children were packing into their cars, getting ready to leave. Matilda picked her way past waste paper, lolly sticks, torn cellophane and remains of picnics, tipped – but not into the wire baskets provided. She wondered whether to pause, collect a few Coca Cola tins and beer cans and put them into the basket, but the jibe "pernickety" still rankled. She kicked a can with her espadrille and watched it merrily roll.

All the way along the cliff path she met weary holiday-makers returning.

"Pop, pop, poppity pop, I shall have the beach to myself," she hummed, strolling neither fast nor slow, carrying the basket with the Brie, the rolls, the peaches and the Beaujolais swinging along downwards, twisting and turning down from the top of the tall granite cliffs to the beach and the sea sighing gently over the sand to stroke the line of pebbles until they rattled. The tide was up, would soon turn and drag itself out across the sand leaving it clean and smooth for her feet.

Matilda paused at the bottom of the cliff path. Three lots of people were getting ready for the long climb up. One group was having a last swim. Matilda had seen them before, knew their routine. They would soon be gone. She walked along the stones enjoying her rope soles. At the far end of the beach she stopped by the favourite rock. Here she would sit in the sun and wait. She put the basket in the shade and undressed, pulling on the bathing suit, deciding to swim before the picnic. It was early yet. It would be light for a long time.

Out to sea a boat sailed slowly across the bay. She could hear the voices of the people on board and a dog barking. The boat had a blue sail.

Not wanting to wet her hair she walked into the sea and swam slowly, breast stroke, no effort, her body received by the wonderfully warm sea. Here so often they had swum, paddling out slowly and chatting with the same closeness as the closeness of bed but unleavened by sex. Matilda, swimming gently, savoured the memory of long swims, the easy talk, the intimacy, remembering conversations wrapped in water, their heads close, bodies floating. A long way out she turned to look at the cliffs which were so like Sounion.

Down the zigzag track came a party of people, young, lithe, noisy. They laughed and talked among themselves. They carried armfuls of rugs, carrier bags, spare sweaters. In jeans and T-shirts they were beautiful and young. Two girls danced down the track swinging a bottle of wine in each hand. Their voices carried across the water.

"Bobby and Vanessa collect the driftwood. We'll get the fire for the barbecue going while you swim."

"Super, it's so warm we can sleep down here."

"Super, super."

"I shan't sleep, I shall watch the moon. Super."

"I shall watch Vanessa."

"Super."

"Let's swim naked."

"Super."

"Not yet, there's someone in the water."

"Oh, bugger, is there?"

"Yes, but she'll soon be gone."

"Oh yes. Oh, isn't it super."

Cold, sick with disappointment Matilda swam for the shore, thrusting her arms through the unwelcome sea no longer hers.

Slowly, bitterly she dried herself. The barbecue party had settled fifty yards away. Fifty yards and the beach was half a mile long.

"I'd meant to use that flat rock she's on as a table but she's on it. It's got useful dips which hold the food. I mix the salad in one of them."

"She'll be gone soon, don't worry. It's a super rock, just the job, super."

Matilda slowly rubbed her legs, pushing the towel down to her ankles, up, then down again.

"I thought we'd have it to ourselves, it's always empty at this time, everyone goes home," the boy arranging the fire grumbled.

"We will. It's super. She won't be long, she's drying herself, look."

Matilda rubbed her arms, looking out to sea where the boat with the dog on board sailed slowly, the sail turning purple. The barbecue party moved continuously, bringing driftwood, fidgeting, throwing their long young limbs about. Their inane voices carried in the clear air.

"Shall we swim now or later?"

"I want to swim naked."

"Super! Why not?"

"Well—"

"She'd go more quickly if we stripped."

"Super. Do strip Bobby – go on."

Matilda pulled off her bathing suit and dried herself standing on the hot rock, baked all day in the sun.

"Christ! She's stripped. D'you think she heard us?"

"No, of course not. She's old, she can't have."

"Old people aren't necessarily deaf." The girl called Vanessa spoke crisply.

"Oh Vanessa, you are so witty, why don't you strip?"

"I'm not beautiful enough or old enough not to care."

She meant me to hear that, Matilda thought, sitting down on the warm rock. That girl would murder her mother without hesitation if she thought she wouldn't be caught. There's no passion in that voice. I bet the Matricide has passion.

"I want that flat rock as a table. I had it all planned." The voice held a whining note.

"She'll be gone soon."

"Yes, poor old bird."

Feeling the rock warm on her bottom Matilda reached for her shirt thinking, "Yes, I'll be gone soon, you despoilers of my beach."

Pulling her shirt on and buttoning it slowly she suddenly wept, remembering this rock with – well, with him her love, he lying back, his hips in one of the hollows, his crane-like legs stretched long and thin towards the sea, grey hair falling back on to the rock, the colour of the granite and the hair merging. Or of watching him stepping slowly along the edge of the water like a heron, unhurried, thoughtful, beaky nose, grey hair, elongated legs, flapping his arms to tease Stub who barked to attract his attention, to make him play, and the children tailing heel and toe along the sand, pressing in toes to form a pattern with Stub's paw marks, Stub who dearly loved swimming and even once with Gus who had become so emotional he'd messed all over the rock and the car going home. Matilda let herself pee allowing the hot urine to flow into a dip in the rock. She stood up, dried between her legs, pulled on her jeans, zipped them.

"She isn't wearing knickers," a girl's voice hissed. "Fancy, an old person like that!"

Matilda picked up her bag and slung it over her shoulder. She remembered she had a sweater in the car and was glad. She took up her basket feeling the weight of the Beaujolais. It would be heavier by the time she got back to the car park.

"Goodnight – there's your table," she said, moving off away from the barbecue party and the rock gently steaming.

"Oh. Goodnight. Thanks. Super."

"Have a good time."

"Thanks, we will."

"Do you think she was listening to us?"

"Of course she was, the old bitch."

Matilda grinned, walking barefoot along the sand.

14

THREE

A long haul up the goat track. That voice – "one more twist, one more turn – nearly there, nearly there now." Voices linger in the mind long after the face blurs. The muscles of her thighs hurt as they always did. Her breath came short, her heart beat. A matter of honour not to stop, however slow one went, until the top. She remembered another very steep path at Le Brusc down to the pebbles in the cove, no sand there, and the hair-raising climb at Pedney Founder where they hauled themselves up clutching at clumps of thrift.

What madness to bring Gus here. Still, he had adored the sea even if he had hissed and honked all the way up the cliff. Stub had barked running ahead and then run back to encourage them. The top at last. Matilda set down the heavy basket, dropped her bag and sat gasping, her legs trembling. Away on the horizon the boat sailed almost out of sight, below on the beach the young people had the fire going, the food laid on the flat rock. Two girls were swimming in water as clear here as in Greece, their hair streaming behind them. They were naked. Their distant voices cried, "Super! Oh, it's super!" Super for some. Would he lay the salad on the rock and would a girl cry, "Oh Bobby, what a super salad dressing. What did you put in it? I've never tasted anything like it, it's super."

Her heart steadied, her breathing slowed. Matilda looked at the view. She was humming a Brandenburg Concerto now. Away to the west were other beaches but all with easy access and car parks. What to do?

Back to the car.

She shouldered her bag, picked up the basket, walked along the cliff, strolling slowly. There was heaps of time. The tide must go out, pause, and come in again. She had to fill in time. That was all. A little more waiting didn't matter. The car smelt of hot metal. Matilda opened the windows, started the engine and drove slowly to the town down the steep streets to the harbour car park. With difficulty she found a place. She locked the picnic basket in the car and set off to wander round.

The town wore its summer face: shops with souvenirs, striped awnings, clusters of buckets, spades, beach balls, racks of picture postcards, the harbour full, every mooring filled. Now was the time for yachtsmen to come ashore, drink long, talk loudly in the pubs, boring on in yard-arm voices. Matilda strolled slowly among the people, observing the fat women in tight trousers or bikinis. They did not seem to mind their bulges burned red by the sun. Nor did the men, their shorts held up by tight belts biting into beer stomachs, mind their shape.

The fat and middle-aged were predominant by the harbour, wandering along with peeling noses, thighs sore from rubbing together. She turned up the main street, glancing in at the shop windows. A group of people stood staring at a television shop. The colour sets were showing the news on BBC and ITV.

"I wonder what he's saying?" A small child holding his mother's hand tugged. "Come on, Mum, I'm tired."

"Just a minute, love, let's see the news."

"You can't hear it—"

"I like that girl announcer, she's lovely."

"I like the man best."

"Oh look, Dad, that must be the Matricide." A teenage girl in shorts pointed. "He doesn't look like a murderer."

"Murdered his mother, a right bastard."

"Oh Mum, I'm tired. Can't we go home?"

"Wait a minute. There may be a new photo."

"They've shown the same photo ever since he did it. You'd think a bloke like that would have lots of photos done."

"I like the way she does her hair. D'you think that way would suit me, Mum?" the girl questioned.

"Ask your Dad, dear."

"I'm tired," whined the small boy.

"I expect with all that money he's had a nose job done by now."

"A nose job?"

"Well anyone would recognise that great hooter."

"Oh." Mum sounded pleased with the idea. "You're clever, Dad." Dad looked gratified.

"Big hooter like that stands out a mile, don't it? So he has a nose job sharpish. That's what I read in the paper anyway, either a nose job or he's done away with himself."

"If he had any decent feelings he'd have done that."

"Oh Mum, I'm tired—"

"Come on, son, I'll give you a ride." The father hoisted the little boy on to his shoulder. "Up you go!"

"Oh look, look, they're shooting! Wait a minute, wait." The child craned down from his father's shoulders to watch a scene of violence, bodies falling, ragged men lying legs astraddle firing guns. "Oh look, that one's dead." He sounded joyful. "Look at the blood."

"So's the Matricide's Ma." The father started up the street carrying the boy who looked back towards the silent television, craning his neck to see death happening.

"D'you think our Mr Antoine could do my hair like that, Mum?" the girl urged.

"Don't see why not, dear. You ask him when we get home. He'll charge, mind."

"Oh I don't mind."

Matilda stood idly watching the man talking and pointing to the weather chart which had circles all over it in which were written "High". Up the street she heard the husband say to his wife, "Bring back hanging, that's what they ought to do."

"Hanging isn't good enough, Dad."

"Got to catch him first, haven't they? Shouldn't be difficult with that great hooter."

Matilda turned back down the street remembering a pub which was relatively quiet. She would sit there and rest.

At a corner shop she bought a paper and strolled along entertaining speculations of that tired child grown up murdering his dreary mother at some future date. Why not? Children like that, perfectly commonplace children, became Guerillas and shot people.

Finding the pub with an unoccupied seat outside she ordered a whisky, sat down to wait and read her paper.

The paper was not one she was used to. She read an article on fashion, another on diet, an account of a footballer's divorce, several accounts of rail, motor and plane crashes, a new earth tremor in Guatemala. On the last page but one the usual photograph of the Matricide, now supposed to have reached Japan. He did not, Matilda thought, seem to have such a very huge nose, nothing out of the ordinary, not much larger than Tom's. The photograph could be anybody. She sipped her whisky, looked at her watch. Still early. A lot of people about, a lot of time to creep by.

Poor man. She looked at the photograph. The country was full of large noses, large cocks too. "My God, I feel tired," Matilda muttered, not even hungry, too tired to eat. What frightful waste of Brie. Mustn't get drunk, she thought, but one more whisky won't hurt me.

She took her empty glass to the bar. As she waited to be served she observed the people sitting round the tables or standing talking. She listened to the topics of conversation. A group of three men and a pretty girl were discussing a couple called Jeffrey and Sally. Sally had upped and left Jeffrey and gone to Ibiza with Johnnie, whose wife Vanessa had moved in with Chris.

"Which Vanessa?" asked one of the men.

"The dark one, you know her, the one they call the Dark Filly."

Everybody laughed and chorused, "Oh, that Vanessa," understandingly.

"But what about Sally when she comes back?"

"She hasn't a leg to stand on. She's been having it off with Charles for a year, everybody knows that."

"But Chris doesn't."

"No, Chris doesn't."

"They only mind about the money. There aren't any kids."

Gossip, thought Matilda, paying for her whisky, never varied much. She edged back to the door, noting three conversations about sailing, two about cars, another husband and wife complex. Nobody, she thought as she regained her place outside, was talking about plane, train or car crashes, terrorists, Guerillas or Earthquakes. They were so saturated with horrors they were immune to catastrophe.

Her watch said 8.30. Time creeping on. She put her whisky on the table, not wanting it now, and sat with her legs stretched out watching the passers-by.

On the whole, she reflected, the human race was unbeautiful although some of the girls in long skirts were lovely, as they passed, holding their lovers' hands, looking up into the ordinary faces of their men who, whether their noses were large, snub or crooked, were transformed by the girls' love to beauty. Matilda remembered Gus's beak and sighed. "A great hooter." She wondered how he was faring among the strange geese and took a sorrowful sip of whisky.

Stub's nose had been long, sad, black, Prissy's a tender pink. Matilda allowed her thoughts a brief recollection of those companions, very brief, for to think of Stub and Prissy made her think of Tom. There, the thought was there. Tom, Tom, Tom, she said in her mind. Tom, Stub, Prissy, all dead. She had said it to herself. Dead, dead, dead, those three and Gus she had betrayed. Matilda had another sip of whisky and looked down towards the harbour.

I am a great betrayer, she thought. That is my sin. I am not a sticker. I betray from laziness, fear and lack of interest.

Beyond the harbour the sea was growing dark, on board the boats were lights and laughter. The sailors had returned from the pubs to cook their suppers.

Matilda stood up, leaving her whisky unfinished, pulled her bag over her shoulder. Inside the bar the musak was turned up and with it rose the decibels of conversation as she started down the street. The voices cried, "Ignition", "It's only the money!", "If we altered the spinnaker", "I really think a Jag is best never mind the Japanese". Matilda went down to the harbour.

She reached the bridge where the river joined the sea. Peering over the parapet she could see that the tide was up, about to turn. A feeling of intense excitement almost made her cry out. She gripped the parapet, stared down at the water, secret, black; soon with the tide running out there would be ripples, as sweet flowed into salt to be drawn out to sea, swing west with the current far beyond the cliffs, round the bay a long way out under the sickle moon.

Suddenly she felt furiously hungry.

She looked at her watch, luminous in the dark. Too late. She felt cheated.

"No Brie, no rolls, no Beaujolais. Damn," muttered Matilda, "Damn and blast!"

She only realised she had spoken aloud when a man, also leaning over the parapet, shifted his feet. She felt fury. What business had he here, how dare he invade her privacy?

Would he go away? He must. There was nothing to keep him here unless, she thought with a sinking heart, he has a tryst. He is meeting his girl. Curse him, she thought. Curse him and his girl. She looked at him sidelong, not turning her head. He looked dreadfully tired. He couldn't be meeting a girl as tired as that. He leant on his elbows, his face in his hands, obviously exhausted. A car passed, driving slowly across the bridge, heading away to the country beyond the town. The man did not move or look up. Perhaps he was drunk. Matilda risked a quick glance. Tall but slumped with depression.

Oh God! Matilda thought to herself, he's going to throw himself over! The selfish brute, he bloody well mustn't. I shall just stay until he goes. She willed him to move, to leave, to push off.

A boy and girl came walking so closely entwined they nearly tripped each other up. They stopped in the middle of the road to kiss, their bodies clenched. Matilda, exasperated, willed them to move on but they continued kissing.

The man paid no attention, leaning lost in thought on the parapet.

Perhaps he's drugged, Matilda thought.

A police car came crawling slowly. The driver gave a little toot. The boy and girl looked up, faces dazed with love.

"Oh piss off," called the girl, moving to one side out of the boy's arms. "Piss off," she yelled.

The constable beside the driver wound down his window. "Now then, Brenda, now then—"

"Piss off."

"I'll tell your dad," called the constable. The driver laughed.

The boy lifted two fingers. "Come on," he said to the girl. "Bloody fuzz."

"Fucking public here. Come on then, Eddy." The girl retwined herself round the boy. They moved awkwardly away.

Matilda's heart beat in heavy thumps. She moved along the parapet closer to the man. Two yards from him she said in a low voice, apologetic:

"I'm dreadfully sorry but I saw your face in the lights of the police car."

"Yes?"

"They'll be coming back."

"I daresay they will."

"Well, I recognised you—"

"Yes."

"Are you going to throw yourself over?"

"It had occurred to me."

"Well, are you or aren't you?"

"I haven't made up my mind."

"Oh."

"I was undecided."

"Well, I wasn't, I'm just waiting for the tide to be right. You are rather—"

"De trop?"

"Yes."

20

The Matricide laughed, leaning against the parapet. "So sorry." He choked with laughter. "So sorry to be in your way. I'll move if you like."

"Put your arm round me. The police car's coming back. Quick." The Matricide put his arm round her shoulders.

"Round my waist, you fool. My hair is white but it looks fair in this light." Matilda pressed her face against him. "I look young in the dark."

The police car crawled by, the constable talking on the car radio. "No, nothing Sarge. Willco. Roger. Out."

"They do dearly love their radio." He bent back a little.

"You haven't shaved—"

"Haven't since—"

"Well, I think that's silly. The first thing they expect is for you to grow a beard and have plastic surgery to your nose."

"D'you realise I killed my mother?" he said gently.

"Of course. Lots of people long to. You just did it."

"Oh."

"Oh hell!" exclaimed Matilda. "I've missed the tide. Damn and blast!"

"I *am* sorry." Sarcastic.

"Well it's too late. I can't now. You have to be exact about these things," she said angrily.

"If you'd jumped—"

"Yes?"

"I would have tried to save you."

"How ridiculous. Interfering."

"You saved me just now."

"That's instinctive."

"What now? I'm in your hands. Hadn't you better take me to the police?"

"If that's what you want you can go by yourself. Are you hungry?"

"Starving."

"Come on then, I've got some Brie in the car – I was going to picnic first. Brie and a bottle of Beaujolais."

"Sounds tempting."

"Put your arm round me and your head against mine."

"I'm rather too tall."

"Don't make difficulties, it isn't far." They walked in a loverly way to the car park.

FOUR

Matilda unlocked the car. "Get in," she said. "I'll get the food."
She reached for the basket on the back seat. "Could you uncork
this?" She handed him the bottle and corkscrew.

"I think so." In the dark he fumbled, holding the bottle between
his knees. Matilda buttered a roll and spread the Brie. The cork
popped.

"Go ahead and drink. I haven't a glass. I wasn't bothering for
myself—"

"But—"

"Go on, take a swig. I'm all right, I've been drinking whisky,
waiting for the tide to turn, for it to get dark."

He drank, tipping up the bottle. Matilda watched his profile.
Not such a very large nose after all.

"The way the papers write about your nose you might be
Pinocchio."

"That was marvellous." He handed Matilda the bottle and took
the roll. "Thank you."

Matilda watched him eat. After cramming in half a roll he ate
slowly.

"There's some salad and a peach. Cyrano de Bergerac too."

"Really?" He sounded amused.

"Yes, really."

"What's your name?"

"Matilda Poliport."

"Married?"

"Widow."

"Sorry — sad."

"One gets used to it. No, that's not true, one never does."

"My name is Hugh Warner."

"I'm glad to know it. I must have heard or read it but for two
weeks you've just been the Matricide on the radio and television.
Have another roll? Your photo's in all the papers."

22

"Thank you." He took another roll. "That your dog? Surely you were not going to leave her behind?"

Matilda looked down. Looking into the car a canine face, paws just reaching the car window.

"Not mine. I have no dog."

"She looks dreadfully hungry." He held out half his roll. The dog snapped at it, gulped, retreated a few paces.

"Now you've done it."

"Done what?"

"Got yourself a dog. Can't you see she's lost? Look how thin she is. If you looked at her paws you'd see they are sore. That's a lost dog."

"We can take it to the police when you take me."

"I'm not taking you, you can manage by yourself."

"Look pretty silly if I walk in and say, 'Hi, Constable, I'm the Matricide and here's a lost dog, will you arrest us.' "

They began to laugh quietly at first then in great whoops. Tears trickled down Matilda's cheeks. She watched him feed the last roll to the dog, bit by bit, luring her into the car until she sat on his knee and licked his face.

"Look at her paws. Poor little thing, oh poor little thing." The dog licked Matilda's face also.

"Well?"

"Well?"

"I'm still frightfully hungry. Will the police feed me, d'you think?"

"Not for hours. They ask questions first."

"Oh dear," he sighed, stroking the dog, tipping up the bottle for another drink. "That was delicious."

"Any left for me?"

He handed her the bottle. She drank, tipping it up three quarters empty, her eyes looking over to the black water in the harbour reflecting the lights from the town. She finished the bottle and reached back to put it in the basket.

"Here's a peach." He ate. The dog watched him.

"You wouldn't like fruit." His hand fondled the dog's tatty ears. "She's a frightful mongrel," his voice tender.

Matilda wiped her face with her handkerchief, tidied up the remains of the picnic. "She's lost and unwanted. I think we can skip the police."

"Ah. You are soft."

"Absolutely—" Matilda began to speak then stopped, remembering Gus. "No, I'm not soft. I don't know what I am. I hate. I hate. I'm full of it."

"Pretty soft sort of hate."

"It would be difficult to resist, just look at her." The dog now lolled between them, her body relaxed, sore paws hanging down, small black eyes moving from one face to the other.

Matilda tried to think. She had failed to carry out the planned picnic. "I've missed the tide," she mewed.

"You can try tomorrow."

"Not with this dog and—"

"And?"

"All that planning gone to waste."

"Carefully worked out, was it?"

"Yes."

"So sorry."

"No good being sorry," Matilda said briskly. "No good us just sitting here." She switched on the engine. "I daresay you'd like a bath."

"A bath would be thrilling. They have them in the nick I understand."

Matilda switched on the headlights, drove out of the car park up through the town. Her passenger did not speak.

On the outskirts of the town Matilda saw a corner shop still open. She stopped the car. "Won't be a minute." She got out, went into the shop and bought several large cans of dog food, two pints of milk, a carton of eggs. "When I get back to the car he will be gone," she thought. "Perhaps he will take the dog. It would be an intelligent thing to do; nobody is looking for a man with a dog. If he's gone I shall go straight back to the cliffs and whether that barbecue is going on or not, I shall swallow my pills and swim out, though washed down with milk isn't as fine as washed down with Beaujolais, but if I swim fast the pills will work on their own. My plan will work after all."

She took the carrier bag back to the car. Hugh Warner was fast asleep holding the dog in his arms. Matilda restarted the car. She sensed her passenger was awake though he did not speak.

They drove out of the town past the bus station, the railway station and the police station. Matilda grinned to herself momentarily, forgetting her resolution.

"It's about ten miles."

"I see."

"You can have a bath and go to bed or you can go to bed and have a bath in the morning. There's food in the house."

"I'd love a bath."

"Okay."

"If you have a razor?"

"Yes."

"A bath and a shave, how civilised. My feet are sore like Miss here. What shall you call her?"

"Folly," said Matilda.

"A very good name."

They drove along the main road. When she reached the turning leading to the hills she said: "I live in an isolated cottage. It is not overlooked. I am a solitary person, people do not often come. You will be as safe as it is possible to be."

"You are very kind."

"I hope you appreciate my tact in not asking you why you killed your mother."

"I do, immensely."

"Good."

"And I hope you will also appreciate my tact in not asking you why you had planned your suicide."

"Oh I do, I do." Matilda began to laugh again. Sitting on Hugh Warner's lap, Folly wagged her tail. Her problem at least was solved.

FIVE

The back door key was under the bootscraper where she had left it. Matilda opened the door and, switching on the light, walked in.

"What a spotless kitchen." Hugh, carrying the bag of food, followed with Folly at his heels.

"It's rather untidy usually." She felt the Rayburn which was still warm, opened its door. In the fire box embers glowed. "I expected it to be out." She threw in sticks and a few larger pieces of wood, opened the damper. The fire flared and she put on coke. "Could you feed Folly? Don't give her too much. The tin opener's on the wall."

Hugh opened a tin. "Is there a dog bowl?"

"There on the shelf." Matilda handed him Stub's bowl. "I bet she's thirsty." She filled the water bowl and watched the dog drink while the man spooned out food. "That's enough. Too much will make her sick."

They watched the dog eat. Matilda sighed and muttered.

"What did you say?"

"I said 'another hostage to fortune' – I had just got free."

He looked at her curiously.

"If you give her a run out at the back I'll get us some food. She may not be housetrained. It's a walled garden. She won't run away."

"What about me?" He snapped his fingers for the dog.

"You needn't run any more tonight. You can eat and sleep."

He went out with the dog.

Matilda went upstairs to switch on the immersion heater and turn down the bed in the spare room. She opened the window and leaned out. In the oak tree up the lane an owl screeched. There was no other sound but the stream trickling over its stony bed. She felt terribly hungry. In her bedroom she opened windows and let in the warm night. The house caught its breath and came to life.

In the kitchen the man sat slumped in the beechwood chair, the dog at his feet, nose straining towards the stove. He said: "She's a good little dog, your Folly." The dog pricked her ears but looked at neither of them.

"She's yours, not mine. I'll get something to eat. Could you manage an omelette?"

"Lovely."

"Salad?"

"Yes please."

"You'll find wine in the larder. The corkscrew's in that drawer." Matilda took a torch from the dresser and went out into the garden, shining it along the rows of vegetables, choosing a lettuce.

The sky was a mass of stars, windless. Were Vanessa and Bobby still on the beach? Had the barbecue been a success? The torch focused on a toad crawling slowly across the brick path, his eyes golden. With concentration he pulled first one long back leg up then the other. He knew his destination.

She laid the table, broke eggs, made a salad, found biscuits and butter, poured the wine, cut bread.

"It's a bit cold."

"It doesn't matter."

The eggs sizzled and spluttered in the pan. She cut the omelette in half and tipped it on to their plates.

They ate in silence. Matilda felt strength return slowly. Their plates empty, they sat looking at each other across the table, sizing one another up.

Matilda saw a man of thirty-five, she knew his age from the radio. Large nose, large mouth, light brown hair, not fair as the papers said, brown eyes, thick eyebrows, stubbled face drawn with fatigue, good teeth, a few definite lines.

Hugh saw a woman in her fifties, blue eyes, very white hair, arched nose, good teeth, slightly runaway chin, sensual mouth.

"You don't look like a Major."

"They confused me with my brother; he is a Major. I expect he will be furious, bad for his image."

"Is he fighting Guerillas?"

"He is actually. Why?"

"Such a lot of fighting. I don't approve."

"Pacifist?"

"I don't like violence."

"I—"

27

"You hit your mother. It may have been justified."

"What makes you think that?"

"The choice of weapon. A tea-tray. Really!" Matilda began to laugh. "Oh dear, I'm drunk. So sorry. It's the anticlimax. I was worked up, was all prepared – I was ready." Folly put her paws on Matilda's knees and buried her face in her crotch sniffing deeply, pressing her jaw against Matilda's thighs. She stroked the dog's head.

"Silky."

Hugh Warner yawned.

"I'll show you where you sleep." Matilda stood up. "This way."

He followed her upstairs.

"Here's your room, the loo, the bath. Sleep well." She left him abruptly. Folly followed her back to the kitchen.

Matilda poured the last of the wine and stood drinking it, trying to think. Her head was looping the loop, with tipsy care she cleared the table, washed up, put everything away, stoked the fire once more and tipped the ashes into the bin outside the back door. Followed by the dog she went upstairs, undressed and got into bed. Without hesitation the dog got up on the bed and settled, pressing into the small of her back. Matilda thought, I shall never sleep, I'm drunk, and fell asleep instantly, her mouth open, snoring.

Along the passage Hugh Warner soaked in a boiling bath, sat up and shaved, then ran in more hot water to soak again. He washed his hair, his hands, his feet, his whole exhausted body until finally, when the water cooled, he dried himself and crawled naked into the bed assigned him and lay listening to the night sounds.

A stream somewhere near.

Owls.

Traffic a long way off.

Snores. "Down the passage my hostess snores." Relaxed for the first time for weeks, he smiled. What folly. He turned on his side and slept.

Half an hour later Matilda sat up in bed screaming, soaked in sweat, trembling. Folly licked her face, wagging her tail.

"He's a murderer, a murderer, he murdered his mother." Speaking this aloud made it true. She shivered, the sweaty nightdress cooling to clamminess on her body.

"Fuck!" She tore off the nightdress and sat hugging her knees.

"Poor little dog." Matilda stroked her. "You will be all right now." She switched on her bedside light to look at the time. "Three o'clock, soon be dawn." She lay back, pulling the sheet round her neck. The dog settled again.

If my picnic had gone according to plan I should be floating by the lighthouse. Time from now on is borrowed. The thought pleased her. She noticed from the taste in her mouth that she had been snoring, got up, rinsed her mouth with cold water at the basin then went back to lie on her side, mouth shut, breathing through her nose. How conventional to wake up and scream, how strong her upbringing. The man must have had a reason to kill his mother. Louise would, Mark could, Anabel certainly. Claud. Not Claud. Something would make him laugh or more probably he would not bother.

Time was I would have killed mine, Matilda thought, only Tom came along. It's all in the mind, she thought drowsily. It is ridiculous to scream about it. Was I not brought up not to scream? Who am I to judge? I was going to kill tonight, suicide is murder.

Hugh Warner was too deeply asleep to hear Matilda's screams. Across the British Isles the police were alert for a man answering his description. At airports and channel ports travellers' passports were examined with care. At 4 a.m. a bored journalist in Cairo filed a message that a man answering Hugh's description had been seen heading south.

Only Gus, the betrayed, shifted restless, unable to settle among the geese, utterly at a loss, anxious, disorientated, lonely.

SIX

Matilda thought best while occupied. Now, kneading dough, her mind came alive.

She and Folly had come down early, Folly trotting into the garden while Matilda made coffee. It was still very hot. Through the open door she could hear the hum of insects, birds singing. Away up the hill a cow cried for the calf recently taken from her. Far off a shepherd was driving sheep – she could hear the harassed bleating, the barking dogs. Folly now sat in the doorway listening.

Matilda heated up the coffee and sat at the table while the dough in its basin rose in the warmth by the Rayburn. Upstairs her visitor slept, she supposed, though he could quite easily have gone on his way while she slept. She hoped he had gone, it would be the best thing. She did not wish to be involved. Sipping coffee Matilda thought, I do not wish to get involved. Then, to be truthful: I would like to be involved and as I am why not enjoy it.

She wore a blue cotton dress, an old friend. Her legs and feet were bare, her hair still damp from washing.

About now the boat crew, probably a mackerel fisherman's, should have caught sight of her body, fished her out to bring her ashore, sent for the police and the ambulance. Matilda frowned, trying to recollect whether drowned people sank for a few days then surfaced, or floated for a few days before sinking. Not knowing bothered her. Why had she not found out this simple fact?

She divided the floury dough into four, smacked the loaves into four, pressed each with the back of a knife and put them in the oven. She would buy another bottle of Beaujolais, more butter, more Brie, another peach.

"I shall take you to the Lost Dogs' Home." Folly twitched her tail. "But I shall have to wait for the tide to be right." The dog wagged cheerfully. "I do not want to grow fond of you." The dog looked away. "You should have gone with him. He picked you up. You are his, not mine." Matilda listened to the silence of the cottage, certain that the man had gone. Not knowing whether the man was there or not, she felt in limbo, not wanting to readjust to living. She felt anguish choking her, cheated, for her mind had been prepared for death. She felt especially angry at the prospect of cleaning the house all over again, all those spiders.

Automatically she took the bread from the oven. If he had gone she would do as before, clean the house, weed the garden, pack her picnic, do it all again in a month. This time there would be no barbecue on the beach; the young people would have gone, their holidays over. If he had not gone she would phone the police. No, not that. They would ask questions. She would be involved. She could just imagine the questions. He would have to go off on his own before anyone saw him. She would ask him to go.

When the telephone pealed she felt fear leap in her throat. She watched the instrument as the bell jangled. Then she picked up the receiver, pinched her nose between finger and thumb and said:

"Ullo?"

"Can I speak to Mrs Poliport, please?" John's voice, crisp and terse.

"She's not here." Only John again.

"When will she be back?"

"She didn't say."

"Has she gone away?"

"She may have."

"Who is that?"

"Mrs 'Oskings"

"Mrs Hoskings who—"

"I clean for Mrs Pollyput. From time to time I clean. Mrs Pollyput she don't like cleaning."

"I daresay not."

"Not's the word. Who shall I say called? I'll write down. You should see the spiders."

"Piers, just Piers."

"Like at the seaside?" Matilda, holding her nose, snorted.

"Yes, like at the seaside. Write it down, please."

"Just a minute. I'll get a pencil – sir—" added Matilda to add credence to her role. "Oh, here's a message from her. Shall I read it to you?"

"Yes, please do."

" 'Dear Mrs Hoskings.' Pretty writing Mrs Pollyput's got, hasn't she?"

"What does she say? Read it."

"Okay. Dear etcetera, you won't want that twice will you? No. Well it says, 'gone away for a change. I'll let you know when I get back. Help yourself to anything you think might spoil from the garden.' "

"Is that all?"

"Yes, that's all, Mr Pier. D'you think she'd mind if took the raspberries, the birds will get them else. Shall I—"

John rang off. Matilda released her nose and sniffed, wriggling it up and down like a rabbit. Piers. How ludicrous John calling himself Piers. Piers rang a distant bell far back in her mind. Piers? No, it meant nothing, recalled nothing, it couldn't. Why this insistence on Piers? Sir John sounded all right. Claud said it was snobbery, that John was a common name. Claud had bet Anabel ten pounds John would be elevated in the Birthday List, not the New Year's, it being the more recherché of the two to enter the lists as Sir Piers in June rather than hustle in in the New Year when everyone was too hung over to notice. Not that he will allow anyone to fail to notice. "He will never get further than a knighthood in his occupation. Decorous recognition for services rendered. No life peerage for the likes of he." Claud's voice in her mind, always that note of affectionate mockery to keep one at arm's length, his arm's length, Claud's. No good trying to get close to that one. A slippery character, Claud, the more lovable for his inaccessibility. Standing with one hand on the rail of the Rayburn, Matilda thought of her youngest child. No hook there to hold her, however tenuously. Why did his saying "occupation" in that tone of voice, almost as though John—

"What a superlative smell." Hugh stood in the doorway looking in.

"You made me jump." Matilda pretended to jump. He grinned.

"No wonder nobody recognised you," Matilda said. "You don't look like your photo at all in daylight."

"I have rested. Besides—"

"Besides what?"

"I told you that photograph is one of my brother. He really has a huge nose but now he's grown a moustache it's not so noticeable."

"The Major?"

"Yes. There's been a mistake, a mix-up."

"Why hasn't he said?"

"He's abroad. He may not know, he might even be loyal."

"She was his mother too."

"He inherits."

"Oh." Pause. "Like some breakfast?"

"Please."

"I was thinking I should call the police."

"Shall you?"

"No." Matilda, getting coffee, had her back to him. Neither spoke for a while. She put a loaf and butter on the table, marmalade in its pot – Cooper's.

"If it were not for your interference I should be happily dead by now." Rage suddenly choked her, tears blinded, the hand carrying the coffee pot trembled.

"It was you who interfered with me, you silly bitch. 'Put your arm round me,' you said, 'put it round my waist.' Like a fool I did. I was going to fill my pockets with stones and go into the river like Virginia Woolf."

"You hadn't made up your mind."

"How do you know?"

"You said so – you implied." Matilda leaned across the table screaming at him, white with sudden fury. "You were shilly-shallying. I had it all planned and you spoilt it. I could kill you."

"Do. It will save a lot of trouble. Poke that knife into my guts, then you can push off and have your picnic, drown the dog as well—" He too was shouting, handing her the knife she had pressed on the dough.

They glared at each other with hatred. The dog whimpered.

"Are we having a row?" Hugh sat back.

"Yes. I'd forgotten what it's like. It's ages since—" Matilda pushed back her hair. "I'd forgotten about Virginia Woolf and the stones. I must remember."

"They would prevent you swimming very far."

"Yes."

"Your plan was probably best for you."

"Was?"

Hugh glanced at the dog who wagged, placating, unsure.

"Eat your breakfast. It's ages since I had a row. Makes me feel sick, my legs are trembling."

"Soon passes." Hugh helped himself to marmalade. "Delicious bread."

Matilda stood by the stove, breathing hard, watching him eat. The kitchen clock ticked. It would need winding tomorrow.

"If anyone comes to see me go through that door into the scullery. It leads to the woodshed."

Hugh looked up, munching.

"If you want to go further cross the garden to the copse. It's thick, nobody can see you by the stream, nobody goes in there, I don't allow it."

Hugh's eyes were on her face.

"I don't allow fishermen or hounds in there. It's mine, private, people know."

"Do they pay attention?"

"Oh yes. Gus found a boy there once and terrorised him. I tied him to a bush and left him for hours. He was scared stiff – told all his friends. It worked."

"Sounds a bit ruthless."

"There's a badger set in there. The boy was planning to bring his friends and bait them."

"I see."

"So you'd be absolutely safe in the copse."

Hugh nodded, helping himself to more marmalade.

"Or if you're upstairs, keep from the windows and go up into the loft."

"The loft?"

"It might be raining."

"You think of everything."

"I'll try."

"Why the hell should you?"

Matilda shrugged. "I meant to be dead by now. It doesn't matter what I do, if it's any help to you."

Hugh looked at Matilda for a long time then said: "You and your husband must have made a formidable pair."

"I betrayed my husband."

"Gus?"

"Gus? Gus is a Chinese Goose, a gander – I betrayed him too." Matilda wept while Hugh laughed.

SEVEN

Hugh looked away from Matilda, finding her tears embarrassing. Betrayed husbands come two a penny, he thought, but a goose – that's different. The dog, sitting with her nose towards the heat of the Rayburn, glanced over her shoulder. She had bright little black eyes. She wriggled her haunches, getting closer to the warmth. He wondered where she came from, who had abandoned her.

"Have you got any money?" Matilda retrieved his attention.

"Not an awful lot. I cashed a cheque – er—"

"After killing your mother?"

"Yes."

Matilda sniffed, whether from contempt or to stop the last tear he couldn't tell. "I have quite a lot in London but—"

"You can't go there, the police—"

"I suppose not."

"They will have your money."

"No, it's hidden in a safe place."

"You sure?"

"Yes, I have a cache."

"I can lend you money. I can cash a cheque, overdraw if need be. I can fetch your money. I'd like to."

"That would put you to a lot of inconvenience, danger."

"I'd like it. It would amuse me. It would be fun."

"Law breaking."

"No more to me than parking on a yellow line."

"An adventure?"

"I suppose so. Have you a passport?"

"Yes. I was going to Greece after visiting my mother. I've got my passport and a bit of money. I left my bag there though."

"How much? Count it."

Hugh pulled his wallet from his back pocket and started counting. "Nearly two hundred."

"That won't get you far. How much do you have in London?"

"Two thousand in cash."

"Well then."

"To get it I—"

"I'll get it. I've told you. Trust me. I'll go to London. You stay here and keep hidden. I'll fix you up with food. Keep out of sight. The rest's easy."

"I need clothes."

"Yes, the whole world knows what you are wearing. There are some of Tom's, a few things of Mark's and Claud's which they left here."

"Your husband's?"

"He wouldn't mind. He didn't die here, he went to stay with a friend in Paris—" she paused.

"And the friend was Death?"

"That's who it turned out to be."

"He must have been very lonely without you."

"Perhaps. No, no, I don't think lonely."

"Dying on his own."

"Don't say that, you have no right."

"Why didn't you go too?"

"I never went to Paris with him. I had responsibilities here, things to do."

"Such as?"

"The children, our animals."

"I thought they were grown up."

"They are. They weren't even here. It was—"

"What was it?"

"What right have you to catechise? What business is it of yours?"

"None. Idle curiosity, I suppose."

"Well," Matilda burst out. "I don't like Paris. I never went there with him. I didn't want to put our dog and cat in kennels. I just didn't want to go. If I had I would have looked after him, not let him drop dead in the street, don't you see? I know I betrayed him, of course I know. They found his pills in his hotel. If I'd been there – damn you, what right have you?" Matilda felt despairing, angry. "I always saw that he carried his pills."

"You saved my life. That gives me the right. Folly and I have every right. We belong to you."

"No."

"Yes."

Hugh buttered another piece of bread, fished in the pot for marmalade. Matilda stood with her back to the stove watching him pour more coffee, drink.

"How do you know I won't betray you? As a good citizen I should."

Hugh grinned. "I don't think you belong to the W.I."

"That's not necessarily respectable."

"Of course it is. You don't, do you?"

"No."

"Well then."

Matilda sighed.

"And these children – where are they?"

"Louise is married. She lives in Paris."

"Didn't you want to see her when your husband—"

"Not particularly. Mark is in business – he centres on Hamburg. Anabel is always on the move, I never know where she is. Claud lives in America."

"Do they come to see you?"

"They telephone sometimes. They don't really want to speak to me or I to them. What would we say?"

"So they won't have to talk to you at your funeral?"

"That's about it."

"So you thought you'd meet the Mutual Friend?"

"It seemed the sensible thing."

"Sensible." He stressed the word.

"Yes, sensible. Without Tom I've no attachment to life. The children don't want me. I was left with our dog, our cat and Gus. The dog died four months ago, the cat was caught in a gin and died of blood poisoning. Gus could live another twenty years. I've found him a good safe home with geese. I've thought it all out, left everything tidy. There's nothing left for me here. I'm off."

"But why? You can get another cat. You've got another dog."

"That dog's yours not mine."

"I doubt it."

"Oh yes, she is. You picked her up. I don't want her."

They both turned their eyes on the dog who sat with her back to them, ears laid back.

"We are embarrassing her." Hugh snapped his fingers. The dog jumped gratefully on to his knees.

Before Hugh could speak Matilda said hurriedly:

"To people like me animals are hooks to hang one on to life.

Think of the thousands of people hanging on because of the dog, the cat, the budgie. Think of all those thousands only hanging on for no other reason as they grow old, miserable, useless, bored. I bet your mother—"

"Her cat died in May. It was a smelly old thing."

"But it didn't murder her."

"No, there is that."

"And she didn't replace it?"

"I tried to give her a kitten."

"And she refused?"

"Yes, she did. She was sentimental about—"

"Old Smelly?"

"Yes. How d'you know I called it Old Smelly?"

"She didn't want to be hooked any longer, not once her company had gone."

"I don't know."

"No, you don't. She didn't want any more hooks. She didn't want old age, arthritis, falling down, losing her teeth, her balance, her hair, her memory, her wits. She didn't want dependence on other people, becoming a bore, growing incontinent—"

"She was very spry for her age, not at all incontinent."

"So am I for mine, but I'm not waiting for all that: it's against my principles; creaking joints, fatigue, clicking teeth, brown spots, wrinkled bottom."

"Bottom?"

"Of course, one wrinkles all over. I'm for the last fling – the ultimate."

"Ultimate what?"

"Adventure. Fun. Experience."

"That's a serious statement if you are talking about death."

"Of course it is. I don't suppose your mother had exactly thought it all out. You saved her the trouble with your tea-tray.

"Her tea-tray, she inherited it from her father."

"How pedantic you are. I was starting off in good shape and got interrupted."

"Sorry about that." Hugh stroked Folly's ears.

"That dog is yours, as Old Smelly was your mother's."

Hugh shook his head. "No."

"What future had your mother?"

"There was nothing really wrong with her."

"And nothing really right." Matilda pounced. "Why should

38

you and the Major bother? You would have put her into an old people's home and forgotten her."

"Probably."

"That's what I can't face; losing my faculties and being put away into a safe place. I am leaving everything tidy, I'm off for my picnic, swimming out while the swimming's good. Now you've turned up and spoilt it."

Hugh laughed. "That's tough."

Matilda's anger switched to merriment. "I think you did your mother a very good turn. One good bang with a heavy tray and Whoops! she's gone. No more worries."

Hugh winced. "She had no worries."

"How do you know? Sure, she had her memories. 'She lives with her memories,' people say. I hear them all the time. How d'you know she liked her memories? People don't necessarily like memories. Christ!" Matilda cried, "of course they don't. Old people are like empty paper bags. You blew yours up, gave it a bang, and pop, that was the lot, her lot anyway."

"And yours?"

"You've interfered." Matilda pulled on her espadrilles. "I'd better stop talking and go to the village, buy the papers, cash a cheque, do some shopping."

"Very practical all of a sudden."

"I am practical. Keep out of sight, won't you? I'll leave your dog with you. Don't answer the phone."

"A loss to the W.I."

"They don't think so."

"Show me the house before you go." Hugh stood up, towering above Matilda. "You are the same height as my mother."

"I don't want to think about her any more. I'll show you round." She led the way. "Here, in this front room if taken unawares you can hide in here or here. They are the old fireplaces, cupboards now for logs for that." She gestured to a pot-bellied stove in the middle of the room. "You can get right up the chimneys to the roof. Claud did once. He got filthy." Hugh stooped and went into one of the cupboards. "Can you stand upright? You are taller than Claud."

"Yes."

"Claud once locked Anabel in one and Louise in the other and went out for the day."

"How did they get out?"

39

"Mr Jones heard their screams. He was passing, luckily for them. You've seen the kitchen and scullery, come upstairs. Mr Jones is my only neighbour. No bother. If you see anyone coming you can hide in those cupboards or in the one in my room, it's huge. Anyway I always know when someone is coming, Gus honks."

"But I thought—"

"Oh God!" Matilda's eyes filled. "I'd forgotten. How could I? He's not here, he's climbing on to all those geese, covering them, whatever it's called, or is that only for horses?"

"I don't know. I believe geese copulate."

"I hope he enjoys it. He's had a sexually deprived life."

"I shall keep my ears alert."

"Yes, do that."

"You do worry about your goose."

"Gander. Yes I do, of course I worry. If you'd seen him in that sack driving away—"

"The cupboard upstairs."

"Oh yes." She led the way upstairs to the room from which he'd heard snores reverberate. "Here's the cupboard. It's deep, it goes on for miles behind those clothes." She pushed an open palm against hangers. "Behind these there's lots of room. It's L-shaped, turns to the right, almost another little room."

Hugh peered in. "What's that?"

Matilda leant forward, her hair brushing his face. "Ah. Claud's fancy dress." She took a hanger off the rail and slipped a caftan over her shoulders. "Look." As she turned her back he saw the back of the garment was painted with a skeleton. "He had casta-nets and clicked them." She began to dance, making the skeleton move eerily. Hugh drew back in vague distaste. "He scared the girls."

"Why should he want to do that?"

"It was Louise, she had—" Matilda pulled the caftan round her.

"She had – what? What had she done?"

"I always think of it as the Postman's Ball. Louise was – poor Louise was going with the postman. She had planned to have him for herself. Yes, I think she had. I know she had. It was to be the postman. He wasn't the postman then. They were all at school together. It's a long time ago. I expect he's forgotten – I mean Claud – the postman wouldn't forget, one doesn't, does one?" She paused, looking at Hugh, pulling the caftan over her shoulders, putting it back on its hanger. She repeated, as she hung the caftan on the rail, "One doesn't forget, does one?"

"Forget what?" Hugh looking down at her, thought that her skin was good for her age, smooth, hardly lined.

"One's first love. One never forgets one's first love."

"I suppose not."

"Claud is homosexual. The postman wasn't even pretty. I don't think he knew until Louise started making jokes, sly digs."

"Not nice of her."

"None of her business, was it?" Matilda shook her head.

"Well, behind that fancy dress there's miles of cupboard. All the garden cushions are in there for the winter. It's very clean, I've just swept it out. I've kept Claud's dress, some of Louise's and Anabel's things too. I borrow them occasionally."

"Do they wear them when they visit you?"

"They don't visit. I have kept them in case they'd like them when I'm dead. Some of those clothes of Anabel's are dateless and Louise always buys wonderful material, she could use it to cover cushions, couldn't she?"

"Yes."

"The boys' clothes are in your room, mixed up with Tom's. I thought—"

"What?"

"I thought I wouldn't tidy Tom away quite as much as myself. It's me they don't come and see."

Hugh said nothing. Matilda closed the cupboard.

"If really pushed, you can go up that ladder to the attic. I even cleaned that."

"Thank you."

"Have some more coffee before I go to the village."

"Thanks." Hugh followed her downstairs, noting that she walked like a dancer, straight backed.

"Are you a dancer?"

"No. I used to do yoga at one time."

"So did my mother. She stood on her head and sat in the lotus position, all that."

"Wasn't brisk enough to avoid that tea-tray."

"She was frightened," Hugh expostulated.

"I bet she was." Matilda, reaching the kitchen, poured the coffee into a pan to reheat.

"Help yourself. I'm off." But she lingered in the doorway,

obviously wanting to say something more. Hugh looked enquiringly over the rim of his cup. "You must think I don't love my children from the way I talk about them."

"You seem a bit – well, casual."

"They will like me better out of the way, the girls especially."

"Why?"

"They think I love Claud best. Those dresses upstairs are dresses he pinched from them. Claud is far more beautiful than either Louise or Anabel, far more attractive."

"You said he is gay."

"In more ways than one." Matilda laughed. "He went to a party in one of those dresses in the days when boys wore their hair long. He snitched all the girls' fellows, quite disrupted Anabel's life – it was a dreadful evening." Matilda grinned reminiscently. "Louise had the big feller – she called him her 'feller' – he went over the moon and as for Anabel's boy – well—"

"What happened?"

"Claud lives in New York." Matilda turned on her heel and went off leaving Hugh sitting at the table, holding a cooling cup of coffee, wondering about her. With the kitchen knife in his other hand he tapped a tune on the deal table, trying to remember his actions of the last days. Then, followed by the dog, he left the house and let himself through the gate into the wood, walking along the stream until he found a patch of sunlight and sat down to watch it cunningly run and circle over the stones. Stroking the dog, who came to loll beside him, he reviewed the jumble of thoughts and terrors which had accompanied him ever since he killed his mother. They could perhaps be looked at clearly now that he had stopped running. He was puzzled that he had run at all. Why had he not stayed? Why take flight, leaving the tray flung down beside her dead body? She had looked peaceful, composed, happier than he had seen her for a long time, certainly happier than during the preceding moments when she had been in a state of extreme terror.

The extraordinary moment with the tray was clear enough, but he was still puzzled by his actions afterwards, his instant flight to his car, leaving his mother, the tray flung down beside her. She was dead. What seemed callous was that he had stopped at the bank in the town to cash as large a cheque as he could without drawing attention to himself. To be overcome by panic was unforgivable. He had driven to London, left his car in Hans Crescent then taken the Knightsbridge tube. Since then he had been on the move, expecting every minute a hand on his shoulder.

The sound of the stream was mesmeric. Hugh dozed. Matilda might not belong to the W.I. but she was capable. "I'll go back presently and they'll be there. No more running."

When Matilda came back with her shopping and the papers she found the cottage empty. Her feelings of relief were equal to her sense of disappointment. She was not used to ambivalence, it worried her. She looked closely in the looking glass above the sink, trying to read her feelings in her face but it was the same face as usual, a mask for whatever feelings or thoughts there might be inside this middle-aged face which was neither young nor old, neither beautiful nor ugly, just her face as usual which protected her from the prying world.

EIGHT

Matilda laid the papers on the kitchen table, put her shopping away, sat down to read. The Matricide no longer rated the front pages. No mention of him in the *Guardian*. She had not been able to buy either *The Times* or the *Daily Telegraph*, only the *Mirror*, the *Sun* and the *Express*.

"Thought you didn't read the *Express*, Mrs Poliport," the postmaster, Mr Hicks, had remarked, taking her money.

"Fascist rag." Matilda smiled. "Very occasionally I like to see it, keeps the mind open to read lots of papers."

"I read the local."

"Yes, that tells you all you want and it's unbiased."

"That's so." Mr Hicks, a stout bald man, gave Matilda her change. "Is there anything else, Mrs Poliport?" He pronounced it "Pollyput" as did most local people.

"Oh, I nearly forgot. I need a dog licence."

"A dog licence?" Mr Hicks had been astonished. "I thought—"

"I know, I said never again. I know I did. I'm weak. It's a mongrel from the Lost Dogs, just a little mongrel."

"Said you didn't want another dog, didn't want to be tied."

"I know. I changed my mind. There it is."

"You were offered that Boxer, pure bred." Mr Hicks could be seen thinking even less of her than usual.

"Well, this is a mongrel. How much is the licence? I forget."

Mr Hicks had found a licence form. Matilda could hear him presently telling Mrs Hicks that Mrs Pollyput got a mongrel from the Lost Dogs when she could have had that Boxer almost free. They would sigh together over her folly.

"I shall call her Folly." Mr Hicks was writing slowly, breathing hard through his well-picked nose, wide-nostrilled. "Hairy as a fernfilled grotto." Tom's voice from the past. None of her family liked Mr Hicks. Louise said he steamed open letters, Mark that he had bugged the call box outside – an unusual flight of fancy for Mark. "How else could he know so much about everything?" She tried to hear Mark's voice but failed. Perhaps one only heard the voices of the dead? Anabel claimed that he had put his hand up her skirts at the school sports, a thick-fingered hairy hand slowly filling in the form. Mr Hicks had all the time in the world.

"Folly, eh? And how is Claud?" Mr Hicks knew all about the postman's reign in Claud's affections and never hesitated to put in a reminding pin. Matilda, waiting for the man to finish writing the few words and find the date stamp, leafed through the paper.

"No sub-post offices robbed lately," she said brightly.

"Busy murdering their mothers." Mr Hicks brought the date stamp down hard on the dog licence. "There's your Folly all legal."

Matilda interpreted this as a quick dig against sex between consenting males. "I don't feel matricide and robbery go together somehow. I haven't seen anything that he robbed his mother, only that he killed her."

"Only!" Mr Hicks, still holding the dog licence between finger and thumb, stared at Matilda through his thick lenses which hid his piggy eyes, "Only! That sort of man doesn't need to rob, he's rich, isn't he? A toff who went to Winchester and New College."

"What a delightfully old-fashioned word – a toff." Matilda regretted the days of long ago when sub-post offices were not guarded by barriers of glass. Mr Hicks, holding the licence in his horrible fingers, was safe. He held her in his power, fixed her with his glittering glasses. She could not snatch the licence and so she must wait for him to pass it through the hatch. Had those fingers pried up Anabel's parts? One could never tell when Anabel was lying, she was a compulsive liar whose highest flights of fancy often turned out to be true.

"Lots of our Trade Union leaders went to New College, Mr Hicks."

"But not to Winchester." Mr Hicks was studying the licence. "That school should be closed. It breeds more commies than any other school in England. I read it in a book." By "book" Mr Hicks meant magazine. Matilda bit her lip.

"Your party too, Mr Hicks."

"My party?" Mr Hicks, fingers holding the licence, rested behind the glass as he leaned on the counter to see her better.

"Fascist – anti-nig-nog." Matilda could just reach and take the licence without seeming to snatch. "Thank you so much, Mr Hicks. Lovely day." She left the shop regretting her anger, for he would know, as he always knew everything, that she was angry and he would wonder why. Very likely he would set about finding out.

She took the licence from her purse and stuck it on a hook on the dresser. If the murderer had taken Folly with him it would be more money wasted. She perused the papers.

Nothing in the *Sun*. She turned to the *Express*. Ah, here was something. *Matricide's car found at Harwich. Search for him intensified in Scandinavia.* Fru Sonja Andersson from Copenhagen had identified the killer on the ship. Why had she not reported her suspicions to the Captain? She had not been sure at first, but now she was asked, as were some of her fellow-passengers, she was sure and so was the friend travelling with her.

Bully for you, Sonja Andersson. The *Mirror* had in its inner page *Matricide in Porn Capital.* Goody! Matilda, hearing a step, looked up.

"I thought you'd gone."

"I thought you'd have a Panda car waiting."

Folly greeted Matilda enthusiastically.

"I bought her a licence," she said shamefacedly.

"*She* trusts us."

"Mm, puts us to shame."

"Anything in the papers?"

"Yes, your car's been found at Harwich and you were seen by passengers on the boat to Denmark. How's that?"

"My car? Where?"

"If you left the keys in it somebody's pinched it."

"That's very helpful."

"Look, *Matricide in Porn Capital.* That's helpful. Nothing in any paper except the *Express* and *Mirror*. Your story is stale; they've run it into the ground."

"Maybe, but the police—"

"They never give up but other things take their time. Look, here's a story of a wife's disappearance. Naked. Just her footmarks in the sand leading inland, uphill away from her clothes and her honeymoon husband."

"Aahh."

"And this one. *Man ate dog for bet. Mr Hooper of Saxon Lane, Hertford, killed his wife's spaniel dog, skinned it, roasted it in butter and ate it with caper sauce. Says it tasted rather strong.*"

"The British public won't like that."

"*Interviewed last night Mrs Hooper said, in tears, I shall divorce him.* Of course she must."

"You're making it up."

"I'm not." Matilda handed Hugh the paper. "Could you manage some bread and cheese and salad? I don't usually eat much lunch."

"When I've recovered from the roast dog story."

"No worse than Matricide. I'll pick a lettuce." She paused in the doorway, her face in shadow. "Incidentally, why did you do it?"

Hugh blushed. "I'll tell you some time, not now." He bent down, embarrassed, stroking Folly's ears.

"Please yourself."

"And you can tell me why you really planned your picnic."

"Easy – but not now either."

Together they shied away from their fear and horror, their pain and remorse.

We have quite a lot in common, Matilda thought wryly as she chose a lettuce, pulled spring onions and radishes.

"How tall are you?"

"Why?"

"Clothes."

"Oh, six foot one or two if I hold myself straight."

"If you've finished eating you had better come up and change your clothes. I'll burn yours."

"Why? I'm not so desperately dirty."

"It isn't the dirt, it's the description. All England, all Europe for that matter, knows you are wearing blue socks, suede shoes, fawn corduroy trousers, a check shirt, red and white, a red scarf round your neck and that you wear your watch on your right wrist."

"How exact." Hugh took off his watch. "There's a sunburn-mark."

"We'll rub in shoe polish. Come on."

Touching Tom's clothes Matilda felt detached. A year ago she could not have opened his cupboard or chest of drawers without gulps of hysteria. Now she picked out a white T-shirt, a blue pullover, pants, jeans, and handed them to Hugh. "Try his shoes for size." She pointed to a row of shoes. "Give me your clothes."

Hugh changed, dropping his clothes on to the floor while Matilda stood looking out of the window.

47

"How do I look?"

"Changed." She eyed him carefully. "Tom was very dark. He was thin like you."

"I think I've lost weight on the run."

"I daresay. Here's his watch. Put it on. It's a cheap Ingersoll, goes like a bomb and tells you the date." She strapped it round his left wrist.

"What shall we do with mine?"

"I'll put it in the bowl in the hall. It's full of unwanted stuff, anything small and broken. We'll hide it under the world's nose."

"How much nose does the world put in your door?"

"Very little. I can't help the occasional person. Nobody comes regularly. Tom and, I put people off. They got the message and left us alone."

"And when he died?"

"One needn't encourage people. Everyone comes to the funeral, then they leave you alone."

"The children?"

"They have husbands or lovers. They came once or twice dutifully. I could see my grief bored them. Mothers are not supposed to be in love with your father – there's something indecent about it. They adore love and sex for themselves but for parents it's unnatural."

"I see."

"Do you?"

"Well, yes, I do. I'm not your child."

"You could be if—"

"Only if you'd been a child bride."

"You flatter me. Actually Tom and I never stopped squabbling in front of the children so they thought my grief hypocritical."

"Quarrels are often an indication of love."

"Tell that to Louise, Mark, Anabel and Claud." Matilda picked up Hugh's discarded clothes. "Found any shoes that fit?"

"These sneakers are fine but my feet are bigger than his."

"Perhaps it will be safe to keep your own." She was doubtful.

"They are a very common make."

"All right, then."

In the kitchen Matilda cut up the discarded clothes and fed the bits into the Rayburn. Hugh sat watching her profile as she worked. What have I let myself in for? he wondered. He tried to place her among the women of his world and failed.

In the afternoon sun the garden shimmered with heat.

"I shall have to water my vegetables. There's been no rain."

"I'll help you."

"You might be seen."

"Couldn't I be a visitor?"

"It's not normal for me to have visitors."

Matilda, putting the last sock into the Rayburn, sat back, her hands folded in her lap, silent.

People do shy away from the slightly loopy, Hugh thought. They don't know what to say. If they are harmless they leave them alone. Watching her lids droop, he wondered whether sitting upright she would snore.

They sat companionably, both tired by the emotions of the past days.

It was Folly who heard the footsteps, first pricking her ears and looking from Hugh to Matilda. Hugh listened. Someone coming – a child on bare feet? Footsteps coming rather slowly from the copse. Was it a trick? A spy? Whoever it was, was coming on steadily. Folly growled. Hugh half rose then sat down again. He was cut off from the passage door by Matilda and could be seen through the open door from the garden. The footsteps were on the flagstones now. Matilda's head jerked up. She cried out, rushed to the door. The footsteps stopped.

"Gus!" Matilda sprang out, swooping down in a birdlike movement. Her arms and Gus's flapping wings made patterns in the sunlight. Gus raised his proud head, honked loud, then laid it across Matilda's lap. She gathered him into her arms.

"Gus, oh Gus! How did you get here? Oh Gus, it's more than ten miles – your feet—" She stroked his neck, his back, his breast. She examined each foot. "You hero!"

Hugh brought a bowl of water. The gander dipped his beak in the water, raised it high, looking at Hugh with an enraged blue eye.

"It's all right, Gus, he's a friend." Gus snipped quickly at Hugh's wrist and dabbed his beak at Folly who backed into the house, tail between her legs. "She's a friend. Oh Gus, I betrayed you." Matilda sat inelegantly, her legs apart, skirt riding up. Gus made throttling noises, weaving his sinuous neck against her throat, nibbling her ears, tweaking her hair.

"He's made a frightful mess on your skirt."

"That's love."

"Will it wash off?"

"It doesn't matter. It's marvellous to have you back. We need you." She looked up at Hugh who was grinning. "We need him to protect us from prying eyes. Mr Hicks, for instance."

"Who is he?"

"The postmaster. He's an inquisitive menace, dangerous."

Hugh noted that Matilda had said "we".

NINE

Watching Matilda with Gus, Hugh wondered whether they were as beautiful as Leda and the Swan. This up-to-date version touched him. Matilda, bare legged, in a crumpled dress, stroking the bird, her hand sliding down his neck from head to breast, her white hair flopping forward over his head while he nibbled at her ears. Now and again the bird stopped his attentions to peer at Hugh and hiss.

"There's some maize in the scullery. Could you find it?" Hugh brought it, holding out a handful to the bird. Gus snipped his forefinger in a painful grip. Hugh kept his hand still. Gus held on while Hugh waited. After a while the bird released him and began to eat. Matilda watched the blood returning to Hugh's finger.

"He won't do that again."

"I hope he won't, once is enough."

"He will terrorise Folly."

"I think she will be all right. She's not very brave, a rabbit scared her in your wood."

"Let's see."

In the room behind them Folly sat anxiously on the chair by the Rayburn.

"I think he will ignore her."

"She will keep out of his way."

"Doesn't he have a new owner?"

"Oh Lord!" Matilda sat up. "He will come over to tell me Gus is lost."

"He may telephone. Couldn't you telephone first?"

"Yes." Matilda was examining Gus's feet. "He doesn't seem footsore."

"Could he have flown?"

"Not the world's greatest flyer. He can fly but doesn't."

"The stream?"

"It goes nowhere near – oh yes, it does, it comes down from

51

the reservoir and he was at the farm at the far end of it. That must be it. You clever, clever Gus."

"So diddums swam and paddled the whole way home—"

"I know I'm soppy." Matilda got up, eyeing the goose mess on her frock. "Frightfully hard to get the stain out. Lucky this dress is old. I'll telephone."

Hugh listened as she went indoors. He could hear her dialling. The dial whined six times. Not 999, not the police. The gander, having finished the maize, began preening. In the house Matilda was talking. After a few minutes the receiver was replaced with a bang. Hugh waited. The gander finished preening and tucked his head along his back, letting himself sink down on the path.

Hugh looked at the watch on his left wrist. Twenty-four hours ago he had got off a train and taken a bus to the port.

"What are you thinking about?" Matilda sat down beside him.

"What did the man say?"

"He said Gus was no good, attacked his geese, killed one. He was rude, said Gus is no gander, no good to him, and will I send a cheque for the damage! I said I would and to bugger off."

"Wouldn't do for the W.I."

"I told you."

"Not a very successful betrayal."

"No. What were you thinking just now?"

"How I was twenty-four hours ago."

"Tell me."

"I had been on the move since I killed my mother. I thought I might get to France, might meet someone with a boat who would take me across. That's what I thought early on. Then I decided it was all too silly. I'd wait until dark and go out with the tide. The police have been no help at all." Hugh laughed. "I've discovered how to run away successfully in this country."

"How?"

"For starters you don't mind whether you are caught or not. You never hurry. You ask the way, if possible from a policeman. He will obligingly tell you. I even went into a police station and stood by a wanted poster of myself and asked the way to the bus station. They gave me a lift in a Panda."

"Where was that?"

"Salisbury, I think. If you run you are chased. If you wander about unworried nobody bothers."

"You were just lucky."

"No. The nearest I ever got to getting caught was when you started helping me."

"Thanks!"

"I do. But now I don't want to be caught. I'm dead scared."

"Oh."

"I keep thinking you will send for the police. I thought when you went to the village that you would get them then, that I would find them waiting when I came back from the wood. I thought just now you might dial 999 not the goose man. I'm sorry."

"Nothing to be sorry about. I'm a great betrayer."

"Not really."

"Half of me is. I hoped you'd be gone, taking Folly, when I came back from the village. I thought having a dog with you would be splendid camouflage. I didn't want to get involved and then—"

"Then?"

"Then I thought I do want to be involved, it's fun."

"Fun? Who for?"

"Me. I've had no fun for years."

"I wondered whether you were mad."

"Menopause?"

"Yes."

"No way – beastly expression – but it applies, it's true. This is fun, let's make a success of it."

"Harbouring a murderer is a criminal offence. Don't be frivolous."

"Don't be so conventional. People are conventional, we can't do without them. In your case, in my life, I've no room for it."

"Oh."

"If you want to go to the police yourself or throw yourself into the sea—" Matilda flushed, getting angry.

"And what will you do?"

"Kill Gus, have Folly destroyed, wait for the tide to be right and swim out as I'd planned."

"Such despair."

"We have equal despair. Your despair could cancel mine, that's all."

"Blackmail now."

"If that's what you like to call it."

They stared at one another with horror.

"We are getting a bit near the knuckle," Hugh murmured.

Matilda nodded.

Feeling their tension, the dog had got down from the safety of the chair and sat between them, managing to press her bony ribs against each of them. She shivered a little, eyeing Gus, but more fearful of losing Hugh and Matilda.

"It's all right." Hugh stroked the dog's head. "Nothing to worry about."

"Sorry to be nervy." Matilda was apologetic. "It's Mr Hicks. There's something very unpleasant about that man. Maybe Anabel wasn't lying."

"About what?"

"She said he groped up her skirts years ago. We couldn't believe her, but I don't know. He frightened the children. Today he made me uneasy. He pries through pebble glasses." Matilda shivered. "A goose walking over my grave. Not you, Gus, not you." She looked at Gus, folded compactly in sleep. "Horrible Mr Hicks was one of the first on Louise and Anabel's list."

"What list?"

"They took a great interest when they were about fifteen and eleven in the population explosion. It was about then Louise joined the Conservative Party. They hung a sheet of foolscap on the wall by the clock and listed people they would eliminate. Mr Hicks was high on the list. They ran out of actual people rather soon or changed their minds and reinstated them, but Mr Hicks and Charles Manson were constants. It became a little macabre. I objected."

"Little girls?"

"Little girls, yes, but I found Tom often agreed with them. They switched from actual people to kinds of people. The list included spastics, lepers, brain-damaged people. Claud wrote in brain-washed, and Louise started it again – the very old, all the handicapped, all Communists. Then Anabel decided Berlinguer was rather dishy and stopped playing. Louise took the list up to her room and carried on alone. A world without weak or imperfect people is, she thinks, she still thinks, a better world. She's a Fascist, my child."

"And your Tom's."

"Yes, of course. Oh well." Matilda shook herself. "Louise is one of the reasons I was picnicking. It would be intolerable to be looked after by Louise, however right she may be about Mr Hicks."

"Have you a terminal illness?" Mention of the picnic suggested this reason to Hugh.

"Haven't we all?" He could see by the set of her jaw he would get no other answer.

TEN

That evening there was a thunderstorm which solved the problem of watering the garden. Clouds gathered about six o'clock while Hugh and Matilda watched the news on television.

The pound was down – the Bank of England had intervened.

The meeting in Brussels—

The E.E.C.—

Unrest in Spain, Ethiopia, the Middle East, Africa – Cambodia—

China—

Students—

The earthquake in Central Asia—

The C.I.A.—

Our correspondent in Beirut reports that the Moslems and Christians—

Mr X, the honeymoon husband of Perranporth told the police that—

Mrs Y, the owner of the dog eaten by her husband, was arrested by the police this morning and will be charged with grievous bodily harm—

Our correspondent in Cape Town reports Hugh Warner, the Matricide, was seen at the races by an intimate friend Mrs Vivian Briggs—

Here the television blanked out, lightning flashed, followed by a clap of thunder.

Matilda got up and tried a light switch. "Power cut," she said and tried the telephone. "That's gone too. Who is this intimate friend, Mrs Vivian something?"

"I've no idea."

The rain came down in noisy torrents. Outside the kitchen door Gus honked, defying the elements. Folly crept under the dresser.

Matilda ran round the house shutting windows against the rain whistling down venomously after holding off for so long. Thunder crashed overhead, then cracked and burst simultaneously with the lightning. She found candles to light the kitchen. Hugh drew the curtains. Gus stood in the doorway and Matilda let him into the scullery and closed the door to the garden. Hugh lit the candles.

Matilda stood with her back to the stove, her arms crossed, hugging herself, her dress stained with goose mess, her feet bare. In turn she warmed each foot against the stove, standing birdlike on one foot. Her hair was swept into a crest. She looked, he thought, like a print he had once bought of a Polish Fowl.

When the centre of the storm had moved a little way off Matilda asked again: "Mrs Vivian something?"

Hugh shook his head. "No idea."

Some girl friend of yesteryear, thought Matilda. Some woman who would enjoy saying at parties, "Oh, Hugh Warner – of course I know him well—" attracting attention to herself by dubious name dropping. It was the sort of thing Anabel did. She let her mind dwell briefly on her daughter and found her wanting. Anabel craved attention, always had, and so too did Louise who got more, being more beautiful than her sister. Two beautiful daughters, two good-looking sons, thought Matilda. They shall find nothing of me to pick over, no surprises. Let them go on with their erroneous ideas. She smiled.

"What's the joke?"

"I was thinking of my children."

"Funny?"

"I have left no secrets for them to pore over – burned my letters, destroyed all clues. I shall leave them nothing but a shed snakeskin."

"You look like a Polish Fowl."

"They are very rare nowadays."

"Yes?" Hugh was delighted that she knew what a Polish Fowl was.

"A white topknot, sometimes known as the Tufted Hamburg."

"Extinct," said Hugh, laughing.

"Like me." Matilda smiled. "I am almost extinct."

"Shall we have a bottle of wine? It would pass the time."

"Okay." Matilda took a candle to the larder. Hugh watched her bend down, reaching for a bottle, and thought that for her age she had good legs, a good bottom. He opened the bottle, poured the wine. Matilda sat opposite him in the candlelight. Overhead and all round the hills the thunder groaned and rumbled. The rain spat down.

"I am an habitual liar," Matilda remarked conversationally. "I find it almost impossible not to embroider. Anabel is as bad."

Hugh nodded.

"When I said Tom went to Paris to meet a friend and you said he went to meet Death I thought that sounded so good I'd let it go. I lied by default. In fact I don't like Paris. Tom knew there was no question of my going with him. When he wanted to go to Paris he went on his own. The friends he was meeting were his friends, not mine. Neither Tom nor I thought he would meet death. That was not in our plans at all. He had a heart attack in the rue Jacob – dropped dead."

Hugh stayed silent.

"The children were all grown up. They had their lives. We were busy still with ours but—" Matilda pushed her hair away from her face, drank some wine. A slight draught made the candles flicker. Her eyes looked dark in their sockets. "But Tom and I were aware of what was coming. Tom called it '*La dégringolade*'. He could not bring himself, as I do, to call it disintegration. You looked surprised when I talked of a wrinkled bottom. However well and fit you are the flesh grows old. We had been young together, loved, fought, had children, ups and downs, a tiring, insecure life but not a boring one. We talked to each other, Tom and I. We decided when we were still in our prime not to allow ourselves to crumble into old age where you are dependent on others, your powers fail, you repeat yourself, you become incontinent. The children try their best, then put you into an old people's home with nothing to look forward to but the geriatric ward. That is what we both minded about age, the keeping alive of useless old people. He and Louise used to have a game: how many children could eat if old people were allowed to die? Millions."

Hugh watched her drink more wine. Presently she went on.

"We decided we would leave no mess behind, nothing for the children to quarrel over. We would leave no messages, we would not let them know us once we were dead. Our children were not interested in how we had lived or felt, so our letters – when we

58

were in love we wrote many letters, people did – we would destroy them. If they are ever interested it will be too late, we said."

"Rather nasty of you."

"D'you think so? We didn't mean it, well, he didn't. Tom was not a petty person. I am. I would have liked the children to have been interested in us but they were only interested in Louise, Mark, Anabel and Claud."

"Are they interesting people?"

"To themselves, certainly."

Hugh was afraid he had interrupted the flow but Matilda went on.

"Sex had a lot to do with it. We thought when sex was no longer fun, no longer essential, we would push off. The great thing for us was to go together, to time it right. Our death must come while we still slept well, ate without indigestion, still made love, while, in Muriel Spark's words we were still 'in possession of our faculties'." She sipped her wine, holding the glass with both hands, her head raised, listening to the thunder. "We were not prepared to put up with terminal illnesses. It seemed to us that the responsible thing was to end our lives at the right moment, go while the going's good."

"Responsible?"

"Yes. Socially responsible in the same way as birth control."

"Wasn't it selfish?"

"Certainly not. We planned to save other people trouble as well as ourselves. It was unselfish."

"I see your point."

"There were other things. We planned not to have another dog or cat when ours died." Matilda cast an irritated eye toward Folly sitting facing the Rayburn, ears cocked, listening. She sighed and made a defeated gesture.

"Suddenly Tom died without me, before we were ready, while we still—"

"Still?"

"Still were enjoying life. We weren't ready. I should have swallowed my pills then, looked sharp about it. But I have betrayed him. I'm still here, damn it."

"You were about to have a stab at it last night."

"You deflate me, mock me. It wasn't just a stab, it was the real thing. I had tidied myself away. In my mind I was as good as dead."

"Okay. What about Gus? What about that heroic bird coming back to find an empty house?"

"It never occurred to me that he would."

"And it never occurred to you and Tom that he would drop dead in the rue Jacob, did it? A fine pair, I must say." Hugh drank his wine, refilled Matilda's glass.

"You are detestable."

"And I murdered my mother."

"How much do you mind?"

"It's difficult to say."

"Why?"

"She wasn't particularly happy. She never had been satisfied with anything. She was a frightened person—"

"I bet she was, with you about to bash her to death."

"It wasn't me she was afraid of, it was—"

From the scullery Gus set up a loud honking. There was a rat-tat-tat at the door. Matilda gestured toward the inner door. Hugh went through to the hall where he stood, heart thumping. Folly barked shrilly.

"Who is it?" Matilda shouted.

"Only me, Mrs Pollyput, only me. Constable Luce."

"She did betray me," thought Hugh. "The crafty bitch, keeping me talking, telling me that tripey tale."

"Came to see if you are all right, been a power cut in the valley."

"Here too." Matilda sounded cool. "Come in. Like some coffee?"

"Powerful honk that gander's got. He's a good watchdog."

"Yes, he is."

"Got a new dog, I see."

"Yes, I licensed her today. Coffee? Tea? Wine? I'll get another glass."

"No, thank you. I must be on my way. Just wanted to see you were all right, you living all alone here. Must be lonely."

"I love it."

"So they tell me. My wife wouldn't do it. She thinks you're brave."

"Or mad perhaps."

"No, no, what an idea—"

"My children think I'm crazy."

"Do they? Well, it's for you to suit yourself, isn't it?"

"Yes."

"Nice little dog. She's only a puppy."

"She might be. I got a licence to be on the safe side."

"Sensible that."

"I've always been scared of you since you caught me with the car untaxed."

"It was duty. I was sorry to do it so soon after Mr Pollyput's death."

"That's what made me forget. Sure you won't have a drink?"

"No thank you, Mrs Pollyput. I must be going. I was going to call in on Mr Jones."

"He'll be hiding under the bed."

The constable laughed.

"Goodnight," Matilda called, watching the policeman get back into his car. She shut the door. "You can come back now, he's gone."

They sat again at the table. Hugh refilled their glasses. "I took mine out of the room with me." He glanced at her sidelong.

"How clever. I didn't think of it. I offered him wine."

"I heard you."

"Where were we?"

"You were telling me about your well-planned death with Tom after your successful loving life together."

"You sound acid."

"Did you love him?"

"Of course I loved him. There was never anyone else. He was my first and only love." As she spoke a puzzled expression flitted momentarily across her face.

"What is it?"

"Something I can't remember."

"Another man?"

"I don't know. How odd. How strange. Why should I suddenly think—"

"What?"

"Some tussle, a sort of thrill. Good Lord, I can't remember. It must be something I've heard or read. It wasn't me, one of the girls perhaps or a friend. Something happened at a party in Bloomsbury. Not important."

Hugh didn't believe her.

"Where did you meet Tom?"

"At a party in Kensington."

"And you fell in love and lived happily ever after."

"Yes."

Hugh tipped his chair back and laughed.

"It's not possible to believe."

"Why not?" Matilda snapped. "Ask around, ask our friends."

"No need," said Hugh. "It's a good story but it won't wash."

Matilda looked blank.

"A person like you," explained Hugh, "with a happy past, nothing but lovely memories does not just walk into the sea."

"I should have thought it rounded everything off nicely." Matilda now was sour.

"Either," said Hugh, watching her, "you had a happy surface life, even deceiving yourself, or you didn't care except for your animals."

"What!" Matilda almost spat at him.

"I've seen you with Gus. That's genuine feeling. You are trying not to let yourself love Folly here."

"I shan't."

"There you go. So passionate."

"Well, animals—" Matilda left her sentence airborne. "Animals are easier to love than human beings. Animals give you their whole heart, animals don't betray. Shall I go on?"

"No. I think I shall get us some supper."

Hugh watched her moving about the kitchen, laying the table, preparing vegetables, rubbing garlic on to steak, grinding the pepper mill.

"I believe your Tom had somebody else in Paris." Hugh watched the hands twisting the pepper pot.

"Oh no."

"I suppose yes. Why don't we tell one another the truth? We met near Death, why don't we tell the truth as good Catholics do on their deathbeds?"

"It would be original." She put down the pepper pot.

"So he had someone else in Paris."

"Yes, he did."

"You could have done something – gone with him, murdered the girl. I'm supposing she was younger than you."

"Much younger."

"He would have got over it. Did you know her?"

"Yes. Yes. I thought so."

"So?"

"I did murder someone once." Matilda looked at Hugh across the table. "I never think of it. It was so quick."

"So why not the girl in Paris?" Hugh wondered if this crazy woman who looked like a bird was lying.

"One could never kill one's own child." Matilda's voice was low.

"Was it Anabel?" Hugh felt shock.

"Louise." Matilda put the steaks under the grill.

"I thought she was happily married," Hugh said stupidly.

"I never said happy. She was only happy fucking with her father. You like your steak rare?"

"Rare, please." He breathed in hard.

"And do you like French mustard or more Truth with your steak?"

"I should like mustard and the story of the murder you did commit."

"All right, as we are into Truth. It's not as interesting as incest."

"But longer ago?"

"Much longer ago, almost forgotten."

ELEVEN

When the telephone rang Matilda lifted the receiver and listened, her jaws working on a mouthful. Hugh listened too.

"Hullo?"

"Matilda, your phone was out of order."

"There's been a storm. What do you want, John?"

"Piers."

"Look, I've never called you Piers in my life. What *is* this?"

"My name is Piers. Call me Piers."

"Okay. What do you want?"

"I've got to go away. I want to know if you are coming to London."

"I might." She swallowed the steak and held the receiver away from her ear. Hugh listened to the pedantic voice at the other end.

"Do make up your mind."

"I can stay somewhere else."

"You always stay here. I'd like to see you."

"That's nice of you, John."

"Don't tease. When are you coming?"

"I'll think. I'll let you know. I have to arrange for the animals."

"I thought the dog and cat were dead."

"They are. Their names were Stub and Prissy, John. They had names."

"Well then? Come on, Matty, don't dither."

"I'm not even going to try to call you Piers if you call me Matty."

"Sorry, Matilda."

"I'll let you know. I'll phone." She grinned. "You wouldn't exactly call this an adult conversation, would you? Think what it's costing you, Piers. Goodnight." She put down the receiver. "I can fetch your money if you like. How would that be?" she asked Hugh.

"Marvellous."

"Will you tell me where it is?"

"Yes."

"My steak's cold. Damn! I'll give it to Fol-de-rol." She cut the meat into small pieces.

"You were going to tell me about your murder."

"So I was. It will give you a hold over me perhaps. John 'Piers' knows about it." She fed the bits of steak to Folly who took each piece delicately.

"Did your husband know?"

"No, come to think of it, he didn't. It never arose. Only John knows."

"What happened?"

"It was that terrible winter after the war. You'd be too young to remember."

"I don't. My mother talked of it."

"I was nineteen, just married. First love. Marvellous. So great it hurt, every nerve raw with love. We had rushed into love, into marriage, headlong. It was gorgeous. I was pregnant with Louise. We were the only people in the world. Then I found he'd had this woman. She was older than him. She was all the things I wasn't. Well dressed, well read, travelled, sophisticated, good looking, sexy, funny, educated. She never let go of anyone she had once had. Once hers he was hers for evermore. She tormented me, showed me up as naïve, unsure, inexperienced, unsafe. Tom used to laugh, said she didn't matter, never had, but I could see there was still a bit left over. If she jerked the lead he'd go back. I saw her do it to other men. Their girls could do nothing." Matilda made a cross with her knife on a smear of butter. She seemed far away.

"What happened?"

"What? Oh! Yes, what happened. London was thick with snow. I was trying to get home to Chelsea from Marble Arch. All the buses were full. I couldn't get a taxi. It was dark, freezing hard, snowing, the ducks standing about on the ice. The snow blotted everything out. I walked through the park. Then, as I walked along the Serpentine towards Knightsbridge barracks, there she was. We were nose to nose in the snow. She laughed when she saw me. Her face lit up with pleasure. 'My Tom's little wifey,' she said. 'Does he let you out alone?'"

Matilda laid her knife and fork side by side and looked across at Hugh. "It annoyed me."

"So?" He studied her face while she paused.

"So I hit her." Matilda was now back there, standing in the snow by the Serpentine. "I hit her as hard as I could. She was taller than me. She slipped down the edge on to the ice, tried to get her balance, slid on out, then, crack, she went through, disappeared."

"What did you do?"

"I waited for her to pop up but she didn't. I suppose she went sideways under the ice. I ran all the way to John's house. He lived off Sloane Street in those days. He was in when I banged on the door. I told him what I'd done. He'd just got in, he was shaking the snow off his bowler and swishing his umbrella. I remember that clearly. He's a fussy old bachelor, wants me to call him Piers now. It suits him, his new job. He's hoping to get a knighthood. Sir Piers would be grander than Sir John. I tease him."

"What did he do?" Hugh suppressed a longing to kick her shins.

"Oh. He made me sit down, gave me a stiff brandy, listened to what happened, then said I was not to tell Tom, ever. He asked me if anyone had seen it happen. I didn't think so. It was snowing so hard I couldn't see more than a few yards, in fact I'd hardly seen her fall through the ice, I only really heard it. Well," she stood up, "that's all. John took me home to Tom in his car, said he'd overtaken me in the street. Tom was pleased to see me. I cooked dinner. It was steak, I remember that, black market. It was delicious."

Hugh allowed the pause to lengthen.

"I suppose the snow covered your footprints."

"I suppose it did."

"When was she found?"

"When it thawed, weeks later. Tom read it in the paper at breakfast. He said, 'Oh look, old Duplex is dead. Found drowned in the Serpentine.' Old Duplex was her pet name, her real name was Felicity."

"What did you say?"

"I can't remember. I remember it being quite obvious he didn't care one way or the other so I had no remorse."

"And Sir Piers?"

"He's like the grave. He's never referred to it. Funny fellow."

"Was he in love with you?"

"John? He's not capable of love. He's cold."

"The police?"

66

"John clammed up and I forgot all about it. I've never told anyone until now."

"It's a good story."

"Yes," said Matilda kindly, "a good story. You see, anybody can commit murder. It's chance really." She could see Hugh didn't believe her or was uncertain.

"You are uncertain of my veracity."

"A bit. It seems odd you should meet this Felicity woman alone in Hyde Park in the snow."

"Not really. She used to follow me to make me feel uncomfortable. One never knew when or where she would appear. She did it to other women whose husbands had lain with her. It was her hobby to make us feel insecure. John told me. I remember now when he gave me the brandy he said, 'A lot of girls will be the happier. You must not let it worry you. Promise.' I'd forgotten that. I promised – put it right out of my mind."

"Can you do that? Put things aside."

"One has to." Matilda looked bleak. "I put Louise aside. How else could I have gone on living with Tom? He needed me, I needed him and Louise—" Her voice trailed, leaving Louise up in the air. She got up and began clearing the table.

"Let's have some coffee and you tell me where your money is hidden. I'll stay a night or two with John and fetch it for you. Is it somewhere difficult to get at?"

"No, it's under the carpet on the staircase up to my flat."

"For everyone to tread on?"

"Yes." Hugh smiled.

Matilda's laugh rang out in delight.

"How original."

"It was my brother's idea, some of it is his. Tax evasion."

"So he—"

"No, he won't. My mother had just heard he was missing in Guerrilla country."

"Dead?"

"For his sake one hopes so."

"Oh, Guerillas/Gorillas. Your poor mother. Maybe I'm right, she was lucky. Did she love him?"

"He was her whole life."

"There you are then, you did the right thing."

"She could have loved me more."

"Too big a risk, I think." He could see Matilda's thoughts

straying where he could not follow. "No more risks for me." Her face was dead-pan. "Bed for me. We can plan your future tomorrow. I will ring up the soon-to-be Sir Piers and tell him I'm coming."

"But—"

"We've had enough for one day." Hugh watched her trail up the stairs. Folly stayed with him until he too climbed up the stairs and, while he took off his clothes, she turned several times around, pulling the duvet into a lump with her paws, waiting for him to get into bed. He held her close to his chest, stroking the silky ears while he tried not to think of Matilda's pain. The dog sighed, breathing warm air into his neck while he lay sleepless, listening to the summer night. He wondered whether Matilda considered God, as his mother professed to do, or whether Death was her only certainty where there would no longer be the possibility of love dying? And did she love Louise, Mark, Anabel and Claud? She had loved her husband. Her voice altered when she spoke the name Claud. He would study it if he had time perhaps. Blood relationships inclined to surprise when there was the inability to communicate.

TWELVE

When Hugh woke the sun was up. Below his window he could hear the gander talk, Matilda answer. The bird stood on the brick path watching Matilda hoeing along a line of spinach, her movements brisk, economical.

Hugh pulled on his trousers and shirt and opened the door into the passage. Matilda's door was open, the bed unmade. Hugh looked again at the cupboard, parting the dresses on the rail to see how large a space lay behind. Satisfied, he prowled round the room, glancing at her things; a silver mirror, a brush, few pots or bottles on the dressing-table. He opened a drawer full of bras and nylons. Remembering his mother's habits, he tried the bedside table, found what he sought, a pile of snapshots. Tom, tall, handsome, fine eyes, hawkish nose, something fanatical about the mouth, a mouth that had kissed wife and daughter. Other snaps jumbled up of children, dogs, Matilda with the children, Matilda holding a puppy, scrawled on the back "Stub – three months". She held the animal with more care than she did the children. Another snapshot – Tom with Louise. The photograph had been crumpled, then smoothed out. Hearing Matilda come into the house he shut the drawer, went down to the kitchen.

"Sleep well?" She looked fresh, healthy.

"Very well thanks. I was prowling round upstairs. I saw you in the garden."

"It's the best time to do chores. I'll get breakfast."

"Have you any photos of your family?"

Matilda looked up. "Try the dresser drawer. There's an envelope on the left, taken before they all flew."

"Flew?"

"Birds leave the nest. It's the best thing."

Hugh opened the drawer, found an envelope. "Is this it?"

"Yes. I don't much care for snaps. It's other things which bring them to mind – smells, sounds, materials."

"Claud's dresses?"

69

She laughed. "Of course, his dresses. That's me. Younger."

A younger Matilda stared at the camera, her hair blown across one eye. That's Louise with Pa." The voice was dry. Louise, tall, exquisite, standing close, too close to her father. "Anabel."

"Oh, Anabel. It's a bit blurry."

"It's very good of Stub and Prissy."

Anabel lay by the dog and cat who stared from eternity with enigmatic eyes. Another of Anabel, a better one – one wouldn't get much change out of her. He put the snap down and picked up the last. Two exquisite girls in jeans, long fair hair, laughing eyes, long narrow legs, the one on the left so beautiful she leapt from the snapshot, so desirable she moved him.

"That's Claud – he's still like that."

"I'm bowled over."

"Everyone is."

"No wonder he made trouble for the girls."

"There's always trouble," Matilda said.

"You love him the best."

"I do." Matilda picked up the snapshots and put them away. "Yes I do."

Outside the house Gus honked. Matilda motioned Hugh out of the room.

"You in, Mrs Pollyput?"

"Yes."

Hugh slid into the hallway.

"Post."

"Oh, George, thank you. Only bills I bet."

Hugh saw a man's shadow, heard steps.

"Looks like Claud's writing."

"George, you are unethical. Like a cup of tea? Postmen shouldn't pry."

"Wouldn't say no." A chair scraped on the stone floor. Hugh risked a quick glance and stifled a laugh. This Claud's postman? Large head, massive shoulders, ginger hair getting thin, a heavy brutish face.

"How is Rosie?"

"In whelp again."

"George, don't be crude."

"She's a bloody bitch, Mrs Pollyput."

"George, shut up! You love her. You are very happy."

"If you say so." George sounded sulky.

"I do say so. It's no use pretending anything else."

"It's just this, Mrs Pollyput. Things might have been different. I feel trapped married, like every other fellow. Now it'll be three kids. I might – well, when I see his writing, I just think, that's all."

"When you see Claud's writing you should thank your lucky stars that Claud left you. God knows what would have happened. Get on with your job, George. You had a sniff of sulphur – be thankful for Rosie."

"You are right. I daresay it was the glamour."

"He's not really glamorous, he's a clown. He says here on this postcard he is hard up. Did you read it? I bet you did. Hard up means he's been chucked out of another job or has quarrelled with his feller."

"Oh, Mrs Pollyput."

"Still owes you, does he? How much?"

"Never mind, Mrs Pollyput. I'm sorry I read the card. It set me remembering."

"Push off, George. Give my love to Rosie." Footsteps faded, Gus honked, Matilda sighed.

"Claud's postman?" She glanced at Hugh. "Rather unlovely."

"He picks them for contrast. Dreadful boy."

"Don't pay his debts."

"Goodness no!" Matilda sighed again. "Now. Let us be clever, make lists and timetables so that you know when to make yourself scarce, where to hide and when you are safe. You must keep out of sight until you have your money and the hunt has died down. Then if you want to move on you can."

"If you really mean it. Tell me your daily routine. I can memorize. For the unexpected I can improvise but I am worried about any consequences for you."

"I've told you," Matilda snapped, "I'm enjoying it. Don't you see, you've given me something to do. A bit of life, for Christ's sake. I was bored stiff."

"Okay, okay, let's make a list then. What happens from morning till night."

Matilda made a list, starting with the postman at the same time each day as she was finishing breakfast so that he could be fairly sure of an offer of tea. "I owe it to him. Claud behaved very badly."

"Was it first love?"

"It was for George. Claud's first love is Claud. He can only hurt himself."

"And your first love was Tom?"

"Yes."

"Are you sure?"

"Of course I am." Matilda was overemphatic.

"There must have been others before him. When you were a child were you not in love?"

"No." Again the emphasis. Hugh waited.

"There is a rota of postmen. When it's not George's turn they come before I am up. I never see them so you won't have to bother about them."

"Okay."

"The milk comes Mondays, Wednesdays and Fridays. You hear the van, Gus honks, you can keep out of sight. The dustbin men come round Thursdays. You hear them miles away. That's about all. I do my shopping in the village or the town."

"Where we met."

"Yes."

"Anyone else?"

"Mr Jones. He gives a shout when he's some way off. He's nervous of Gus. If I don't answer he goes away."

"Sure?"

"Yes. Quite often I don't answer. He can be a bit of a bore."

"Made a pass at you?"

Matilda blushed. "I'm too old." She caught Hugh's eye. "Well, he did, but I took evasive action. One must be kind. He's got the male menopause, Claud says. Louise said the same thing."

"What other neighbours?"

"Few. They wave as they go by, shout 'How are you?' or 'It's a fine day.' Gus keeps them away. Nobody cares to get nipped. Gus will warn you."

"What about exercise for me?"

"I hadn't thought."

"I'll walk at night."

"That would never do. Everyone would know. Dogs would bark. You'd be seen."

"I can't stay cooped up. I'll go mad."

"You'd be cooped up in prison."

Hugh did not rise to this bait. "I'll play it by ear," he said.

"All right." Matilda agreed, then, remembering another danger, said: "Never ever answer the telephone. That would be fatal."

"Do many people ring up?"

"No, but if I go to London and collect your money and you answered the telephone it would be known there was someone in the house."

Hugh was bored by this meticulous planning.

"Suppose you carry on exactly as though I were not here – let me keep out of sight. If someone does come in say I'm a friend of Claud's or something."

"You are not his type. I'd say Mark, a friend of Mark's."

"He has catholic tastes?" Hugh was pleased not to be suitable fry for Claud.

"Mark is straight hetero." Matilda smiled. "No problem there."

"I thought this Mr Jones fed Gus for you when you go away—"

"He thinks I've given him away."

"Won't he find out?"

"Damn! Of course he will. When I go you'll have to avoid him."

"I expect I shall manage. What would you be doing if I were not here?"

Matilda glanced at the kitchen clock. "I'd go to the village, do a little shopping, come home, have a snack, work in the garden, snooze in the sun, go to the sea if it's fine."

"Then why don't you do just that?"

"There's you."

"Don't bother about me. Let me manage. I'm not half-witted. If you go to London I will be deeply grateful. I swear I won't be seen. Why not go and do your shopping – carry on as usual?"

Matilda looked doubtful, then agreed. Hugh watched her drive down the lane with relief, glad to have the house to himself. The fuss she was making was tedious, all the more irritating since he felt he should be grateful.

He sighed and set about exploring the house. He felt it imposs-ible to believe Matilda had really swept herself away. There must be clues to her character that she was unconscious of leaving. He remembered exploring his home as a child, his discoveries among his parents' possessions. The thought of his mother, lovely, young, made him pause. She had been old looking up from the sofa, really old. The recollection of her sitting there, eyes full of terror, rid him of any wish to pry on Matilda. He would do it later, in a better mood. He wandered back to the stream in the copse, Folly at his heels. If he stared long enough at the running water he would stop seeing his mother's hands, rings loose on old fingers. The rings, in his childhood, had fitted tight. She had pulled hard to get them off. "Try them on your thumb, my love," she had said. "Try them on your thumb." He looked at his hands. None of those rings would fit now. He sat watching the water flow past, the dog beside him, companionable, alert, quizzing a black and green dragonfly zipping up and down the water.

Presently Gus floated past, proudly paddling.

"Goose murderer," Hugh called to the bird. "Goose assassin." Gus barely turned his head, floating on to land further down to crop grass on the bank.

"Thinks he's human," Hugh said to the dog. "Thinks himself like us, free to take life." The dog looked up at him briefly, then lay in a ball against his thigh, her nose under her tail, the warmth of her body consolatory.

Gus finished cropping grass, crossed the stream and waddled back to the cottage past Hugh who heard him honk as a car passed along the lane.

The gander set up a different honking when Matilda returned. Hugh heard her voice raised in greeting. Followed by the dog, he went to meet her.

"I've bought stocks of food for you for when you're alone. Tins and dry stuff. You won't have to shop. I won't be away long. D'you think you can manage with cold food?"

"Oh yes."

"If you have the fire the village will see smoke and if I'm away someone may come and look."

"I'll be all right."

"It's rather drear but—"

"Less drear than the nick."

"There's that. Oh, by the way, Mr Jones – he sees UFOs."

"What?"

"UFOs. He's given up telling the police because they laugh but he still tells me. It's just possible that he may appear suddenly then—"

"What do you do about it?"

"I pretend to take an interest. Tom did. He always took note; it's a neighbourly act."

"Do I hide?"

74

"He can appear silently on bare feet. It's awkward. Even Gus has missed him on occasion."

"It's a hazard I must take."

"Yes."

Gus honked. "Telephone." Matilda ran to answer it.

"Hullo? Oh darling!" – a cry of joyful greeting. "How lovely to hear your voice. Where are you? In England . . . how long for? Oh . . . shall I see you? Oh, I see . . . yes, of course, too busy . . . no, no, of course you must . . . yes . . . no . . . no, of course not . . . yes, I'm well, of course I am . . . yes . . . no . . . really? . . . well, best of luck, it sounds a brilliant idea, quite honest too . . . what? . . . I said quite honest . . . too must rush . . . goodbye." He heard the telephone ping as she rang off. Several minutes passed before she came outside.

"That was Claud."

"Too busy to see you?"

"Yes. He has a new venture. So like Claud. It's brilliant. I hope it makes him lots of lolly."

"I talked to my mother like that." Hugh watched her.

"Me too, but I hated mine and she me, whereas Claud—"

"Is too busy."

"I had to be quick to be the first to ring off."

"I noticed."

"I used to drag on until he said, 'I must go now, Mama.' I've learned. I've learned to be the first to ring off." She looked side-long at Hugh for approval. "It's hard learning not to be a bore. I damn near invited him to my funeral but—" She began to laugh.

"What's the joke?"

"His new venture. He's buying up old gravestones with beauti-ful inscriptions to sell to Americans. He's going up to Yorkshire where they are turning several graveyards into car parks."

"Who sells them?"

"Oh, I wouldn't ask!" Matilda broke into cheerful giggles. "An impoverished curate perhaps? The Church of England doesn't pay well, so—"

"If you found some round here?"

"I'd see him then of course. He might even stay the night and charge up the County Hotel to an expense account."

Hugh said nothing.

"It does prove it's time to be off." Matilda sounded almost pleased as she reversed disappointment to hope.

"To London?"

"To the next world."

"Will he phone again?" Hugh found himself hating Claud.

"No, no, that's my ration."

THIRTEEN

Two days passed. The weather stayed hot. Her feeling of trepidation subsided; Matilda grew calm. Hugh gave no trouble. He ate sparingly, slept a lot, spent hours out of sight in the copse with the dog. In a conscious effort to act normally Matilda worked in the garden, shopped in the village, read the papers, watched television, went to bed, got up at her usual time, cleaned the house in a desultory manner and cooked meals for herself and Hugh. She decided on action.

"I must ring up John/Piers, he always gives me a bed in London. Tom and I always stayed with him. He was my friend but became more Tom's. I'll telephone tonight and fix it. It's a very comfortable house. Perhaps you know him? John seems to know everybody, he's very social."

"No, never heard of—"

On the line from London John was warmly welcoming. Of course she must come. When? Soon? "Come soon, I'm going away, come before I go. I'm very busy but we can have the evenings together."

"That would be nice."

"How long can you stay?"

"Oh, not long, a night or two."

"Nonsense, you must stay at least ten days, get back into your London ways. Mrs Green will give you breakfast in bed. We will cosset you."

"Would Monday be all right?"

"Of course. I shall expect you in time for dinner. You'll take the usual train?"

"I expect so."

"Monday evening then." John rang off.

Matilda looked at Hugh. "Did you hear him? He has a very loud voice, always has had."

"Every word. What does he do?"

"Some branch of the Treasury. He wanted the Foreign Service. He was disappointed. We met when we were young. His aunt was a friend of my mother's. He's rich, rather an old woman, likes his comforts, won't ever come here, it's not grand enough. He likes birds and fishing. Tom and I could never decide whether he liked girls or boys or neither. That side of him is non-existent, he's sexless."

"Or it's carefully hidden."

"That's what Tom said – carefully hidden. He always pretends he is something to do with Intelligence, it's his sort of snobbery."

"What form does it take?"

"He talks as though he knew about spies, defectors to and from Russia, the C.I.A., French Intelligence, even Chinese. To hear him talk he might be all the M.I.s rolled up in one umbrella. He carries an umbrella, wears a bowler." Matilda laughed. Hugh liked to see her laugh; she had small teeth, unhorsey.

"He's an odd man," Matilda went on, "good looking in a way. He always talks as though he knows me better than I know myself. He also knows the children better. He knew Tom better, too."

"Differently, perhaps?"

"Perhaps that's it. Another side to the side which was mine? People are so much more difficult than animals."

"You love animals best?"

"Oh yes," she said quickly. "I trust animals."

"Not Tom? You didn't trust Tom?"

Matilda flushed.

"I'm sorry," Hugh said quickly. "I'd forgotten."

"I didn't trust Tom before I found him in bed with Louise. There was a part of Tom I never knew and John, in an odd way, knew it. He knows more about Mark, Claud, Anabel and Louise than I ever shall."

"Why does John want to be called Piers? Does he hate his name?"

"No." She shook her head. "He wants to be Sir Piers, it's more elegant."

"Are you afraid of him?"

"He is a bit creepy. Claud says he's creepy. When the children were small he pretended he knew all about Burgess, Maclean and Philby. The children called him 'Beclean filthy'. A silly joke."

"How well does he know you?" Hugh wondered whether Matilda would tell this man about himself.

"We've known each other since we were tots. I don't tell him things, not since I killed Felicity. I've been very careful since that episode."

"Maybe there's some other thing?"

"What could there be?" Hugh watched her puzzled face and a minute breeze of fear flickered in her eyes. She also seemed puzzled. I'm getting to know this woman, he thought then. "Let me tell you where the money is."

"Yes, do."

"If I give you my latchkey could you get me a pair of my own shoes?"

"Of course."

"What else shall you do?"

"Get my hair done, shop."

"Don't let them spoil it!"

"If I go looking like this John won't take me to good restaurants. He'll say nothing and take me to cheap, poky places, hide me."

"Nasty man."

"Just vain. He likes to be seen with presentable women."

"Not Polish Fowls."

"Certainly not."

"He doesn't like animals best."

"I don't think he likes animals at all, or people. He is the sort of person who likes power. Poor old boy, it would be nice for him to be Sir Piers. That would give him a certain power. Sir Piers first, then after a few years Sir Piers will shift into another gear. Who knows – KCMG? I think he would like that."

She is being malicious, Hugh thought and wondered whether Matilda knew she did not like this man or whether she had buried her feelings too deep to germinate.

"Shall you see friends?"

"I have so few left in London."

"That's no answer."

"We, or I, have changed. There isn't much left in common."

"Your other children?"

"Neither Anabel nor Mark are in London." She straightened her back. "I wouldn't know if they were."

"Surely?"

Matilda grinned. "Did you keep your mother posted?"

"No," he said. "I did not bother."

"She had her cat." Matilda's unkindness was intentional.

"You need not invite me to your funeral either," he said.

"Love all." She pursed her lips.

FOURTEEN

When Matilda set off, respectable in her London clothes, Hugh sighed with relief. He intended a voyage of exploration. He was still sure that he would find some clues about to amuse him during her absence.

In the dressing-table drawers were the photographs – Louise, Mark, Anabel and Claud from babyhood to adolescence. He turned them over. Sometimes something was written on the back – "Mark in Berlin'" or "Picnic near Helston". In a good-looking family Claud's beauty was outstanding. He was like Matilda, but beautiful. He put the photographs aside, feeling that he knew Claud, would not care for Louise, would like to fuck Anabel, be bored by Tom and really dislike Mark who had a priggish expression. He searched for letters but was not rewarded. He put the snapshots back. There was a space in the drawer where probably Tom's letters had lain – now destroyed? No sign of any in Matilda's writing. At the back of the drawer a yellowed postcard of Trafalgar Square. "Come at the same time. I'll take you on to the party. It's in Guildford Street." No signature, but Hugh was reminded of the voice on the telephone, "You will take the usual train." The postcard was in an authoritative script. He put it back.

Hugh prowled, felt the bed, a deep mattress. He examined her books. There had been a poetry phase. Then, rather surprisingly, the Russians: Chekhov, Dostoevsky, Tolstoy. Then Camus and Sartre. The flyleaf of each book was initialled and dated. She had tried Bertrand Russell but not got far, had read Thomas Mann, left Jane Austen untouched but managed Shaw. Graham Greene and Muriel Spark were read and reread. In Ivy Compton-Burnett she had written on a flyleaf, "needs more concentration than Dostoevsky." In Margaret Drabble's first novel, in Claud's hand, "Darling Mama, try this, she knows about your kind of despair."

Hugh opened Matilda's drawers. The clothes were not the clothes of a woman who felt the need of sexy knickers. She wore Indian cotton shirts as nightdresses, Jaeger wool tights in winter.

81

The clothes were rather worn, unglamorous. In the middle dressing-table drawer a note: "Have put jewels in the bank, listed for each of you. Don't quarrel – take what's given. I flogged the pearls." That wouldn't make much difference with Matilda dead, Hugh felt. There was an envelope with a bent corner as though it had been stuck in the corner of the mirror. Hugh tried it. The crease fitted. He went downstairs and put the kettle on to steam the envelope open. Inside on a plain sheet of paper dated the day he had met her was a note:

Darling Louise, Mark, Anabel and Claud. I have had enough. Please have me cremated and scatter my ashes over the stream. I love you all. I am in full possession of my faculties. My Will is at the bank. Goodbye. I love you. Don't feel guilty. Your loving Mother.

Hugh wondered why she had said twice that she loved them. It tinged of doubt. He stuck down the envelope and went back to the room to replace it. He closed the drawer and lay down on Matilda's bed. Folly, who had kept silent company, got up and lay sighing, pressing her nose against his neck, her breath warm and damp.

"She must be about fifty." Hugh put his arm round the dog. "She hasn't quite swept herself out of the house," he whispered to the dog. "She left her anxieties about their subsequent behaviour. Poor fare." Hugh sighed and repeated "poor fare" which made him feel hungry. Matilda would be arriving in London about now. "Let's get some food and then get out." He stroked the dog who was making a draught with her tail.

Downstairs he fed her, made tea and ate a tin of tuna fish with pepper and raw onion, then lay again on Matilda's bed until it grew dark.

He let himself out of the back door, locked it and set off across the fields, desperately in need of exercise.

He walked up the valley, taking his bearings by the stars. The air was clear, the country very still. Walking across the fields, trying not to disturb sheep and cattle, he zigzagged to find gates, kept on uphill. Cars drove occasionally along the lane but he kept below the skyline, gaining confidence as he walked, feeling his unused muscles working easily. Near the top of the valley he came to the village – a post office, one pub, a church, scattered houses, two farms in the village itself. He debated whether to try and skirt round but decided to walk through. It was September, there would still be holiday people about, he would not be conspicuous. The pub was surrounded by parked cars, a cheerful hubbub came out of open windows. Dogs barked as he passed the farmyards. Folly closed in on his heels. From the houses came the sound of television, music and loud laughter. Beyond the village a stretch of road, then a wood, a stile, a path sign-posted. He climbed the stile and followed the path, disturbing a pair of lovers. It led through the wood, over a stretch of moor to the top of a hill, turning left downhill. He stopped to get his bearings. Below and behind him lights from scattered houses and farms, the headlights of cars probing along the main road, far off the red glow of the town. To his right, away from the patch and below it was a long reservoir, silver from the rising moon slicing the black water. He jogged downhill to the water's edge. Folly drank. Hugh felt the temperature of the water. He listened. There was no sound other than faint rustling in the reeds.

His mother, he remembered, as he crouched with his hand in the water, had told him that in her youth, sent to Germany to learn the language, she had swum at night in the lakes. He remembered her voice.

"We swam naked, darling. If we rode we took off the saddles and swam the horses. We held on to their manes and they drew us along. It was poetry."

Hugh had been delightedly shocked, unable to imagine his mother so.

"Naked?"

"Yes, darling, naked boys and girls. Of course our parents thought we were all in bed."

"Together?" Hugh had asked. His mother had said:

"Don't be improper. Of course not."

"Wasn't the swimming improper then?"

"It didn't feel it. They were all young Nazis, Strength through Joy and so on, handsome creatures. Their father was a Graf – very pro-Hitler for a while."

"But Grandfather!"

"Your grandfather sent me there to get a good accent. When I wrote to him about the Strength through Joy he came at once and fetched me home. He'd never bothered about the quarter of Jewish blood in my mother before, never thought about it."

"Poor mother."

"Well, the swimming was lovely, you should try it some time in a lake at night."

He took off his clothes and waded into the water, trying not to make a splash. Folly followed. They swam out together. The dog came too close and scratched his shoulders. Hugh swam out to the middle of the reservoir, thinking of his mother, trying to visualise her swimming in Germany, but it was Matilda he thought of who, having had enough, had been about to swim out to sea. He turned back to find his clothes. He dressed while Folly shook herself and rolled in the rough grass by the water's edge.

He walked back slowly, astonished at the distance he had covered on his walk. His mother was right, the swimming was good. He decided to do it again. There was no need to tell Matilda, who would worry and push her hair up in a crest. What had she had enough of, he wondered? Loneliness? People adjusted to being alone. Was she bored? Certainly not ill. She appeared to have the wherewithal to live without undue worry. Guilt? Not guilt – she barely remembered killing that woman – he was half inclined not to believe it. What then? What? He was very tired when he got near the cottage, anxious for food and sleep. In his scullery Gus honked loudly. Hugh stopped. Gus could not have heard him yet. Folly pricked her ears. Hugh stood at the edge of the copse. A figure was creeping round the cottage, a short thickset man with a beard. He peeped in at the windows, funnelling his eyes with both hands to look in, moving from window to window, trying the back door. Gus honked.

"All right, all right, I hear you. She out or something? Not like her to be going out." The voice was faintly Welsh. "She can't be away or she would have asked me to look after you." He was now peering in at the scullery window, standing on an upturned bucket to look in. Gus flapped his wings.

"All right then, all right. I'll be round again tomorrow, eh?" The visitor stepped off the bucket and set it right way up. Hugh watched him walk away, waited for him to be well out of sight before letting himself into the house. Gus throttled in his throat in greeting.

"Mr Jones, was it? Seen a UFO or something? I'd forgotten about him."

Not daring to put on a light in case the man came back, Hugh felt his way about the kitchen, finding the bread, butter, a bottle of beer in the larder, cheese.

He sat at the table munching, still thinking of Matilda. Despair? Self-hate? Maybe. Hugh shrugged his shoulders, climbed the stairs. He went into Matilda's room, got into her bed with Folly. She had not changed the sheets, they were rumpled, the pillow smelled of her hair. He felt comforted. It was on this pillow she snored open-mouthed.

FIFTEEN

The ringing telephone woke Hugh. He had overslept; it was late, nearly ten.

He let the thing ring. He had promised Matilda not to answer it. They had arranged a code. If it rang three times and stopped it would be Matilda. She would do this twice. The third time he would answer, otherwise he would let it ring unanswered.

When the phone stopped Hugh went down to let Folly out and feed Gus his mush by the back door, which he propped open with the bootscraper. He made toast and tea, got out marmalade and butter. He stood eating, watching Gus guzzle his food then move slowly across the grass, cropping.

Hearing a car in the lane he hurried into the hall. Folly joined him. The car stopped by the gate; he heard voices. He looked out cautiously. The man he had seen prowling round the cottage was getting out of a police car. He slammed the door.

"Well, thanks, Constable. Thanks for listening anyway."

"That's all right, Mr Jones. Any time."

"I'll just tell Mrs Poliport."

"You do that. You tell her. She and Mr Poliport were always interested I understand."

"Oh yes, he was particularly."

"A nice gentleman. Goodbye, Mr Jones. See you."

"Goodbye." The car drove off, footsteps came up the path. Hugh retreated up the stairs to the landing.

Gus honked.

"Hey, Gus, where's Matilda then?" The man came to the kitchen door, calling.

"Matilda, hey Matilda, where are you?" He thumped the back door, walked into the kitchen. Hugh slipped back into Matilda's room, caught up Folly into his arms and dived into her hanging cupboard, bending down, pushing between the coats and dresses to the back where he sat down on a heap of cushions.

Mr Jones moved noisily about downstairs, talking to himself and the gander.

86

"Where is she, then? I came early this morning. She wasn't here, boyo, not here to see Jones. There, there, don't honk so. You know me. You honked this morning but she's fed you since. Ah, kettle's hot. She's had her breakfast, not put away the butter nor the marmalade. Don't come in boy and make a mess, you know what she's like."

There was a listening pause. "Matilda? You ill or something, Matilda?" Then steps on the stairs. Mr Jones was coming up. Hugh held Folly's nose lightly.

"Matilda, you in there?" Steps in the room. "Not made her bed. Funny. Gone out in a hurry." The springs of the bed were bounced. "My, what a comfortable bed she has." Hugh held his breath. The cupboard door opened suddenly, letting in light. "Not in there either. Hardly be hiding in her cupboard. Must look in the garage." Then a loud shout as the footsteps retreated down the stairs. "Matilda! I know I bore you, woman, but there's no need to hide. I told you I won't do it again, I told you!" There was anger and pain in the voice, frustration. Mr Jones in the kitchen called for the last time.

"Matilda?"

Hugh crept out of the cupboard, keeping well out of sight, looked down on Mr Jones. Short, thickset, a forest of a beard, thin strands of hair trained over a large head from ear to ear. From Hugh's view-point the top of Mr Jones's head looked like Spaghetti Junction. He stood looking about him with one hand stroking the strands into place. Presently he moved off to the garage, his feet slapping on the stone path. Hugh heard him say, "Gone out then. Where's she gone, Gus? Ah me, poor Jones, I should have known better. I should never have tried." The gander honked and flapped dismissing wings. Mr Jones reached the gate. "You tell her, boyo, I'll be back." The gander resumed his cropping, unmoved by the rather affected Welsh voice. Hugh swore. Damn the man, when would he be coming back? Obviously he'd got a lech for Matilda. He tidied Matilda's bed. Fine thing if Jones had come in to find him in it. He sat on the edge of the bed considering what to do, idly thumbing through the book she must be reading at the moment. Rosamund Lehmann's *The Ballad and the Source* – notes in pencil on the flyleaf in Matilda's hand, but shaky:

I think only people like me do this. I get heightened perception. I'm insecure. I'm pissed on pot, Claud darling. I found it in his overcoat, him of all people! He made me safe. This perception is awful. *I found it last night, I wonder if* – no not last night last year *Claud, it's made me remember* – it was at a party—

The writing straggled and stopped. Hugh sniffed the book. I'm not a trained Labrador, he thought. Then he remembered the overcoat at the back of Matilda's cupboard, crawled back in.

In the pockets of an overcoat he found a sizeable amount of cannabis and a packet of heroin. He flushed the heroin down the lavatory and pocketed the cannabis. It would be interesting to know why Matilda had left evidence of Tom while sweeping herself out of the house before her picnic. And the note to Claud? Perhaps Claud was the only one she could talk to. Hugh walked thoughtfully downstairs.

Mr Jones was standing in the kitchen.

"I thought there must be someone here," he said. "Who are you?"

"My name is Hugh Warner."

"The Matricide, eh?"

"Yes."

"Mine is Jones."

"How d'you do."

"Matilda usually asks me to care for Gus when she goes away."

"I'm doing it."

"Good." Mr Jones looked hesitant. "Do you know when she will be back?"

"No."

"Oh."

"I've just flushed the heroin down the loo—"

"Oh de-arr!"

"I suppose it comes in the UFOs."

"Clever you are."

"Matilda seems to have found out."

"Oh de-arr."

"Shall we ring the police separately or together?"

"Whatever for?"

"You can tell them about me and I can tell them about you."

"No."

"No?"

"Too upsetting for Matilda. When did she find out about Tom, then?"

"I don't know."

"I bet she's strangled the knowledge." Mr Jones teased his

hair carefully. "She does that, it's her gift. She won't remember anything she wishes to forget, if you catch the drift."

"I've caught it."

Mr Jones laughed.

"How much heroin was there?"

"One packet."

"Good, that's what I missed. Ah well, not to worry. Since Tom's untimely heart attack all that's over."

"But you reported a UFO this morning."

"So you were listening? They don't come any more, not since Tom's demise. I just go on occasionally reporting one. You should never stop anything suddenly, it makes the police suspicious." The Welsh accent had returned. Hugh began to laugh.

"Do you play chess?" asked Mr Jones. "Tom was a very good player. I miss it."

Hugh nodded.

"Good. Did you sleep in her bed last night? It was warm when I felt it."

"Yes."

"In the cupboard were you?"

"Yes."

"It would be nice to sleep in that bed with Matilda."

"I hadn't thought of it."

"But I have." Mr Jones sighed. "I suggested it. Fatal. She was offended. Took offence."

"Poor Mr Jones."

"Yes, poor Jones, poor Jones."

"I suppose," Mr Jones said later as he took his leave, "you were missing your mother."

Hugh made no reply.

"I was referring to your sleeping in Matilda's bed, obliquely of course. It is Freudian."

"Of course."

"And what do you know about UFOs?"

"Nothing."

"Hah! Nothing he says. They came up the creek, a little seaplane it is, was, I should say."

"Where?"

"On the river. They cut out the engine and landed on the water. So easy it was."

"Your idea?"

"No, no, man, Tom. Tom's idea, his organisation, a sideline."

"Well, I flushed it down the loo."

"Couldn't flush your mother. Had to leave her on the sofa. That was messy."

"Heroin's worse."

"A point there. Do you mind the pot?"

"No, I'm not averse. I think it's harmless."

"So is death. The newspaper said she could not have known much. It is you that do the knowing."

"Oh, bugger off."

"All right I will, but presently we can play chess and share a joint while Matilda's away?"

"All right." Hugh felt inclined to like Matilda's suitor. Heavily bearded, paunchy, squat, he had beautiful liquid black eyes.

Mr Jones walked crabwise along the path. "I will bring my chessboard. It is nicer than Tom's. It was my Da's. The feel of the ivory is good to the fingers, engenders thought."

"Goodoh." Hugh was amused.

"And yesterday's paper. You were seen in Rome at the airport changing planes, it says. It says in the *Daily Mirror*, look you."

"Jolly good, Dai Jones."

"My name is not David, it is also Huw, but HUW not HUGH." Mr Jones paused to let this sink in, then, "Not to worry, it is the disappearing bride from the beach they are on about. The poor husband is frantic, naked she is, wandering."

"Ah yes, I'd forgotten I had competition. What about the man who ate his wife's dog?"

"Ah that!" Mr Jones paused, one foot slightly airborne. "That woman is clever, oh she is. She said the dog had rabies. The poor husband is in an isolation hospital having painful injections in his greedy stomach. He is under observation, look you, daren't take the risk."

"Are you really Welsh?"

Mr Jones laughed. "Never been there. Born in Tooting. It's the fashion, that's all. Gives me class."

"Of course."

"Not like Winchester and Oxbridge but it's cheaper to obtain." Mr Jones reached the gate. "See you for chess then." The gate clicked shut and he was gone.

SIXTEEN

Matilda arrived in London in the early evening, taking a taxi to Chelsea. She put the window down so that she could hear and smell London, the roar of the traffic, heels clicking on pavements, engines revving as they waited for lights to change. The constant chat on the taxi radio, blare of musak from open shops, exclamations in foreign languages, people of many nations hurrying across before the lights changed. Just as she thought she could bear no more the taxi turned into John's cul-de-sac on the border of Chelsea and Fulham.

John came out to meet her, paid the taxi, took her case, bent to kiss her.

"Lovely to see you, Matty, absolutely great. Come in and have a drink." He was using a new shaving lotion she noticed and was glad. Up to now he had used the same as Tom. She wondered whether this was tact or chance. He led her into his sitting-room. "Sit down, Matty, you must be tired. What will you drink? Whisky? Vodka? Sherry? Gin? I'm drinking vodka, suits the weather. Vodka and tonic?"

"Yes please." How like John to offer a choice but do the choosing.

"You've altered the room." She accepted her vodka with a slice of lemon. He must have had that lemon sliced, she thought, doesn't want it wasted.

"Yes, do you like it? I've got this new sofa. I sold the old chairs. They fetched a very good price."

"They were a bit rickety." Matilda felt the need for assertion. This was London she had just sniffed, one must be sharp.

"Yes, need a bit spending on them. They've gone to America."

"So much does."

"So much does, yes. I've changed the house round a bit, hope you will like it. I sleep at the back now. The spare room is at the front."

"Oh good, how clever of you. It must be almost like a new

house." Matilda sipped. "What frightfully strong vodka. Might I have a little more tonic?"

John took her glass. There would be no memories of Tom in the new spare room, she thought, looking at John's back, so young for his age, such a good figure. She knew he did exercises. John poured in a little tonic. He wondered how much she still grieved for Tom.

"I thought we'd dine at home tonight and go out tomorrow, unless you have plans." He handed back her glass.

"No plans. Dinner here will be lovely. I'd rather not be seen until I've had my hair done."

"You look very nice, as always."

"My hair looks like a chicken." She could not say "Polish Fowl" and, as she withheld it, wondered why not.

"A ruffled hen." John smiled. Goodness! Matilda thought, he is bland.

"You *know* you like your women well dressed. I shall have my hair done and wear a decent dress. I have a new one." He wouldn't know she would be wearing a cast-off of Anabel's and shoes that had been Louise's.

"What are your plans?" John, sitting opposite, quizzed her. She wore well, he thought. He hoped the dress would be Anabel's as he didn't care for Louise's taste. The elder of Matilda's daughters dressed rather loudly. Anabel, whose very appearance was a call to bed, had the quieter dress sense.

"What are your plans?" he repeated.

"My hair, some shopping, any exhibitions I may fancy, nothing much, just a sniff of London." As though searching for a handkerchief, Matilda felt in her bag for Hugh's key.

"I'll give you a latchkey. You must come and go as you please. Another drink?"

The man's got sixth sense, Matilda thought. Christ! I must be careful. "No, no more. May I have a bath before dinner?"

"Of course. The supper is cold. Take your time. There's no hurry."

Matilda looked at him. "Dear John, it is good to see you and you look so well, such a marvellous figure."

"Piers. I play squash. Try and remember Piers. And I garden—"

She went upstairs. He followed, carrying her case. "I hope you will be comfortable."

"I'm sure I shall."

How stilted we are. He behaves as if he's being careful too. I must be crazy. Matilda turned on the bath, began unpacking, hanging Anabel's dress in the cupboard, throwing her nightdress on the bed, putting her few clothes away in the chest of drawers. She lay in the bath. I must be very careful, she thought. When I've used that key I'll post it back to myself at home. It was silly to be afraid of John but it would be sillier to risk anything. Better to humour him, call him Piers if that's what he wants.

At dinner John gave her a run-down of new books, plays, films, exhibitions, current affairs. The fishing season good on the Test in spite of the long dry spell, birds at Minsmere, mutual friends. Matilda listened, saying "Yes?", "No!", "Oh really?", "How extraordinary and how very interesting!", while she ate delicious iced cucumber soup, salmon mousse with a ratatouille, which she herself would not have served together, and mountain strawberries with Kirsch. She would have preferred them plain but exclaimed with delight over them. John's choice of wine was impeccable – a Niersteiner. She refused brandy, accepted coffee.

Without asking whether she minded, John turned on the radio to listen to a concert he wished to hear. She's not musical, she can put up with it, he thought. Matilda, who happened to know and like the particular symphony being played, listened until the end and, when he switched it off, remarked:

"I love that one, so much prefer it to the sixth, don't you?"

"Oh yes, the sixth is played far too often." The bloody bitch, John thought, looking at Matilda's chin, slight and undecided. "More coffee? A brandy now before bed?"

"No, Piers, no thank you. Have you been away?"

When she smiled the chin altered, stopped being weak. He wondered why, as he often had before, liking to know people exactly.

"I was going but then this Warner affair blew up. I shall go next week, it's a small delay, that's all."

"Where are you going?" Matilda kept her voice steady by refusing to hear the name Warner.

"Czechoslovakia."

"Fishing?"

"No, no, this is work. The fellow is, it seems, in Prague, which complicates things slightly."

"What fellow?" Her voice steady, lifting up her coffee cup, looking across at John/Piers the future knight.

"Hugh Warner, the man they call the Matricide. You must

93

have read the papers. Killed his mother, smashed in her skull with a tea-tray."

"Oh, of course." Matilda hoped her heart could not be seen thundering against her ribcage. "Of course I've read about him. I'm more amused though by the man who ate his wife's dog. He must be some sort of pervert, don't you think?" She put her cup down on the table beside her, triumphant when it did not rattle.

"He's not a pervert."

"Oh John – to eat a dog!"

"I'm talking about Warner. The 'ate wife's dog' man must have done it for publicity. No, I'm talking about Warner."

"What's he to do with you?"

"The office is interested. The assassination of his mother was just a cover."

"It must be very serious to have such a desperate cover." Matilda affected eager interest. "Tell me more – what's it about?"

"I can't, Matty." She hated him calling her Matty. "You should know by now I don't talk."

"Another Burgess and Maclean? A Philby? They didn't murder their mothers, did they? Goodness me, reading the papers one would never guess."

"Don't be silly, Matty. It's a sort of – let's call it a parallel."

"Call it anything you like, Johnnie. How do you know he's in Prague?"

"I can't tell you that but he is. Why d'you call me Johnnie suddenly? You never have before. Call me Piers."

"You call me Matty and I hate it. Are you going to Prague to see him?"

"I can't tell you that either. Don't pry, Matty. I shall call you Matty. I want to, I always have. It would be difficult to change now."

"I'm sure I asked you not to. I must have."

"No, no never." John well remembered the occasion when she had, the intonation of her voice. It was all a long time ago but clear.

"It must have been someone else, then. What a fascinating life you lead. Off to Prague to meet the Matricide. Will you say 'Boo' or will he?"

John laughed. "Keep it under your hat."

"Of course I shall." What a comical old bugger he is, thought Matilda. This is a real Beclean filthy. "The papers keep saying he's been seen in a new place every day but they haven't mentioned Prague yet. Why d'you think he went there?"

"I can't discuss it any more, Matilda. You know me."

"I wonder whether I do. What did he do? What was his profession? The man who ate the dog is a builder."

"I don't think there's any connection." John got up and poured himself another brandy. How these London people put it away. Matilda shook her head when John made a mute offer.

"Just the Silly Season." Matilda smiled. "What was his profession?"

"He was in publishing, lived not far from here." John mentioned the address Matilda had memorised, the house whose key lay in her bag.

"Oh really? Not a bad area now. It's grown quite smart. Our mothers thought it beyond the pale, poor old snobs. Have you been there?"

"Of course not. The police let my people have a look. Nothing to see, naturally."

Matilda yawned, putting her hand up to her mouth. "What an interesting job you have, absorbing," repeating herself.

"Not bad." John looked at her hand. Hands showed age more than faces. She was six months younger than he, or was it a year?

"I must go to bed." Matilda stood up. "A long day tomorrow."

"Shall we meet here, then, for dinner?"

"Yes please."

"Would you like to dine at Wheelers? They have oysters. I have rung them up."

"Dear John, I should love it. Sorry – Piers." Matilda held up her cheek to be kissed. "Goodnight, bless you."

John kissed the proffered cheek – quite hard, not flabby. "Goodnight, bless you."

"How easily we say 'bless you'. Do we mean it?"

"Of course we do, Matilda. What can you mean? One always blesses an old friend."

"I was joking, Piers, joking." Matilda went steadily up to bed, determined not to hurry. In her room she pulled the ribbon off the top of her nightdress and, stringing Hugh's key on it, wore it round her neck, pulling the duvet up to her chin. It was like John to have the most expensive duvet from Harrods. She missed the weight of sheets and blankets and, with a sudden pang, missed the pressure of a dog in the small of her back. She must not think of Stub, it was weakening.

Sleep did not come easily. She listened to John moving about downstairs, locking and double-locking the front door, bolting the windows. If there were a fire, she thought, we'd never get out. The key lay heavy between her breasts. Hearing John's footsteps on the stairs, she held it tight in her hand.

"You all right, old girl? Got everything you want?" he called from the landing.

"Yes, thank you. Lovely new duvet."

"Harrods. Sleep well."

"Thanks, same to you." She turned on her side, away from the window, disturbed by the light from the street lamp. For what seemed hours she lay wakeful, worrying. Would Hugh be careful – keep out of sight? Would Gus be safe? The dog? Had she forgotten anything? The unaccustomed rich food was taking its time settling in her stomach. She got up and tiptoed to the window. It only opened a little way, not enough for even a thin burglar to climb through. She knelt down and breathed the street air, listening to the roar of the city which never quietened.

In childhood she had listened from her grandparents' house, heard trains shrieking in the distance, tugs tooting on the river, taxi doors slamming, the creak of cowls on chimney pots as they whirled in the wind, turning this way and that like the heads of armoured knights. The Clean Air Act had put paid to them. She remembered, too, how once when she was very small she had heard sheep and seen a flock driven through her grandparents' square to Hyde Park. She wanted to remember that dawn, was comforted that she did. I will get his money tomorrow, she thought, and then forget all about him while I am here. She fell asleep, holding the latchkey in her hand, her mouth open, snoring.

Across the landing John, roused by his bladder, stood in his bathroom. He thought crossly that in youth he would have lasted the night. Then he cocked his head. God almighty, how she snores. Nothing wrong with my hearing anyway. How could Tom have put up with it all those years? A bit uppity calling him "Johnnie". Menopausal cheek, must make allowances. She'd seemed a bit edgy somehow, something on her mind. Probably still missing Tom. It had been a pity, that heart attack.

SEVENTEEN

In the morning Matilda sat in bed eating breakfast brought up by John's housekeeper. Mrs Green was a woman who while modern in appearance could create a Mrs Tiggywinkle atmosphere if she so wished. The tray placed across Matilda's knees held coffee, boiled eggs, toast, butter, marmalade and a linen napkin.

"It's lovely to see you. It's ages, isn't it? You are spoiling me."

"Far too long, Madam." Matilda knew well that the "Madam" bit was a joke, that she was referred to by her Christian name behind her back.

"This is delicious. Dinner last night was a dream."

"I'm glad you liked it." Mrs Green smoothed Matilda's duvet. "He would have the ratatouille with the mousse, said it had to be eaten up. Getting a trifle mean, our Mr Leach, doesn't like anything wasted."

"It was a very good ratatouille."

"I just thought I'd mention it. I wouldn't like you to think it was my idea."

Matilda crunched her toast, poured coffee, topped her eggs. There was more to come.

"It's his age, Madam."

Matilda raised an eyebrow, glanced at Mrs Green.

"The male menopause, Madam."

"Go on—"

"True, Madam, Mr Green has it too."

"Wow!"

"Of course Mr Poliport wouldn't have—"

"Didn't live to have it, Mrs Green."

"Oh, Madam."

"Don't let's think about it."

"No, Madam, of course not. But I just thought I'd mention it in case Mr Leach seemed a bit funny."

"No funnier than usual."

"Oh good. Of course I took Mr Green to the doctor. He takes pills now. That settles him."

"Female hormones?"

"Oh, you know about them." Mrs Green was disappointed.

"I don't really think Mr Leach needs pills, not yet anyway. But he's got you to keep an eye on him, lucky fellow." She could see that Mrs Green also considered John fortunate.

"Would Madam like the telephone? I can plug it in for you."

"Oh, I would. I've got to do something about my hair."

"I took a chance. I made an appointment for you at Paul's for eleven."

"Mrs Green, I could kiss you."

"Also your friends Lalage and Anne are in London, but Mrs Lucas and Mrs Stern are away, Madam."

"You've been spying for me!"

"Anticipating your desires, Madam."

"Stop the 'Madam', Mrs Green. You know you call me Matilda to your husband and everyone else."

Mrs Green laughed. "I'll get the telephone. D'you want your dress for tonight pressed?"

"No, it's that black thing of Anabel's. D'you think I shall look all right in it?"

"If Anabel does, you will. You are the same size."

"Have you seen Anabel lately?"

"No," said Mrs Green, who had, and thought Anabel a selfish good-for-nothing tart to neglect her mother so.

"Nor have I. She seems to like living in Germany."

Mrs Green made a non-committal noise and went to fetch the telephone. "Don't be late for your appointment. You know that Paul—"

"All right, I won't." Matilda telephoned Lalage.

"Lalage? It's me. Lunch tomorrow?"

"La Green warned me," shrieked the telephone voice. "Of course, sweetie, lunch tomorrow. Come here. Anne left a message. Lunch with her the day after tomorrow. La Green rang her up. All right?"

"Sure."

"See you tomorrow, must rush. I'm having my face done, late already, 'bye."

"She's having her face done, Mrs Green."

"Wait till you see it." Mrs Green showed her teeth.

"Oh, Mrs Green, up again? Really?"

"Yes. Cost a thousand, I believe. Her husband's made of money
– diamonds – a new car too."

"None of that envy now. I must get up. I have to see to my
hair. Just look at it."

"Her hair is blonde now."

"Thank you for warning me. What's Anne's?"

"Same old red."

"Ah."

"You keep yours as it is."

"I shall, I shall. Can't do anything else in the country even if
I wanted to."

Matilda put on her frock, several years old but dateless. She
had bought it with Anabel's help for Tom's funeral. She had
barely looked at the garment when Anabel had taken her to buy
it, her mind had been full of the horror of meeting the plane
carrying Tom's coffin. The coffin had lain in the sitting-room for
the time it had taken to arrange the cremation, buy the dress,
wait for Louise, Mark and Claud to arrive. Louise had said:

"Why here, for God's sake, Mother? Why can't it be in the
crematorium chapel?"

"I want it here. He would be lonely in the chapel, out of place.
He had no beliefs." Then Claud had said, "Shut up," to Louise,
and Mark, who agreed with her, had shut up too. Matilda zipped
up the dress.

"Do I look respectable?" she asked Mrs Green.

"Very chick." Mrs Green pronounced her "chic" as in Chicago.
She had heard Matilda say this when younger, happier.

"It's not new. I'm mean about clothes. I live in jeans in the
country."

"You look fine." Mrs Green watched Matilda go out into the
street. "Don't let that Paul ruin your hair."

"I won't."

Matilda caught a bus, rocked and roared along the King's Road,
up Sloane Street, lurching round into Knightsbridge, grinding up
to Piccadilly. She walked through side streets to Paul's.

The silence as she went into the hairdresser's was a relief after
the racket in the street. Paul met her.

"Hullo, Paul."

"I've got a job ahead of me I see. Evie, shampoo Mrs Poliport
then bring her to me. Just got to cut a slice off a Frog visitor then
I'll be with you."

"She'll hear you, Paul."

"What if she does? These Frogs and Krauts only come once or twice. It doesn't pay to bother, I haven't the time."

"He doesn't change, does he?"

Matilda submitted to a brisk shampoo, feeling relief when Evie finished and turbanned her head in a towel.

"Now what have we got here?" In disgust Paul flicked Matilda's wet hair upwards. "Who cut it last? Been nibbled by a mouse?"

"You cut it."

"Never."

"You did, when you came to do that demonstration at the Grand Hotel."

"Oh, I remember. It wasn't my day. Robert and I had had a row."

"Be more careful this time. I hope you haven't had a row lately."

"We split up. I'm ever so peaceful now, living with a gloomy Dane."

"Good news."

"Wouldn't you like a rinse?"

"No, I wouldn't."

"All your friends have them. Needn't be red, you know. Just a bit of gold in with the silver. It would suit you."

"No thanks."

"Honestly? Why not tart you up a bit?"

"Honestly, Paul, leave it alone."

"How right you are. All the old Fraus look years older than you, your hair looks terribly distinguished with your skin. How do you do it?"

"Come on, Paul. Concentrate. Snip, snip, but don't get carried away."

"Very well." Paul's tired eyes met Matilda's in the glass. "I'll take great care. You don't come often but I'm glad when you do."

"What a nice thing to say." Paul snipped, concentrating, combing her hair this way and that, snipping off tiny bits, the scissors, razor sharp, flickering between his fingers.

"Have you seen Anabel or Louise lately?"

"No, Paul. I think they have their hair done abroad. They haven't been over for ages."

"No." Paul, who had cut Anabel's hair a few days before,

agreed. "They've got lovely hair like you, though I don't think either of them will go your colour."

"Why not?"

"All those rinses. Girls forget the colour they were born with. Very few white heads these days. There, how's that? Suits your head." He held a mirror so that she could see. "Janey, blow Mrs Poliport then bring her back to me."

Janey led Matilda away and brushed and blew.

"That's better." Paul gave a final snip or two. "Be all right now."

"Thank you. I feel ready to face the world."

"See you soon?"

"I don't know when I shall be in London again, if ever."

"Goodbye then—" Paul was already hurrying to another customer. Matilda was forgotten. She paid the astronomical sum asked, tipped the girls, walked downstairs into the street, strolling slowly along to Green Park Tube.

As she went down the steps the hot air blowing up from below lifted her new hair and blew it every which way. She bought a ticket to Gloucester Road and went down into the bowels of London. It was time to find Hugh's money. She wanted the job over, behind her, so that she could forget it.

Sitting in the train, which was bursting with young foreigners carrying parcels, shouting to one another above the noise of the train, Matilda breathed deeply to calm her nerves and repeated Hugh's instructions to herself to be sure she had them right. She got out at Gloucester Road and walked to Hugh's flat. Long before she rounded the corner into the Gardens she had his keys in her hand, one for the street door, the other for the flat.

The police would no longer be watching the flat but John's fantasies of the night before made her nervous. If there were suspicious-looking people in the street she would walk past the house. But who was or was not suspicious? The few people about looked ordinary enough. When she reached the house she fitted the key in the door, opened the door and walked in.

The hall was dark and drab, the stairs steep and badly carpeted. She counted them as she made a slow ascent – eighty-five, eighty-six, eighty-seven. Eighty-seven brought her to the small landing and the door which still had a card by the bell which said "Hugh Warner".

Matilda listened.

No sound. Nobody coming up or going down. Hugh had said that nearly everyone in the house went out to work all day every day. She ran her finger under the left hand edge of the landing carpet and found the string. He didn't lie about this, she thought. She pulled. From under the carpet came the envelope. She put it in her bag. Two steps down in the fold of carpet over the step another string brought a second envelope. Two steps more, another tweak and she had the rest of the money. She was breathing hard. Should she or should she not go into the flat? It was not really necessary; he could manage without shoes. Curiosity won. She let herself in quickly, closing the door behind her. The flat looked undisturbed though there had been a search by the police. She did not believe in John's Beclean filthy people.

She looked curiously round Hugh's home. Books. He was considerably more erudite than he appeared. Some good pictures. A stack of records, a very nice record player. A bathroom she envied. She looked wistfully at a Greek sponge, decided to leave it. Clothes she must leave too. The bedroom was comfortable. She felt the big bed gingerly. The flat was friendly. A snapshot of a woman smiling at the camera from a garden chair, a black cat in her arms – unmistakably his mother, the nose feminine but large. "Well, Mother." Matilda looked at this version of Hugh. "You were not afraid that day." In the street a car door slammed. She heard voices, the insertion of a key in the front door. She looked around for a hiding place, moving out of sight of the door. Footsteps pounding up the stairs, a man and a girl talking.

"My God, what stairs! How much further? My legs ache."

"Top floor, I'm afraid."

"Ooh!" in a squeak. "You didn't say the Matricide lived here."

"I did, stupid, you were too pissed to hear. Come on."

"It's scary."

"Don't be stupid. He isn't in there."

The footsteps went on up the stairs. Matilda let out her breath. She snatched up a pair of shoes from the rack, let herself out of the flat and ran down to the street. In Gloucester Road she bought a carrier bag and put the shoes in it. The shop girl looked at her briefly, then away to the next customer while she held out her hand with the change.

She asked in a fruit shop where the nearest post office would be and walked steadily along the pavement towards it. She was sweating with retrospective fear. Her feet hurt in their thin soles on the London pavements. She hoped she looked unobtrusive among the throng of foreigners pushing and barging towards the tube.

"*Qu'est qu'elle fait ces jours, Madeleine?*"

"*On dit q'elle fait le trottoir.*"

"*Pas vrai, elle s'est bien installée avec un Suisse?*"

"*Elle doit s'ennuyer!*"

Perhaps Madeleine's feet had hurt on the *trottoir*? Matilda pushed into the post office, joined a queue edging slowly towards the counter. Her feet swelling unbearably, she waited, holding Hugh's keys in her hand. As she moved slowly up the queue she took the keys off her nightdress ribbon, putting the ribbon back in her bag. When at last she reached the counter she found herself face to face with an Indian, whose sad eyes looked through her.

"A registered envelope please, medium size."

Delicate fingers pushed the envelope towards her. She paid. He would not know her again, this man imprisoned behind the counter, so infinitely more dignified than nose-picking Mr Hicks. Mr Hicks feeling superior with his itchy nose and putty-coloured skin would call him a nig-nog or coon.

"Next please." The Indian waved three fingers just a trifle. She was holding up the queue staring.

"Sorry." Matilda blushed, hurried to a counter and addressed the envelope to herself, put in the keys, first wrapping them in a telegraph form, licked up the envelope, closed it firmly, pressing hard, then posted it. Overwhelmed with relief she went out to the street and waited to take a taxi which was disgorging some Arab ladies outside an hotel. After giving John's address she sat back, easing her feet from their tight shoes.

That evening at Wheelers she greedily ate a dozen oysters and a sole and listened with pleasure to John's description of a day's fishing on the Test, conscious that with her hair properly cut she looked more than presentable in Anabel's dress and glad that Louise took shoes a size larger than she did.

"London pavements are death to my feet, John dear, does it show in my face – Piers, I mean."

"You look younger than I've seen you look since Tom died, if I may say so. You look splendid, Matty. What are you doing these days?"

"Just living, John – Piers."

"It's been very hard for you, you two were so close."

"Dreadfully. I wished for a long time to be dead, in fact I wish it still."

"The children should be considered."

"Louise, Mark, Anabel and Claud have their own lives."

"They come and see you."

"No. One visit each after the funeral, then away they went."

"I should have thought—"

"None of them lives in England. They are all busy people."

"Do you go to see them?"

"I haven't so far."

"Really? It's three years since Tom died. I should have thought—"

"I don't particularly want to go. The States are so far. I hate Paris. I don't like Frankfurt either."

"Tom liked Paris."

"I never went with him."

"Yes, I know that."

"How?" Matilda asked sharply. "How did you know? We were pretty well inseparable."

"I suppose he told me. Yes, yes that must have been it." John looked slyly at Matilda. "There's no harm in telling you now. I knew you never went with him. He told me so, naturally."

"What do you mean, naturally?"

"Tom used to do little jobs for my department. They paid for his trips."

Matilda flushed. "John, you go too far with your fantasies. Don't start telling me Tom was a spy. It's too bad of you."

"My dear girl—"

"I'm not a girl, yours or anybody else's. I'm too old to play silly spy games with you. It used to be funny, but bringing Tom in like this isn't. It's indecent, it's worse than rotten taste."

"I'm sorry if I—"

"I should hope so. We laughed at you over Burgess and Maclean, and Philby and you made me laugh last night over your date in Prague with the man who murdered his mother." Matilda prevented herself from saying "Hugh". "But I tell you, John, it's not funny when you insinuate Tom was a sort of agent; it's revolting."

"Sorry, my dear. It's a foible. Forgive me." John signalled to the waiter to bring his bill, looking away from Matilda, pleased to find she knew nothing, suspected nothing. He had not been sure these three years that Matilda believed in Tom's heart attack. It had been unfortunate. Nice to make sure of Matilda's ignorance. They had been close, those two.

Matilda watched John pay the bill and thought, the cost of this meal would keep ten third world families going for months. She was still angry.

"It's a dangerous foible, John, and hurtful."

"I apologize, Matty, I am truly sorry. How can I make amends? Tell you I am not going to Prague to meet this mother-murderer, that I'm only going for the fishing?"

Matilda looked at him doubtfully. She had enjoyed the Prague fantasy; it had made her feel safe.

"I don't think you know truth from fiction and it doesn't matter but you should be more careful. You hurt me."

"Matty, I am sorry. Shall we go? Finish the apologies."

"Let's walk a little. I'll tell you a secret. I'm wearing a pair of Louise's shoes. My feet swell on these pavements."

John took her arm and said cheerfully, "And I will tell you one too. I sleep with a revolver under my pillow – always have."

Matilda burst out laughing. John laughed too, though he was still a little annoyed with what he considered her prissy reaction over Tom. "I showed it to Tom on one occasion and he said, 'Never tell Matty, it would scare the pants off her.' "

"He never called me Matty."

"No, of course he didn't."

"And I don't believe in the revolver."

"There is no need for you to."

Matilda thought this answer ambiguous and decided to cut short her visit. London suddenly seemed too large, too noisy, too much for her altogether. Too much for her feet.

"I shall have to go home very soon."

"You've only just arrived."

"There's nothing for me in London, John, not any more. Piers, if you like."

"It's lovely to see you. Don't hurry away now you're here."

"It's such a pity there's no fishing near me. Wouldn't it be nice if there were?"

She's taken offence, thought John. No matter, she's saved herself a heart attack which would be boring for me to arrange. I don't want to stay with her anyway.

"When must you go?"

"In a couple of days, if I may stay that long."

"You know you may. I'm not going to Prague until Saturday. Today is Tuesday."

"I shall go on Thursday then."

"Why don't you ring up?"

"There is nobody to ring up. I live solo."

"Yes, of course."

"Don't advise me to marry again."

"I wouldn't dream of it."

"Louise, Mark, Anabel and Claud have."

"Fools."

"And you're an angel."

"With foibles." They had reached John's house and he reached for his key. "A nightcap? Brandy?"

"No. Bed for me. Thank you, I've had a lovely evening." Matilda left him and later in bed wondered whether he did or did not sleep with a revolver under his pillow. She felt anxious and disturbed, wishing she were at home.

In his room John read for a while, checked that his revolver was correctly placed before turning off the bedside lamp. He lay smiling. Matilda was splendidly naïve. He thought and wondered, without being more than mildly amused, what sort of fellow she was shacked up with and why she should be toting his shoes around in a carrier bag. Larger feet than Tom's, not Mark's or Claud's style. It was probably somebody quite unpresentable. He switched his mind to his trip to Prague. There were various conundrums which might be clearer after a night's sleep. It was aggravating that he had to do so many little jobs himself. Tom Poliport had proved irreplaceable, small cog though he had been.

Restless and unable to sleep, Matilda remembered Hugh's shoes. She had left the carrier bag in the hall. My Christ! What stupidity, she thought, tiptoeing down to fetch them. What a daft thing to do, though Mrs Green would not be in until morning.

EIGHTEEN

Matilda was in good spirits at breakfast. John put his head round the door.

"Dinner tonight?"

"Yes, looking forward to it, Piers."

"What are you doing today?"

"Lunching with Lalage. Some shopping. We won't lunch till late, knowing her."

"Give her my regards."

"I will."

Later she set off, taking a quick look round Habitat and Peter Jones before taking a bus to Piccadilly. She crossed the street, looked in at Hatchard's on her way to what Tom called "St Fortnum's, Piccadilly". They had bought one another presents there when courting but today the memory did not bother her. She had discarded yesterday's high-heeled shoes and strode along in espadrilles. She bought a pâté for Claud, arranging to have it sent to his New York apartment. The salesman gave her a card on which she wrote: *Eat this in memory of me. Mama.* He would eat it with his lover if it had not gone bad, which she rather hoped it would. She paid by cheque.

A short step into Jermyn Street, the careful choosing of a shirt for Louise at Turnbull and Asser. Louise would prefer something else and lend it to her husband whose colouring would be better suited to the shirt than Louise's. Matilda knew Louise would wonder whether her mother had chosen the shirt with this in view and tell herself her mother was not sophisticated enough to do anything so mean. She paid by cheque and had it sent to Paris.

She walked briskly to Liberty's where she chose two scarves for Anabel to match her most frequent moods, lust and satiation. Anabel would know what was meant. Here too she paid by cheque. A taxi to Foyle's where she bought the latest Russian poet in translation who had defected to the West and had it sent to Mark who would put it on his coffee table. She paid by cheque.

The shopping elevated her spirits to the necessary pitch to meet Lalage with a fair degree of calm, arriving for lunch a calculated ten minutes late.

"Darling, you are late! What on earth have you got on your feet?" Lalage kissed the side of Matilda's face, managing to look her over from head to foot. "Darling, come in. I see you've been to Paul's. His prices are getting more astronomical every week."

"Pretty steep," Matilda agreed. "How does it feel to be blonde then?"

"Oh sweetie, it's my natural colour. You must remember that. Your father used to call me Blondie."

"That 'thirties cartoon?"

"Don't be naughty. Come in and tell all."

Over lunch Matilda listened. Lalage chattered, her mouth full, about herself. In the time spent on drinks and the first course she told Matilda in immense detail about her face lift, each stitch, each pleat, and the price.

"I thought after the last lot you would not need to have it done again. That's what you said."

"It didn't work out that way. I had a gallop. Swear you won't tell? It got damaged."

"Who should I tell?"

"You might tell John, you're staying with him."

"I won't if you don't want me to."

"I don't mind really. It's just who I had the gallop with. After what he did my face fell so I had to have it pulled up again."

"Who was the galloping Major then?"

"Not the Major, sweetie, the brother. The one who killed his mother. You must know him – Warner."

Matilda swallowed her soup and laughed.

"Lalage, come off it. He murdered his mother four weeks ago. You can't have been sleeping with him, had your face done and recovered in that short time."

"You've got your dates mixed. How do you know, anyway?" Lalage, her expression limited by the amount of slack taken in, managed to look cross.

"I read the papers, watch the box, listen to the radio."

Lalage, not put out, grinned. "I'll use that one in a few months. All right, it was someone else. I did meet Hugh Warner once. I thought him very dishy. The huge nose is so sexy. Have you ever met him? His brother's a bit of a bore."

"I don't think so."

"I fear he's dead, must be or he would have been caught."

"They don't catch them all." Matilda was pleased by the steadiness of her voice. "They never caught Jack the Ripper."

"Well, he went for tarts, that was different. I don't suppose they really bothered. One's mother is different."

Matilda grunted. "Who were you galloping with then?"

"Ah, he's at the German embassy. He knows Anabel." Lalage's glance was barbed.

"Lots of people know Anabel. She hasn't necessarily slept with them. She isn't a tart."

"Steady on, love, I never said she was."

"You implied by voice."

"No, darling, no. Anabel's lovely. She gets around a lot. She's so pretty people are bound to talk about her. It's a pity about her hair."

"She's young, it doesn't matter what she does to her hair." How fast, Matilda thought sadly, one catches the breeze. What am I doing here talking to this spiteful old bag, she isn't my friend at all.

"I always loved Tom's hair, the way it flopped forward." Lalage was removing their plates, fetching the next course. "The same colour as Anabel's exactly, wasn't it?"

Lalage had her back to Matilda who sat forcing herself to be quiet, forcing herself not to get up and hit that freshly lifted face that knew that Tom's hair only flopped forward when he bent over making love. Then it flopped, but at no other time. She was surprised how mild her feelings were at having what had been a suspicion verified. So what? If he had slept with Lalage it didn't matter. Once she would have tried to kill Lalage; now she would not even slap her.

They finished the meal to the tune of Lalage's other affairs, her new fur coat, her new car, a hoped-for diamond. As she combed her hair in Lalage's bedroom Matilda, her feet comfortable in their espadrilles, was able to say with easy laughter:

"Everything new, darling, face, clothes, car, lovers, everything except old moneybags. You are so clever to hang on to him."

"My husband's not just an old moneybags, Matilda. You are a bitch."

"Yes, I know. Thanks for the lunch. Take care of yourself. Give him my love. I suppose he's a veritable Kojak by now, poor Bertie."

Matilda crossed Oxford Street and walked down to the Curzon

cinema where there was an erotic German film showing. As she settled in her seat she thought idly, Tom must have been sloshed to sleep with Lalage. There was no doubt in her mind that he had. She was surprised she did not care. She dozed off after the first half of the film, took a taxi back to John's house, soaked agreeably in a boiling bath before dressing to go out. If Tom had slept with her friends then life was a little diminished. Time to go, time for the picnic.

"Would you like to have dinner at the Mirabelle or The Connaught?" John's voice called from the landing.

"You choose, John, Piers I mean."

"The Mirabelle then, and The Connaught tomorrow."

"You spoil me." Matilda ran more water in the bath. Staying with John was like having a rich, undemanding husband, though perhaps as a husband he might have demanded more? Somewhere at the back of her mind Matilda knew what he would demand. She decide to entertain him during dinner with a spiced-up version of lunch at Lalage's.

John surprised her by taking her to a concert at the Festival Hall before dinner.

"You can rest your tootsies while I listen to music."

"I do like music too you know—"

"You never used to." He drove well, nosing his car easily through the traffic.

"Since Tom's death I've listened a lot to the radio. One can't help getting to know, recognise, love music."

"Very bad for your ear unless you have a really good radio."

"I haven't. All the same I've learned some music and a lot about current affairs. Sometimes I listen all day, it helps me."

"Helps what?" John was parking the car, hoping Matilda wouldn't drop off during the concert.

"Helps me keep alive while I must."

"Of course you must. You are not a suicidal character."

That's what he thinks, poor old sod. Matilda was glad the concert was to be Mozart, a great cheerer-upper. Beethoven, John's favourite, was inclined to depress. She did not wish to drip tears on to Anabel's frock. She annoyed John by sitting alert and upright through the concert without nodding her head or toe-tapping, making several knowledgeable and intuitive remarks about the conductor. When at the end she turned and gave him a huge smile of thanks he was astonished to find how touchingly like she was to the Matilda he had known before her marriage. Driving her to the restaurant he felt kind and indulgent. She wasn't bad company; certainly tonight she looked presentable.

Eating dinner Matilda told John what Lalage had said or hinted about Anabel.

"She's like that, I shouldn't pay any attention. She's jealous of you, that's all."

"Jealous of *me*?"

"Yes. Poor Bertie is the dreariest of bores. No wonder her face falls and has to be lifted."

"But so rich."

"I grant you that. He's disgustingly rich, does nothing interesting with it, just makes more money for Lalage to spend."

"No need for her to pick on Anabel. How could she be sleeping with this German when he's in London and she's in Frankfurt?"

"There's that modern invention the aeroplane."

"So it's true, then?"

"What if it was?" John, having seen Anabel with the German quite frequently, was not prepared to deny.

"I shouldn't mind." Matilda looked around the restaurant. "She's a beautiful girl. For aught I know she sleeps around a lot. She should be here, not me, it's a good setting for her. I don't belong any more. The pavements are a disaster to my feet and I feel out of place. Anabel belongs, I don't."

"Did Lalage suggest she had slept with Tom?"

"No," said Matilda, too quickly, reinforcing John's knowledge. "Have a brandy?"

"No, thank you, it would keep me awake."

"Did you sleep well last night?"

Matilda wondered whether he had heard her creeping down for Hugh's shoes. "Oh, I always use Claud's cure if I can't sleep."

"What's that?"

"Composing letters to *The Times* about the Queen's hats. You have to write a letter which is not derogatory to the Monarchy but expresses your distaste for her headgear. Without appearing unpatriotic it's not possible. In despair you drop off and snore." Matilda laughed as John grinned at her.

"Sure you won't have a brandy? D'you mind if I do?"

"Of course not. A brandy will suit you sitting there in your super pin-stripe. The onslaught of years has made you very distinguished, Piers." Matilda liked serving the occasional flattery.

"You are looking very pretty yourself."

"It's the brief whiff of London you are treating me to."

"Stay longer. Aren't you lonely in your cottage all on your own?"

"I've got a dog and a gander. I am a country bumpkin."

"But not a lonely one?" She's being very secretive about this chap, John thought as he ordered brandy. I expect he's good in bed but drops his aitches.

"Not lonely at all. I won't mind going home on Thursday."

He must be good, thought John. When I have the time I must find out who he is.

What a boring conversation this is. I prefer Gus any day. Matilda swallowed a yawn. It was long past her bedtime.

"You used to have a cat."

"She died."

"I'm sorry."

"No use being sorry. Death is death. Tom's dead and our cat's dead. It won't be long before I'm dead too. Most of me died when Tom died. We had planned to die together."

"Death control."

"Yes. Did Tom tell you?"

"He must have. He wanted to go while the going was good. He got his wish." John sniffed his brandy. If Tom had wished to die young the heart attack in the rue Jacob was really of little consequence. If I felt guilty which I don't, thought John, I should have no need to.

"Well, it was our wish. I got left. It's bloody hell," Matilda snapped, anger making her look rather beautiful.

Whoever fits those shoes is lucky, if you like that sort of thing, which I happen to know she does. John watched her colour rise, pleased that Matilda believed in the heart attack, that there was no need to arrange one for her.

"You and Anabel are very alike." He swallowed the brandy.

"Anabel and I? Goodness no."

"Not in looks perhaps."

"What an extraordinary—" Matilda paused.

"Accusation?"

"Yes. I never slept around."

"You might very easily have gone that way if Tom had let you out of his sight."

Matilda let that pass, relieved that John was about to pay the bill.

"I'm lunching with Anne tomorrow. I wonder what she will have to say."

"She will pick on Louise, you had Anabel today. Louise is also very beautiful, though not as sexy."

"I shall try and be ready for her."

"I'd let the girls protect themselves if they were mine."

But they are not, thought Matilda, feeling sorry for John, unmarried, childless, sexless. What did he do on long winter evenings?

"You are an enigma," she said later when she kissed his cheek goodnight. John felt complimented but not pleased and before going to bed checked his engagement diary and was annoyed to find there was no way of getting down to see Matilda until November. Big Feet must wait, he thought, switching off the light, feeling for his revolver.

In her room Matilda was not composing letters to *The Times* but congratulating herself on the fact that by the time the cheques she had written that day had bounced she would be dead. Let Mark worry. It would do him good to feel he had always been right in his opinion of his parents as unworldly, feckless people. As for her host John, if he had thought earlier of calling himself Piers a feast of confusion and derision would have been lost to anyone interested in her entourage, such as Claud. Matilda liked the words "interested in her entourage" and mulled them over gently before snoring.

Listening to the snores, John lay thinking about Matilda, remembering their youth. It had been too late to hold her, even if he had wanted to, when she had come running to him after killing Felicity. He had been glad she had killed Felicity, who was a nuisance. Desperate Matilda, so upset so long ago. "I was so frightened I peed in the snow. It was so cold—" She had minded the cold more than killing. He had made her drink brandy, taken her along to Tom. And now, he thought, she's past fifty and snores like the devil.

NINETEEN

On her way to lunch with Anne, Matilda strolled from Chelsea to Harrods. It had occurred to her to surprise Anabel by leaving a really beautiful dress worn only once. She would choose a dress which would suit both Anabel and Louise. They would find it, be aware of its cost, both want it. They would quarrel over who should have it. Anabel, the more ruthless and determined, would get it. Adrenaline would flow, brisk up the funeral. Later Louise would make her husband buy her an even more expensive dress and the anger would spread to him while Mark, who by this time would have visited the bank manager, would be furious. Only Claud would be delighted. Of all my children I love Claud the best, Matilda thought, as she walked into Harrods by the Hans Place entrance and strolled through the men's department to the lifts.

She enjoyed trying on and making up her mind. She was helped by an assistant who was not yet unkind to middle-aged ladies. Matilda confided that the dress was to be for Anabel after she had worn it once.

"I shall wear it tonight, then my daughter can have it."

Matilda decided against white or black, havered a bit over a lime green which would suit Anabel but looked distressing with her white hair.

"There is a deep rose which would suit you."

"Let me see it."

The rose dress did suit. "I shall have it. Anabel will look marvellous in it."

"What about the length?" Matilda was wearing her espadrilles. "It will be rather short with heels."

"I loathe heels, they hurt. I'm wearing these things to save pain. What shall I do?" She was distressed. She wanted the dress. With heels it would look ridiculous, too short.

"If you tried in the shoe department you might find a pair of dancing shoes. They are quite flat. I wear them often after a long day at work. My feet swell."

"Do they at your age?"

"Yes."

"Shall I go at once and find out, then come back if successful and pay for the dress?"

"Of course, Madam."

"Will you take a cheque?"

"Of course."

Successful with the dancing shoes, Matilda left Harrods carrying the dress and shoes, light in heart and lighter by one cheque for several hundred pounds. She walked through Montpelier Square to the park on her way to Anne in Mayfair.

Strolling along by the Serpentine she passed the spot where long ago she had biffed Felicity out on to the ice to her death without even the vaguest recollection of the event. She was filled with the euphoria of spending money she had not got. She enjoyed the crowds of young people walking, sitting, lying on the grass, in one case openly copulating. She liked the boats, ducks, prams, small children running. She enjoyed the shouting and screaming from the Lido, the flying of kites, orange, blue, red and green kites soaring and swooping in the late summer sky, reminding her for a moment of the blue sail she had seen on the sea during her abortive picnic. Next time she would surely be alone.

Anne lived in Mayfair; not for her Chelsea or Kensington. It was known that if she had consented to move to one of these areas her husband would have taken her on more holidays, given her a cottage in the country.

"I can only live in Mayfair, nowhere else," had been her cry. "It's so near the shops." It was said she could be seen shopping in street markets as far away as Lambeth, wearing black glasses and a headscarf – a rumour unconfirmed.

"Lovely to see you, darling." Anne kissed Matilda. "What have you got on your feet, for heaven's sake?"

"Espadrilles."

"Darling, you can't be seen like that, people will laugh."

"Suppose they do?"

"Oh, you've been *shopping*! Let's have a peep." Anne's voice was the tone of a daily communicant who has caught a lapsed friend coming out of Mass. It combined surprise with forgiveness.

Matilda showed her the dress and dancing slippers.

"It's not you, you know, is it the new mode? Those baby shoes?"

"Yes. I lunched with Lalage yesterday."

"Darling, she mostly talks about her face, you know."

"I noticed. How is the family?"

"All right. Peter's in Greece, Humphrey is sailing. So boring, and death to one's hair. He always asks me to go too but it's not on, is it?"

"Why not?"

"Well, one feels sick, one gets bored, one's hair goes the most dreadful carrot, you know, and it's difficult to get back to normal, you know."

"How would I know?"

"Well, love, you can wear it white but at this moment in time one can't, you know."

"How is Vanessa?"

"Vanessa has some dreadful man in your part of the world. You probably know him, Bobby something. She's been on the bed thing with him, someone said she even does it on the beach. She wants to marry him. You know what girls are like, you've got two."

"Oh yes, the penny's dropped. I saw her on the beach. They were going to have a barbecue. She swam naked and kept saying everything was super, super." Matilda accepted an offered sherry.

" 'Super' is her latest word. How one hates these expressions! At this moment in time its 'super'. One never had these verbal tricks oneself, one was prevented by one's parents."

"Have you been seeing a lot of Princess Anne?"

"Why should I? We don't move in those circles, though one's not far off, you know. How is Claud?"

"I thought you might ask after Louise."

"Why? One's more interested in Claud. So like Tom, isn't he – his manners, habits, you know."

"What habits?"

"One supposes it's the genes, you know. Claud has inherited Tom's – you must have noticed – it's all genes." Matilda listened for an unspoken "you know" hovering at the end of the unspoken sentence. What am I doing here? Who is this dreadful woman? Where is the Anne who was once young, pretty, full of life. Who is this bore?

"Claud lives in the States. I never see him."

"One couldn't very well go and see him, could one? One sees that."

"Sees what?"

"One sees in Claud what you never seemed to notice in Tom. You carried it off marvellously. We all thought so, you know."

"Are you implying Tom was a bugger?"

"Matilda!"

"Well, Claud is, 'one' knows that. You seem to imply Tom was too."

"Didn't you know?"

Matilda grinned. "No, and nor did you. I bet you tried to get Tom into bed and he refused, so now you say he was a bugger."

"If you weren't one of one's oldest friends—"

"How old are you, Annie?"

"Well—"

"Same age as me."

"A good deal younger. I married when I was sixteen."

"Anne *don't*! Not with me. Please. We are old, nearer death than birth, time to get ready. You can't go on dyeing your hair, using silly expressions like 'one' instead of 'I' or 'we' and mischief making."

"I should think," said Anne, her face clashing with her hair, "that living as you do has softened your brain. You should come up to London oftener and keep up."

"Keep up with what?"

"Life, of course. Life, you know."

"I am more interested in death, so should you be. You haven't much time left to be nice to poor old Humphrey. Why don't you tie up your hair and go sailing with him? Why don't you go to bed with him now and again? Have a good romp."

"At this moment in time I don't want to."

"Not during lunch but when he comes back from the Solent? Why not be like Vanessa? She has fun, I've seen her. Sexy."

"You always had a vulgar streak, even at school."

"That's like the old Anne. I'm going now. I can't take any more. I'm sorry. I don't belong any more. I'm off—"

"Leaving London?" Suddenly aware of Matilda, Anne caught her hand.

"London and life. Give my love to Humphrey." Matilda picked up the dress in its Harrods bag.

"Don't get uptight, Matilda. You know you—"

Matilda kissed her quickly. "I'm sorry, I must go, really sorry."

117

Her lunch unfinished, Matilda got into the lift and down into the street, conscious of behaving badly in her need to get away. Fool, I didn't go to the lavatory, she thought, walking quickly along the hot pavements to Piccadilly, into the Ritz where in the calm of the cloakroom she assuaged her need, washed her hands which were trembling and combed her hair. He may have slept with Lalage but he was not a bugger.

Matilda stood at a basin letting the cold tap run over her hands, wondering how to fill the afternoon until she could go back for dinner with John. The running water made her want to pee again. Sitting on the lavatory seat she remembered periods at parties when nobody had wanted to talk or dance with her and she had spent much time in cloakrooms. There had been one party which was different. She tried to remember why, in what way it had been different. Where was the party? When? What year? The memory escaped. I can't sit here the whole afternoon. This is ridiculous. She left the lavatory, washed her hands again then sat in the hall to collect herself. She felt angry that yesterday Lalage had sniped and hit and today Anne. They had attacked like birds when a member of the flock is wounded. They wanted to kill me, thought Matilda. How shocked they would be if they knew I mean to kill myself. I am already extinct, a Polish Fowl, a Tufted Hamburg. She smiled and caught the eye of an old man who was sitting near by. He winked infinitesimally. He was listening to his daughter. She must be his daughter since she addressed him as "Papa", speaking French. Papa was to sit here and rest while she did her shopping at Fortnum's and Elizabeth Arden and Liberty's. He could rest, order tea, she would be back in an hour. Meanwhile he must rest. She went off with a cheerful wave, high heels trotting.

"Is being old very boring?" said Matilda in French.

"Je m'emmerde, Madame."

Matilda moved to the chair beside him.

"May I tell you what I am going to do about it for myself?"

"Je vous prie," politely.

"I am not going to get old," said Matilda. "I am going to kill myself."

"You have cancer, perhaps?"

"No, no. I just refuse to suffer the horrors of age. I have had all I want. I have decided to stop."

"How will you stop?"

Matilda outlined her picnic.

"I wish I could accompany you," said the old man, "but I have waited too long. I cannot walk without help, I can do nothing without help. It is undignified. Only my cat understands. I have a cat in Paris."

Matilda told him about Gus.

"That presents a problem."

Matilda agreed, thinking of Gus, his honking and his feet slapping on the path. She had forgotten Folly as she had forgotten Hugh.

"My daughter has gone to the shops. I must sit here and wait. I can no longer go myself. I am a prisoner of age."

To amuse him Matilda told him about her shopping, her choice of presents for her children, of the dress she had bought that morning for the girls to quarrel over.

"That does not sound like a death wish."

"All my cheques will bounce."

"And you will be gone when they do?"

"That's the idea."

"*Quelle révanche.*"

"It is my eldest son, he is such a respectable man—"

"Like his father, perhaps?"

"No, not a bit."

"What is called 'a sport'?"

"Yes, just that. Here comes your daughter. Thank you for listening to me. I should have liked to tell you about my two women friends."

"The one who said she had slept with your husband, the other that he was homosexual?"

"How did you know?"

"That is an old trick. Have a happy death."

"Goodbye."

Matilda left him and, feeling cheered, took a taxi to the Hayward Gallery and thence, on her way back to John's house, to the Tate. She would have liked Claud to meet that old man. She made a quick little prayer for Claud, ejecting it from her mind like a cartoon bubble. If there was "anybody" about to hear it, perhaps he would do something for Claud?

As she waited on the pavement outside John's house for the taxi driver to give her change she began to hum,

> "There's a small hotel
> By a wishing well
> I wish that we were there, together."

"My Mum and Dad used to sing that song." The taxi driver counted the change into Matilda's palm. "Said they danced to it."

"I did too." Matilda separated the change for the tip.

"Stood up hugging?"

"Yes, we hugged as we danced. We hung on to one another."

"Shocking, you does that—"

"In bed?" Matilda laughed. "We did a lot of hugging upright. I don't see the point of dancing separate from your partner." She gave him her tip. He drove off laughing. "Funny old girl."

TWENTY

If Matilda had known that Hugh was spending the nights walking the countryside and swimming in the reservoir she might have worried.

He came in before dawn, slept until lunch when Mr Jones came to feed Gus, a task he had taken upon himself, and to chat. What Mr Jones wanted to chat about was Matilda.

"I love the woman." Huw Jones sat at the kitchen table, resting his beard in his hands.

"Does she reciprocate?" Hugh was making a pot of tea.

"She does not. She was in love with Tom, that is what she thinks."

"She wanted to die because she can no longer live without him."

"That is the uppermost version."

"Oh, what's underneath?"

"Who knows? Does my Matilda know herself?" Mr Jones threw out a dramatic enquiring hand. "She has a great talent for putting matters out of her mind."

"Your Matilda?"

"Alas not. There was an attempt, a brief scuffle it was but—"

"But what?"

"She pushed me downstairs. I might have broken a bone. I tried to clasp her in my arms but she pushed."

"What were you doing upstairs?"

"It was the ballcock of the loo. She had asked me to mend it. I saw her great bed in her room, the bed you slept in, desecration that. I thought it would be lovely to roll on the bed with Matilda so I – but she pushed and down I went. She laughed! Laughed," he groaned.

"When was this?"

"Several years ago. Since then I keep my place."

"But you love her?"

"Yes. Silly, isn't it?"

"Depends."

"Of course it's silly. She is mad. She wants to die. She does not want to grow old and clutter the earth. I love her. I would look after her."

"You would be old too."

"Ach! We would be old together but she hates old age, refuses it. She wants to push off. It is arrogant!"

"What about her children? Can't they stop her?"

"Her children!" Mr Jones held up a finger. "Louise, beautiful, married, two pretty tots, husband with money, lives in Paris. Louise, she is grand, she is the cat's whiskers. She has a lover, all very discreet. Then there is Mark." Mr Jones held up a second finger. "A right bastard, a pompous pillar of the establishment, always at conferences. I read his name in the paper. Then there is Anabel. She is flighty, a tart, hard, beautiful of course." He lifted a third finger. "Ah, Anabel!" A fourth finger went up. "Claud. The youngest, a cissy, a poof. And none of them," Mr Jones thumped the table so that Folly barked and Gus honked, "none of them bothers to visit their mother."

"Perhaps she does not encourage them."

"True, but they should try. I visit my mother in Tooting and very boring it is too." Huw Jones laughed, tears leaping from his black eyes to flow into his beard. "She is so boring," he cried joyously, "but I go. She whines, she cries, she is lonely."

Hugh laughed with him, pouring the water into the teapot, putting the pot on the table.

"I constantly visited my mother."

"But you murdered her."

"I know, but she wasn't boring."

"Tell old Jones about it." The black eyes stopped twinkling, the laughter died.

"No thanks."

"Okay. So now we have an embarrassed pause while we think of something else to talk about." Mr Jones was huffed.

Making toast, Hugh asked, "And Tom, what was he really like?"

"Matilda's Tom?"

"No, yours."

"Mine? An amusing man. Loved Matilda as well as he was able. I only knew the UFO side of him."

"And what was that?"

"He had experience in the war, see? Brought people over from

France in boats to the estuary here and in a little seaplane. So later he started smuggling, not very often, just now and then. He was a mysterious man. I think he did some work for that chap Matilda is staying with, but I'm not sure."

"Does she know?"

"Oh no, no, no. Tom also brought in pot. He liked to smoke it just as I do. But just before he died he was cheated. Whoever sent the pot sent heroin too. Tom said he'd been double-crossed, that someone wanted to incriminate him—"

"Why did he not destroy it?"

"He did, he destroyed it, flushed it down the loo just as you did. But he told me he was keeping one packet to confront—"

"Confront who?"

"I don't know, do I? Tom went off to Paris and never came back. There have been no more little boats or little seaplanes, nothing."

"But you go on reporting UFOs?"

"Yes I do. The police think I am harmless, so I am safe."

"Did Matilda know of this?"

"Nothing. I think she knows nothing."

"So she is bored."

"Matilda is lonely, she has cranky ideas. She is middle aged, has nothing to live for so she falls in love with death. There you are," Huw Jones exclaimed. "I am brilliant! Talking to you has discovered for me what Matilda wants. She wants death because she wants something she has never had, a splendid deduction." Mr Jones looked enchanted.

"But we all get it. Death is the one certainty."

"But we don't all love it, do we? It is love she wants."

"I thought she'd had love."

"I think," Huw Jones said sadly, "that she has discovered she never really had it."

"That can't be true."

"She could love me but she won't even try. I love her. I look after Gus when she goes away. I would die for her. I have never betrayed Tom to her. I lie at her feet and I don't get a sausage."

Hugh gathered up the tea things, took them to the sink.

"That woman loves Gus, she does not love poor Jones."

"Shall we play chess?" Hugh hoped that playing chess would distract his visitor. He found this talk of Matilda painful.

"Okay." Mr Jones set up the board. "We will play chess, stop talking about Matilda who thinks old people should not be encouraged to live, that weak babies should not be put into incubators. I think she secretly thinks it's a good thing when a lot of old people are suffocated in a fire in an old people's home, when faulty brakes fail on the buses on old people's outings, when they catch the 'flu and die by the score. She is a horrible woman, just like Hitler, and I love her and I hate her and her Death. I want to hold her in my arms and roll about in that bed." With tears coursing down his cheeks Huw Jones set up the board. "Your move." His voice was desolate.

Hugh moved his Queen's pawn. I could not comfort this man, he thought, he loves his grief.

When the telephone pealed, which it did occasionally, they watched one another, counting the rings then waiting for it to stop.

"The machine is broken."

"I taped it up for her. Stub knocked it over, he hated its noise, poor old dog."

"She could have a new one. It looks untidy."

Ruminating over his next move Huw Jones muttered, "She is not a tidy woman. The house is usually a mess. She feels a mess, so death is logical, tidy."

Thinking of his mother, Hugh exclaimed harshly, "I don't find it tidy."

Aware of Hugh's thought, Huw moved a threatening Bishop.

They did not hear the lorry roll to a stop in the lane, though Folly pricked her ears and Gus honked.

"Hullo," said Claud. "Where's Mama?"

"In London." Hugh looked up.

"I telephoned." Claud looked from one man to the other. "An hour ago. I thought she must be out. She never goes away."

"She is." Hugh took in the full beauty of Claud in tattered jeans, worn suede jacket, Gucci shoes, dark brown eyes in sunburned face, improbable yellow hair, Matilda's mouth.

"She is away, she's staying—" began Mr Jones.

"With loverboy Sir Piers to be."

"He's not her lover." Mr Jones spoke crossly, jealously.

"No? Why didn't you answer the phone? Were you here?" Claud looked from one to the other. "Oh, I *see!*" he exclaimed. "The Matricide. Is Mama hiding you? Rather brave of her, sporting, jolly sporting. When will she be back?"

"Day after tomorrow." Mr Jones's voice did not disguise dislike. "Why are you here?"

"I wanted to show her my find. I've a lorry of the *most* exquisite Delabole and Serpentine headstones. She'd like them. They were in a place I heard of in Cornwall."

"Pinched?"

"No, Jonesy, not pinched. They were being – er – moved, lined up. Car parks now not graveyards. We move with the times, move to the New World."

"She'll be back."

"I can't wait, have to get them packed in the container. Pity. She would have liked them. She never goes away this time of year. Sorry to miss her. Must get them shipped."

"She—"

"She hung up on me when I phoned, cut me off. I was about to say I might be around, couldn't be sure." He looked Hugh over, grinning slightly, Matilda's mouth, Claud's expression. "Well then, another time. Give her my love. This her new dog? She can't live without animals." He stroked Folly's head as she stood on her hind legs, feet braced against his thigh, tail wagging. "Taken old Stub's place, then?" Patting the dog, he looked from one man to the other, the question "taking my father's place?" in his eyes. "How's her terminal illness?"

"Her *what*?"

"How's her life? Bet you've cheered her up." He looked at Hugh. "I shan't tell. A good lech is what she needs; a lot better for her than her infatuation with—"

"Who with?" Mr Jones's voice betrayed fear.

"Death, chap with a scythe. That one – spells it D-E-A-T-H. 'Bye then."

They listened to his quick step, the slam of the lorry door, the engine starting up, dying away.

"Bastard! He might have told her he was coming."

"He expected her to be here."

"Took it for granted."

"He did telephone. We didn't answer."

Mr Jones was furious. "Young sod!"

"It will be better not to tell Matilda," Hugh said quietly, putting the chessmen away.

"Oh, much better," Mr Jones agreed, "much better, if better's the word."

"Worse would be her disappointment. I've done the same—"

"Your mother wasn't like Matilda, you killed her."

"Oh shut up about my mother, you improbable fool."

"One thinks another time will do, you are right, I do it too. But my mother's so boring, so lonely, she whines at me."

"Sod your mother." Hugh tipped the chessboard on to the floor.

TWENTY-ONE

John liked the new dress, Matilda saw at once. He seldom commented on her clothes. Walking to The Connaught from Berkeley Square where he had parked the car, she noticed too that wearing flat shoes not only allowed her to walk comfortably but made John look taller, more distinguished. Tonight he wore a dark grey flannel suit, a cream shirt and black tie. He held her arm lightly, steering her towards the restaurant.

They sat at a corner table and had a drink before ordering. Matilda told John about her day. He laughed.

"You should not take Anne and Lalage seriously."

"But I do. They make me suffer. It is a fine art with them."

"Rubbish."

"They have perfected the detection of the weak point."

"You should be safe against pinpricks."

"I am not. I used to be better at it when Tom was alive, better in London. Now it exhausts me. I have lost my vitality."

"I would hardly say that." John had been amazed by her itinerary. "You never crammed so much into two days. You would have used up two weeks in the old days."

"Old age is creeping in."

This irritated John, who picked up the menu. "What will you eat?"

Sensing his irritation, Matilda obediently studied her menu, flushing slightly at his tone. Immediately John was sorry. "You look ten years younger than our age." There was so little between them he could safely say this.

"Our age. Yes." Matilda flashed him a grateful smile. "I have always envied you your assurance."

"I always thought Tom a very lucky man."

Matilda stifled a yawn behind the menu. Why must they talk such balls? After a lifetime knowing each other, she thought, we might have at least one absorbing topic in common. She looked at the menu and longed to be home with Gus, eating a bowl of onion soup, reading a book propped up against the teapot.

"I shall eat mussels, then salmon. I never get decent fish living so near the sea."

"Shall you be glad to get home? Aren't you lonely?"

"No." Matilda looked John straight in the eye. "Not a bit." It occurred to her that John thought she had a lover. "I like living alone, I am used to it now. You know what it's like. Of course I'm not lonely."

John ordered grouse. "Why don't you change your mind and have grouse? There are no grouse in your part of the world. Oysters first."

"All right. I gather you want to drink red wine. All right, oysters first."

"That's about it, you read my mind."

They ordered grouse with matchstick potatoes. John ordered a second bottle of wine. Matilda drank more than she used to, he thought, watching the way she drank, not one mouthful at a time, but two, even three, emptying the glass frequently. The wine enhanced her looks. He told her about a very beautiful villa where he had stayed that spring.

"In France?"

"No, Italy. Marvellous wild flowers in April, one can still find so many different kinds of orchids."

"I'd rather you didn't come to my funeral, John, Piers I mean."

"What?"

"I said I'd rather you didn't come to my funeral."

"I was telling you about Italy. Weren't you listening?"

"Only half. I'm obsessed by death."

"All right, we'll talk about it. Why don't you want me to come?"

"You get too close. You think I have a lover."

"It occurred to me."

"Mr Jones made an advance."

"That fellow with a beard, that fat bald chap? What cheek."

"No it wasn't. He isn't fat, he is square. He can't help being bald. It was very sweet of him really."

"Sweet!"

"You talk as though—" Matilda stopped, realising the unwisdom of what she was about to say. I do not belong to John, she thought. He mustn't get that idea in his head. She drank more wine.

"I'm verging on tipsy." But John was looking towards the entrance. Matilda followed his glance.

"Oh Christ!"

Strolling in, cool, young, exquisite, came Anabel, followed by a very tall black man with quite extraordinarily beautiful features. Anabel was laughing up at him, her teeth, larger than Matilda's, flashing, her face alight with the joy of conquest.

"What a wonderful young man. Who is he?" Matilda had jerked into sobriety.

"Quite a sizeable fish at the U.N."

"Is his wife beautiful?"

"Yes, a very brilliant woman."

"Poor Anabel."

But Anabel had seen them. She came forward in a rush.

"Ma! How super to see you! No wonder I couldn't get you on the phone, you were up here with your beau all the time. How are you, Piers darling? This is Aron, Ma, isn't he exquisite?" Matilda shook a firm hand. "Oh, Ma, what a dress! You do look wonderful, doesn't she look wonderful?" Her great eyes swivelled from John to her escort. "Wonderful!"

"Won't you join us?"

"Oh, no, darling, we can't. We only came in for a drink. How is home? How is Stub? How is Prissy?"

"They have both been dead for a long time." Matilda felt no anger.

"And Gus?"

"He's alive."

"He'll be next then, won't he?" Anabel let out the words with a yelp of laughter.

When Anabel and her man had gone Matilda began to laugh. "It's the surprise! The surprise I have every time I meet her that I in my belly created that girl."

John grinned.

"How long has she been in London? You always know everything."

"About three months."

"Little bitch. Couldn't get me on the phone. I suppose the others have been over too?"

"Not Claud, I haven't seen him."

"His teeth are better than Anabel's and he doesn't go about with his mouth open. He telephoned me, you needn't cover for him."

"Don't be a cat, Matty. Anabel probably has adenoids. You're her mother, you should have seen to them. How long is he here for?"

"Girls with protruding teeth always get men, it makes them look amiable. Oh, Claud – he went to Yorkshire."

"Have another drink."

"I see why people become alcoholics. They learn to accept. No thank you, no more."

"You must learn to accept your children."

"Why should I?" Matilda was suddenly extremely angry. "Why? I don't like any of them except Claud. Let them come to my funeral. I don't want you but I do want them. How dare she not know about Stub and Prissy?"

"Perhaps you didn't tell her."

"I'm sure I didn't."

"Well then."

"Well nothing. I want to go home."

"We will." John waved to the waiter. "I'll take you home."

"Not yours, mine. I must get back. It's nothing but stab, stab, stab in London." In an unconscious gesture Matilda cupped her breasts in her hands, then folded them in front of her on the table.

"D'you know that someone somewhere put his hands over my breasts and said 'Chimborazo Catapaxi has stolen my heart—' "

"I should think lots of chaps did." John was signing the bill and counting money for the tip. "That was one of the poems our generation quoted like *A Shropshire Lad* and one or two particular sonnets we'd done at school."

"How bracing you are." Matilda stood up. John followed her out thinking that after all that wine she was wonderfully steady on her pins.

Arriving back in Chelsea, Matilda's mood changed. She hummed and sang snatches of Cole Porter. John joined in.

"A lovely evening, so educational." She watched him lock the car, standing in her flat shoes on the pavement, still warm from the long hot summer. John opened the door and they went in.

"A nightcap?"

"An Alka-Seltzer more like."

"I'll get you one."

Matilda kicked off her shoes and spread her toes.

"You and your feet." John stood in the doorway, holding the Alka-Seltzer, smiling indulgently.

"My country feet." She pulled at the toes of her tights, easing the constriction.

"Have you seen my bedroom?"

"No."

"You are wonderfully incurious, Matty. Come and look." Matilda followed him across the landing.

"New curtains."

"Very pretty. Where did you get that stuff?"

"Paris."

"They are not like you somehow—" She was puzzled. "More Tom's sort of thing."

"He got it for me."

Just one more prick in the heart, thought Matilda, keeping her face blank. Trust John.

Pulling the pink dress over her head she was dazzled by the momentary darkness. Whoops! I'm tipsy! Carefully she put the dress on a hanger, turning it this way and that to see whether she had spilled food on it. She took off her knickers and bra. Her head was singing, it was difficult to focus. In the bathroom she mixed Alka-Seltzer and drank the noxious mixture, sitting naked on the edge of the bath, expecting to throw up.

After a few minutes she put on her nightdress and got into bed. She kept the bedside light on. If she turned it off her head would whirl.

She said a little prayer asking for sleep.

No sleep.

She lay thinking about Anabel. So beautiful. A horrid girl on the whole. She had never been able to communicate with her, nor with Louise or Mark, only Claud, and even then only on occasion. It is my fault, she reproached herself. I cannot reach them any more than my mother could reach me. I am not wanted. What could I have said to Anabel? Something warm, loving, maternal. I felt none of those things. I felt resentful. She never comes near me. I should have made friends with that man, he would then be kinder to Anabel, dispose of her less lightly. I don't mind her going about with a black man. Why should I? Stub was black.

That's it. Matilda drunkenly saw her nature revealed. I can only get on with animals. I only trust animals. Stub, Prissy, Gus, all the animals in her past, as demanding as children but never nasty. Wow! Black, brown, multicoloured animals. Ah! She loved them.

Gosh, she thought, I'm never going to sleep. She put on her dressing-gown, put out the light, opened the window and leant out. Somewhere in London lovely Anabel lay in that man's arms. I envy her. I hope he will not hurt her. It will make her take it out on someone else, some white dolt. Anabel, so self-assured, no great animal lover she. Matilda remembered Anabel drowning a rabbit in a bucket. Bloody child. In a way she was like Tom. This unforeseen thought caused Matilda to weep. She walked up and down the room weeping. "Tom, Tom, oh poor Tom, did I love you?"

Matilda felt so uncertain she became distraught. I must walk, she thought, putting on her slippers. She wrapped the dressing-gown round her, took her latchkey, tiptoed downstairs, letting herself out into the street.

Roused by the slight sound, John looked out on to the landing, wondering what the hell Matilda was doing now.

"What on earth is going on?" he called querulously.

"I'm going for a fucking walk." Matilda slammed the street door.

"If anyone behaved like that to me," Matilda said aloud in the empty street, "I'd never have them in my house again." She walked weeping along the pavements, composing nice things she should have said to Anabel, clever intelligent things she could have said to the beautiful black man. Aron – a splendid name – balanced, biblical, dignified. My word, she thought, he was sexy, no wonder Anabel – do hope she enjoys it, lucky girl.

She walked briskly, passing the Royal Hospital, far from John's house. The Alka-Seltzer was working. She turned left through Burton Court, into Smith Street, along the King's Road. A middle-aged widow, she saw herself walking down the King's Road in her dressing-gown, sober now. It was a pity that she liked animals best, but there it was. At some moment, she could not remember when, she had nearly loved human beings. It must have been a moment of passion. Passion was something so tremendously rare. Animals were better, safer, Now she was nearly back at the cul-de-sac. The latchkey? She had it in her hand. I couldn't bear to wake him again, she thought, letting herself in quietly. He may have owned Tom but he doesn't own me. She shut the door and crept up to bed.

TWENTY-TWO

In the train Matilda leafed through *Harper's*, a luxury bought for her by John with *The Times* and the *Guardian*. He had found her a seat, kissed her goodbye and left before the train started, putting her out of his mind before he reached his car.

Matilda, too, had forgotten John, it dawning on her that for four days in London she had not listened to the news or read a paper. This had happened to her before. Usually she found she had missed nothing and what news there was was fresh and interesting.

She had hardly thought of Hugh since visiting his flat. Now, skipping through the *Guardian*, it seemed silly to have bothered to snatch him a pair of shoes. Any man in his senses would have long since left and be far away. He had no real need of the money. A man ingenious enough to keep a cache under the communal carpet of a house full of flats would be clever enough to have moved on. The probability was there and as the train moved out into open country she hoped it was a certainty.

Matilda laid *Harper's* down. Its contents were a catalogue of the shops she had visited. The train, gathering speed, rocked along by the Kennet and Avon canal. Harrods, Fortnum's, Habitat and Liberty's seemed to her more like museums than places where persons like herself shopped. She was glad she had sent her children presents and that from a flower shop in Knightsbridge she had arranged for an exotic fern to be delivered to John with a note of thanks. She would write an apology too. A group of geese crossing a farmyard seen from the train made her feel intensely anxious. If Hugh had left would Gus be starving when she got back? Normally if she went away she would ask Mr Jones to keep an eye on Gus, but Hugh did not know Mr Jones and would have left Gus to his own devices. Nervously, as though the action would make the train go faster, she felt in her bag for the keys of her car. For the rest of the journey she held them in her hand.

Anxiety bunched her stomach. She shook her head when the attendant came down the corridor calling "First Lunch," then "Second Lunch," then "Coffee, Tea, Ices." All she could think of was Gus starving. She had shown Hugh the maize bin. Perhaps he would have gone off leaving a large basin of maize and a bucket of water. If he had let Gus out to fend for himself the neighbourhood fox would have killed him.

Then again perhaps Hugh was still there. He had food for some days. All he was short of was milk. She had made him promise to be careful, to keep quiet, to keep hidden. She wondered how she had got herself into this situation, it was lunatic. Obviously, she thought, clutching the car keys, by now something would have happened to alert the police. The dog would have barked, Hugh would have been seen, arrested after a chase, be "helping the police with their enquiries". Why had she not read the papers or listened to the news?

Of course John was joking when he said he was meeting the Matricide in Prague. He read the papers, would have taken it for granted she did too, would have made his joke. Oh God, thought Matilda, he must think I'm mad. Perhaps I am. It's high time I replanned my picnic or I shall end my days in a bin. Too boring for Louise, Mark, Anabel and Claud. I care for them enough not to inflict that on them. The car keys bit into her palm.

She made an effort towards calm and how to react to the police when they told her they had found Hugh. It would be best to be flustered, astonished, indignant. Then, remembering Hugh's shoes were in her suitcase, she thought, how incriminating, I must throw them out of the window, and stood up to reach for her case on the rack, when she noticed the train slowing down. She had reached her destination.

134

TWENTY-THREE

The car was where she had left it, exactly the same, just a bit more dusty. Somebody had written in the dirt on the back windows:

The driver of this car is a sex maniac.

Matilda put the key in the lock. The car was airless. She opened the windows, starting the engine, letting it idle. The palm of her hand felt sore from clutching the keys. As the engine livened she thought she would never know whether those hints dropped about Tom were true. As she drove out of the station yard she told herself she didn't care whether he had been a part-time spy, slept around or been a bugger. It made no difference now.

Driving through the town she saw faces light up with laughter as people read the message on the back window. It's great to look respectable, she thought. Then she thought it must even soften the hearts of the police who would be waiting for her. If Hugh has any gratitude he will have broken a window to make it look like a break-in, messed things up a bit, not too much, just enough.

She stopped to buy milk, then drove fast along the road bordered by bristly cornfields waiting for the plough, pheasants gleaming in the stubble. She felt hot and sticky after the train, looked forward to changing into old clothes. It felt warm enough to swim, make a trip to the sea. As soon as she had dealt with the police she would go.

In the three miles of lanes from the main road to her cottage, late holidaymakers were sticking firmly to the middle of the road, determined not to scratch their paint against the tall banks of this alien countryside. Their care was alarming to Matilda, used to judging the width by a whisker.

She opened the gate, drove into the garage. She switched off the engine. Silence, then a loud honk and the slap of Gus's feet as he came to meet her.

"So you are all right my handsome, my gorgeous brute." Gus flapped his wings, excreted.

"All alone?" She stroked his neck. Gus honked louder, walked slightly ahead towards the back door. Matilda listened. Not a soul about, no Panda car, no surprises. She felt a sense of loss. Hugh had gone just as she had thought he would, as she had hoped he would.

My Christ, Matilda said to herself, what a fake I am. I am sadly disappointed. What shall I do with his shoes and his money? He might have waited, might have trusted me.

Crossly she felt for the key under the scraper and opened the door. The house was orderly and empty, as empty as when she had closed the door and set off for her picnic.

"Damn, blast and to hell with that barbecue," she said to Gus, who craned his neck in at the door, blue eyes meeting hers. "That bloody girl Vanessa and her Bobby."

"I wasn't expecting you back so soon." Hugh, followed by Folly, walked in past Gus. "Hullo there." He bent and kissed her cheek. Matilda burst into tears.

"What's up?" Hugh stood back while Folly leapt up, wagging her tail in ecstasy, scratching Matilda's London clothes. "What are the tears for?"

"I was expecting the police to be waiting for me. I was all ready."

"All keyed up?"

"Yes."

"No police, sorry. Were you hoping?"

"I thought you'd gone."

"Sorry, I haven't."

"I brought your money and a pair of shoes."

"Oh good, I need shoes. Well done."

"But I absolutely felt you'd be gone or that they would have caught you. I saw it all in my mind."

"So you're disappointed."

"God, no, I'm—" Matilda pretended to herself she did not know what she was feeling.

"Don't tell me you're pleased."

"Very," Matilda whispered. "Very pleased."

"Ah." Hugh took her face in his hands and gently kissed her mouth. "Nice to see you back, sex maniac."

Matilda giggled. "Some naughty child."

"Did you have a good time?" Hugh was filling the kettle,

putting out cups while Matilda, in her London clothes, watched him.

"Not really. No. I had good meals, went round the shops, saw people—"

"Friends?"

"They used to be friends."

"Not any more?"

"One suggested Tom was a bugger, another that she'd slept with him and the friend I was staying with had the nerve to hint that Tom was a spy."

Hugh laughed. "Strong or weak? India or China?" He held a tea-spoon in one hand, a caddy in the other.

"Strong Indian."

Hugh made the tea.

"It's been pretty boring here without you. If it hadn't been for Mr Jones I might have left."

"Have you met him? Oh my!"

"Yes. Day after you left. He came to tell you he'd seen a UFO. He and I play chess."

Matilda kicked off her shoes, sat at the kitchen table.

"He used to play with Tom."

"So he says."

"Has he told anybody you are here? Who does he think you are?"

"He says he never sees anybody except you as they think he is barmy. I like him. He plays a very odd game."

"Tom said he cheated."

Matilda took from her bag the envelopes, handing them to Hugh. "What made you think of hiding it in such a public place?"

"My brother and I used to dream up places, have competitions between ourselves when we were children."

"The Major with the nose?"

"Yes. Life was simpler then. We trusted each other. It was like Mr Jones. He trusts me. I trust him."

"When did he see the UFO?"

"Day you left. He's coming presently for a game and supper."

"It's not safe."

"I can't tell him not to come. It would upset him."

"A secret between two people is a secret, but not between three. More than three, I daresay. He's really crazy."

"No, no," said Hugh comfortably. "He is eccentric. He likes to talk, he's lonely."

Matilda groaned, put down her cup and went up to have a bath, running the water very deep, almost hotter than she could bear, to wash away insinuations about Tom. She came down to find Hugh and Mr Jones lying on the grass, chatting in the dark.

"Mr Jones, Huw, how nice."

Mr Jones scrambled to his feet, short, square with his beard grey on the chin, brown at the sides, his black eyes observant and bright.

"I brought a bottle with me." Mr Jones held Matilda's hand between both of his, squeezing it reassuringly before letting it go.

"Oh, how kind." She tried to enthuse.

"Not dandelion, whisky." Mr Jones smiled shyly. "From the pub."

"I'll fetch some glasses." Hugh went into the house.

"How was London?" Mr Jones asked politely.

"So, so."

"Nice to get home then?"

"Yes."

"I was delighted to find Hugh here when I came to see you. I would have been disappointed to find the house empty."

Hugh came out carrying a tray with water and glasses. Mr Jones ignored him. "It is important to help Hugh."

"Help? In what way?"

"Oh, give him a lift." Mr Jones reached out to take a glass from Hugh and passed it to Matilda. "I am interested in the extreme."

"What do you mean?"

Mr Jones took the glass Hugh offered. "Just a little water. It's extreme to kill your mother." He sipped his drink, eyes downcast.

Matilda couldn't see Hugh's face. She let out her breath. "You sly old boots."

Mr Jones swallowed a gulp of whisky. "I am neither sly nor mad. I listen to the radio and read the papers. I mind my own business. You should know that, Matilda. Hugh knows it."

"After all these years I certainly should."

Mr Jones looked gravely at Hugh then at Matilda. "It seemed to me no business of mine to inform on your visitor and Tom never informed on me so fair dos, I thought, finding Hugh Warner here, fair dos."

"We, I mean I, never believed—" Matilda hesitated.

"Never believed in the UFOs?"

"Well, not really."

"Just as well, nobody else does, so in return I do not believe in the Matricide. You *cannot*," Mr Jones leaned forward to put a hand on Matilda's knee, "you cannot believe all you read in the papers or hear on the radio, that's a fact."

"It is."

"Mind you," Mr Jones laughed, "I don't suppose he ever told you."

"He didn't. I only found out after his death."

"Well then, you know now. Sorry."

"For the last few days almost everyone I've met has been hinting at a Tom I didn't know. I thought that was spiteful London but now you do it too." Matilda paused. "He hid things from me."

"Not telling is not necessarily hiding. He knew and I knew if he upset me about the UFOs I'd take umbrage. I would have stopped him, so he said nothing, that's all." Mr Jones finished his whisky, put his glass down on the grass and sprang to his feet without using his hands.

"We'll play chess another day," he said to Hugh, shook Matilda's hand and walked off jauntily.

"Well!" Matilda sat back on the grass, stretching her legs, "I'm blowed! What a simpleton I've been. It never dawned on me he and Tom were partners."

"You look shocked." Hugh gathered Folly into his arms. "You must have had an inkling."

"None. It was after Tom's death I found—" She hesitated.

"Evidence." Hugh was smiling, his teeth foxy. "Pot and heroin."

"You've been prying."

"Surely you didn't expect me not to?"

"Rather ungentlemanly." Matilda's voice was tart. Then she giggled. "What did you find?"

"Heroin. I flushed it away. What did you do with the pot?"

"Smoked it."

"All of it?"

"No."

"Where is it?"

"In the bank."

"And you say under a stair carpet is imaginative."

"I didn't have much left. I packed it into a silver cigarette box of my grandfather's and left it for Claud. He likes it."

"How much did you use?"

"Don't know. It lasted some months after Tom—" She sat up suddenly. "D'you think Tom really had his heart attack in the rue Jacob or d'you think it was in Louise's bed? She lives just round the corner, she could have pushed him out."

"Don't be vile," Hugh shouted at her. "Don't imagine worse than you need. He was probably on his way to see her." He was very angry.

"Yes, I expect you are right. One thinks such dreadful thoughts. That's why I smoked pot. The hallucinations are mostly nice."

Hugh refilled her glass, put it in her hand. "Tell me about Louise."

Matilda did not look at him. She sat, the glass in one hand and with the other hand stroking Gus, who had come to stand beside her.

"She was our first child, a love child. Tom was crazy about her. I was pregnant when we married. I don't like babies much. I prefer animals." Gus sank down beside her, his neck twisted, blue eye looking up at her. "Tom looked after the baby better than I did. He changed her nappies, washed her, fed her, had her in bed when she cried, cuddled her, was marvellous really. She adored him. It was always Tom she loved, not me. I suppose in the event they were so close nappy changing evolved into fucking. I should not have been surprised."

Hugh said nothing, watching her face, as did the gander.

"I loved Tom," she said quietly. "They didn't see me when I found them in my bed, well, our bed I suppose. I went for a walk and had a think. I couldn't stop loving Tom. I loved Louise, not as much as Claud but I did love her, so I decided half Tom was better than no Tom. I never told him I knew."

"Go on."

"I thought when Louise married it would stop."

"Did it?"

"No it did not." She flushed. "It became more so. Tom brought home lots of new bedtime tricks. I pretended I didn't notice." She glanced at Hugh. "I enjoyed them. I felt a bit funny learning new aspects of sex from my daughter but it's true, I liked it." She grinned at Hugh. "I tell you everything, don't I?"

Hugh felt he had had enough of Louise, that it was better to leave Louise while she was tasting good. "Tell me about Jones. Have you slept with him?"

"Does he say I have?"

"No, but I wasn't sure."

"I haven't. He wanted to and there was a time when I might have. He is such a contrast to Tom, all that hair and short legs, but Anabel – oh!" Matilda gave a shriek of laughter which she tried to stifle, putting her hand across her mouth.

"Anabel?" Hugh probed.

Tears of laughter oozing from the corners of her eyes, Matilda gasped. "It's so unkind to laugh. Anabel had come. It was after Tom had been dead some time, a year perhaps. Mr Jones was being helpful, so kind, weeding the garden. I'd let it go dreadfully. Anabel was with me in the kitchen. She'd just said in an arrogant, bossy voice, 'Ma, you should brace up. What you need is sex. It's very bad to stop suddenly and give it up altogether. You've tried pot,' she said – I don't know how she knew – 'you've tried pot and it doesn't do anything for you, you must have sex. Why not,' said Anabel, fixing me with those great brown eyes, 'have old Jones? Do him a favour. You know he pines for you.' " Matilda wiped the tears with her finger. "We looked at him. He was crouching there wearing wide khaki shorts and his balls were hanging down over the carrot leaves. Oh!" Matilda's eyes filled again. "I've never been so close to that girl. She said, 'They look like nutbags you hang out for the tits. Sorry I spoke.' Poor girl. She laughed until she threw up and Mr Jones came in and made us a resuscitating cuppa. He thought we were crying over Tom. That was the last time she came here. I saw her in London. She came into The Connaught looking lovely with the most beautiful man. John, Sir Piers to be, knew him. She wasn't expecting to see me. She carried it off rather well."

"You didn't know she was in London?"

"No. She had not wanted to see me. I might have asked her to visit me. It's a risk." Matilda shook her head. "Poor Mr Jones." Hugh felt it safer to leave Anabel sick with laughter.

"So Mr Jones' UFOs?"

"Why are you changing the subject?"

"That's the art of conversation – edge. Did you know about the UFOs, what they were?"

"Not until I found the drugs after Tom's death. While he was alive it all went on under my nose so . . ." She seemed unwilling even now to say more.

"So?" Hugh pressed.

"So if he was a smuggler and I didn't know, it may well be true that he slept with Lalage as well as Louise and that he was one of the next-honours-list Sir Piers's spies. But I cannot see him as a bugger, as Anne suggests."

"Would you have loved him less?"

"No. I loved him. If you need proof there's Louise. No divorce."

"You couldn't cite your own daughter."

"I don't see why not. I thought of doing it but it wouldn't have altered anything. Louise is married to a man I like, it would have broken him, whereas you—"

"Whereas I, who have killed my mother, can understand, is that it?"

"I suppose so."

"Tom and Louise didn't kill anything or anybody."

"How d'you know?"

"What are you suggesting now?"

"Louise's second child is abnormally like Tom."

"You repellent woman! It's well known children take after their grandparents. Louise would never have let herself—"

"Conceive her father's child?"

"That's what I mean."

"You don't know Louise."

"She sounds very like you." Hugh's voice expressed disgust.

"She's very like me, very like indeed. Tom always said so." Matilda laughed. Hugh joined in the infection.

"The Egyptians, the Pharoahs." Matilda grinned at Hugh. "If they did it, why not Tom and Louise?"

Hugh left the question unanswered, setting himself to opening the envelopes and counting the money.

"How much?" Matilda watched him.

"Quite a lot. Enough to get away. When my brother gets back, if he ever does, he will find the cache gone. He'll know."

"But he won't tell."

"Money is funny stuff, it does things to people. If he is needing a couple of thousand and it's gone, he may well be irked. So—"

"So you'd better go."

"Yes,"

"How?"

"Like everyone else – train and plane on a busy day. Passport Control are very pushed, all those faces just become a blur."

"Why not a boat? One of the UFOs?"

"That has stopped. I wouldn't involve him anyway. I like him."

"What about me? I'm involved."

"Like you say, you're a dead woman."

"And you don't like me. Repellent, you said. Evil."

"Truthful. Truth may be a laughing matter but it is quite refreshing. Shall you miss me?"

"I shall plan my picnic." She would not answer directly. "You can stay as long as you like," she added quickly.

"What about Gus."

"I love him."

"That's true, an uncomplex love to you, easy, but the poor bird's so twisted he kills a goose when put with one."

Matilda wasn't listening to him. She tapped her teeth with her empty glass.

"John, Sir Piers to be, was in this somewhere. I believe he was in on the smuggling thing. I think he and Tom worked together or Tom worked for him. I had the impression in London that he was trying to find out if I knew. No, that's not right; I have the impression now. He said he was meeting you in Prague."

"What did you say?"

"I pretended to believe him, played along. I didn't exactly want to tell him you were here. He's sinister."

"Maybe my brother is one of his minions infiltrating the Guerillas or some ploy of that kind. They train in Prague."

Matilda stood up suddenly, startling Folly. "All I really mind," she said bitterly, "is being left out. I feel such a fool left out of the *fun*."

"Hurt pride."

"Of course my pride's hurt, battered."

Hugh said nothing, finding no word of comfort.

Matilda lay in bed that night hugging the bedclothes, full of suspicions. The annihilation of her pride was complete.

TWENTY-FOUR

Equally perturbed, for he had no reason to hurt her, Hugh woke Mr Jones in his bungalow, inviting himself in for a drink. Pleased to be needed, the lonely man arose, wrapped an old kimono round his hairy person, took the whisky from its cupboard, found glasses and set up the chessboard.

"Your mind is not on the game," he presently said, checkmating Hugh too easily.

"I have hurt Matilda."

"She is vulnerable."

"How did her husband manage?"

"He had the knack. She is not all that bright."

"Bright?"

"That is what I said. She is young for her age, she believes what she wishes to, always deludes herself."

"I think she is getting over it."

"A pity for her."

"Why?"

"Well," Mr Jones looked uneasy, "it is far better for her to remember Tom as she liked to have him."

"You are ambiguous."

"Tom had her caged where he wanted her. She never knew he was a rogue, dishonest you might say, but there you are, she loved him."

"She loves that goose."

"It's the same thing. Her gander is a fantasy, so was her husband, but she was satisfied, thought they'd live and die together. It was tommy rot, romantic. Tom would not have killed himself before he got old to save people trouble. My God, he would not. No, no, he would have had Louise, Mark, Anabel and Claud belting round waiting on him in his invalid chair."

"And Matilda?"

"He would have let her die first, worked her to death and made her enjoy it."

144

"It sounds just as well for Matilda he died in Paris."

"I don't think so." Mr Jones yawned and scratched his hairy chest. "She is finding out more about him, liking him less, getting disillusioned, it is a pity."

"She will find a *modus vivendi*."

"Not Matilda. Whatever anyone does she will remain what she is. She and the gander are well suited."

"I think she will kill herself. She should have some fun first though, take a lover, go abroad—"

"She has no wish to go abroad. She has the goose."

"Gander."

"Okay. Now what did you wake me up for in truth?" Hugh laughed.

"Can you, if I give you the money, get me some foreign currency?"

"Sure, of course I can." Mr Jones did not add that he had a trunkful of German marks and Swiss francs as he did not think Hugh would believe him. "How much have you got?"

"A thousand."

"Bring it to me tomorrow. Do you want to go over in the UFO? Nice boat. It's in the harbour."

"No. I shall go from London Airport, it's the most crowded."

"Very good, you do that. That is how your murdered mother would travel."

Hugh answered shortly, "There is no need to harp."

"Takes all sorts. Louise, Mark, Anabel and Claud would not kill their mother, only want to."

"Poor Matilda."

"She has the goose." Mr Jones had begun to look sleepy. Hugh got up.

"I will bring the money tomorrow in cash."

"I will have the currency ready for you in a few days."

I bet he has it stashed around the bungalow thought Hugh. He said goodnight and walked back to the cottage.

Gus, recognising his step, gave a token honk from the scullery. As he climbed the stairs Hugh heard Matilda's snores. By morning, he thought, she will have forgotten her unease, have buried the discoveries about Tom in her unconscious.

He stood in the dark, looking out of his window at the moonlit countryside, thinking of his mother, remembering her face looking up at him in terror and hearing her voice. "Oh Hugh, quick, *please*." Her eyes large, stone grey, fringed with, for an old woman, ridiculously long lashes, haunted him. He recollected how, as a boy at school, homesick, unable to sleep, he had tried to bring her face and voice to mind for comfort in the alien environment of his dormitory. He had had trouble in those days to see her clearly; now he both saw her and heard her voice. "Oh Hugh, quick, *please*." She would travel with him whether he willed it or not.

TWENTY-FIVE

Hugh made his arrangements without consulting Matilda. While she was shopping he tried on Tom's clothes, looking at himself in the glass, wearing various garments. Tom's taste in dress was unlike his own. He felt unnatural in most of the clothes. From a store of trousers, jeans, suits, shirts, jerseys, he made a final choice of pale corduroy trousers, a tweed jacket, red socks. He hesitated whether to wear a polo neck jersey or a shirt, settling for the shirt as more respectable. He put aside, for packing, jeans, T-shirts, spare pants, a shirt or two, swimming trunks and sweaters. Ranging round the house he found several pairs of black glasses.

He dressed himself and waited for Matilda, listening for her car, standing out of sight in the hall. When the car drew up Gus honked from the back door and slapped his feet as he ran to meet her. Listening to her voice greeting the bird Hugh thought she sounded younger, happier, altogether more cheerful and full of confidence.

She dumped her parcels on the kitchen table. "Wait, Gus, wait," she said to the bird. "I'll get you some maize." She kicked off her espadrilles. Her feet were barely audible on the stone floor. "Here," she said, "here, Gus, my love, eat this." She put the bowl on the step and straightened up. Catching sight of Hugh in the doorway she gasped.

"Hullo," she said, "were you looking for me?" Hugh came forward a step. "Or my husband?" Matilda's voice tightened. "He's around somewhere, I'll call him." She raised her voice and called loudly, "Tom. Darling? There's a man here to see you—" She edged towards the telephone.

"Matilda." Hugh stepped forward. "It's me, don't be frightened."

"Oh!" Matilda whispered. "My God, you scared me. I nearly wet my knickers. How d'you do it? You've changed yourself completely. I thought you were the police." She sat down abruptly.

147

"It's good, isn't it?" Hugh turned around so that she could see him. "What do you think?"

"Those trousers were Mark's."

"Not Tom's?"

"No, and the jacket was Claud's until he took to wearing suede. Where did you find the glasses?"

"In the hall cupboard."

"Those were Anabel's when enormous lenses were in fashion. They make your nose quite small. What's this in aid of?"

"I want to get out. I'm getting claustrophobia. I feel like taking you out to lunch and a swim. What do you say?"

"Risky."

"I have to start some time. Come on, it will give me confidence if I'm with you."

"We can't start off together, nobody knows you are here."

"Very well. I'll go through the copse and meet you at the bus stop."

"I must change my clothes, get my bathing things. I don't think you should risk it."

"Come on, Matilda, try."

"Wait a minute then."

Matilda went upstairs and snatched up a cardigan, put on a clean shirt, combed her hair, excited.

"Okay, I'm ready."

"Give me ten minutes' start." Hugh left the house.

Ten minutes gives me time to ring the police. Ten minutes gives me time to make a plan with them. She watched the clock jerk its minute hand. "Ten minutes is a life," she said to Gus as she filled his bowl with maize. "Why does he tempt me with ten minutes?" She locked the back door, put the key under the scraper, went to the car and sat with her eyes on her watch until the ten minutes had passed.

Hugh sat on a stile by the bus stop, Folly beside him. He got in beside Matilda. Folly sat behind.

"First mistake was to bring Folly. She's been seen with me. People think she's mine. You mustn't do that again."

"Right, I won't."

"You shouldn't have given me ten minutes. I might have phoned the police."

"But you didn't?"

"No, but please don't do it again. I thought of doing it."

Hugh laughed. "There are two Matildas, one who phones the

police and one who is kind and loves Gus. For all I know there are many more; those are just the two I've met."

"How many of you?"

"Count."

"There's you hunted, about to go out with the tide. There's you with Folly. There's you with Gus. There's you with me. There's you—"

"Killing my mother."

"I wasn't going to say that."

"You were. Be honest, stay honest. We are near death, both of us."

"All right, there's you killing your mother. End of conversation."

Angrily, Matilda trod on the accelerator and drove fast on the main road.

"Don't drive so fast, there's a Panda car behind you."

Matilda slowed, letting the police car overtake them. "I'm frightened every time I see them. I was brought up to like them."

"So was I." Hugh looked at her profile. "Where's the best place to eat?"

"We'd better go somewhere quiet."

"No, I want a busy place. I don't want a quiet place, as though I were hiding."

"All right. The best place is the Crab Inn if we can get a table."

"Does it have a bar?"

"Yes."

"Right. Take us there."

Matilda parked the car. They made their way to the restaurant along the crowded street. Hugh held Matilda's arm, liking the feel of her skin, glancing about him at the people.

The Crab Inn was crowded. They agreed to wait for a table.

"Let's sit outside. Can we eat out, it's pleasant."

They were told they could. Hugh ordered drinks, sat facing Matilda who, with the sun in her eyes, screwed up her nose and sneezed.

"I forgot my dark glasses."

"Stay here. I'll get you some. Sit in my place." He did not offer Anabel's glasses.

"I'll come too."

"Wait here. If there's a free table, take it, start ordering. I shan't be long." Hugh loped off up the street. He bought a plain pair of dark glasses for Matilda, guessing at the fit, then went to a travel agency. He enquired the times of trains to London before strolling back to Matilda.

"They are just getting us a table overlooking the harbour."

"Nice." He handed her the dark glasses.

"Thank you." She put them on.

A waiter brought the menu. Hugh asked for the wine list.

"What's good here?"

"They do a delicious smoked trout pâté. The crab's always good. Sometimes they do a lovely goat cheese with garlic, blows your head off."

"We could finish with that. I shall have the trout pâté. What's the steak like today, waiter?"

"Well – sir—"

"Okay, not steak then. I'll have the gigot of lamb, the pâté first and the goat's cheese. What will you have, Matilda?"

"Just the gigot, the cheese and salad."

"And a bottle of No. 17 please." The waiter scribbled on his pad.

"It's a nice place and Folly can sit with us." Hugh smiled across at Matilda who looked at him anxiously. She made a tiny sideways gesture with her thumb. Behind his dark glasses Hugh let his eyes swivel without moving his head. A rather vacuous girl sat at a table with her parents who were stolidly eating their pudding. The girl had finished eating and was idly flipping through the *Express*.

"It says the police have a line on the Matricide, Mummy, and they are charging the dog-eater."

"The what, dear?"

"The Matricide, Mummy, he's been seen in Paris on a barge on the Seine."

"Can't think why they haven't caught the fellow."

"Oh, Daddy, he's clever, grown a beard, it says here, a red beard."

"Have they arrested him, dear?"

"No, Mummy, it says here one of his best friends recognised him."

"Can't be his best friend if he tells the police."

"Oh, Daddy, he'd have to! He did murder his mother after all."

"Bribed I expect."

"Who's bribed?"

"Someone's bribed the police. What the hell do I pay my taxes for, I'd like to know, if they can't catch a simple murderer. Waiter, my bill."

"I don't think he's so simple."

"Don't contradict your father, dear."

"I wish you wouldn't call me 'dear', Mummy. My name is Inez."

"I know, dear, we chose it for you."

"There you go again, *dear*! It's common to say 'dear' all the time. Why can't you call me Inez or 'darling'. 'Darling' is all right."

"So you call your mother common do you? You'll be murdering her next."

"Oh Daddy, I'd never."

"Call me Dad. Dad's common. This is a bloody expensive lunch."

"Poor man, I expect he regrets it now. Such a large nose. Rather an attractive man from the photograph."

"Mummy! Your taste, really!"

"Well, dear, you can be both, dear, attractive *and* a murderer. D'you want to powder your nose before we go to the car?"

"I want to piss." The girl got up, dropping the paper.

"Who's being common now?" Her father tipped the waiter and roared with laughter, his stomach joggling as though it had a life apart. Matilda let out a sigh as the party left. Hugh was choking with laughter.

"How can you laugh?" Then she joined him, enjoying the food and the wine, the pleasure of being taken out to lunch, sitting in the sun.

"I'd never thought of you as attractive to stout matrons." Matilda looked across at Hugh. The sun had caught his nose, turning it red. "If you go on sitting in the sun your nose will peel."

"Mustn't have that. Have you got any sun stuff? I can't afford to draw attention to it."

Matilda fished in her bag, found a tube of Ambre Solaire. "Try that."

Hugh squeezed a blob on to his finger and applied it to his nose. "Thanks." He gestured to the waiter for the bill. "Let's go and swim. Will you take me to your death beach?"

"It's a long walk."

"Our lunches can settle before we swim, then we won't get cramp."

Driving to the cliff, walking down the steep path to the beach, Matilda felt a surge of happiness. She called cheerfully to Folly who raced up and down the path, passing so close to their feet that she nearly tripped them.

"It's a golden afternoon."

Hugh nodded, enjoying the moment, the pretty dog, the sun, the sea. Matilda ran barefoot on the sand at the cliff bottom, racing along to the flat rock she considered hers. They sat in the sun before undressing and Matilda, remembering the young people's barbecue, told Hugh about it.

"There was a girl who kept saying 'super', everything was 'super'. They wanted me to go away so that they could use this rock. If it hadn't been for them I shouldn't have met you. I had my picnic with me, I was going to swim out."

"From here?"

"Yes. See that smooth bit of water? That's the current. It carries you out past the lighthouse. Tom was caught in it once. He was lucky, he was picked up by a boat."

"What was the plan? You've never told me."

"To eat my Brie and rolls, swallow my pills, wash them down with Beaujolais, then I reckon I could just make the water. The current would have done the rest. The tide has to be exactly right."

"Drowned people look disgusting."

"Not like Ophelia?"

"Not one bit. The body bloats."

"I shall be picked up long before I swell up. One of the fishing boats will find me."

"Horrible for them."

"Oh rubbish," said Matilda. "They'll enjoy it, tell their friends about it in the pub. I reckon my carcass is worth lots of rounds of drinks."

"Have you ever seen a dead body?"

"I don't think I have. Let's swim." Hugh ran down the beach into the water and swam.

"Put my foot in it," Matilda said to Folly. "He's seen his mother's. Sit by our clothes, there's a good dog."

Folly wagged humbly and stayed watching anxiously as Matilda walked down to the water.

Matilda swam, watching Hugh's head moving away from her. "Dear God," she said aloud. "I've put ideas into his head, he won't come back, he's gone." She called loudly and waved her arm. "Hugh, come back!" He swam on, his head growing smaller on her horizon. A small wind sprang up, flipping the sea into waves. "Hugh!" Matilda called. "Hugh!" A wave filled her mouth, making her gag.

Matilda was further from the beach than she thought. She swam back, her arms and legs tiring. She could see Folly down by the water's edge, advancing, then retreating from the waves, giving small anxious barks.

"Damn him, damn him, damn him!" Matilda cursed Hugh as she pushed her arms through the water. "Damn him, oh damn him!"

"The wind's getting up." Hugh swam alongside. "Sea's getting quite choppy."

Matilda did not answer. When her feet touched bottom she waded ashore, spitting out the taste of salt, pushing her hair away from her face with wet hands.

"Now what's she on about?" Hugh greeted Folly who jumped and cavorted in the shallows. "Think we'd get drowned, did you, you foolish little creature." He watched Matilda walking up to the rock, reach for her towel, rub her face with it, pressing it against her eyes.

"Lovely that was." He joined her. "This rock's quite hot." He sat down and let the water run down him. Matilda, angry with herself, did not speak rubbing herself dry. "Look the other way. I want to strip," she said tersely.

Hugh, leaning back on his arms, looked out to sea. He could hear her pulling down the bathing dress and the rubbing of the towel. He glanced along the beach.

"Here come our lunchtime neighbours." He looked round at Matilda standing naked beside him, rubbing her hair with the towel. With her arms raised her breasts looked quite girlish. She had a flat stomach.

"Oh Christ! Not them again!" Matilda grabbed her knickers. "I'm used to having this beach to myself. Nobody ever used to come here."

"I bet fat Dad saw your bush, it's very pretty."

"Don't be common." Matilda imitated the girl's voice. "It's common to talk about bushes. I have grey hairs in it."

"Distinguished. I didn't note your wrinkled bottom."

"I'm wrinkled all over. Neck, face, hands, bottom, all wrinkled through to my soul."

"I must be short-sighted."

Matilda struggled into her shirt and jeans. "Put your glasses on, for God's sake. That woman thinks you're attractive in your photographs, she'll recognise you."

"Does it matter?"

"Don't let's give her the pleasure."

"The father and mother are sitting down. The girl's going to swim."

"Let's go. Do get dressed."

"All right." He stood up.

"D'you think they heard me calling?" Matilda was suddenly anxious.

"Did you call?"

"Yes. Didn't you hear? I thought you were going out too far."

"I didn't hear. What did you say?"

"I shouted, 'Hugh, Hugh, come back.' They could have heard."

"Suppose they did?"

"That woman knows you are called Hugh. Do hurry."

"Hurrying would be the stupidest thing. You go ahead if you're nervous."

"All right." Carrying her towel and bathing dress in one hand, her shoes in the other, she started along the beach, taking a line which would bring her close to the family party.

The father lay back, his head on his arms, eyes closed, his stomach a mound above skinny legs. The mother sat upright, glancing about her. The girl carefully oiled her arms and legs. She had rather bony knees.

Matilda, walking silently, strained her ears.

"No, dear, I don't suppose so. I only said it's funny he should be called Hugh, that's what she was calling, dear, she was calling 'Hugh'. I told you. Hush, here she comes."

"Oh Mummy, don't keep saying 'dear', can't you say 'darling' or Inez?"

"That Dereck you are going to marry is supposed to be so democratic. Why should he mind if I talk common? If I want to call you 'dear' I shall. 'Darling' doesn't come naturally to me, you know that. You used to say it was the thing to be common."

"Oh Mummy, that was in Nigel's day."

"I only said it was a funny thing that that man over there who looks like the Matricide should be called Hugh, dear. That's all. It's his name, Hugh Warner, it's been in all the papers."

"Hardly likely he'd be using his own name, is it?" Dad looked up at the sky.

"The *Express* says he's in Paris and has grown a beard." The girl had turned sulky.

"You can't believe all you read in the papers, dear."

"Oh Mummy," the girl almost screamed in desperation. "Must you say 'dear' all the time?"

"Now then, Inez, don't you be rude to your Ma." Dad sat up and glared at his daughter. "We've been 'dear' to each other all our lives and 'dear' we shall stay. We may be common but we are dear to one another and you are dear to us. Eh, Ma, how's that?"

As she pulled on her espadrilles, Matilda listened anxiously.

"It's a very common name." The girl poured oil into her palm and massaged her throat upwards. "Think of all the radio and TV Hughs, Hugh and Huw."

"You contradict everything I say, dear. It's becoming a habit."

"I wasn't contradicting, I just said—"

"Did your paper say what the chap who ate his wife's doggy-woggy is being charged with?" Dad spoke with his eyes shut. Matilda blessed him.

"Eating dogs isn't a chargeable offence. I asked Dereck."

"Your Dereck knows it all."

"Dereck says that bride who vanished from the beach had probably been murdered. That's what Dereck says."

"Beaches aren't all that safe then. Better be careful when you honeymoon on the Costa what's it, Inez girl."

"Oh, Daddy."

"Call me 'Dad' like you always have. I don't like this 'Daddy' bit, it stinks."

"Yes, dear, call your dad 'Dad'. No need to change all of a sudden now you are engaged to Dereck. Call him 'Dad' like always, dear."

"Oh, Mummy," the girl whined in exasperation.

"Just because he works in a solicitor's office and talks posh doesn't mean he knows it all. Call your dad 'Dad', dear."

Matilda, moving away, detected hurt in the mother's voice, then suddenly aggression. "I'm not saying anything against your Dereck, but we all know people can take elocution lessons." Matilda risked a backward glance at Inez's angry mother. "You call us Mum and Dad like you always have. Dear."

Matilda moved on, her heart thumping. She started up the cliff, daring to look back. She was appalled to see Hugh talking to the family party.

"Is he quite crazy?"

Presently they all laughed and Hugh walked on towards her, followed by Folly.

"Are you quite mad?"

"No. The mother accosted me, said I looked like the Matricide, was I often mistaken for him."

"Christ! What did you say?"

"I asked, in my best German accent, who was the Matricide? They told me. I made a joke and we all laughed. That's all."

"They must have heard you talking English at lunch."

"I doubt it. We never raised our voices. I was on the far side of the table. We listened to them, not they to us."

"I pray you are right."

"Don't be so panicky and spoil the afternoon."

"Sorry. It's been lovely." Hugh stood looking down at the beach.

"My mother would have loved this beach. She adored places like this."

"Your *mother*?"

"Just because I killed my mother doesn't mean I don't know what she liked," Hugh said coldly, looking at Matilda with dislike. "I know very well what gave her pleasure – pain, fear."

"Let's get back to the car." Matilda shivered. "I'm afraid. That woman heard me call 'Hugh'. I'm afraid."

"Yes, she mentioned that. I said 'Hugo' was my name. Sounds much the same when shouted. My mother used to call 'Hugh-o'? A sort of yodel."

"You loved your mother?"

"Of course I did."

"I'm afraid."

"That's life. All your claptrap about death is rubbish."

"No, no, it isn't, wasn't."

Hugh walked ahead to the car. His back view expressed annoyance. Matilda cheered up on the way home, and sang as she drove.

> "I paid a shilling to see
> A tattooed Lady
> Ta ta-ta ta-ta ta

I can't remember the words. D'you know them?"

"No."

"I remember, it ends like this—

> On her hips were battleships
> Oh my, but they were fine,"

Matilda sang, "and

> Right down her spine
> Were the King's own guard in line.

Oh, I have it all wrong. I wish I could remember. Joyce Grenfell sang it at a troops' concert in 1939. I don't suppose you were born."

"Not quite. Go on singing."

"I'll try and remember the words. My Pa was in the Territorials. Ma took me to their concert."

"It sounds Edwardian. Go on singing. I like it."

"I forget the words, just as I forget my life, huge chunks of it."

"It will all flash before your eyes out by the lighthouse."

"Maybe. That's something I hadn't thought of. Surely I shall think of something more profound than tattooed ladies?"

"You will think of your lovers, perhaps." Hugh, lolling beside her, thought of her standing naked, arms raised, on the beach. "You must have had plenty."

"No, I didn't. Vague experiments, then I married Tom."

"But surely—"

"I was faithful."

"Prig." Hugh teased. Matilda frowned.

"I was, I promise. No chance of anything else. Tom was a jealous man, he chased other men away. We lived like swans. They mate for life," she said, knowing she lied.

"Swans," Hugh jeered.

"I know, I've found out, haven't I? But I don't suppose I would have been any different if I had known it all."

"But since his death?"

"I'm too old. No one. Well, a glint in Mr Jones's eyes soon doused."

"Well I never." Hugh thought of the tussling Mr Jones in bed. "I daresay he'd put up a creditable performance. Maybe you're not keen though."

"Keen on what?"

"Bed."

"I adore fucking," Matilda said intensely. Hugh raised his eyebrows, looking at her sidelong, full mouth, small chin. She opened the mouth and sang, repeating the words she could remember.

"I paid a shilling to see
A tattooed lady,"

then, breaking into a piercing whistle she turned the car off the main road and drove through the lanes to the cottage.

"It's been a lovely day. Thanks."

"I enjoyed it."

"Here we are. Where's Gus?"

"Can't see him." Hugh gathered up their bathing things. "I'll hang these up."

"Okay. Gus, Gus, where are you? Gus? Sometimes he goes down the river. He always comes back."

"You sure?"

"Yes."

"I have to see Mr Jones. I won't be long."

"Don't let anyone see you."

"Of course not." Hugh went up to his room, took his money from the dressing-table drawer. He counted a hundred pounds in notes, put them in his wallet, then counted the rest. Matilda was in the garden picking vegetables. From time to time she called, "Gus, Gus, come on boy," in a high voice.

"He'll come, he does this sometimes. It's his way of asserting his independence."

"You sure?"

"Yes, quite. Don't be long. I'm hungry."

"Not long—" Hugh walked along the stream, through the copse, followed by Folly, to Mr Jones's bungalow. Mr Jones was sitting in his porch smoking.

"I didn't know you smoked."

"Pot." Mr Jones offered the cigarette to Hugh who drew on it deeply. "Improves the view," Mr Jones said, "makes things twice as clear, if you want clarification."

"I've brought the money." Hugh gave back the cigarette, handed over the envelopes. Mr Jones counted, then said, "Okay, fine. I have francs, dollars, deutschmarks, that do you?"

"Yes, thank you."

"Hold this." He gave Hugh the joint. "Won't be long." He went into the bungalow. Hugh smoked quietly until Mr Jones came back.

"Here you are." He handed Hugh an envelope. "That should keep you going for a while. When are you off?"

"Soon."

"Right. No need to tell me. Does she know?"

"Matilda?"

"Yes."

"I haven't told her. I'm just going to be there one minute, gone the next."

"That's the best way." Mr Jones nodded. "The *Express* says you've been seen in Paris, the *Mirror* says East Berlin, they're always keen on East Berlin, it's not easy to check."

"I shall leave the dog."

"Sure. Something to remember you by."

"She won't want to remember me. It's her husband she remembers."

"That's an illusion." Mr Jones spat, drew on the last dregs of pot. "She's conned herself all her life, that woman."

"She doesn't seem to have had much life. I must go." Hugh stood up quickly. "She's cooking supper. It's getting dark."

"Autumn's here—"

"Yes, nearly."

"Where shall you go?"

"East Berlin."

Mr Jones waved as Hugh left. As he walked away he could hear him chuckling.

The cottage was strangely still. Hugh paused, smelling danger. Matilda was silent. There was no car by the gate but something had gone wrong. Hugh gestured to Folly to run ahead. The dog trotted along the brick path and in at the kitchen door.

Inside the house Matilda made a noise, just a noise barely human. He ran into the house. Matilda looked up at him. "The police—"

Hugh felt his heart constrict, sweat break out, pins and needles in his fingers. "Where? When?"

"They saw him from their car, they tried, one of them went into the water and got wet. There was nothing they could do. His head was bitten off."

"What are you talking about?"

"Gus. He's dead. A fox, they said. A struggle by the river. His body was in the water. Feathers on the bank, they said. He must have put up a fight."

Hugh let out his breath. "Where is he?"

"They took him away. I wouldn't want to see him like that, they said. He pecked one of them once. I thought they were coming for you, but it was Gus. What shall I do?"

Hugh moved, picked up Matilda in his arms and held her close.

"Shut up. Don't speak." He carried her upstairs. She was lighter than she looked. He pulled off her clothes, snapping buttons, yanking her arms out, unzipped her jeans, pulled them off.

"What are you doing?"

"Undressing you."

"Why?"

"Shut up." He kicked off his shoes, tore off his trousers, "Come here, hold on, open your legs—"

"I—"

"You like fucking, you said so, shut up." He put his hand over her mouth. "There, be quiet, just move a bit – there."

Matilda came alive, gasping, struggling, fighting, joining in, holding him, her response sudden, silent. Then she sighed.

"It hurt, it hurt, you raped me."

"I didn't mean to rape you. I meant to console."

"Like your mother," Matilda murmured.

"What?"

"Nothing. It hurt nicely."

"You haven't for so long. It will be better next time." He held her, stroking her back. Outside the room Folly yawned and stretched then, with a sigh, fell asleep. They would remember her dinner in time. She wasn't all that hungry though it was late.

Owls on their silent hunting zoomed over the fields. Holiday-makers drove along the main road, making for the motorway and urban life.

Matilda lay in Hugh's arms. "You will flash before my eyes," she murmured.

"Hush." He kissed her mouth gently.

"I am old enough to be your mother." He kissed her, running his tongue along her teeth as a child rattles railings with a stick.

"A good joke. Sleep now, it's not the moment to say so."

"Would I have liked your mother?"

"I think so. Sleep." He kissed her.

He slid out of bed, dressed, crept downstairs. His wallet was on the kitchen table. He crept up again for his passport and small bag of clothes, stood by Matilda's door listening.

Matilda snored.

Downstairs Hugh fed Folly, scooping dog meat from a tin, watching her wolf it.

"Quick now, have a run." He let her into the garden to pee. "Hurry up." She came in. "Stay now. Take good care of her. Be a good dog. Go to your basket." He pointed to the basket. The dog went to it, sat uneasily, watching as he swallowed a quick sandwich and drank milk. He patted her once. "Lie down, be good. Take care of her."

He let himself out by the kitchen door, closing it gently. If he walked fast he could catch the 11.30 to London. Then who knows, he thought. Who knows where my dollars, deutschmarks and francs will take me. From London I can take the tube to Heathrow, into the world, back to life. Walking fast across country, Hugh thought bitterly of his mother and of Matilda. She always hoped I'd find a woman I could love. Now, he thought, pausing by a gate, leaning his head in his arms, thinking of Matilda, now I can't have her. They shan't find me, not now, not ever, for her sake they must not. He hurried on, across the main road, down a side road to the town, to the station. He was engrossed by Matilda, her body and his joined, smelling her, hearing her, feeling her. He did not hear the squeak of brakes or the yelp as a car driving fast clipped Folly on the head and killed her, tossing her body to the curb. He was so absorbed by Matilda that it had not occurred to him that Folly would leap out of the kitchen window and follow.

I will write from wherever I may be, he thought, thinking aloud as people do under stress. I will tell her everything and she will laugh. It will be good for her to remember me with laughter. She needs laughter.

At the station he bought a ticket to Paddington and fell asleep as the train drew out of the station.

Folly's body was hit by two more cars before she was found by the police, squashed flat. "Poor Mrs Pollyput," said the constable. "First that gander, now this. She isn't in luck exactly."

TWENTY-SIX

Waking, hearing the birds, Matilda stretched, then curled up again. She wanted to prolong her sense of ease. She felt as though each bit of her body was free from the tension which had been there so long. She felt the bed beside her. Hugh had gone. It didn't matter. A wren sang loudly in the garden. He would come back. There would be more. She tried to remember whether it had ever been like that with Tom. It hadn't. Good but not perfect. Hugh was so much younger than she, it couldn't last. He would go away, indeed he must go away otherwise sooner rather than later he would be in prison. She slept a little then woke, thinking of Gus.

No more honking, no more slap of feet, no more throttling noises, no more messes. She felt calm now, her horror and grief over his death had raised her emotions to the pitch which had allowed love. By Gus's death I am complete, she thought. It was pleasant to stretch her legs without disturbing a dog. Since Stub's death she had slept alone. Folly had slept lately with Hugh, she was his dog. Matilda hoped Hugh had fed her during the night. She remembered him leaving. He would have fed her surely. The police had been kind about Gus, nice of them to come and tell her, they might easily have telephoned or done nothing. It was lucky they had not run into Hugh, that he was out when they came.

Matilda remembered the two policemen. She had guessed that Gus lay headless in their Panda car. She had guessed too that one of the policemen would give the body to his wife and that Gus would be roasted and eaten. She was not shocked or angry about this, it seemed natural. She thought again of Hugh and, turning away from the light, thought he must be sleeping deeply after so much – she searched for the right word – expenditure. Yes, a great night of spending. She smiled, pulling the sheet up over her eyes, dozing, conscious of happiness. She must guard it.

At the police station the two constables from the Panda car made their report. The sergeant made notes.

"Okay, just an ordinary night."

"Do we still keep an eye open for the fellow who killed his old mother?"

"Nothing come through to the contrary. That missing bride is more urgent."

"Seems a waste of time."

"Putting the public's back up. Every man with a large nose is feeling awkward," said the younger constable.

"You've got a large nose, Sergeant," ventured his mate.

"I know that. That's why the public has my sympathy for once. The moment I'm in civvies I feel awkward. My wife says people stare."

"They stare because you're such a fine upstanding man, Sergeant, not because of your hooter."

"Enough of that."

"Okay, Sarge, what about the dog, then? What do we do?"

"The goose was last night, wasn't it?"

"Yes."

"You passing her way as you go off duty?"

"No, we aren't."

"Well, pass her way, take her the dog, tell her before you go off duty."

"That's overtime."

"No it isn't." The sergeant wrote up a note. "That's paying for the goose. It's my guess one of you is going to eat it."

"Very well, Sergeant." The two policemen went out.

"Crafty bastard. My Annie says with an old bird, boil it first, then roast it slow and it will taste like a young one. She knows a thing or two. She was brought up on a farm."

"Lot to be said for country lore." The second policeman, who was courting a secretary in the Council Offices, slipped the car into the gear. "Seems stupid though to me."

"What does?"

"We keep the bird and you eat it but the dog, which is much more of a mess, we return."

"You don't license a goose and you can't eat dog."

"They do in China."

"I know that. Let's get it over with. I hate this kind of job. Who is this Mrs Pollyput anyway?"

"They've lived here a long time. He died a few years back. She doesn't mix much. Got grown children. They never come to see her. He ran some sort of travel business from home. Never been any trouble there apart from the odd motoring offence. She doesn't belong to the W.I. or go to church. She's not above the occasional coarse expression. Talks to herself and sings too. It's her time of life, I suppose."

"My mum's having hot flushes."

"There you are then."

"And here we are. You carry the dog and I'll do the talking."

"That isn't fair."

"Isn't it? Afraid of messing your uniform? It's in a sack, isn't it? Hold it well away from you so it won't drip. You carry the dog, you're eating the goose."

"We could share it."

"Oh belt up. I don't fancy it."

Matilda heard a car door slam and, shortly after, a knock on the door. She got out of bed and looked from her window.

"You again? I'm asleep, can't you bugger off?" Her voice rose high.

"Sorry, Mrs Pollyput, but—"

"Wait a minute, I'll come down." She withdrew her head.

"You're right, she is coarse."

"Told you so." They stood patiently.

Matilda's knees trembled as she pulled on Anabel's dressing-gown, ran a comb through her hair. She looked at the clock.

"Christ, it's late. What an oversleeping."

She took a deep breath, put the comb down, pulled the sash of the dressing-gown tight and left the room. Before coming down she looked into Hugh's room, her finger on her lips. It was empty, the bed made.

"Taken Folly out. Please God keep him away while they are here." She ran downstairs and opened the door.

"What is it?"

"Mrs Pollyput, it's—"

"What is it?"

"Is this your dog, Mrs Pollyput? Found her on the main road. Can't have known what hit her."

Matilda said nothing.

"Must have been following somebody, she was nearly in the town."

"Following somebody?"

"That's what the sergeant thinks."

"Who?"

"Who what, Mrs Pollyput?"

"My name is Mrs Poliport."

"Yes, Mrs Poliport."

"Was she seen following somebody? Who would she follow?"

"It was just his idea. We only found her."

"When?"

"Coming off duty we—"

"You were coming on duty when you found my gander."

"Yes Mrs Pollyput, Poliport.

"Yes, she's my dog." Matilda put out a hand to touch the mangled body. "She's cold."

"Er, yes."

"This is an idiot conversation. Where did you say you found her?"

"On the main road by the turning to the station."

"The turning to the station. I see." Matilda was quite still. The policemen stood embarrassed.

"You all right, Mrs Poliport?"

"Would you be?" Matilda started at him. "Give her to me." The younger policeman made a protesting noise.

"Give her to me." Matilda took hold of the body in the sack, holding it close.

"Following somebody."

"Or running away. She may have been frightened. Dogs get scared on roads, Mrs Poliport."

"Yes."

"You all right, Mrs Poliport? Would you like us to make you some tea?"

"No thank you. I must buy some Brie and a bottle of Beaujolais."

"What, Mrs Poliport?"

"Cheese and wine—" Matilda stood staring at them, her face white, "not tea."

"Oh. You sure you're all right? We could—"

"You couldn't do anything. Just bugger off." She turned into the house, shutting the door in their faces. The two men exchanged glances, one of them took off his hat, resettled it on his head. The other straightened his tunic. They turned to go.

Matilda opened the door and shouted, "He'll make very tough eating," and slammed it again. They heard her scream, "*Cannibals!*"

"Phew!"

"Holy Cow!" They drove off.

"Hot flush or no hot flush, she's put me off my dinner. Bugger off, is it? The sergeant can go himself another time."

"Funny her being in bed this time of the morning. She's usually up at dawn, everybody knows that."

"Perhaps she had some fella for the night."

"Don't be daft – at her age?"

"Daresay it was just shock. She hasn't had that dog long, only bought it a licence the other day, she told me. I told her it wasn't yet six months and not to worry."

"Wasted her lolly then."

TWENTY-SEVEN

When her arms began to ache, Matilda put the sack down on the kitchen table. The clock said midday. She went across the room and wound it. She felt dizzy and put out her hand to steady herself against the Rayburn. It was cold. She looked in the firebox. The draught she made opening the stove stirred the embers. As she straightened up she saw the mess on her dressing-gown. She took it off and wrapped it round Folly's body. The rather tarty chiffon and lace garment which had once belonged to Anabel made a neat wrapping. Realising she was naked she went upstairs and ran the bath very deep and hot. She washed thoroughly and shampooed her hair, ducking under the water to rinse it.

She dressed in the jeans and shirt she found on her bedroom floor. There was only the top button left, the others twinkled up from the carpet. She pulled on a sweater, combed her wet hair, put on espadrilles, went back to the bathroom to clean her teeth. As she brushed them she noticed that Hugh's shaving things were gone from the shelf, that his sponge was gone and his toothbrush.

She looked at her reflection in the mirror without recognition.

From the garden shed she fetched fork and spade and dug a deep hole by the rhubarb bed where the ground was soft and free of stones. When it was deep enough she fetched Folly and laid her in the hole, covered it with earth and trod it flat. Her espadrilles were full of grit and she had hurt the sole of her foot, digging. She took off the espadrilles, shook out the grit, then walked awkwardly to the tool shed, carrying the shoes in one hand, the fork and spade in the other. Her hand was not large enough to hold the tools; she dropped the spade with a clatter, bruising her foot. She hung the tools on their hooks and closed the shed door.

"Matilda. I heard. I came to see whether I could help." Mr Jones stood a few yards off.

"Excuse me, I've just had a bath. My hair is wet."

"I heard about Gus and Folly. I wondered—"

"Yes?"

"Is there anything I can do?"

"Do you have a large flat stone?"

"I can bring you a slab from my path, one of the paving stones."

"Could you bring it at once?"

"Yes, of course. You look strange. Shall I make you some tea?"

"Not tea!" Matilda exclaimed harshly.

"I'll get the stone at once."

"Please do."

"I'm sorry."

"Sorry to be rude. It's just—"

"I know. I'll go and get it."

Mr Jones broke into a trot, running towards his bungalow. Matilda thought he looked ridiculous from behind. Short, fat, middle-aged men should not run.

She went back to the house to wash her hands at the sink, cleaning the earth from under her nails with an orange stick. There was a stain on the kitchen table. She wiped it with a wet cloth.

Waiting for Mr Jones, Matilda wandered round the house. Everything was in its place. The spiders were back slung across ceiling corners. She left them alone.

In her room she made the bed, smoothing the stained sheets, pulling up the blankets, puffing up the pillows. She held her breath so that she would not smell what was there, covered the whole with the patchwork bedspread Claud had sent from America. "Pretty." She stroked it. "Sweet Claud."

Hugh's room was empty. She inspected for traces of his occupancy. There were none.

Mr Jones came with a stone slab in his arms.

"Will this do? It's Delabole slate."

"Yes, it will. Thank you."

Together they went to the dog's grave.

"Where shall I put it?"

"Here, across here." Matilda pointed.

Mr Jones laid the stone, rocking it to level the earth.

"Thank you," she said again.

"It's nothing. Can I do anything else?"

"No thank you. I have to go out and shop."

"Could I not do it for you? You should rest."

"No thank you. I'm going for a swim."

Mr Jones stood looking miserably at Matilda.

"I know Hugh has gone."

"Yes."

"He meant you to keep Folly."

"She was his dog. She followed him – naturally."

"He wouldn't have wanted her to."

"I daresay not. I don't think it matters now what he wanted, not any more, not now."

"He would have wanted to leave you happy."

"Don't talk drivel."

"I'm sorry. I – I wanted."

"You *what?*"

"I wanted to tell you I love you, Matilda. I always have. I want to comfort you. I'd like to begin by making you some tea."

"I don't want tea, Mr Jones. It's very kind of you but I don't need comforting. I don't think you do love me, it's just an idea, all in the mind."

"It's not only in my mind, it's in my balls." Mr Jones found himself shouting at Matilda, longing to hit her.

"It makes no odds to me whether your love is up or down, Mr Jones. I'm sorry, I have to go out." Matilda moved towards the house.

"I chose the wrong moment. I thought we could live here in your house or in my bungalow—"

"Oh, fuck your bungalow!"

"All right. I'm sorry. I'll go."

Mr Jones turned and went. Matilda watched him out of sight, fetched her towel and bathing dress from the line, noting that Hugh had even remembered to take his swimming trunks, which had belonged, she thought resentfully, to Tom.

She looked in her bag to see if she had any money. Hugh might have taken that too, but her purse was full. She put it in the beach bag with the towel and the bathing dress, went out, locked the door, put the key under the doorstop, got into the car and drove off to the town.

It was market day so she had trouble finding a place to park the car, finally leaving it on a double yellow line.

She made for the wine shop where she bought a bottle of Beaujolais, then to the baker where she bought rolls. At the delicatessen she persuaded the girl behind the counter who was more than usually busy to butter the rolls while she chose some Brie.

"What d'you want to do that for? A whole crowd of people are waiting," the man who owned the shop hissed at his assistant as she buttered the rolls.

"She had a funny look in her eye. I didn't like to say no."

"Don't let me catch you at it again. Here you are, Madam." He handed the Brie in its paper bag to Matilda. "Glad to be of assistance."

"I don't suppose she'll ask me again, she never has before." The girl watched Matilda leave the shop.

"Did she pay for the butter?"

"Paid for half a pound and only wanted what I used on the rolls. I think she's a nutter."

There was a ticket under the windscreen wiper of the car. Matilda handed it to a passer-by, who examined it, puzzled, then shouted, "Hey!" as she drove away without looking back.

Parking the car at the usual place, she sauntered along the cliffpath, looking down at the sea, which was calm but grey. The beach was empty, the season over. She was glad she had her sweater, wished she was wearing socks. It was chilly and her foot bruised where she had dropped the spade. She sang softly going down the cliff path:

> "I paid a shilling to see
> A tattooed La-a-dy."

Reaching the sand, she kicked off her espadrilles, leaving them to lie, hurrying barefoot to the far end of the beach to the flat rock.

> "And right down her spine
> Were the King's Own Guard in line."

The rock was cold when she sat on it. She shivered, unpacking the rolls and Brie, standing the Beaujolais carefully so that it would not topple over. She felt in the bag for the corkscrew.

"Oh Sod! I've left it behind." She began to weep. "It's got to be there—" She tipped the bag over, shaking it. No corkscrew. A sheet of paper slid to her feet.

Darling Matilda. Hugh's writing, a little blurred by the damp towel. *I love you. I can't impose my life on yours. I must go away. I love you. You are the kind of woman my mother would have loved. You are what I have wanted, what she wanted for me. I thought she knew nothing of love, was old, naïve. Christ, this is an impossible letter to write. Forgive me. Folly will look after*

*you, hook on to her. She belongs to us both, just hook on. Killing
my mother was an accident. She was terrified of mice. Don't laugh.
There was a mouse on the sofa. She cried to me for help. I smashed
at it with the tray as she moved. I've been too embarrassed to tell
anyone. Please don't laugh, though I love your laughter. Hugh.*

Matilda tore the letter, letting the breeze scatter the pieces. She
undressed, pulling on her swimsuit, goose pimples on her legs.
Sitting on the rock she reached in her bag for the pills, spilled
them into her hand. She knocked the neck of the bottle against
the rock, crammed her mouth full of pills, choking them down
with the wine. The jagged glass cut her mouth. She poured in
more pills, more wine.

The tide was just right, on the turn, the sea waiting. Matilda
stood up.

"Folly?" she called, feeling dizzy. "Belongs to us both?" She
fell on her knees, crawling down the beach on all fours. "Gus?"
She retched, keeping the pills down with an effort. "We all belong
to you," she whispered, reaching the water. "I'm coming."

A gull swooped down to snatch a roll from the rock, followed
by others, screaming, fighting, white wings beating, yellow eyes
glinting, beaks snatching.

The sea caught Matilda as she began to swim out. She did not
wish to get her hair wet.

It's late in the year for swimming. She pushed her arms out
mechanically, turning the grey water pink with the blood from
her mouth. A memory came tentatively. She had read or heard
that people shit as they die. In distress she pulled off her swimsuit,
getting her hair wet as she did so. She let the thing drift away.

At least I shall die with my body clean. She swam more slowly
now. I should see my past life flash before my eyes. Her wounded
mouth smiled. A memory which had so long eluded her came
uselessly back. John/Piers in Trafalgar Square, his bowler, his
umbrella. Whose party had he taken her to? Some place in
Bloomsbury. I got drunk, she remembered, swimming very
slowly now, never been drunk before. He had taken her into a
bedroom. She had smelled his hair oil from Trumpers.

She had pushed it out of her mind. "Hugh," she called in the
cold tide, "Hugh, I want to tell you—" John/Piers next honours
list had pushed her on to a bed, pulled up her skirt, hadn't even
pulled off her knickers.

"This will be a new sensation." That voice of his.

"Death, you are new too," she said to the tide.

The fishing boat found the body floating by the lighthouse.

"Looks as though she's laughing," the younger man said.

"Cut her mouth on the rocks," said his father. "Haul it in. Cover it with a bit of tarpaulin, 'tisn't decent, not as though she were young."

"Buggered up a day's fishing, this."

THE CAMOMILE
LAWN

to James Hale

ONE

Helena Cuthbertson picked up the crumpled *Times* by her sleeping husband and went to the flower room to iron it.

When she had suggested they should buy two copies of the paper, so that each could enjoy it in its pristine state, Richard had flared into rage and his accusations of extravagance had gone on for weeks, made worse when she had pointed out that it was her money that paid the paper bill.

Ironing the paper, a self-imposed task, she inclined to regret her period of widowhood after the war when she had read *The Times* whenever she pleased and not had to wait. Replacing the sheets in their proper order, she considered it ironic that any man could take so long reading the leaders and the Hatch, Match and Dispatches and reduce the paper to hopeless disorder. She looked round the flower room; it was far from tidy. Something should be done about it, but not now. Helena let herself into the garden, walked round to the camomile lawn, sat down in a deck chair and settled to read the paper. Richard would sleep for another hour before fussing as to whether he or she should meet the evening train, and to which bedrooms his nephews and nieces should be assigned, as though they did not always decide for themselves. Richard attributed his temper and fussiness to being gassed in the trenches. Turning the pages of the paper, Helena rather wondered. She laid the paper down and, closing her eyes, lifted her face to the sun. There was no good news these days and although Richard had touching faith in Mr Chamberlain it looked as though Calypso, Walter, Polly and Oliver were in for the next bout of gas. Sophy, too, of course. She tended to forget Sophy, so small, so quiet, so young compared with the ebullient others. Helena knew she should make an effort about Sophy. She had never had a child of her own, neither had Richard. Calypso, Walter, Polly and Oliver were Richard's siblings' children. Calypso was the only child of Richard's elder brother John Cuthbertson, a dim country solicitor with a vapidly pretty wife.

Polly and Walter were the children of his younger brother Martin Cuthbertson, a surgeon and rising star, and Oliver only child of Sarah, his elder sister, married to George Anstey, a prominent civil servant.

Richard resented clever Martin's success, felt contempt for John, and was not only rather afraid of his sister Sarah but also jealous. Poor little Sophy was his half-sister's child, an error which had killed the half-sister, leaving Sophy solo. Helena admitted to herself that had she known about Sophy when Richard had pressed her to marry him she would have thought twice. The others were all older and only came for visits, whereas Sophy of necessity was always there, though thank God fairly invisible.

Lying on her stomach along the branch of the Ilex tree overhanging the camomile lawn, Sophy looked down on her aunt. She was trapped until Helena chose to move. She had a foreshortened view of Helena, relaxed, legs apart, cotton dress riding up her thighs, lolling. A perfect view across the lawn to the cliff running down to the cove, and of the path winding along the contours of the coast a few feet from the drop to the sea, calm this hot August day. She wondered whether Oliver would have the Terror Run as he had for the last three summers and whether she would be old enough to join in. The Terror Run was run by moonlight along the path from the headland below the coastguard station. The first year Walter had sprained an ankle and last year Polly had been badly scratched by brambles. Oliver so far held the record. Calypso always came in unscathed, her exquisite face no pinker than usual, her breath only lifting breasts the better for the boys to gaze at. As Sophy watched the coastguard walk along the cliff path, going on duty, she wondered what it would be like to have breasts, what it would be like to be loved as Calypso was loved. Aunt Helena's breasts were packed into a garment called a bust bodice which made Calypso and Polly laugh. They wore Kestos brassières.

The coastguard reached his station. Uncle Richard limped through the French windows saying "Ah, there you are" in a surprised voice, as though his wife never sat on the lawn. Helena pulled down her skirt.

"Would you like some tea?" She wished he would not limp so obviously. There was no need.

"Yes indeed, why not? Shall I ask Betty?"

"It's Betty's day out. I will get it, it's all ready."

Helena sighed and rose to her feet. Above them Sophy edged backwards along the branch to her window.

"I'd get it if it weren't for my leg." Richard Cuthbertson always said this. The leg was somewhere in Flanders, a place he talked about with nervous affection.

"You rest it." Helena always said this. Oliver had once been heard to say: "When I drove through the battlefields of Flanders with Mother the thought of Uncle's leg double-trenched among the beet made me give up sugar with my tea." That Helena had overheard him he was unaware. Calypso had laughed her chuckling laugh.

"Imagine in bed! Poor Helena! I mean, as they, well – as they – there it is, the false one, propped against the wall, as often as not still in his trousers. I couldn't, I simply couldn't."

Oliver and Walter had laughed too and increased their laughter when Calypso had added: "They don't, of course. It was twin beds and now he sleeps in the dressing-room."

When Sophy asked, "Don't what?" Walter had cried: "Sweet innocence of youth", and Sophy had angrily blushed.

As Sophy eased herself over the sill into her room she saw Jack from the post office pop up the path leading to the lawn.

"Telegram, Major, for you." She watched Uncle Richard tear the envelope with his thumb, read, then glare at Jack. "Damn the boy!" he exclaimed, staring at Jack, who retreated a couple of steps and asked: "Any answer, sir?"

"No, no thank you. Damned inconsiderate."

Jack disappeared down the path to his bicycle.

Uncle Richard shouted, "Helena, Helena, I say."

"What is it?" Helena came through the French windows, pulling a trolley. "I thought tea out here would be nice. What is it?" she asked, bringing the trolley up to the deck chair. "I'll get another chair," she added, as her husband sat in the one she had vacated.

"It's Oliver. Has an appointment in Harley Street, isn't arriving until the midnight train. He is inconsiderate. It's inconvenient, means meeting two trains. I ask you."

"Calypso can meet him, she can drive."

"Not my car." Uncle Richard helped himself to a scone. "Any cream?"

"On your left." Helena poured tea. "She can take mine, then." Helena passed her husband his cup. She seldom allowed herself to refer to the fact that not only the car but the house and nearly all their possessions were hers. It was a pity Army pensions were so small, a good thing her first husband had left her well off.

"Oliver has been wounded in Spain. I expect George wants to make sure he is all right."

"George is a fool. Why did he allow the boy to get mixed up with those dagos?"

"I don't suppose Oliver asked, he just went. They are lucky he has come back. The Turnbulls' son has been killed."

"At least he was fighting on the right side."

"Do you mean right or Right?" Helena spread jam on her scone.

"If you are going to start up again with that attitude I refuse to discuss this – this scuffle in Spain. Where is that child Sophy? Should she not be here for tea? Sophy?" He raised his voice to shout as he would have liked to shout at his wife if he had not been afraid of her.

"Coming." Sophy wiped the tear she had spilled in disappointment, combed her hair and called again, "Coming." Perhaps Calypso would let her go to meet Oliver, although it was all too probable that she would be sent to bed long before midnight. That she loved Oliver with all her heart and always would was Sophy's burden.

TWO

Helena met the London train, taking Sophy, who seemed quieter than usual. Sophy was small, ten, and her appearance had a touch of the Orient, not what Richard would call the Tarbrush, but the Orient. Her cheekbones could be called Slav but not her eyes. Helena hoped that she would improve. She had never enquired precisely what and who Richard's half-sister had been up to with or where.

The London train snaked into Penzance. Calypso, Walter and Polly sprang from it with zest, kissing Helena, hugging Sophy and crying, "Well, well, how are you? Isn't this lovely? Isn't this wonderful? What air after London! Let's grab the luggage, find a porter. Where's the car? How's Uncle Richard? How's his leg?" Their anxiety always seemed to be addressed to the artificial limb, which indeed went wrong oftener than the active member.

Calypso was breathtaking. Helena was freshly surprised. At nineteen she was still gangly. Her dreadful red mouth and nails and excess face powder could not spoil her beauty. Walter at eighteen had broadened. He was a dark version of his father and uncle except for his nose, which he had broken when small. Polly, on the other hand, favoured her mother with a square jaw and startling green eyes with long lashes. Her teeth slightly out of kilter, like a false step in a chorus line, gave her smile a particular gaiety. At nineteen there was already beauty.

"Did you hear about Oliver?"

"Oliver is coming on the late train." Helena watched the young people pile into the car. "And nobody is to mention General Franco." She settled herself at the wheel.

"Oh, Aunt Helena, you spoilsport. Here, Sophy, sit on my knee." Calypso clasped Sophy round the waist and kissed the back of her neck. "Nice to see you." She squeezed the child. "Come and meet Olly with me? May I meet him, Aunt?"

"If you like, but Sophy should be in bed."

"Oh, Aunt, just this once."

"She's a growing child, she needs her sleep. She can see Oliver tomorrow."

"Mother talked to Uncle George and he said Oliver had a near miss. The bullet grazed the side of his head." In the back with Polly, Walter leant forward to talk to his aunt, who was driving recklessly. "What do you think of the war, Aunt?"

"Which?" Helena jammed on the brakes to avoid a van. "What your uncle calls 'the scuffle in Spain' or the coming one?"

"The coming one. I shall join the Navy."

"But you are always sick." Polly closed her eyes as Helena increased speed. "Even in a dinghy."

"I shall get into submarines. You can't be sick under water."

"You are too young," said Helena.

"I am eighteen, I've left school."

"What about Oxford?" Helena changed down and set the car up the steep hill out of the town.

"Either it will have been destroyed or it will wait. Besides, I haven't got a place like Oliver. I wonder whether he will go now."

"Uncle George didn't at all like him using his waiting year to fight in Spain. He wanted him to learn German."

"He wouldn't have liked Germany. I was there at Easter. It was vile. All those *Sieg Heils* and *Juden verbotens*. A filthy Brownshirt was rude to me in Munich because I was wearing shorts." Calypso flinched as Helena rasped the gears at the top of the hill.

"Let's not discuss politics or war. This may be our last summer holiday ever." Polly spoke with urgency. "We can't stop it now."

"Your uncle does not think there will be a war. I would rather you did not discuss it in front of him."

"Oh, Aunt, really!" Calypso threw back her head and laughed, then, seeing Helena's face, stopped abruptly.

"He wants the last one all to himself," Polly muttered to Walter, "and Aunt lost her first husband completely not just a leg and an eyeful of gas."

"Here we are." Helena swung the car into the drive, which led to the back of the house and the entrance protected from the prevailing wind. "When you've seen Richard will you choose your rooms?"

"Shall you get full up with evacuees, Aunt?" Walter hefted the suitcases.

"Uncle's leg will prevent that." Polly slid out of the car. "Oh damn, I've laddered my stocking."

"Polly, please—" Helena felt inclined to slap.

"Sorry, sorry, Aunt. Hullo, Uncle Richard, how are you? Father and Mother sent their love."

Polly and Calypso kissed their uncle. Walter held out his hand, too old now to kiss and comment on whether or not his uncle had halitosis.

Waiting for the midnight train, which was late, Calypso shivered as she walked along the platform. She remembered Polly's suggestion that this might be their last holiday. She and her cousins had been coming every summer for ten years, ever since Helena married Richard and bought the house, square and ugly but in a marvellous position.

Every August since she was Sophy's age she had come with Polly, Walter and Oliver to bathe, climb cliffs and over-eat at Helena's expense, treating the house as their own, then vanish like a flock of starlings, leaving the house for Uncle Richard and Helena and, for the whole year, Sophy, who could speak of winter storms and violent seas, of driving rain, wind she could not stand up against and fog. Calypso hugged her cardigan close and hopped from one foot to another. "Come on, train, come on, Oliver." Would he be changed? Would beautiful funny Oliver, who planned all the games, be the same? What had he seen and done in Spain in this war people felt so passionately about?

Oliver stepped stiffly from the train and looked about him. Calypso ran.

"Oliver, darling, how brown you are! You look like Suzanne Lenglen. Does it hurt?" His head looked strange bandaged. Oliver put his arm round her shoulder. It was all exactly the same, nothing changed, same porters, same ticket collector, same cab rank, harbour, water lapping at high tide, tired train.

"Does it hurt?" she repeated.

"No, I can take the dressing off tomorrow. Are you driving? Where's the car?"

"Usual place."

"D'you think there'd be a pub open?"

"It's far too late. Have you taken to drink?"

"Just wanted to delay arriving."

"Why?"

"All the questions."

"There won't be many. Helena says we are not to talk about Spain or the war. How soon will it be, Oliver? How long have we got? They are all in bed by now."

"Could we stop on the cliff before we get to the house?"

"Of course." Calypso, vaguely embarrassed, drove fast through the sleeping town on to the cliff road. "Will this do?" She stopped the car. Oliver got out, walked across the rough ground and stood looking down at the sea. He seemed to have forgotten Calypso, who sat in the car watching him. He did not move so she joined him.

"The Terror Run." She pointed to the cliff path. "Shall we run it this year? Polly says this may be our last holiday."

"May I fuck you? Now, at once? Calypso, I want to marry you." She said nothing. "Well?" Oliver looked down at the sea. "Well, can I?"

"No, darling. I'm a virgin. I'd have a baby. I can't marry you. I want to marry somebody rich, you know that."

"To keep you in the state to which you wish to become accustomed?"

"Yes. I do love you, Oliver, you know that. Besides, we are only nineteen."

"Nineteen!"

"Nineteen is too young for a man to marry. You have to go to Oxford."

"Oxford, Christ—"

"Don't spoil our holiday."

"All right, we will have the Terror Run." He walked back to the car. "God, I'm tired." Calypso got in beside him. "The smell. I can't tell you what it's like."

"What smell?" She started the engine.

"Death."

"Bits of people, like Uncle's leg?"

"Exactly. The poor sod, and we mock him."

"You have changed." She tried to speak lightly.

"I've only come out of my shell, woken up, grown up."

"Here we are." Calypso stopped the car by the house. "I'm so sorry, Oliver."

"Goodnight. Which room am I in?"

"The red room."

"Thanks." Oliver went up the stairs without looking back and into his room. He undressed without putting on the light, pulled on pyjamas, crossed to the window to pull back the curtains, found Sophy.

"Sophy, what are you doing here?"

"Aunt Helena wouldn't let me meet you. Calypso wanted to take me to the station."

"She did?"

"Yes, she suggested it, but Aunt Helena said I must go to bed and could see you in the morning. Are you cross?"

"No. You are cold. Come here." He picked her up. "Let me warm you." He carried the shivering child to his bed. "Let's warm each other. Get in with me."

"Does your head hurt? How did you get shot?"

"No, it doesn't. Lie quiet. Perhaps we can hear the sea."

"Oliver, you are crying." She touched his wet face. He held her close in her Viyella pyjamas. She smelt of soap.

"Just let me cry—" He wept for the horrors in Spain and Calypso's rebuff.

THREE

"May we ask the twins over?" Walter addressed his aunt.

"Of course." Helena glanced fleetingly at her husband's fingers and balding top, which was all she could see behind the outspread *Times*. She watched the fingers tighten their grip. "Ask them to lunch tomorrow or Friday."

"I am out on those days." Richard Cuthbertson doubled up the paper with a sweep of his arms, tearing the top sheet. Helena winced and Walter and Polly exchanged a smile.

"Telephone and ask them." Helena spoke towards Polly without moving her head. "Such nice boys."

"Extraordinary, considering their father. The fellow's a conchie. I hear he's filled the Rectory with Germans. What's he going to get away with next?"

"Actually, the Erstweilers are Austrian. He played the organ quite beautifully on Sunday, even though it needs repairing. It was so nice of him."

"Playing for his supper, that's all. The fellow's a Jew, I hear."

"Presumably that's why they are here." Walter helped himself to more butter than he needed.

Polly reached for the toast. "Are there any young Erstweilers, Aunt?"

"One, in a camp. The Floyers say the Erstweilers are worried stiff."

"Brace him up, do him good. The General says they are splendid places. His friend at the Embassy offered to show him round one when he was over there. Of course he knows it's all propaganda."

"What's propaganda?" Calypso came sleepily into the room. "Forgive me coming down in a dressing-gown, Aunt. Good morning, Uncle."

"Concentration camps." Walter swallowed his toast.

"Father says General Peachum is the most gullible man he's ever come across. Any kedgeree?"

"I ate it." Polly got up from the table.

"All of it?" Calypso whispered.

"There wasn't much. Sorry."

"That's all right. I'll eat an egg. Calypso sat beside her uncle. "I didn't think it worth dressing as I intend spending all day in the sun. Oliver's marvellously brown."

"We are going to ask the Rectory twins to lunch tomorrow," said Walter.

"If they are conchies like their father I won't have them in my house," said Richard aggressively.

"It's Aunt Helena's house, Uncle, and Father says we should all admire people like Mr Floyer. If there had been more like him in 1914 we should all be living in a better world."

"Walter," said Helena quietly. "Stop it. He will wreck *The Times* if you tease like that!" The three young people gave a whoop of laughter. Helena suppressed a smile. Richard Cuthbertson left the room.

"Aunt Helena, he's worse than ever." Calypso laid a hand on her aunt's.

"He doesn't want another war." Helena patted Calypso's hand. "He won't admit it's coming. Here's Oliver. You are up early, that's not like you." Oliver came in through the French windows carrying a towel.

"I've developed new habits, Aunt. Not all of them good. I've been swimming in the cove with the twins. Is there any coffee left for us?"

"Come in, twins, we were talking about you. We were going to ask you to lunch." Polly went to pour coffee. "Don't just stand there."

David and Paul came in shyly, muttering "good morning", "thank you" and "hullo". Tall, with startling yellow hair and brown eyes, indistinguishable, they sat down, their eyes fixed on Calypso, by whom they were fascinated.

"Uncle was suggesting you will be conchies if there's a war." Polly handed them coffee.

"No, no," they said. "Not this war. One should fight for the Jews."

"Two should." Calypso, aware of their eyes, mocked them.

"Two will," said David.

"Two are joining up at the end of the holidays," added Paul.

"Oh," said Walter eagerly, "what in?"

"Air Force," they said.

"Long distance killing." Oliver looked at them. "Heard of Guernica?"

"Of course we have. Picasso."

"Just as awful as close to. I shall go into the Navy as soon as they will take me." Walter spoke eagerly.

"Oh!" cried Helena, rising from the table. "Do stop, children. There may not be a war. It may not happen. All that over again. I can't bear it." She left the room, closing the door.

"Poor Aunt Helena." Oliver buttered his toast. "She will not face the fact that in all of us, even in her, there is the person who is capable of killing, you, you and you." He pointed round the table with his knife. "Every one of us is capable of killing other human beings. Let's have that game for this year. As well as the Terror Run we will have the Killing. What do you say? Draw straws? Not afraid, are you? Let's have a killing, to take any form you choose. We'll include Sophy. That makes seven of us."

"You are mad, Oliver." Calypso was looking excited.

"It's a mad world. Are you on?"

"I'm on." Calypso smiled across the table at Oliver. "I'm on."

Nobody else spoke until Sophy, who had followed Oliver and the twins into the room, said: "What does it matter if there's going to be a war, anyway?"

"Out of the mouths—" said the Floyer boys in a tone of relief and Walter said: "All right, let's make it that the killers kill within a time limit of five years. That should include us all. Sophy doesn't really count."

"But I do. I do count, don't I, Oliver?" Sophy screamed suddenly at Oliver.

"Yes, yes, you count," Oliver said soothingly, not taking his eyes off Calypso. Calypso stared back, remembering the coarseness of his words the night before, her hasty refusal more from habit than inclination. Oliver back from Spain had a new dimension.

FOUR

Richard Cuthbertson smoothed his hair with the ivory brushes Helena had given him when they married, brushing the grey hair along the sides of his head. He laid the brushes in exact alignment with the bottle of hair oil in symmetry with the matching clothes brushes, and glanced as he always did at the photograph of his first wife Diana, posed looking away from him, her arm round her dog, a sensible smooth fox terrier, not one of those rough-haired things one saw nowadays with oblong snouts and trembling legs. He had no dog now that his retriever had died. Helena had objected to the smells when it farted and the hair shed on the carpets. She was happier without a dog. She would not prevent him replacing his old companion but difficulties would be made, hints dropped. Two can play at that game, he thought. "It would be good for Sophy." His eyes travelled past his first wife's photograph – had she really looked like that? – to the group photographs of his fellow officers, a splendid lot, mostly dead. He ran over their names, a familiar litany. They looked so young. Peter a stockbroker now, Hugh a brewer, Bunty secretary to a golf club, Andrew farming, their commanding officer now retired a general, chairman of the local bench of magistrates, Master of Hounds, rich.

"And I live on my wife's money and have one leg." Richard looked closer at the regimental group of 1913, young men without fear. He wiped a tear from his right eye with a fastidious handkerchief, a perpetual tear due to gassing just before the loss of his leg, an embarrassment and a nuisance. He would get a dog, to hell with Helena. He settled his tweed jacket squarely on his shoulders, tweaked his trouser crease into correct line down his artificial leg and turned to leave the room. As he did so he glanced out of the window and caught sight of his nephews and nieces running from the house across the lawn, carrying towels and bathing suits and accompanied by the parson's twins.

"Wait for me!" Sophy's high-pitched scream halted Oliver,

who with Calypso made the tail end of the procession. "Wait,
wait!" Irritating child. He watched Oliver pause and noticed with
a frown that he and Calypso were holding hands. Oliver had taken
off the ridiculous bandage he had worn at breakfast, showing off,
of course. Oliver dropped Calypso's hand and, catching hold of
the child, swung her on to his shoulders to sit astride. The child's
gingham dress flew up and Richard saw that she was wearing no
knickers, bloody little bastard exposing her bum.

"Helena?" Richard shouted, limping downstairs. "Helena,
where are you?"

"Here."

"Helena, I don't often interfere in your department, but this
time I must insist — "

"What?" Helena was in the drawing-room, putting roses in a
bowl he had won at polo before the war. She did not look round.

"That bowl needs cleaning."

"If we polished the silver according to your directions there
wouldn't be a silver mark left. What is it, Richard?"

"That child Sophy is wearing no knickers."

"How on earth do you know?" Anxiety showed in Helena's
eyes.

"I saw Oliver pick her up."

"Is that all?"

"All?" He was nonplussed. "It's indecent. I ask you."

"Richard," Helena laughed, "she's only ten, she never wears
knickers if it's hot. What are you fussing about? She's gone bathing with the others. A little girl of Sophy's age can't be indecent."

Helena's laughter infuriated Richard.

"Your friend the General wants you to ring him." Helena
always referred to the General as "your friend".

"What about, did he say?"

"He's going to put the hounds down, thought you ought to
know as you are on the Hunt committee."

"Good God!"

"He says if it's war it's total. No more hunting."

"Good God! So *he* thinks there will be a war?" Richard was
shaken.

"Yes, dear, he does."

"Helena — " he took the hand she held out to him. "Helena, I
am useless, useless."

"Nonsense, Richard. There will be masses of things for you to
do."

"Such as what?"

"Organisations, ARP, things like that."

"Answering the telephone? I ask you. I'm not a bloody clerk."

"Ring the General. Have a talk with him, he will be in the thick of things."

"I have only one leg."

"You don't answer the telephone with your legs," Helena said brutally. "Now I must get on, if Cook and I are to feed your army of relations."

"What about Sophy's knickers?"

"There's going to be a war. What the hell do Sophy's knickers matter? If you are interested I don't wear knickers in very hot weather. Knickers are a Victorian innovation." Helena picked up the flower scissors, brushed stalk ends into the wastepaper-basket and left the room. Oh, why must I be so awful to Richard? she asked herself. If Anthony had only lost a leg instead of being lost altogether would I be so beastly to him? Getting no answer to her hypothetical question Helena dismissed her first husband, whose bones lay somewhere in France, from her mind, and went to discuss meals in the kitchen. It was amazing what a lot of food Calypso, Walter, Polly and Oliver consumed; not only breakfast, lunch, tea and dinner, but continual snacks from the larder. Remembering the last war she speculated on the return of food rationing, one of the chief topics of conversation among her friends and relations of that time. The shortage of potatoes. The occasion when one of her aunts had had her butter ration stolen on a bus, blown up into an epic, treated as a tragedy almost equal to the loss of a dear one in the trenches. Helena stood in the doorway leading to the kitchen, remembering the telegraph boy bringing the news, "killed in action", and the physical shock in her chest. "Now all's to do again."

"What, Madam?" said Cook.

"Oh, nothing, Cook. I was just thinking. What shall we feed the Major's crowd on?"

"Something filling." Cook said this every August. Helena was horribly aware of the end of the life to which she had grown used, afraid of what a drastic change might do to her uncertain equilibrium. Women entering what is euphemistically called "the change of life" were not famous for making the passage of others' lives pleasant.

I must, she told herself, speak to Mildred, she is a rock, and she smiled at Cook as she thought of Mildred Floyer, barely five feet tall but with the strength required to cope with a High Church parson husband in a parish which was essentially Chapel and Low.

"Poor Mrs Floyer has two sons," she said.

"Coming to lunch, are they?"

"Going to war."

"Then we must see that they get a good lunch," said Cook, who had the talent of living in the moment.

FIVE

"When is the full moon?" Polly, lying on the rocks beside Oliver, watched him watching Calypso swim out from the cove with Walter. Oliver closed his eyes and lay back.

"Thinking of the Run?"

"Yes. Shall we let Sophy do it? She does so want to."

"I don't see why not, if she practises a bit first."

"Will you tell her? It will fill her cup of happiness."

"A full moon ago," said Oliver, "I was on the Ebro." Polly said nothing.

"One of my friends, a Czech, was killed, never made a sound, shot through the jugular. He and his friends burned a priest, made a bonfire and burnt him. What good did that do? The joke was it turned out he was one of us, or had been."

"Joke?"

"Atrocities are jokes, you can't survive otherwise. We all committed atrocities, their side and ours, made this pit, built a fire in it and pushed them in to frizzle."

"You did?"

"I stood by. It comes to the same thing. I don't remember whether I actually pushed anybody in but I think I helped."

"Think?"

"We were all drunk, Polly. If it wasn't wine it was fear or rage or just wanting some action. There's an awful lot of waiting about. To fill the time you burn, rape, pillage."

"Rape?"

"Yes. Well, actually she was more than willing and later I thought, oh God, I may get clap."

"Did you?"

"No, I was lucky. I didn't."

"Just the once?"

"No, sweet, every time I got the chance." Oliver laughed.

"So that's why you say we are all capable of killing. You've changed."

"Who would you like to kill?" Oliver leant on one elbow, looking at Polly stretched beside him, her body nearly as beautiful as Calypso's.

Looking down her nose at the bobbing heads in the cove, Polly said, "I don't think I know anyone I want to kill, but I'd like to have the power to make people suffer," she lied, speaking lightly, for there were times when it would be nice to have Calypso out of the way. "What's your killing game to be?"

"It's just an idea. I must plan it. Look how far out the twins are. They've got Sophy with them."

"They won't drown her. D'you know, Olly, their father was a stretcher-bearer in the war?"

"Jolly brave. He's never talked about it. He's not a war bore."

"Poor Uncle. I hope none of us will become like him."

"The Somme, the Marne, Wipers, the BEF, General Haig, General French, trenches, conchies, war profiteers, yankees, comradeship and what does it produce? Cotton poppies and two minutes' silence. Christ Almighty!"

"I don't feel, somehow," Polly was laughing, "that he'd call you officer material if he heard you now."

"Too true. I'm for the ranks."

"Really? After all that OTC at school?" Polly was intrigued. "I should have thought you'd go straight into the Guards as an officer."

"Not after the International Brigade."

"I suppose not. Was there comradeship there?"

"Lots of comradeship."

"Making bonfires?"

"Yes, yes, yes. Now let's plan the new game. Sophy!" Oliver shouted through cupped hands towards the twins who were swimming to shore, Sophy between them, a hand on each twin's shoulder. "Like to join the Terror Run this year?"

"What?" The child scrambled up the rocks. "What did you say?"

"I said would you like to join the Terror Run this year?"

"Yes, please."

"You'll have to practise."

"I know the path. I know it better than any of you."

"Not in the dark, not by moonlight."

"Yes, I do."

"Well, you must let me see you run it so that I'm sure."

"I'm sure. There's a man with a snake on it. Will you watch the whole way?"

"Yes. We'll watch both ends and the middle and see how you do."

"Oh, thanks, Oliver."

"See what it is to give happiness."

Calypso sat beside the twins, who watched Oliver, who watched the drops of water run down her legs into her groin.

"Will you run?" Polly invited the twins.

"Yes," they said. "When is it?"

"Full moon, whenever that is."

"And the Killing Game?" Calypso looked round. "You both in on that?"

"Yes," they said, surprising the cousins.

"That makes six of us," said Walter.

"Seven," said Sophy. "It's me, too."

"Oh, Sophy, you're too small to kill anyone."

"Oliver said, he said." Sophy looked from face to face, distressed. "Besides, I shall grow up."

"Oh, let her." Calypso wiped the salt water from her arms with fastidious movements. "I think we should include Aunt Helena and Uncle and Betty and Cook and the Rector; make it more of a lottery."

"Not Father," said the twins.

"All right. Aunt and Uncle then, not Betty or Cook."

"Why not? Because they're village, not our class?" Walter jabbed at Oliver. "I thought all you Comrades were classless."

"Far from it," said Oliver, laughing, "as you'd know if you'd been there. No, Betty and Cook might get ideas."

"Above their station?"

"No, you fool. They might easily go full tilt, might take it seriously."

"Go to the police?" Polly grinned.

"Oh, forget it. Just don't include them."

"I thought the whole idea was that it *is* serious." Calypso stared at Oliver maliciously. "Wasn't it?"

"May I do my practice run soon? Will you watch me?" Sophy put her pale face close to Oliver's so that he squinted into her large black eyes. He put up a hand and pushed back her hair, black too like a cat's and silky.

"Puss." He caressed her as he would an animal. Calypso and Polly watched, amused.

"Why not this afternoon? How would that be?" Oliver patted the pale cheek dismissively.

"We shall have to see that she doesn't cheat." Walter stretched his arms to the sky.

"It's so hot." Polly turned over on to her stomach.

"It won't be hot if we line along the top of the cliffs. We will get the breeze. It's Sophy who will get hot." Calypso closed her eyes, lifting her face to the sun. "Is my nose getting red?"

"Put a leaf over it." The twins spoke in chorus.

"Clever. Find me one." Calypso lay with a leaf shading her nose while they all cooked gently on the rocks.

The only flaw in her looks, thought Polly, observing her cousin, was that both sides of her face were symmetrical, her expression masklike. Most people had two sides to a varying degree, good and evil, happy and sad. Walter was particularly varied, as though he had been sat on at birth, and she herself had a slightly bent nose, while Oliver had the trace of a squint.

They lined the cliff that afternoon, Walter and Polly starting Sophy off from the headland under the coastguard station, the twins stationed above the path halfway along the course, Calypso and Oliver waiting at the finish. For most of the course Sophy would be visible, only out of sight where the path ran through dense thorn or at one point just above the sea, where it twisted sharply round high granite boulders.

Up on the cliff that afternoon the twins sat with their backs to the fence which prevented straying cattle from falling over.

"She's off. Walter's unleashed her." They looked down at Sophy leaving Walter at a run to tear along the path.

"I wonder what it will look like from the air."

"We've never flown. D'you think they will let us keep together?"

"Surely they won't separate us?" Paul looked at David aghast.

"It may happen."

"My God, I hope not."

"Death may."

"Not us. We shan't get killed."

"Hi, we've forgotten Sophy. I can't see her."

"She must be among the thorns."

"Or the boulders. She was going lickety spit. You don't really think we can get split up, do you?"

"Father says the authorities are bound to. He may be right. Think of the confusion at school."

The other twin laughed. "Whatever happens we've had fun."

"If you die, I die."

"Oh, gloom! It hasn't started yet. Where the hell is Sophy?"

"She may have hurt herself. We'd better follow her. Remember Walter's ankle."

They scrambled down through the gorse and heather to the path, unusually tall young men, loose-limbed as puppies, their maize-coloured hair flopping over brown eyes fringed with feathery lashes, their looks the more noticeable because duplicated. They brushed their hair back from brows untouched by experience and ambled along the path.

"Where are Walter and Polly?"

"They must have gone back by the short cut."

At the finish Calypso sat with Oliver, holding his hand.

"I tell you what, Olly, even if I won't marry you I'll sleep with you. Have you ever done it?"

"Yes, I have."

"Is it nice?"

"Nice." Oliver looked at Calypso and repeated "nice". How could "nice" be a word applied to Calypso? "I want to have you to myself. I'll wait."

"If there's a war I'll sleep with you before you get killed. That's what maidens did in books and I am a maiden."

"How you carry on about your virginity. Virginity's nothing. You can lose it riding a bicycle."

"I never knew that. I must be careful. I'm going to ride a bicycle in London. Pa says petrol will be rationed."

"And virginity not. How shall you find your rich prince from a bicycle? It's so bourgeois."

"I will find him. If you want something hard enough you get it, and I want a very rich husband, always have."

"Oh, Calypso, don't." Oliver put his arms round her. "Oh, my love, I will get rich, very rich. Then you will marry me."

"What's that?" Calypso drew away from him and sprang up. "Somebody screamed. Sophy."

"Something's wrong." They ran down the path to meet Sophy, who approached them in a rush, hurling herself into Calypso's arms, sobbing wildly.

"What is it? What happened? Are you hurt? What's the matter? Stop it, Sophy, stop it." But Sophy, clinging to Calypso, could not stop. Her sobs turned to screams, her fingers dug painfully into Calypso's neck.

"Sophy, you are hurting." Oliver pulled the child away and smacked her face. "Stop, Sophy. What happened?"

Through white lips the child said, gasping, "Pink, pink snake."

"What?" Oliver stared at the child, her tears splashing white cheeks. "Speak up." But Sophy neither could nor would.

"Did it bite you? She said 'snake'." Calypso looked anxiously at Oliver. Sophy, silent now, said no more.

"Our word, you made good time. What's happened?" The twins came trotting up the cliff path out of breath, flushed.

"She's been frightened, something about a snake. Did you see anything?"

"No," they said. "Let's see if she has been bitten." The twins examined Sophy's legs as she lay across Oliver's lap, giving an occasional exhausted hiccup. "Nothing, not even scratched. Let's see your arms." They examined the child. "Surely you ought to wear knickers," they said, pulling down her skirt.

"Oh, leave her alone. She's been scared by something and she's not going to tell us." Calypso stood above Oliver and the twins. "Come on, Sophy, it's over now, time for tea." Her voice was adult, she held out her hand, Sophy took it, letting go of Oliver.

"Sorry." The child looked round at their kind faces. "I'm sorry."

"You did the run jolly fast," said the twins.

"Record time." Oliver smacked the child's bottom in friendly fashion as he stood up.

"Did I really?"

"Yes, I shall have to look to my laurels."

"Oh, good. I'm even quicker by moonlight." She sprang away from them towards the house.

"Something happened." Oliver watched her go. "I wonder what."

"Well, she's not going to tell." Calypso put a full stop to the incident, feeling that Sophy wished to draw attention to herself.

SIX

On the evening of the Terror Run Helena invited Max Erstweiler
and his wife Monika to supper. They walked with the twins
across the stubble on the top of the cliff.

"So peaceful," Monika said. "A year ago in the country at
harvest time we were full of fear."

"We are full of fear still. But not for ourselves any more."

"I find it worse to be safe and Pauli not, he must follow us.
God will help us and our friends."

"*Gott mit uns?* Don't be ridiculous," Max sneered.

"Father says we must not lose God," said David, walking
beside Monika, "but we already have. We lost him when we
slipped our cartilages playing rugger. We lost the match as well.
We really had prayed."

"How old were you?" Monika smiled.

"Twelve," said Paul, laughing.

"And you dropped him just like that?"

"We've never told Father," said David gravely.

"Your father is a saint," said Max. "I say this in case there are
saints, though personally I doubt it."

"You go to Father's church, you play the organ for him."

"That is the least I can do for your father and mother. Also
you boys are fortunate."

"We are," said the twins, grieving for the Erstweilers' anxiety.
"It will be all right, Monika, you wait and see. We are going to
fight for him."

"How?"

"The Air Force. We are off at the end of the month to join up,
fight for all you people. We will get your son for you."

"In a casket," said Erstweiler bitterly. "They send you a casket.
Our son is a musician, you cannot play the piano in a casket."
The twins fell silent, showing their awkwardness by stiffening
their legs as they walked.

197

"What is this game you play?" Monika felt the hurt in their silence.

"We race along the cliff path. Oliver called it the Terror Run because he is afraid of heights. It is a bit scary in places but even Sophy can do it now. It's an institution. We run by the light of the moon."

"May we watch?"

"Of course. The elders sit on the camomile lawn and gossip while we run."

"And this new game? Did you not say there is another game?" asked Max.

"Yes, a secret, a dare. We are going to draw lots, you and Monika too, if you want."

"Even if we don't know what for?"

"Yes. We know and the cousins and if any of us draws the card we shall know what to do but if you and Monika join in it makes it more exciting for us. There are only three marked cards so it's much better if you and the Major and Mrs Cuthbertson join in. That makes eight blanks."

"And the result is secret?"

"Yes."

"It sounds like life," Max said grimly as he rang the bell in the Cuthbertson porch.

Walter came to the door. "Come in," he said, "come through the house. We've persuaded Aunt to let us dine on the lawn." He led the way. "Look," he said, "isn't it terrific?"

"Ach!" exclaimed Monika. *"So schön."*

The cousins had carried out the dining table and chairs. The table was set with a white cloth on the camomile lawn, the setting sun and the sea a backdrop.

"Isn't this fun?" Calypso came to greet them.

"Lovely," the twins admired, "brilliant idea."

"It was my idea." Calypso led Monika up to her uncle.

"Uncle Richard, this is Monika Erstweiler and Max Erstweiler, who are staying at the Rectory."

"We met briefly in church." Richard limped forward to shake hands. "My wife allows my nephews and nieces a very free rein. May I offer you a drink?"

Helena came out wearing a long dress which gave her dumpy figure dignity. She admired Monika's looks and was struck by Max's charm. "This is a party we have every year," she said. "It may be the last. When the war starts we shall have to black out our windows, show no lights."

"Every year out of doors?"

"Never before, but tonight it seemed safe. It's fun for the children."

"The children are talking of fighting, are they not men?"

"I suppose they are." Helena looked at the twins, at Oliver, at Walter. "Men—" her voice trailed.

"You have a son," Richard broke the silence heartily, "in a camp, I believe. My friend the General says they are doing all these people a power of good."

Max Erstweiler gasped and uttered a word which sounded alien on the lawn above the English channel – *"Unerhört—"*

All the cousins started talking at once and Helena said: "Shall we start dinner? The sun is almost set. Light the candles, somebody. Mrs Erstweiler, will you sit here, and you beside me, Mr Erstweiler."

"What did the fellow say?" Richard hissed at his wife, who had kicked his good shin painfully. "Can't understand his accent."

"It's what you said." Helena spoke from the corner of her mouth.

"Oh, did I drop a brick?"

Helena was already chattering to Max, and the agony passed as they ate and talked while the sun slid into the sea and the light from the candles lit their faces so that eyes shone from mysterious sockets. The girls grew more beautiful and Sophy, sitting still beside Oliver, who held Calypso's hand on his other side under the table, registered the scene in her mind.

When the moon came up like an outrageous balloon they fell silent, watching her rise red, gold then silver into a taffeta sky.

"The moon." Oliver held his glass high.

"And absent friends." Richard rose, steady on his good leg, smiling down at Monika. "Absent friends," he repeated as they all drank.

He can be splendid, thought Helena. I must encourage him and not crush.

"Thank you." Monika smiled at Richard, her eyes wet. He is a sensitive man, she thought, noticing the tear in his eye, and one can't deny these Semites have looks, thought Richard, wiping the tear with his habitual flick.

"Shall we draw lots before or after the Run?" Polly enquired.

"Let's do it now." Calypso let go of Oliver's hand. His was dry, hers growing sticky.

"Uncle Richard, shuffle the pack."

"Very well." He picked up the cards. The Cuthbertsons, the Erstweilers, the nephews and nieces and the twins all drew, Sophy last. "Whoever draws a marked card keeps it secret."

They looked at the cards and threw them back into the bowl.

"That's done," said Oliver. "Now for the Run. Bags I go first."

"Me next," said Calypso. "Will you time us, Uncle Richard?"

"Very well. Got your torches?"

"Yes."

"Right. Same rules, I take it – flash the torch when you start?"

"Yes."

"Off you go, then." Richard settled in a chair beside Monika. The young people moved off.

"Isn't Sophy rather small?" asked Monika.

"She is running with the twins keeping an eye on her. She'll be all right," said Helena.

"And this other game for which we have drawn lots?" asked Max.

"I have no idea. Oliver dreams up something new every year. It's no good asking, they won't tell us."

"So we do not really take part?"

"Possibly, but not consciously." Helena laughed.

"It sounds like a gamble."

"Yes."

"Our son is involved in this sort of game. He was to follow us but the Brownshirts came to the University and took every fourth boy. It is terrible being a mother."

"I have always regretted missing out on that experience." Helena sought to comfort Monika.

"Personally I think you've been spared a lot of bother," said Richard. "Think what the Virgin Mary went through."

Helena burst out laughing. Max looked puzzled and muttered to his wife, *"Herrlicher Humor?"* Before coming to England he had heard much of this English trait and wished to cultivate it himself.

"They have reached the start." Helena pointed. "See their torches."

Across on the headland the Cuthbertsons and Erstweilers could make out the group of young people above the sea, the rocks black and stark, the moon now quite high. Below the cliffs a calm sea and at the top of the cliffs the coastguard station white and functional.

"Isn't it dangerous? I can see no path." Monika was interested.

"They all know it very well." Richard was lighting a pipe. "If I had my leg I would think nothing of it."

Helena guarded her tongue.

"Where is the finish?" Max filled the brief silence.

"Below us, out of sight. We hear them shout when they reach it. I time them. I have my stop watch and my word is final."

"Oliver is starting." Helena pointed. A torch flashed three times and Richard started his watch. They saw Oliver bound down the cliff, running hard along the narrow path which twisted through the bracken and heather, then close to the cliff edge past clumps of thrift and sea campion, through short grass which in spring was full of squills, past gorse still in flower, mixing its sweet smell with the heather.

Oliver ran feeling exhilarating fear. If he ran fast enough he would outstrip terror. He had never let the others know the extent of his fear of heights, of the vertigo which would paralyse him if he looked down. He ran a race against his weakness.

As he doubled and jumped past the rocks he thought briefly of Sophy's snake, then his feet pounded on grass and the scent of Lady's Tresses came sweetly up and he knew it was over.

"*Spiranthes autumnalis,*" he cried, exulting, flashed his torch and sat down panting to wait for Calypso.

Within minutes she had run the course straight into his arms.

"Was I fast, Olly? Shout for Uncle Richard, I have no breath left."

Oliver held her close and they stood face to face, he holding her against him so that he felt the rise and fall of her breasts as her breathing steadied.

"Who is next?"

"Sophy, then twin, twin, Polly and Walter last."

Oliver stroked her hair then ran his hand down her back, holding her close.

"Oliver, what's that?"

"What?"

"This." She touched him.

"Me. My cock."

"Oliver!"

"What is it?"

"It's enormous."

"It's quite ordinary. I've got an erection."

"A *what?*"

"An erection. I want to poke it up you. Have you never seen a man with an erection?"

"No." She turned in his arms and stood with her back to him. His hands covered her breasts.

"So you really are intacta."

"What does that mean?"

"Virgin. I didn't believe you."

"You embarrass me." Calypso leant back against him, covering his hands with her own. "Is it true? Wouldn't it hurt me frightfully?"

"No, you stretch. After all, you must stretch to let a baby's head get out. You know how babies are born, or don't you?"

"Of course I do." Calypso closed her eyes against the moon.

"I love you." He kissed her neck. "I always shall."

"I don't think you will." Sophy arrived beside them, scrambling up the last slope silently. "What time did I take? Flash the torch for me and shout, please."

Calypso raised her voice in a long cry, then said: "Why won't he love me for ever?" But Sophy knew better than to answer when Calypso used that tone of voice. They waited, flashing the torch and shouting up the cliff towards the lawn as Paul, David, Polly and Walter joined them. Then they sat for a while looking at the moon-path on the water.

"Never again," said Polly. "This time next year where shall we all be?"

"Under the sod," Walter grunted.

"Lying in some distant field forever England," misquoted Oliver, "like Uncle's leg. I hate that poem. I prefer the one 'and is there honey still for tea and crumpets with my strumpet'. Three of us had a bowdlerising competition in a ditch a few months ago."

"Who drew spots and who drew blanks?" Sophy, thinking of the new game to distract her mind from Oliver and Calypso, tried to catch them napping.

"That would be telling." Walter rolled her over on the grass. "There were eleven of us, so eight will be innocent and most of the eleven wouldn't know what to do if they did draw a black spot."

"Makes it very exciting. Did you say five years for a time limit,

Oliver? That's rather short for something so important."

"Make it ten," said Oliver grandly, "then Sophy, if she's drawn a spot, can wait till she's twenty."

"The war will be over by then."

"Or we shall be dead. Come on, up, up the cliff. Like a ride on my shoulders, Sophy?"

"No, thank you."

"What will the old people do in the war!" Polly climbed beside the twins.

"Compare it with theirs," said Walter over his shoulder.

"Watch and wait," said the twins, thinking of Pauli Erstweiler trapped in his concentration camp.

"Mourn," said Calypso. "They know how to."

"No doubt we shall learn," said Oliver drily.

"Uncle Richard wants a dog," Sophy exclaimed, apropos of nothing.

"How do you know?"

"He is mourning old Farticus."

"Then we shall find him one. Helena won't be pleased."

"It's about time we stopped always considering Helena," said Polly. "She gave him a pretty hefty kick before dinner."

"He deserved it, he and his General. Down with all Generals, I say."

"And especially Franco."

"That's right."

"It's going to be awkward for the General," said David.

"Why?" asked Polly sharply.

"Because when he was invited to the Nuremberg Rally, and introduced to Hitler by his Nazi friends, he came back to tell us it's all a damn good show which puts a bit of backbone into the youth of the nation. He was full of it last year after Munich."

"The General told my father it would be a good show if the pansy youth of England were put into the Hitler Jugend." Calypso laughed. "That was because he thought all you boys needed a haircut and Oliver's suede shoes got up his nose."

"He's being very patriotic now," said Polly. "I hear he's organising air raid precautions and urging all his tenants to join up."

"Oh, blow," said Walter, "you put me off. When I'm in my submarine it won't be for his sake, not bloody likely."

"It will be for the Pauli Erstweilers of this world, I know." Polly turned to Calypso. "What shall you do?"

"Find a glamorous job where there are lots of rich men."

"I really think she means it," said the twins, laughing. "Won't you comfort the troops?"

"I shall do that, too." Calypso smiled sweetly. "Impartially," she added, looking sidelong at the twins and Walter. Did they too get erections? She must consult with Polly, who knew about sex since she had access to her father's gynaecological books, without if possible betraying her own sexual ignorance.

As they reached the lawn Polly called out: "Did Oliver win, as usual?" but the elders were in the drawing-room, an anxious group talking in low voices. Helena stood in the doorway white-faced.

"It was your father," she said to Walter and Polly. "His hospital is to be evacuated tomorrow."

"War," said Polly. Nobody contradicted her.

The fear in the room was tangible. Monika reached for her husband's hand. Helena found herself exchanging a glance of despair with Max. Looking round at the young people she read on their faces fear mixed with a sexual combustion she was to remember later. Walter's eyes were clouded. Polly stared questioningly at the twins, who held her gaze. Calypso looked up at Oliver.

"Well?"

Sophy tugged at Oliver's hand: "What about the new game?"

"Scrub it." He stared at Calypso, ignoring the child. "We've all drawn marked cards now."

Sophy muttered mutinously. Oliver shook his hand free.

Richard limped into the hall to tap the barometer. "Weather's set fair," he said cheerfully. The tableau melted.

"We should be going," Monika said gently.

The Erstweilers said polite goodbyes. The cousins and the twins went and sat on the lawn, staring out at the sea. Helena called from the house: "Sophy, go to bed. It's long past your bedtime." The child trailed into the house without saying goodnight.

"Shall we try and get through to Mother?" Walter and Polly went to telephone.

"We'd better go." The twins left sadly. "Shall we tell them tonight or wait till the morning?" They considered their parents.

"We've had a good time there." David looked back at the house standing square to the winds. "What an ugly house. I suggest we let them sleep and tell them in the morning," said David, feeling protective towards the innocence of good people. "They are as vulnerable as Sophy."

"Differently." The brothers exchanged a glance, each seeing his concern for their parents mirrored in the other, and their joint fear.

SEVEN

Helena undressed, brushed her hair, cleaned her teeth, rubbed cream into her face, then sat on the edge of her bed listening to Richard going through his familiar routine in the dressing-room.

"Richard."

"Yes, my dear? A good party. Thank you for your trouble."

"It's no trouble."

"Sorry I dropped a brick with those Jews."

"You made up for it. Richard, I don't think I can sleep. Could we talk a bit?"

"What about?" Her husband stood in his shirt and trousers, his braces hanging down at the back.

"The war."

He said violently: "It's another false alarm. There isn't going to be a war."

"The hospitals and doctors are being evacuated and the children too. Martin knows—"

"It's just another exercise. The General says—"

"The General is killing the hounds."

"He hasn't done it yet. Good God, Helena, there won't be a war. Don't be so panicky." Richard's face grew scarlet.

"I can't talk to you." Helena was filled with bile.

"What do you mean?"

"I can't. If you deny what is happening how can I talk to you? All those children will be in it, all the horrors will happen again, only worse. Richard, I can't stand your head-in-the-sand attitude. I'm going to London."

"What on earth for?"

Helena looked at him helplessly, unable to say "To get away from you", which was her uppermost feeling. She said: "To do some shopping."

Richard closed the door of the dressing-room. She heard him get out of his trousers, prop his leg against a chair, hop to the

206

bed, scrabble into it, and the wheeze of the mattress as he lay down.

Oh *God!* Helena changed her clothes, packed a case and left the house. This is the most terrible row we've ever had and nothing said. She carried her case to the car, got in and drove down the hill. When she reached the level road at the bottom of the hill the engine coughed, choked, moaned. She had forgotten to fill up with petrol. She laid her arms across the steering wheel, her head on her arms, and wept with frustration.

In the warmth of the late summer night Oliver and Calypso lay on the scented lawn. Oliver held Calypso's hand, lying on his back with his free arm across his eyes.

"*Now* will you marry me?"

"No, no, no."

"But war changes everything."

"Does it?"

"Of course it does. I must have you if I am to fight."

"You could get a safe job. They say there's no need for so many men in this war. There are to be reserved occupations."

"I've got to fight. I'm committed."

"Who to?"

"Myself, you."

"I'm not asking you to fight. I didn't ask you to rush off to Spain in that silly way. I'm not asking you to fight for the Jews."

"Against Fascism, against the Nazis."

"Oh, that. It's just a tag. Some of them are awfully nice. All that lot we met skiing. I loved that lot in Kitzbühel."

"They liked you, I remember. Did you kiss them?"

"One or two."

"Calypso, look at me. I'm serious. Will you marry me? At least let us be engaged."

"If I've said no once I've said it a hundred times. No. I will comfort you, as they say, but marriage, no. I'd only make you unhappy," Calypso snapped.

"I'd risk that. I'm unhappy already."

"Well, then, you've a taste of what it would be like." Calypso stood up yawning. "I'm so sleepy, Goodnight, Olly."

"I'll hold you to the comfort bit."

"You do that." Calypso drifted into the house.

Oliver rolled over and lay on his face. Above him Sophy edged backwards along the branch, her pyjama trousers rucking round her waist.

"Sophy, were you listening?"

"Yes."

"You shouldn't eavesdrop."

"I happened to be here. I often am."

"Come down. I'll catch you." He held out his arms, catching the child as she jumped.

"There. Let's just sit for a while."

They sat with their backs to the tree, listening to the sea slapping against the rocks.

"It's high tide," she said.

"War tide."

"I'm frightened, are you?"

"Yes, very."

"Worse than the Terror Run?"

"Oh much, much worse. This is real."

"In what way?"

"The noise, the smell, the filth."

"I shall run again in your honour."

"Funny little thing. You should be in bed."

"Let me stay a bit."

Oliver sat, his arm round the child. In the east the false dawn. He kissed the top of her head. "I'm going, Sophy."

"When?" She was startled.

"Now. The sooner the better. There's nothing for me here. The war's waiting."

Sophy looked at him, tears on her cheeks. She longed to say, "I am here, I am not nothing." She followed him into the house, watched him push his clothes into his rucksack, followed him downstairs and out of the door, hopping beside him barefoot across the garden. At the gate he stopped.

"Say goodbye now and pop back to bed."

"I would comfort you," Sophy cried passionately.

Oliver laughed and bent to kiss her.

Sophy flung her arms round his neck. "Will you come back? Promise."

"Perhaps. Let me go now." She dropped her arms and watched him lope down the road, the pack on his back turning him into a monster. The first seagull of the day set up its wailing. She was cold in her pyjamas and wanted to pee. Her desolation was great.

At the bottom of the hill Oliver found Helena in the car, asleep with her head on her arms.

"Are you all right?" He wondered what she was doing at this hour.

"I've run out of petrol."

"I'll walk on and get you some. The garages will be opening soon."

"Leave your pack with me." She asked no questions.

He returned carrying a can. "Where are you going?" he asked.

"London."

"Me too."

"I can drive you there, we can take turns."

"All right." He got in beside his aunt.

"Are you staying with Mother?"

"I hadn't thought."

"She'll be glad to put you up. If we stop for breakfast in Truro I will ring her up."

"Thank you, Oliver."

Forty-five years later, driving down the surgical motorway, Helena remembered with nostalgia the journey she and Oliver made. Breakfast at the Red Lion in Truro, bacon and eggs and marmalade eaten in silence in an empty dining room, reading the papers. Then on through central Cornwall, catching glimpses of the sea on the north coast, through Bodmin on to Bodmin Moor, past Jamaica Inn to stop in Launceston for a drink at the White Hart before lunching at the Arundel Arms at Lifton, where the talk at neighbouring tables was of the state of the river and the prospect of catching a fish. On through Somerset where farmers were cutting the corn, the machines clattering behind plodding horses, past Ilchester and Ilminster along the road bordered by stately elms, the late summer foliage dark green, to Mere where they stopped to dine at the Old Ship. Then the last hundred miles over Salisbury Plain, watching the moon swing into a cloudless sky as they came down into Hampshire where the corn stood waiting for the reaper. On through Andover and Camberley, past the Cricketers' Arms at Bagshot, past Virginia Water and Egham, to be caught in a jam of traffic in Staines until at long last they reached the street where Oliver's parents lived, within easy reach of Harrods and Peter Jones. What had they talked about that long day, she and Oliver? Speeding down the motorway Helena could not remember. What had they discussed? Not Richard, not Calypso. War? Books? Music, perhaps? Travel, very likely. She remembered describing Greece. Swimming in warm seas and clambering over rocky hills in autumn where yellow crocus sprang from the rock itself and pink cyclamen.

They had also remembered the villages decorated with flags all the way from London to Penzance only two years before, when a party of them in different mood had fled London and the King's Coronation crowds, driving through the night along deserted roads. That was a happy night she remembered, thinking, Of course he was happy, he was not in love with Calypso then.

"You must be exhausted," Oliver's mother called down to them from the balcony, leaning over the trailing pink geraniums. "I'm coming down."

Oliver lifted Helena's case from the car. Sarah Anstey put her arms round Helena and kissed her.

"Sarah, I had to come up. I hope you don't mind. I can go to an hotel."

"Don't be absurd. George will be in soon. They've hustled him into the Admiralty, he's terribly busy, overworked already. I am glad to see you."

"I can't make up my mind in Cornwall. I never can."

"No, of course not. I understand."

Had Sarah understood? Of course she had not. She was fortunate, in love with George, always would be; worried of course about Oliver and the war, but how could a woman like Sarah, who always got everything right, understand Helena, whose talent was to get things wrong?

She remembered, speeding down the motorway, Sarah had put her in the spare room on the floor above her own, had sent her maid, who later became something rather grand in the Wrens and called them all by their Christian names, to help her unpack, turn down the bed and make a welcoming fuss. Helena remembered a long soak in a hot bath and the relief of getting into a bed out of earshot of Richard.

"I should have been ashamed," said Helena, speeding down the M4.

"Ashamed of what?" The driver of the car kept an eye on the road, driving in the fast lane.

"Ashamed of myself," said Helena recollecting, "but I wasn't. It was such a relief to be in London."

"When was that, then?"

"At the outbreak of war."

"Oh." He accelerated, overtaking a Lancia, making it swerve. "Pity about the elm disease," he said, making conversation as she appeared to be awake. "Must have been lovely once, this countryside."

"No, I wasn't ashamed, I was just bloody relieved." Helena hoped to shock her driver and succeeded. "Oliver thought I was past it then," she added.

"When?"

"Forty years ago – more."

But she had been ashamed, for it was shame as well as pity for the animal which had caused her to buy Richard a puppy in Harrods' pet shop a few days later.

"How Sarah laughed."

"Who was Sarah?"

"Sarah was Oliver's mother."

"Oliver Anstey?"

"Yes."

"He was quite well known. I didn't know you knew him."

"He's still alive, very much so."

"Oh. I didn't know. I've read his books, of course. Always seems to be looking for something, doesn't know what it is."

"You are very perceptive. Would you mind not driving quite so fast? I am not afraid of death but I am afraid of being mangled in a pile-up," and the driver, who had offered a lift from kindness of heart, reduced speed, regretting his soft-heartedness. Another time he would know better, though on second thoughts his passenger looked frail and might not have many more times.

"I thought you might be in a hurry to get there."

"Oh, no. I have never been in a hurry. Indeed at one time I came close to leaving altogether."

"Oh really, when was that?"

"Mind your own business."

Helena's driver pressed his foot on the accelerator.

EIGHT

"Sarah." Helena sat with Oliver's mother at the kitchen table that September Sunday morning. "I am thinking of leaving Richard."

"I thought as much." Sarah felt no surprise. "Why did you marry him? We've always wondered."

"I don't really know. Could it have been because he had known Anthony? Because I needed someone to look after? Because I was lonely? Pity? Because he was lumbered with orphan Sophy? It wasn't love."

"Not love, of course not." Sarah went on peeling potatoes. The world might be about to end but her husband expected Sunday lunch. "I am so unused to cooking," she muttered, peering into the oven at the joint of beef. "Do you think it's doing all right?"

"I expect so." Helena looked up at the feet passing by the area railing. "He had a fine war record. That seemed to matter. Shall I do the greens? I know how."

"Yes, please, be an angel. Here's a knife."

Helena picked up the knife and a handful of spinach. "I've suddenly realised why I married Richard."

"Why?"

"His leg, it was his leg."

"But surely that's why you are leaving him." Sarah's eyes, brilliant as Oliver's, caught Helena's worried ones. Both women burst out laughing, an outburst of hilarity which filled the kitchen. George's voice shouting down the stairs was drowned. He repeated himself, running down the stone steps followed by Oliver.

"What did you say, darling?" Sarah wiped her eyes.

"You missed the announcement." George looked at the laughing women. "We are at war."

"Bother, I'd meant to listen to that jackass."

"In a way it's a relief." Helena had stopped laughing, drew in her breath. Sarah and George had a son. "Oh God," she said, "dear God."

"I thought you didn't believe any more," Oliver pounced on her.

"In time of stress—" If she had been able to say more Helena would not have been heard. The first siren of the war started its whoop. They went up to the balcony to look at the sky, standing in a row behind the geranium-filled flower-boxes.

"Take cover, get your gas masks," a hurrying warden shouted up at them.

The calm of a London Sunday continued. An owl hooted some distance away in Thurloe Square. "Must have been woken by that filthy noise. Nobody seems to be taking cover." George thrust his chin forward to ease his neck. He had been changing while listening to Chamberlain and tied his tie too tight. He felt half throttled.

"Loosen your tie, darling, you will choke. Oh, look!"

A taxi. Calypso's head craned out of the window, looking up at the sky. Calypso, Polly and the twins got out.

"Any bombs?" shouted Polly.

"Gas?" called the twins. "Any gas?"

"Seven and six," said the taximan.

"Want to take cover?" George called down from the balcony.

"Nah. Thanks all the same."

"Let them in, Oliver." Sarah looked up at the sky, innocently blue.

"Where's Walter?" Helena leant over the balcony.

"Got off at Plymouth to join the Navy. Marvellous smell of beef."

"Oh, my God, the joint!" Sarah fled down to the kitchen to switch off the oven.

It was later, while they ate an overcooked lunch, that Oliver told them he had enlisted in the Army. "I'm in the ranks but having been in the OTC helped a bit. I fixed myself up before I went down to Cornwall."

"What about Spain?" asked a twin.

"They didn't ask, so I didn't tell."

"We must hurry. I wonder where we go. Any idea?" They looked at George.

"Try the Air Ministry." George was preoccupied.

"There will be posters, let's go and look. Our country needs us."

"Where are you all staying?" Sarah looked round the table.

"With me," said Polly. "Mother and Father have got rooms near the hospital in the country. They said Calypso could stay and the twins until they are fixed up."

"What are you girls going to do?"

"Jobs? Any ideas, Uncle George?" Calypso looked beguiling.

"I can give you some introductions, I suppose."

"I've got a job," said Polly. "I fixed myself up months ago."

"Oh, lucky you. Is it glamorous?"

"I hardly think so, just War Office."

Richard telephoned that night. When was Helena coming home?

"I must do my shopping." How lame that sounded. "There will be shortages. I am going to stock up." This sounded reasonable.

"It's very inconvenient without the car."

"Get the General to drive you."

"He's very busy organising things."

"Get him to give you a job. You will be needed."

"Helena, he put the hounds down, can you believe it? I ask—"

"Poor Richard. What do you feel?"

"You may be right about Hitler."

"Richard, are you all right?"

"Of course I am. The General thinks so too."

"Thinks what?"

"Thinks Hitler's a jumped-up cad, only a ranker could behave like that."

"Richard, that's the best joke you've ever made."

"I wasn't joking."

Helena heard him replace the receiver, cutting her off.

"Are you going back?" Sarah looked troubled. "Not yet. I have to think."

"What about? Sophy?"

"Sophy is what a lot of it's about. It's not altogether the leg, it's Sophy too. Sarah, I don't like Sophy—"

"I know," said Sarah. "I know. Why don't you send her to school?"

"In wartime?"

"Helena, life's not stopping, it's going on, war or not. Find the child a school, send her away, you will both be much happier."

"Do you think so?" Helena respected Sarah.

"Ask Polly. She was quite happy at her school. They might take Sophy. Calypso's wouldn't do, she was expelled, supposed to have flirted with the gardener."

"But Polly's was near Cambridge—"

"There are such things as trains. Ask Polly and check with her mother. They will help you. Why don't you make a list? Start it with Leg, then Sophy, then your shopping. You can cross out Leg straight away since there's nothing you can do about it." Anxiety made Sarah sarcastic.

"I knew you would help." Helena reached for a piece of paper and wrote on it "List", which she underlined, then underneath she wrote "Leg" and ticked it, followed by "Sophy? Food and clothes". "What shall we run short of?" she asked, but Sarah was busy and left her.

It was the following day after an exhaustive spree in Harrods that, taking a short cut through the pet department, she bought a dachshund puppy. Her attempt to get the price reduced on the grounds that it was German met with contempt. She was, though, able to make arrangements to have it sent to Richard by train. "I was mindful of your carpets," she told Sarah.

"Carpets aren't going to matter much. I have telephoned Polly's mother about Sophy for you."

"And what did she say?"

"Said it's a good school, send the child and she can stay with Polly when she has to pass through London or for half terms."

"You've done my job for me." Helena was huffed.

"You can visit the school, here's the address. Telephone tonight. Get it done, Helena."

"You are rushing me."

"There is a rush. Being hated at Sophy's age isn't right."

"I never said I hated her."

"But you do."

Helena went to visit the school. When she got back to London she found a message from Richard to ring him urgently. "Something has happened to Sophy," said Sarah.

"What?"

"He won't or can't say. He sounds desperate."

"All right, I'll go." Helena gave in.

This time alone, Helena had an unpleasant drive down the winding roads. From now on, she thought, petrol rationing would restrict what freedom the car gave her.

Richard came out to meet her, carrying the dachshund puppy in his arms.

"So you got my present."

"It chews everything, it's eaten my best cardigan."

"Where is Sophy?"

"In bed at the Rectory."

"Why? What happened?"

"Child won't or can't speak. The Rectory offered. It seemed better for her to be with a woman. I can't do much with my leg. Monika Erstweiler sits with her. The doctor said to keep her quiet."

"But what happened, for God's sake?"

"Don't know." Richard put the puppy down on the grass and watched it make a puddle. "Good little chap. Nice thought of yours."

"What happened to Sophy?" Helena felt furious impatience.

"Went out for a walk. You know how she wanders. I don't know where. I've been stuck here with my leg—"

"Damn your leg!"

"Yes." Richard looked at his wife with sympathy. "Must be as trying for you as it is for me. Sorry. Must ignore it. I hear there's a chap with no legs who flies, chap called Bader trying to get back into the Air Force with no legs, I ask you."

"Sophy?"

"The Rector found her wandering on the cliff road. Thought she looked odd, offered her a lift and she passed out in his car. She hasn't spoken, just lies there. It's unnerving."

"Any bumps or bruises?"

"Nothing, had some sort of fit, I'd say."

"Rubbish."

"Well, yes. The doctor says shock, but round here, it's ridiculous, how could she get a shock?"

"We'd better go to her." Helena opened the car door and Richard got in holding the puppy.

"Doesn't even respond to the puppy. You'd think she'd like it."

"Did the doctor say, I mean has he—" Helena hesitated.

"Not interfered with. Nothing. Can't have seen anything of Penrose either. Wrong place, wrong time."

"Penrose? Who is Penrose?"

"Coastguard chap, you know him. The Army are wiring off the path against invaders, I ask you. Hitler's not going to invade up perpendicular cliffs. Of course with my leg I never walk along it. Oh, sorry, mentioned it again."

"It doesn't matter." Helena drew up at the Rectory. "What about Penrose?"

"Fell over the cliff. Drunk, I suppose, or suicide, moody fellow his wife says. Anyway the Army found him, saw him floating. The police are being quite active, gives them something to do. If I had my leg I'd—"

Helena got out of the car and rang the Rectory bell. The Rector opened the door. Helena kissed him on the cheek.

"Like to go straight up? Monika's with her. The room at the top on the left. Mildred had to go out."

Sophy lay propped on pillows, eyes dark in a face no paler than usual. Monika sat by the open window sewing.

"Hullo, darling." I never call her darling, thought Helena, feeling embarrassed. "Hullo, Sophy, I've come home. How are you?"

Sophy did not answer; her eyes looked at some point other than Helena.

"While I was in London I bought that puppy and I bought you a lot of clothes, too." No response. Helena looked at Monika, who smiled encouragingly and pointed at a chair near the bed. Helena sat.

"Polly's got a war job and Calypso is looking for one. Walter is joining the Navy, the twins the Air Force. Oliver has got into the Army, in the ranks, he doesn't want to be an officer." The child lay limp, eyes unblinking, disconcerting. Helena felt her sense of exasperation rise. Why couldn't the child answer? She looked at Monika for comfort.

"Aunt Sarah and I thought you might like to go away to school, so I went and saw Polly's old school near Cambridge. I think you will like it." Monika nodded approval. "There will be children of your age, games, and so on. Polly says you can stay with her on your way through London. What's that noise?" Monika was looking out of the window.

"Police," said Monika Erstweiler. "Police."

"Oh, yes." Helena dropped her voice to a whisper, which Sophy heard perfectly but Monika not, since she was leaning out of the window. "I hear there was an accident to a coastguard, so unfortunate."

"For us." Monika turned back into the room, white-faced.

"Not the coastguard," she said. "Your kind brother-in-law warned us. We are to be interned. We are enemy aliens."

"How totally absurd," said Helena, speaking loudly from anger.

"I must find my husband." Monika came close to Sophy. "Be brave, my child." She bent and kissed her. "These are English police not the Gestapo."

Sophy sat up abruptly. "We will get you out, write to our Member of Parliament, write to *The Times*." She scrambled out of bed. Helena and Monika, taken aback by this adult attitude, began to laugh.

"Sophy, I love you." Monika put her arms round Sophy and hugged her.

It would make my life easier if I did, thought Helena, watching them.

"Uncle Richard can write the letters." Sophy had run down the stairs calling loudly, "Uncle Richard, Uncle Richard, please!"

"And he did write," said Helena to her driver. "He wrote to *The Times*, to all the Members of Parliament he could think of, he became very passionate about it."

"About what?" Her driver overtook a large lorry, causing Helena to wince.

"About the wrong aliens getting interned."

"Like Arthur Koestler?"

"Yes. He was well known, but the Erstweilers were hardly known in those days. He wrote to Calypso's husband, got him interested. He was quite helpful, very helpful really."

"My father?"

"I'm sorry, I'd forgotten for a moment that Calypso is your mother."

"That's quite all right."

"It gave Richard something to do, made him forget his leg."

"What was wrong with it?"

"He lost it in Flanders."

"Wouldn't have stopped him writing, surely?"

"It didn't. The injustice gave him a lift."

"Did he get them out?"

"Yes, eventually."

"Then he remembered his leg." Helena's driver considered himself a student of psychology.

"Yes, yes, he did." Helena sighed. "He remembered the bloody thing."

Helena's driver, Calypso's son, raised his eyebrows. In his book middle-class old ladies did not swear, not in their eighties.

"Of course, looking back, being among the first to be interned was a great help to Max."

"How was that?"

"His name became familiar in the papers, favourably compared with Furtwangler who had stayed in Germany. He wasn't Jewish, of course, like Max, and very pro-Hitler. Monika and Max were released just when all the others were gathered in. He got a head start professionally."

"Became famous in this country."

"I've always believed it was the General's doing."

"What General?"

"General Peachum, a friend of your great-uncle's, a neighbour, loathed Jews, an admirer of Hitler and Ribbentrop, rather a silly man, Master of Hounds, urged the local police and coastguards to watch for spies, a typical 'country gentleman', a good man. They do a lot of harm."

NINE

Calypso's marriage to Hector Grant, during the early days of the war, when for months nothing happened except a tremendous freeze, came as welcome entertainment. One day she was working in the glamorous secret job she had found for herself and the next inviting everybody to her wedding at Caxton Hall.

Hector Grant, a tall, elegant Member of Parliament for a Scottish constituency, had been married before with no issue and was extremely rich, with a house in Westminster and a castle in the Highlands. The trouble in the eyes of Calypso's parents was that he was the same age as Calypso's father; indeed it was he who had introduced them.

"How could John have been so stupid?" cried Sarah, on hearing the news.

"I don't suppose it occurred to him," replied George. "The man is supposed to be uncatchable. How was John to know the advent of war made Hector determined to beget a son and heir?"

"But he's had a wife."

"Who wouldn't or couldn't oblige."

"Perhaps Hector can't."

"We shall see, won't we?" And George had gone gloomily off to his office, leaving Sarah to telephone what she called the Cornish Contingent, Helena and Richard.

Richard refused Calypso's invitation, excusing himself on the grounds of pressure of work. "I've written to Hector of course about the Erstweilers, knew him in the war, splendid chap, got a very good DSO." Richard had received no decoration for losing his leg. Sarah suspected that Richard resented this. She asked to speak to Helena, putting this point to her.

"Don't be absurd, Sarah," Helena had said briskly. "His leg blew off when he had his back to the enemy and was drinking a mug of tea. He remembers it perfectly. He never expected a medal. He really is busy."

"Will you come, then? Stay with us."

"I'd love to. I've never been to a registry office wedding."

"The reception is at the Ritz."

"I daresay he can afford it. I gather he's paying for all of us to have lunch."

"Yes. He won't allow Calypso's parents to spend a penny."

"They have no pennies, that's their trouble. Calypso wants money."

"Helena, you will bring Sophy, won't you?"

"She's at school."

"They might let her come. Try."

"I'll have to see."

See that she doesn't, Sarah thought, but did not say, and Sophy did not come. In the event George, too, was too busy. Sarah and Helena sat with Calypso's mother, watching a stony-faced John give his only child to Hector, magnificent in a morning suit with hardly a grey hair in his thick thatch, his black eyebrows like moths' wings meeting above his nose.

Calypso shone triumphant in a white coat and skirt, satin shirt, a wreath of gardenias on her sleek head.

"I've never seen anyone look so smug," one twin in Air Force uniform whispered to the other. Polly, overhearing, grinned. Walter arrived in time for the luncheon, a scrubbed and healthy Able Seaman. Oliver came late but in time to kiss the bride, hugging her against his rough khaki uniform.

"How prickly you are."

"Am I still to get my comforts?"

"Oh, that!"

"I may claim them soon. I am hoping to get to Finland."

"Hector says that's all collapsing."

"There will be other campaigns."

"I wish you joy of them —" She looked at him with fear.

"Well, you've got what you wanted." Oliver made no effort to lower his voice. He turned away, caught Walter by the arm, "Come on, old sod, let's go and get drunk."

Hector raised eyebrows, murmuring, "He seems halfway to his goal," and, holding Calypso's arm, steered her away. "Come and meet some of my friends from the House. Then we must go, if we are to catch our train."

"Even you were young once," Calypso said brightly, thus setting the tone of their future relations. "I'll keep my word if you'll keep yours," she whispered up at his darkening face.

"How fond she is of him." The wife of a junior minister tried to open a conversation with Helena, who was watching.

"Fond? Oh yes, fond." Helena, who had drunk more champagne than she should, let the conversation abort.

Later that evening Polly steered the twins to the York Minster in Soho, where they found Oliver and Walter sunk in alcoholic gloom, and amazed them by leading them on to the Gargoyle, a haunt Oliver had heard of but never visited, where Polly appeared to be quite well known. Amused by their dazed expressions she said: "I have not been letting the grass grow. I work for half the literati in London in my dump." Oliver grew sober as she pointed out Cyril Connolly, Philip Toynbee, Erica Mann, Robert Newton, Brian Howard and various other figures of the older generation.

"My bosses know them, I don't," she tried to console Oliver. "When's your train?"

"Midnight, Paddington."

"Walter, too. We'll put you on it. The twins are staying until tomorrow."

"She's quite a girl, your sister," Oliver gasped when he and Walter had struggled on to the train, pushing their way into an overcrowded carriage.

"Not stupid," agreed Walter.

"Very pretty, really – pity old Sophy couldn't make it."

"That's the most uncomfortable wedding I've ever been to." Sarah climbed into bed with George that night. "I've never seen so many unhappy faces. Oh, my poor Oliver."

"Lucky escape, if you ask me."

"Perhaps. I wonder what's going on in the night train to Inverness."

"Night of the long knives, by the bride's looks."

But George was wrong. Hector had whisked Calypso off to the Savoy, where her joy at finding a telephone by the lavatory seat had set the tone for an enjoyable wedding night.

"I did appreciate that," she said at last. "I can't tell you how I was dreading it."

"I thought as much." Hector was pleased. "Would you like some oysters?"

"In the middle of the night?"

"Why not?"

"Build up our strength for your Highlands? I'm dreading them, too."

"Wait till you see them."

"All right, I will. They'd better be good."

★ ★ ★

222

"You are driving too fast again." Helena, sitting ancient in the bucket seat, turned her head to look at Hamish, watching his mouth tighten with annoyance as he obediently reduced speed. "You are very like your mother."

"Oh, am I? I'm glad to hear it. I thought I took after my father."

"You do, but you often have your mother's expression." Helena undid her safety belt, letting it wind back, to Hamish's alarm.

"You really should wear that belt, Great-aunt. She must have been very beautiful."

"Not if you drive at a reasonable speed. Of course she was beautiful. She still is. Much improved since her stroke."

"What could you mean?"

"Calypso's face was too regular, both sides were the same. Since her stroke she looks human, lopsided. I don't suppose it's changed her character."

"She seems to have made a good recovery except for her face. She drags a foot sometimes. How well did you know her when she was young?"

"My dear, I was just an onlooker. She and the others came every summer. All the men were in love with her; she took it as a matter of course, as far as one could see."

"How far was that?"

"I don't know." Helena turned to watch the landscape flashing past. "She never made any bones about what she wanted."

"Oh?"

"She got it, too. Money, a good time, nice houses, clothes, jewels, yes, she got what she wanted."

"Did she want me?"

"Of course she did." In her eighties Helena's voice was better than it had been in her forties. "Of course she wanted you," she repeated. Was he not part of the bargain? "I don't believe she wanted more than you. She had a bad time when you were born."

"So she always says."

"Well, it wasn't your fault, my dear. She would insist on staying in London. Air raids and childbirth are not compatible, but you don't want to hear about the war."

"Why did she have me in London?"

"She loathed Scotland, that was a flaw in her marriage. Your father wanted her to have you in Edinburgh."

"He adored Scotland. I do, too."

"He took her up there on their honeymoon. She found it cold.

How she complained when she got back! The train got stuck in a snowdrift."

"I expect they had a sleeper." Hamish tried to visualise Calypso young and beautiful in a sleeper with his father. "I suppose they had sleepers in the war?"

"Oh yes. Paddington to Penzance. Euston to Inverness. We had them when we could get them. Your father, being an MP, had priority."

"My mother must have liked that." Hamish drove faster.

Helena resigned herself, closing her eyes. "I don't believe it made up for the cold."

"So you don't think I was conceived in a sleeping car?"

"Not until much later, my dear. At this speed we shall arrive early."

"We can have a drink or two."

"Yes, of course."

"I don't take after my father in that."

"I wasn't suggesting you did."

"Do you think he got drunk in the sleeper?"

"I wouldn't know," said Helena, who had often wondered the same thing.

TEN

Getting no nearer Finland than a brief interview in London, Oliver went to his parents' house for a bath.

The house was empty; in the bitter cold the water either turned off or froze. After wandering round the empty rooms he telephoned Calypso, writing her name in the dust as he waited.

"I am in London for the night. Any chance of seeing you?"

"We are going out, you just caught us. Hector's already on the doorstep, we are due at a party." She sounded breathless.

"Can't I come too?"

"It's not your sort of party, so sorry. Another time give us some notice. There are so many parties. London's great fun."

"My camp isn't."

"I suppose not. Why don't you try Polly? Coming, Hector, coming." She rang off.

Oliver walked through the snow to Polly's and rang the bell, stamping his feet in their heavy boots.

The door flew open.

"Oliver!"

"Sophy, what are you doing here? I thought you were at school."

"I've got a week off because I've had German measles. Polly's out with the twins. Come in, don't let the ice indoors."

"You've grown. D'you think I could have a bath?"

"Of course."

"Anything to drink?"

"There's some gin in the kitchen. I was just going to have my supper. The twins are up for the night."

"I'll take you out to supper when I've had a bath." The child looked peaky. Helping himself to gin, Oliver tried to remember what his mother had told him. Something had happened to Sophy. What?

"Any news of the Erstweilers?"

"Uncle Richard is trying to get them out. I had a letter from

225

Monika. It was censored. Isn't it stupid?" Sophy flushed.

"The whole bloody war is stupid." Oliver swallowed his gin. "Boring, too. Polly shouldn't leave you alone in the house, there might be an air raid."

"I'm all right. I'm used to being alone. There have been no raids."

"There will be." Oliver had a bath and emerged feeling better.

"Where shall we have dinner?" The child looked a waif with her black silky hair unbecomingly cut, eyes wary.

"Anywhere."

"I'll take you to the Savoy. I'd like a good dinner."

"I've never been anywhere in London."

He took her to the Savoy. "My father used to give me lunch here at half term. Why didn't you go back to Cornwall?"

"Aunt Helena said it was too far for such a short time."

"Do you mind?"

"Not really." Sophy looked evasive.

"Do you like school?"

"It's all right."

"Not like Cornwall?"

"Not a bit. What's it like being a soldier?"

Oliver tried to tell her, watching her eat, gradually relax after drinking a glass of wine.

"You weren't at Calypso's wedding."

"Aunt Helena didn't want me to miss school."

"I see. Going back to Cornwall for the holidays?"

"Yes. Perhaps Uncle Richard will have got the Erstweilers out by then. She said they are hoping in their letter."

Oliver refilled her glass. "Drink up."

"Won't I get tipsy?"

"I'll look after you."

Sophy drank. "I don't like it much but it makes me feel warm." She pressed her flat chest then, leaning towards Oliver, she whispered: "I ran the Terror Run."

"What?"

"It's wired off now but I ran it the day before they put the wire along it to prevent the Germans invading."

"Oh, the Terror Run. I'd forgotten. Seems a long time ago. What was the other thing going to be? Something idiotic. We drew lots, a killing, wasn't it?"

"Yes," she said slowly, "but you cancelled it."

"What's the matter, Sophy? You look funny. Seen something in the woodshed? Did the Terror Run frighten you?"

"Fear lent me wings. I met, I mean I saw, I—" Sophy stared at Oliver, who stared back, thinking, She's going to be lovely one day with those eyes. What did she see that day? "Yes?" he said.

Sophy drew a deep breath. "I met the Rector, he was very kind and took me home." She rearranged the knife and fork by her plate. "Oh, look," she said, looking across the restaurant. "There's Calypso."

There indeed was Calypso, dining with a man in Naval uniform, not Hector. By the look of their table, they had reached the brandy stage. They had been there some time.

"Bloody, bloody bitch – 'London's great fun'. How long have you known she was there, Sophy?"

"I saw her when we came in. I'm not a bloody bitch."

"I meant Calypso, not you. Waiter, my bill, please." She did see something in the woodshed and she's not going to tell me, Oliver thought as, choked with jealousy of the unknown Naval man, he paid his bill and led Sophy out past Calypso who, deep in talk, had not seen them. "Comforts for you, old chap?" He addressed the stranger, who looked startled, as he pushed Sophy on ahead. Calypso laughed. In the Strand the cold bit deep. Oliver took Sophy by the hand. "Let's go for a walk."

All her life whenever there was a full moon Sophy remembered walking the empty streets, her hand in Oliver's greatcoat pocket, their feet crunching the snow, a full moon casting black shadows from tall buildings, the frozen air painful to breathe, walking in silence all the way to St Paul's, where they stood looking up at the dome and listened to the starlings fighting for roosting places on the cathedral, whistling, high-pitched, aggressive.

How long had they stood there? Long enough for Oliver to regain his composure, long enough for Sophy to get thoroughly chilled, long enough for a solitary policeman to get interested and pace slowly towards them.

"Monika said the police were not the Gestapo when they came to fetch Max and her. I hope they get out soon." She shivered in the snow.

"Sophy, you are freezing, why didn't you say?"

"I'm all right." Her hand at least had been warm, held in his pocket. That, too, she would remember.

"The Erstweilers will be released. Come on, I must get you back to Polly. We never left a note, she will think you have vanished."

"She's out with David and Paul."

"They may be back by now." In later years Oliver was to wonder why the whistle of starlings always gave him a sensation of sexual jealousy. He quite forgot St Paul's by the light of the moon before the bombing.

The twins and Polly had been dining more modestly at the Royal Court. Polly had pointed out Augustus John at the bar. They looked older, more confident, more alike than ever in uniform. Oliver wondered whether he had chosen the wrong service.

"How's it going, Oliver?" Polly, too, had aged. Her face had thinned so that her eyes seemed larger, her lashes longer, mouth wider.

"It's going nowhere. I've been trying to get in on the Finnish war but they say it's nearly over. I'm bloody bored and cold in my camp. You look fine."

"I'm busy. I think I'm doing something useful."

"Secret?"

"Not so that you'd notice. Well, it is really."

The twins laughed, watching her.

"We saw Calypso," said Oliver to test them.

"We've rather gone off her." David glanced at his brother for confirmation. "She's become grand and social, not too keen on old friends – has other fish to fry."

"She was dining with one tonight." Oliver was still angry. "She said she was going out with Hector when I telephoned."

"He's in the House most nights, she can't be expected to sit at home alone." Polly came to Calypso's defence.

"No need for her to lie."

"Well, that's Calypso. She will be free another time. Try again, you may have better luck."

"She's no Penelope." David exchanged a glance with Polly. "We went to her house last time we were up. Have you been there?"

"No." Oliver noticed the change in the twins' attitude. "You two used to sit there drooling. She loved it."

"You did too. She liked you better than us."

"Or Walter," Polly remarked. Then, noticing Oliver's expression: "She's married, got money, a lovely house, she entertains, is the wife of Hector Grant, she isn't one of us any more."

"Is she happy?"

"I think so. Next time you get leave give her notice. The twins did."

"How did you get on?" Oliver looked from Paul to David. "Was she glad to see you?"

"I suspect she prefers officers." David was ironic.

"You'll get commissions. Tell me about yourselves." Oliver suddenly wanted to drop the subject. "Where are you stationed? What are you doing?"

"We are near Cambridge at the moment. We are escorting Sophy back to school tomorrow. We tried to get into bombers but they are training us for fighters. We could have been together in bombers, we thought in our innocence."

"How long before you are trained?"

"Another month, less."

"And I am kicking my heels square bashing. God!"

"Walter's full of grumbles, too. They won't have him in submarines. He says the Navy are sadists, that he'll spend the war being sick." Polly yawned. "I've got to work tomorrow. I'm off to bed. If I'm gone in the morning before you wake don't worry, come again whenever you like. There's plenty of room. I'm in Mum and Dad's room, the twins have got the spare room, you can have Walter's. Sophy's in mine. Goodnight."

Oliver looked after her. "It's not only Calypso who's changed."

"We all have," the twins said. "Who would have thought a year ago we'd all be sitting round a kitchen table in fancy dress, the camomile lawn days over?"

"You know I still can't tell you two apart, can you, Sophy?"

"No." Sophy grinned. "Nor can Polly."

"Nor the RAF. It's like school. Perhaps the war will make some distinction."

Sophy looked at the twins across the table, troubled. "Wound." She spoke in her clear voice. "Or kill."

The twins looked at her. "You never know," they cried cheerfully. "Anything left to drink?"

"There's someone at the front door." Oliver stood up. "Who, at this hour?"

"Go and see. Don't wake Polly, she really works very hard." Oliver opened the front door, peering out. "Good Lord, Uncle Richard! What are you doing here?"

"Looking for shelter." Richard limped indoors. "Got lost in the bloody blackout, difficult to see the numbers, what do they want a blackout for with a full moon, I ask you?"

Oliver shut the door. "We are in the kitchen. Polly's gone to bed."

"Went to your house, found it shut up, nobody there. What happened to your maid?"

"Joined the Wrens."

"Women in uniform, I ask you."

"Lots are. Why are you here, Uncle? Come down and have a drink or something. The twins are here and Sophy."

"What's she doing here? Run away from school? No, don't tell me, half term."

"German measles, actually." Oliver led his uncle down to the kitchen. The twins stood up politely.

"Hullo, hullo, not conchies, then? Nice to see you. What's this about measles?"

"German." Sophy pecked his cheek. "Why are you in London? Aunt Helena never said—"

"Germans, child. Well, they say they are Austrian but it's all the same thing. Enemy aliens, I ask you, it's ridiculous. Quiet respectable violinist, law-abiding. I told them. Cut your bloody red tape, I said, and let them out, costing the taxpayer a packet. The Rector and I will take care of them. What's this? Gin? Oh, all right, if it's all you've got. Been at the Home Office all the afternoon, absolutely bloody people, positive Huns in their methods, wound in red tape, can't tell a simple violinist who can play the organ and wouldn't hurt a fly – they've called up Tompkins, by the way, so we need him – from an enemy agent. Any more gin? Thanks. Not taking your last, I hope? Well, I got nowhere at the Home Office, didn't do my leg any good, they passed me from one buffoon to another. Why aren't they in the forces, I asked them. They didn't like that, I can tell you. Go and lose a leg as I did, I told them. In the last war we didn't sit on our bums in the Home Office, we fought. I saw six of the buggers. I ask you. Got nowhere, absolutely bloody nowhere. What are you all laughing at?"

"Nothing, sir."

"Well, where was I? Oh yes, nowhere, so I didn't give up, I'm not German, not that they've given up but they will, mark my words. I went along to the House of Commons and found that chap Calypso married and two friends of his. Good bar they've got there, by the way, and bingo, what do you think? This fellow, member for some Home County or other, tells me the Erstweilers are being released and arriving in London the day after tomorrow and none of those fellows sitting on their arses wound in red tape had heard, I ask you, what is the country coming to? Any more of that gin?"

Oliver poured the last of the gin into the outstretched glass. "So you've got the Erstweilers out?"

"That's what I said, made myself clear, didn't I? I may have lost my leg but not my wits. Can't see what's so funny. Can't think why you are all laughing." Putting his empty glass carefully on to the table, Richard Cuthbertson leant back, slid from the kitchen chair on to the floor and lay prone.

"Mind the leg." Sophy hopped behind Oliver and the twins as they carried the unconscious figure up to bed.

ELEVEN

"Try and relax." The lady doctor smiled down at Polly.

"That was my idea in coming here." Polly lay on the couch.

The lady doctor stood warming her hands. "There, my hands are warm. I have always thought touching patients with cold hands the height of cruelty."

"Our doctor always made us jump as children."

"A man, I suppose."

"Yes. He gave us disgusting medicines, too."

"There, my dear, how's that? Feel comfortable?"

"Will it stay in?"

"Goodness, yes. Now try it yourself, don't hurry, remember what I said."

Polly tried. "That right?"

"Perfect. Do it again to make sure. I don't want you getting home and panicking."

"I don't think I'll panic."

"I expect not. How old did you say you are?"

"Nineteen."

"Are your parents pleased?"

"I haven't told them yet. My father's a doctor. He's been evacuated with his hospital, Mother's with him."

"You seem the sort of girl who knows her own mind."

"I am."

"I hope you will both be very happy. It's two people's job to make a success of it."

"I realise that." Polly got off the couch. "Thank you very much." She smiled warmly. "The war doesn't help," she added.

"The war shouldn't be allowed to destroy values." Seeing Polly's face, the doctor added, "That's my only bromide."

"I'm hanging on to my values." Polly held out her hand. "Thank you very much for your help."

The older woman looked thoughtfully at Polly's green eyes, bright hair. They shook hands. Her values are not the usual run of the mill, the doctor thought. She rang for the next patient. While she waited she watched Polly skip down the steps into the street and run a few yards before crossing the road. Rather a monkey, that one. She wondered what Polly was really up to. She had not seen any reason to tell her that she had trained with Martin. Any child of Martin Cuthbertson's would be likely to manage her own business.

Polly went alone to see *The Wizard of Oz* and was singing "Somewhere over the Rainbow" when she let herself into her parents' house. She shut the street door and fumbled her way round the house, drawing the blackout curtains before switching on lights. A musty smell of tobacco and alcohol seeped down from the floor above her parents' room, which she had made her own since there was a telephone beside the bed. She cursed Oliver and the twins who had disturbed her on their way up the night before. She had left without waking them that morning. She ran up to Walter's room to fling open a window. A bitter wind blew in then sucked out the sour air. A lump on one of the beds groaned. Polly spun round. Unable to see, she tripped over an obstacle wrapped in cloth and fell full length on the floor.

"Curse it!"

"Who is that?" A grumpy voice she recognised as her Uncle Richard's emanated from the bed. Polly disentangled herself from his trousers, drew the curtains and switched on the light.

"Uncle Richard, what are you doing here? I fell over your leg."

"Arrived last night. Must have overslept. What time is it?"

"Sevenish."

"I'll be up for breakfast."

"Supper. It's seven in the evening."

"Oh." Her uncle dragged himself into a sitting position. Polly had never seen him grey and unshaven.

"We were celebrating. I remember that. I wonder how I got here?"

"I heard Oliver and the twins making an awful noise going to bed. I suppose they were putting you away."

"Where's Sophy?"

"The twins took her back to school this morning. That was their plan. They were all asleep when I went out."

"She was pleased about the Erstweilers."

"What about them?"

"They are out, getting out. What day is it?"

"Wednesday."

"Tomorrow they get to London."

"How thrilling! Did you do it?"

"Pulled strings, made a fuss, got drunk, I remember now, brandy with Calypso's Hector, gin when I got here, haven't been drunk since 1918, not like that, what will Helena say, I ask you?"

"No need to tell her. Why don't you have a bath? I'll see what I can find for supper. There's a razor of Father's somewhere."

"Feel woeful." Richard Cuthbertson lay back with a groan. "Woe, woe."

"I'll mix you some Alka Seltzer. When you've had a bath come down and have supper. I live in the kitchen nowadays." Polly went for Alka Seltzer and stood over her uncle as he drank it.

"My God, how disgusting."

"It helps." Polly waited while he drained the glass.

"I remember now, I had a few whiskies before going to the Home Office. You won't tell Helena?"

"Of course not."

"They all laughed last night when I told them what I'd said to those bureaucrats, found it funny. Helena finds me funny too, can't think why, I never make jokes, do you find me funny?"

"Not at the moment. Come down when you're ready, Uncle. I'll make some soup." Polly left him.

In the kitchen she laid places for two and started preparing a meal, humming Judy Garland's tune as she worked. She was disturbed by a ring at the front door. She called up the area steps: "Who is it?"

"It's me, Calypso. Can I come in?"

"Of course."

Calypso felt her way down the area steps.

"We are far more likely to break our necks doing this than get bombed. I've laddered my stockings tripping over the kerb."

"That's not like you. Come in. What's the matter?" Polly looked at her cousin. Something was wrong. "What's up?"

"Just felt I'd like to see you. Hector's in the House, thought a chat would be nice. I've hardly seen you since I married."

"What with your marriage and my job it's not easy. What's wrong?"

"Nothing. Oh, are you expecting somebody?" Calypso looked at the table. "I don't want to butt in. Shall I go?"

"It's only Uncle Richard. He's got a hell of a hangover, he

seems to have been boozing with Hector. He's in London getting the Erstweilers out from the Isle of Man. I found him in bed when I came in. Last night Oliver and the twins who were here put him away. I only just found him."

"Are they here now?"

"No, they took Sophy back to school on their way to their station and Oliver had to be back in his camp."

"What fun. I wish I'd seen them all." Calypso sounded wistful. Polly made no comment.

"The twins did come one evening and Olly rang up but I was doing something else. What a pity."

"They can always come here. I'm alone. I've given them keys. Walter has his, of course."

"Polly—" Calypso took a deep breath. "I've got to tell somebody."

"Fire away. Stay to supper, won't you?" Calypso looked awful, hunted, her normal bright confidence gone.

Richard came into the kitchen. "Hullo, girls." He kissed Calypso's proffered cheek. The girls exchanged glances, the moment for confidences passed. During supper Richard told them all he had done for the Erstweilers, finishing his account with a compliment. "Damn good chap, your Hector. Couldn't have managed without him, you're a lucky girl."

"Yes," said Calypso. "Yes, of course."

Helena telephoned from Cornwall. Polly called Richard to speak to her. The girls listened.

"Yes, of course I'm here, couldn't get in at Sarah's house, they've shut it up. What? Tomorrow I'm meeting the Erstweilers and will bring them down with me, tell the Rector. What? When? Who? How ridiculous. One of those buggers must have done it to annoy, sitting there swathed in red tape – I told them – what? Not till tomorrow week? How did you find out? They telephoned Floyer? Why not me? I'm the one who's on the spot. I'm the one who's made all the running, well, not running, not with my leg, how could I? Polly fell over it. What? Oh all right, I'll come home. Yes, tonight. I—" He turned to the girls. "Cut off, goddammit. They aren't getting out until tomorrow week and travelling via Bristol, I ask you. They get a train pass. Helena seems to want me home, didn't know where I'd got to. I'd better catch the night train." He spoke forlornly.

Polly said, "It's only one more week, Uncle, you've done marvels. It's thanks to you they are getting out."

"I'll take you to Paddington. I've got Hector's car round the corner," Calypso offered.

"What about—" Polly began to speak but Calypso shook her head. "It was nothing, nothing important."

Presently Polly watched Calypso, driving Hector's Lagonda, their uncle beside her, vanish in the blackout.

"Poor Calypso," said Polly out loud in the freezing street. She had never felt sorry for her cousin before. "I wonder!" Indoors she went to the telephone and dialled thoughtfully.

"Sorry I couldn't ring before. I found my uncle here in bed." The telephone crackled. "Not my bed, one of the spares." She listened, then; "Well, I'm rather depressed. I came in full of zeal, went to see *The Wizard of Oz*, was all cheerful and relaxed, but not only was there Uncle Richard, you know who I mean, one leg, I tripped and fell over it. How? In the dark. No, not particularly funny, no, it just wasn't. Then Calypso came along, yes, the beautiful cousin you want to meet. No, she was not at her best, she looked terrible, well, worried, fraught. She was just going to confide when Uncle interrupted us so we couldn't talk. No, she clammed up. No, I can't imagine what it is, she's got everything. Well, I know she's not got you. Yes, I promise you shall meet her, blast you. Yes. No, what I'm trying to say is not tonight. Because I'm feeling sad. Oh, really – do you think so? Cheer me up? Does it? All right, then, come along. I see I've got a lot to learn. Don't forget I've got to clock in at my office at nine. All right, all right. No, I'm not joking. I can't see it as funny."

But forty years later, on her way to the funeral, Polly laughed out loud and her daughter in the back seat asked: "What's the joke, Ma?"

"Only something in my distant past. You wouldn't find it amusing, just something I learned."

"You always said you were dead bored at lessons."

"Not on that occasion." Stifling her laughter, Polly snorted like a horse.

TWELVE

When Calypso had her stroke in 1979 she was completely para-
lysed for two days, unable to speak but able to see and hear.
Bored by what she heard – everyone within earshot was cagey –
and only able to see part of the room where she lay, she nerved
herself to think back while she could and remember what had
happened. She had long been aware of self-deception and wilful
forgetfulness, a self-preserving double standard. As a convert
to Catholicism, she was aware of her deceptions even in the
confessional, of making her sins sound droll, therefore less serious. She was always angry when the priest could not share her
view. Now, convinced she was dying, she cast her mind back to
the moment she had realised that she had grown up and must
manage by herself. When she made a rapid recovery her first
words addressed to Hamish, who was sitting by her bed, were:
"It was the night I put Uncle Richard on the night train. I got
him a seat but I couldn't get him a sleeper." Her speech was only
slightly slurred and that left her after a few days. All that remained
was a slight stiffening on one side of her face and a small limp.

"I'm not dying," she had added, watching Hamish's
expression. "It takes three." Hamish, at a loss, had said: "Three
what?" looking at his mother with pity. Calypso answered,
"Strokes," and drifted into a healing sleep.

It was a struggle to get Richard on the train, carrying his over-
night bag in one hand, holding on to his arm with the other. The
station swarmed with soldiers, sailors, airmen, a large proportion
drunk. They overwhelmed the civilians and smelled different.
Calypso supposed the materials their uniforms were made of
absorbed the smells of beer and tobacco differently from civilians.
She dragged her uncle along to the First Class carriages. "Get in
here, Uncle Richard, I'll find you a seat." She pushed and shoved,
popping her head in and out of carriage doors. "Is there room

for my uncle? He's lost a leg, he can't possibly stand all the way to Penzance."

Taken aback by her beauty, made to feel guilty about the leg, a competition took place to surrender hard-won or booked seats. Calypso thrust Richard into a corner seat, crying: "Thank you, thank you, how kind of you. He's not feeling very well, so it's 'specially kind. Come and see me when you're in London, won't you? Oh, I am grateful." She kissed Richard, hissing in his ear, "Don't you dare give them my address. Goodbye, Uncle Richard, goodbye," and leapt from the train as the guard blew his whistle. Watching the overladen train snake away into the dark she stood feeling totally alone, frightened but defiant. Now, she had thought, and remembered it all those years later, now I must live.

And if Uncle Richard hadn't interrupted us and I'd asked Polly's advice and taken it my life might have been entirely different. She thought, recovering from her stroke, that it was better that she had made her own decisions. There was nobody to blame but herself. Waking, she saw that Hamish still sat beside her bed. He must be anxious. He was also easily bored, taking after her.

"Why don't you read a book?"

"Wouldn't you mind?" He hated the twist in her lovely face. "Why should I mind?"

"Seems a bit insensitive."

"I'm not sensitive but I keep my promises."

"Of course. Don't tire yourself talking."

"It's wonderful to find I can. You are a promise."

"What?"

"Glad I made it." His mother's eyes smiled. He felt closer to her than he ever had. Perhaps she was dying? Hamish bent and kissed her.

"Not dying yet." Her twisted mouth smiled. "Not this time."

She had gone home after putting her uncle on the train, taking the Underground from Paddington to St James's Park, then walking through the dark streets. She put her key in the door and pushed it open. Hector was standing in the hall.

"I thought you were visiting your constituency." Calypso was suddenly very tired.

"I decided to go tomorrow instead."

"Oh." Calypso walked past him and up the stairs.

"I wanted to say I'm sorry."

She stood on the stairs looking down. "Do you behave like that often?"

"I thought you'd walked out on me."

"Do you behave like that often?"

"Not very often. Darling, I wanted to say I'm sorry."

"Now you've said it." She started on up the stairs.

"Calypso, I've said I'm sorry. Will you forgive me?"

"No."

"Calypso, I'm sorry, darling, I'm sorry."

"Why didn't you warn me?"

"If I had you wouldn't have married me."

"Oh yes I would."

"Why?"

"For your money."

"Bitch." Hatred stretched between them, tangible, horrible. They stared at one another across the chasm. "It's my fault," he said.

"Mine too, now." Infinitely tired, Calypso held the banister. "I've been putting Uncle Richard on the night train."

"Oh my God, it started with him, stupid man trapped me in the bar."

"So I gather." Coldly she spoke, she felt numb with misery. "I'm cold, tired."

"It won't—"

"Oh yes it will. I may be only nineteen but I know it happens again and again. I know that much – I'm twenty next week."

"Twenty. Oh God, Calypso, don't leave me."

"I'm not leaving you."

"Why not?" He stood in the hall looking up at her, eyes strange under the thick eyebrows. "Daphne left."

"I'm not Daphne."

"I didn't love Daphne. I do love you."

"It doesn't matter whether you do or not. I'm not in love with you. To be honest, I don't think I'm the sort of girl who can love. I married you for your money and to give you an heir. That's the deal, whatever way you wrap it up. I'll keep my word and I hope you won't get drunk and violent too often. I promise I'll keep it. I only hope he's not a sod like you."

"We'll make a fine pair of parents," Hector shouted up the stairs. Then – "What the hell are you laughing at?"

"I left your— Oh Hector, I left your precious car at Paddington. I took it to go and see Polly then I took Uncle Richard to Paddington in it. Oh!" she wailed. "Your precious car. I came home by Underground, forgot I'd had the car. Oh!" She gave a whoop of laughter. "It's by Platform One."

"And the keys are in the ignition, I suppose?"

"Yes, they are. Why are you laughing?"

"Because you are so funny. I'll ring the police about it, then I'm coming to bed."

"Not with me you're not. I'm not keeping that promise tonight."

"I wouldn't ask you to. I'm too bloody tired. I've been working like a dog all day with the most diabolical hangover."

"And bad conscience."

"That, too."

"It was months later," Calypso whispered to Hamish.

"What was? Don't tire yourself."

"Months later I kept my promise. I never let him promise, it would have been too humiliating."

"What would have been humiliating?" Hamish wondered whether her mind was affected by her stroke.

"Never mind," she said and reached for his hand. "Look, I can move my arm. I shall get well."

THIRTEEN

Oliver telephoned. "Can you have dinner with me?"

"When?" Calypso lay on the sofa.

"Tonight. Please. I'm going away."

"Where?"

"I'll tell you when I see you. I'll come round at once."

She met him at the door. "Darling Olly." She hugged him.

"I'm going to Norway."

"Oh, my God! Hector says it's ill-fated. Why you?"

"They want people who know mountains. They are even flying chaps from India who've done mountain warfare. I'm being given a commission."

"What about your principles?"

"No commission no action, so I take it. I've been so bored doing nothing, it's demoralising."

"Where shall we go? Hector's in the House, won't be back till late."

"Berkeley?"

"Fine. I'll dress."

"No, don't waste time."

"Talk to me while I tidy, then."

Oliver followed her to her bedroom. "You do live in style."

"Nice, isn't it? I'm changing the house quite a lot. Hector doesn't mind what I do here as long as I don't interfere in Scotland."

"What's that like? Antlers and kilts?"

"It's Hector's place," she said drily.

He watched her brush her hair, touch up her face, put on a coat, move about the room. He kept his eyes away from the bed. Hector's bed, her rich husband.

"Polly's got a bigger one." She stared at him from the mirror, a finger smoothing her eyebrows.

"Bigger what?" She'd noticed.

"Bigger bed. She's moved into her mum's room to have the

telephone near her. It's not so high up if she gets bombed."

"I suppose there will be raids some time. Hurry up, Calypso, I'm starving."

"I must just telephone."

Oliver waited impatiently. Calypso appeared to be breaking an engagement. She rang off.

"Who was that?"

"Just someone I was having dinner with tonight. I can go out with him any time."

"Like that sailor?"

"He was only in London for a night."

"Like me."

"I didn't know him like you. Did you take Sophy out *faute de mieux*?"

"Polly left her alone."

"I bet she enjoyed it. Sophy is going to be a beauty. She adores you."

"She loves us all because we are so much older."

"We represent glamour."

They walked along the street. Oliver held Calypso's arm. She wore an expensive fur coat, smelled of scent, clipped along in high heels. He remembered holding her on the cliff, the feel of her breasts. He stopped a taxi. They got in.

"You smell different."

"So will you when you get your new uniform."

They sat side by side in the restaurant. Calypso knew people at other tables. She waved.

"Tell me about your rich husband."

"He's busy. He's clever. He's ambitious. He's doing well. He will do better. He visits his constituency. He lets me do what I want, within reason."

"Are you happy?"

"I've got what I want."

"That's not the same thing."

"When do you go to Norway?"

"I wouldn't be allowed to tell you if I knew. I leave London tomorrow, tonight, really, at dawn."

"I see."

"What about my comforts? You swore you'd sleep with me."

"Did I?"

"You know you did. I'm off to war."

"I keep my promises. Where shall we go?"

"I'm not staying anywhere. I telephoned from the station. Not your house."

"Where, then?"

"Mine? My parents are away. I have the key. Let's go there."

"All right." She was docile. They drove to his home. The house was dark, the flower-boxes on the balcony empty. Oliver put his key in the lock and pushed. A bit of newspaper rustled in the hall. No light came on when he pressed the switch.

"It's empty. They've moved the furniture. You knew?" He held her arm.

"Aunt Sarah told me. They've taken a house in Bath near your father's war job, moved everything there."

"You bloody bitch. I shall fuck you on the floor."

"Not in this coat you won't. Hector said if I bought mink I must make it last."

"Damn and blast Hector."

"Oh, well."

"Come in. They may have left something, a sofa, a bed, a carpet." He pulled her into the house, slamming the door. Holding hands they climbed the stairs, their feet loud on uncarpeted boards. They stood in the drawing-room, empty, the long windows black, the trellised balcony just visible.

"How damnable."

"You explore. I'm afraid of breaking a leg. I won't run away." She listened to him walking about the house, his feet stamping in their Army boots. He came back.

"You can lie on my uniform."

"That scratchy thing!"

"I'm randy as hell."

"I'm not. I'm cold."

"You promised."

"I know I did. Let's go to Polly's, see if she's in." She took his hand. "Come on, Olly, have some sense." He pressed himself against her, pushing her against the wall.

"Not a tuppenny upright!"

"All right, we'll go to Polly's. I bet she's out or having a party. This is bloody hell." He slammed the door. They were out in the street walking.

"I've got a large sofa."

"I don't want a sofa or your rich husband's bed."

"You are hoity-toity."

"No I'm not. I suggested the floor."

"And I refused." They walked along, he holding her arm. "It's not that I'm unwilling, Olly, it's just, well, I do like a bit of comfort when I make love."

"You don't know what love is."

"I don't think I do."

"This is the street, isn't it?"

"Yes." They stood and rang the bell, looking up at the blacked-out windows.

"She's very particular about her blackout is Polly." He could see her neck as she looked up at the house white against the black mink collar. "But she doesn't answer the bell. Polly's out."

"What's the time?"

"One-thirty. What about an hotel?"

"I haven't got enough money."

"I've got money."

"I don't want your rich husband's money."

"My sofa?"

"Your husband will be back."

"Probably, but he'll be asleep."

Oliver put his arms round her, holding her close to him. "You used to smell of camomile and salt."

"Oh Olly, dear Olly, that was so long ago."

"Last August." He kissed her hard. "I'll walk you home. I'm not randy any more."

When they reached her street she felt very tired. Her feet were hurting. "Better luck next time."

"I may not come back."

"We'll arrange it better. Take care of yourself. Of course you'll come back."

Oliver gave her a push and watched her until she reached her door and let a shaft of light escape as she opened it. Then it closed and he began a long walk to the station, to the train, to the camp, to the war which for him was beginning at last.

Calypso got into bed beside Hector, who sleepily put an arm round her.

"Where have you been?"

"Having dinner with Oliver. He's off to Norway."

"Poor devil. It's a crazy mission."

"He's got a commission."

"So have I."

"What?" She sat up.

"Lie down, you are letting the cold in. Snuggle up." He smelt of cigars.

"I hate cigars. What did you say?"

"Got a commission, it came through today. In the Guards. Can't leave it all to the young boys. It's a nice surprise for you."

"Oh, no!"

"Aren't you pleased?"

"No, I'm not. You'll go away."

"You won't mind."

"Yes, I shall."

"You'll get used to it, sweetie. I'm forty-four. I don't suppose they'll let me do anything dangerous. If I'm sent overseas I'll send you up to Scotland where you'll be safe."

"Oh no you won't. I'm staying here, whatever happens. I'm quite fond of you," she said, snuggling up. "How nice and warm this is." She thought of Oliver and sighed. Hector slept, turning away from her.

Oliver sat, crushed among others, sleepless in the train taking him back to camp. Soldiers sang in the next compartment. Wryly Oliver thought how bad their songs were compared to the last war's.

FOURTEEN

When the Erstweilers reappeared from internment the Rectory was full of evacuees. Helena, using Richard's leg as a pretext, had escaped her quota of unwilling London children but was glad to welcome Monika and Max as paying guests. In camp the Erstweilers had not been idle. In a way they had rather enjoyed it. While Max found friends with similar interests, Monika discovered a cousin in international banking who was prepared to chance his arm and help them financially. They were no longer humiliatingly penniless. Max, using introductions from musical friends, started a cat's cradle of correspondence which was to lead first to employment in orchestras up and down the country and soon to playing solo in London.

Helena, tone deaf and uninterested in the arts, had not realised the Erstweilers' former position in Vienna, Prague and other European cities and found herself playing second fiddle to Richard, who emerged in the guise of a lover of music, a taste she had never suspected he had. His knowledge of the subject was, she discovered to her annoyance, considerable.

Max's English was poor. Richard made himself busy translating his mittel-European letters into plain English, bought a typewriter and became Max's secretary and adviser.

With Monika's help Helena adjusted to the changes brought about by the war. Her first hurdle was the disappearance of domestic staff. It had never occurred to her to manage the house on the cliff with less than three servants. Daisy, the parlour maid, was the first to defect, giving in her notice and going home to her parents' farm to become a land-girl. Janey, who had housemaided for years without complaint, left to join the ATS. When Max and Monika arrived Helena was managing alone with Cook, a placid woman fond of Helena, agreeable to Richard, devoted to Sophy and exhilarated by the annual visits of the nephews and nieces. Whereas Helena was relieved to be spared the threat of evacuee children by the advent of the Erstweilers, she was not prepared for their effect on Cook.

Monika, eager to make herself useful, helped in the house, proving better and quicker at sweeping, dusting and polishing than Helena, clever at ironing, quick to make labour-saving, comfort-enhancing suggestions which Helena would never have thought of. It was when she moved into the realm of food that clouds gathered.

It began on the two women's walks together. Monika picked herbs and berries and brought them home. She acquired a clove of garlic and showed Helena how to grow it.

"If you grow herbs and garlic, darlink, we will transform the rations."

"Richard won't eat garlic, he hates it."

"Do not tell him, he will not know. I will tell Cook."

"Do you think that wise?"

"Helena, she must learn. I find her throwing away sour milk."

"Well, if it was sour—"

"She must make cheese! She must use it for cooking."

"I don't want to upset her."

Monika smiled. "All right," she said, "don't worry, I am going to the woods. Also yoghurt!" she called over her shoulder as she set off inland with Richard's dachshund, sadly in need of exercise. Helena waved and called after her, "Yoghurt."

"Helena is learning German." Richard looked up from the letter he was translating.

"It is food." Max's brow was furrowed. "I need a music stand, a piano and a stool. I cannot work without."

"I'll ring the General. He had a piano at one time, his mother's."

The General refused to part with the piano. "I'm not lending it to the enemy."

"Look here, old boy, he's not the enemy. He's a refugee working for us, I ask you."

"Call that work? Why doesn't he join the Home Guard, not that they'd have him. Chap's a spy, making a fool of you. Get him to do something useful. You heard what's happened to the hounds."

"You put them down."

"So I did, but the farmers have collected others, formed their own pack, not going to be done out of their fun. It's mutiny."

The General laughed. "Rather enterprising. Showed the proper spirit, even had the nerve to ask me for a subscription."

"Did you give them one?"

"Said I'd think about it. I'm rather in favour of a mounted Home Guard."

"What for?"

"Get an allowance of corn. Be able to keep my horses. Damn good idea, if you ask me."

"What about that piano? It's in a good cause."

"What good cause?"

"Entertaining the troops, boost morale. Let me bring Erstweiler over to look at it. You never use it, it just sits in your house. There's a war on, I ask you."

"Oh, very well," the General grumbled.

Max got the piano and had it tuned. The Rector found a music stand. Monika returned from the woods full of hope for the autumn crop of fungi to enrich their diet, but long before the autumn Cook left. Monika was making yoghurt. Cook went to Birmingham to work in a factory, a move she had been planning for months. Helena wrung her hands while Monika moved smoothly into the kitchen to produce Continental meals both delicious and nutritious and still found time to accompany Max on the piano when needed.

"She's taken over everything," Helena wailed down the telephone to Sarah in Bath. "I'm left with nothing but the shopping and driving the car."

"You should be thankful," said Sarah. "You hate cleaning and can't cook. Consider yourself lucky. I wish I had some Erstweilers."

"But the drawing room's become a music studio. I can't go in without appearing to interrupt."

"You will find some solace. Our three minutes are up." Sarah, with no news of Oliver in Norway, had little sympathy for Helena. Where was Oliver? Dead or alive? News gleaned from the wireless was of retreat. Desperately anxious, she telephoned Calypso. Could Hector get news?

"No, Aunt Sarah, he knows no more than you. Try Polly."

"What good would she be?"

"She works in an office which is in the know—"

"But she's not allowed to tell."

"There is that. If I hear a whisper from any quarter I'll give you a ring."

"If there's any news he'll get it to you, he loves you."

"I did get a letter," Calypso admitted.

"What did it say? Quick, tell me." The line from Bath was faint but Sarah's anxiety strongly conveyed.

"Nothing much. It was censored. He just said, 'This is worse than the Terror Run.' "

"That game you all played? What does it mean, for God's sake?"

"I don't know. Don't worry, he'll be back safe." Calypso knew well enough what the message meant. Oliver was afraid. She telephoned Polly. "Polly, Aunt Sarah's having kittens about Oliver. Have you any tit-bit of news in your office?"

"Nothing good." Polly was cagey.

"The radio says they are retreating and Hector is pretty glum about it."

"I can't tell you anything, it's no use asking me. I don't know and if I did I couldn't tell you."

"Damn and blast!"

"Come round and have supper. Are you doing anything?"

"Twiddling my thumbs."

"Come to supper. I've got a friend here who wants to meet you."

"Would I like him?" Calypso was doubtful.

"Yes. Light entertainment. Just the job."

"All right," said Calypso, "but I can't stay late, Hector said he'd be back tonight."

"There you are, she's coming." Polly turned to the man beside her. "I promised you should meet her, didn't I?"

"You did." He grinned.

"Mind you are nice to her."

"I always am, surely." He looked pleased.

"You can take her home after supper. I want an early night."

"But Polly—"

"But Polly's had enough, so off you go."

"Are you giving me my congé?"

"Yes. That was the arrangement. It's worked very well, now it's over. Thanks a million and all that."

"You are a cold-blooded bitch."

"No, no," said Polly, laughing, "just practical."

"I've grown very fond of you. You've used me."

"Yes," said Polly, "I have. You've been an investment, a tutor."

"You've behaved like a young man in a brothel!"

"And why not?" said Polly who was ahead of her time.

"Polly was ahead of her time," Helena said to Hamish years later, driving down the motorway. "And if you go on driving as fast as this you will cut your time short."

"She must have been a very attractive girl." Hamish slowed down a little. "Irritating, too," he added, knowing that Helena liked to gossip.

"Yes, she could be irritating to some people but only if they were too pleased with themselves, got too big for their boots."

"Like me?"

"I daresay yours fit a bit tight, you are your mother's child."

"Was she pleased with herself?"

"I wouldn't say that. She just knew, how could she not, that she was the most lovely girl around."

"I bet she gave a lot of pleasure. Did she ever suffer? I've often wondered." Calypso's son probed.

"I wouldn't know, my dear. Your mother is as proud as she is beautiful." Helena closed her eyes. I must pretend to doze, she thought, else I will be disloyal to Calypso and damage her child. She never really loved, so how could she suffer? "I stood on the sidelines and watched." Helena glanced at Calypso's son. "They were all so young. Mine was the older generation. Not that I was altogether idle," she added, half to herself, and Hamish wondered what so ancient and shrunken a creature could have been like when his mother was twenty.

"She was twenty when I was born."

"About that. She got her figure back instantly, I remember. Slim, she was."

"She still is."

"I was plump." Helena thought back to the days when Hamish was born. "Some men like women plump. I was the same age as your father, of course, not that he ever looked at me," she added as the car swerved slightly. "A very attractive man, your father. He liked slim girls."

"Who liked them plump?" Hamish played along with reminiscence. "Apart from Great-uncle Richard, I mean."

"Poor Richard. He knew a lot about music, or so he thought."

"You are using my father as a red herring," said Hamish, using guesswork.

"You are not stupid." Helena was amused in her eighties, remembering what she had gained when she lost her drawing-room. It had not occurred to her, until she found herself on her back in the daffodil field, to consider Max Erstweiler as a lover. Having been married so long to Richard she had thought herself past that sort of thing.

FIFTEEN

Sophy and other girls crossing London at the end of term were escorted to Liverpool Street by a mistress who handed them over to their relatives. Helena informed Polly of the times of arrival and expected her to meet Sophy, keep her for as long as necessary and put her on the next convenient train to Cornwall. Helena ignored the fact that Polly worked and might not be able to take time off.

To overcome this difficulty Polly had given Sophy instructions to pretend to recognise anyone who approached her with glad cries of "Sophy, how *are* you?" so that any suspicious mistress would be deceived. "If I can't come myself, ducks, I'll send a friend." Rather apprehensive to begin with, Sophy learned to enjoy the variety of her escorts, in the event mostly men. She was met by soldiers, sailors, airmen, Free French, Dutch, Poles, on one occasion a turbanned Sikh and latterly by Americans. It never occurred to her to wonder how these strangers recognised her. If she had thought she might have supposed Polly had shown a snapshot. She never knew that Polly's orders were, "Look for a thin chinky child with black hair and slant eyes who looks like a Siamese cat. She stands out among the goosey English."

At half term in 1940 she was met by the twins, who greeted her with cries of "Hullo, Soph-ophy-ophy, give us a kiss. You're not to go home, you're to spend half term with us."

"Oh, goody, where?"

"With Polly. We are building her a shelter. You can help," said Paul.

"She says she'll never go down to a shelter so we are reinforcing her bed."

"When are these raids, then?" Sophy had learned to be sceptical.

"They will come, never fear," said the twins, bundling her into a very old car they had bought for five pounds. "We can't have our Polly in more danger than she need be."

"She hasn't noticed," said David to Paul. "She hasn't noticed our elevation, have you, Sophy?"

"What?" said Sophy.

"You haven't noticed us."

"You look exactly the same, more so than ever. Oh, I see," she exclaimed. "You've become officers. How grand!"

"What else?"

"Wings. Oh gosh, you've got wings!"

"Pilot Officers with wings on leave. We're posted. We've been home, now we've got three days in London."

"Any news of Oliver?" Sophy did not want to ask but did.

"No," they said soberly. "No. He'll be all right, bound to be."

They showed her the shelter, a corrugated iron canopy above Polly's bed, strongly supported by struts and stays. "A wartime four-poster."

"Is she pleased?"

"She doesn't know. You can paint it while we finish it off. We could only get moss green; it doesn't look too bad. We want to get it finished before she gets back from her office."

Sophy enjoyed that hot June day making sandwiches, answering the telephone when Polly called to find out whether she had arrived and later telephoning Calypso, asking her to come round and see the twins.

"I can't. I'm in bed with a throat, can hardly speak. Give them my love."

The twins opened the windows to lessen the smell of paint and sent Sophy to Harrods to buy ribbon. As children they had built a tree house in the Rectory garden; reinforcing the bed recaptured for a day their childhood delight. When Polly came home the canopy was overhanging the bed, the struts bound around with pink and yellow ribbons. She said: "Oh, twins!" She put her arms round them. "You darlings! I love it and I love you."

"We must have you safe," they said, hugging her.

"Christ Almighty! What is going on?" Walter, carrying a bottle of gin, appeared from nowhere.

"Walter, I thought you were in Portsmouth." Polly hugged him.

"I was. I'm on my way to Plymouth to another bloody destroyer. It's total hell, sadistic bastards."

"Who?"

"The Admiralty. Can I stay the night? I'll take you all out to dinner."

"It's your home as much as mine." Polly was indignant.

"I keep meeting people who've stayed the night. I just wondered whether there was a bed."

"They are often your friends."

"Let's go out while the smell blows away. Sophy, you've grown."

Sophy felt happy with Polly, the twins and Walter with his squashy face. She was glad Calypso couldn't come, glad a sore throat kept her away.

Walter rang her up. "Says not to come near her, she feels rotten. Must be, she's missing some do she was going to with Hector. She had been looking forward to it, says she hopes he'll be all right on his own. Quite the little wife, our Calypso."

"Yes," said Polly, "er – yes." Then, "Come on, Sophy, put on a pretty dress, I'm going to."

Calypso answered the telephone in a husky croak when it rang beside her bed.

"Can I speak to Calypso?"

"Oliver! We all think you're dead, it's months—"

"I'm not. I got back a while ago but I've only just got to London. What's this sexy voice?"

"I'm very ill – tonsillitis. Nearly dead."

"Coming to dinner with me? You promised."

"I can't. I'm in bed. Doctor's orders."

"Oh come on, I've booked a table."

"I'm very ill. Hector's had to go to a party without me."

"Good."

"And I couldn't go out with Walter, Polly and the twins. They're all there with Sophy. I'm stuck in bed."

"Get up and come out. Dinner with me won't kill you."

"I mustn't. The doctor says—"

"You bloody well must—"

"I've got a temperature."

"I don't care. Meet you in half an hour at the Berkeley."

"Feeling rich?"

"Nothing to spend my pay on in Norway. Half an hour. Look sharp." Oliver rang off.

They held hands through dinner. Calypso felt ill. Oliver refused to talk about Norway except to say it was "awful, bloody awful. If the War Office hadn't interfered all the time we might have managed something." He was bitter.

"How long have you been back?"

"Several weeks. I've been in bed, too."

"Wounded?"

"Very slight. The trouble was fatigue. Retreating, as they call running away, is tiring."

Calypso said nothing. This was another Oliver, very different from the Oliver who had come back from Spain. That man had been furious but intact. She said: "If you hadn't been retreating in Norway you might have been in France. Incredible how many got back. Hector was sent down to Dover to meet them."

"How nice for them. Being met by Hector would be the last straw."

"Now, now."

"Norway's forgotten now. All I hear about is heroic Dunkirk. Paddle steamers and dinghies helping the British Navy. Was Walter there?"

"Polly says he was. He rang up to say he hadn't been sick because it was calm. I haven't seen him because I'm so ill."

"He's obsessed with seasickness. Wasn't he terrified by the bombing?"

"Polly didn't say. She was just glad he was all right."

"Like me."

"More cheerful than you. He wanted me to go out tonight, he sounded quite normal, said he was passing through London – like you – just tonight. I'm glad I'm not in Paris, it must be horrible. You wouldn't think anything had happened if you'd been in London lying in bed trying to swallow—" Calypso rather wished she was back in bed. Oliver was poor company. He looked strained. Shell-shock was a state she had read about but never seen. She said: "Were you, I mean, are you shell-shocked?"

Oliver laughed, his taut expression relaxing. "Only demoralised. I've got a room in Half Moon Street, let's go there for a sex shock."

"What, now?"

"Yes. I'm not hungry. You're not eating anything, either."

"I can't swallow."

"That won't prevent—"

"Oliver, I can't, I'm infectious."

"Try not to be silly, stop prevaricating."

"Have you told your mother you are back?"

"Not yet."

"You must, she's in agonies of anxiety."

"I will. Soon."

"Do it now. Then I'll come with you to your room." She led

him to the telephone. "I'll get the number for you." Calypso watched Oliver's strained face as she got through to Sarah in Bath. "Aunt Sarah? It's me, Calypso. No, only tonsillitis. Aunt Sarah, Oliver is here—" She handed the receiver to Oliver, who listened a moment.

"Yes, I'm all right. Yes, I'll come down tomorrow. No, don't. I'm quite recovered, it wasn't serious. Tell Father I got a medal, he'll like that. What for? What medal? Oh, an MC for being the last to leave. Couldn't run as fast as the others. See you tomorrow." He rang off. "Why do mothers cry?"

"It's relief." Calypso held his hand as they walked along the street. "I wonder whether I shall cry for my child?"

"Are you pregnant?"

"Not yet. I've put it off. I shall put my mind to it soon. I promised Hector."

"You promised me my comforts long before you met Hector. Here we are."

"Why didn't you tell me you'd got a medal?"

"I was looking forward to this." He led Calypso into his room. "Hope you don't mind, it's the only room I could get at short notice. Landlady's a tough old bird." Oliver took off his coat and helped Calypso out of her dress. "Come on, my love, hurry up."

"The zip's stuck." Calypso stood with her arms above her head. "Not down, you fool. Pull it up and start again."

"I believe you are doing this on purpose."

"No I'm not. Oh God!" Calypso gave a yelp of pain as the zip pinched flesh. At the same moment the howl of the air raid siren began. "Oh my God, an air raid! Hector will kill me if I get caught out in this." She pulled the dress down and stood looking at Oliver with her hair tousled, mouth open. A heavy hand banged the door.

"Let me in, sir, there's a raid."

"I know. I can hear."

"I've got to see that the blackout is all right."

"It *is*," shouted Oliver, drawing the curtains.

"I must see for myself and in the bathroom. Let me in," the angry voice cried. "Our warden's a terror."

Calypso stepped swiftly into a hanging cupboard. Oliver opened the door. "I was just going to bed," he said angrily.

"You alone? I thought I heard voices. I don't allow my lodgers to bring ladies in."

"Just fix the blackout and push off."

"Aren't you going to take cover?"

"No! All well now? Had a good peek round? Goodnight, then. Have a good raid." He closed the door after her and pulled Calypso out of the cupboard. "What d'you want to hide in there for?"

"It's Hector."

"It was my nosy landlady."

"I have to be careful because of Hector. If he found out he'd kill me. Oh, look at my hair." She began to comb it. "Goodness, I feel ill. Will you take home, Olly, please. I don't think I can be of much comfort—"

"You do sound a bit hoarse, now I come to listen."

As they walked across Green Park towards Westminster the All Clear sounded.

"I don't think the Furies want me comforted."

"It's midsummer night. Do hurry, Oliver. It won't be all clear unless Hector comes home to find me safely in bed. I don't want to get myself divorced."

"Don't fuss, it's not late. What's midsummer night got to do with us?"

"Nothing. I just thought – well, Hector said this morning that it's midsummer day and we've had the most wondrous summer so far. Hector loves hot weather."

"Damn and blast Hector, may he fry in hell."

"I forgot to tell you. He's in the Army now, got a commission in the Guards."

"I hope he gets killed. Here's your street."

"Oh good, he went in the car and it's not back. We don't seem to be very lucky, do we?" She put her arms round Oliver's neck and kissed him. "I'd better run or he'll be back before I am in bed." She fled down the street. Oliver watched, leaning against a lamp post, until some time later the Lagonda drew up and, resplendent in Blues, Hector stepped out, locked the car and let himself into the house. Unwilling to go back to Half Moon Street, Oliver walked across the park and down Knightsbridge until he found himself outside his aunt's house. Looking down the area steps he saw a chink of light and heard laughter. He ran down. Round the kitchen table sat Polly, Walter, Sophy and the twins.

"Oliver!" they cried, surprised and joyous. Oliver sat down at the table, rested his head on his arms and wept. Sophy came to stand by him, he put out a hand and she held it between hers.

★ ★ ★

257

On her way to the funeral years later, Polly remembered that night. "What a fool Oliver was," she said aloud. "Such a fool."

"I should have thought that was the last thing one could say about him," said her son, who was one of Oliver's admirers.

"I'm entitled to my opinion," said Polly, "he was a fool." Then, sensing her son's disagreement, she spoke with the irritation she had felt all those years before. "He was obsessed – crazed."

"About what?"

"Calypso."

"Well, I never!" said Iris, Polly's daughter. "She's so artificial."

"That's because she had a stroke, idiot," said her brother.

"No, it was a face-lift," said Iris, knowing best.

"She's had both a lift and a stroke," James persisted, knowing better still.

"Stop wrangling, you two," Polly flared up. "How horrible you are." She switched on the car radio to drown their voices and drove faster. She shouted above the pop music – "She is honest." Polly's son and daughter, sitting on the back seat so that Polly's mongrel could sit beside her, looked at one another in an effort to deduce what exactly their mother meant by honest in relation to Calypso.

SIXTEEN

Max Erstweiler was so excited by the success of his first wartime concert that he was unable to sleep. He telephoned Helena, who was staying with Polly. "I want you to come out with me, I am restless."

"But Max, I am just going to bed. Polly has made us a hot drink, we are tired."

"You must walk with me. You do not know the musical soul."

"Can't you walk alone?"

"Don't be feeble, Aunt," Polly whispered in her ear.

"If I am stopped I might be interrogated. I must have you to translate. I need to find calm by walking. I come at once." He rang off.

"Aunt Helena," said Polly, rinsing her cup at the sink, "that man is making use of you."

"He needs me. He is an alien."

"I quite see he needs moral support, but dragging you out now! We've been to his concert, we all clapped until our hands were sore! Why didn't Monika come?"

"She is afraid of the air raids."

"Aren't we all. There's no raid tonight. She could have come. Lots of us live with them, work through them. Why is she so terrified?"

"She just is. He will be round in a moment."

"But you're tired, Aunt."

"Not really, no."

"He's treating you as though you were his mistress. Oh!" Polly caught Helena's expression. "Are you?"

"Don't be ridiculous." Helena was blushing.

"Oho, I see."

"No, you don't." Helena was quick to deny a situation which was already established but which she was not prepared to discuss with Richard's niece. "The poor man is highly strung, he needs —"

"An audience. I shall go to bed. I have to be up early." Polly kissed her aunt.

"I suppose you realise it's two in the morning." She opened the door to Max.

"What about it?" Max came in. He did not at that time much like Polly, who resisted his charm. "I like to see cities in their sleep. Come, Helena," he called down the kitchen stairs and Helena obediently called back, "Coming, Max."

Polly got into bed resolving to telephone Calypso next day, for Calypso, watching Helena helping with the preparations for the concert, had said: "Aunt Helena is having a canter with Max Erstweiler."

Polly had mocked this theory on the grounds that their aunt was too old.

"She is a year younger than Hector," Calypso had said.

"But he is a man, that's different."

"I bet you I am right. I wonder how it began? If Sophy had not been sent to school she would know."

"She wouldn't necessarily tell us."

"She would if we asked her indirectly."

Remembering this conversation Polly curled up under the corrugated iron canopy and slept, so tired that she did not hear the siren wail to alert London to attack. There had been no news of Walter for weeks, and no sight of the twins since the beginning of what was later known as the Battle of Britain. All she knew was that each had been shot down once and survived. For all their cheerfulness when they telephoned, they sounded tired and frightened. That Helena should be having an affair with Max Erstweiler afforded light relief in a world of black anxiety.

"The war was very romantic," said Helena all those years later, driving down the motorway with Calypso's son Hamish.

"Surely not, Great-aunt."

"Surely yes. Why, Max and I went to Covent Garden at dawn and he bought flowers as they were unloaded from lorries. He filled a taxi with roses and carnations. He was exhilarated by his first concert in London. What a success! Those flowers! I can remember the smell now. We drove back as it grew light to Polly's house, where I was staying. It wasn't so romantic when we got there."

"Not enough flower vases?"

"No. Someone had just woken Polly to tell her her parents had been killed by a stray bomb. They were somewhere near Godalming, near the hospital. Her father was a doctor, you know."

"I didn't know."

"They can't have known anything about it, but it was sad for Max after his concert."

"Did he know them? Worse for Polly, surely."

"No, but think of the embarrassment of all those flowers, and Polly so upset."

"What happened to the flowers?"

"We told the taxi driver to take them to a hospital, but I expect he sold them. I kept some roses for Polly."

"Not so romantic, then."

"It was when he bought them. It is those moments one remembers. Oh, yes."

"Nice to look back." Hamish knew old people lived in the past. He was glad poor old Helena found it enjoyable.

"Nicer to think of him extravagantly buying flowers than to be on our way to his funeral. I'm not sending any flowers."

"Have I done the wrong thing? I ordered a wreath," said Hamish.

"Wrong? Right? You must do as you please. If it helps you to order a wreath, do. It can't help Max. A wreath isn't a lifebelt."

Hamish resented his passenger's snappy tone. In an effort to remain agreeable he said: "Max Erstweiler must have loved you very much."

"I suited him. He grew to rely on me. I taught him English manners and customs. I don't know about love. I loved him, I don't know whether he loved me as much."

"What happened to his wife?"

"Monika? She worried, grew very thin. Max liked women plump. I was plump. Yes."

"What was she worried about? You?"

"Oh no, no, no. Monika was quite used to Max's ways. She used to say he was worse than Furtwängler. Monika worried about their son."

"Oh. Should I know him?"

"He was in a concentration camp. Pauli. You must have heard of him."

"Oh dear. Yes."

"News filtered through from Switzerland and poor Monika

simply faded. Made no fuss, but she nearly died of anxiety."

"Poor woman."

"Well, it didn't help Max. Or suit him," Helena added. "No."

"But you did." Hamish's tone was congratulatory.

Helena smiled. "Yes," she said, looking back. "Mind you, musical souls – you will remember he called himself 'a musical soul'?"

"Yes, I remember, like Thomas Mann."

"They can be extremely boring."

"To the non-musical," Hamish teased.

"To anybody. Those mittel-European tantrums. I never stood for them. I used to clap my hands and say, 'Stop that, Erstweiler', and he did. Over-excitement made him play badly, not that I would have noticed, but that's what I was told, so I stopped him when I saw him working himself up. I'd say 'Stop it, I say, stop it!' and he would laugh and call me his '*Kleine* British Phlegm'." Helena laughed in ancient reminiscence.

"Not a very endearing pet name – Phlegm. I never heard him call you that. Nobody ever mentioned it."

"It was private. He used it in bed, too."

"Oh." Hamish ruminated, allowing a motorcycle to overtake him. "Why in bed, Great-aunt?"

"Does nobody ever tell you to stop?" enquired Helena with asperity.

"Sometimes," said Hamish, laughing.

"Well, then." Helena smiled, pressing her lips together, a habit she had formed when forced to have false teeth.

"It's very interesting to have you for a great-aunt," said Hamish, seeing her face in the driving mirror, "a great, a famous man's – er—"

"Mistress," said Helena. "No need to be coy, everybody knew then and now. Yes."

"Now we are on our way to his funeral."

"It's a bit thick." Helena used a colloquialism of her period.

"What is?"

"To be the last of my lot. It's a bore. Yes."

"You bear it very well."

"Not inside," said Helena, rummaging in her bag for a flask. "D'you think you could slow down while I have a swig? Max envied me this flask, it was my first husband's."

"Great-uncle Richard?"

"No, dear boy, I was married to a man with two legs, he was

killed in 1916. You must get your facts right. Richard came next. He rather envied this flask, too. I shan't offer you any as you are driving." Helena tipped the flask and swallowed. "That's better."

Hamish accelerated, moving smoothly down the M4. "What was your first husband called?"

"Anthony. He was beautiful. I never had to tell him to stop. No."

Hamish tried to imagine dried-up Helena as a sex object. Perhaps his mother or Polly had photographs. He must ask them.

"He was stopped almost before we began. Girls should comfort their men before they go to war." Helena's voice sank to a mutter.

"What did you say? I didn't hear."

"I said 'however uncomfortable'." Helena put the silver flask back in her bag. "Whatever the discomfort of comforting to the comforter. I did not fail there. No."

"I'm sure you never failed."

"Ho!" Helena laughed, exposing her teeth. "Of course I failed. I was not expert like your mother."

"My mother?" Hamish looked sidelong. Helena's face was wrinkled, like a Cox's Orange Pippin in January.

"I think if you don't mind stopping I shall buy some flowers, after all, when we get to Penzance. There's a good shop in Causeway Head."

"It's a very narrow street."

"But it has the best flower shop." She would go no further about Calypso.

SEVENTEEN

It was during the bombing in the autumn of 1940 that Helena bought two adjacent houses in Enderby Street. The price was low, the owners anxious to get away from London.

"You must be mad," Richard yelled on the telephone from Cornwall.

"I am using my own money."

"Throwing it away!"

"They are convenient for Harrods and Peter Jones."

"They will be bombed, I ask you."

"Not necessarily. No."

"The General says you should see a psychiatrist."

"So do my lawyer and my bank."

"Why can't you stay in Sarah and George's house?"

"They have moved to Bath."

"With Polly, then, as you are doing now? Buying houses in London is lunacy. That street is jerry-built. Not even solid. I ask you."

"The houses are an investment. Our three minutes are up. Goodbye." Helena turned to Polly. "What's so funny?"

"You and Uncle Richard. Your three minutes were not up."

"He was too cross to notice."

"I know why you are buying those houses. Shall you have a communicating door?"

"What a good idea. Do you know a reasonable builder?"

"We can find one. You know, Aunt, you can always stay here."

"Thank you, but this house is for the young. I want my own house. I shall enjoy furnishing it."

"Why stop at a door? The two front rooms knocked together would make room for a grand piano. You can have musical soirées."

"I think not. He's ruined my drawing-room for me in

264

Cornwall. Monika bangs away for him, it's no longer mine. Richard encouraged it. Oh no."

"Then where will Max have a piano?"

"He has the use of a piano in Pont Street. He can go on using that, it's only a minute away."

"You are tough."

"Pont Street won't get bombed."

"Why not?"

"It's too ugly. I refuse to have a piano in my house. No."

Helena moved fast, finding a builder who was willing to decorate and plumb. By the end of October her houses were ready, sparsely furnished but comfortable. The communicating door was disguised as a bookcase. Monika, should she overcome her fears, could stay with Max with propriety.

On the evening when Calypso visited Polly, arriving on her bicycle before air raid time, she found Helena and Polly discussing furniture.

"What have you bought so far?" Calypso was interested.

"Beds," said Helena, "the best from Heals."

"Very important. Hector had a frightful thing. He had slept in it with Daphne. It sagged in the middle. I bought a new one."

"I thought they weren't close."

"They weren't. Hector slept in his dressing-room. Daphne's Great Dane slept with her. That's what Hector says, one can't be sure."

"I shall collect furniture from damaged houses. Prices will be astronomical if we survive the war. I shall pick up antiques."

The girls looked at one another, amused. "Rather a gamble," suggested Calypso.

"Worth taking," said Helena. "Goodnight, girls."

"There's a lot more in Aunt Helena than I'd thought possible," said Polly. "What do you think Max is like in bed?"

"Better than Uncle Richard. By the way, I told Tony he could pick me up here when he comes off duty at eight. Is that all right?"

"Perfectly," said Polly coolly. "He seems to enjoy being a fireman. Who would have thought it?"

"You don't mind?"

"Why should I? He doesn't belong to me."

"I rather thought he did."

"I introduced you, didn't I?" Polly said equably.

"So you did, but I rather thought, well—"

"Only for a short time. Just long enough, actually."

"Long enough?"

"Yes. Darling, do you imagine if he were mine that I'd allow you to meet?"

"Tony says he doesn't understand you."

"Of course he does."

"D'you think that's him? There's someone at the door. Are you expecting anybody else?"

"No."

"He can see me home."

"Is Hector away?"

"Yes, Aldershot. I haven't seen him for a week. I'll let him in, shall I?"

"Don't show a light." Polly tidied the kitchen as Calypso ran upstairs to open the front door. She heard her exclaim and men's voices. Then Calypso came in, looking rather pink, followed by Tony and Oliver.

"Can you house me for a couple of days? I'm on embarkation leave." Oliver kissed Polly.

"Of course." Polly looked over his shoulder at Calypso. "Did you meet Tony on the steps? Tony's a fireman. Are you going on duty or coming off, Tony?" Her smile showed her slanting teeth.

"Coming off," said Tony, eyeing the girls, his expression conveying the words "as well you know". He said: "I saw your bicycle, Calypso. Someone might fall over it out there in the street."

"Yes. Well, I'm just leaving."

"I'll see you home," said Oliver.

"My bicycle."

"I'll wheel it, or run beside you."

"Oh Olly, like a faithful dog."

"Shall we go?"

Polly and Tony listened to them leave.

"Did she know he was coming?" he asked suspiciously.

"No, Tony, and nor did I."

Tony laughed. "I shall have to wait till his leave is over."

"I suppose so. Would you like to meet our aunt?"

"Your *aunt*? Not particularly."

"Helena. Max Erstweiler's chum."

"That aunt. Yes, I would. Is she here?"

"Just gone upstairs. She's bought two houses near here. She's
– well, you'd better meet her."

"I saw her at his concert. She didn't look musical. A dumpy
figure."

"She isn't, but she's learning all sorts of tricks."

"How do you know?"

"Not bed tricks, tricks of speech. She's taken to ending her
sentences with yes or no, like *Ja* and *Nein*. Her life, once so dull,
is now far from it."

"Lead me to her."

"Tony Wood became a great friend of Helena's," Polly later told
Iris and James as she drove them to the funeral.

"Really? Tony Wood? How did that come about? Isn't he
homosexual?"

Polly took a hand off the wheel to stroke her mongrel dog.
The dog continued to gaze ahead without acknowledgement.
"Well, he is, but at one time he was a great one for the girls. I'd
call him ambidextrous."

"Was he a friend of yours or Calypso's?"

"I introduced him to Calypso. We all shared him. Hector found
him amusing. Walter liked him, even Oliver grew to like him, I
believe, later, but it was Helena who really caught his fancy. He
was older than us, just that much nearer to Helena. She made use
of his sophistication, he taught her a lot, it helped with Max."

"I should have thought," said James, "that in the war, with
the bombing and so on, there wasn't much time for private life."

"That's where you are wrong," said Polly. "We all lived
intensely. We did things we would never have done otherwise.
It was a very happy time."

"What about fear? What about anxiety for your loved ones?"
Iris leaned from the back seat to speak to her mother.

"I was frightened and anxious all the time, but it made the
delights all the more so, the surprises more surprising. People
like Oliver, Walter, David and Paul appeared and disappeared, it
was wonderful that they were still alive. My parents were killed.
I thought they were safe in Godalming. In London I survived.
Calypso survived. If we were in love it was acute. We had fun.
I know Calypso did. I did and Helena, who had never had fun,
grabbed it. Tony, who was in London all the war, watched
us, was amused by us and in his way loved us. All the other

men came and went but Tony was always around."

"What about Oliver?"

"I saw him towards the end of 1940. Calypso had come to see me. He walked her home pushing her bicycle. She had a bicycle."

Holding Calypso by one hand, Oliver pushed the bicycle with the other. Calypso used her torch with care. "The wardens get awfully ratty if one flashes it about."

"Is Hector in London?" Oliver asked stiffly.

"No. He may turn up but I don't think so. I haven't seen him for weeks. I'm alone. I'd come round to see Polly and find out what Aunt Helena is up to."

"Who is that man?"

"Tony Wood. Friend of Polly's."

Oliver, holding Calypso's arm, now said: "I'm on embarkation leave."

"Again? Where are you going this time?"

"I don't know. Not supposed to tell."

"Egypt, I bet."

"How do you know?"

"Hector and his friends talk. He was at Dunkirk, you know."

"You said Dover last time I saw you."

"Well, he went across to collect the French from Dunkirk, then further along to Cherbourg. Some of them are awfully jolly."

"Jollier than me?"

"Much." Calypso chuckled as they walked in the dark. "One of them, a buddy of Hector's, rowed himself across to Dover, then got sent back to France only to have to bunk again. Lots of bunking, isn't there? Look at you in Norway."

"Is this your street?"

"Yes." Calypso was silent as they reached her house. "Would you bring the bicycle into the hall?"

Oliver propped the machine against a radiator and took Calypso in his arms, kissing her neck gently. "My darling."

"Darling Olly. Nice sofa. Come." She led him to her drawing-room. "I must pull the curtains. Take off your scratchy uniform. Oh, it isn't, I'd forgotten you'd become an officer, but take it off, I hate being squashed against buttons. Hector's make quite a pattern in groups of three, or is it four?"

"Being snobby about buttons won't put me off. You'd better unzip yourself this time—"

Calypso laughed, kicking off her shoes. Oliver watched her
undress, then walk naked across the room to put logs on the fire.
"One of my luxuries, having a log fire. We get the logs from a
friend of Hector's in Berkshire."

"Stop talking. Come here."

"I'm nervous."

"No, you're not. Here. There." He held her, stroking her back.
"Relax. Remember the camomile lawn – magic."

"Helena planted it for our games, our plots."

"Hush, pay attention."

"Oh, Oliver, Oliver."

"You didn't enjoy it. My God, you didn't enjoy it. Oh, damn
and hell and blast."

"I didn't say—"

"You didn't need to." Oliver was collecting his clothes, pulling
on his trousers, buttoning his shirt, tucking it into his trousers,
putting on his tie, putting on socks and shoes in bitter concentration.

Calypso sat naked on the sofa watching him, her eyes in her
pale face thoughtful. Below them the street door opened with a
bang, then slammed shut. There was a clatter of collision with
the bicycle, a man's voice: "Whoops!"

Calypso snatched her dress, pulling it over her head, zipping
it up. "Hector." She pushed her underclothes behind a cushion.

"Whoops-a-daisy." The bicycle clattered again. Hector broke
into song: "And when I'm dead don't bury me at all." He kicked
the bicycle. "Out of my way, weighy! Just pickle my bones in
alcohol."

Calypso, who had been listening intently, grinned. "He's in a
good temper. Thank God."

"Is he often drunk?"

"Sometimes." She was evasive.

"Violent?"

"I think you'd better go." She went out on the landing and
leaned over the banisters, looking down. Hector lay entangled
with the bicycle. "He's passing out," she whispered.

"Shall I help you put him to bed?"

"No, no. I'll see you out from the kitchen, he's blocking the
front door. Come on," she said impatiently.

"Are you sure? Surely I can—"

"No. Please, Olly, go." She took his hand, leading him down
to the basement, through the kitchen, up the area steps.

In the street he took her shoulders, looking into her face. "Goodbye."

"It was small comfort, I'm afraid. Better than none, I hope."

Almost, Oliver thought, she minded. "Better to know." His voice was neutral. He kissed her lightly and was gone, his steps diminishing fast in the quiet street.

Calypso noticed the Lagonda at an angle to the pavement, its lights still on. She parked the car properly, switched off the lights. Back in the house she disentangled Hector's legs from the bicycle, fetched cushions to prop his head and blankets from the dressing-room bed, making him as comfortable as possible, unbuttoning his tunic.

"What a pattern of buttons!" The affection in her voice surprised her. Hector opened his eyes, focusing carefully, squinting up.

"I'm drunk."

"I know. Come to bed when you can."

"I'm not. I'm not – er – er – what do I want to say? Calypso, don't leave me, stay here."

She lay down beside him. He put an arm round her while she pulled the blankets up to cover herself.

"Come close."

"Your buttons hurt."

"Never mind."

"I'm terribly uncomfortable."

"Go to sleep."

"D'you think you could get up to bed?"

"All fours."

"I'll help you. Come on, try."

"So drunk."

"Yes. Try harder."

Hector suddenly reared to his feet and headed up the stairs at a run. As she propped the bicycle against the wall she heard a crash and Hector laughing. She helped him undress, levering him out of his trousers. "There, lie still."

"The room's going round and round and it comes out here."

"I'll make us some coffee."

When she came back with the coffee Hector was asleep. Calypso drank coffee, watching Hector. He looked vulnerable, eyes closed under his thick eyebrows. She smoothed them gently with a finger and then ran it along his lips, which were slightly rough. Outside the All Clear sounded. She had not realised there was an alert. She put the light out and drew the curtains to look down at the street. Was it possible Oliver was still there? The street was empty.

As she stood looking down a special constable strolled round the corner. He was joined by an air raid warden. She saw them laughing. They walked along to Hector's car and admired it. The warden patted the bonnet as though it were the nose of a horse. Calypso turned to look at Hector whose eyes were open watching her.

"Hector?"

He pulled her down. "Does my breath smell?"

"No." She sniffed. "Yes."

"Get in with me. Would you mind?"

"No. What's the matter?" She slipped her dress over her head and got in beside him. "What's the matter?"

"I'm on embarkation leave."

"You too?"

"Who else?"

"Oliver."

"Was he here?"

"Yes, he walked me home from Polly's."

"He's in love with you."

"He *thinks* he is."

"And you?"

"No. I like all those boys. They are cousins, might be brothers."

"There's incest."

"Not for me."

"I might be your father."

"My father never behaved like you. Wild."

"Ah me. Do you think there's any Alka Seltzer?"

"Yes. And coffee." She brought him coffee. He drank and lay back with his arm round her shoulders.

"Will you go to Scotland? Stay there?"

"Oh no!"

"Would be safe."

"But lonely. I hate it. I'd die of melancholy. When are you off?"

"Two weeks. Put my affairs in order. Get lightweight uniform."

"Egypt?"

"Probably. I must do a dash north, will you come with me?"

"Of course I will, just for a day or two, not more."

"I wish you'd stay there, safe out of London."

"If London gets too bad I'll go to Cornwall. I'll take care of myself."

"Promise?"

"Yes."

"That man Tony Wood is in love with you too."

"It isn't love, it's lust."

"Do you know the difference?"

"I know lust. I don't think I know love." Calypso leant her head back, closing her eyes.

"Lucky you, oh lucky, lucky you."

"Why? I thought I was missing something."

"You are, you certainly are."

"What then?"

"Pain, lots of pain."

"You do talk rubbish." Calypso chuckled.

"If you say so," said Hector drily.

"I don't even know anyone who is in love. I don't think it exists."

"Quite apart from me, it's under your lovely nose."

"Who, for God's sake?"

"Helena, Polly, Sophy."

"What a buffoon you are. Perhaps that's why I put up with you, apart from your money."

"That reminds me, I must make my will."

"What filthy bad taste."

"I'm a hard-headed Scot."

"You hurt me."

"Good. Another time," Hector's voice was turning nasty, "please leave your bicycle where I won't fall over it." They laughed together, relaxing.

"My mother says she and my father used to laugh together," Hamish said conversationally to his passenger.

"Yes, they did. Calypso had very little humour, but then she had no love either, poor girl."

"They say my father had humour."

"He also had love."

"Did he love my mother?"

"He adored her and he knew her."

"What do you mean? You sound a bit," Hamish hesitated, "a bit, well, as though you didn't like my mother."

"I like her, she's always been very nice to me, she's not a giver, that's all. She can't help her character."

"She gave my father me."

"You were part of a bargain. For his money an heir."

Hamish pulled across to the slow lane and stopped the car.

"What's the matter? Something wrong with the engine?" Helena watched Hamish get out and stand with his back to her. He reminded her of Hector at his wedding long ago, tall, towering above Calypso, who was a tall girl.

"Did he love me?" Hamish got back into the car.

"He loved you very much."

"Are you sure? I never really knew."

"Quite sure. He was very happy about you. You are very like your father, less endearing, though."

Hamish laughed. "You are a wicked old woman."

"I know I am." Helena nodded. "Evil."

EIGHTEEN

Polly answered the telephone. "Oh, hullo, Monika, how are you? Can you speak louder?"

"Polly, we only have three minutes, can you find Helena, it is urgent."

"There's a raid on, try to speak louder."

"*Mein Gott!* I want Helena. She does not answer her phone."

"She's gone to Max's concert in Liverpool."

"There are raids there too, *lieber Gott.* What is that noise?"

"A bomb." Polly crept under the table, taking the telephone with her. "Sophy and I are under the kitchen table. What do you want Helena for?"

"Richard is ill. I think and *der General* and *der Rektor* thinks she should come, and *Frau Rektor.*"

"I see. I'll try and get hold of her. She will be back in London tomorrow. How ill is he? What? I can't hear you," Polly shouted.

"It was flu and now pneumonia."

"Poor old boy. Gosh, that was close."

"What did you say? Polly, are those bombs?"

"Yes," yelled Polly. "I'll do what I can. Don't worry, I promise."

"We have bombs too in Penzance."

"Yes, I heard about them."

"They hit *der* wine merchant, your uncle got his chill trying to rescue his wine."

"His *what?*"

"His wine. He had tree dozen clarets. They got bomped." Monika's voice faded. Polly clutched Sophy as she replaced the receiver.

"His claret!" The girls shrieked with laughter.

"You girls got hysterics?" Tony Wood came in from the street. "It's quite lively tonight."

"Aren't you on duty?"

"Just on my way, came to see if you were all right. What's Sophy doing here? You all right, Sophy?"

"Yes, thanks. My holidays have started."

"If we can find Aunt Helena you can travel down with her."

"I'd much rather go alone, thank you."

"Safer with Helena. Plymouth has raids too, you have to go through it."

"People always help. I'd rather be alone—" They all cowered, listening to the sound of a bomb coming down. "Ouch, that was close."

"Somewhere near the Brompton Road."

"Wish I could leave my tin hat with you. Here comes another." Tony put an arm round each girl. They listened. Not far away an anti-aircraft gun fired, pom, pom, pom – pom, pom, pom.

"*And* another. What time are you on duty?"

"In half an hour. Must leave you, I'm afraid. I brought you some whisky."

"How good of you. Do be careful."

"I'll be all right. And another! I always think of Peter Pan—"

"Captain Hook's trousers tearing."

"Of course. Goodbye, girls, must be off." Tony kissed the girls. "Keep under that table." He was gone.

"Nice of him to come, it's out of his way. Lovely whisky."

"I wish Oliver was here. Have you heard from him?" Sophy came as close as she could to Polly.

"Aunt Sarah had a letter, he's in the Middle East. Safer than Walter on the Atlantic run. He says it's awful, sick all the time, non-stop."

"Polly."

"Yes?" They huddled together.

"You remember the Terror Run?"

"Of course I do. Yes, let's think of that. The sea, the moon, the camomile lawn."

"I'm scared. I wish – I must tell."

"It will be over soon. We will all be back there one day."

"Polly, on the cliff path I—" The sound of a bomb very near drowned Sophy's voice. It fell close by and Sophy finished her sentence on a high note of fear, " . . . so I – it was just a push," but Polly listened to the falling masonry and glass tinkling into the street and failed to hear what Sophy heard, the cry of a man, the sound of seagulls. She was concerned that Sophy wept and trembled in her arms. "Don't, Sophy, that one was further away, it will be over soon. When the All Clear sounds I'll make some tea and lace it. There may be people hurt out there, we must help them. Tony's whisky will be welcome."

"I tried to tell you."

"Of course you did. Naturally. Listen. No guns, no planes. Ah, the All Clear. Pop up the steps and look, while I put the kettle on. I shall have to get hold of Aunt Helena if the telephone's working."

Later, leaving Sophy to dispense tea to an assortment of bombed-out neighbours with tales of lucky escapes, Polly managed to get through to the hotel in Liverpool where she knew Max Erstweiler was staying.

"'Allo. Erstweiler *hier*."

"Max, do you know where Aunt Helena is? I'm trying to get hold of her. Monika rang up from Cornwall."

"Monika?" Max's voice conveyed distrust. "What she want?"

"She wants Helena."

"What for she want Helena?" Max switched on the bedside light and prodded Helena, asleep beside him. Helena woke, saw Max's finger to his lips, the other hand holding the telephone.

"It is five in the morning."

"I know it. Can you find Helena? Monika says Uncle Richard is very ill. She and the Rector and the General think Helena should come."

"I find her, *ein Moment*." Max stuffed the telephone under the pillow. "It is Richard, is ill, you should go to him."

"Oh damn." Helena pushed her hair back and pulled a shawl round her shoulders. She held out her hand for the receiver. "Helena here. What's the matter? I only just got to sleep. There was a raid after Max's concert. It was a great success, the concert."

"Aunt Helena, Monika tried to find you, Uncle Richard is very ill."

"I knew he had flu."

"Well, now he's got pneumonia."

"How did he get that?" Helena listened to Polly's voice shouting eerily from London, a garbled explanation.

"His claret? Trying to save his claret? It is my claret. I thought we might run short, can't get rice either now. No, not mice, rice. No."

Polly's voice suddenly sounded clear and angry. "While you are waffling he may be dying. I'm putting Sophy on the ten o'clock train. If you can get to Bristol you could join it at Exeter."

"Sophy?"

"Yes, her holidays have started. She's here but it isn't healthy. I have to work. I can't leave her in the house alone."

"I'll leave as soon as I can. Can you get through to Cornwall? I can't. I tried last night. Max wanted to tell Monika about the concert," Helena lied. She put the telephone down. "Why does one lie?"

"Instinct." Max was watching her, pink, amply rounded, blonde, the type he liked. "You look like a Greuze."

"What's that?" Helena was angrily brushing her hair. "How inconvenient this is! Oh, do be of some help, find out about trains while I pack. Buck up. Just like Richard to rush out in the rain with flu. I bet all the claret was running down the gutter. Oh, why do I have to behave badly in times of crisis?" Helena wailed with frustration.

"*Nimm deine Ihre Arschbacken zusammen,*" exclaimed Max.

"What's that?"

"A coarse German expression. I will enquire for trains."

"I'd forgotten Sophy's holidays, lost my head as well as my heart."

"You do not love me."

"Not at the moment. *Do* go and ask about trains. There will be some terrible cross-country connection. Hurry up and do it."

Sophy from her corner saw Helena puffing from another platform at Exeter to join the train. She huddled back, hiding her face with a book, having no wish to endure Helena's company on the train, which stopped at every station from Exeter to Penzance. She hid, even though she suspected Helena had no more wish for her company than she for Helena's.

Crammed into an over-full carriage Helena reproached herself for neglecting Richard, all too aware that since the incident in the daffodil field she had discarded her former life, left the running of her household to her lover's wife, the care of Sophy to a school, with help in the holidays from the Rectory. In her mind she saw herself and Max making love under a blue sky surrounded by golden daffodils, ecstasy in the midst of war. She ignored the truth, which was that the daffodil season had long been over, the leaves withered to a dull straw colour, that there were weeds among the bulbs and that while slipping off her knickers she had been stung by nettles. What was true was that the encounter with Max had produced the first orgasm she had ever experienced and in return she loved him with an aggressive devotion he found touching and useful. It wasn't until now that Richard was ill that she considered his feelings and felt regret, tinged with guilt, about her new mode of life. She had no intention of changing it. Another woman, a good woman, would stand by Richard just because he was boring, just because he had lost a leg, just because he'd been gassed. "Not me," said Helena aloud, to confirm the course of her life. "Not for me." Her neighbour, a fresh-faced Wren, looked at her in surprise.

"I said there's no tea," said Helena, "no tea on this train. No."

"Oh. Shall I get you a cup at Plymouth? I get off there. There is usually a buffet, unless the station has been disrupted by a raid."

"It's very kind of you, but I think not, no." The Wren went back to sleep. Helena planned ahead for her life in London. It was fortunate that Monika was terrified of raids and that Richard loathed London, only visiting it once a year to stay at his club for his regimental dinner, to meet his few remaining contemporaries. Now, with the war, there were no dinners for retired Majors, but opportunity for adultery for their wives. Helena considered the situation with wry amusement.

She had recently met Hector in the street and he had taken her into the Ritz bar. As they sat in the bar he had pointed to the people around them. "Look at them all, not one with a wife or husband. All hell let loose. War makes people fearfully randy. It may not apply to you, or does it?" He had appraised Helena, sharp-eyed under his eyebrows. She had blushed. "Well, good luck to you, old girl. Now I'm in the Army Calypso's out every night. She says she goes round to Polly but that's all my eye. She's picked up a friend of Polly's, that's true, Tony Wood, entertaining fellow, and she meets Oliver there. He's in love with her."

"They were children together."

"*Ceci n'empêche cela!* The poor chap's crazy about her."

"She isn't about him." Helena knew this in her bones.

"Maybe. Then there's Walter and those twins. Wouldn't blame her there. What a handsome pair! If one had a brougham and they were horses—"

"Those three are over Calypso."

"Really? Nice to know. But look at the choice she has. All the most enterprising Frogs, Dutch, Belgians, Poles, you name it. They'll be around sniffing and God help us husbands when the Americans make up their minds. No, no, this is one hell of an opportunity for licence." Hector drained his glass and signalled to the barman, "Same again."

"No, thank you. You and I are not particularly licentious." Helena in her role as Max's mistress heard herself making remarks she would never have made until recently.

"No – though – well, what I mean is when I am overseas, as I shall be shortly, I'm not fool enough to imagine Calypso sitting at home, tatting."

"And what shall you do?"

"I shall be propping up the bar with a popsy, as I'm doing now."

"Not with such innocence, I daresay." Helena's martini had gone straight to her head.

"You have your fiddler—"

"How—"

"News gets around, it gets around, good news and true."

Helena wondered why she had made no denial and decided that she was proud to be pointed out as Max's mistress. It was the only thing that got her through the intolerably boring concerts. "Are you fond of music?" she asked Hector.

"Yes, but not night and day. I bet you feel the same." He had stood up to leave, settling his Sam Browne belt at his waist. They had exchanged a glance before parting which Helena was to remember. It said "Were it not for Calypso" and "Were it not for Max". Sitting in the train on her way back to her husband Helena gave a little laugh. The soldier opposite her sized her up, thinking her a bit touched. He was very young, as yet unaware of the extremes a woman of forty's pent-up sexuality could lead to. Helena had tried to conceal her ignorance from Max, but he had noted and played on it, enjoying her pleasure as one would enjoy a volcanic eruption. Not being at a safe distance added spice to his practised palate.

When at weary last the train drew in Helena roused herself, snatched nervously at her suitcase and stepped out on to the platform, half-consciously searching for her old self, her old pre-occupations with Richard, her household, her garden, her friends in the neighbourhood. Ahead of her she caught sight of Sophy, a semi-familiar figure walking lopsided because of her suitcase, grown since she had last seen her, almost into that stage which is now called teenage but which Helena termed awkward. She felt a spasm of anger as a young man in uniform overtook Sophy and took her heavy case, smiling down as Sophy looked up with laughing profile. Then she saw Sophy wave an arm and break into a run to greet Monika, holding the dachshund on a lead. Sophy and Monika embraced, the dog leapt up barking, the young man carried the case to the car, saluted and went on his way. "My car, what's she doing with my car?" Helena knew she was being unreasonable as she watched Monika question Sophy and Sophy shake a negative. Monika looked worried, got into the car and Sophy, holding the wriggling dog, followed. Monika started the engine. Helena called out loudly: "Hey! Monika!"

Monika looked relieved and jumped out of the car, leaving the engine running. "Sophy said you were not on the train. What a relief you are here." Sophy looked secretive.

"I joined it at Exeter. I didn't see you." Helena accepted Sophy's help with her suitcase.

"Nor I you," Sophy lied.

"Poor Richard will be so glad," Monika said gently. "Perhaps you should drive, yes?"

"No, you drive, I expect you can manage." Helena was ungracious, angry with herself. "And how is he? Much better?"

"Not better, oh Helena, he is not better."

Helena sighed a sigh of exasperation. "We'd better be getting along. Can't you keep that animal still, child," although the animal sat perfectly still in Sophy's arms. Helena met its beady eyes and glanced away from Sophy's black ones. Sophy smiled.

"You must be so worried." Monika headed the car out of the town.

"Of course I am. Max sent his love," she added cruelly.

"He has so much." Monika, used to this kind of attack, rather enjoyed it. "How was the concert?"

"Splendid. How lovely the sea smells." Her pre-war self was roused. She consciously tried to get back to Helena, the aunt by marriage of Richard's nephews and nieces, churchgoer, member of the Women's Institute.

"That is where the bomp fell." Monika slowed the car as they drove through the town. "Poor Richard *unt der General* were very upset but no people hurt at all."

"All that lovely wine! I'd asked them to keep it for me. We will win this war, but think what the Germans will have drunk meanwhile. Any news of your son?"

"No." Monika increased speed. "None," choking back her anguish.

"Can I get out before we get to the house? I'll give Duck a run." Monika stopped to let Sophy and the dog out. "She loves that dog and so does Richard. You are a good woman, Helena."

"Oh no I am not. No."

"Come, Duck, run." Sophy raced up the hill with the delighted dog, arriving abruptly on the camomile lawn. She ran round it, brushing the turf with her feet. It was the wrong time of year and the scent was faint. She stopped running and looked at the sea, rough and grey, sea horses turning into rollers to crash against the cliffs. She looked along the path, blocked by barbed wire, to the coastguard station once so bravely white, now camouflaged dirty green and brown. "It's all gone," she cried miserably to the dog, who whimpered, feeling the wind sharp and cruel on his thin coat.

Helena went upstairs, leaving Monika to manage the luggage. Richard lay passive, propped on pillows.

"Poor fellow. How d'you feel?" Helena bent to kiss his forehead. "You've got a temperature. What's the doctor doing about it?"

"Given me M and B." Richard's voice was weak.

"Hope it works. Who changed the room round?" Helena looked disapprovingly at a change in the order of furniture.

"Monika. Easier to nurse me. She is very good."

"She called me good just now." Helena laughed and Richard smiled a conniving smile. "You'll be all right." Helena's voice was confident.

"Now you are here."

Helena felt a pang of guilt. "Sophy was on the train. We didn't see each other until we arrived. Polly posted her off from Paddington. I was in Liverpool with Max when I heard you were ill."

"No need for you to bother."

"Probably not. All the same, it wouldn't look well if I didn't come."

"What would the neighbours say? I ask you."

"Are you joking?"

"Of course not." Richard's voice was hoarse. "Must think of the General and Monika. Not that she cares." His voice dropped to a mutter. "She's used to it. Used to it! I ask you." He began to cough.

"Shall you get used to it?"

Richard nodded. He looked feeble and unattractive. Helena looked round the room for his leg and, not seeing it, caught his eye.

"She put it next door."

"Oh." Helena experienced a rush of friendship for Richard, smiled at him warmly, then sat beside him holding his hand. She felt they had briefly exchanged the truth and grown closer. The dachshund scratched at the door.

"There's your dog. He loves you."

"Yes." Richard watched his wife walk across the room to let the dog in. Her walk was different.

"I can't bully you any more," he said, coughing.

"You never really succeeded." Helena watched the dog jump on to the bed and settle its head close to Richard's, looking at her down its long nose.

"She's moved the kitchen furniture and you are to sleep in the spare room."

"Oh." Helena was surprised into annoyance. "Why?"

"You might catch my flu."

"And if I did?"

"You'd stay longer." He laughed, then coughed, getting very red in the face.

"So that's how it is." Helena watched him cough, trying to speak between spasms. "What did you say?"

"A straight swap," he gasped.

"But it isn't, is it?" she queried.

"No." He held the dog's absurd nose loosely in his hand, its wet black tip showing between thumb and forefinger, its eyes peering across his veined fist. "But it's all right."

Helena was furious, insulted. He was her husband, he should mind.

"You've got bronchial pneumonia," she said, wondering whether he would die, whether if he did she would mind.

"Not dying, though." The bout of coughing stopped. He lay back.

"Uncle Richard?" Sophy came in, hurried up to the bed and kissed him, then stood back holding his hand, looking down at him.

Richard's eyes lit up. "Sophy."

"Am I glad to see you!" the child exclaimed. Helena was surprised. Sophy had never shown Richard affection.

"Thanks for your letters," she said. "They make school bearable."

"Good," he said, holding her hand. "Good."

He loves her, Helena told herself, loves her. Sophy sensed something and, turning to Helena, said: "He writes to me about the garden and the birds and what's happening in the village and what the General thinks and the Rector and all that, so that I know it's all here, that I'm not just homesick for an idea. I always end my letters, 'Love to the camomile lawn'." She paused and looked at Helena. "You planted it, didn't you?"

"Yes," said Helena remembering. "They all said it wouldn't grow."

"But it does." Sophy felt warmth for her aunt, for a brief moment they liked each other.

"You've grown." Richard held on to Sophy's hand. "One day—" he began to cough again, a hard, racking cough. "Bugger this cough, got pneumonia too, doctor says 'Being gassed didn't help'. The Huns didn't do it to help us. I ask you! Did it to kill us. Sloppy use of the English language."

"Time you stopped talking." Monika sailed into the sick room carrying an inhaler. "Swallow your pills and then you inhale, yes?"

"Whatever you say, my dear."

His dear! Helena raised her eyebrows.

"He has talked too much." Monika dismissed Helena gently, Sophy too.

Helena followed Sophy downstairs. "He doesn't write to me," she said.

"You don't need letters. You've got so much. Oh, how wizard!" Sophy admired the new arrangement of the kitchen. "Uncle Richard said I'd like it. You like it, don't you?" She turned to Helena.

"Yes." Helena looked at the transformed kitchen. "I admit I do."

"Much cosier than in Cook's day, quite Viennese, isn't it?"

"Yes."

"She's enjoying the factory."

"Who? What factory?"

"Cook."

"How do you know?"

"We write. She's engaged to the foreman, he's called Terence and is a widower."

"You do keep in touch."

"I must. Otherwise I—"

"What?" Helena stopped staring at the unrecognisable kitchen and looked at Richard's niece.

"Nothing." Sophy patted a cushion which had appeared from another part of the house to soften an upright chair. "Otherwise I should get lost," she said to herself, "disappear."

NINETEEN

"I shall have to stop to let Jumbo out."

"You can't stop on the motorway, Ma." Iris and James spoke together, knowing best.

"I wasn't born yesterday. I can turn off at the next junction."

"Junction 17 is two miles on," James and Iris chorused.

Children! thought Polly. "Travelling in the war was quite different," she said. "There was no petrol except for short runs and the trains were full to bursting. People like Calypso managed to get sleepers. She used to press ten bob into the attendant's hand, look him in the eye and say, 'I am the Member of Parliament for Hogmanay' or whatever Hector's constituency was. It worked even when she went to Penzance."

"He was an MP, wasn't he – Conservative?"

"Yes." Polly turned off the motorway. "All right, Jumbo, I'll let you out in a moment. When he went off to war some other member looked after his constituency. He came back to vote Labour and chuck politics." She stopped the car, let Jumbo out on to the grass verge. "Don't take all day," she said to the dog. "Hector had more constituents in the Highland regiments than anywhere else."

"Charging across the desert with bagpipes?" Iris watched the dog defecating. "He did want to be let out."

Polly whistled. The dog, who had not finished, ignored her.

"I can't somehow see Calypso in the Highlands." James snapped his fingers at the dog, now scratching the grass, sending little clods of turf high.

"She went once on their honeymoon and once just before Hector went overseas. Catherine came from his place, Hamish's now, of course. Catherine had him up there when he was an infant and later for his holidays. Calypso found it dreary and isolated."

"Not her style." Iris pulled the dog into the car. It jumped on to the front seat beside Polly.

"Not her style at all." Polly drove back on to the motorway. "Of course Hamish—"

"Hamish behaves as though he had no drop of English blood," Iris agreed, "totally Highland."

"And yet he is Calypso's child."

"If anyone had told me this would be enjoyable I would have told them to get their head examined." Calypso, held tight in Hector's arms, rocked with the train. Hector held her, pressing his feet against the foot of the bunk.

"I rather like the rhythm," she whispered in his ear. "It says, 'Fuck fuck-fucker fuck fuck fuck-fucker fuck.' "

He turned his head to find her mouth. "Improper words."

"Not for a wife."

"Another go?"

"Another go. Don't fall out of the bunk."

"I'll try not to."

"What time do we get to Euston?"

"Just shut up for a while."

When she slept he held her in his arms. The train roared south through the night. The engine shrieked eerily.

"Are we nearly there?" she said sleepily.

"No, not yet."

"We are too big for this bunk."

"Do you want me to move to mine?"

"Not if you can bear the discomfort."

If I tell her how happy I am she will laugh, he thought, gritting his teeth against the agonies of cramp.

"Oh, I must stretch, you are squashing me." She was suddenly fully awake, pushing him on to the floor. "D'you think there's any whisky left in that bottle?" She pulled a jersey on and sat up.

He had stood up, swaying with the train, to reach up, find the whisky, pour her a drink.

"D'you think the puppy is all right?" Calypso fumbled under the bunk to peer into a basket where crouched a small brindled cairn with a black face. It wagged its tail. "Yes, he's all right." She closed the basket. "He's a lovely present." She took the whisky from Hector, who watched her sitting swinging her long bare legs, wearing her jersey. Hector poured himself a drink and sat beside her, putting his free hand to cover her warm stomach, feel her hair.

"I shall call him 'Highland Fling' but 'Hamish' for short." She tossed back the whisky. "It's a family name, isn't it?"

"Not for a *dog*," he shouted at her in sudden rage.

"I didn't mean the dog." He could not read her expression. "You are on embarkation leave, aren't you?"

"Darling—" he stared back at her.

"Yes. With any luck. It'll keep me busy. Oh, Hector, do I see a tear?"

"I can't help it – I love you."

"Is it so painful?" Her wry smile made him laugh.

"Agony," he said. "You wouldn't know."

"Glad I don't."

"Calypso had a dog in the war." Polly increased speed.

"I thought she didn't like animals," said James, who did.

"She liked that dog, horrid little thing. It bit and was never properly house-trained. Hector gave it to her. It slept on her bed."

"Is that the animal that bit Tony?"

"Must have been, she never had any other dog."

"So Tony isn't telling tall stories when he says he slept with Calypso," James remarked.

"Shooting a line, they said at the time," Polly agreed. "I hope we aren't going to be late. It's wrong to be late for a funeral. You wait for it all your life and when people are late it seems rude."

"He won't know, Ma. It's not as though it's a concert. Anyway, the funeral is tomorrow."

"There was always another concert."

"Oh really, Ma! Try not to fuss."

"You can cough and sneeze and cry at funerals but you mustn't be late," said Polly sadly.

"Oh Ma, just drive carefully or we will be having a mass do."

Calypso watched Hector pack.

"Shall you grow a military moustache? It would make you very unattractive."

"Would you mind?"

"I shan't be there to see it."

"Calypso, darling, will you have Catherine?"

"Who is Catherine? What for?"

"You know perfectly well. Her father bred the puppy, she will look after the baby."

"And me?"

"Yes."

"But I don't know yet whether I am having a baby. Shan't know for weeks and weeks."

"If you do I want you to have Catherine."

"All right, I will, but only when it's born. Why isn't she in war work? Why isn't she an ATT or a Wren, is she wanting or something?" Watching Hector pack made Calypso disagreeable.

"She's lame."

"Poor girl. Sorry. But I don't want one of your people spying on me."

Hector smacked Calypso's face quite hard. "You fool, do you think I like going off like this, leaving you with no one to look after you? You won't go to your parents because you'd be bored, you won't go to Scotland, you'd be bored there, you insist on staying in London, you may get bombed. I worry."

"No need to hit me. That's much more of a worry."

"Don't let's get sour."

"All right, I'll send for Catherine if anything happens."

"Hector went off in a filthy temper." Calypso sat on the edge of Polly's kitchen table swinging her legs. "All the rush of packing."

"Shall you miss him?"

"I don't intend to. It's lovely having the house to myself, working when I want, going to bed when I want."

"With whom you want."

"I didn't say that."

"You didn't, of course." Polly wondered who Calypso intended going to bed with, whether Tony had yet staked a claim.

"If you get lonely you can always come here."

"Thanks. Any news of Walter?"

"Not for ages and ages."

"The twins?"

"They are alive. They come up when they get a night off."

"Always together?"

"Usually one at a time. They get awful nightmares, Calypso. They scream."

"So would I if I were shot down. It's hard to take in, though.

Hector says you look up and if someone's missing from breakfast in the mess it puts you off your nosh; you think it may be you tomorrow. That's what Hector says. It may be quite different for the twins. Hector's experience was in the last war."

"Like Uncle Richard. Funny that Hector is as old as that. They won't let him near any fighting, will they?"

"He's awfully aggressive, he might be very good at it."

"Walter says they take ages to get there and they might be torpedoed."

"Thanks a lot, you're very cheering. I don't know where 'there' is, Cairo or Crete or the Suez Canal. Hector won't like being stuck on a ship, he hates inactivity. Polly, d'you hear things in your office, real news?"

"You can read the papers, listen to the wireless."

"But can one believe one word? Look at Dunkirk. Hector says it was a shameful shambles."

"Does he? We thought so in our office but we didn't dare say so. Goodness." Polly looked thoughtfully at Calypso respecting Hector. "My boss thought we'd be invaded by the end of June, he even knew the date."

"And what was that?"

"June 24th. I remember because it was Midsummer Day. Why are you laughing?" Polly was startled by Calypso's giggles.

"Nothing, oh nothing. Poor Oliver. I had tonsillitis. I wonder where he is now? He went off in a temper, too."

"I think we should ring up the old people while we are together. Aunt Sarah's a worrier and I haven't heard anything from Cornwall for weeks. Helena behaves as though they didn't exist."

"She's having such a good time." Calypso spoke with admiration. "I never would have thought it of her, would you?"

"Not in my wildest dreams."

"We kept in touch by telephone," said Polly, speaking over her shoulder to Iris and James. "In the war," she added, catching James's expression in the driving mirror. "This drive, this funeral, thinking of Max, Uncle Richard and all of them brings it all back."

"You seem to remember it all very vividly." Iris leaned over from the back seat to stroke Jumbo.

"Vivid, yes. London on fire. The House of Commons, the Guildhall, the East End. Some nights we climbed on the roof to watch. Turner couldn't have done better. Other times we hid under the kitchen table."

"You make it sound beautiful and exhilarating, fun even."

"It was. One should be ashamed. Before it started we all swore we wouldn't become War Bores like Uncle Richard. Gosh, he was boring. On and on about comradeship, courage, carnage and—"

"Clap?" suggested James.

"If his generation caught clap it wasn't mentioned. Poor old fellow."

"You never talk about your parents, Ma."

"I know, I don't know why." Polly shifted in the driving seat. "One day they were there, Father in his hospital, Mother doing war work, and the next they were whooshed away by one stray bomb. Walter couldn't get to the funeral, he was at sea. Aunt Helena and Aunt Sarah and Uncle George came. It's an awful thing to say but I simply seemed to forget about them. There was so much going on."

"Oh," murmured Iris and James, wondering whether in the event of Polly's sudden demise they would take it so calmly.

Of course they would have objected to what went on, interfered, thought Polly to herself. "Divine Providence is pretty quirky," she said aloud. "We used to telephone. We were rationed to three minutes and had to cram all the news into that."

"Any news, Aunt Sarah? Any news? How are you and Uncle George?"

"We are well, my dear. How are you?"

"I'm well. Hector's gone overseas."

"My dear child, are you alone?"

"I'm with Polly at the moment."

"You shouldn't be alone."

"I like it. Any news of Oliver?"

"We had a letter. He's in Egypt."

"How d'you know? I thought they weren't allowed—"

"He said the weather's lovely. Lots of old friends call. They just toot and come in."

"How naughty of him!" Polly took the telephone from Calypso. "Not that it does much harm. I've no news of Walter, he's at sea. We are going to ring the Cornish lot."

"They've got someone they don't like planted on them. I couldn't make out what Monika said, you know her accent. I didn't talk to your uncle, he was out. I know you are busy, but could you get Calypso to go down and see them? Helena has just deserted. This love affair's gone to her head."

"Not only her head," said Polly. "Damn, that's the three minutes."

They waited patiently to get through to Cornwall. The telephone was answered by Richard.

"Ah, Calypso, just the girl. I want to talk to your Hector."

"You can't, he's gone overseas."

"Then give him a message."

"I can't get hold of him, Uncle."

"My dear you must, the bloody Army's put a gun under my nose. I ask you, a gun!"

"What sort of gun?"

"Anti-aircraft. It makes us a target. The Hun will shoot us."

"Surely it's camouflaged?"

"Right under my nose. I won't put up with it. I said so. All the bloody jumped-up joker said was 'There's a war on', as if I were not aware. I lost a leg in the last one, I told him. I'm not going to have my lawn ruined in this. Hector could get it moved along the coast."

"Couldn't they put it on the General's land?" Polly took the receiver and joined the conversation.

"They tried, silly buggers. They tried but he pulled rank, said he was a General. Wouldn't hurt him to have a gun but if they fire the damn thing they will frighten the cow."

"What cow?"

"Monika's bought a cow, pretty beast, keeps it tethered, says that's what they do in Austria. If they fire, the poor beast might try and run away and strangle itself. It's too appalling to contemplate. Hector could get it moved."

"The cow?"

"Don't be dense, girl. The gun. If the Huns machine-gunned St Mary's. We are quite unprotected."

"Was St Mary's machine-gunned?"

"Yes. They say they killed the village idiot but people will say anything these days."

"I didn't know about St Mary's."

"Supposed to be a top secret. They dropped a bomb on that secret place on Goonhilly Downs, missed of course, made a bloody great crater. We've no defences. The buggers just fly up and down the coast as though it were Bank Holiday, nobody to stop them, all our Army's gone to the Middle East, I hear."

"You seem to hear an awful lot, Uncle Richard."

"Monika listens to the German news, it's much clearer than ours. We get jolly good concerts too, no atmospherics. Pretty efficient lot, those Germans, you must grant them that. They wouldn't plant a gun on my front lawn."

"Is it really on the lawn?"

"Poetic licence. Try and get Calypso to get hold of Hector, there's a good girl. We'll never win the war at this rate, first Dunkirk and now this. Try and—" The telephone crackled then fell silent.

"We've been cut off." Polly replaced the receiver. "Could you go down and see what's going on, Calypso?"

"I was thinking of going back to my job now Hector's away to war."

"Couldn't you go down there first? It sounds as if Uncle Richard is in a fix."

"All right. We owe it, I suppose. Come, Fling." She picked up the puppy. "Goodnight, sweetie, see you soon."

"Keep in touch. I'd like to know what's going on, and do tell Uncle not to careless talk."

"Fat lot of good that will do."

"He will get into trouble if he's too indiscreet listening to the German news."

"It's Monika. She can't do any harm."

"Monika is a victim. When shall you go?"

"Soon. It will take my mind off things. Goodnight, discreet cousin."

"Why do you call me that?"

Calypso went off laughing without answering.

"Oh, darling," said Polly in bed later. "I am so happy. Will Calypso be all right alone in that big house? Will she be afraid in the raids?"

"She can put out her hand, feel Fling and pretend it's Hector's hairy chest."

"Perhaps she likes hairy men." Polly was half asleep.

"She has catholic tastes."

"Are you speaking from first-hand knowledge?"

"Guesswork and hearsay. Roll over—"

TWENTY

"It is good of you to meet me," Calypso climbed into the car beside Monika, "when you are rationed for petrol."

"That's no matter. The General told us what to put on the form for the ration. The General knows all these things."

"Oh, what did you do?"

"Richard asks for petrol for shopping, yes? Petrol to go to church, yes? Nobody goes much to church. Then to get Sophy to her school. He 'forgets' to cancel now she is at boarding school. Then petrol for Max's concerts, that is war work. Petrol for Richard's ARP when he goes to his post, and of course petrol for Richard's leg. That is useful, no?"

"Very." Calypso was impressed. "I never thought the General was so fly."

"War sharpens the intelligence," said Monika grimly.

"What's this about a cow and a gun?"

"The cow is war work. I buy her from the General. I make the butter and the cheese and we have milk."

"But what does it eat? Uncle Richard and Helena have no fields."

"I tie it by the road, it eats what they call 'the long pasture'. The old men in the pub they tell me that."

"Is it legal?"

"In Austria they do it. The gypsies do it. The grass is waste if the cow not eat it."

"Goodness. Where does she sleep?"

"On the lawn or if it rains in the garage."

"The camomile lawn?"

"The cow does not like the camomile."

"But we do." Calypso felt outraged. "It must make an awful mess."

"I gather the mess for the vegetables."

"And where is the gun?"

293

"On the cliff where you and Oliver were sitting, where Mrs Penrose's husband fell over drunk."

Calypso asked: "Who is Mrs Penrose when she's at home?"

"She lives in the village, but she works three days' housework for the Frau Rektor Floyer and three days for me."

Calypso noted the way Monika referred to Mrs Penrose as working for her.

From outside, the house on the cliff was the same as ever, crouching glum over the sea, but once inside Calypso sniffed. No whiff of Helena's roses and pot-pourri but an aroma of Continental cooking. She did not immediately note other changes as Richard's dachshund sprang, snarling, and pinned Fling screaming to the ground. As she tried to rescue the puppy Richard came and buffeted the struggling dogs with his artificial leg.

"Lay off, you filthy Hun. Can't you see the poor little brute's only a baby? Hullo, Calypso, my dear, good of you to come." He kissed her. "We'll have tea by the fire, Monika."

Calypso, holding Fling out of Duck's reach, followed him to the drawing-room.

"You spoke to her as though she was a servant," she said.

"She doesn't mind. She's Hebrew. Slaves in Egypt and so on. Got to keep my end up. Just look around and see what she's done. I ask you, just look."

Calypso looked. The furniture was changed round. The pictures re-hung, the old curtains swathed with elegance, the furniture polished.

"Same all over the house," Richard snorted.

"But it's lovely."

"That's the trouble. She's got bloody good taste. They say Jews are an artistic race."

"But—"

"You must see what she's done outside. There's the cow. There are hens. They actually *lay*. She grows vegetables, she knits, she sews, she cooks. I have to speak to her like a servant, she's so bloody competent." Richard Cuthbertson sat down and began to laugh, his tearful eye spurting. "She's even got me a new leg, it's got a hinge." He pulled up his trouser leg and showed his new contraption. "The old one got a gremlin in it."

"A new mode of speech too."

"Parson's twins. Gremlins. Prangs. Burtons. Wizards. Practically incomprehensible."

"Er – what does, er—" Calypso hesitated.

"What does Helena say? Suits her. She's changed too, you may have noticed. She's become flighty."

"May I go and choose my room, Uncle Richard?" Calypso felt Helena had become thin ice as well as flighty.

"You'll have to ask Monika." Richard Cuthbertson roared, "Monika!"

"Richard?"

"Where's Calypso to sleep?"

"Might I have the red room?"

"I put you in what was the spare dressing-room."

"Oh." Calypso followed Monika upstairs carrying the puppy, her suitcase picked up by Monika.

"Richard sleeps here now and Helena there. Max has to have their old rooms because of the piano – he has to have one at night for his inspirations. I sleep here, Sophy in her old room and this is the guest room for guests. You I put in this room, your dog can sleep in the scullery."

"No, it can't."

"No? Is it safe? Does it mess?"

"Sometimes. You seem to have been awfully busy, Monika, you seem to have taken an awful lot on your shoulders. You have changed Aunt Helena's house completely, taken over, I mean moved in, moved everything. Apparently you cook, sew, clean, garden, run a farm, run Uncle Richard. It's all very well, but should you? I'm sure it's all very beautiful and in perfect taste but Fling shall not sleep in the scullery and should you have done all this, Monika, should you? What's the matter?" Calypso stared at the tears pouring unchecked down Monika's face. "I'm sorry, Monika, you poor thing."

"It is Pauli. If I do not work I go mad. You have no child so you would not understand, perhaps I am mad already." Monika's tears dropped unchecked on to her jersey, caught like dew in a spider's web. "I am sorry. I invented all those jobs for myself. I wanted to thank Richard and Helena but I have spoilt your childhood. I am so sorry."

"It's all right." Calypso put the puppy down and found a handkerchief. She wiped Monika's tears. "It doesn't matter. I am grown up now." She stood embarrassed in front of the older woman. "Poor you. Is Max as worried?"

"No, he has his work, his success, he has Helena, she suits, he likes the plump, the phlegm." She smiled wanly.

"You have Uncle Richard. Blow your nose, *do*."

"The poor man. The cow, too, I have the cow. If you like I move things, put you in the red room, it won't take a minute to change it round."

"Oh, Christ, no." Calypso snatched up Fling, who was off adventuring. "I shall be perfectly all right. I haven't come here to cause trouble. We thought, or rather Polly thought, Uncle Richard, and you of course, would like a visit, that you, that I, that, oh blast! I've put my great foot in it, and honestly Monika I don't usually bother to notice or care where I put them so you are one up there."

Monika's mouth twitched. "You are so beautiful the feet do not matter."

"You make me feel awful. I thought I was coming here to help, or, to be honest, Polly thought of it."

"You can help. The Floyers' sons come tomorrow, you can help with them."

"Paul and David here?"

"*Ja.* Frau Floyer is too full up with evacuee children, a new lot arrived last week. I said the boys should sleep here."

"Oh goody, how splendid, but a lot more work for you."

"They make your uncle happy."

"But you do that, Monika, he is thrilled with what you've done, the cow and everything."

"I make him comfortable like a good servant."

"Come and have a drink, Calypso," shouted Richard from the hall. "Isn't it time you put the cow away, Monika? Take the dog with you when you go out, he needs a run."

Calypso accepted a glass of sherry. "Pretty filthy stuff, I'm afraid, South African, you heard the wine merchant got bombed? Absolute tragedy losing all that claret. Helena should have had it delivered here, silly woman. Had her mind on other things. We shall get bombed now we have that bloody gun. I ask you. What fool would do such a thing? In my day the War Office would have, oh well, they might have done something worse. Hi, Monika, you didn't take the dog. Go on," he said, opening the door and shooing the dachshund out, "go on out. Now then, got your drink, good, good. See the look he gave me? Looks like Monika. Long Jewish nose, liquid eyes, reproachful. She looks like the cow too, it's a Jersey."

"Jerseys don't have—" Calypso spluttered.

"I know they don't, but it's the eyes, the liquid dark eyes. I don't know what will happen when they fire the gun; anti-aircraft's pretty noisy. By the way, careful what you say. The General's taken rather a shine to her, offered to have her with him, I ask you."

"The cow? Wouldn't that solve—"

"No, no, Monika. I couldn't possibly allow that. Between ourselves – I can say this now you are a married woman – the General's rather a chap for the girls."

"An old lecher?"

"So I'm told, only gossip of course, can't stand gossip but can't risk Monika. She worries about that boy in the camp, dead by now if you ask me, Hitler won't be wanting useless mouths. Did you bring your ration book by the way? Give it to Monika if you did. Just thought I'd ask, though we grow so much ourselves nowadays we shall send you back to London laden. I'll show you the gun after dinner and get you to bewitch the officer in charge."

"I hear the twins are coming."

"Yes, their mother has a horde of lousy children crammed in the Rectory, Monika goes over once a week to help the district nurse wash their heads. They are crawling, I ask you. Infesting the village. Now in the last war we had our heads shaved and my batman ironed my uniform when I came out of the front line."

"Ironed?"

"Lice don't like a hot iron, kills them double quick. I must tell that Pongo fellow, give him a tip or two, he seems pretty green, only a Territorial not the real thing."

"When shall I see him?" Calypso sipped her sherry and looked round for a handy vase to tip it into.

"If you don't like it," said Richard, noticing, "tip it in the soup. Monika makes very good soup. The Pongo is coming to supper. Fellow called Brian Portmadoc."

"What a grand name."

"Called after the village where he was born, if you ask me. A Taffy. I'm depending on you to get that gun moved. Charm the fellow, take him to see the General's flower fields, that should do the trick, romantic."

"Couldn't the twins?"

"No, no, no. Wrong service, wrong sex. There's no love lost between the Air Force and the Army, you should know that. It takes a woman to do this sort of thing."

★ ★ ★

"What d'you do in real life?" Walking down the valley to the General's flower fields Calypso edged towards the subject of the gun, which crouched above the sea like an obscene animal covered with camouflage netting.

"Insurance." Brian Portmadoc, hopelessly ensnared since he set eyes on Calypso, repeated the word sadly. "Insurance." Hardly a job to interest a creature of such beauty, married to a romantic-sounding and martial Member of Parliament. "Insurance," he said again, studying Calypso's profile.

"What about the windows?" She let her beautiful eyes meet his. He was not bad-looking, rather stubby fingers and short legs but otherwise presentable, the Welsh lilt rather attractive.

"The windows?"

"When you fire your gun they will break. As an insurance man you should know. Cause a lot of ill feeling. Surely you can get it moved? It's awful for Uncle Richard."

"I have my orders, I didn't choose the spot." Calypso continued to gaze. "When it's fired once we have to move it along the coast, so that the Germans think there are lots of guns," said Brian, embarrassed.

"How silly. Shall we go and see if we can snitch some of the General's violets? Follow me." Calypso spoke coldly. Brian felt the chill. "Here we are. I shall sit while you pick a bunch." Calypso sat on a rock and waved towards the violets planted in long rows. Obediently Brian picked, and as he picked he wondered how he could please this girl. The scent of wet violets roused his senses intolerably. Bending over the flowers he considered furiously how he could please her without getting himself court-martialled.

Calypso, having planted the seed of an idea, was happy to leave it to blossom.

The flower farm, a spread of tiny fields bounded by stone walls, was a delight for Calypso whose visits had always been in barren August. Presently they met the General bullying his work force of old men and boys. She asked to be taken on a tour. Brian fell in behind, listening sulkily to the General showing off his fields of violets, anemones, narcissi and daffodils.

"Help yourself, my dear, any time, take as many as you please. A pity the Scilly Whites are not ready yet."

"Are you selling?"

"Good gracious, yes, trade's never been so good. We will be sending away trainloads in a few weeks."

"Doesn't the war interfere?"

"No, less to buy in the shops so people spend on flowers. The more they are bombed the better for trade. They buy them for funerals. From my point of view the war is a bonus. Air raids have their sunny side. I am averaging fivepence a bloom."

"Oh," said Calypso. "I shall think of your profits when I'm in a raid."

"A girl like you must get bunches the whole time." He put his arm round her waist but she moved away.

The twins arrived in the evening complaining of the journey, the intolerable stops at every station, the crowded train. "People have become boorish." They had spent the previous night in London, gone to a show, had a bad meal in a restaurant.

"Did you see Polly?"

"Stayed with her. She sent you all her love." They put their suitcases in the guest room and went to spend the evening with their parents.

Calypso called her puppy and the dachshund and strolled down to the cliff. Memories of holidays came to mind, summer days spent on the rocks and swimming in the cove. Down there in the dark was the place they all sun-bathed, where she had lain in the sun conscious of Oliver's eyes on her. Here where she stood Oliver had said "I want to fuck you." She remembered her feeling of fear and excitement. She stood in the dark, hugging her coat round her, remembering the Terror Run, the games, the laughter, Oliver scared of the drop to the sea. The dogs found a rabbit hole and Duck was frantically digging, lying on his side paddling at the earth with his absurd paws. She watched her puppy, ignorant but eager to join in. The breeze coming off the land brought the smell of ploughed earth and the sound of soldiers' voices by the gun. The war seemed as far away as her childhood, so effectively swept away by Monika's rearrangement of the house. Even the lawn has stopped smelling, she thought resentfully, blaming Monika for the time of year. "I know it *doesn't smell in winter*," she muttered. "Sophy told us." She called the dogs, who ignored her. She went on her knees to reach into the hole and catch the dachshund, trying to get a grip on its tail. The dog went on digging, the puppy yapped. In the sky a familiar drone. Busy with the dogs, it took minutes to recognise the sound of a German bomber. Above her by the gun orders barked excitedly. The drone grew nearer. She looked up, chilled, listening to the far-away sound of sirens in the town. The plane flew closer and she heard the tearing sound as a stick of bombs dropped screaming. She grabbed the puppy and crouched low by the rabbit hole. The gun fired pom, pom, pom, pom and again, banging a futile threat. The sound of the plane receded and Calypso sat up holding the puppy. The dachshund was still digging, pounding the earth with its paws. She reached in, caught its tail, dragged it out. Carrying both dogs, she started up the cliff. She could hear shouts and see lights. She tried to run, her legs weak, heart pounding. In the house her uncle was shouting.

"Bloody fool, look what he's done! Monika, she's gone. Right through the house, bust the windows, I told him it would happen, look at the mess, I ask you."

"Uncle, are you hurt? Did it hit the house?"

"Of course it didn't. They can't aim straight. It's that Pongo fellow. The gun frightened the cow, look what she's done. Came bursting through the French windows, she's broken the glass, torn the curtains and now there's the telephone." He limped to answer the telephone shrilling in the hall. "Showing a light, am I? What of it? Bloody Boche, nothing better to do than frighten my cow. Of course I'm showing a light. The poor beast broke in through the blackout, broke the window, frightful mess. Nobody hurt, of course not. Turn out the light? Very well, if you insist. Oh, damn your regulations, have a heart. The plane's miles away."

"Chased by our gallant few." David and Paul came hurrying in. "There's a lovely row of craters across the plough. Anyone hurt, any damage?"

"The cow took off through the house."

"She's all right." Monika came quietly into the room. "She is in the kitchen. We must block up the windows; you are showing a light, Richard."

"God damn it, I know I am. How is my cow? Will this stop her milk?"

"No, no, a little cut on her nose, a mess in the kitchen. I clean it up. I will put her in the garage with some hay. Yes."

Calypso watched Monika lead the cow out of the house, then helped the twins block up the French windows as best they could.

"Hector is afraid of me staying in London," she said, steadying the steps as David nailed up the torn blackout curtains. "He wanted me to go to Scotland."

"They get random bombs there, too." Paul swept up the glass.

"I shall tell him so when I write." Calypso suddenly missed Hector. "I feel sick," she said, sitting down on the sofa, "and sweaty."

"That's fear, we all get it."

Calypso looked at the twins. "I didn't realise. I thought it was just me." She felt admiration.

"Sophy will be sorry to have missed this." Richard limped in to join them. "Monika says leave all this mess and come to the kitchen, she has some soup for us. Make a change to have some lively news for the child, my letters get a bit boring."

"There's someone at the front door." Paul went and opened it. "Hullo, Mr Hoskings." An old man wearing an ARP helmet came into the hall.

"They was trying to bomb Coverack, thought you'd like to know, Major. Any damage here, then?"

"Coverack's thirty miles away, need their heads examined. As for you, young fellow" – Richard Cuthbertson suddenly noticed Brian Portmadoc standing sheepishly behind the air raid warden – "hope you're pleased with your night's work."

"Very, very sorry, sir. We shall be moving on now, can't fire it twice from the same place."

"And how's Jerry to know that?" asked the warden nastily. "You foreigners coming down here with guns, interfering, ach."

Calypso showed Brian Portmadoc out.

"What does he mean, foreigner?" Brian asked, aggrieved.

"Anyone who isn't Cornish."

"I suppose I shan't see you again?" The young man lingered, a prey to mixed feelings, proud to have fired his gun, angry with the air raid warden, infatuated with Calypso.

"Come and see me in London," she said casually. "I'm in the book."

"May I really?"

"Of course. Night, then." She closed the door and went to the downstairs lavatory and was sick.

"I'm never scared in London," she said, rejoining the party in the kitchen, "I must have agoraphobia," but her uncle, Monika and the twins were not listening. They were gathered round the wireless to hear the news in German with Monika translating.

Presently there was the sound of a car outside and the General came in.

"Hear you had a spot of bother," he said, looking round the kitchen. "Nothing serious, I hope."

Richard regaled him with a list of damage and complaint. The

General was wearing battledress with Home Guard insignia.

"Thought if you were in trouble Monika might like to take shelter with me, and anyone else of course. How about you, Calypso?"

"No," said Richard Cuthbertson, "let it not be said that the Hun chases my guests away, mustn't allow any hint of defeat. Cow's upset, of course. The only thing I want moved is that infernal gun. Stupid fellow in charge fired the damn thing, even I know it's a million to one chance of his hitting anything in the dark. Just fired it for the hell of it, if you ask me."

"He did come to apologise," said Paul. "Fair's fair, sir."

"Let's go and see if he's packing up." David signalled to Calypso, who was watching Monika edge away from the General as he put an arm round her waist.

"Like to come, Monika?" asked Paul. "Get a breath of fresh air before bed?"

They took Monika round the house and stood on the lawn looking down at the gun. There was activity, sounds of talk of a grumbling nature, a hearty oath. Somebody started a lorry engine. Side lights were switched on, engines revved up and lorries drove away, bumping across the grass.

"It would have amused Sophy." Calypso took Monika's hand. "Are you all right, Monika? Hector says we aren't as incompetent as we appear, he talks as though we shall win the war. What do you think of that, twins?" She chuckled.

"We do our best," they said gravely.

Monika let out a long high cry which echoed down the cliffs, chilling their blood. A howl of anger, frustration, despair.

TWENTY-ONE

By the time Sophy came home for Christmas the saga of the gun had grown. Enemy planes, Sophy heard in the village, had attacked the Scillies, killed several people and sunk an MTB. Some said it was a destroyer but others said no. Lord Haw-Haw said an MTB. The planes had continued on their way to bomb Helena and Richard's house and it was not the anti-aircraft gun but Mr and Mrs Erstweiler who had been the target. Had not the General said they were German spies? He was wrong – the village knew. Mrs Erstweiler was harmless, her son a prisoner of war. Not in a real prison camp but a concentration camp. What's the difference? If Mrs Penrose worked for Mrs Erstweiler at the house on the cliff she couldn't be a spy. Mrs Penrose also worked at the Rectory. All those London kids, disgusting, really. Mr Erstweiler's a nice gentleman, pity one couldn't understand his accent. The papers said he was a famous violinist, so there you are, no spy he, whatever the General said. Luckily the Floyer twins had run to the rescue when the bombs fell, nobody hurt bar the cow, funny Lord Haw-Haw made no mention. They'd swept on, those bombers, plucky really after being fired at, to bomb Penzance, did some damage there, Lord Haw-Haw mentioned that, then on to Plymouth. Getting bombed a lot, Plymouth.

"I came through Plymouth, the station's a mess," said Sophy.

There, now, it just goes to show. Sophy listened at the post office, at the shop, got hot news at the garage and best of all the truth, she swore it was the truth, from Mrs Penrose who was entitled to know. Had not her husband fallen over the cliff, pushed by a German spy, just before the war began? Mrs Penrose had a fascination for Sophy, who watched her scrubbing floors on hands and knees, her large bottom high, refusing to use the squeezy mop which Helena had bought on her last visit. Sophy followed Mrs Penrose round the house, watching her dust and make beds and in the kitchen with Monika. While Monika worked silently

Mrs Penrose talked, describing her life with Penrose, as she referred to her husband. Penrose had spent his early days at sea before joining the coastguards. Penrose did not like the station on the cliff, Penrose had been happy on the Longships cut off from the drink, for Penrose drank. Never on duty, but when he came off duty he reached for the bottle. Mrs Penrose, having her mid-morning tea, would reach for the teapot in illustration. "Penrose often went on duty half seas over. No wonder he couldn't be a proper husband, poor soul."

"What's a proper husband?"

"Never you mind." Penrose's superiors never knew of his weakness. "Why, he would walk along the cliff to work as straight and upright as you please. He would sit by the cliff path before going on duty and stare at the sea. He loved the sea, the sea and the drink. He should never have married, he couldn't be a proper husband, could he? Penrose must have been drunk or he would have seen the spy who pushed him over."

"Did anyone see the spy?"

"Nobody, spies were sneaky people who worked unseen. Then thump, push, over he goes, and Mrs Penrose was a widow, not that he was ever a proper husband, otherwise—"

"What?"

"Well, I'd have kids, wouldn't I? Not that I like kids, look at the worry they cause. You poor dear have all that worry. If Mr Erstweiler, well, if as I say he'd been like Penrose there wouldn't be all this worry over your Pauli, would there? Now," Mrs Penrose would say, taking her cup to the sink, "you mustn't keep me here talking. I must get on with my work," and Sophy and Monika would smile, both too careful to ask the other what she knew or thought she knew of Penrose.

"Are there people like Mrs Penrose in Vienna?"

"Cornwall is not like Vienna," Monika would answer, "but Mrs Penrose is a universal character."

"In the Middle East, will Oliver meet people like her?"

"Surely." Monika frowned over a cookery book, striving to follow the recipe for Christmas pudding. "Do you write to him, Sophy? This pudding will be indigestible."

"No, I don't. I think they are meant to be indigestible. It's just so difficult to imagine them all now. Walter at sea. The twins flying Spitfires. Aunt Sarah told Polly Oliver's in Egypt. I expect he is all right," said Sophy, who expected all the time to hear that Oliver had been killed and, if he was, whoever killed him would kill her too.

"Child, you look sad, help me with these pies. Christmas is a happy time."

"I don't think so," said Sophy, looking at Monika. "I don't think you do."

"You must be happy, your aunt arrives this evening."

"She is not my true aunt and she does not love me."

"Of course she does, we must make her welcome. And Max comes also, he will be tired after his concerts."

"A proper husband," said Sophy, mimicking Mrs Penrose. Monika laughed, thinking of her proper husband in Helena's house in London, and that probably over Christmas he would wake in the night and ask her to accompany him on the piano, a chore which was impossible for Helena.

"I wish they were not coming. It is much nicer here with just you and Uncle Richard."

"My child—"

"I suppose it will be nice for you, having Max."

"Of course."

"Aunt Helena always stops things. You'd think she'd never enjoyed herself."

"Perhaps she has changed," said Monika drily.

"Like Mrs Penrose, only the other way round?"

"You are very observant."

"Do you think Mrs Penrose loved her husband, even though he was not proper?" Monika wondered whether this sort of conversation was good for Sophy. "Are you able to love?" Sophy pressed on.

"Yes, I am able, and so are you." Monika sang a West Indian song one of the evacuees at the Rectory had brought from the East End.

"It's love and love alone
That caused King Edward to lose de trone.

"I am sorry you missed Calypso and the twins," she said.

"I don't mind," said Sophy, who preferred not to see Calypso so loved by Oliver. "None of them ever came in the winter before the war."

Helena came down full of good resolutions, bearing gifts for

Richard and Monika, books for the Floyers, a pretty dress for Sophy and a heavy package of gramophone records for Max, who pretended he did not know the contents of the package he carried.

They stepped off the train and stood waiting for a porter, surrounded by their suitcases. Max wore a black overcoat with an astrakhan collar and an Anthony Eden hat; he carried his violin case in his arms, protecting it from the jostling crowd of servicemen hurrying off the train. Helena wore a new fur coat and very high heels, which made her calves bulge. Her hair now waved softly round her face, she smelled expensive. She tendered a cheek to Monika.

"Ah, Monika. Ah, Sophy, you have grown. Is Richard well?"

"Just gone up the street to get some cigs." Sophy appraised this new Helena. "You look wonderful," she said.

"Have to take trouble now our clothes are rationed, though lots of people seem to have no trouble over coupons. Don't you think it's very immoral, Monika?"

"Morality is elastic." Monika kissed Max on both cheeks as he stood holding his violin case and the parcel of records.

"Let me help," said Sophy, taking the package.

Max surrendered the records and put his free arm round his wife. "Ow goes it, *Mein Schatz?*"

Schatz? What is *Schatz?* thought Helena. He never calls me *Schatz.* "Dear Richard," she exclaimed, seeing Richard limping down the platform, and broke into a trot to kiss him brightly.

"Well, well," said Richard, surprised, wiping his tear. "What's this transformation? Quite the Londoner these days." Helena took the remark in a kind spirit.

"You are walking better," she said as they moved towards the car. "I always thought you made too much of your leg."

"Absence of. This one's new."

"What?" Helena stopped in her tracks. "What d'you mean, new?"

"Monika got me fixed up. Took me to Exeter. Look, it's got a hinge." He bent down and pulled up his trousers. "See? I press it and bingo, the knee bends. Shan't be tripping so many people. It's an easier job altogether. I use the old one to poke the fire. I go to bed in this, sometimes, just for the hell of it. Wonder what that Bader chap does at night, now he's a prisoner of war."

Helena said nothing; no use feeling furious, she'd left him alone with Max's "*Schatz*", she'd asked for it.

"D'you mind? You look bothered."

"Good heavens, no." She took Richard's arm. "Why should I mind?" They walked towards the car. "I should have thought of it myself, it makes me feel—"

"She wrote to the spare part place, sort of St Dunstan's for legs and arms. Imaginative girl, old Monika, thinks of everything, must come from years of looking after an artist. Just wait and see what she's done to the house, we don't even sleep in the same rooms. It's all changed, quite a performance, you'll never recognise it."

"Oh," said Helena, angered. "I can't wait."

They drove to the house, Richard sitting beside Monika, Helena and Max in the back with Sophy between them. Arrived, Monika said to Sophy, "Show your aunt her new room, darling."

Helena cried out with genuine pleasure at the bowls of hyacinths on the hall table and in the drawing-room, filling the air with bitter-sweet scent. "Monika, how gorgeous."

"I like them for Christmas." Monika smiled at her. "I have moved you into the red room, Helena, so that Max can have his piano with him." She indicated Helena's old room. Where once her dressing table stood was now an upright piano.

"You will be quieter and more peaceful where I have put you. As you probably know, Max likes to play at night."

"Not the piano." Helena came into the open. Monika ignored her.

"He calls and I come to accompany him. He is at his best at night. The most inspired. I sleep next door in Richard's old dressing-room."

"Why did you interfere with Richard's leg?" Helena's fury burst out like an angry terrier.

"Are you jealous of something which irritates you profoundly?"

"Yes," admitted Helena. "I am. I shall miss it."

"But he still has it for spare," said Monika, friendly and calm.

"As Max has you – for spare – his *Schatz*."

"He always calls me that, it is his pet name for me. Has he yet a pet name for you?" Monika looked amused, ignoring Helena's jibe of "spare".

"No." Wild horses would not make Helena confess to *Kleine Phlegm*. "This will do very nicely. Thank you, Monika." She inspected the red room. "I like this room, it is one of the children's favourites. Any news of Pauli?"

Monika knew Helena hoped to unbalance her. "No news whatever."

"Oh, curse this war!" Helena put her arms round Monika. "Curse it, curse it! I am a horrible, selfish creature, Monika, please forgive me." She held the other woman's shoulders, shaking her to and fro.

"You do no harm." Monika kissed her lightly. "We are partners, *nicht*?"

"You are generous." Helena was briefly humble.

"I try to survive. We shall make a nice Christmas, yes?"

"What have you planned?" Helena sat on the bed looking up at Monika, her eyes clear blue, her hair fair and fluffy, her pink complexion a total contrast to Monika's olive skin and sleek dark hair, drawn back into a knot, accentuating her dark eyes and Semitic nose.

"You are beautiful, Monika. You look like Nefertiti."

"I have a Jewish face even more so than Max."

"I never thought about Jews before the war." Helena looked down at her trim ankles as she kicked off her high-heeled shoes.

"You did not have to."

"I thought they were just other people. Richard's nephews and nieces told me about the Nazis and I became interested when I realised the war was coming. You have no idea how irritating Richard was, he believed everything that boring old General told him. He liked Nazis."

"He no longer does. The General is very keen on the war, he sends his young workmen to enlist. He is *der Patriot*."

"I bet they don't want to go," said Helena.

"He tells them their jobs will be waiting when they come back – if they come back."

"Do you like him?"

"He tries to be kind. He is useful." Monika shrugged. "He does no harm."

"Like me?"

"Ah, Helena, you and I are friends, yes? We work in a team like the English are supposed to. You make Max happy."

"Don't you *mind*?" Helena stared at Monika in agitation.

"No," Monika said lightly, "I do not mind, so I hope you do not either."

"Richard?" Helena was puzzled. "Poor Richard."

"I make him less poor."

Helena sat looking at her feet. Less poor, she thought, less poor meant richer . . . a caring woman, a new leg, of course he was less poor. She found it hard not to feel resentful. "What about Christmas plans?" She changed the subject.

"A party in the village hall for the London children. The village children they do not mix, but perhaps Christmas will help? Church. The Rector asks if Max will play his violin if I play the organ. Sophy has helped me make a pudding. The General sent a turkey, he asks us all to go and sing songs on Boxing Day at his house, everybody to choose their favourite tune and for us to sing together."

"I hope there will be plenty to drink," said Helena, linking her arm in Monika's and leading her downstairs. "I never used to drink but since the war I've taken to it. I believe it's the threat of shortage which makes me want it. Tomorrow we die."

"Of course," said Helena, all those years later, "we didn't die. Here we are driving to Max's funeral. Some of us are dead but not me. That was a priceless party!"

"What party?" Hamish lent an ear. Helena's voice was sometimes creaky with age.

"A sing-song at the General's. He had a stroke which did for him in 1948. He made a fortune out of flowers but didn't live to enjoy it."

"What happened at the party?" Old people wander, thought Hamish.

"Had his stroke in a public lavatory. He wouldn't have planned that. He planned the party so that each of us hummed our favourite tune and the rest of us sang the words if we knew them."

"Sounds quite a harmless idea." Helena's laugh made him turn round and look at her. "What went wrong?" Hamish had a theory that old people liked recalling disasters.

"The General hummed a marching song he'd picked up at the Nuremberg Rally in 1938."

"The Horst Wessel?"

"Yes. As you can imagine Max and Monika were not pleased, especially as only they knew the words."

"Did that finish the party?"

"It was Sophy's choice which put the kibosh on it."

"What did she choose?"

"The Internationale. She sang it from beginning to end. She said Oliver had taught it her. I thought the General would have a seizure. She made things worse by saying, 'The Russians are our allies and yesterday was Christ's birthday, he was the first Communist.' She was at a difficult age. I found out later Max had been giving her drinks. As parties go," said Helena, enjoying her reminiscences, "it was a flop, though I remember the evening ended well."

"That must have taken some doing. How could anyone be so naïve as your General? It's unbelievable."

"There was quite a strong minority like the General, Conservative people who admired Mussolini for his trains. They didn't want to hear about Abyssinians being thrown out of aeroplanes. Max found it hard to believe the General was really honourable and patriotic. Richard gave us all a nightcap when we got home and we went to bed. It was so funny!" Helena, sitting beside Hamish as he drove down the motorway, chuckled delightedly, tiny tears squeezing out among the wrinkles. "I shouldn't really tell you."

"Go on," said Hamish, driving steadily, "tell me, do."

Helena paused in agreeable recollection. Then: "I undressed and went to bed. I forgot Monika had changed all our bedrooms. I found myself in bed with Max, as though we were in London. When I realized my mistake I was too tipsy to care and presently who should join us but Richard, scrambling in on my other side."

"A threesome?"

"My dear boy, he had his leg, it was—" Helena paused in recollection.

"His artificial leg? What did you do?"

"Threw it out. Threw it out of the window. I thought he thought I was Monika."

"And then?"

"Max was furious, told me to go and fetch it. I didn't, of course. I moved in to sleep with Monika. In the morning those two men were asleep in that bed in perfect friendship. I always say one can never know what men will do next."

"Perhaps they were tired."

"Drunk, we were all drunk. After today," said Helena thoughtfully, "they will be at it again."

"What do you mean?"

"Side by side in a bed – of clay this time. You won't forget I want to buy flowers, will you, dear?"

"No," said Hamish, treading on the accelerator.

TWENTY-TWO

Brian Portmadoc, posted to an anti-aircraft battery in London, telephoned Calypso, inviting her to dinner.

"I'd love to as long as you don't keep me up too late."

"I won't do that."

"I am working. They have taken me back in the job I was in before I married."

"Oh, what's that?"

"Top secret," Calypso said. "I'm not allowed to tell you what I do. I don't understand the half of it."

"Shall I fetch you at your office?"

"Not allowed to tell you where I work. Come to my house."

Brian arrived bearing flowers.

"How beautiful. How kind." Calypso held the flowers to her nose and looked at Brian.

"You look beautiful." He blushed.

"Good," said Calypso. "Where are you taking me to dinner?"

"Where would you like to go?"

She thought this tiresome. He should choose a place he could afford, he should say as Hector would, "We are going to the Savoy or Lyons Corner House." How could she tell how much money he could afford? Men all looked alike in uniform.

"We could try Soho," she said. Brian looked grateful. The flowers had been expensive. He found a taxi.

"Hector has hidden his car in the country," she said, "otherwise I would drive you. It eats petrol."

"What is it, a Rolls?"

"Near enough. He doesn't want it bombed, it's his dearest possession."

"What about you?"

"I am not his possession. I am his wife." Brian did not know what to say to this.

Difficulty in finding a table in the first restaurant they tried humiliated him and he felt worse when Calypso was effusively

311

greeted at the second and led to a corner table, made much of. She was known and pampered. She knew several other diners. A Frenchman came and talked in French which Brian did not understand until he kissed her hand on departure, saying, *"Alors, à demain."* Other men came up to her during the meal. Brian felt inadequate, that she would prefer to be with someone else, someone smarter, more glamorous.

"Do they all tell you how beautiful you are?" he ventured.

"Some do. I know I am beautiful, now *you* tell me something I don't know. Tell me about insurance."

"You are laughing at me." Brian gulped some wine. "I would insure every hair of your head," he said. "I think it is what they call ash blonde."

Calypso nodded.

"I would insure your blue eyes and long black lashes."

"They are real," she said encouragingly.

"I would insure your nose, your mouth, your teeth, your ears."

"Good, good. What about my body?"

Brian drank a full glass of wine. The bottle was now empty. "I don't know about your body," he muttered, "I can't—"

"We shall have to correct that. Shall we go? Can you take me home?"

As they left the restaurant she said to the Frenchman, "See you tomorrow" and "Let's meet on Thursday week" to two men dining together. Brian took her hand and held it in the taxi. He was afraid to kiss her. When they reached her house she said, "I must give my dog a run, then you will come in for a nightcap." The dog jumped with joy when it saw Calypso, then ran excitedly up and down the pavement. "Hurry up," she said, "don't take all night. He came from the Highlands, shouldn't really be in London. Do you notice there are no dogs nowadays, no children, either?" She held Brian's hand like a mother as she watched the dog lift its leg, sniff the railings, trot back wagging, look up at her with beady eyes. "I hide him under my desk in my office," she said. "My boss pretends not to know."

Brian stood beside her rather drunk, uncertain what to do next.

"Come on in then. Let's correct your ignorance," she said.

In her bed, his face buried in her hair, Brian said, "I love you. I love you."

"I don't know what love is." She rocked him in her arms. "I like this, though, you are nice. You don't really love me."

"I do. If you don't know what love is how can you be sure I don't love you?"

"You have a point. But it won't last, you can't insure it. You can't insure an emotion, it's a pleasure like eating or drinking."

"It will last with me."

"That's your affair. I can't help it, can I? Now, you should get back to your gun and I must get some sleep."

She watched him as he dressed, putting on his uniform, doing up his buttons.

"Shall I see you again?" He stood by her bed.

"I expect so. Telephone. Can you let yourself out?"

She listened as he went downstairs, waited until she heard the front door slam. In his basket the little dog whimpered.

"Oh, Fling," she said, "I am so lonely." The dog jumped up on the bed. She lay face down, trying to sleep, then reached out and switched on her radio, twiddling the knobs. Over the air came ghostly voices speaking in German, French and English. She wondered what the hell was going on in the world. What was the time in Egypt, where Oliver was supposed to be? What was Hector doing and where? She had had no letter for so long and only a BFO address to write to. What could she write about? He would hardly be glad to hear she had slept with Brian Portmadoc and intended sleeping with his French friend. He would get no pleasure on hearing that she quite often slept with Tony when he was not on duty at his fire station. Were most grass widows faithful, were girl friends true? She could write to him, she thought, about her visit to Cornwall and the carryings-on of the older generation, but then she could not, she thought, since Helena and Hector were of much the same age.

She slept and dreamed uneasy dreams which turned to nightmare. She was running through the streets of a town she did not know to escape she knew not what. Her legs would not move, her breath came in gasps, she tried to wake for she knew she was asleep and if she could wake she could tell Hector of her fear. She reached out her hand to wake him, her hand pushing into his hair. Then she screamed, for she felt not his warm cock but something cold and wet. Her terror was so great that she clutched at the hairy thing, which was wet and cold, and it yelped with pain for she squeezed Fling's nose instead of Hector. Instead of Hector to wake her from nightmare there was a frightened little dog.

"Oh," she said, consoling Fling. "I did not mean to hurt you. Oh, Fling, my Highland Fling boy, I feel sick." Sweating and greasy she got up and went downstairs to make tea. When she had drunk it she was very sick indeed and felt so faint she had to lie on the bed until she felt better.

In the morning she telephoned Polly.

"Polly, I haven't seen you since I went to Cornwall."

"How were they all? Come to supper and tell me about it. Come tonight."

"I can't come tonight, I'm going out with a Frog friend of Hector's. What about tomorrow, if I'm well enough?"

"Are you ill?"

"I don't know. I've eaten something, I feel sick and nearly fainted just now. Come to think of it, I was sick in Cornwall when they fired the gun. I thought it was just fright. It must be some bug I've picked up."

"Have you missed the curse?"

"I'm bad at counting."

"Well, count. I am late for my office. You for yours too, for that matter."

"I must look at my diary."

"See you tomorrow. Goodbye."

"Goodness." Calypso looked at her diary. "Goodness," she murmured, looking at the small pages, "goodness gracious me. I meant it. But it seemed a sort of joke," she muttered as she went to clean her teeth, which made her sick again. She telephoned her office and asked leave for the day as she felt ill.

"Seen a doctor?" said her boss briskly.

"Just going to make an appointment."

"Well, mind you try and get here tomorrow, you know how busy we are. You're the only one who knows that file on—"

"I know, I know. I'll be there."

"And don't let me catch you lunching in the Écu de France with some Frog."

"Is that where you're lunching?"

"No. I shall be at my club."

Calypso telephoned Hector's doctor for an appointment. Then thoughtfully she dialled again: Helena's number. Max answered.

"Listen, can you give me lunch today? Dutch, if you're feeling poor. I'm in need of moral support."

"Where would you like to meet?"

"Écu de France."

"It'll have to be Dutch."

When she left the doctor she took Fling to Hyde Park, walking on the grass, watching him run. Men and women in uniform walked briskly along the asphalt paths, barrage balloons rocked at anchor. Crossing Mayfair she found a post office, found a form. She wrote Hector's name and rank and his alien secret address. She wrote "Hamish en route Calypso" and handed it to the clerk.

"Better write in English," he said.

"Why?"

"Looks like code. Is Calypso a ship?"

"No, Calypso is my name."

"Better put your surname, then."

The message "Hamish on the way Calypso Grant" looked chilly. She tore up the form. "He's not a trunk," she said to the clerk behind the desk. "I will write."

"Please yourself," he said. Then, finding Calypso pretty, smiled.

She went out into the street. "It's a commercial undertaking," she said to herself. "I shall have to put it in writing."

Early for her lunch appointment, she strolled through the streets, noting here a gap and there a gap where bombs had struck. Nobody stood to stare or paused as they went by. Calypso paced slowly, with Fling on his lead trotting sedately. At the Écu de France she said to Max: "I'm feeling generous, I'll stand you lunch."

"Ta very much." He switched his gaze to the more expensive dishes on the menu. "What are you celebrating?"

"A private joke."

"May I hear it?"

"Some time, perhaps. What do you think is the best thing to eat?"

They discussed, chose, gave their order.

"Did you tell Helena you were lunching with me?"

"She is out shopping."

"Who taught you to say 'ta'?"

"Isn't it snob?"

"Who taught you, come on, Max, tell me."

"A young woman I know."

"You are being unfaithful to Helena."

"And to Monika. I am not a faithful man just as you are not a faithful woman."

Calypso grinned. "I went to bed with you, Max, in a purely exploratory fashion. I wanted to find out whether my aunt is on to a good thing, whether you will break her heart."

"Dear Calypso, would it be too much to ask you to mind your own business?"

"Promise you won't hurt her? Don't let her find out you are sleeping around. We are all very fond of her and Uncle Richard. They are part of our childhood."

"'Our' meaning you, Polly, Oliver, Walter, Sophy and those twins?"

"Yes."

"I will not hurt her, I am a sensitive man. Under that British phlegm your aunt is also sensitive."

"Is she really?" Calypso was thoughtful. "I would never have known it."

"There is a lot you do not know, for instance your Hector."

"What about Hector?" Calypso was instantly on the defensive.

"Your Hector is sensitive."

Calypso laughed. "Oh, come on! Hector isn't sensitive, he's a great big hunting, shooting, aggressive politician."

"And oh so rich."

"That's why I married him, for his money and in exchange—"

"Yes?"

"In exchange he has a pretty wife." Wild horses, Calypso thought, feeling the blood rush to her face, wild horses will not make me tell Aunt Helena's lover that I am bearing Hector's child. I am keeping my promise, and he's got to be the first to know. Why should I tell Max, who isn't great shakes in bed anyway, one single thing about Hector's baby? Hector's baby, she thought, not mine, why should it be mine when I don't even like children, what on earth shall I do when I've got it?

She remembered the chugging train and Hector's voice telling her "You must have Catherine" and again his voice saying curtly, "She's lame." The rocking movement of a lame person would lull the baby as she carried it.

"May I come back to your house this afternoon?" Max liked copulating in the afternoon before a rehearsal.

"Sorry, no, I have to write letters. Why not Helena, why not the girl who says 'Ta'?"

"Your voice is cruel, your letters can wait." Max was persuasive.

"How could you know? Will you ask for the bill, please, Max."

He signalled to the waiter while Calypso fished in her bag for money.

"Did you not enjoy our afternoon together?"

"It was all right, but I think I shall stick to your concerts for Helena's sake."

"You are very considerate suddenly." He looked at the bill, which the waiter had put by him folded on a plate.

"Today is a day to be considerate," she said gravely, as she put money on the bill.

"Shall you perhaps reconsider?"

"I think not. Now," she exclaimed lightly, "thank you for your company. Give my love to Helena, see you soon, goodbye." But as she gathered up her bag a man who had been sitting at another table came across the restaurant. He excused himself to Calypso, drew up a chair, leant across the table and talked to Max in German.

Not understanding a word Calypso watched the two men. The newcomer was large, well dressed and expensive, his shiny hair brushed back in wings. He smelled of cigars, wore a heavy gold watch. Listening, she heard and understood odd words – America – concert – dollars. Monika's name was mentioned. Max was shaking his head, speaking rapidly, gesturing with his hands. His expression lost the look she rather despised of wishing to please and assumed one of pride. He finished what he had to say in English: "No, I cannot and I will not."

The stranger turned to Calypso. "Forgive me, please, Max did not introduce us." He looked at Max, who stared back, making no effort to do the polite conventional thing. "I am trying to make Max accept a wonderful offer."

"And what's that?" Calypso was not taken by the stranger, whom she found too opulent.

"I offer him a contract in the States, a passage to America for himself and Monika and he refuses. In America they will be safe and make lots of money. There is no necessity for them to stay where they are in danger. In America Jews are safe."

"Safe here, too," said Calypso.

"Only until the Germans come, then they are in terrible danger."

Calypso opened her mouth but Max laid a hand on hers and said: "I must speak for myself, Calypso. This man was German. Now he is American, you understand. He is trying to make me run away and I will not. I have run far enough. Here I can work."

"For less money," put in the stranger.

"*Ja*, for less money maybe but I work for people who shelter us. I will try to repay their kindness with my music."

"I've not been particularly kind," said Calypso.

"Your country has and for that I will pay in the only way I can, with music." Max sounded pompous, Calypso thought, but his air of pride carried it off. She looked from one man to the other, sizing them up, liking Max.

"Oliver would say you are paying with an idea."

"Ideas are his speciality." Max relaxed and laughed.

"Who is this Oliver?" asked the stranger suspiciously. "A conductor, perhaps? Amateur?"

"A young man who fights the Nazis, fights for the Jews. So do the twins and the other boy Walter."

"Who are these people? An orchestra?"

"Nothing you would understand. They also have ideals."

"Do they play the violin?"

"They play with death."

The prosperous stranger laughed, settling his broad bottom on the chair. "Listen," he said. "England is losing the war. Soon Rommel will be in Egypt. The British Army is retreating. Hitler invades this country after a bit more bombing and then it is goodbye to your talent, goodbye to Jewish refugees. I am here at great risk to find you and others and bring you to the United States. Be sensible, think of your art, your talent, do not waste it. It is no use your listening to this Churchill, who I admit makes good propaganda, but England will starve very shortly. I know you eat a good lunch today but for how long? Do you know what the U-boats are doing, do you hear of the millions of tons which are being sunk? In a matter of months it is all over in Europe, whereas in America I offer you a future. Even to bring your mistress."

Calypso, watching the two men, became conscious of a Max she did not know. Helena's lover, charming, talented, light-hearted, fairly good in bed, changed into a steely creature who made her shiver. She had seen anger, she had seen rage, everyday emotions compared to what Max was experiencing. He began to speak in a low hard voice in German, staring into the eyes of his enemy, for she guessed that if the stranger had not been an enemy before he was one now. He spoke with bitterness. The stout man tried to interrupt with sneering remarks. Max suddenly spoke in English.

"Now will you go? Get out, leave this country where you are
not even worthy to shit, get back to your safe America. I hope
the U-boats you so admire will sink you on the way. Get out,
get out, you *Dung*—"

The stranger pushed back his chair and went away. People at
neighbouring tables, who had overheard, stared after him then
back at Max. Calypso stared back at their disconcerted faces.
They looked away. She took Max's hand.

"Have a brandy? Who was that creep?" She signalled to the
waiter. "Brandy, please."

"A German producer. American now. He makes and breaks in
the music world."

"Well, he didn't frighten you, did he? Here's your brandy, sip
it slow."

"I hate that man. Have I been vulgar, as vulgar as saying 'Ta'?"

"As I don't understand German I can't say, but you sounded
good and rude."

"Good." Max's colour was creeping back. He squeezed
Calypso's hand. "Friends?"

"I feel," she said, "that I have grown up several years. I was
beginning to grow up this morning. Will this scene upset your
music, spoil your concert tonight?"

"I shall play better than ever, for me anger works better than
an orgasm."

Calypso laughed, stood up to leave. Max found her a taxi. As
she travelled through the streets made shabby by war she mulled
a thought, new for her, that she had no need to go to bed with
Max because now she was his friend. She wondered whether she
could put this into words in her letter to Hector and decided it
was too difficult. As she stood on the pavement outside her house
paying her taxi, Max drove up in pursuit.

"You forgot your poor Fling. You left him tied up in the ladies'
cloakroom."

"People like me are not fit to have a dog." She took Fling from
him and watched him drive away. "And as for being fit to have
a child, God only knows," she said to the forgiving dog. She
went into the house, where her bicycle was propped against the
wall in the hall. How long could she go on riding it without
harming the baby? She sat down at her desk and began her letter:
"Darling Hector—"

TWENTY-THREE

Enduring school, Sophy depended on Richard's weekly letters, a factual account of life in Cornwall. News of the dog, the cow, the hens was far more important than history or mathematics. Every Monday Richard's plump white envelope brought the news which would enable her to survive the week. He wrote about the Home Guard and what the village thought of it, he wrote that the General was bossy. He wrote about the Rectory evacuees returning to London when there was a lull in the air raids, only to hurry back when the raids started up again. He wrote about the wrangle as to whether a mounted Home Guard was feasible in Cornwall, the jealousy of Home Guards who were said to be mounted on Exmoor. He wrote about the Belgian fishing fleet in Newlyn and of how the Cornish fishermen were called up into the Merchant Navy. He wrote of the harvests, the flowers on the General's farm. He told Sophy when Monika made jam and how she saved up the sugar. He wrote about bartering Monika's butter for meat and swapping eggs for fish. He told her which boy had been called up from the village to which regiment, and who was fortunate to be in a reserved occupation. He wrote that Monika and Mildred were shocked that it was possible to buy clothing coupons under the counter from the village shop. He told her which hen was destined for the pot. He wrote about rabbit pie and blackberries, the weather, rain, fog, wind, sun, all recorded in faithful detail, his new leg and Calypso's visit, the gun and the firing of it. He wrote that the pits made by the stick of bombs would become useful ponds; wild duck would come to them.

Sophy put the letters in the locker by her bed to re-read during the week. Every night, homesick and wakeful, she visualised Richard and Monika sitting by the fire, Richard writing his letter, Monika sewing or knitting. She dreamed of summer days when Polly, Walter, Calypso and Oliver had lolled on the camomile lawn, laughing and joking. She treasured the evening she had spent with Oliver in London. Whenever she was cold she remembered the icy streets by St Paul's. She remembered Oliver weeping and her holding his hand when something terrible to do with Calypso had happened. He had let her hold his hand for several minutes before dropping it to blow his nose. Every night before she slept she wished herself back in her bedroom; from there she could climb out along the branch of the Ilex above the camomile lawn and sniff its scent, mixed with the salt smell of the sea. With pain she remembered Oliver loping down the hill to the war.

Once a week she wrote to Richard of her school life, what she was learning, how she hated the cold and the games, what they were allowed to listen to on the radio, the News, *ITMA* and *The Brains' Trust*. Occasionally, if Richard wrote asking permission for her, she was allowed to listen to one of Max's concerts. She longed for the holidays. She never wrote of her unease with Mrs Penrose, nor could she mention Richard's habit of putting his hand up her skirt, which when she was small had not bothered her but now was distasteful, though small cost to keep in touch with the only home she knew. She would find a way round these troubles without causing embarrassment to Richard, who was her only link with Oliver. For Richard would sometimes, among the minutiae of his daily life, write that there had been news of the others. He wrote when Polly and Walter's parents were killed, "Can't have known anything about it, nice way to go." He wrote that Sarah had heard from Oliver now fighting in the Desert, "Jolly good show." He wrote that Hector, old though he was, forty-four, might also get in on the action, another jolly good show as there was "No real need for him to take risks." For Walter on the North Atlantic run he had no praise, "Foolish fellow not to get over his seasickness, look at Nelson." He occasionally noted that the Rector and Mildred had heard from the twins, "Now separated, which only makes sense". He wrote praising Mr Churchill and criticising the generals, he wrote that like it or not one had to agree that "this Hun General Rommel is the best general in the war, he would get defeated though it was hard to imagine how" and that, awkward chap though he seemed to be, "this General de Gaulle fellow is the only Frog to stand up and be counted." In those days Sophy grew almost to love him. She forgot in her loneliness the revulsion she felt for his dismemberment, her horror of his smelly breath, the disgust she felt when he touched her, patting her thigh as he had patted stinking old Farticus, now long dead. He did not pat Ducks but fondled his ears, muttering, "Only good thing to come out of enemy territory." She wove round Richard's weekly reports the substance which kept her heart alive. She was too young to find it ironic that Richard, whom she had never liked, and who had never liked her, should be the only person to bother to keep her in touch with base.

But when the holidays fell due Sophy travelled to London with her school to be met by whoever Polly persuaded to meet her, spend the night and catch the train to Penzance. By the time Monika met her at the station a metamorphosis would have taken place. She would arrive at the house on the cliff as shy and reticent as ever, finding it possible to talk to Monika and the Floyers but impossible to communicate with Richard. For his part Richard seemed to find this natural and would wait till she was back at school to resume the intimate terms they arrived at on paper.

At the end of an Easter term it was Tony who met her train.

"Hullo, Sophy. Polly is away, she asked me to meet you."

"Where has she gone?"

"I don't know, somewhere to do with her job. Walter is in London on leave, he's very fed up at missing her. He was still asleep when I looked in before coming to the station. How is school?"

"Horrible. I shall be glad to see Walter. How is he?"

"Tired and fed up. Not only is Polly away but Calypso's gone tripping up to Scotland, so he can't see her either."

"Whatever for? She hates Scotland."

"She had all her windows blown in so she went up there while the workmen put them back. Said she had a job to do, something to do with Hector."

"She'd never put herself out for Hector."

"You know a lot for your age." Tony spoke reprovingly. Criticism of Calypso from this child, however apt, was galling. Arriving outside Polly's house he put her suitcase on the doorstep and rang the bell. "You all right if I leave you? I have to be at my fire station in a few minutes."

"Yes, thank you." Sophy watched him go, feeling ungrateful. Walter opened the door.

"I was just going to get breakfast. Are you hungry?" He kissed her heartily.

"I had mine before leaving school."

"You could do with another. Did he tell you the girls are both away?"

"Yes."

"Terrible. I get the first leave for ages and no sister, no cousin."
He led the way down to the kitchen. "Like fried potatoes?"

"Oh yes."

"And a spot of bacon? Right, you sit down out of the way
while I cook. D'you think they'd mind in Cornwall if I came
down? There's nothing for me here."

"They'd love it. I would, anyway. Monika will be pleased and
Uncle Richard."

"Really think so? I don't want to impose. Where is Aunt
Helena, somewhere with Max, or don't you know about them?"

"Of course I know. I'm not a baby any more."

"No," said Walter, "you're not, you seem quite a bit bigger.
Right then, we'll catch the night train. I haven't been down since
those last summer hols." He dished out fried potatoes and bacon.
"You get stuck into that and then you can bring me up to date
with all the changes down there."

The night train was unbearably crowded. They squeezed into
a carriage full of sailors travelling to Plymouth, who filled the
carriage with cigarette smoke and drank from beer bottles. Walter
pushed Sophy into a corner and squeezed in beside her. The
blacked-out train chugged steadily, stopping at dimly lit stations
where the guard shouted the names of the towns. Walter dozed
while Sophy sat wakeful, watching the sailors and listening to
their talk. She was too uncomfortable to sleep and there was not
enough light to read. When she prised a chink in the blind she
could see the moon with clouds racing across it. At Taunton more
people crowded in, standing in the corridor, smoking, muttering,
shifting from foot to foot. Posters in the dim light said, "Be Like
Dad Keep Mum". Walter fought his way out of the carriage to
find a buffet. The train went on again and Sophy became anxious,
fearing he had been unable to get on again. Her anxiety was
reaching fever pitch when there was a jostling in the corridor and
he appeared, elbowing his way, carrying a cup of tea in each
hand, stepping over the legs of their fellow occupants.

"Thought this might keep us alive." Sophy took the cup gratefully. "Afraid a lot's slopped."

"Doesn't matter," she said.

"Filthy stuff, really." He squeezed beside her. "It'll be funny
to be there without the cousins. We always came together."

"I'm your cousin."

"So you are." Walter put his empty cup under the seat. "You've
always seemed too little to be a cousin."

"I'm larger now."

"Much." He put his arm round her. "That comfortable? It won't be the same, no Oliver to boss us, no Calypso, no twins. Lovely times, weren't they? Do you remember those last holidays before this began, d'you remember the Terror Run? Weren't you bitten by a snake or something and crying in Calypso's arms?" He remembered Calypso's expression of anxiety and exasperation. The reflected light from the sea had made her eyes quite a new colour. "What did you say?"

"I said I wasn't bitten, it was something else."

"And that other game we were going to play, we drew lots. What was it? To kill somebody, something like that, one of Oliver's barmiest ideas."

"He said all of us were capable of killing, but he cancelled it."

"Well, as things turned out we are at war and doing our best." Walter with his arm round Sophy felt dozy. Their companions in the carriage were snoring, mouths open, sprawling. Sophy gave a loud sob. "Hey, what's the matter? Tell old Walter. 'Ere, 'ere, have a handkerchief."

"I tried to tell Polly but she didn't take it in. I told her in an air raid, we were under the kitchen table. I don't even know if she heard."

"Tell me, then, I'm all ears." Walter gave a colossal yawn, nearly dislocating his jaw. "I nearly dislocated my jaw. What did you say?"

"I pushed him over."

"Pushed who? Pushed over what?"

"The coastguard. He used to hide behind a bush on the cliff path. He had a pink thing – it looked like a snake – in his pocket."

"Oh." Walter was waking slowly. "A flasher."

"What's a flasher?"

"Never mind, go on, ears flapping. I'm awake, tell. Stop crying, do, you snuffle so I can't hear. Jumped out from behind a bush, did he?" Walter held her quietly, his eyes roving over the sleeping sailors.

"He didn't exactly jump, he just appeared from behind the bushes. You know where they are, near the rocks?"

"Yes, go on."

"Well, that's what frightened me when we did the Terror Run, and made me scream."

"I remember." He remembered Sophy hysterical, Oliver slapping her face.

"When it happened again I tried to push past him and he went over." Sophy's voice was almost inaudible. "He was found in the sea, I was ill and the police came and took Monika and Max off to be interned."

"What had they got to do with it?"

"Nothing, nothing. Oh, Walter, what shall I do? D'you believe me?"

Walter said nothing, holding her close while the train chugged slowly, the sailors slept and in the corridor a party of soldiers began singing mournfully but in tune.

"They must be Welsh, they are singing in tune." He rocked her gently, his chin touching the top of her head. What silky hair. Polly said Chinese. He felt the tension slip out of her body and knew she slept. He wondered whether to say anything. The subject is beyond me, he thought.

"You do believe me, don't you?" Sophy spoke sleepily.

"Yes, yes," he said quietly. "Yes, yes."

"Polly didn't." She slid back to sleep. Walter sat holding her as the train drew into Plymouth. The sailors woke, gathered their luggage and lurched off the train, their places taken by newcomers.

The train carried on, stopping at every station through Cornwall, and still Sophy slept, until at last he heard the cry, "St Erth change for St Ives", let up the blind and it was early morning. "Wake up, Sophy, nearly there." The sun sparkled on Mount's Bay and St Michael's Mount rose from the waves. "Wake up, wake up, you are home. Gosh, I'm looking forward to this leave."

"Isn't the sea lovely? I hope Monika's there to meet us." Sophy combed her hair, tightened the laces of her shoes, looked out at the sea with her oriental eyes. "I could eat a horse," she exclaimed.

"Some people pull legs better than others," Walter muttered to himself as he lifted their suitcases off the rack. "A word with Polly is what I need."

"What was so dreadful," said Polly to Iris and James, driving to Max's funeral all those years later, "was that I was in Portugal when Walter had his last leave. I never saw him again. If I'd known I'd have got out of it somehow and seen him."

"But you wouldn't have known he was going to be killed,"

said Iris, who had heard her mother say the same thing so often she knew it by heart. "You couldn't have had last words or anything, as you didn't know."

"It taught me to treat everybody's leave as perhaps the last. He might have wanted to tell me something. They said he had something on his mind. We only had each other, our parents had been killed by a bomb."

"I know," Iris had often heard this too, "and Helena and Max arrived with a taxi full of flowers from Covent Garden."

"I bore you as Uncle Richard bored us." Polly was resentful.

"Oh no, Ma, you don't, it's just—"

But drowning in the North Atlantic three weeks after his leave, Walter had a vivid recollection of Sophy weeping in the train. He opened his mouth to shout for Polly and drowned that much quicker.

TWENTY-FOUR

It was Calypso and Brian Portmadoc who were the first to hear about Walter. They had dined together. Instead of inviting him back to her house, as he had hoped, Calypso said she must go and tell Polly what she had been doing in Scotland.

"Won't it wait?" Brian longed for Calypso's bed with Calypso in it.

"No, I have to see her."

They took a bus which crawled through the blackout. Calypso rang the bell and waited impatiently. "I must get her to give me a key, everyone else seems to have one."

The door was opened by a slight dark girl with curly hair. "Who are you?" Calypso stepped inside, pulling Brian after her.

"Elizabeth. I'm a friend of Walter's. You must be Calypso." The girl was shy and awkward. "He gave me a key, he said Polly wouldn't mind."

"Is she here?"

"She's away somewhere. Walter said—"

"And where is he?"

"He's gone back. He was on leave a few weeks ago but I—"

"You a girl friend?"

"Well, I was, I—"

"What are you doing here if you're a 'was'?"

"We made it up. We talked on the telephone, he said to come here to Polly. Anyway, what business—"

"Oh, it's no business of mine, I just want to see Polly."

"Oh." The girl called Elizabeth looked discomfited by Calypso's hard tone.

"Any clue as to when she'll be back?" Calypso began looking through a pile of letters addressed to Polly on the hall table. "What's this telegram?"

"I don't know."

"Might be urgent." Calypso opened the telegram and read it. "Oh," she said, "Oh," and looked at Brian and the girl called

Elizabeth. "He's been killed," she said. "Why him? Why not somebody nasty? Did you love him?" she asked the girl, who gave a moan, turned and ran upstairs. Calypso watched her go.

"Let's find a drink." Calypso started down to the kitchen. Brian searched, she stood by the table.

"Weren't their parents killed?"

"Yes. Buck up with that drink."

"So Polly's alone?" He found some whisky.

"Not exactly alone but no family now. Thanks." She took a gulp of whisky. "How bloody, how absolutely bloody."

"That poor girl."

"She'll find someone else. What's her name, anyway?"

"Elizabeth."

"Elizabeth what?"

Above them feet pattered through the hall, the front door opened and slammed shut. They heard high heels clatter away in the dark.

"We shan't know now." Calypso swallowed whisky in a gulp.

"Was Walter? Did you—"

"No, I didn't. Wish I had. Can't now. Oh, bloody, bloody hell, why him? He never hurt a fly. I think you'd better go, Brian, I'll stay here, she might get back any moment. Awful for her to be alone."

"Can't I—"

"No. Listen, if I give you my key will you fetch Fling for me? Bring him here. There's a dear. Then I'll be here if she gets back."

"But I hoped I—"

"I know you did, but I wasn't going to anyway. I meant to tell you but you were so nice at dinner. Please, Brian, just fetch my dog."

"Clothes?" He swallowed, trying to conceal his disappointment.

"I'll manage with Polly's."

"I've got to go away on a course tomorrow."

"I know, you told me. Not much luck tonight for either of us."

When he had gone Calypso re-read the telegram from the Admiralty. She noted it was dated four days earlier. "How bleak," she murmured, "how bleak. Already four days." She sifted through the letters and found a sheet of paper with a note in Walter's handwriting. "I've given a key to a girl called Elizabeth, be kind to her for a night or two. Have been in Cornwall,

remind me to tell you about Sophy. See you next leave." Near
the letters the girl had left her key. Calypso put it in her bag. She
wondered how many girls had loved Walter. He had been secretive about love affairs. She thought of him in Able Seaman's
uniform at her wedding, going off with Oliver, drunk. Where
now was Oliver and what doing and for that matter Hector, what
was he up to?

When Brian came back she thanked him for bringing Fling.

"Can't I come in?"

"Brian, no! Can't you see I want to be alone?"

"But you weren't in love with him."

"He's part of my life, my cousin. I feel robbed."

"But you weren't in love, it's not the same. That poor girl
who ran off was."

"I don't know what love is. Just go, Brian. Please. Leave me
with Fling."

When he was gone she fetched some blankets, lit the fire in the
drawing room and settled herself with Fling on the sofa. By the
light of a table lamp the room looked dusty, deserted by her aunt
and uncle snatched by a wanton bomb. In this room there had
been parties, children's parties with games, impromptu dances,
the rugs rolled up, dancing in Walter or Oliver's arms to the
gramophone. She remembered laughter and cries of pain when
the boys trod on her feet, cocktail parties as they grew older,
windows open on hot summer evenings. Now it was dead and
dusty. She would wait for Polly.

Drawing the blankets round her, holding the dog close, she
found herself wishing that Hector was there. He could help Polly,
he would do it much better than she. She was surprised at her
thoughts, and began to think back to the week she had just spent
in Scotland and the friend she had made, of some of the things
she had been told about Hector, aspects of his life he had been at
pains to conceal. She had meant to spend the evening talking to
Polly about herself, and was irritated that instead she must stand
by for Polly's grief, put her own needs aside. Sleepy, she tried to
keep awake, wondering if it would have been better if Hector
had been killed or Oliver or the twins. Oliver loved her, she
enjoyed his adoration. Hector? She would have his money
whether he lived or died. The twins seemed since the war to have
lapsed in their adoration and Walter, too. She tried to think of
Oliver dead instead of Walter and smiled sleepily, remembering
him saying of Hector, "I hope he gets killed." She thought she

could do without them all. Cuddling Fling close she laid her head back and closed her eyes.

Polly was at her feet when she woke, holding the telegram. Their eyes met.

"I stayed to be here when you got back." She sat up.

"Thank you." Polly was very still.

"Where have you been? You are all sunburned."

"Portugal. Lisbon. It was lovely and hot."

"Your job?"

"Yes. It won't happen again. It seemed an opportunity. My boss needed me. I'm not supposed to talk about it."

"Polly, there was a girl here—"

"Elizabeth. He left a note. Elizabeth who? Did she say?"

"No, she ran off crying."

"In love with him, I suppose. Several girls were, I shall have to tell them."

"Why him? Why Walter? Why not Hector or Oliver or the twins?"

"Not the twins." Polly gave a gasp, glancing at Calypso. "Why are you here, anyway?"

"I came to see you. I wanted to talk to you. Then I saw the telegram and read it and thought I'd wait. You'd be all alone—"

"Kind of you. What did you want to see me about?"

"I'm having a baby. I wanted to tell you."

"Hector's?"

"Of *course!*"

"That's all right, then. I guessed you had morning sickness not food poisoning, didn't I?"

"Yes."

"Have you told him? He'll be terribly pleased, won't he?"

"I've written. He should know by now. He wants an heir. I've got one of his people to be its nurse. I've been up in Scotland. Hector said if I had a child Catherine must look after it. She's small, lame, plain and reliable. I went up there to see her. She will come when I'm ready, she can look after it."

Polly listened to Calypso, holding the telegram in her sun-burned fingers.

"Perhaps it will make you happy."

"But I am happy."

"That's not happiness that's money." Polly's voice was bitterly nasty. She recovered herself quickly. "Sorry, Calypso. I must have a bath. D'you think you could ring them up in Cornwall, and Helena and Aunt Sarah?" She put the telegram on the table by Calypso. "I don't think I can do it, so will you?"

"Of course." Calypso shook herself free of the blankets. "I'll just give Fling a run. You go and have your bath."

Standing on the doorstep watching her dog trot to and fro in the early morning street, Calypso found herself weeping, tears splashing on to the pavement. In the house Polly would be lying in the bath, her sobs drowned by the sound of the water taps. Presently she would appear puffy-eyed and grim, refusing to discuss her loss, insist that she was all right and go off to work and snap at anybody who showed her sympathy. Calypso went in to telephone.

"Aunt Helena, it's Calypso. Aunt Helena, Walter's dead. Yes, a telegram. Yes, quite sure. Yes, she knows. No, she's in the bath – well, you know Polly. Yes, I was here. Actually I opened the telegram. What? Not open people's telegrams? Let her read it herself. She did read it herself. I fell asleep and she came home and found it. What has Uncle Richard got to do with it? Oh, your first husband – sorry. It helped to open the telegram your-self? Really? Well, it's too late now. Yes, I'll tell her, she's in the bath. Aunt Helena, I must go now, I have to ring Aunt Sarah. Yes, yes, I will, of course I will. Yes, I'm sure she will. Yes. Goodbye."

Calypso dialled trunks and asked for Sarah's number in Bath.

"Aunt Sarah? Calypso here. Aunt Sarah, Walter's been killed. Yes, quite sure – a telegram from the Admiralty. Well, you know Polly, she's crying in the bath. Yes, I'm crying here – oh, and you are crying there. In Bath. I suppose that's funny. Well, not funny. Why Walter, why him? Why not someone who could be spared? Yes, I'll tell her. Yes, I'm sure she would like it if you came up. Yes, I've told Aunt Helena, she was angry that I'd opened the telegram. What? I found it and read it, Polly was away. Aunt Helena carried on about opening the telegram about her husband. I'd forgotten she had one. Oh God! Three minutes! Goodbye—"

Calypso slammed down the receiver, wiped her eyes and went down to the kitchen to give Fling some milk. From upstairs she heard the rush of water as Polly pulled the plug in the bath. Hurriedly she dialled trunks on the kitchen extension and asked for the Cornish number.

"Sophy? Is Uncle Richard there? Well, is Monika there? When will they be back? Not till late. Oh God! Sophy, listen, there's bad news. No, no, not Oliver, it's Walter. Walter's dead. Yes. What did you say?"

"He was the sweetest," Sophy's clear voice all the way from Cornwall.

"Well, darling, will you tell them? Yes, please, Sophy. Yes, of course I will kiss her for you. She's – yes, she's in the bath, actually. I heard the water running away just now so – yes – well, goodbye."

Polly came into the kitchen puffy-eyed.

"Have you told them?"

"Yes. Sophy said he was the sweetest."

"He was." Polly tightened her dressing-gown belt. "I must have some coffee and then rush or I will be late for work."

"I'll get it while you dress."

"Thank you, but I'll make you late."

"My office doesn't mind."

"Mine does. My boss isn't at all obliging."

"But surely today he—"

"You aren't suggesting I should tell him, are you?" Polly suddenly spat at Calypso, then, seeing her expression, said, "Right, then. Come to supper tonight and tell me about your baby."

"Hector's."

"All right, Hector's." Polly's face was pinched with misery; she looked almost ugly. "Not that Hector's baby is much of a replacement."

"Nobody could replace Walter!" Calypso put her arms round her cousin, feeling her stiff with reserve. "I would give myself, darling, if it would do any good, but who am I? I love money and a good time, I'm enjoying the war, I find it exciting and frightening. I enjoy the raids, I like all the men taking me out. I like being a grass widow, at least I think I do." She felt Polly relaxing in her arms. "But when something like this happens I hate it, Polly, I hate it, and now I shall stop having a good time and blow up into an awful balloon and nobody will want to sleep with me for months and months. D'you think I'll ever get my figure back? Polly, what are you laughing at?"

"You." Polly pulled away from Calypso, took her face between her hands. "You're so utterly selfish." She kissed Calypso gently. "There. Don't worry. Whatever shape you are all the men will want you. Walter only gave up trying because he thought it was a waste of time. He didn't think he was attractive enough. Think of Oliver—" She kissed her cousin. "I must go, I hate being late."

She turned and ran upstairs to dress. Calypso followed slowly.

"Can I come this evening? You are so comforting, though I thought I would comfort you."

"Of course." Polly was pulling on her stockings. "Of course you must come. I want to hear all about the baby. What shall you call it?"

"I haven't thought," Calypso lied, feeling protective towards Hector, who must be the first to know. I'm only a vehicle, she told herself. This boring child is his.

TWENTY-FIVE

"Why the fuss?" exclaimed Max. "What does it matter? A telegram is not private like a letter. Anyway, it was not for you."

"It's the principle of the thing. When Anthony was killed I saw the telegraph boy coming. I opened the telegram myself. The message was for me. Anthony was my husband, Calypso had no business—" Helena was excited.

Max put his arms round her. "Helena, where is your calm? The girls do not worry. Calypso has not behaved badly, she—"

"She always behaves badly. I hear she is having affairs all over the place since Hector went overseas. She—"

"Opening the telegram and having affairs are two different things. Maybe she thought she was doing right to open the telegram. You are old-fashioned, my Phlegm, you—"

"Old-fashioned?"

"No, darling, it is my bad English. I am Continental. I do not think poor Calypso behaved—"

"Poor! That girl's rich, not only Hector's money, she's rich in gall. You be careful of her, Max. Before you know where you are she'll be scrambling into bed with you."

"Ach, Helena." He stroked her hair, thinking of Calypso's peach-coloured body, relaxed and cheerful before rehearsals. "She will not make a scramble, as you call it." No such luck, thought Max. "What can we do for Polly?" he said, regretfully remembering Calypso's recent refusal to sleep with him any more. "We should do something. Go and see her, telephone first, she was not thrilled to see us when her parents had been killed."

"That was different. Poor Polly. What a lovely time we had, the taxi full of flowers. I shall never forget that morning in Covent Garden." Helena kissed him as she had learned, open mouthed.

"We telephone presently, my darling." He pushed her back on the bed. "We telephone later." He ran his tongue along her teeth.

"We've only just had breakfast," said Helena, yielding.

"You still think love is only for between ten thirty p.m. and midnight?"

"Not any more. Come, ruin my make-up. What time is your rehearsal?"

"Shush, *meine Kliene*—"

Later Helena told Sarah on the telephone: "We rang up but she did not answer. I think she must have gone to work. How much do you think she cares, Sarah?"

"Terribly, I should think. Let's let her be. I offered to come up but she put me off for a few days, said the Floyer twins are coming on leave for two nights. I shall come when they are gone; perhaps it's better for the young to be together. She said Calypso's being very helpful."

"That will be the day," said Helena. "Calypso never helps anyone but herself."

"Oh, I don't know," said Sarah, remembering that Calypso had made Oliver telephone when he returned from Norway. "She's a dark horse. I've known her unselfish."

Helena, repairing her make-up, wondered whether Sarah had been giving her a small dig. Nobody could call me unselfish these days, she thought, creaming her face. Here am I, making up for lost time, so happy. I must go to Hatchards, she thought, and choose some books for Richard and send something nice to Monika, who looks after him as I should be doing, cares for Sophy in a way I could never manage. How extraordinary it is, thought Helena, wiping the cream off and starting again, that with all the dreadful news from the Middle East, with Walter dead, with the war spreading all over the world, I should be so happy and Calypso, so different from me, looks as though she is thoroughly enjoying herself. Were it not for Hitler I should never have met Max, were it not for the war Hector would not have decided to marry again. The Jews may be enslaved, thought Helena, powdering her nose, but I am free of boring, boring Richard. If the telegraph boy had not brought me the telegram to say Anthony was killed, what sort of woman would I have become? Certainly not Max's mistress. I still think, Helena told herself, that Calypso was wrong to open that telegram. It was addressed to Polly. Carefully applying lipstick, Helena tried to recall her feelings in 1917 when she grieved for her young husband. She had been wearing a grey herringbone tweed skirt, a white blouse and a woolly cardigan which dipped where she overloaded her pockets. She remembered that she had a cold which weeping made worse, that her period had started the night before she got the news. She remembered being thankful that she was not pregnant. That her mother-in-law wept, exclaiming, "He was the flower of the flock", she being left with two other sons, both black sheep. Helena stared at her present-day face in the glass. After Anthony's death she had met Richard. A bit unfair when the Great War had left three million surplus women that she should find another husband and now have a lover; a fresh lease in this new war.

A little later, stepping out into the street, Helena met the post-man. A bill and a letter in Richard's writing for herself. She put the bill on the hall table then opened Richard's envelope. Richard wrote that, things being what they were and clothes rationed, he was coming to London to visit his tailor and would be staying with Helena in her new house while he had his fittings. This would not take more than a few weeks. He was sure, wrote Richard, that Helena would agree it was wise to buy the best and make the most sensible and lasting use of one's coupons. Also, wrote Richard, it would be nice while he was in London to see a few shows. He hoped Helena would accompany him. It would be an excellent opportunity to attend one of Max's concerts. Since Monika was reluctant to leave Cornwall – there was really no one she could entrust with the cow and the hens – she was giving him her list of shopping and "I've told her that of course you will be only too delighted to help me with it."

Helena stood in her hall with the street door open, feeling a fog of intolerable boredom engulf her. How dared he enter her new world? She knew she could not stop him. She re-read the letter. There was no escape. There was a postscript: "I thought we might go down and take Sophy out from school." Helena crushed the letter in both hands. "You might," she muttered resentfully, "I won't." That afternoon she telephoned Sarah again.

"Sarah, could you not come and spend a few nights? You can visit Polly and help me at the same time."

"What help do you need?" Sarah sounded harassed.

"Richard is proposing himself to stay for weeks. Don't laugh, it's not funny."

"I'll see what I can do, how long I can be spared."

"I shall be so grateful," said Helena. "He could, he may—"

"I'll come. He won't spoil anything for you, I'll see to that."

Helena, conscious of the fragility of her happiness, felt a rush of gratitude.

Driving down the motorway with Hamish all those years later she said: "One did not feel safe at that time."

"When was that then?"

"During the war."

"I should imagine not, the bombing must have been pretty frightening."

"Oh, I didn't mind the bombing, it was my husband—"

"I never knew him." Hamish was puzzled as he drove fast, pushing a button to squirt water on his windscreen, switching on the wipers to clear the dust. What had been wrong with this old creature's husband? Come to think of it, had she not had two?

"What?" said Hamish, trying to find something to say. "Why?"

"He barged in at a delicate period. Of course later on nothing mattered. Max and I were as established as H. G. Wells and Rebecca West—"

"Didn't he keep trotting off with other ladies?"

"Of course he did. So did Max, but he always came back to me and Monika."

"Who was Monika?"

"Monika was his wife, she died. You must have met her."

"Of course. What did your husband do?" I must get these relationships straight, thought Hamish. They are of historical interest.

"He bored," said Helena in her old voice, sitting beside him. "He was handicapped by being a bore. Now Max, with all his faults, never bored anyone."

"Well, no," said Hamish, grinning at the road ahead. "I never knew him well but I found him a very lively person, also very courageous."

"That's what your mother said. She maintained Max was extremely brave, that he could have taken himself and Monika off to America and been safe. Extraordinary of her to think that. After all, they were perfectly safe in England."

"Jews," said Hamish.

"Of course they were Jews, but we won the war. There was no need for them to bother once they were here."

"We might have lost it." Hamish had read history. "Very nearly did."

337

"It never occurred to me that we would." Helena stuck out her jaw. "Never. People like your father called Dunkirk a disaster and talked of touch and go in the Middle East, and Oliver used to carry on about Norway, I believe. That was a bit of a set-back but apart from the occasional losses—"

"Singapore? Burma?"

"We got them back. There was no need for the Jews to fuss. Max was no braver than anyone else."

"Oh."

"Your mother showed courage, I realise that now. At the time we all thought she was being tiresome and selfish."

"What did she do that was so special?" Hamish was ever ready to talk about his mother, with whom he had never achieved intimacy.

"At a time when children and pregnant women were being sent to the country she sat tight in London. She refused to go to her parents, she refused to go to Scotland, she paid no heed to anybody, she stayed in the London house quite alone apart from a daily woman, alone except for that dog. She wouldn't budge, said the country in wartime frightened her. She thought Max brave and she ganged up with Polly and called Richard heroic."

"How interesting. Was he some special kind of boffin, risking his life and limb? Secret war work? That sort of thing?"

"Richard was no *boffin*." Helena gave a cackle of laughter which ended in a fit of coughing. As she grew mauve in the face Hamish slowed the car and drew on to the hard shoulder. Stopping the car, he patted Helena gently on the back until her wheezes subsided.

"Perhaps you'd better have another swig," he suggested, and helped her unscrew her flask. Still rather choky she took a swallow.

"Ah, that's better, much. It's comical now but I was angry at the time – yes."

"I find it very interesting how the English all pulled together in the war and worked."

"I wouldn't call Richard's behaviour work." Still chuckling, Helena put the flask back in her bag. "You'd better drive on, we shall be late for the funeral."

TWENTY-SIX

Using the key the girl Elizabeth had left, Calypso let herself into Polly's house. She let Fling off the lead and went into the dining-room to take a sheet of writing paper from the desk.

"Darling Polly," she wrote. "I haven't told Pa and Ma that I am pregnant. They will want me to go home and I could not bear it. The fuss. The boredom. Help me. Tell them London's safe, that I need to be near my doctor, something plausible. Love. C." She stuck the note in an envelope and put it on the hall table. "Come on," she said to the dog, who was sniffing at a pile of coats on a chair. She looked closer. RAF caps, overcoats, gas masks. "The twins must be here, how lovely." She started up the stairs. Outside Polly's room the dog pressed his nose to the door and snuffled. Calypso picked him up and walked in. Dim light slanted through the cracks in the blackout curtains. In the bed Polly slept, her dark hair covering one cheek, her face serene, long lashes on sunburned cheeks, sad mouth relaxed; on either side of her lay David and Paul, each with an arm across her body.

Calypso held her breath. They looked peaceful, beautiful. They moved gently, enjoying in their sleep a respite from grief and war. She stepped back, closed the door, tiptoed downstairs, clipped the lead on to the dog's collar and let herself out into the street.

For the moment Polly was out of the question. She remembered the night she had come for Polly's help and been interrupted by Richard. She had since been grateful to him. She glanced up at the curtained window, then started walking towards Helena's house. If Polly had discovered what her life was about so, in her way, had Helena. A call was in order. She paced slowly, recollecting the night Oliver had walked her home, his anger, the aridity she had felt, her relief when she heard Hector crash into her bicycle, saving her from difficult talk. Now both were in the Middle East would they meet and speak of her? She put her thumb on Helena's bell, wondering which twin Polly had slept with first. She was smiling when Max opened the door. He came out quickly shutting the door behind him.

"Come on," he said, taking her arm. "I am going to the cinema, you come too." He started walking her along.

"But I came to see Helena."

"In a bad mood. Better to leave her alone for it, *ja*."

"But I don't want to go to the cinema, I want—"

"You want to see the Marx Brothers in *A Night at the Opera?*"

"I saw it with Hector. It was on in Leicester Square."

"Now it is in Kensington High Street. Laughter will do you good, you look like you need it. I need it severely."

Calypso allowed him to propel her along at a brisk clip. "Why?"

"Ach, Helena is in a foul mood. Your uncle comes to London, she does not want him, she has no talent for living her lives, she wants the compartments separate."

"So would I," said Calypso sharply, "in her shoes."

"You are grumpy, my Calypso." He looked at her closely. "Ach, you are pregnant, *nicht?*"

"How did you guess?"

"It shows in your eyes. Are you sick?"

"I'm in a permanent state of nausea."

"It will pass. The child is Hector's?"

"Of course it is Hector's."

"No of course. I might be honoured and who else, one asks? One sees you with others paying court, one hears—"

"Pig."

"I am teasing. Is Hector pleased? He will now have his heir. In Hector's boots I should be delighted. Did you know that at Harrods one can buy boots with rubber soles called 'Desert Boots'? You should send some to the proud Papa."

"He's got some."

"Well, then, he has an heir en route, he has boots, the brothers Marx will cheer up Mama, she will forget her nausea, we will go back sweet-tempered to Helena and her malaise."

"Is Uncle Richard coming to London to snoop?"

"*Nein.* He says he comes to buy clothes but I think there is something else, I do not yet know what."

"Aunt Helena will try to stop him."

"So. I shall succeed in stopping her stopping him. Come, jump on this bus."

As the bus careered along Max shouted: "And Polly, have you

seen poor Polly? She must mourn her brother, a lovely fellow, how will she console herself?"

"She has her work."

"That will not be enough. We must rally round, as you call it, try to blunt the horrors of grief, keep her mind occupied with pleasant things. What can we do for her, what do you suggest?"

"I—"

"A lover is what she needs, a good lover to occupy her, but one does not find him just like that. We must—"

"We must mind our own business," said Calypso tartly. "Were you going to volunteer?"

"Oho, is like that, is it, *das ist sehr interessant.*"

"You—"

"I shut up." Max smiled wolfishly. "Come, we get off here for our healing laughter."

In the cinema Max's immoderate laughter proved infectious and Calypso laughed more than she had when she had seen the film with Hector. When the lights went up she found herself quite feeble and sat waiting for the cinema to empty.

"Thank you, Max, I loved it." She smiled at him warmly.

"We should have brought Polly, perhaps."

"Perhaps not." Calypso grew sober. "Of course Walter would have adored it—"

"We will go and tell Helena what she has missed."

"Did you ask her to go with you? I bet not."

"Mind you," said Helena to Hamish as they drove, "Max could be difficult. He used to go off on his own and not tell me what he had been doing. Once he came home from the cinema with Calypso, said he had met her there. I didn't believe him. It was when Calypso was having her baby, she felt sick all the time."

"So she tells me," said Hamish drily.

"It was you of course. One forgets. The baby was you, rather a pretty child you were, not that I like babies."

"Nor does she."

"She isn't a pram drooler. Where was I?"

"Max and Calypso at the cinema."

"That's right. They had seen *A Night at the Opera* and came back to tea. Calypso told me she was pregnant; it was a surprise. Of course I was pleased for your father. I had a soft spot for him."

"He rather liked you."

341

"I believe he did. When Calypso told me I congratulated her. I remember it well, said I supposed she would go and live with her parents. D'you know what she said?"

"No." Hamish kept his eyes on the road, intending to be punctual at the funeral.

"She said, 'Not on your Nelly, not bloody likely.' Max was surprised, too."

"Oh."

"Her parents, your grandparents, were dim and boring. That was one thing I agreed with Richard. Conventional, puritanical, rather badly off. They had no conception of how to treat a girl like Calypso. She had very little fun. All they ever did was repress and try to prevent her doing almost anything. Put ideas in her head, if you ask me. It was lucky for her she found your father. She might so easily, given her nature, have—"

"What?"

"Become promiscuous." Helena chuckled. "'Wild' would have been your grandparents' euphemism. Anyway, she said she had no intention of being bored and did I know what her mother said when she found her reading T. S. Eliot?"

"What had my grandmother said?"

"She said, 'Oh, reading that man who doesn't write poetry.' Max went into fits. He cried with laughter. I didn't see anything funny. He said of course Calypso couldn't go to your grandparents, it would psychologically upset the baby. Your mother said, 'It's not the baby I'm worried about, it's me.' Anyway, she stayed in London."

"Did nobody try to stop her? Surely it would have been sensible to go to the country."

"She called her mother philistine, she made T. S. Eliot an excuse. Mind you," said Helena, watching the wide ribbon of the motorway, "I couldn't say much at that time. I hadn't read Eliot either. I sneaked off to Harrods and bought his poems. That was one good thing about the war."

"What was?"

"Lots of books. We couldn't buy sanitary towels but there were plenty of books published. People like me took to reading, our minds were loosened as well as our morals."

"It's difficult to imagine you loose."

"Well-brought-up girls like Polly and Calypso had such opportunities and I became quite a butterfly."

Hamish was silent.

"I may look like a chrysalis now," said Helena angrily, "but in my forties I flowered. The war even inspired Richard. When he came to London he cramped my style. Your mother egged him on. If left to himself he would have bought his clothes and gone back to Cornwall, but she and Polly encouraged his wild ideas, they were mischievous, those girls."

"I wish I'd known you all in those days. I've seen photographs, of course."

Helena snorted. "Photographs! Polly looking as though butter wouldn't melt when she was selfish, greedy and flouting convention. She got away with it because nobody could believe what she was up to. Her parents would have put a stop if they'd been alive, or at least tried. Your mother did exactly as she pleased, turned a deaf ear to advice and encouraged Richard to make a fool of himself, said he needed a bit of fun."

"But what did he do? What was so awful?"

"I felt his behaviour reflected on me. I was annoyed with those girls, your mother in particular, and really upset when Oliver's mother took Richard's side." Helena took another sip from the flask. Glancing sideways, Hamish surmised it held half a bottle of whisky and wondered what Helena would contribute to the funeral.

"I used to take this flask to Max's concerts; it helped me through many an evening." Helena screwed the top on tightly. "People thought I had a weak bladder, those constant trips to the cloakroom, ho-ho."

"When does Uncle Richard arrive? No, no sugar, thanks, Aunt, it makes me queasy."

"Next week. I have asked Sarah to come up to see Polly. She can help, well, help with Richard. I'm so busy."

"I'll ask him to take me out to lunch. I'll take him off your hands." Calypso knew that her aunt knew she knew how unwelcome Richard would be in Enderby Street.

"But you are at that office of yours all day."

"I'm leaving it this week."

"Don't they want you any more?"

"It's not that. I'm sick all the time. They are getting a bit cross with me, say it wastes valuable war work time."

"Oh my dear, is it—" Helena looked at Calypso in alarm. "I mean—"

"It's Hector's," said Calypso stuffily. "Do I have such a wild reputation?"

"No, no, of course not. I was going to say is it wise in wartime to have a baby?"

"Hector wants one, especially if I can grind out a boy. That's what—"

"What a way to talk! Aren't you pleased? Hector will be."

"Hector doesn't feel sick all the time, he won't swell up like a balloon. His part was easy, it's a part he plays with enthusiasm, he—"

"That's enough, darling, not in front of Max, you'll embarrass him."

"He doesn't look embarrassed, he's laughing. All right, let's plan how to keep Uncle Richard out of your hair."

"Oh, Calypso." Helena began laughing too. "Richard will enjoy seeing you. He is so fond of you girls, he will be so glad to see you and Polly. Perhaps you could go with him to visit Sophy, I simply haven't got the time."

"Oh." Calypso was unbelieving. "Really?"

"I have joined the Red Cross, that takes up my mornings and—"

"Why the Red Cross, isn't it full of snobs?"

"It's useful for Max. Red Cross charity concerts advertise his name and names are what matter. It doesn't matter if they can't tell one note from another, I can't either."

"I bet Max knows Sir Thomas Beecham."

"But not Lady Cunard. So you see, darling, I am busy."

"Aunt, you have changed."

"I just have more scope. More tea?"

"No, thank you."

"She has asked me to call her Emerald."

"Oh my, you fly high. When does Uncle Richard arrive? I'll meet him." Calypso watched Max liberally buttering a scone. "Where d'you get all this butter, Aunt?"

"Monika sends a hamper on the train every week. I send it back empty. It's a bit of a nuisance having to go to Paddington to collect it but it's very useful."

"What else does she send?"

"Cream, eggs, vegetables, fruit. She sent a lobster last week. She hadn't tied its claws properly, I got nipped."

"Oh, Aunt!"

"Not badly."

"Isn't it black market?"

"It's my house, my garden, my produce. Monika is my guest."

"Grey?" suggested Max. *"Le marché gris."*

"Nonsense, Max, you need the food."

"I like the food. I shall also meet Richard when he arrives, he will be bringing compôtes and such."

"I will come with you," Calypso volunteered.

"I won't have you raiding the hampers."

"What an idea, Aunt."

"You should show a bit of enterprise and get Hector's people to send you grouse and venison and herrings."

"They would go bad."

"Kippers, then."

"I'll think about it."

Richard arrived with several hampers and settled into Helena's spare room, unpacking his ivory brushes, the photograph of his first wife, his toothbrushes, sponge and pyjamas, arranging them in orderly fashion in their new surroundings. Within half an hour he looked, thought Helena, ominously settled.

The following morning he limped out to make a preliminary visit to his tailor, then took a bus to the City and the East End to view the bomb damage.

"Really most impressive," he said to Calypso, who had turned up at tea time. "I saw a lot of rubble in France but nothing like this. There's no mud and no dead horses. Those ARP chaps seem efficient at finding the bodies. One misses the smell, a sort of haunting odour of wet dead. What's it been like round your way?"

"I lost all my windows when Parliament was hit."

"That all? Have you seen the City?"

"No."

"Good Lord, you live in London and haven't seen it? I'll take you tomorrow, you must see the Docks and the City. I'll take you on a tour. The best way to see it is from the top of a bus. One should walk of course, but with my leg—"

"Even your new one?"

"Not the same as flesh and blood but it will not prevent me from dancing."

"Dancing!" exclaimed Helena and Calypso in chorus.

Richard smiled with satisfaction. "I have, or rather Monika has, enrolled me in a course of lessons at a school in Soho."

"How many lessons?" asked Helena suspiciously.

"Twelve, two a week, so in six weeks I shall – where's she gone?" Helena, carrying the teapot, had left the room, her lips compressed.

"Did Monika suggest this course, Uncle?"

"Yes. Fact is she gets kicked when I dance with her and one gets a bit weary of dancing with a chair."

"A chair?"

"Yes. I turn back the carpet and dance with a chair. It can't complain if it gets kicked but it's not like dancing with live flesh. But Monika complains about that too."

"Why?"

"Keeps her awake, scraping noise on the parquet. What with that and the music she loses sleep. She has to get up early to milk the cow, says it can't wait, I ask you, she should train it. Anyway the upshot was she came up with this plan. I paid in advance, start on Wednesday."

"A brilliant idea, terribly brave."

"What's brave?" Helena came back carrying the teapot. "More tea, anybody?"

"Uncle Richard learning to dance is heroic."

"How long will this pantomime take?" Helena looked coldly at Richard.

"Six weeks, my dear. I told you."

"My God!"

"I won't be a bother. I have my club, my tailor, Monika's shopping and I'm told there's a place called the Windmill."

"That's for dirty old men."

"No it isn't, Aunt Helena. Hector met someone who'd been there. He said it was good clean fun."

"Did he go himself? No, I can see he didn't."

"Hector would have no need," said Richard, looking at Calypso.

"It's naked girls." Helena sighed.

"You are in no position to talk." Richard held out his cup for a refill.

"Now, now," said Calypso, "don't squabble."

"Not that one would call you a girl any more," pursued Richard. "More in the class of Monika, 'femme d'un certain age' fits the bill. Now you've abandoned me and taken to this life in London you have beauty—"

"Thanks," said Helena, interrupting.

"Of course Monika is sensitive. She has a lot to put up with, not knowing whether her son is alive – dead, if you ask me, but women go on hoping – and Max carrying on with you and again, if you ask me, others as well. What d'you think, Calypso?"

"I wouldn't know."

"Of course you know, fellow's got an eye for the girls and it's not only his eye." Richard, watching Helena, burst into a guffaw. "Anyway, who am I to grumble, Monika puts up with it. Life in Cornwall seems to suit her. She did offer to teach me herself but I preferred the chair. A chair does what you want, doesn't try to lead, it bloody goes where you push."

"What do you do for music? There aren't many dance records in the house."

"That's a point, clever of you. There's a late-night programme of dance music on the wireless, that keeps her awake too, then she starts thinking about her boy, I daresay."

"Yes," said Calypso, "she probably does." She remembered Monika's anguish.

"Well, now, suppose I trot round and see Polly? Back from work by now, I expect. I want to ask her to come down and see Sophy. I've never seen a girls' school at close range."

"I'd ring up first," said Calypso hastily.

"Really? Like that, is she? My word, you've all changed. I'll probably find Sophy doesn't want to be taken out."

"Of course she does. I'll come with you. Let's make a day of it, unless you want to go, Aunt Helena?" Helena shook her head. "Fling will love a day in the country. Let's have a picnic."

"All right. I'll telephone the school."

"I'll tell her I'm having a baby. I wonder what she'll say to that."

"There's a cooked chicken in one of the hampers, the one they called Jane. Sophy was rather fond of it but it's stopped laying so Monika gave it the chop."

"What brutality."

"You sure Polly wouldn't like to come too? Take her mind off Walter. The Floyer boys are stationed somewhere near, it might be possible—"

"They've been moved to another station now they are on ops again."

"Pity, we might have combined – seen them lately, have you?"

"No," said Calypso obliquely, "no."

"They are known as the 'High Floyers' in the village. Baptist minister having a dig at the Rector's High Churchmanship. Jolly good joke until they got shot down. Perhaps Sophy has some little friends who'd like a blow-out. That's what children like when they are at school."

"She won't be a child much longer." Helena eyed her husband thoughtfully.

"All the more reason I should do a bit more than just pay the bills. I write, of course, and she writes back, but when she's at home I sometimes wonder—"

"Wonder what?" Helena voiced anxiety.

"Whether she's quite normal. Not a tear when Walter was killed, left a note on the hall table and disappeared on some long walk, it was a shock for Monika and me. 'Calypso phoned, Walter is killed. "Just like that, I ask you. It was cold of her."

"I expect she was glad it was not Oliver." Calypso looked thoughtfully at Helena. "She loves him."

"Rubbish, a child doesn't know about love. What she'll mind is if she discovers what she's eating is Jane," said Richard sarcastically.

"You dolt," said Helena viciously.

TWENTY-SEVEN

"Well, one hopes one gave some pleasure." Richard fumbled for the hinge of his leg through the material of his trousers. "Sophy's little friends were a lot more forthcoming than she was. She was more interested in the grub than in us, if you ask me."

"She was glad to see us."

"You quite sure? I got more change out of her little friends, not that they gave me much information about Sophy."

"She says she hardly knows them. They aren't in her form. She was sorry for them because nobody takes them out."

"Really? That shows a proper spirit. I was wrong about Jane. 'Is this Jane?' the girl asks, biting into the drumstick, then, with her mouth full, 'Can I have a bit of breast?' And then haggled as to who should pull the wishbone. I told you she was cold. Well, we've done our duty." Richard eased his leg into position and shook open the evening paper. The guard blew his whistle. The train started towards Liverpool Street with a clang.

Calypso pulled down the blackout blind and, leaning back, closed her eyes. Thinking of Sophy's ivory-coloured face, watchful eyes, full-lipped vulnerable mouth, she could not think of her as cold, nor was she unloving, Calypso thought, with a pang of envy.

It had been a crisp blue and gold day and the Backs had looked their best. She and Sophy had walked slowly, following Richard ahead with the two guest girls, one redheaded, one fair. She had told Sophy about her impending child.

"What will you do with it?" Sophy had known instinctively that Calypso could not, would not cope.

She found herself telling Sophy of her visit to Scotland and the plan she had made. Sophy perfectly understood that Hector's castle would receive the baby with joy. She told Sophy about Catherine, the lame woman who would take charge of the infant and bring it up. Walking and talking with Sophy she described the Scottish environment objectively. Sophy needed no explanation or excuse as to why it was not an environment she could bear but would be perfect for Hector's child.

"I suppose Catherine loves Hector?"

"I believe she does."

"Is it Hector's fault that she is lame?"

"He feels responsible but she says the accident was not his fault, would have happened anyway."

"Is that true?" Sophy watched her uncle limping ahead. Now and again he touched one of the girls, putting a hand on arm or shoulder.

"She doesn't elaborate."

"He would feel guilty if he does not love her. What have you arranged?"

Calypso explained that when the child was due Catherine would come. "I have booked a room in a nursing home in Wimpole Street."

"And then?"

"Then she will take it up to Scotland and bring it up in Hector's nursery. The place is full of Commandos but there's a comfortable room in the nursery wing, above the kitchens."

"Won't you have milk?"

"Milk?"

"Won't you feed it? People do. I've learned about it, it's called 'breast-feeding'."

"I couldn't bear to." Calypso shuddered, unconsciously raising her hands to her breasts. Sophy said nothing, watching the figures walking ahead. Then she said carelessly, "Of course not, they are private. What else?"

Sophy broke into her rare laughter, laughing at Calypso who began to laugh too.

"I haven't told anybody. Hector left me to find out for myself. The bastard. His family are Catholic, all his people up there are Catholic. He's in disgrace for divorcing Daphne, they don't think of me as his proper wife."

"Will they think the baby is—"

"Blood's thicker than religion in its case, and while they can't take to me they'll love the child."

"You've never bothered about religion."

"Of course I haven't, none of us does, look at the twins. Mr Floyer's a parson but you'd never know from their behaviour. It appears Hector's is one of those very old Scottish families who survived Henry VIII's mob. It's rather smart. I am mugging them up."

"I suppose he thought you might not marry him if you knew."

"Of course I would have. I married him because he's rich, everyone knows that."

"I hope he's not going to put his hand up their skirts," exclaimed Sophy suddenly.

"What?"

"Uncle Richard. That's what he used to do to me. He keeps patting Valerie and stroking Miranda."

"Then let's walk faster and catch them up." Calypso increased her pace.

"Didn't he do it to you and Polly?"

"I suppose he did, in a mild form. Oh Sophy, how awful, hurry."

"It's not awful," said Sophy. "It's just boring, but they wouldn't understand. Uncle Richard!" She let out a shout. "Wait for us." Ahead of them the two girls turned innocent faces alight with enquiry. "Calypso wants to see King's Chapel, it's the other way."

"Then we can have tea in a tea shop if we can find one," said Calypso to Miranda the redhead.

"That would be nice," said Miranda. "Could we go to a lavatory before King's Chapel?"

"I'll wait for you in the Chapel," said Richard. "Rest my leg."

Watching him asleep in the opposite corner Calypso felt affection. He had played his avuncular part. All those two girls had been interested in was gobbling the picnic lunch. Why should he not put his hand up their skirts? she thought indignantly. They wore elastic in their knickers. She had observed the blonde Valerie wrapping a fairy cake in her handkerchief and stuffing it up under her gym tunic.

"Come to me sometimes on your way through London," she had said to Sophy.

"May I? I would love that. Polly often gets very full up."

And what, Calypso thought, did Sophy mean by that? What did she know?

"Not bad little friends, those two of Sophy's." Richard woke suddenly. "Quite pretty and appetising in their way. Pity Sophy's growing up so fast."

"She's going to be a beauty."

"D'you think so?"

"Yes. Those eyes, like jet. Who was her father, Uncle Richard?"

"Well may you ask! Better not to enquire, I never did. Wouldn't have been much use if I'd wanted to. Her mother was dead by the time I reached her and I was left holding the baby, I ask you. Fortunately I had persuaded Helena to marry me, not that she has ever taken to the child. She is not a child lover."

"Nor am I."

Richard laughed. "Find a wet nurse."

"I've found a nurse. It can have a bottle."

"Well then, there's nothing to it."

"I still have to bear the thing."

"Strong girl like you." Richard Cuthbertson snapped his fingers. "Nothing to it. My poor sister was the runt of the family."

"Oh? I know nothing about her."

"Brains though, she had brains, and this mania for travelling, couldn't be content with her own country, always off abroad somewhere. I couldn't keep up with her travels."

"Did her husband?"

"She didn't have a husband, good Lord, no. Would have tied her down, stopped all that drifting round the world. She came back to base to have Sophy – a British passport matters even to people like my sister – just in time, she was practically born in the docks. She ran it fine."

"Where had she been?"

"Your guess is as good as mine. By the time I got the letter the child was born, and my sister dead."

"Oh. Was there—"

"Nothing. Padre chap had given her the last rites and she died. If the stupid fellow had stopped to think he might have gleaned a shred of information, but he was high like Floyer, keen on spiritual matters, RC now I come to think of it. Supposed he was doing the right thing. Fellow said, 'Your sister died in a state of grace.' How did he *know*? Said she gasped out, 'Tell my brother', then kicked the bucket. I've been wondering ever since what the message was." Richard Cuthbertson lifted the blind and peered out into the darkness. "Getting into London by the look of it. Indo-China."

"What?"

"Looks as if she came from Indo-China. Now what's happened? Why are we stopping?"

"Some delay."

The train sighed, hissed, then all was quiet. Calypso tried to catch the words from a conversation in the next carriage. There was a long pause.

"Life isn't easy, is it?" Richard looked at his niece.

"Not really."

"I saw you today. I can't help liking little girls, they are so pretty."

"Uncle Richard, you needn't—"

"I never hurt them. Didn't hurt you or Polly, did I? Now Sophy's growing up, growing away. People say Ruskin was a stinker but I don't suppose he could help himself, probably had only looked at pictures and statuary. 'Art' was different in his day, poor fellow was a virgin like as not, then when he married he got the hell of a shock. Were you a virgin when you married?"

"Of course I was."

"No of course. Bet you got a shock."

"Actually—"

"Ah, the train's starting. Unexploded bomb on the line, do you think?"

"There haven't been any raids for ages."

"Nor there have. Funny effect trains have, one finds oneself talking as though one were in limbo, voicing private, er, really private ideas. Just ideas, of course."

"Of course, Uncle Richard."

"That's all right, then. The extraordinary thing is that I don't mind it on Monika, actually like it, and she doesn't shave her armpits like you girls."

"That's Continental." Calypso began to laugh.

"What are you laughing at?"

"You, Uncle Richard, oh-oh-oh!" Calypso wiped her eyes with the back of her hand. "Ah-ah-ah oh!" she moaned. "Oh!"

"I wish I knew what's so funny. You children make a mock of me. I'm just a one-legged misfit in this bloody war." Richard suddenly felt rage. "I go to my club and it's full of every conceivable ass in uniform and I am totally useless. Helena has a lover, a well-known violinist, she's sick of her boring one-legged husband. I've never ever been able to make love to her, I ask you. I never liked women until—"

"Monika?"

"Yes. Why am I talking such tommy rot, it's being in a train, what's the matter?" Calypso had moved to sit beside him, putting an arm round his shoulders.

"You're brave, Uncle Richard, you are contributing so much.

Look what you've done to my morale. I was depressed. You are wonderful." Calypso was between laughter and tears.

"No, no." Richard looked embarrassed.

"Yes, yes, awfully brave. We all love you, you know we do."

"Rubbish." Richard grew red in the face.

"It's true," cried Calypso, making it true for herself at least. "Without you all our lives would be different. Think how you rescued Max and Monika from internment – marvellous."

"We are getting into the station, let's see if we can find a taxi." Richard was embarrassed.

Calypso combed her hair and applied lipstick. When the train stopped she took Richard's arm as he limped up the platform.

"Will you be godfather to the baby, Uncle Richard?"

"I don't think I'd be much good. I'm not rich and don't believe in God. Kind of you to ask, though."

"I mean it."

"In that case, thank you. I will think about it."

"Here's a taxi, we're in luck. Get in, quick."

Richard scrambled in, dragging his leg. The taxi wound its way through dark streets and Richard sat silent. Then said: "Wish I'd been in those raids, a fellow feels a bit left out."

"I expect there will be more. Will you drop me at the next corner? I'm practically home."

"Tell the driver. Thank you for coming with me."

"I enjoyed it. Goodnight, Uncle. This will do." Calypso opened the taxi door.

"Goodbye, my dear. She did offer to shave her, er, you know—"

"What? Who?" Calypso was half out of the cab.

"Monika, her pussy, but I said – well, take care of yourself. Enderby Street, driver."

There were two letters from Hector on the mat. Calypso shut the door and drew the curtains before sitting down to read. That he had not yet heard of the baby was clear. He wrote in his neat script of the people he knew now gathered in Cairo, an old school friend who drove a dog cart to save petrol, of swimming at the Gehzira club, tennis, visits to the pyramids, the ill-feeling emanating from King Farouk, the constant round of parties, the wives who had managed to join their husbands, his doubts as to whether it would be safe for her were she to wish to come. He wrote about the light and the smell and that some day he would love to bring her to Egypt. Then he wrote of his plans for peace and several paragraphs Calypso skipped, of his political views, how they were changing. Then rather stiltedly the letter ended, leaving Calypso wondering whether she missed this man, this political animal, a man as old as her father. At least, she thought, he is interested in women, not pining after little girls. Still in the second letter Hector had not heard of her pregnancy. She frowned. Hector wrote that he planned to buy land in England and plant trees.

Seeing all this desert makes me crave for trees. There was once a forest along the shores of North Africa. The Romans felled the trees and never replanted, hence the soil erosion which caused the desert in which we fight. I write metaphorically. My part in the fighting so far is from an office desk. Perhaps I can remedy this. Back to my dream. I shall plant woods of oak, beech, chestnut and among them flowering cherries. I will plant the cherries in curves and circles so that when some future airman flies over them he will see the name Calypso spelled out in blossom. I was in hospital with a fever when I made this plan. I met your cousin Oliver in a bar yesterday, on leave. He has desert boils, disagreeable but not fatal, love, Hector.

Calypso sat with the thin sheets of airmail paper in her lap. This was a Hector she did not know. There were few trees in Scotland. Pines, birches and rowans. It had been cold on their honeymoon, cold when she had travelled up to see Catherine. She had walked along the track by the river. Catherine, the ghillie's daughter, had limped along, speaking in her lilting voice, stopping to point out the rock that Hector had bullied her into jumping from when he came home from school for the holidays, forcing her to leap so that he could catch her, boasting of his strength. "There," she had said, pointing with her sharp chin. "There we fell and my leg it was that broke."

"And left you lame," said Calypso, shocked.

"Aye." Catherine smiled. "To remember him by."

They had stood looking at each other, the older woman's clear blue eyes looking into Calypso's heavily fringed, greenish blue in the Highland light. Then, laughing, the older woman had closed the episode. "Yon Daphne was no leaper such as you, and our Hamish will love the glens, do not worry. He will stride the hills."

Sitting alone in battered London Calypso thought not of Hector but of the mountains and rushing streams which were his

355

background, the scudding clouds and driving rain which had turned to snow, of Catherine coming to stir the fire in her bedroom and put another eiderdown over her in Hector's bed, where she felt an alien. She felt grateful that Catherine, like Hector, made no effort to make her love that savage beauty, accepting her as a Southerner, respecting her for not pretending like Daphne to acceptance by Hector's people. By hints and casual references Hector's people had made it clear that, though Daphne was still in God's eyes Hector's wife, in their hearts they regretted it.

Calypso telephoned Polly.

"What are desert boils?"

"No idea. Why?"

"Hector says Oliver has them."

"Poor Oliver. Ask Aunt Sarah, she is due in London soon. Are you coming round? The twins are here."

"Not tonight, I'm quite busy."

"Doing what?"

"Nothing. It takes all my time."

"Are you all right all alone?"

"I have Fling. I prefer to be alone."

"That's not like you."

"Ah, well." She put down the receiver.

"Pregnancy is making her unsociable," said Polly to David, who was peeling potatoes for their supper.

"She was always a bit unpredictable," murmured the other twin. "A solo artist."

"Not like us," said his brother. "But we were fated, born as we were."

"After all these years I still don't know which of you is the eldest." Polly paused in her task of laying the table.

"Nor do we know," said Paul. "Our parents took the attitude that the first shall be last and the last first. Father living up to his churchy principles and Mother with her idea of fair play."

"Oh."

"Rather like you, darling. Will these be enough potatoes?"

Polly blushed, looking from one brother to another. "I think they are right," she said. "You give me a seed of hope."

"Will you go and see them when we are gone?"

"Gone where?"

"Overseas, darling. The way things are going we are bound to be posted. All the action is in North Africa now. One or both of us may find ourselves in Malta."

"Oh God, no!" Polly burst into tears.

"As bad as that, is it? We rather guessed." They faced Polly, who stood in her kitchen apron, an oven glove in her hand, tears streaming down her cheeks.

"Don't cry, sweetheart, think how good the sun will be for us."

"We can't leave it all to the Pongos. Hector and Oliver have been out there for ages. Nothing has happened to them."

"Oliver's got boils, Calypso told me." Polly's tears seemed limitless.

"And Hector has an office job, I know." Gently they held her, patting her, wiping her tears, stroking her brown hair away from her face. "There," they said, "there. Better now."

Polly gulped strangled words against David's shoulder, laying her head against him, reaching a hand for Paul.

"It's Walter."

"That was months and months ago."

"I know, but it's still—"

The brothers exchanged smiles across her tangled hair.

"Come, blow your nose. You may not have to weep for us."

"When are you likely to go?"

"We have guesswork, that's all. You probably hear more in your office."

"Hence the tears." Polly dried her eyes, trying to subdue her fear.

TWENTY-EIGHT

Left on her own in Cornwall Monika increased the production of food. To hens she added ducks, letting them stray round the flower garden to eat slugs. She bought two rabbits and put them on the tennis court where, wired in, they lolloped, oblivious of the fate in store. The General came and examined the pretty creatures.

"You realise, Monika, my dear, that you have two bucks. You have been sold a pup."

"I do not understand."

"You will never get young with two bucks. You must kill one of these and get a doe."

The upshot was a rabbit stew such as the General had not imagined possible. He invited himself to come again, to the delight of the villagers who followed his every movement, as reported by Mrs Penrose. Bets were laid as to whether the General would entice Monika into his bachelor household before Richard returned from London or Max visited again. At the Rectory Mildred Floyer remarked to her husband that village gossip might have some foundation and that Monika was strangely naïve.

"She is tormented by fear for her son. Anything that takes her mind off him is a good thing," said the Rector. "The WI should have gone in for rabbits. They should not wait for Monika to set an example."

"She is not a member."

"Why not?"

"Because she is a foreigner, not even of the English variety. Her delicatessen infuriate them."

"Dear God! Women!" The Rector felt safe to protest to God in his own kitchen.

"She will," said Mildred, laughing, "go too far. They are shocked by the fungi, disgusted by the garlic, furious that without a trace of black market she produces so much. They hope she will come to grief."

"Has she not enough grief?"

"They hope that she will alienate the men as well."

"You are usually right," said the Rector. "Poor woman. We, at least, know more or less what our High Flyers are up to."

"More or less," said Mildred. "Though sometimes it seems to me they perch rather often in Polly's house."

"They have known Polly all their lives. It was Calypso who struck me as a potential menace before she settled down."

"And how settled is that, one wonders."

The Rector did not reply but went to struggle with his sermon, to preach peace which he believed in yet give comfort to the parishioners who had sons at war.

Sophy, home for the holidays, borrowed Mrs Penrose's bicycle to go to Newlyn harbour where, although entrance to the quays was forbidden to anyone without a pass, she had found that a blind eye was turned to a child, especially if the child brought eggs to barter for fish.

Sitting on an upturned lobster pot above a Belgian trawler tied to the quay, having swopped her eggs for a langouste, she listened to the fishermen talking with savage glee of the night's trawl in incomprehensible Flemish. Men drifted in twos and threes to join the group and slap backs, every now and then breaking into laughter. Willy Penrose, a second cousin of Mrs Penrose, came and sat on a bollard.

"What's going on, Willy?"

Willy glanced around, then said: "They made a funny catch last evening."

"Oh, what?"

"Not for me to say. Ain't you getting a bit big to be coming into the harbour?"

"What happened, Willy?"

"Cross your heart?" He squinted at her.

"Cross my heart, Willy."

Willy bent forward, putting a cigarette in his mouth, cupping his hands round the match.

"Jerry plane came down between Land's End and Scillies. Jerry pilot bales out. Belgian picks him out of the drink, ties a rope round his feet then trawls 'im behind. The Belgians ain't fond of Jerries."

"Oh, Willy!" Sophy stared aghast.

"Crossed your heart, didn't you? No need to believe what I say, plenty don't."

"Oh, Willy."

"You stop coming into the harbour where you don't belong to be then. Take your lobster home and don't come again. You're a big girl now, too big to creep in."

Sophy found her bicycle, put the langouste in the basket and half an hour later, obsessed by the picture of the pilot's body trawling through the sea, skidded on a patch of cow dung and crashed, barking both knees. She was sitting in the road examining her wounds when voices from a nearby cottage drifted through the air. She limped to the cottage and knocked. When a woman opened the door she mutely pointed to her knees. She was led in, sat in a chair, had her wounds painfully bathed, was given a cup of tea and told she would be taken home as soon as Dad came with his car.

"The bicycle." Sophy shivered from shock.

"Our Tom, go and fetch it."

A mutinous-looking boy went out and clattered the bicycle, propping it against the gate.

"Mrs Penrose's bike, ain't it?"

"Yes, she lent it to me. Is it hurt?"

"Nay." The boy sat angrily at the kitchen table, putting both hands protectively over a cardboard box.

His mother glanced at him and, continuing the argument Sophy had interrupted, said: "You take them straight back to that John."

"Can't. He won't give me back my knife."

"Do as I tell 'ee."

"I can't."

"What you can't is keep those things here." She looked at Sophy sipping her tea. "Tom's swapped his knife for guinea pigs, proper pests. I'll throw them out."

"Do then. I don't want them." The boy thrust the box towards his mother and slammed out of the house.

"He brings animals home and lets them die," said his mother.

"Really?"

"Pups, kittens, birds, they all die, as though our lads getting killed weren't enough."

"Have you got a son in the forces?"

"No, but this war aggravates me. You from Cuthbertsons' up on cliff?"

"Yes."

"Lost your cousin. Drowned, I suppose."

"Yes."

"You have the guinea pigs then. Tom's dad gets angry with all he brings home.'Tisn't as though the child cared."

Presently Tom's dad dropped Sophy, the bicycle and the guinea pigs at the house and Monika put them in with the rabbits. That evening the General called, bringing a bottle of cheap sherry.

"If you don't like it you can use it for cooking."

"Of course I shall like it. Come and see what Sophy was given today." Monika led the way to the tennis court.

"There," she said, pointing proudly.

"By Jove, takes one back, used to keep guinea pigs as a boy. Trouble is they breed faster than rabbits, used to drive my mother mad." Putting his arm round Monika's waist the General gave it a squeeze.

"Reminds me of Peru," said Monika, moving away. "Max did a concert tour of South America and from Lima we went up into the mountains to see the villages."

"Women wear bowler hats, I hear. Heard about the German plane? Limping home, lucky shot by some ack ack in Bristol I daresay, ditched off Land's End, Belgian trawler picked up the pilot, dead when they got him to Newlyn."

"How dreadful." Monika looked at the General in distress.

"Germans, Monika, they were Germans. It was an enemy plane, nothing dreadful about that."

Monika frowned and went into the house.

"If one didn't know she was worrying about her son one would think she was pro-German," the General said to Sophy in disgust.

"She doesn't like anyone getting killed."

"Womanish rubbish. Don't you start. Can't have a war without killing, wouldn't do at all."

"She didn't want a war."

"Can't understand her attitude, such a pretty woman, such a good cook."

Upstairs, face down on her bed, Monika lay wishing Max would come to her for a few days, speak to her in their native tongue, relax for her the constant strain of being an alien in a land at war with her country. She had let them believe her fear of air raids kept her from London. It was convenient, while Helena created an establishment where Max could invite fellow musicians and get into the English scene, easier for him with Helena. Once acclimatised she knew Helena's ascendancy would weaken. Monika lay listening to the waves breaking against the cliffs. She feared the sea and at times she loathed the English, with their obstinate courage, their patronising kindness. Her heart ached for Viennese jokes, for the smell of hot chocolate and Continental cigarettes. Max had told her of the bribe to get them to America, a country she liked even less than England. She was thankful he had refused. She opened the drawer of her bedside table and allowed herself to look at a snapshot of Pauli. He frowned in sulky reproach, filling her with guilt.

"Is that your son?" She had not heard Sophy come in. "I did knock."

"I was a long way away. Yes, that is Pauli if," she added, "he is still alive." Monika put the photograph back in the drawer.

"The General left. Said he'd come back another day." She exchanged glances with Monika. "He has a shine on you."

"What's that?"

"He's falling in love with you, like Uncle Richard." They laughed. "Are you very unhappy?"

"An attack of homesickness, that's all."

"That's enough," exclaimed Sophy. "I have it all the time at school. Do you hate it here very much?"

"Only sometimes. What I miss is my mother tongue."

"Oh."

"Max says that we must always speak English, learn to think in English, sometimes I rebel. I was thinking just now of the smells of home. Do you understand?"

"Yes, I do. At school I think of the smell of the camomile lawn. What did Pauli smell like? I hope I shall meet him. You won't rush straight back, will you? Will you go and find him, or will he find you?"

"We will never go back. Jews move on."

"Then he will come here and I will meet him. I wish," said Sophy, looking out at the scudding clouds, "I wish they'd all come home. Walter won't. Oh Monika." She threw herself into Monika's arms, told of the Belgian trawler and what Willy Penrose had said.

Presently comforted in Monika's arms she said, "Don't let's tell anybody."

"It would be no use. Only the other side commits atrocities," said Monika drily.

"But—"

"You think Oliver would not, nor Hector nor the twins?"

Monika spoke bitterly. "They will be given medals. Gongs, as they call them."

"It's not the same," Sophy sobbed. "The fishermen weren't English."

"But the man who told you was pleased, *nicht*? He approved, *nicht*? He was English."

"Yes, I suppose – well, Cornish."

"Then what is the difference? The Nazis are not the only ones."

"They started it."

"By the time this is finished none of us will care who started it." Monika smoothed Sophy's hair. "Come," she said, "help me pack the hampers for our brave family in London."

"All right."

"Will you take some eggs to Mrs Floyer for me, and some butter for Herr Floyer? He does not eat enough."

Sophy propped the bicycle against the porch and walked into the Rectory without knocking. From the kitchen area she heard Mildred Floyer's voice, "Not so loud," almost drowned by the sound of children singing a breathless version of Fred Astaire's "Putting on my top hat", as they tap danced round the big iron boiler of uncertain age and horrible temperament which heated the bath water.

"Monika sent you these eggs and the butter is for Herr Floyer." Sophy handed over her basket.

"She behaves as though I starve him. He has always been thin, he eats like a horse. Oh, children," she raised her voice. "Not quite so much noise, *please*." The racket subsided slightly. "Come into the kitchen, darling. The Herr Floyer will be most grateful, he will probably pass it on to someone he thinks more worthy. Don't tell Monika."

"Of course not. Your evacuees seem to be flourishing. How are the nits?"

"We have them under control."

"They all seem very settled."

"Yes. Some went home, but if the raids start again they will be back."

"None for ages. Have you heard from Paul and David?"

"Yes, coming on leave, both of them."

"How lovely."

"Not lovely, it's embarkation leave." Mildred Floyer looked anxious.

"Oh, where?"

"I don't know. Why is it worse to have them overseas? They are in danger, anyway. It's their second or third tour, I'm losing count."

"No telephone. A long time for letters. Not being able to imagine the place, I suppose. I try and—"

"Yes?"

"I try and imagine Hector when I see Calypso and Oliver, of course, when I see Aunt Sarah." And, Sophy thought, at all other times. "Perhaps they will all meet out there and think of home."

Mildred stood by the kitchen table holding Monika's basket. "It's so difficult to realise what's going on. There is so little sign of war. People training, of course, those Commandos round St Ives and now the Americans, but we never actually see anything happening."

In her mind's eye Sophy saw the body towed behind the Belgian trawler. "Monika says both sides commit atrocities."

"What a funny thing to say. She's foreign, of course."

"Well?"

"Poor Monika. Her son. There seems no way for people like Monika to find out. You'd think the Red Cross—"

"She says the Red Cross have no access to concentration camps."

"I think, I hope Monika exaggerates. It really is hard to believe that even Hitler – surely our propaganda – I mean that exaggerates too. I am sure when the war is over she will find her Pauli is quite all right and has been doing something useful all the time." Mildred clutched at her Christian ethics.

"I think he is probably dead."

"Sophy, what an awful thing to say."

"Why? He wouldn't be suffering as he is now."

"Not if he's in a good job."

"He is a pianist."

"Well, then, he is probably entertaining the troops. They can't be all that different from us."

"But he's a Jew, not allowed to work."

"Oh." Mildred put the eggs away. "None of us knows anything and now the boys are off overseas I don't know what to think. We listen to the news but it doesn't really tell us anything, does it? All those names . . ."

"Tobruk, Cairo, El Alamein, Malta," said Sophy.

"Don't say Malta. I think if they are sent there I shall go mad,

She put the butter on a plate and moved to the larder. "I can't afford to go mad," she added. "I have too much to do, all these children. Tell Monika that I will have the boys here this time. I'd like them to be under their own roof as it's the—" Hopelessly Mildred began to cry. "Sorry to be so silly."

"It won't be the last time," said Sophy stoutly. "Don't cry, Mrs Floyer." She handed Mildred a handkerchief.

"I think it's that tune," said Mildred, "those children have been singing it non-stop for six weeks. It's on my nerves."

"It's the best one to tap dance to." Sophy found herself singing the tune as she pedalled home along the track through the fields. At the top she looked out across the sea, flecked with white horses. Below her the cliff path was overgrown by bracken and brambles. Were it not for the barbed wire there would be no trace of the Terror Run. "Putting on my top hat," sang Sophy, pedalling into the wind. "Tra-la-la my tails." Her eyes stung in the cold wind, which snatched her voice, to drown it among the gulls lower down the cliff.

TWENTY-NINE

Arriving early and leaving late, Polly immersed herself in her work. She forced herself to listen, to write, to talk of nothing but her work. She surprised the people she worked with by joining them for cups of tea, or lunch, and accepting offers of drinks or meals which normally she would refuse. Once home she turned on the radio or telephoned friends, catching up with people she had let drop. She widened her circle but avoided people close to her, busy filling her life with trivia so that she did not know what might be happening to Helena, Calypso or Sophy. None of this prevented her from waking in that dead hour when it is too early to get up and too late to sleep again, from hearing over and over again the falsely cheerful inanities David and Paul had shouted on the telephone from the air station from which they had flown to North Africa. Both had been drunk and both frightened. They were to be piloted by an American. They were averse to anyone but themselves being at the controls. If Polly had asked herself which she had spoken to last, David or Paul, she would not have been sure, any more than she had been sure of which she had made love with first. To her they were one man, multiplied by one, her lovers. She wanted them both.

For weeks after they left she worried and mourned in agony. Brought up in the conventional mould of her class, nothing had prepared her for the position in which she found herself. She grew thin and short-tempered, she made mistakes at work, she was sent for by her boss.

"Are you ill?" He eyed her with care.

"No, of course not," she said defensively.

"Worried by something? I don't want to pry." He looked away.

"No, thank you," she said stiffly.

"Missing your parents, your brother, it's hard for you—"

"No, I'm glad they – I'm glad they are – well, they would only interfere – I—" She looked at her boss with loathing.

"I think you had better take some leave." In love with a married man, no doubt. "Go somewhere quiet. You like Cornwall, don't you?"

"Not there. God, no."

"Try Dartmoor. Do you know it? No? Well, go and walk on a bit that hasn't got troops training in it. Walk yourself into a coma and see what your subconscious comes up with."

Polly permitted herself a brief expression of surprise.

"Didn't think of me reading Freud and Jung, did you? Well, go to Newton Abbot, take a taxi and – here, I'll write it down – stay in this pub. Can you ride?"

"Yes."

"When you're tired of walking you can hire a horse, the landlord has several. I'll bet you come up with the answer after ten days or so. Go tomorrow."

"Thank you." She took the slip of paper and left him. He wondered whether she was pregnant, couldn't quite ask her. Married men were just as potent as bachelors.

Polly left the office, leaving her work mates jealous and irritated. "She's his pet, he took her to Portugal. Why not me? I speak the language."

"Oh, shut up. She came back to find her brother had been killed."

"Really? She never said—"

"Somebody who knows a girl friend of his told me, a girl called Elizabeth."

"Her mother and father were killed, weren't they?"

"Yes, earlier on. Bad luck."

"I don't know, she's got their money and house. Nice, in a way. I should like it – my family are always interfering with my life."

"My mother's so busy she never bothers. If my bowels are working and I'm not pregnant she's happy."

"There." Polly changed gear as they reached the top of the hill. "I love this view. The promised land—" The rolling hills of Dartmoor lay ahead stretching to the horizon in the west.

"Why don't we take the road across the moor, and picnic up there?" Iris leant over from the back seat. "Give the old boy a run." At the word "run" the mongrel stood up on the front seat, wagging his tail.

"It's longer," said James, "but beautiful. Have we time?"

"The funeral is not until tomorrow."

"We always miss the moor, we are always in such a hurry. Do you know it, Ma?"

"Not really. I spent a few days' leave there in the war. Walking and riding."

"Sounds nice. Where did you go?"

"It was somewhere between Haytor and Manaton. I'll try and find it. Sit down," she said to the dog. "I must concentrate."

Later, sitting in the sun, their backs to a rock, they ate their lunch, munching brown bread, cheese and pickles, gulping wine. The dog ran joyously in the bracken, leaping up to see over the golden fronds, bouncing high. They could see his tail in the waving fern. The autumn sun was warm on their faces.

"This is lovely." Iris lay back, stretching her legs, lifting her face to the sun. "Why don't we come here oftener?"

"Always in a rush to reach Cornwall." James lay propped on his elbow, a mug of wine in his hand. Two years younger than his sister, he had much the same colouring: chestnut hair, but whereas Iris's eyes were brown his were green like Polly's. His teeth too were out of kilter.

"Who did you come here with?"

"I came alone. I was at a low ebb—"

"Why?" James looked interested. His mother seldom spoke of her private life.

"When was this?" Iris enquired casually, afraid of stemming any slight reminiscence.

"I walked," said Polly in recollection. "I walked across these moors and clambered over that tor over there. I was trying to tire myself so that I would sleep. I had not been sleeping, it was in the war, I was worried. I had to make a decision." Brother and sister exchanged a glance. "I thought—" Polly was speaking now as though to strangers. "I thought I had to give them up, that I could not marry one and leave the other. I thought that if one of them was killed the decision would be made for me. I was unhappy. Girls like me were brought up to be respectable. The atmosphere of the war shook that, but the shaking hurt. People like Calypso did not seem to worry, but I wonder. I've never known Calypso deeply, she won't allow it. There were dozens of girls who went on being virtuous, but we broke out."

Polly put out a hand to stroke the dog who had come back to join them. "Good boy. Having a nice time?" Iris and James said nothing, looking away from their mother across the moor, purple and brown in the distance.

"Then I hired a horse and rode. I could get further into the moor. I rode right across there." Polly pointed. "I picked my way round that very rocky tor and not terribly far on the other side there was a moorland farm, green fields fenced in by stone walls around the top of a valley with a stream at the bottom. Emerald fields, blue sky, larks singing, I particularly remember the larks. Then suddenly round a corner came a herd of llamas, white against the sky. My horse reared up terrified, the llamas spat, the horse bolted, I lost my stirrups, the horse jinxed, I fell off."

"Llamas!" James and Iris were laughing. "Llamas? Why did you never tell us? What were they doing there?"

"Evacuated from the Paignton Zoo, I heard later." Polly stroked the dog's head, her eyes on the distant tor, now in sunlight, now in shade, as clouds coming up from the west blocked the sun. "I was concussed. A farmer found me and brought me back. They put me in the cottage hospital where the people were kind. They didn't know about the llamas, they thought I had DTs or something. The doctor found it was true, the llamas were there, only nobody knew, nobody could have foreseen me on a horse, could they?"

"I should have thought—"

"It was wartime. People were so tucked into their little lives they didn't necessarily know what was going on in the next parish. That's why I often think the Germans who say they did not know about the concentration camps may be telling the truth. Anyway—" She gently pulled the dog's ears as he gazed dreamily into her face.

"Anyway?" suggested Iris, almost whispering.

"Anyway," said Polly, "I found I could talk to the doctor. I told him my dilemma. He was a nice man, kind." Polly thought back to the cottage hospital bed. Iris and James exchanged glances of exasperation as she paused. "He did not give me advice. He sat on my bed and talked about Nepal. He told me about polyandry, he had been on some expedition there. Then one morning he said I was well enough to go back to London and—"

"And?" Iris sighed, drawing out the word.

"He shook hands with me and said, 'What you are about to do is not illegal.' He had guessed that I would not give up either. So," Polly looked at her son and daughter for the first time since she began her tale. "So that's how you two came about. Now," she said, standing up, "I must pee, then we must push on." She walked away behind some rocks.

"I suppose it would be too much to ask which of us is whose child, or whether one or both?" said James to his sister.

"Much too much. There are permutations. I don't believe she knows. We have discussed this often; we will never get any further. I too must pee." Iris waded away into the bracken. James collected the debris of their meal, packing the remains into the basket. Polly came back, casting her shadow across him as he knelt. He looked at her and her heart lurched at how like he was to the twins. He stood up and kissed her. "Greedy." His voice was full of affection.

"That's what they all said."

"What did they say?" Iris came back, pulling her sweater down over her lean hips.

"That I was greedy and selfish."

"Good job, too." Not denying, Iris gave her mother a quick kiss on the cheek, adding, "We don't think so."

"There's a storm brewing, look at that sky." James pointed westward. "Funeral weather. I wonder who besides us will make it. I suppose," he said, "if you had married one of them you would have made everybody miserable."

"Of course."

"It's good of you to tell us even a little. I suppose you think now we are middle-aged it's—"

"Middle-aged?" Polly protested. "Hardly."

"I'm nearly thirty—"

"I don't know when middle-age is. Look at Helena, nearly ninety, her middle-age must have come pretty late." Iris packed the picnic basket in among the luggage.

"That generation was tough. Yours, too."

"Tough, greedy, selfish, all that," said Polly lightly. "We were under stress, people react differently under stress. We had an awful lot of fun—"

"And funny adventures. Why did you never tell us about the llamas?"

"It was private." Polly started the car. "Private," and they knew she was not referring to the llamas.

"Was there a great hullabaloo among your stuffy relations?" Iris had often wondered.

"They did not notice for ages. Then it had been going on for so long when they did, other people were so much more interesting. Calypso captured attention, and Monika. Then there was the Rectory's attitude and, oh, I don't know, somehow or other they were all aware and used to it before it occurred to them to be shocked. Nobody was hurt, so why bother?"

"I daresay it was your craftiness."

"Perhaps it was. Yes, quite likely it was that."

"A loner?"

"In some ways. Mind you, Calypso is a loner and Sophy turned out a super loner. It was our rebellion against our upbringing."

"And you had fun." James, lolling on the back seat, enjoyed the view.

"Yes," said his mother, "we certainly did."

"Look, lightning." Iris pointed ahead. "And it's going to pour."

"Sophy used to tell us about autumn storms when we were young. The wind howling and waves crashing into the cliff and heavy sheets of rain. I hope we don't all catch our deaths and join Max."

"Wasn't he a great womaniser?" Iris, brought up on a legend, sought the truth.

"Well, I don't know. In trouble some men reach for the bottle; Max reached for the nearest girl, and if the girl was in trouble he was a great consoler. No, I wouldn't say he was a womaniser, just busy." Polly, driving into the storm, smiled reminiscently.

"Did he ever console you?" James dared question.

"I didn't say so." Brother and sister smiled at one another.

"It will be interesting to see whether anybody turns up in this ghastly weather. Look at it!"

The rain, slanting from the west, poured on to the windscreen. The dog got down off the seat and crouched under the dashboard while Polly, surprised, suddenly remembered a Sunday afternoon during the invasion of Normandy when Max, finding her alone, had led her to bed and made love to her, assuaging her pent-up anxieties with skill end affection. "I do this, dear Polly, for the twins' sake. You worry and I worry for Monika and Helena. Worry makes me what you call randy with Monika and Helena. Alas they shut up shop. You open the legs, *nicht?*" Polly, increasing the speed of the screen-wiper, laughed joyously in her sixties.

"What's the joke?"

"I was thinking back to the Normandy landings—"

"The twins were there, weren't they?"

"Indeed they were. I was worried sick."

"Cause for laughter?" asked Iris, puzzled.

"Max cheered me up. His genius was to make everybody feel better. You should know, you've been to his concerts."

"You weren't laughing as though you remembered a concert . . ."

"What else could it be . . ." Iris muttered so that only her brother could hear. They smiled complicitly on the back seat, amused by their mother and her life.

"And what was Max worrying about? His career rocketed during the war." Iris tried to visualize the white-haired old man, whose funeral they were about to attend, in bed with her mother.

"He had plenty to worry about. His career went marvellously but the war was agony for him. He worried about Monika worrying, he was nagged by fear for Pauli. He hardly hoped he would ever see him again. He used to talk about him and what a pianist he would be if he survived."

"How much did people know?"

"Rumours. News trickling through via neutral countries. If we'd known the size of the horrors we couldn't have borne it. Refugees like Max used to hear things from people who got letters through Switzerland or Sweden. Max always played better when he'd heard some ghastly rumour. Sorrow fed his genius, his emotions went to his bow." Polly paused, peering ahead.

"And his balls." James filled the pause.

"To be honest, yes." Polly's mouth twitched. "This is hardly a suitable recollection of the dead."

"You so rarely talk to us about your private self, we enjoy it."

"I thought we were talking about Max."

"In connection with you."

"We were all interconnected." Polly's tone indicated the end of the conversation, such as it was. She kept her eyes on the road and the driving rain, thinking that tapes and records would never replace the tall thin man who had once played for her in the basement kitchen when he had news of the death of a great friend. "They say he died in a hospital, that is what they say, but I hear they are gassing thousands of people."

"I cannot believe it," she had exclaimed in disgust, "it is too revolting." He had taken his violin and played so piercingly sadly that she had wept for his friend, whose name he had not told her, and on that occasion it was she who had reached for him.

"You sound a caring group," said Iris, Polly's daughter, who concerned herself with good works to assuage her conscience, which had nothing to be guilty about, she having been born good.

"Not caring enough, as was proved with Calypso. Not that it wasn't her fault, a more secretive character it would be hard to come by."

"I wonder whether she will turn up by the grave?" James spoke enquiringly.

"Hamish is driving Helena down, so it looks unlikely," said Iris.

"Hamish wants the glory of bringing the headmistress," said her brother, who had offered and been refused. "Besides, he has the best car."

THIRTY

Helena looked forward to the end of Richard's dancing lessons. A gleam at the end of the tunnel of boredom now shaped her days. True, he despatched the empty hampers from Paddington and fetched back the full ones. True, he was out every day lunching at his club, where he watched men younger than himself now high ranking, men he had served with in the Great War. True, he stayed out most days until dark, but he always came back in time for tea at five and stayed in from then on to talk to her, if she would listen, to Max, if he was home, and tirelessly to Max's musical friends, who frequently stayed to supper, sampling the pâtés, compôtes and cooked meats with fresh vegetables with which Monika stuffed the hampers. Her ample supply of eggs and butter assured Helena of many a convivial evening, when all her soul longed for was to be alone with her lover.

"You are impatient, my Helena."

"He's got his new suits, he's shopped for Monika, he should go home."

"He is enjoying himself. He is out all day, I am not. Why don't you come nicely to bed now? I have a rehearsal about three, there is just time. Max held her against him, stroking her back, kissing her neck, glancing at his wristwatch over her shoulder. One forty-five. "Come, *meine* dumpling." He nuzzled her neck. "You smell nice."

"He might suddenly come in. He comes back and goes out again."

"So he goes out again. Let me in." He pushed her back on to the sofa.

"Max!" Her token protest. "Really!"

"*Ja, ja*, relax and enjoy—"

"There's the telephone, oh—"

"So let it ring, we make symphony to its ringing. The telephone has no soul but I try and conduct. There, that was good, *nicht?*"

"For you." Helena wept with fury.

"*Du bist nervös.*" Gently he held her. "Where is your phlegm?"

Helena pulled down her skirt. "I wish you wouldn't call me that, it makes people laugh."

"People don't know."

"Sometimes you forget and call me – er – call me that in front of your friends."

"*Kleine.* Jewish refugees do not know what it means. They think I call you heroine, they think phlegm is like spirit of Dunkirk or Rule Britannia or some such, *nicht?*"

"All the same—" Helena kissed his ear, relenting.

"I must go. They will be waiting for me at the rehearsal." He kissed her briskly. "If I bring some few friends is there food? I make an omelette. Ludwig's wife makes omelettes with dried egg, Eno's salts to make the egg powder rise and salad dressing with medicinal paraffin. He has never been so healthy." Max smoothed his hair, straightened his tie, bent to kiss her while buttoning his flies.

"Richard collected a hamper this morning," she said stiffly.

"Good. *Auf Wiedersehen.*" On the doorstep he met Richard. "My dear fellow, would you be amused to come to my rehearsal? I go this minute."

"Delighted," said Richard, and turned to walk with him. "D'you know, I saw General de Gaulle in Piccadilly walking past the Ritz, looked lonely, poor chap, carries that big nose high."

Resentfully Helena watched them, heads together in interested talk until they turned the corner. It annoyed her that they were friends. "Damn, damn, damn!" she shouted in her empty drawing-room. She plumped up the sofa cushions and went to unpack the hamper, arrange a cold supper. Max never came back from rehearsal without two or more friends. If he calls me "phlegm" tonight I shall hit him, she told herself, or deny him my favours. She was laughing when the doorbell rang. She opened the door to her sister-in-law.

"Sarah, my dear, how lovely."

"I telephoned. You must have been out."

"No, no, I heard it, we were, I was in the lavatory. Come in, come in."

"I was wondering if you were visible."

"What d'you mean, visible. Here I am."

"I meant busy," said Sarah, who had wondered whether Helena had been in bed with Max. "Are you busy?"

"I was seeing about supper. Max has taken Richard to his rehearsal. Oh, Sarah, d'you think he will ever go home?"

"Why ever not?"

"He's enjoying himself. He says he's seeing the war at first hand."

"I thought he came up to see his tailor and shop."

"Can you stay to supper? He's finished with his tailor, he's done his shopping, he's been to the cinemas and the Windmill, he's nearly finished his dancing lessons but he shows no signs of leaving. I tell you he is enjoying himself."

"Isn't that a good thing?" Sarah, having followed Helena to the kitchen, helped her unpack the hamper. "What a lot of goodies!"

"Monika's clever. Doesn't think me much of a cook, sends lots of cooked stuff. She's right, of course. Could you carve those things and put them on a dish? I never know how many people Max will bring home. It's a good thing the hamper came today. Richard fetches and sends back the empties, at least he does that chore."

"What are these?" Sarah searched for a knife.

"Chickens, rabbits, mix them up. There's a pâté too. We are rather short of drink, though."

"I brought you a bottle."

"Oh, Sarah, wonderful! So hard to get."

"What is the poor old boy doing then?"

"Getting on my nerves. Just joint those things, here's a dish. He goes to his club and counts generals. He knew a lot of them in his youth. Then he prowls the streets."

"What d'you mean, prowls?" Sarah exclaimed anxiously.

"He prowls about clubland, Sarah, and Whitehall, he's like a child. He's thrilled if he sees General Eisenhower or Brooke or Alexander, anyone in the news. This morning he saw General de Gaulle. I heard him tell Max."

"Seems quite harmless to me." Sarah looked relieved.

"He's your brother, you know he is harmless. It's me that's suffering. I want him to go home. He assumes that just because I bought these houses he has the right to live in them." Helena began to cry stormily. "I want to be alone with Max. God knows I seldom am, he's dreadfully sociable, always asking people here. If I can't be alone with him at night when can I be? Don't laugh, Sarah, it's not funny."

"It is, though. What about Monika? I thought Richard and she—"

"So did I, but she sends all this food, she keeps the Cornish house going far better than I ever did and she seems very matey with the General, the Floyers and the village."

"Why don't you ask her to come up?"

"God, no. Besides, she can't leave the hens and the cow. No, Sarah, he's got to go, he's ruining my life."

"I'll try and think of some ploy. By the way, I have to see Calypso. She won't go near her parents, they are worried stiff."

"No need, she's another who's enjoying the war."

"She's pregnant."

"*Ceci n'empêche cela.*"

"Really?"

"From what I hear. Never in. Lunching, dining, dancing with French, Poles, Americans, Belgians, Australians. She was even seen with a Sikh, it will be a black man next."

"There are no black officers."

"Just as well. She's no longer working so she has all the time in the world and that delightful house."

Parting with her lunch companion, a Free French officer with the pseudonym of a Paris Métro station, Calypso rode on the top of a bus towards Kensington noting, from her elevated viewpoint, Uncle Richard walking along Knightsbridge with Max, limping nimbly beside the violinist who was restricting his usual stride to accommodate the older man. The bus rocketed along Kensington Gore. She got out at the Broad Walk to give Fling his walk across the parks. The giant avenue of elms was touched by misty green almost invisible against the pale sky, still cold from winter. On the north side of the park barrage balloons bobbed sulkily. She headed across the grass past Watts' "Physical Energy" to the Serpentine, where the ducks hopefully congregated to be fed by nannies and children long since evacuated to the country. She appreciated the wide stretch of grass, bare since the outbreak of war, empty of pekinese, dachshund and poodle. Fling barked at a squirrel, sleepy from the long winter, exploring a paper bag. The gardens looked blousy and unloved, park chairs tipped over and in need of paint, restless bits of paper scurrying in the chill wind. Nostalgically she doubled back to the Round Pond but nobody raced toy boats, no model yachts sailed. Some vandal had thrown a park seat into the water; a row of gulls perched along the back. Here, once, Oliver had pushed her in. She had sat waist deep in icy water screaming, while Walter, infected, had pushed in Polly, then given her nanny a shove as she leaned to the rescue, hoping not to get her feet wet. Calypso remembered the row when they got back to Aunt Sarah's house, followed by hot tea and crumpets. The gulls rose shrieking and drifted west. A soldier wandered along, meeting no girl, having no tryst. She walked faster, making for the Dutch garden. There, pacing between the pools, peering to see whether coot or duck were yet nesting, busy in their tiny world of reeds, Fling leaned to catch sight of his whiskery reflection and jumped back barking. Hands in pockets, she turned back to the Serpentine to walk along the north side, watching mallard in pursuit of duck skitter along the water, then rise high in flight across to St James's Park, their quacks diminishing in the evening sky. Down in the Dell she stood by the railings. A moorhen walked jerkily from the bushes and rabbits hopped slowly across the grass, impervious to the war. Hector had told her to be careful Fling did not squeeze in and give chase; he had once had a lurcher who had leapt the railings and caused havoc. She walked up to the Row, shabby and sad, robbed of its railings. Hector had been angry, asked questions in the House, unfashionably blamed Lord Beaverbrook for the desecration of London's parks and squares by the uprooting of railings made from the guns of the Peninsular War and Waterloo. She thought of dancing with him in the "400", held close against him, feeling his cock rise in desire against her body. Now, standing by deserted Rotten Row, she felt an answering pang. She stared in disgust at the growing mountain of rubble from bombed buildings heaped on the Guards' football ground. Were there bones of people unaccounted for in the rubble, precious furniture, objets d'art? She crossed Hyde Park Corner dodging the traffic and, tired now, walked down past the Palace into the maze of streets round Petty France. Near the Underground she was amused to see Polly wheel her bicycle from an office building and pedal towards Knightsbridge. She looked at the ugly block which housed Polly's secret work. Her own job had been two doors down. Both were sworn not to disclose the whereabouts of their offices. We could have met for lunch, she thought, and mockingly remembered the many documents marked Top Secret which often contained information equally available in the *Daily Mirror*.

The telephone was ringing as she put her key in the door. "Hullo," she said. "Hullo."

"Telegrams."

"Yes?"

"Calypso Grant Mrs?"

"I am Calypso Grant. Yes, please read it – yes, I've got that. Yes. No – yes, a confirmation copy. Yes, please. Thank you." She replaced the receiver and bent to take Fling off his lead. In her haste to reach the telephone she had left the door open. In the street the plane trees dappled shadows on the pavement, a tug hooted on the river. She closed the door and listened to the silence in the house. Then she went into the cloakroom and was sick. She splashed her face with cold water and rinsed her mouth, expelling the haunting taste of bile.

"What the hell was he doing?" she said to the dog. "I thought he was safe in Cairo." She dried her face, looking round the cloakroom. Umbrellas, a shooting stick, Wellington boots, an old country hat, a Spy cartoon of his grandfather on the wall, a faint whiff of hair oil and tobacco. She sat on the bottom stair. Fling sat beside her, pressing his rough little body against her legs. She leant her head back against the banisters, waiting for strength to flow back. When she opened her eyes it was night. She felt a peculiar fluttering sensation in her belly. "Ah," she said grimly, "it's you, is it? He won't be here to welcome you and I don't much want you."

THIRTY-ONE

"What a good party." Sarah helped Helena clear the table. "Feeding nine of us. It reminds me of pre-war, delicious food."

"I couldn't do it without Monika." Helena carried a tray to the kitchen, stepping carefully down the precipitous basement stairs. If the houses survived the war she intended a drastic remodelling. She navigated a chair in the passage where the men had heaped their overcoats, brushed past Ludwig's cello case propped against the umbrellas. She cursed Ludwig's instrument, also his wife Irena who had a way of sitting cross-legged on the floor which annoyed her. "Let someone else have the chairs, I am so small I take no room."

Sarah joined her in the basement. "That's the lot. Let me wash up, you dry."

"All right." Helena reached ungraciously for a tea towel.

"What's the matter?" Sarah turned on the hot tap.

Helena did not answer but stood waiting for the wet plates.

"Cough up. What's the matter?" Sarah handed her a plate.

"It's difficult to explain. I'd rather not try."

"Very well." Sarah washed the plates, stacking them to drip. "I have to telephone George. There might be a letter from Oliver. We worry. There's been so much fighting in the Western Desert."

"The telephone's in the drawing-room. It will be a good excuse to get them to leave early." Helena brightened.

"Don't do that. They are enjoying themselves."

"But you want to talk privately."

"I'll go back to Polly's, it's only a step. I don't want to break up your party."

Helena sighed, wishing that Sarah would break it up, wishing the party over. She blamed herself for not objecting long ago to Max inviting his friends to eat her food, drink her drink, sprawl in her drawing-room. When first she had bought the houses she had welcomed his friends, but now she felt differently. She did not grudge them the food, she grudged them the long hours they stayed, discussing their music, behaving, as many of them gratefully told her, as though they were at home in Vienna, Prague, Berlin or Budapest. They treated her with affection, apparently unaware that she wished them, their music and their laughter gone, so that she could have Max to herself, be in bed with him, feel his whip-thin body against hers and rejoice in the miracle which had befallen so late in life.

"I'll trot round to Polly's, then. Back in a few minutes. Are you all right, Helena? You look funny."

"No, I'm not all right," Helena shouted.

"Why not? Are you ill?"

"No. I wish they'd all go. I never seem to see Max now Richard is here. I'm never alone with him. I thought—"

"If you become possessive you will lose him. Try and be like Monika, let him off the lead."

"Like Monika?"

"They've been married years. She never tries to change him. If you listen to those people you'll find they are all her friends too."

"Then why isn't she here?"

"I should think that's pretty obvious."

"Because I am?"

"You and air raids. Although I don't know her, I think she is doing what she can for him, taking care of Richard, sending up food, running your house."

"I wish Richard would go back to her."

"You'd still have all the friends."

"I suppose so." Helena groaned.

"They are his life, like his violin. You can't have just the one thing . . ."

"Bed?"

"You've got to realise he is more than bed if you want to keep him."

"You mean go to all the concerts, listen to all his friends for ever?"

"If you want to keep him," Sarah repeated.

"I love him."

"Then think on it. I'm going round to telephone from Polly's. Shan't be long."

Helena sat by the kitchen table listening to the talk and laughter from the room above, trying to catch Max's voice from among the many, hearing Richard's laugh, sharp cries of appreciation

381

from the women, feeling anguish. Could she ever fit in with this cosmopolitan crowd, she who was tone deaf? Was love enough? Irena found her. Irena so small, who took up so much room with her ebullience, her brilliance, her enthusiasm.

"Helena, what you do sitting alone?" she cried.

"Nothing." Helena was ungracious.

"Come up, we miss you, do not leave us."

"You don't need me," she said grumpily.

"But we do. You are our cement, we cannot do without you."

"*I am tone deaf,*" Helena said to Irena in a hard flat voice, hoping to shock her into throwing her out of Max's life, his music, his love. She felt at that moment that Irena or any of Max's friends was capable of casting her out. She would go meekly to the square house on the cliff, back to her former life. She felt desperate facing Irena. Irena laughed.

"You are ridiculous." She cried with merriment, not questioning Helena's statement, laughing so that Helena laughed too, recognizing her curmudgeonly jealousy for what it was. They linked arms and climbed the stairs, jostling each other in the narrow space. In the hall they met Sarah coming back from using Polly's telephone.

"Any news?" Helena asked, not caring in her happiness whether there was news or not.

"George had a letter from Oliver. He read it to me. He says Hector—"

At that moment the telephone in the drawing-room rang and its news blotted out any news Sarah might have.

Richard, answering the telephone, exclaimed: "Mildred old thing, you all right? Your voice sounds—" The telephone crackled and Richard held it away from his ear with an expression of unbelief.

"She wants to speak to you." He handed the receiver to Max. "Called me maladroit. I ask you, what's got into her? Says Monika—"

Max took the receiver. "Max *hier.*" Everyone in the room listened, trying to make sense of Max's responses. "When – where? The cliff – 'ow did she? What pigs? We never eat pigs. The General he say *that*? Crazy old *Dummkopf*! Where is she now? The coastguard – I come at once to kill that man. I get the first train." He replaced the receiver, eyes blazing. "She threw herself over the cliff," Max shouted, "my lovely Monika. Why have you left her so long?" he yelled at Richard. "I have to work, you are my friend, you should look after her."

"Is she dead?" asked Helena, bravely asking the question on everyone's mind.

Irena burst into stormy weeping and threw herself into Ludwig's arms. "Monika is *tot*."

"No," cried Max, "but I kill that swine General, that mother-fucking Nazi."

"What happened? Stop shouting, Max, tell us." Helena peered up into his face, gripping his hands.

"You bloody English!" Max shouted, distraught.

Helena smacked his face, reaching up on tiptoe. "Tell us what happened instead of abusing us, you great oaf."

"It is your hampers, your *verdammt* hampers of food. She puts in pigs."

"Are you mad?" cried Helena, getting excited. "Chickens, rabbits, butter, eggs: you know perfectly well she has no pigs."

"Guinea pigs, my Phlegm, she has been breeding guinea pigs. We have been eating them and your swine General says Monika is a spy, a foreigner, a Jew, and eating habits in England do not permit guinea—"

"I kept guinea pigs as a boy," Richard broke in. "Charming little—"

"Shut up," said Helena.

"Wogs eat songbirds," Richard continued.

"Shut up," said Helena. "Max, try to be calm and tell us."

Max sat down suddenly on the sofa, clutching his head.

"And the Frogs eat frogs, but guinea pigs, I ask you, that's a bit steep," Richard carried on.

"Shut up, I tell you." Helena silenced him. "Now, Max, please, try and tell us what Mildred—"

"She said—" Max took a deep breath. "She said some fool gave Sophy those pigs. She gives them to Monika, *ja, und* Monika breeds them with her rabbits which we eat, probably we eat them tonight?" He looked round the room.

"Delicious," said Ludwig calmly, stroking Irena's shoulder, holding her as tenderly as he held his cello. "Delicious and original."

"And?" Helena resented Ludwig's interruption.

"She gives this *schrecklich* old man supper. He asks what it is he eats, so gourmet, so unlike the filthy rations. Monika tells him and then—" Max's voice rose again, "this disgusting old man abuses her and Monika cracks, runs out and throws herself over the cliff."

"Oh no, no, no," moaned Irena and another girl, "oh, no, no, no," in chorus.

"But," said Max slowly, "she sticks on a ledge and the Floyers and the coastguards they pull her up."

"Is she hurt?"

"How do I know? Mildred says she has the breakdown."

"We'd better catch the midnight train. Quick – somebody go and find a taxi, hurry. Max, I will come with you." Helena, suddenly calm, British and practical, took charge.

"I'll come along too." Richard limped out of the room. "Won't take a minute to pack. Most of my stuff is ready, I—"

But nobody listened. Sarah, aghast at the whole scene, took her leave and started back to Polly's house, not wishing to get involved in such foreign turmoil. As she reached the corner of the street Irena and Ludwig were waylaying a taxi which was disgorging its passengers.

"Sorry, luv," said the taximan. "I'm shot to bits, dead tired, going 'ome."

"This is *sehr important*," begged Irena.

"Sorry, luv, not tonight."

"It is only to Paddington," pleaded Irena.

"Sorry, luv—"

"It is for the exiled King of Greece," cried Ludwig. "He lives here. It's of vital importance he catch the train."

"King of Greece?" The taximan was incredulous.

"Top secret," said Irena, lowering her voice. "So urgent. So secret."

The taxi driver opened the door. Irena and Ludwig sprang into the taxi and waved to Sarah as they drove past with gleeful faces. Sarah, while disapproving, was impressed by their ingenuity.

Driving with Hamish to Max's funeral, Helena remembered her dinner party.

"Did you ever hear the saga of the guinea pigs?" she asked Hamish.

"Yes. That is one aspect of your war which has impressed me." By his tone Hamish made clear the impression was not a good one.

"When you consider the horrors of war, it's remarkable that it was guinea pigs which gave Monika a breakdown. Max blamed me. He wasn't really loyal over those guinea pigs and yet it was during that period I became really fond of Monika."

"How was that?"

"If you really love somebody," said Helena in her steady old voice, "you see the people they love through their eyes. Monika would have bought him flowers if she were here and I not."

"Would she?"

"Yes. He hated chrysanthemums. I can't buy those. They made him sneeze."

"Me too."

"Lilies? A bit banal. Why not violets? On the way to the night train he saw a flower barrow being trundled along the street, stopped the taxi and bought a basket of violets for Monika. Nearly made us miss the train."

"Oh."

"Silly really," Helena chortled, "when you think they'd been grown in Cornwall. Come to think of it, they may have been grown by the old idiot who had upset Monika, made her try to kill herself."

Hamish was silent, visualising the scene.

"We were pretty crazy that night. We were in such a rush to catch the night train we left the door unlocked."

"Were you robbed?"

"No. Some time during the night Sophy turned up. She'd run away from school. We never found out why."

"Poor kid." Hamish's experience of Sophy was of a later date. "She doesn't strike me as the running away kind," he said thoughtfully.

"How well do you know her?" Helena enquired, glancing at Hamish's profile, finding him handsome. I may be old, she thought, but I dearly love a good-looking man.

"I wouldn't say well, not well at all." He thought back to the year he was sixteen when, in the South of France, in a mutual friend's house, Sophy had gathered him into her bed and relieved him tenderly of his virginity, setting him a standard for the future. He had thought himself in love with her. There had been no pain in their relations. "Was she unhappy?" he asked Helena. "Was she in pain?"

"Waste of time worrying about what that child felt. I never asked her. She's just the same now, doesn't have any feelings.

People say she is enigmatic but I wonder whether there is anything there."

Disliking his passenger Hamish said: "Perhaps you never bothered to find out."

Helena was silent, rebuked by Calypso's son. She liked men to approve of her. Max had given her this luxury; from now on she must live with less approval, less of everything. "It would be nice if I could find violets," she said. "He loved violets."

"Wrong time of year," said Hamish, hoping to hurt, thinking of Sophy. "No violets."

Sophy's flight was unpremeditated. Suddenly she could bear no more. The insidious horror had begun towards the end of the previous term, started again on her return to school, grown over the weeks to unbearable proportions. If she had known what it was about she might have fought back, but she could do nothing about sniggers from her peers, nothing to protect herself from the sarcastic innuendoes of mistresses, nothing against the prick of snide remarks, nothing against the incomprehensible envy, disgust and veiled accusation which wrapped her in a frightening fog. Instead of doing history prep she took her pocket money, put on her outdoor shoes and overcoat and caught a bus to the station. Her money bought a single ticket to Liverpool Street and from there she walked, arriving outside Polly's house in the early hours footsore, hungry, elated at having escaped her prison. She looked forward to telling Polly how she had crossed London through the blackout, alone.

No one answered the bell. She stepped back in the street to look up at the windows. The ground floor was shuttered; she could see by the light of the moon that the upper floors had curtains drawn. She remembered Polly writing, "Sometimes I go to Bletchley." This must be one of those times. Her elation evaporated. She was too exhausted to walk on to Calypso in Westminster. Helena was only round the corner. She made her way to Helena's house. She hoped Richard or Max would open the door, be there to protect her from Helena's disapproval. Arriving, she stood hesitating to ring the bell. How could she explain to Helena a mystery with undertones of indecency and disgustingness? She pressed the bell. She was poised for flight should Helena appear, but as at Polly's nobody answered, nobody came. She leant against the door in defeat. It swung open.

Coming off duty from his fire station, looking forward to a few hours' sleep, Tony Wood, passing Helena's house, noticed the front door open and a light showing. He went to investigate.

"Hullo? Hullo? Helena? You there? Your front door's open, anything wrong?" There was no answer. Puzzled, he put his tin hat and gas mask on the hall table, shut the door, investigated. Strong smell of cigarettes and liquor, signs of a party, cushions crushed, chairs awry, music sheets loosely stacked on a side table, no people. He went down to the kitchen, found Sophy standing petrified with terror, a glass of milk in one hand, a piece of meat in the other.

"Christ," he said, "what the hell are you doing here? Where's Helena?"

Sophy leapt into his arms, clutching him round the neck, gasping incomprehensible sentences. "Couldn't stand any more – nobody here – hungry – walked from Liverpool Street – they said – I can't – it was horrible – I'll never go back – please, Tony – please help – I won't – I can't – I had to run away." Her thin arms clutching him in a vice reminded him of a terrified cat up a tree.

"Steady on," he said. "It's all right, calm down, let a chap breathe." He tried to prise her from his neck but she clung tighter, her face pressed into his neck, her hair stuffed up his nose. He held her taut body, patting her back, stroking her. "Calm down, try and tell me what it's about." He managed to free his face from her hair. "There, now, let's find somewhere to sit." He led her to the drawing-room, sat her on the sofa, put his arm round her. "Try and tell me what happened, poor child, tell now—" But she's not a child, he thought, she's a girl and a bloody attractive one. "Oh," he said, "been in trouble with some man, been writing notes to a boy? My sister had that trouble at her school. Is that it?"

"No!" Sophy screamed, pulling away from him. "No. They said – they thought – they – they – it wasn't men, they said – they said I was – I was in love with Miss Stevens."

"A woman? One of the mistresses?"

"Yes."

"Silly cows." Light glimmered in Tony's perplexed brain. A schoolgirl pash.

"How could I be in love with a *woman*?" She looked up at him, her eyes enormous in her white face, her expression one of profound disgust.

"It happens."

"A woman in love with a woman? I can't believe it." She looked incredulous.

"Perhaps she fancied you?" Tony suggested.

"Oh God." Sophy shuddered. "Revolting."

"Men love men," Tony found himself saying.

"That's different." Sophy pulled away from him. "That's all right, I know that happens, but women, ugh."

Tony laughed, pulling her towards him. "Try and forget it, it's over now."

"Not if they send me back."

"I don't suppose they will." But Tony thought: They probably will. Helena wants her out from under her feet.

"Oh God," Sophy began to cry. "Oh God, if they knew what it's been like."

Tony kept quiet, holding her against him, letting her cry, handing her his handkerchief to mop the tears which spilled the fear of the indefinable from her system. He guessed she would tell him no more, that probably she couldn't.

"It's not against the law," he said, "what women do. Chaps, that's different. Found out and you go to prison."

"Why?"

"I've often wondered," said Tony, who frequently found his own sex attractive. "The laws of sex are rather obfusc."

"I wish I knew about sex. Nobody tells one anything and what the girls at school say is patently untrue."

"I long to know."

"I shan't tell you, you'd laugh. Oh God," she said suddenly, "I'm so tired."

"Bed then." He took her hand and led her upstairs. "You'd better get into Helena's bed. She's vanished somewhere, and Max too."

"Don't leave me." Panic sounded again.

"OK, but go and wash and get undressed." He yawned, fatigue catching up with him from long hours on duty. Sophy took off her school jersey and skirt and laid them on a chair. He watched her as she stood with her back to him, thin legs in black lisle stockings protruding from grey school bloomers. He counted the knobs on her spine before she turned round, breasts showing small under her wool vest.

"D'you think I could borrow one of Aunt Helena's nighties?"

"Sure." He yawned again.

She searched in a chest of drawers. "Gosh!" she exclaimed. "What undies, silk, look!" She held up a pair of pink cami-knickers. "Wow, what a change falling in love with Max has made. She used to wear liberty bodices and, oh, look at this." She held up a brassière.

"Buck up, find a nightdress."

"D'you think I could borrow this?" Sophy whispered as though in church as she held up a white satin nightdress trimmed with lace. "It's awfully bridal." She began to giggle. "Aunt Helena, of all people. She's so old."

"Hurry up, Sophy, I'm whacked."

"All right." She disappeared into the bathroom carrying the nightdress. Tony scrubbed his hand over his jaw feeling the bristles. From the bathroom he heard small exclamations, the sound of taps being turned on and off, the clatter of glass on the glass shelf. "Hurry up," he called, "I'm half dead."

Sophy came out of the bathroom on a choking wave of scent, her black hair brushed, wearing the white nightdress. She held it up on one side like a ball dress. He stared at her, taking in long arms and legs, black eyes, black hair, the shadow of her small bush through the white silk, her hand outstretched.

"What do you think this is?" She reached out to him. "She's got gallons of Chanel 5 in there and Elizabeth Arden make-up. What d'you think it can be?" She handed him a Dutch cap. "What is it for?"

"You'd better put it back where you found it."

"Oh, is it medical?"

"You could say that."

"Something like a truss? For a bosom?"

"Buck up and get into bed. Put that thing back first, though."

"All right."

"Now get into bed and go to sleep."

"Don't leave me." She was afraid again.

"I'll be downstairs."

"Can't you wait until I'm asleep? Mrs Floyer does. Kiss me goodnight like her."

"Who's she?"

"Our Rector's wife, the twins' mother."

"I'm not the Rector's wife," said Tony through gritted teeth.

"She sits on the end of my bed."

Tony sat on a chair at a safe distance, feeling her school skirt and bloomers bunching under him.

"Won't you kiss me?" She held out her arms.

He bent over her and kissed her mouth. "You stink," he said.

"I didn't mean to use so much." She lay back in the bed. "Why don't you lie here, if you're so tired?"

"For Christ's sake go to sleep," he yelled at her, exasperated.

"Sorry." She closed her eyes and, as he watched, relaxed suddenly like a cat and slept. Presently he stood up and looked down at her full mouth, short thick lashes. He pressed his hand against his genitals, grunting with anger and need.

Downstairs he stood by the telephone, the receiver on the table, dialling with one hand while he fingered his flies with the other. He got no answer from Polly and the telephone rang disregarded in Calypso's house. "Bloody little sexual hazard," he cried out loud. "Under age, too," he muttered in anguish. "Miss Stevens, indeed. What about me?" He lay face down on the sofa, blotting out the feel of Sophy's mouth against a cushion while he wooed sleep.

THIRTY-TWO

Sarah, hoping to find Helena's daily help, rang the bell in Enderby Street. She was surprised when Tony Wood, dishevelled and sleepy, opened the door.

"Who are you?" she asked. "You were not at the party last night." She sounded aggrieved.

Tony explained himself, brushing his hair back with his fingers, straightening his loosened tie.

"I am a friend of Helena's. I met her through Polly and Calypso."

"My nieces." Sarah eyed him with chill.

"Then you must be Sophy's aunt. She's upstairs."

"Sophy's at school."

"She's asleep in Helena's bed, or was when I last looked. She ran away."

"Perhaps you can explain. Do you mind if I come in?" Sarah crossed the threshold. Tony hastily buttoned the top of his trousers and reached for his coat.

"Has there been a fire?" Sarah sniffed the atmosphere in the drawing room, wondering what a fireman was doing in Helena's house. "Where's Helena's daily?"

"I don't think she comes today. Would you like some coffee or something?"

"I will make you some," said Sarah, taking charge. "Open the windows and get rid of this fug. While I make coffee you can explain."

Guiltily Tony obeyed, throwing wide the windows, letting in the chill air. He joined Sarah in the kitchen.

"Why did she run away? Is the child in love with you or—" He could see the phrase "something silly" freeze on her respectable lips.

"I wish – I mean, no. She came here because she couldn't find Polly. She—"

"I must have missed her. I got in late from Helena's party. Perhaps you had better tell me what you know."

"Do you know where Helena is?"

"By now she should be arriving at home in Cornwall."

As she made coffee Sarah gave Tony a bare account of Helena's departure with Richard and Max, but not all the reasons for it. In his turn Tony told of finding the lights showing, the door open and Sophy in the kitchen. He did not tell her why Sophy had run away.

"Why did she run away?"

"I think she'd better tell you herself, she was very upset last night. She doesn't want to go back."

"Wouldn't have run away if she wanted to stay," said Sarah crisply. Tony recovered his equilibrium. He had not, he told himself, done anything. Well, not much.

"Helena will be put out," said Sarah.

"Yes. Thank you." He took the cup she tendered.

"I'll see what I can do. I have to go and see Calypso. I can take Sophy with me."

"I tried to phone her in the night; she didn't answer. I tried Polly's number first."

"Polly's away. I sleep very deeply. I am staying in her house."

"Oh," said Tony neutrally. "Oh." They sat on either side of the table. Tony drank coffee. Sarah watched him, wondering where he fitted into the scheme of things, whether he was trustworthy.

"So you are a friend of my nieces?"

"Yes." She sounded coldly inquisitorial. Next she would be enquiring whether he went to bed with them. He felt disinclined to tell her that whereas he and Polly had slept together they no longer did, that when he had last invited himself into Calypso's bed she had refused him on the feeble pretext that she had not enjoyed herself the last time. As for Sophy, it was a case of thought more than deed. At some later date he hoped he would rectify the situation. He smiled at Sarah, putting on the charm.

"You must be Oliver's mother."

"Yes."

"How is Oliver?" Blast his guts, he thought, remembering Oliver snitching Calypso from under his nose, so confident, so handsome.

"Oliver? Did you say Oliver?" Sophy came eagerly into the kitchen. "Aunt Sarah, how are you, how is Oliver?" She hugged Sarah. "I am glad to see you," she said sincerely.

"Go and put a dressing-gown on, then I'll make you some breakfast. You'll catch cold in that thing."

"Isn't it beautiful? Aunt H has got some terrific clothes. Where does she get the coupons?"

"I don't know, darling. Go and wrap up." Sarah was startled by the transparent garment.

Tony carried his cup to the sink. He wondered whether Sarah, who had followed Sophy from the room, believed he had left Sophy's virtue intact. It would seem unlikely. Helena's silk night-dress made her look much older than she was, more desirable. He called up the stairs, "I have to go, Sophy. I'll ring up and find out how you are. Where will you be?"

"With Aunt Sarah at Polly's." Her cheerful voice came down the stairs. "Or with Calypso."

"Thank you, Mr Wood. We'll let you know." Sarah leant over the banisters. He knew that she suspected him of malintent. "I will take care of her now." She was dismissive.

"I will be off, then," he said. "Goodbye."

"Goodbye," said Sarah. "Thanks again."

Tony walked down the street feeling empty. For a few hours Sophy had turned to him; now she had her robust tweed-suited aunt. Oliver's mother, rather a dragon.

"When you are dressed," said Sarah to Sophy, lying in the bath, "we must go to Calypso. There's been a letter from Oliver. I gather something has happened to Hector."

"If he's dead Oliver will be delighted."

"What a dreadful thing to say."

"But it's true," said Sophy. "Nothing would please him more."

"Sophy!" Sarah was shocked.

"It doesn't please me, though." She reached for her school vest and bloomers. "And I hate these clothes," she said viciously.

"Can you tell me why you ran away? Is it serious? What happened? What did you do?"

"Nothing happened. I didn't do anything. It's serious to me. I am not going back." Sophy's face was closed. Sarah was realistic enough to know that Sophy would sooner part with her back teeth than oblige with information. Quietly she thanked her God who voted Conservative and was on the side of the Allies that she was not blessed with a daughter. She sat watching Sophy put on her school skirt, tie, jersey and sensible shoes, obliterating the brilliant image that had appeared in the kitchen.

"We can catch a Number Eleven bus if we walk to Sloane Square," she said.

"Of course." Sophy looked as pleased as though Sarah had said Pumpkin Coach.

Presently they stood on Calypso's doorstep and pressed the bell. Inside the house Fling barked furiously, running to the door, his nails clicking on the tiles. Nobody came.

"She must be out."

"I'm sure she's in." Sophy rang the bell again, holding her thumb hard on the button. Fling barked crazily, choking with excitement. Sophy pushed open the letter flap and tried to peer in. The door opened suddenly.

"Hullo," said Calypso. "Come in." She picked up the dog with one hand and scooped letters off the mat with the other. "Come in," she repeated. "Nice to see you." She kissed her aunt and Sophy and began sorting the letters vaguely. "Mostly bills," she said, laying them down. "Shut up, Fling, be quiet now. He's made a mess, mind where you put your feet – he hasn't been out yet."

"I don't suppose he could last, it's long after ten." Sarah, prepared to lavish sympathy, was furious with herself at her implied reproach.

"I'll clean it up presently. Mrs Welsh doesn't like him. I thought you were at school, Sophy."

"I've run away."

"I don't blame you. I was asked to leave mine, accused of flirting with the gardener, I ask you, as Uncle Richard would say. A spotty youth. It was an insult to my intelligence. I was about as ignorant as a newborn baby." Calypso made a faint choking sound, thinking of her ignorance so brilliantly enlightened by Hector. "Come to the kitchen. I'll make tea or something." She walked down the hall, her body unbalanced by her pregnancy.

"I had a letter from Oliver, darling." Sarah watched Calypso fill the kettle, wondered when the child was due.

"Told you Hector was dead, I suppose? He must be pleased."

"Oh no, darling." Sarah was shocked.

"How are his boils?"

"What boils?" Sarah was caught off balance.

"Oliver's. Hector wrote that Oliver had desert boils. Didn't he tell you?"

"No." Sarah wondered how to get through the barrier of indifference Calypso wore. "I came, I came," she said bravely, "to see whether there is anything I can do."

Calypso watched the kettle. "Thanks, Aunt Sarah, there's nothing at all."

Sarah asked: "When did you hear? Why haven't you—" She paused.

"Why haven't I told you all? Rather be alone, I suppose." She spooned tea into the pot and poured from the kettle. "Except that I'm not alone, there's this bloody baby. I can't wait to get my body back to myself. Roll on the ninth month."

"Naturally you are upset." Sarah flinched at her inadequacy.

"Why can't they tell the truth? What's the use of 'missing believed killed'? They only say that because they haven't found the body. They didn't find Walter's. They only say it to prolong the agony." Calypso blazed with anger. "D' you like milk and sugar?" Her expression snapped back to normal.

"Just milk, please." Sarah sat on a kitchen chair, her back stiff. "It's the most terrible shock when you are in love with—"

"I don't know what love is," Calypso said. "Sugar, Sophy? I married Hector for his money. I've got his money. He made a generous will, everything to go to the baby after me. I can marry again if I want to and still keep the money for my life. The child is provided for separately." She sipped her tea, smiled wryly. " 'Separate' being the operative word. Once this lump and I are separate everything will be OK. That about wraps it up. There isn't any 'in love', Aunt."

"I'll go and clear up that dog mess and give him a run." Sarah stood up, too horrified to speak.

"His lead's on the table." Calypso watched her aunt leave the room with the dog, then grinned at Sophy. "She can walk him round Parliament Square and cool down," she said. "Why don't you stay with me, Sophy, love, while they get used to the idea that you won't be going back."

"D'you think they will let me?"

"Yes, I do. Monika tried to kill herself. Tony rang me up before you came. Don't worry, she didn't succeed. Aunt Helena will be busy smoothing things down in Cornwall. I'll take charge. Aunt Sarah can't have you in Bath, she is dreadfully busy with her WVS. You stay here for a while and amuse me."

"If only I could."

"You can, we'll fix it. Have to get you some clothes, you can't go around looking like that."

"Coupons?"

"Mrs Welsh has an inexhaustible supply at a pound each from the *Marché Noir*."

"A pound! Gosh!"

"I'm rich, so what's a pound?"

"What did you say about Monika? Aunt Sarah said she was ill."

"She would. I daresay she is ill. All Tony knows is that she tried to jump over the cliff. I think the war is affecting people's minds. Do you know what Hector's letters have been about? Trees, planting trees, 'designing' is the word he used, designing woods. You'd think he had no interest in anything else."

"She wouldn't fall far," said Sophy, who wasn't listening. "The Army have blocked the Terror Run with barbed wire."

Sarah, her equanimity recovered, came back into the kitchen with the dog.

"What does Oliver write about in his letters, Aunt Sarah?"

"Oh, darling, he writes that the desert is cold and gritty, that he is bored, that he is tired, that he is—"

"Frightened?"

"He doesn't say so but no doubt he is. He can't write what one wants to hear because of censorship. It's all so horrible." Sarah sat down and stared at her niece anxiously.

"Hector wrote about trees. Before that he wrote about politics, that the whole Army will vote Labour next time and so would he and that he was going to give up politics. Well, it doesn't matter now."

"He's only missing, darling." Sarah spoke gently.

"Believed killed," Calypso replied steadily. The two women stared at each other, then Calypso said brightly: "I've asked Sophy to stay with me. She can keep me company. Will you deal with her school, say she's not coming back?"

"Helena should deal with the school. Perhaps Sophy should go back, I don't know why she left."

"I do," said Calypso, who had been told by Tony. "She can't possibly go back. Why not leave it to me?"

"But—"

"They won't know I'm only twenty, they won't know it's me. I can be awfully toffee-nosed. I will deal with them, tear them off a strip. I will enjoy having Sophy here, she will take my mind off things."

"If you think—" Sarah began weakly.

"I do, Aunt Sarah, I know. This will be good for us both. Sophy will care for me, won't you, Sophy?"

"Yes."

"Well, for the moment. Just for a short time time . . ." Sarah in her country tweeds looked worriedly at Calypso wrapped in a lace dressing-gown which did nothing to hide her shape. "If I could have her I would." She stood up, feeling she must leave. "I shall talk to Helena and Richard."

"The bulge and I will be very glad to have her," said Calypso.

"I'll see you to the bus," said Sophy.

"Can't I get you to a taxi?" Calypso kissed her aunt, mentally speeding her off.

"No, a bus, Number Eleven." Sarah kissed Calypso. "Look after yourself, darling." She felt inadequate, shut out.

"I will. And Sophy." Calypso was cool and firm.

"I wish I knew whether I was doing the right thing."

"Don't worry, Aunt. Don't fail to tell us news of Oliver."

"I'm sure he writes to you oftener than me."

"Oh, no," cried Calypso, waving from the doorstep, "of course not." She waved again, then gathered the letters from the table where she had laid them, among them one from Oliver.

"I bet he's gleeful, the bastard," she muttered. Slitting the thin air mail letter open she read: "Now that you are a widow, my darling, we can start making plans for our future in case I survive this bloody fucking war. I calculate we can live very comfortably on your late lamented (not by me) husband's money while I write my first novel, after which all will be plain sailing into the sunset. Talking of fucking, we are very deprived here in the desert so get set to make up for lost time when—" She screwed up the letter and threw it on to the floor. "The shit," she muttered, "shit, shit, shit." She watched Fling pounce on the letter and tear it to shreds, growling and shaking it like a rat. Coming back into the house Sophy said: "What is he eating?"

"A letter from Oliver."

"He told Aunt Sarah about Hector. I suppose he is pleased."

"Don't sound so desolate. Oliver may get killed, and the twins, and that will be the end of our lot, not that Hector belonged—" Her voice trailed.

Sophy asked: "Has Oliver really got boils?"

"So Hector said. Let's go and light the fire in the drawing-room." Calypso led the way up the stairs. "I hope Mrs Welsh has laid it." She struck a match, held it to the paper, watched the flame creep and take hold. "Don't tell me about school if you don't want to. I can guess. Was Tony kind?"

"Very, but he said I stank." Sophy described Helena's bathroom, her soaps and scent. "I used too much. He kissed me goodnight." She touched her mouth unconsciously. Calypso smiled.

"He will fall in love with you."

"Nobody will do that. The girls at school call me—"

"What?"

"Eurasian. They say none of their brothers—"

"Bugger their brothers. You don't need that kind of girl's brother. Sophy, you are lovely, beautiful, didn't you know?"

"Me?" Sophy stared at Calypso in astonishment. "You are just trying to be nice."

Calypso grinned. "Nice is not a word much applied to me. I am going to dress. You read these while I have my bath, then we will go shopping and buy some clothes for you." She handed Sophy a batch of letters and left the room.

Sophy held the letters, turning them this way and that. Letters from Hector, written on air mail paper. She began to read, unfolding them carefully, refolding each one as she finished it. When she had read them she laid them on a side table and sat staring into the fire, where Calypso presently found her.

"I wish someone would write letters like that to me."

"About trees," Calypso scoffed. "What was he thinking about, what did he mean by it? There's nothing, absolutely nothing about the war or what he's doing. The nearest we get is Oliver's boils."

"Perhaps he didn't want to think about the war. The letters are all about after the war and things he wants to do for you, with you—"

"I haven't read them properly." Calypso was defensive.

"He wanted to plant a forest with your name spelled with wild cherry trees."

"You make it sound poetic. It is wasted on me. Let's go shopping. I don't want to talk about Hector, Sophy. He isn't like that, he's a tough who gets drunk and—"

"So do Oliver and the twins, so does Uncle Richard, so did Walter."

"Was Tony drunk last night?"

"No."

"You were lucky." If he had been drunk, thought Calypso, Sophy wouldn't be sitting there looking so virginal. "It's the war. Everybody's drinking, even Aunt Helena."

"Really?"

"Yes, she is. People say it's fear. I think it's because people think there's a shortage. They soup it up in case the next person wants it. The war's driving us to drink. At the moment. It makes me sick. As soon as I am delivered of this lump I shall go on a bender."

Filling in the time before the funeral Sophy walked along the cliffs in the wind, which stung her eyes. She remembered the time spent with Calypso while here in Cornwall Richard and Helena had cared for Monika, each solicitous for a different reason, Richard because he was truly fond, Helena because she wanted to get back to London. Max had travelled to Cornwall whenever he could leave London, deeply concerned for Monika. He would come and sit with Calypso, bringing presents of books or flowers, and talk about life in Vienna before the war and on rare occasions of Pauli, his son, hinting with perplexity at a stormily aggressive character who might or might not, if he survived, become an artist, a youth who somehow frightened his parents into an excess of guilt, giving the impression of some dire force which made him unlovable. Then he would pause, rub his hands together, shake his shoulders, laugh and change the subject. Similarly Calypso rarely mentioned Hector, and Polly, who came often after work, never mentioned the twins except casually and jokingly as the High or Hoi Floyers.

As she strode along the path, neatly signposted by the National Trust, Sophy remembered those months in London as months of happiness. Calypso taking her shopping, buying her pretty clothes, teaching her how to care for her hair and nails. Max, Brian Portmadoc, Tony Wood and other friends of Calypso and Polly came to spend evenings, talking, joking, cooking supper in Calypso's kitchen, sharing bottles of wine which one or other would bring. They had all, Sophy thought, shied away from anxious subjects like Hector, Pauli, Oliver and the twins and turned to her as a person they could share communally in safety without awkwardness. They had taken her to the cinema and out to lunch. Once or twice Max had taken her to a concert, several times Tony had smuggled her into a pub. She walked Fling in the parks with Brian. It was generally understood, though not underlined, that presently, when Monika was well again, when Helena came back to London, Sophy would go back to Cornwall and help with the cow and the hens, go to day school perhaps. The attitude seemed to be that there was no hurry, things would work out, meanwhile forget beastly school, have fun, grow up. Ah, thought Sophy, walking over the short cliff grass in her green gumboots, those were the days when I grew up, when we chattered and gossiped and phoned occasionally to the old people, Helena, Sarah, Uncle Richard and Monika, none of them, except perhaps Uncle Richard, as old then as I am now.

They had discussed war news, shortages, the unexploded bomb which had lurked for months under Knightsbridge while the buses trundled over it, the flooding of London by the Americans, who got noisily drunk and were so helpful and polite, giving nylons to the girls, nylons, nylons. Sophy tramped over the cliff, hearing the gulls' high-pitched crazy cry, as they had always cried over the grey sea. She tried to remember what Calypso had said to her school, that nightmare place, and failed. We were all in love, she thought, stopping on the headland, looking out to sea, Uncle Richard with Monika, Max with Monika and Helena, Polly with the twins, Helena with Max, I with Oliver. Oliver and all the men with Calypso, who said she didn't know what love was.

Sophy wondered what Calypso looked like now she'd had a stroke, recovered, they said, except for her face. It was some years since she had seen her. She wondered whether she dyed her hair, and what she would look like with her face twisted, though someone had said it was twisted only a little. I remember, Sophy told herself, I shall always remember what she looked like when the news came that Hector was a prisoner of war and not dead at all.

THIRTY-THREE

Turning back towards the house, the wind nudging her along with threats of winter stinging her ears, she could see across the fields the church tower rearing above the squat little village, protecting as it had for centuries the bones of the dead, among which lay Uncle Richard, the Floyers and Monika, where tomorrow they would lay Max with whom she had spent the day that Calypso was given the news that Hector was no longer missing but a prisoner of war.

With the wind bringing colour to her high cheekbones, Sophy remembered that day, or thought she did, for she knew well enough that memory plays false, that mind and emotion build on memory. The picture which is not clear at the time becomes lucent with recollection.

Max had taken her to a rehearsal of Yehudi Menuhin. She had sat listening to the talk, watching Menuhin and other musicians, and then the unearthly sounds of Menuhin's violin drew her up to a new plane of existence. She was aware that Max had left the hall to talk to a stranger. Coming back he sat beside her, held her hand until the music stopped, then said, "We must go," and led her out. He had not said goodbye to any of the people. He had said, pushing her into a taxi, "Stay with me, try not to talk." On the way to Enderby Street he had held her against him, sitting taut, just holding her until they arrived, fumbling for money, paying the taxi, not speaking, pushing her ahead of him into Helena's house. He had told her in the drawing-room or Helena's bedroom that in the concert hall the man who had access to information, no one knew exactly how, told him that Pauli had died in the concentration camp. I have lost my son. What can I say to Monika? Why did we not stay? Why did we run away?" He had rocked her in his arms, holding her against his bony body. She had responded, holding his head against her breast, consoling him with all the emotion set in train by Menuhin, and then Sophy delved back into that traumatic afternoon in Helena's bed, to the tender love-making of a deeply sorrowful man. She had lain beside him as he slept, glad of what he had done. He had woken, kissed her. "Did I hurt you, child?"

"Very little," she had said honestly.

"I am glad you were there," he said, consoling her.

"I am glad, too," she had answered, comforting him.

Sophy, remembering the comfort of Helena's bed, the hardness of Max's ribs, was glad that she had been there while he endured the agony of his loss – not unexpected, no deaths were unexpected. Later they shared the bath, using Helena's bath essence, wrapping themselves in her enormous white towels with "H" stitched on the corners in red.

They dressed and walked from Enderby Street to Calypso's house. Max had held her hand all the way. On the cliff-top Sophy smiled, for now he was dead she was the only one left who knew that they had been lovers. She had happened to be there at the right moment for him to reach for.

In the dusk they had stopped to stare at a bombsite, each noticing, neither commenting on the weeds growing in the cracks of what had once been a house. They had reached Calypso's house as it grew dark, letting themselves in. Fling had rushed to greet them and Calypso had called from upstairs, "Is that you?"

She was sitting in the middle of the sofa, heavily pregnant, legs apart, holding the telegram. Sophy remembered Calypso's eyes and she remembered Max's face as he read the telegram held out to him.

"What joy," he had said, kissing Calypso, who put her arms round him, laying her face against his. His eyes catching Sophy's had signalled "No", and neither of them had breathed a word about Pauli.

Max had said: "Bubbly, *nicht?*" being very keen on using what he called "English argot". They had trooped to the basement to raid Hector's precious cellar and Calypso had telephoned Aunt Sarah, her parents, Helena and Richard. Polly had come round with Brian Portmadoc, Tony Wood and a Frenchman who knew Hector. There had been quite a party. Probably, Sophy thought, it was the best thing for Max, who did not break the news until weeks later to Monika, waiting until she was quite well, no longer likely to throw herself over the cliff, as she had tried during the guinea pig scandal. It must have been about here, Sophy thought, peering over. There was the ledge she had fallen on. If it had been anyone other than Monika one would think she had known she couldn't fall far. As she peered over, aware of the sea, the wind, the crying gulls, measuring the drop to the ledge, one of the many impertinent cliff foxes poor Ducks used to chase zigzagged along the slope. Sophy felt a rush of tears for the dog, for Max to be buried tomorrow, for her virginity given him so carelessly. Lucky, she thought, that she didn't conceive a replacement for Pauli, and she remembered what she had long forgotten, Calypso's glance exchanged with Max, the way they had smiled complicitly, then Calypso's change of tone.

"Perhaps he'll stay long enough in prison to get the news that I am pregnant."

"You make him sound like a shop," Polly had said with implied reproach.

"He is very distant," Calypso had answered. "Hard to imagine when he isn't here."

Sophy climbed the last bit of cliff arriving breathless on the camomile lawn. She looked at the house, quiet now, its rooms empty, the windows sightless. The Ilex tree stood as it always had, protecting the eastern side; the branch she had climbed along as a child darkened the drawing-room. Here Helena had sat in her deck chair, here Oliver, Walter, Polly, the twins and Calypso had lolled chatting on the summer evenings of their youth. Here she had stood whistling and calling Ducks when he had gone hunting the cliff foxes when Uncle Richard lay ill with pneumonia. He had fretted for his dog. She had spent hours whistling and calling, her voice mingling with the gulls. On the third evening the dog had appeared, paws sore with digging, coat ingrained with earth, eyes bunged up with sand, so tired he crawled to Sophy's feet and lay feebly wagging. She had carried the dog into the house, given it water, tempted it with food and carried it up to Uncle Richard, who gasped for breath against his pillows. Coughing, he had said, "Give him to me, put him here." The dog had lain in the crook of his arm, his long nose on the sleeve of Richard's striped pyjamas, his eyes closed in exhaustion and Richard had slept for the first time for days. Monika had sat up with him, sending her to bed, anxious for Richard who was iller this time than ever before, not responding to the M and B pills prescribed by the doctor.

Mildred Floyer had come to sit with Richard. Sophy had listened to the two women discussing penicillin, which could save Richard but was only issued to the forces. Unable to sleep, she came down to the kitchen to join them drinking cocoa.

"He was so anxious for the dog, he will get better now he is found."

"One hopes," Monika had said. Monika, who no longer had hope for Pauli, no longer flushed at the mention of guinea pigs. Monika, who had in her sorrow strength to lavish on Richard, who loved her, had said, "He may try to get better now, perhaps he will try for the dog's sake." She had asked to be allowed to sit with Richard and they had agreed. Mildred left to get a little rest, her face etched with anxiety for the twins in Italy now, for the war had taken its turn for the better and the German armies were moving back, albeit slowly.

Standing on the lawn Sophy remembered Richard and sitting by the bed listening to his breathing, his snorts and snuffles. Repelled by the sickroom smell she sat bolt upright, unable to relax, watching Richard's grey face, his mouth slackly open, his every breath an effort. He opened his eyes and said: "I'm buggering off."

"What?"

"Come over here." She got up and stood by the bed.

"Dog's done for too." His breath whistled.

"What?" She could barely hear him for the fear she felt.

"Can't move his legs, poor little brute."

She had felt the dog, picked him up, put him on the floor where he rolled over, his eye catching hers, listless.

"Put him back." Richard coughed, fighting for breath, gasping, wheezing, his face a dull purple.

She eased the dog back into place. "He's not old," she had said defensively, feeling the dog criticised.

"But done for."

"I'll get the vet as soon as it's light."

"No good, both dying." Richard's eyes on her face, the dog staring, daring her to move it again, its teeth bared.

"He loves you," she had said, adding after a pause, "we all do."

"Love," Richard gasped, an expression of weary contempt on his face. "Used to love Helena." Sophy had leant close to hear. The dog growled, threatening to snap. "Love Monika now. Your mother said she loved, priest said she said." His chin sank on his chest. "Some Chink, I ask you. A coolie, shouldn't be surprised, lucky we're winning the war, the Huns would see you're not pure Aryan." His voice had trailed into a coughing fit. She remembered holding the glass of water so that he could sip, and hating his breath. He gripped her hand.

"I ask you, Sophy. It is Sophy?"

"Yes," she had said. "Yes, it's Sophy," repelled by him. "Come closer."

Holding her breath so that she need not breathe the odour she feared, she had leant closer.

"See that they bury him with me."

"At your feet?"

"In coffin. Promise." His anxious eyes close to hers echoed the dog's expression. "I ask you—" His grip on her hand faded, his chin sank on to his chest, she could hear the bedside clock ticking where Monika had moved it on to the chest of drawers. She stared at the dog and the dog stared back. She closed Richard's eyes, able to touch him now without dread. She remembered waking Monika and that Monika had lifted the dog from the bed, saying in a matter of fact voice, "Put him in his basket," that she had carried the dog to its basket in the dressing-room, reached for something to cover it and the nearest thing was a pair of trousers. She had pulled the artificial leg away and wrapped the trousers over the animal.

Sophy remembered standing where she stood now the morning Richard died. She had wept for the dog, who was dying. She had run back into the house where Monika was telephoning the doctor and Helena and found the dog dead. It was Max who helped her smuggle it into the coffin where Richard lay in a dark suit, his wispy hair brushed neatly back, his face wearing the mortician's idea of dignity. Ducks joined his master, his lip curled in a snarl, body stiffly bent. Max tucked him in beside Richard and called to the undertaker to put the lid on the coffin. Standing on the lawn, looking up at the house, Sophy wondered how large a tip had been pressed into the undertaker's hand, how Max had ensured the dog's burial would remain secret. When she stood by the grave with Helena, Monika and Mildred Floyer, Mr Floyer reading the burial service, his surplice flapping in the wind, the coffin resting in the deep pit, Max had caught her eye across the open grave and smiled. The old devil, Sophy thought, turning to look at the sea, where later strange shapes which were bits of Mulberry Harbour were towed past in the spring of 1944. How Uncle Richard would have loved the Normandy invasion, she thought, even though both the High Floyers were wounded and several men from the village never came home. He would have gloried, watching American bombers fly over the coast to bomb France. Without his enthusiasm the war had become dull, something to be finished as quickly as possible, for Richard had represented the audience. All the rest of us, she thought, who had gathered in 1939 on the camomile lawn, played small parts. She bent to look at the texture of the lawn. It was amazing it had survived. She ran her palm over it, sniffing the elusive scent evocative of other times, other loves. Someone tapped on the glass of the French windows. She had thought the house empty and was startled. The light, tempered by racing clouds, shone in her eyes. She could see a shadowy figure behind the glass, who tapped again then backed out of sight.

Sophy crossed the lawn and stared in at Monika's meticulously furnished drawing-room, all trace of Helena obliterated. When Max bought the house in the fifties Helena had finally settled in London. She tried the windows, found them locked and walked round to the front door.

"I'm in the kitchen," Calypso called, "making tea."

"Oh." Sophy felt mixed emotions: anger at being disturbed in her nostalgic trip, gladness at hearing Calypso's voice.

"Come along, darling, it's only me."

The two women embraced, each hiding her face against the other's cheek.

"You still use Mitsuko," said Sophy.

Calypso stood back, holding Sophy's shoulders, smiling.

"Not a grey hair. Not even a rinse! How many years?"

"What are you doing? The funeral is tomorrow." They spoke together.

"I thought I'd collect my thoughts. I haven't been here for years." Sophy returned Calypso's crooked smile.

"Doesn't show much, does it? I thought I'd come the night before the wake. I've got a carload of booze. Any idea who's coming?"

"The neighbours, I suppose, friends, other artists. Hamish is bringing Helena, you know."

Calypso laughed. "At her age, crikey."

"She enjoys funerals, she's strong. She was at Richard's, Monika's, both Mr and Mrs Floyer's. She even turned up at General Peachum's."

"Seems excessive. Were you at all of them?"

"No, no, only Monika's and Uncle Richard's. Felt I owed it. Why didn't you come?"

"I was abroad. Besides if you mean what I think you mean, I don't know that I—"

"I always imagined you qualified."

Calypso chuckled. "I expect Polly will come, don't you?"

"Yes." Sophy watched Calypso search for cups, find sugar, warm the pot. "I wanted to look round the house."

"I'll come with you, unless you want to be alone."

"No."

"I suppose it will be sold now, Pauli won't want it."

"I am sure he doesn't."

They left the kitchen, strolling through the hall – "D'you remember Monika's hyacinths?" – into the dining-room. "Those holiday breakfasts, Uncle Richard crumpling *The Times*."

"Monika made this room look lovely." They stood in the drawing-room.

"Helena had no real idea."

"The bedrooms were always comfortable."

"Cold in the winter."

"Not since they put in central heating."

Companionably they climbed the stairs. Sophy noticed that Calypso dragged a leg.

"This room had the finest view." Calypso opened a bedroom door.

"Uncle Richard died in it."

"Oh Sophy, look, did you know?"

Propped on stools Max lay in his coffin. Calypso crossed herself. Sophy took her hand.

The afternoon light was kind to Max. He seemed to be listening, his springy white hair swept back, arched nose, mobile mouth, bottom lip slightly pouting, brow lined but serene, paper-thin eyelids hiding the black observant eyes.

"I never realised he was so beautiful," Calypso whispered.

"Because he was busy making us feel beautiful." Sophy spoke in a normal voice. "No need to whisper," she said.

"He doesn't look his age. He's as old as Aunt Helena."

"Not quite." Sophy bent to kiss the still face. Calypso watched her.

"I couldn't do that," she said. "I couldn't even kiss Hector goodbye. What are you laughing at?" She turned on Sophy, who had sat back on the bed giggling.

Sophy told her of Max smuggling the dog into Richard's coffin. Calypso let out a yelp of laughter.

"The old rogue."

"He had compassion," said Sophy.

"What a philanderer," Calypso grinned.

"But faithful to Monika and Helena," said Sophy.

"If you like a *ménage à trois*," said Calypso.

"They did. Country wife and town wife. They were happy."

"Mistress," said Calypso.

"If you must split hairs," said Sophy, who had never married.

"Shall we make that tea?" They went downstairs. "I will gee up the kettle. I wonder why they haven't closed the coffin, why he's alone, why the house is empty."

"We'd better stay and keep him company."

"I don't want to," said Calypso. "I've got a room at the Queen's."

"I shall, then. Somebody should until Pauli comes—"

"Of course that's why it's open. I'd forgotten Pauli." Calypso made the tea.

"People do." Sophy watched Calypso pour water into the pot.

"He isn't one of us, is he?" Calypso poured. "Lapsang Souchong sounds better but doesn't taste as good as Earl Grey." She handed Sophy her cup. "Sugar?"

"No, thanks."

"Come and spend the night at the Queen's. I'll pay."

"No, thank you, Calypso."

"Come to dinner, then, we have so much to catch up on – do. It's so many years."

But Sophy refused. "No, thank you, love." She had so very nearly married Hamish. What would Calypso have been like as a mother-in-law?

"Tell me something." Calypso sipped her tea, reading Sophy's thoughts.

"What?" Sophy was wary. "I always think you know everything."

"Did Hamish want to marry you?"

"I was there when he was born."

"That's no answer."

Sophy laughed. "I am nearly old enough to be his mother."

"You haven't answered me." Calypso was watchful. "You would have been rich, didn't that tempt you? I like being rich, always have."

"So you always said. You said, too, that you didn't know what love was. You lied."

408

"Oh?" Calypso was non-committal. "What makes you think that?"

"When Hamish was born you gave yourself away."

"How?"

"Your voice."

"I don't remember saying anything. I remember yelling a lot."

"When you saw him, when you looked at him you said, 'His balls are as big as Hector's' – your voice."

"I'd never seen a new-born baby, it gave me a shock."

"You sounded as if you loved Hector."

"You are fanciful." Calypso sipped her tea, watching Sophy. "You still haven't answered my question."

"It wouldn't have worked."

"So he did want to marry you."

"He was only a baby."

"Too young to know his own mind?"

"Of course."

"He has never married anyone else."

"There's time enough," said Sophy stoutly.

Calypso laughed. "What a birth that was, put me off having another."

"You didn't want another."

"Right. Hamish is enough. We might have got on, you and me. You could have provided me with a grandchild. Hector would have liked that."

"Cousins."

"Not too close. Walter was too close and Oliver." Calypso let Oliver's name hang in the air. "Does he ever come to England?"

"I wouldn't know." Sophy's neutral voice was steady. It would be unbearable if Oliver turned up.

Both women sat thoughtfully holding their teacups in the kitchen which had become so exclusively Monika's.

"You were extremely plucky when Hamish was born. I've never really thanked you. I didn't see you after I was whisked off to hospital. What happened to you?"

"Brian put me on the train to Penzance."

"Not Max?"

"No, Brian. They had arrived together to find you. Max went with you to the hospital."

"Oh."

Calypso and Sophy remembered the solitary air raid, the bomb which had demolished Calypso's house, trapping them in the basement, the shock bringing on premature labour, the long hours while rescue workers frantically dug.

"How Fling barked!"

"How I yelled. You must have been terrified."

"I was until the baby came out."

"You wrapped him in glass cloths."

"There was nothing else."

"You found Mrs Welsh's apron, you used that."

"So I did."

"It was wonderful when they got us out."

"Wasn't it!"

"Even more wonderful when Catherine came and took him off to Scotland so that I could be free. I wonder who sent for her?"

"I did."

"Really? Clever of you."

"I telephoned her and she came right away. She was furious. She said you'd been irresponsible."

"So I was." Calypso laughed, not minding the criticism. "But there was no need to fuss. I was quite all right."

"It was Hamish she was worried about," said Sophy drily. "Not you."

"Hector's baby," Calypso agreed. "So long ago, it doesn't seem real, does it?" She stood up. "Sure you won't come to the Queen's? It's comfortable." She gathered her bag, put on her coat not expecting a reply. "See you tomorrow in church. Goodbye, love." She laid her cheek against Sophy's in token affection. Sophy watched her get into her car and drive out of sight, then went and stood by the drawing-room window and looked out. She folded her arms, hugging herself, remembering how in the bomb-blasted kitchen in London she had held new-born Hamish screaming his objections to this horrible world. She had crouched, holding the infant, listening to the curses of the rescuers as they dug through the rubble to reach Calypso, buried they knew, injured they thought, unaware that she had Sophy with her, unaware that she had given birth to Hamish. She had crawled about the kitchen still amazingly intact. The ceiling had not completely collapsed until after they were rescued. She had seen the telephone, tried it, found it wonderfully working, said to the operator, "Get me through to Scotland." She supposed the number had been written up somewhere, or had she asked Calypso? She could not remember. Catherine had answered – she could recollect Catherine's voice, clear from the Highlands – "I can hear him greeting." She had wrapped Mrs Welsh's apron more tightly round the sticky, screaming baby and, crouching beside Calypso, had waited for release.

"D'you think they will get us out?" Calypso had been wonderfully resilient.

"Of course they will." Sophy listened to the picks and shovels, the grunts of the men trying to reach them, guided by Fling's high-pitched barking.

"Hector will kill me for this" – Calypso had sounded pleased, crouching in the shattered kitchen – "when he gets to know. I really believed he was dead."

"I know. I wonder what it's like to be a prisoner of war. At least he's safe."

"He still writes about trees," Calypso had complained. "Nothing about his camp or me."

"If he wrote love letters he would not want someone other than you to read them. I expect he feels private. I would."

"D'you think that's it? I hadn't thought."

"Of course. For flowering trees read whatever he says when he tells you he loves you." Calypso had laughed.

"Clever Sophy. Guess what he says when he loves me."

"I couldn't. I know, though, that he loves you."

"He loves my rump and, well no, I can't tell you what he says, you would be shocked."

"Perhaps."

"I'll whisper. We mustn't let the baby hear what its pa says." She whispered in Sophy's ear. Both girls were laughing when the first of their rescuers broke through, bringing with him a shower of rubble. There was so much laughter at that time, Sophy thought, and Hector had not been safe in a camp but winding his way down Italy in an intricate escape. She had been back in Cornwall when he got home to Calypso. Hamish had grown up in Scotland. Hector had joined the Labour Party and taken up forestry. Calypso had lived on, beautiful, remote, adored. Hector had died some time in the fifties. Calypso had not remarried and Oliver presumably went on loving her, for though he had married she had never heard he was happy.

Looking out at the grey unfriendly sea, Sophy remembered the last period of the war, living with Monika, helping with the cow, the hens, the garden, Mr and Mrs Floyer, village activities, and of how she had longed to be back in that dreadful school for the sake of the brief moments passing through London when she had felt part of Helena's, Polly's or Calypso's lives, with news of Oliver, glimpses of the twins, moments with Max, talk of Hector, a feel of belonging, of being part of the group which had dined on the lawn on one of the last days of August 1939, sitting round a table lit by candles, with the moon rising over the sea.

I was alone then, she thought. I'm alone now. Oliver, bane of my life.

THIRTY-FOUR

"Curious that they have both died in that house." Helena had not spoken for some miles, Hamish thinking her asleep.

"Who, what both?" he blurted in surprise.

"My husband Richard, my lover Max are 'both'." Helena's accent was tart. "I sold it to Max after Richard died. I am said to have smothered him with a pillow. It has become folk lore. I wasn't sorry when he died, though."

"Oh." Hamish had heard the legend. "Oh." He felt uncomfortable.

"I could not have smothered him, I was in London with Max. Richard smothered me until I bought my present houses. Sound investment, though not thought so at the time. I paid two thousand pounds for the two."

"It's unbelievable. As little as that?"

"Richard said they were jerry built. They will last me out." Helena paused, thinking of her houses. "I like risks," she said. "Polly's was hit by a doodle bug, only her bed survived. Your mother was caught in a raid, too."

"So she tells me. Brought on her labour."

"She can be boring about it. She had Sophy with her to make herself useful. One could say she was the midwife."

"I never knew that." Hamish thought, I must remember to quiz mother about Sophy being there. Helena may be inventing.

"If anyone smothered Richard it would have been Sophy. She was with him when he died."

"Why on earth should she?" Hamish was surprised at the amount of ill feeling the old woman could arouse.

"Richard wasn't what you'd call safe with little girls, though I thought at the time Monika had weaned him. Perhaps she had, perhaps I am wrong about Sophy." Helena stared thoughtfully at the road ahead. "Mind you, she was secretive as a child, still is. When Richard died she was in her teens, revenge perhaps. Something odd happened in the early days of the war." She paused then went on, "Well, what does it matter, it's so long ago. I was busy with Max. Falling in love left me no room for anything else. You wouldn't know, perhaps."

Oh, wouldn't I, thought Hamish, grimly remembering Sophy's body, silky hair, slant-eyed tenderness. What a bloody old woman Helena is, he thought. What possessed me to come to this funeral anyway?

Helena was speaking again. "I may be wrong. At the time nobody else thought so, it was only a hunch so—"

"What was only a hunch?" Curious in spite of himself, Hamish questioned his passenger.

"Just that one of the coastguards fell over the cliff. I wondered whether Sophy might have pushed him."

"Jesus Christ!"

"Not Jesus Christ. Sophy. It was only an idea. The child had some sort of seizure. I thought if she'd given the man a push it would account for it. Then Max and Monika were interned and of course one couldn't think of anything else." Helena laughed her old person's laugh. "The war kept us all busy, even if we didn't actually take up arms like your dear father and all those boys, Oliver, Walter, David and Paul, beautiful young men. Oldish now, of course, except Walter who had no time to deteriorate."

"But Sophy—" Hamish betrayed himself, Helena noted.

"Sophy was much younger. Far too shy to push anyone over anything. That I even thought such a thing shows the state war got us into, not that I didn't enjoy the war, I would be a liar to deny it. Sophy wouldn't hurt a fly," said Helena with force, not wishing to hurt Hamish, Calypso's son. "Sophy had a vein of something which attracted people. Even before her sort of looks became *comme-il-faut* Max was—"

"Max?" Hamish was unaware of the jealousy in his voice but Helena noted it, confirming her suspicion that Hamish loved Sophy. I must not be garrulous, she admonished herself.

"Max was fond of the child, said she would have a success with some types of men."

"Did he really?" Hamish felt relief. Helena smiled. Not you, my lad, I shall not tell you what I never told anybody, that I found black asiatic hairs in my bed and minded when I never minded any of the other women. She cried out, sitting in Hamish's car on her way to Max's funeral.

"I *mind*! God, how I *mind*!" Helena's voice was strong.

"What?" He felt her pain embarrassing.

"Max dying." She sighed, lying.

"Let's see if we can find violets," Hamish said, repenting his anger, but Helena's grief was not to be assuaged.

She said bitterly: "Just because I am very old does not mean I have forgotten about loving."

Hamish drove on in sulky silence, wishing that curiosity to see something of his mother's contemporaries had not lured him to come to the funeral.

"I trust this performance will not be the most fearful cock-up," said Helena, using an expression that had been a favourite of Max's, who had learned it from the twins. "Cock-up," she said, looking at Hamish's profile, "was one of his expressions."

"Whose?" Hamish felt he would never get used to his passenger's use of the English language.

"Max's. He was so keen to learn English slang. He learned 'cock-up' and 'pull your finger out' from David and Paul and used them in the wrong context."

"When was that?"

"In bed. I never undeceived him. I overheard a woman at one of his concerts tell a friend with considerable indignation that he had lured her into bed then said, 'This is a cock-up, isn't it.' Ah-ha-ha-ha." Helena laughed merrily. "He tried so hard to be English. Ah-ha-ha-ha."

Glancing at Helena Hamish suddenly saw the years fall away. "You sound as though you had fun."

"We did, we did, a lot of fun. Max and I, Max and Monika, Monika and I. We had many a good laugh."

"I've never understood Monika's attitude," said Hamish, who held the rather puritanical views of some cradle Catholics.

"Quite simple," said Helena. "We were fond of each other. Once Monika took to country life she reigned in Cornwall. I was his town wife. We travelled with him in turns. It wasn't anyone's business but ours. After Richard died it worked very well. When poor Monika died I carried on. Max needed two women just as Polly—"

"Polly?"

"I was going to say needed two men. She was greedy, she wanted, got and kept the twins. My word, if you'd seen her as a girl!"

"What was she like?"

"Pretty, reserved. Gave the impression she was conventional, that no one should dare question her life. On the whole nobody did. Her sheer effrontery silenced her critics and gained the admiration of her peers. It came in useful when she decided to have James and Iris."

"Do you know which twin is Iris or James' father? I often wonder."

"I presume they do too. I have never asked because I do not think Polly knows herself." Helena laughed her ah-ha-ha-ha laugh, appreciating Richard's niece Polly, and added, "It worked, it still does. There you are, dear boy, two cases of it takes three to make a marriage. Why don't you try it?" she asked cheerfully.

"The Church, my upbringing."

"None of us allowed our upbringing to interfere with our mode of life."

"Well—"

"Your nurse Catherine! Your mother! My! My! Your mother converted to annoy your father, who had lapsed. Then, like Saint Paul when he fell off his horse or whatever he did, found she liked it. Your father was flummoxed."

"He didn't mind."

"He was like putty in her hands."

"He adored her. They had awful rows," said Hamish, remembering his childhood.

"When he was drunk, only when he was drunk. He blacked her eye."

"My mother can't have liked that." Hamish was shocked.

"You'd be surprised what people put up with when they are in love."

"Are you suggesting my mother was in love with my father?" Hamish's tone of disbelief delighted Helena.

"Of course she was. She never let on."

"My God!" Hamish whispered. "My God!"

"Why do you imagine she never remarried?" Helena left her question to penetrate Hamish's mind. I can't bear dense men, she thought, how can I endure life without Max? She fumbled in her bag for her flask and unscrewed the cap. After drinking she said in a new tone of voice: "If you see a suitable pub please stop, so that I can refill my flask and go to the lavatory."

"And if I die in the attempt I shall find you violets." Hamish felt a surge of gratitude towards Helena for her betrayal of Calypso. "I won't tell her you told me," he said.

416

"Much better not," Helena agreed, casting her mind back to the return of Hector, escaped from his POW camp in Italy, and Calypso's efforts to conceal her joy.

"She tries to protect herself, *unsere* Calypso," Max had told her. "She pretends she cannot love, it is her camouflage."

"If your father had not loved your mother so helplessly he would have returned to the Church," said Helena thoughtfully.

"How come? I'm not with you."

"It would have changed her idea of him, he couldn't risk that."

"If I fail to find violets what other flowers did Max like?"

"We will find violets," said Helena, liking Hamish, Calypso's son, who reminded her of Hector, his father. Then, feeling warmth for Hamish, she said: "As you know, your mother had quite a reputation for sleeping around." Hamish winced. "But I never heard a whisper after your father came back from the war. Max said she stopped looking at any other man because she found she had the best of both worlds."

"When she joined the Church?"

"Tcha! She married the world of money, found it held a world of love. The Church was for you, I imagine, as much as for Hector. Let's call it a sauce."

"My parents being the goose and the gander?"

"There's a pub about a mile ahead, we can stop there," said Helena. "Your Church had a thumping Requiem Mass for your father when he died. I went with Max and Monika – most impressive. Calypso manoeuvred it. You were there, quite a nice little boy, same hair as your father's."

"I can't think that there was any manoeuvre," said Hamish defensively. "The Church isn't like that."

"But Calypso is." Helena snapped her bag shut as they drew up at the pub. "Oh, look," she said, "that's Polly's car. She's driving Iris and James down. Hoot."

Hamish obediently tooted his horn, pulling in beside Polly's car. James came out of the pub.

"Hullo," he said, kissing Helena's cheek as she got out of the car. "Mother and Iris are in the loo."

"Good." Helena drew herself up straight. "Get this filled." She handed her flask to Hamish. "I like Vat 69. We can all arrive together."

Hamish and James watched her enter the pub.

"She's got hollow legs," said Hamish.

"We wondered whether there would be anything to eat. We stocked up at that mini-Fortnums in Tavistock. We spent the night there." James was amicable.

"Great-aunt Helena has been reminiscing," said Hamish.

"So has Mother." James grinned. "That is what happens at funerals."

"Any cats out of bags?"

"Not exactly, more a tiny clarification." James walked with Hamish into the pub. "About our backgrounds."

"Our stable backgrounds," said Hamish. "What will you drink?"

"Nothing, thanks, I'm driving the last lap."

Hamish ordered himself a whisky and asked the barman to fill Helena's flask with Vat 69.

"Considering our backgrounds," said James, "yours and ours, I'd say we were remarkably stable."

"What are you on about?" Hamish was not particularly fond of James, preferring his sister who had tact.

"We have two fathers, you have none," James asserted with pride.

"I had one to start with." Hamish was huffy. "He died. They weren't divorced or anything. Yours never married your mother."

"How could they?" said James angrily.

"Now, now," Iris had come up behind them. "For God's sake, let well alone. The less we disentangle relationships the better. You forget I am married and have two small children who will soon be asking questions."

Hamish laughed, for indeed he forgot Iris was married and had two children, her husband and style of life being so respectable and happy no attention was ever attracted.

"And what shall you tell them?" Hamish sipped his drink, smiling at Iris, who was less beautiful than her mother, far less beautiful than Calypso.

"I don't think they are going to be interested," said Iris, "it's all so long ago. We are only interested on occasions like this when the funeral stirs up Mother's memories."

"And Helena's," said Hamish.

"Yes, I daresay. Poor old thing, but when she's gone—" her voice trailed.

"There's my mother, there's Sophy, your – er – your fathers. Are they coming, by the way?"

"They may not be back in time, they are in Vichy. I don't think they can make it."

Hamish remembered that Paul and David seldom turned up at family gatherings, using their arthritis as an excuse.

THIRTY-FIVE

Pauli Erstweiler drove up to the house in his Mercedes. He slammed the door of his car. Sophy heard his heavy steps in the hall. He paused by the hall table then went to look at his father, who had been in England while he, Pauli, had been in the concentration camp. She could feel Pauli's bitterness sweep into the house with him, wrap its icy silence round her like a shroud. She shrank back into the nearest room and stood behind the door. She heard his heavy tread come down the stairs, heard him lift the telephone, dial, speak, ordering the undertaker to close the coffin. Then: "Thank you. *Ja, Ja.* Two-thirty tomorrow. What?" He listened. "Yes, yes, the house will be for sale. Do you know of a buyer? Tomorrow then, thank you, tomorrow will do," his heavy accent.

He went into the drawing-room, his tread the tread of ownership. He lifted the lid of the piano, played a few blurred chords with fingers crushed by the camp guards, their music expunged from his life. He let the lid slam and again heavy footsteps to the door, the door opening, slamming shut, the car door slamming, the engine revved, the crunch of tyres, the sound of the wind drowning the sound of the car, rain sheeting against the window.

Poor Pauli, so full of bitterness, she had thought, lying in his arms. How can you love when you are filled with hate?

How could he believe he would have been a musician when he had no love? He had made himself a millionaire, they said, wheeling and dealing in tanks, planes, guns. She went back to stand by Max, lying silent, his music stilled, his grief for Pauli over. There had been such joy over Pauli's survival. She remembered the skeletal young man, Monika and Max's joy turning to fear, pain, sourness.

"He needs love," Monika had said.

"He needs love," Max, too, had said.

"He needs rest," the Floyers had said, "and peace."

"He needs a good smack," Helena had said.

They had watched Pauli grasp at life and use it, careless of the hurt he inflicted, greedy, cruel, selfish, worldly.

"He was a cruel, selfish young man," she said to Max lying in his coffin. "I made a fool of myself trying to wake love in him. Calypso was right when she called him 'the sow's ear'. He is still those things. Calypso when she first met him had said, 'He is not one of us.' Polly had said, 'He is not the Jew the twins fought for,' and Helena sized him up immediately, saying it would have been better for Max and Monika if he had died, leaving them with their memory of him unscarred."

Gently Sophy stroked Max's face with her finger, feeling the cold cheek, the mobile mouth. It would have been better to bury Max without Pauli's arrogant presence.

Made restless by the wind, uneasy by Pauli's abrupt visit, she wandered the house, refurnishing it in her mind as it had been in her childhood. She went up to her bedroom and, looking along the branch of the Ilex tree, she remembered the years when she had dreamed of Oliver, Oliver who loved Calypso. She tried to pin down a time when she had not loved him, or the time she had ceased to love him, and failed. She could not remember when she had last seen him, or where it had been. Long years ago, another life, she thought, moving into Uncle Richard's room. Poor old man, too ill to wipe his tear. Why did I not do it for him, why let him die with a smeared cheek? she reproached herself.

"Sophy." Calypso's clear voice. "Are you still here? Are you mad?"

"I thought I'd better stay with him tonight." Sophy went to meet Calypso on the stairs.

"Morbid, but please yourself. Can you give me a hand? I've brought the booze for tomorrow. Can you help me unload the car?"

Sophy followed Calypso out. "Goodness, champagne."

"He liked bubbly. D'you remember he called it bubbly? D'you remember when we heard Hector was not killed we celebrated?"

"I remember well."

"So I thought," said Calypso, moving towards her car, "we'd have bubbly tomorrow, he'd like that."

"He would."

"Guess who I saw in the town – Pauli."

"He's been here. I hid."

"Don't blame you, he's a right sod. I think he's a changeling.

When you think of Monika and Max you think he can't be theirs."

"Almost."

"Not almost. Quite. Quite not theirs. D'you know – can you carry all that, it's heavy – d'you know he made a pass at me once."

"I slept with him."

"How could you? What *possessed* you?"

Sophy laughed at Calypso's astonished expression. "I thought I'd teach him how to love," she said wryly.

Calypso put down the case she was carrying and let out a shout of laughter. Momentarily she looked as she had long ago before the war. "But darling, you love Oliver, you always did, nobody else ever mattered."

"As a child. How did you know?" Standing in the rain and wind, holding the champagne, Sophy grasped at her privacy, trying to protect it.

"We all knew." Calypso pushed open the front door. "Your enigmatic little face, your eyes. Where shall we put it?"

"In the kitchen." Sophy, carrying the case of champagne, led the way, glad to turn her back on Calypso. "In the larder it's cool, let's put it there."

"Oliver's such an ass. Have you seen him lately?"

"Not for years."

"Both his wives. Awful."

Sophy said, "Are there more cases like this?" wishing to drop the subject of Oliver.

"Yes, in the car. He got over me years and years ago when the penny dropped," Calypso persisted.

"What penny?"

"The penny that said Hector."

"I always knew you loved Hector."

"No, no, not love. He suited me, nobody else did."

"That's your version." Sophy sniffed.

"When we've finished unloading I'm going to take you off to dinner."

"I thought I'd stay the night here."

"Why?"

"Max is all alone. He always needed one of us there."

"Very well, we will have bacon and eggs and I'll keep you company. You can't stay here alone, Pauli might come back. Why d'you think he came?"

"To look at Max. I heard him tell the undertaker to close the coffin and that the house is for sale. It's his now."

"Doesn't let the grass grow. Not that it matters, it will never be the same. I always think of it as Richard and Monika's. In the war when Brian fired the gun."

"Monika and Max's. Latterly Max alone, with Helena visiting."

"Of course, but our roots are on the lawn. D'you think it smells now?"

"Faintly." Sophy smiled at Calypso, glad she had come back.

"Let's finish unloading, then we can have a bottle with our supper. He would approve."

"I don't like leaving him in the dark."

"Candles, then. Electric light wouldn't look right. Wish I had some holy candles."

"The only time he used holy candles was during power cuts. He'd make a dash to the Oratory. Helena was shocked."

"I'm sure the Church wouldn't mind." Calypso rummaged in a cupboard. "Here we are, pity they are red."

"The light is much the same." Sophy took them from her and led the way upstairs. "We'll use the candlesticks we had at his first dinner party here before the war."

"D'you remember that?"

"Yes, the full moon. You held Oliver's hand."

"You noticed?" Calypso laughed.

"And Uncle Richard toasted absent friends, meaning Pauli," said Sophy.

"And the lawn smelt delicious after the heat of the day and Max looked us all over." Calypso struck a match to light the candles.

"Aunt Helena wore a long dress and kicked Uncle Richard when he was tactless about Pauli." Sophy set the candlesticks by Max's head.

"And Monika's eyes were huge as she sat thinking about Pauli left behind in Auschwitz. Why do you think they left him behind?" Calypso, lighting the last candle, stood with the lighted match looking across at Sophy.

"A friend they trusted had sworn he could get him out and send him to join them. It didn't come off. The friend ended in a camp too."

"Ow!" Calypso dropped the match which had burned her fingers. It fell on to Max's chest.

"Look out, you'll set fire to him." Sophy snatched at the match.

"You've singed his suit." She brushed at the dying match.

"Horrid smell, pooh." Calypso blew on her fingers. "Monika was very clever," she said thoughtfully, looking across Max's body at Sophy. "She and Helena ended by adoring each other. Attraction of opposites? Mutual interests? She was clever. Good, too."

"Also artful. When the guinea pig scandal was on she moved into the General's house." Sophy smiled in recollection.

"But he started it, horrid old thing," Calypso exclaimed. "What d'you mean 'moved in'?"

"She packed a small case, walked across the cliffs to his house and put it to him that as the press were on to the story, as an English gentleman it was up to him to protect her, give her asylum."

"Oh my, how crafty."

"She knew and he knew he'd look pretty silly if the press got the story, so he stifled them. I thought it quite fly of Monika."

"I bet Max put her up to it."

"No, no. Max, Helena and Uncle Richard arrived here to find her holed up with the General."

"I never knew."

"No one did. She put him on his mettle to do the English gentleman bit," said Sophy.

"Always putting his arm round our waists for a squeeze. How did you find out?"

"David and Paul's mother. She said she thought it a just punishment for his pro-Nazi views."

"Oh, yes. One forgets." Calypso looked thoughtful. "Used he not to make passes at Monika too?"

"Yes, he did, but never after the guinea pig affair. I wish you could join in this conversation." Sophy looked down at Max. "I don't think the burn will show."

"Let's open a bottle. We'll remember even more after a drink or two." Calypso moved towards the stairs. "If we weren't so old we'd be off on a moonlight run. My goodness," she said, catching hold of Sophy's hand, "we were an ignorant lot in those days."

"Very."

"Who did you sleep with first? Who was your first lover?" Calypso bit her tongue, seeing Sophy's face close blankly shut. "Mine was Hector," she plunged on. "Nobody believed it but Hector was my first, and it didn't take me long to find he was the best, too." She watched Sophy relax warily. "They thought I grew stuck-up when I married, perhaps I did. Being rich went to my head." The danger's passed, she told herself. "Let's crack a bottle," she said, moving down to the harsh light of the kitchen, where she looked quite old but a lot more human since her stroke than the girl on the camomile lawn.

THIRTY-SIX

Too early for the service, Sophy strolled in the churchyard in her green gumboots, the wind whipping her skirt round her knees, her head wrapped in a shawl.

Among the local Penhaligans, Boscences, Penroses, Tremaynes and Tredinnicks she sought the Floyers, Uncle Richard and Monika. She read the Floyers' names, the dates of their births and deaths. Rector of this Parish RIP. Someone had planted the grave with daffodils. In spring they lay under a yellow duvet. Others had planted colchicum. Now, in the rain, the Floyers rested under a shocking pink spread which reached across to neighbouring graves as their spirit had enveloped the parish. Sophy marvelled that they had never criticised or interfered with their sons and Polly. Their acceptance of an unusual situation had silenced waspish tongues as effectively as foam suffocates fire.

Richard Cuthbertson lay apart, his grave planted with spring and autumn cyclamen, fluted pink heads thrusting up through marbled leaves.

"Uncle Richard, salute, and Ducks." Sophy ran her hand over the cool leaves. Richard, tap dancing with the Rectory evacuees round the hot water boiler, had overheated and caught a chill leading to pneumonia and death. "Putting on my top hat—" Where, when the time came, would they put Aunt Helena? It seemed a pity to disturb the cyclamen so well established.

Sophy, holding the shawl close under her chin, observed the pit dug ready for Max, dark earth piled to one side, a pit which already held Monika, now lined with plastic grass. Was there room for three? Sophy suppressed a smile as she walked back past the Penhaligans, Boscences, Penroses, Tremaynes and Tredinnicks. Which among the many Penroses was the Penrose who had not been a proper husband, who had exposed himself to a terrified child, who had fallen or been pushed over the cliff? In the church porch Sophy took the shawl off and shook the rain from it. The lingering memory of a man's shout flipped away with the raindrops as she looked across the fields to the cliffs and the grey Atlantic raging in from the western approaches. Replacing the shawl, Sophy moved into the church, her eyes adjusting to the semi-darkness.

The church was a blaze of colour, red, yellow, pink, orange, dahlias, lilies, chrysanthemums, michaelmas daisies, blue, green, pink and white hydrangeas, stooks of corn, stacks of vegetables, pots of jam, sacks of potatoes, bunches of carrots, vegetable marrows, pots of chutney, baskets of fungi, strings of onions, ropes of garlic, oranges, bananas. Harvest Festival tomorrow.

Outside the wind screamed and battered. The rain slanted vicious rods from bulging clouds. Rainbow weather.

In front of the altar two coffin stools waited to receive Max. Sophy sat at the back of the church to wait the hour. Soon they would all be gathering, the friends, the colleagues, the lovers, the curious, to bury the alien, the refugee, the man who had made this place his own, who had earned the right to rest among them. After nearly fifty years even Monika was forgiven her alien ways, *vide* the ropes of garlic, the baskets of fungi, mute testimony of quasi-acceptance. Sophy sneezed, breathing in the pungent smell of chrysanthemums, the earthy reek of potato sacks. Feeling chilly, she moved to the space under the tower where the bell ringers gathered, and danced a jig to whip up her circulation, her gumboots slapping on the stone floor. When she heard voices in the porch she sat down again, panting, well back in the shadows.

Three or four pressmen gathered, pushing back the hoods of their parkas.

"Won't take long, there's to be a memorial service in London. Only worth a paragraph or two."

"Depends who comes. Won't be many celebrities, this weather."

"Never know. There are two coppers to direct the traffic. I saw several faces in the pub worth a mention."

The village came in twos and threes, middle-aged women with umbrellas, men in sober suits. They sat at the back near Sophy.

"Looks lovely this year." They viewed the harvest decorations with pride.

"I see Lorna Tremayne's put three jars of her pickle by the font. That's not like her."

"She'll take un back after service. She'm so mean she won't

give you the drips off her nose if so be you might want them."

"Parson will have to look sharp if he wants 'em for the hospital."

"Mrs Floyer always made a list, no flies on Mrs Floyer. New parson needs a wife."

"He'm too high. Higher than High Floyer ever was."

"Ah. Miss them when they're gone, new chap don't seem to have what it takes." The voices dropped to an inaudible whisper and suppressed laughter shook the row.

More footsteps in the porch. The pressmen asked for names. A posse of well-wrapped women followed by their consorts in overcoats and hats, pausing a moment to give their names to the press, then moving in to find a seat, settle their haunches, look around, wave discreetly to friends, admire the Harvest Festival flora, peer at the vegetables.

A group of young people carrying musical instruments came in a shy rush, the girls tossing back long hair, the young men ill at ease in formal clothes.

"His master-class," said a well-informed woman in front of Sophy.

"There's to be music then. Ah."

Polly, followed by Iris and James. How fat Polly had grown; she looked funny wearing a brown hat, handing James her umbrella to shake, settling with her son and daughter in the third row from the front.

An elderly man, rather shaky on his pins, with a large healthy consort. Sophy recognised Brian Portmadoc. Another vaguely familiar figure, hair trained from a low parting to cover his baldness, asking fussily, "Where shall we sit? Which side shall we go?" By his voice Sophy knew him. Tony Wood, brave fireman, true friend.

"Doesn't matter, it isn't a wedding, sit where we can. Here will do." Tony's friend: he had finally settled for a male lover. They ran an antique shop in Brighton.

Two identical figures, bald heads with a frill of white hair, both paunchy, both lame, both heavy on their feet. They looked about them, spotted Polly, Iris and James. Polly looked up and waved.

"I didn't know you were coming." Polly looked delighted, smiling her contagious toothy smile.

"Move along a bit. We came by train. You'll have to sit in the next row, James." Inflexion of parental affection.

428

"No, no, it's all right, nicer all together." Affection there, too.

"Bit of a squeeze." Paul sat down smiling.

"How was Vichy?" Iris welcoming.

"Did you do anything about a wreath?" David vaguely anxious.

"Of course I did. Shush . . ."

People came in a steady stream. The young musicians put up their music stands, one or two notes tentatively played on the organ, a scrape on a violin, a twang from a cello. Sophy, breathing in the damp smell of autumn flowers, dreamed of camomile, the dry aromatic smell of her youth. In the porch the pressmen stood aside to allow Helena, wafting into the church in an aura of whisky, to walk steadily up the aisle to the front pew, where she sat alone on the left hand side close to the coffin stools. The whispering in the church stopped; all eyes were on Helena, boring into her back. Swiftly behind her Calypso in white overcoat, black hat, gloves, stockings and shoes, her lovely face composed, Hamish beside her lightly holding her elbow. They sat immediately behind Helena. Hamish leant forward to put a cardboard box beside her. Helena nodded her thanks.

The church was full, every pew filled except for the front pews, where Helena sat on the left, the right-hand pew empty, waiting for the chief mourner.

Above the whispers of the congregation the wind bumped and buffeted the church, whining round the finials on the tower, growling over the lead roof. Helena took the flask from her bag, unscrewed the top, tipped a liberal swig into her mouth, swallowed. "Shall I ever be warm again—"

The congregation stood. Slow steps on the gravel path grated.

"*I am the resurrection and the life, saith the Lord—*"

The new parson's bass voice, carrying through the gale, led the coffin up the path to the church. The newsmen drew aside as he stood for a moment in the porch, a giant wearing a black cloak billowing out in the wind to display its red lining.

"*We brought nothing into this world and it is certain we can carry nothing out*".

The words rolled out in splendid cadence.

"You carry my love," Helena muttered mutinously, and Calypso drew in her breath while Hamish glanced quickly at her, wondering whether his mother prayed and what her prayers might be. She always looked particularly beautiful in church.

"I mind, God how I mind." Helena watched them steady the

coffin on to the stools. She did not hear the Rector's sonorous voice, she did not listen to the service or the music played by Max's pupils. Max's spirit was not in the coffin, far too ornate, chosen by Pauli, Pauli who had followed the coffin into the church and now sat across the aisle alone in the right hand pew. How could he be Max's son, how could he have been conceived by Monika, so lovely, so sweet, so good without being boring? Helena turned to stare at Pauli, who looked ahead. What business deal was he dreaming up, this financial wizard spawned by Max? "I bet you are never frivolous in bed," Helena muttered, for yes, it may have taken time, but she and Max had had many laughs. "What shall I do without his jokes?" her old heart cried.

The service rolled inexorably on. Automatically Helena stood, knelt, sat and behind her, her mind straying as it always did at Mass, Calypso thought of food and sex and of Hector. The texture of his skin, his nutty smell, his laughter, his passion, his rages. Max had made jokes too. Briefly she paid attention. Max would enjoy the sight of Helena and Polly, Sophy hiding at the back of the church and herself attending his funeral and goodness knows, thought Calypso, how many more of us in here lay with him. Hector always said Max would impregnate this corner of Cornwall with a shot of musical spunk. She wished she could in decency lean forward and ask Helena for a swig from that flask. She took Hamish's hand and squeezed it, enjoying his quick smile, so like Hector's.

"Soon be over."

"Yes."

Helena was glaring at Pauli, Pauli risen from the dead to hate, make money, hate again, make more money. He had no love for Monika and Max, no understanding and, quite extraordinarily, no music. Max, unable to understand his lost son found again, had wept and Monika had nearly thrown herself over the cliffs, blaming herself for the accidents of fate.

"Not again, *mein Schatz*, you cannot do it twice. For the guinea pig was enough."

Helena smiled broadly at the parson, remembering Max's voice, the easing of tension, the laughter. Without being drunk I could not get through this, she thought.

The parson, seeing her broad grin, hesitated in mid flow, missed a beat but carried on bravely, glad that his training enabled him to perform without much thought. He was glad too that he had put on warm socks. It would be cold by the grave.

How Helena hates Pauli, thought Calypso. How could Sophy have slept with him? Wish she had married Hamish, being older wouldn't have mattered. The trouble with Sophy was that she thought a bit of love was a cure-all. What was it Hector said? "She's deliberately wasting her gifts." Oh Hector, my darling, you did not waste yours, the woods you planted spell my name in spring. I wonder whether Pauli has provided any food to soak up my champagne. I should have thought of it sooner, not in the middle of the service. Her reverent expression pleased the Rector, who looked past Helena, resting his eye on Calypso with approval. Wonder what he's like in bed, thought Calypso from force of habit. Did parsons need a little boost, as Max had before rehearsal? How he laughed in the cinema. What had been the film? She frowned, trying to remember.

"Was Max a Protestant?" Hamish whispered as they knelt.

"Haven't the foggiest," Calypso whispered behind clasped hands. "He must have been born something."

"If he was a Catholic this is all wrong."

"Too late now. Shut up."

"I'll ask Helena. Helena," he leant forward, his head on a level with Helena's as she sat in front of him, having found that kneeling hurt. "Aunt Helena, was Max a Protestant or a Catholic?"

"Jew. Why do you ask?" Helena's voice rang clear.

"This funeral service. Surely—"

"Not practising. He didn't practise religion, only the violin. Women too, of course."

"Hush," whispered Hamish.

"You started it, hush yourself." Helena stood up as the choir prepared to sing.

"O God our help in ages past."

She cleared her throat, recognising the words. There would not be many more ages, she thought with satisfaction, as she picked up the cardboard box and prepared to follow the coffin to the grave. He never minded that I am tone deaf, she consoled herself, he thought it funny.

Oliver, drenched from his long walk from the station, wished he had not come. First the shock of finding Penzance harbour, where water had always lapped in greeting by the train, filled in to form a car park. Now, arriving late, crushed in the crowd at the back of the church, having to endure the spectacle of Polly grown fat and stodgy, flanked by children who must be at least thirty. Calypso, squired by a younger version of Hector, looking so preserved. Preserved for what? He had heard she had had a stroke. She looked trim, *"tiré à quatre épingles"*, the epitome of everything he disliked: classy bitch preserved in money. Well, that was what she had wanted, she had been honest about it. What a fool one was in youth. And there the twins, couldn't be anyone else. Those godlike giants grown stout, bald, lame. Probably had piles, all pilots had piles he had heard. Couldn't put that in his novel, not very well. Well, why not, anything goes these days. Stupid idea, though, to think he'd get copy from Max's funeral. Funerals in books and plays were *vieux jeux*. That fearfully old woman, could it be Helena? Must be, must be about a hundred, mummified, what a survivor and glaring at that fellow in the other pew. Pauli, of course. Pauli risen from the heap. Well, I never, so that's Pauli. Well! Oliver remembered Max telling him of his own and Monika's dodgy escape from the Nazis and the dismal failure of Pauli's expected follow-on. "We shall always feel guilty. We shall always feel we should have died with him." Well, he hadn't died. That looked like a vicuna coat. Do people still wear vicuna coats? I must check, though none of my characters wears that sort of clobber. Oliver gingerly moved his legs in their damp cord trousers, hunched his shoulders in his heavy storm-proof parka, wished he'd put on another sweater. The woman in front of him wearing gumboots, with a shawl round her head sneezed. She wasn't dressed like all these respectables. None of them wore gumboots. High-heeled leather boots, plastic boots towards the back here with zips. No, no good for the novel, thought Oliver, so I'll sit back and enjoy the music when it comes. Those pupils of Max look ready to play their hearts out, not that one would hear very well with the bloody gale blowing.

"What are they going to play?" he asked a neighbour. "D'you know?"

"Mozart, I believe, and Bach while they go to the grave. We could move up the church when the front pews empty."

"Thanks." Oliver realised he had not been attending to the service. A white-haired man was finishing the reading:

"—and all the trumpets sounded for him on the other side."

Oliver felt furious. Trumpets. How did they know? How outrageous! They are fooling us, how do they dare think of trumpets? There is earth. I saw it in Spain. I saw it in the desert, earth, earth, no bloody trumpets, just holes in the ground. I don't write these illusions, I write about uncomfortable things, that's what

432

sells. Oliver felt a jet of pleasure douse his bitterness, glad that from callow boy he had evolved to successful writer.

The church part of the service was ending, the splendid parson in his theatrical cloak preparing to lead Max out to his grave. It would soon be possible to move up closer to hear the music. Oliver, looking over his half-moon spectacles, watched the procession form, Pauli behind the coffin, broad, plump, Monika's eyes, lardy cheeks, no trace of Max's whippy body or humorous face. Helena shrunken, all her weight in the middle, carrying a cardboard box, her blue eyes vague, hair faded to dust colour. Calypso in vivid white coat, eyes shaded by black hat, Hamish a new version of Hector. The twins stoutly limping with sticks and their middle-aged children. Polly in spectacles, her hair a sort of quasi-henna. Elizabeth, surely that woman was the girl Elizabeth who had loved Walter and married Brian Portmadoc. Walter would laugh at this crew. And there Brian talking to Tony Wood, must be, couldn't be anyone else, and all these people, who were they? Where did they come from? Oliver felt hysterical laughter rise in his chest as the procession passed him. Soon he would be soothed by violins and cellos. A man he recognised as probably the best music critic in the business laid his hand on Helena's arm.

"Dear Helena. Just to say I am so sorry that Max, that – so sorry about Max's death."

"There's a lot of it about." Helena focused old eyes on the man for an instant and walked steadily out into the porch. Calypso, Hamish and the twins closed round her. Forgetting the violins and cellos Oliver followed the little group, pushing his spectacles further up his nose, pulling his collar round his ears. The rain had stopped and shafts of afternoon sun struggled through the hasty black clouds.

"There will be a rainbow." A boy's voice broke through the sound of shuffling feet.

"Mind where you put your feet, never mind the rainbow." An anxious mother snatched at her son as he trampled on to wreaths and sheaths of expensive flowers heaped near the path by undertakers' minions, their beauty blinded by cellophane wrapping. "You clumsy lout."

The woman in gumboots sneezed despairingly, "Aaachoo, aaachoo."

"D'you need a handkerchief?" Oliver offered.

"Got one, thanks."

They were lowering Max into that bosom of green plastic.

"Man that is born of woman hath but a short time to live."

Good Lord, thought Oliver, the sneezer is Sophy. What a surprise.

"—whom may we seek for succour but of—"

When had he last seen Sophy? Years and years. He racked his brain. She sneezed again, pressing her handkerchief over her nose to drown the sound. The parson's rich voice rolled on and from the church a burst of Mozart.

"—I heard a voice from heaven saying unto me 'Write'—"

All very well, thought Oliver, saying "Write" like that. Writing is damned hard work without voices from heaven interfering. And now the Lord's Prayer. Oliver muttered with others, resenting as he always did the "Lead us not into temptation" bit. If God were God, supposing he existed, he wouldn't do a thing so damn stupid.

"—The grace of—"

Oliver looked across the grave at Helena. What was she up to? What was that box?

"Be with us all evermore. Amen."

"Amen," said Calypso and Hamish, crossing themselves. Of course, he'd heard she'd gone over to Rome, old Hector was some sort of Papist.

"Amen." Helena opened the cardboard box and with a hand bony and veiny with age, mottled with brown death marks, began dropping its contents into the grave: violets, their scent, as they fell down on to the coffin, filling the wet air.

Hamish and the twins threw token clods of earth then followed Calypso and Polly, who walked slowly on either side of Helena to shake hands with the parson in his cloak, and wander towards the cars.

Oliver came up behind Sophy, took hold of her elbow.

"Can you give me a lift?"

"Of course." Sophy looked at Oliver, startled, her oriental eyes taking him in, stooped, thinning hair, spectacles, very tall, very thin, wet, perfectly recognisable.

"I walked from Penzance." He held her arm.

"A long way." She moved away from him.

"They've filled in the harbour," he said angrily.

"Yes. A very long time ago."

Pauli standing by the gate. Impossible to avoid him.

"Sophy. You will come back to the house, of course." A command.

"Well – I—" Sophy looked distressed.

"You must come. Calypso has provided drinks, Polly food."

"This is Oliver Anstey."

"I have of course heard of you. You will come too. Helena will be there, I suppose—" Pauli had authority, confidence.

"Yes, we'll come." Sophy walked quickly to her car, followed by Oliver.

"He looks so pleased," she burst out.

"What Uncle Richard would call a bounder."

"The camp *didn't* do him good." Sophy burst into nervous giggles. "Oh my God, my feet are freezing. I must change my shoes." She pulled off her boots and sought shoes. "They're on the back seat. Oh, thanks."

Oliver stared at her. "You haven't changed. All the others—"

"We've grown old." She was keeping her distance.

"It's not that, it's—"

"Aunt Helena is drunk, we'd better get to the house." She started the engine. "I think I've caught a cold."

"I noticed you sneeze."

"Inviting her to her own house—"

"Is it still hers?"

"She sold it to Max years ago but she was constantly here. She just happened to be in London when he died."

"So it's not Pauli's?"

"Technically, but—"

"What?"

"He doesn't belong. Max was ours, not Pauli's."

"You don't like him?"

"I don't think he likes us." Sophy stalled the engine. "Damn."

"Listen." Oliver put a hand on her arm. "Roll down the window."

A lull in the storm, a burst of sound from the church as violins and cello reached their climax. Oliver put a finger to catch the tear rolling down Sophy's cheek.

He licked his finger. "How salt your tears are." She started the engine and drove following the procession of cars. "I suppose we have to go to this wake."

"I want to see that Aunt Helena is all right." Sophy was anxious.

"Aunt Helena is made of sterner stuff than us, she's tone deaf. D'you know," Oliver leant back in his seat, stretching his legs, "a friend of mine watched her read the whole of *War and Peace* during a performance of *The Ring*."

"Bully for her. Where on earth shall I park? I'd no idea so

many people would come. Look at all those cars." Sophy sounded desperate.

"Leave it here. Let's walk." Oliver was calm.

They left the car by the side of the road and, climbing a stile, approached the house from the cliff path.

"I haven't been here since our last holidays before the war. Where was it we ran?" Oliver peered over the edge.

"The path was wired up during the war and became overgrown. This path is a new one."

"I had vertigo. I was terrified."

"I was frightened too. I ran to show off, to gain attention."

"Let me give you a hand." He helped her up the bank on to the lawn. "Does it still smell?"

"Of course." Her voice was distant. She was looking towards the house. She let go of his hand and he watched her run across the lawn to the French windows, tapping on them for admittance, slipping in, a little dark shadow as James let her in, leaving him outside. Oliver felt a rush of emotion and wondered what it could be. Fear. Am I afraid? he questioned. In which case what am I afraid of? She ran off, she left me. Why the hell did she do that? He stood on the lawn while the wind rose again, lashed him, clouds covered the brief sun and the rain poured down aslant. Hamish opened the French windows and waved a champagne bottle.

"You'll get soaked. Come in, for heaven's sake, come in and have a drink before it's all gone." Hamish had had a few drinks and his careful nature was expanding.

"Is Sophy married?" Oliver peeled off his wet anorak.

"Good Lord, no, of course not. Not for want of—"

"I wondered. I've been abroad so long I'm out of touch. Oh, thanks." Oliver accepted a glass thrust into his hand by a stranger.

"I'm a great admirer of yours. I've read all your books." Hamish beamed at Oliver, pinning him against the window. "I suppose you can't come home because of tax—"

"Tax?"

"Income tax." Hamish still beamed.

"I'm not that kind of a writer. Surprised you can read." Feeling suddenly hurt, Oliver wished to wound. "Are you Calypso's son?"

"Yes. Yes I am." Hamish looked wounded.

Oliver felt perverse pleasure. "Saw your father run over by a tank in the war. Didn't kill him, though. I was upset at the time, seems a joke now. I liked your father, a man of imagination. When Calypso married him I thought, we all thought—"

"Thought what?" Hamish stared at Oliver through an alcoholic haze. The rush of champagne on an empty stomach was having a malign effect.

"We thought she was wrong to marry for money."

Hamish aimed a blow at Oliver and hit the curtain beside him. As he strove to regain his balance Oliver put out a hand to steady him.

"Now, now, what's going on?" Calypso appeared beside them. "Are you two squabbling? Can't have that."

"He said—" Hamish tried to speak.

"I said you married for money," said Oliver.

"So I did." Calypso spoke lightly. "Wisest thing I ever did. Married for money. *Then* fell in love." She looked from Oliver to Hamish.

"Why did you never tell me?" Hamish suddenly roared at his mother. "Why did you keep it so bloody secret? Why did you never let on? Why did you let me suffer?"

"You are drunk. Go and eat something oily, you are making an exhibition." She waved Hamish away. "Have you got any children, Olly?"

"No."

"But you married."

"Twice."

"Twice. Goodness, I'd forgotten. Are you married now?"

"No." Oliver's eyes searched the room.

"Are you happy?" She watched him. He looked lean but had worn well.

"Are you?" His eyes came back to her face. "What's happened to your face?"

"I had a little stroke. Yes, thanks, I am happy. Well, as happy as it's possible to be. Where do you live?"

"Abroad." Oliver was noncommittal.

"All right, don't tell me."

"Polly's grown very fat and respectable."

"Spread. She's happy too—"

"Who is the father of—"

"James and Iris? I've never asked. Why don't you? We don't dare." Leaving him apart Calypso moved back into the crowd, most of whom now held glasses of champagne. Oliver stood by the window watching the pattern of the party, two moving circles, the nearest moving up to and round Pauli, greeting, not lingering. The second circling round Helena sitting in an arm-chair, Polly and her children posed protectively, filtering, without seeming to, the guests who wished to speak to her. Calypso in white moving through the crowd. Corks popping and laughter from the kitchen where the twins opened bottles to fill glasses carried on trays by the young musicians who, offering with shy smiles, received congratulations on their performance, thanked with the kindness of youth the compliments of the old.

"Fancy you turning up." Tony Wood shook Oliver's hand. "Remember me, Tony Wood? We first met on the doorstep of Polly's house."

"Yes, I remember." Time had done something terrible to Tony Wood.

"We've all changed, of course. Old age has crept up on us." Tony noticed Oliver's expression with malicious pleasure.

"Yes, indeed."

"Have you seen Sophy? Helena wants her." Iris kindly enquiring.

"No." Oliver realised that what his eye sought was Sophy. "She was here. We came back from the church together."

"Oh, did you?" Tony Wood's bright eyes investigated. "What an exquisite girl child she was, one almost—"

"Almost?"

"Succumbed. Ah, here you are, have you met Peter? Peter and I have a shop in Brighton, antiques and objets. Peter, this is Oliver Anstey, you love his books."

"Do I, darling?" pouting at Oliver.

"Yes, you do. What about another drink and some of that lovely nosh Polly brought?" Peter allowed himself to be led away by Tony. Oliver elbowed his way after them through the crowd. "Didn't think then you'd become a writer." Tony looked at Oliver over his shoulder.

"Didn't think you'd turn into an elderly poof."

"Oh, screw you." Tony let out a high gleeful laugh.

Oliver paused to listen to Pauli, who had succeeded in button-holing a stranger.

"If I add a wing for a restaurant and build a pool it will sell very well as an hotel in this situation."

"Oh," said the stranger. Oliver stopped to listen. "Of course."

"My father's name will attract people. He had his master-classes here, you know."

"Yes, very wonderful."

Pauli waved his twisted fingers. "As I say, the situation above the sea is unique now the National Trust try to buy the whole coast. One heats the pool, it goes without saying."

"Of course," the man agreed, smiling.

Oliver thought the man did not look like a friend of Max. Was Pauli merging business with funeral meats?

"Dig up the lawn, pave it with those warm-coloured slabs, have a terrace." Pauli gestured out towards the lawn saturated and discoloured by the storm.

"Put fake plastic chairs and tubs of flowers." Oliver shouldered into the conversation. "Something that doesn't smell."

"Admirable suggestion," Pauli thanked him, "and of course garages, a sauna, haute cuisine, it goes without saying. One gets planning permission."

"It will make a nice property," said the man. "How much are you thinking of asking?" He refrained from looking Pauli in the eye, glancing casually out at the water-logged lawn.

"I must cost it." Pauli was thoughtful.

Oliver moved to join another group, thinking he must say goodbye to Helena, feeling sickened, wanting to leave.

"Has anyone seen Sophy?" Polly's voice, not much changed.

"It's getting late. Helena wants her before she leaves. I can't see her anywhere."

"I'll look upstairs." Oliver ran up the stairs two at a time.

Sophy was standing by the window of what had once been her bedroom, looking out through the branches of the Ilex tree which shivered and creaked in the gale.

"Sophy, Helena wants you," he said harshly.

"What does she want?" Sophy looked likely to take flight.

"Are you leaving tonight?" He came close to her, moving slowly, as though she were a nervous animal.

"Yes, very soon." She moved towards the door. "Why are you here? You were not at the other funerals." She was wary.

"I thought I'd get some ideas for the book I'm writing. It was stupid of me." She hadn't grown much, he thought, compared with the other girls. She was a very small woman. "Why are you up here?"

She looked away from him. "I used to climb along that branch."

"In your pyjamas, and eavesdrop."

She glanced at him sidelong. "What does Helena want?"

"You jumped down and I caught you. Will you give me a lift? I came by train. We could have a meal at the Red Lion in Truro." He followed her on to the landing.

"They've pulled it down. It's gone." She sped down the stairs.

"Oh no!" He hurried after her in distress.

"Oh yes." She had reached the hall.

"Pauli is going to dig up the lawn." He caught her arm.

"It belongs to him now." Her voice was expressionless. "You should not have come back," she said, looking at him with pain. "It's worse for you."

"The lovely harbour's been turned into a bloody great car park." Oliver's anger grasped at lesser sorrows. "We used to step off the train and hear the water slopping against the quay."

"I know, I know." Gently, she took his hand away from her arm. "I must go to Helena."

"She planted the lawn." He gripped her arm again.

"I know, I know. Please, Oliver—" She turned and went swiftly to find Helena, slipping through the crowd like an eel.

"What do you want me for?"

Helena gripped her hand. "Listen, Sophy, bend down close." Helena spoke urgently into Sophy's ear. Oliver, joining them, heard her say, "Promise you'll do that for me."

"Of course I will. Have you told your lawyer, put it in writing?"

"Of course I have. I'm not senile yet. I hope to die first."

"That's all right, then." Sophy stayed close to Helena, surrounded by Polly, David, Paul, Iris and James.

"What's the secret? Don't keep moving away, you used not to be so elusive."

"She wants her ashes dug into Max and Monika's grave."

"Good Lord." Oliver was taken aback.

"It seems reasonable."

"What about Uncle Richard?"

"He's got his dog, didn't you know? It's what Max and Monika would want. Uncle Richard wouldn't want her."

"Good Lord," said Oliver again.

"It's obvious, it's right. Uncle Richard would be the first to — what are you laughing at?"

"It's so peculiar." Oliver looked at Sophy. "We were such an ordinary lot of people at that dinner party."

"You remember it, too?" she said. "Max's first appearance."

"So conventional," Oliver insisted. "We *were*."

"Calypso's conventional." Sophy spoke defensively.

"What will that splendid parson say?"

"I shan't tell him."

"How then will you manage?"

"I shall be planting rosemary or something on Max and Monika and just pop Helena's ashes in too. No need to say anything or tell anyone, just do it. You can come and help if you like." Sophy was defiant. "*You* used not to be so conventional."

"Oh, but I was, that was my trouble," said Oliver, staring at Sophy, suddenly realising what he had been like as a young man. "If the Red Lion's gone, how about oysters somewhere near the Helford River. We could—"

"I don't know." Sophy was in retreat again, he noticed.

"You don't know what?"

"I don't know anything any more. This was my home. It's gone, it's crumbling away." She looked near tears.

"We'll go somewhere we've neither of us ever been." She was edging away from him. "You are upset." He felt inadequate. Sophy sneezed violently.

"I've caught a chill. I must go."

"I'm coming with you. We can't go before Helena. I'm still conventional enough to know that."

"Poor Helena." Sophy looked distraught. "She's getting up, she's leaving."

Oliver was holding Sophy by the wrist.

"Let go," she whispered.

"No, I won't." He tightened his grip as she twisted to get free.

"You are hurting me."

"No I'm not. Look, she's gathering herself up to go." Oliver held Sophy, who gave in and stood quietly. "Look, she's having a last swig. I didn't know Helena drank. That flask must hold half a bottle."

"She doesn't really drink. This is a special occasion."

"I'll say!" Hamish was standing beside them. "I refilled it on the way down and I found her violets. Wasn't that marvellous? I mean, violets in October! She didn't want anything else for Max." Hamish sounded amiably drunk.

"I will drive Helena." Calypso came up to Hamish. "You had better sit in the back."

"What about my car?" Hamish was truculent.

"I've arranged for your car. You don't want to get breathalysed, do you? Here she comes."

They watched Helena making her progress out of the house.

"Where's your wife?" Sophy snatched her hand free.

"What wife?" Oliver grabbed it back.

"I thought you were married." Sophy, not wishing to make a scene, left her wrist in Oliver's hand.

"I married twice, Calypso look-alikes, neither worked. Haven't been married for years. What about you?"

"No, no." Sophy sounded miserable.

"Lovers?"

"Yes, yes."

"I heard rumours about various—"

"I daresay you did," she said stiffly. Then – "Will you let me go. We aren't children." She twisted her hand.

"Sixty and more, and you?"

"Fifty and more. Oh, look." Her wrist in Oliver's grip, Sophy watched Helena.

Helena's progress was slow. She shook hands or kissed the guests saying, "I am glad you came, it was nice for Pauli. Thank you." She said the same thing to each person so that the words "nice for Pauli" became the most important: "Thank you. Nice for Pauli." She walked quite steadily, flanked by Polly and Calypso, through the crowd of guests all preparing, as she was, to say goodbye to the inheritor, Max and Monika's son, stout, prosperous, able to pull off a business deal in any circumstances, his soul uncluttered by musical nonsense.

Not much nonsense about Pauli, thought Helena, as she reached him and stood looking up into his face.

Holding Sophy's wrist, drawing her close to him, Oliver watched Helena, as did all the guests, making ready to leave, to thank their host, to say goodbye, to condole once again on the loss of his father, to reach their cars, to drive away sighing with relief, to catch their train, to return to normality, to life, to forget this brief interlude until the next, the next funeral, maybe one's own.

Helena was speaking now. It was amazing that such an old woman should have such a clear voice. Her voice in the wet evening air – it had stopped raining, there would a beautiful sunset – carried to all the guests in the house, on the steps, in the drive.

"Goodbye, Pauli, I am sorry—" she hesitated. "I forget what I was going to say," she said, looking at him carefully, searching for some small trace of Max and finding none. She turned away,

assuming vagueness, taking Calypso's arm and walked to the
waiting car.

I am sorry, thought Helena, that so petty a thing as his intention
to dig up the camomile lawn should make me wish he had died
in his concentration camp, never come back, been made into a
lampshade. "I cannot help my thoughts," she said much later to
Calypso. "They rage."

As the guests dispersed a flight of starlings homing to roost
blackened the sky, the sound of their wings muffling all other
sound. Oliver tucked Sophy's hand into his pocket and walked
her to the car.

Watching them go Polly said to the twins, "I hope the old boy
hasn't left it too late."

In Calypso's car Helena turned to Hamish in the back. "Run
after them, dear boy, and give them this." She handed him her
silver flask. "It will help them over those awkward moments."
Then, seeing him hesitate, for his baser nature hankered after the
flask for himself, she added, "And look sharp about it."

So Hamish obediently ran, catching up with Sophy's car as she
started the engine. He watched her drive off without a backward
glance, then plodded back to Calypso and Helena.

Sophy drew into the side of the lane and sat staring ahead.
From time to time she sneezed, her whole body shaken by the
spasms. Oliver watched from the corner of his eye. He felt
immensely tired, drained of anger and resentment.

The funeral guests drove past, their tyres hissing on the wet
road, spattering the windscreen with mud.

Polly, her family all talking at once, the dog barking, a sudden
cacophony of cheerful noise which Oliver took to be their norm
and briefly envied as he watched other cars bearing Max's friends,
colleagues, neighbours. Then Calypso in her white coat glimpsed
in profile driving serenely. Helena beside her, old, exhausted,
spent. Hamish on the back seat, mouth slightly open, face blank.

Finally Pauli's Mercedes nipping along, lights on, indicators
blinking, horn sounding in frenetic haste. Then the procession
was over, leaving the sound of the wind, the sea in the distance,
gulls crying, fresh rain tapping on the glass.

Oliver looked at Sophy's profile, tiny face, high cheekbones,
immense black eyes, full mouth. She threw up her nose to sneeze,
her thin fingers clutching the steering wheel, a tear forced from
the corner of her eye.

"Oh." She laid her head on her hands on the wheel. "Oh my God." He counted white hairs among the black, observed the wrinkles round her eyes and mouth. Picking up Helena's flask he unscrewed the cap, swallowed a mouthful of whisky and said: "You?"

"No, no thank you." She did not look at him.

"Once," he said, staring ahead at the empty road, "you hid behind the curtains of the red room and I took you to bed to warm you. You smelt of soap. Rather nice soap. I wonder what it was."

"Rose geranium." Sophy turned her head away in protest.

"When you were still asleep I put you back in your own bed, d'you remember?"

"No." She shook her head. "No."

"Liar." He gulped some more whisky. "A funny little girl you were."

"Over forty-five years ago," Sophy whispered.

"So now we have whatever's left to catch up. What d'you say to that?"

"We can't." She turned to look at him in despair.

"Why not?" He stared at her, letting her see his thin lined face, receding hair, bright, slightly squinting eyes.

"I am terrified," she said.

"What makes you think I am not afraid too?" Again he offered the flask. "I am just the same inside," he said defiantly, "as I was then." He forbore to say he might be wiser. He wondered whether she would refer to Calypso. She took the flask, tipped it, swallowed a mouthful. He watched her throat working.

"I don't feel anything any more," she said, averting her eyes. "I don't know you now. I am old and so are you."

"I admit there's a considerable gap in our relationship." Still he watched her and she did not answer. "If you are thinking of Calypso," he said tartly, "it was like loving Greta Garbo or Marilyn Monroe. It wasn't real, it was a sort of measles."

"A very long attack," she said sharply.

"All right, a very long attack." Oliver was patient, which went against his nature, holding back annoyance.

"You slept with her."

"How do you know?"

"I guessed."

"Just once. She made it clear she didn't enjoy it. It was humiliating."

"Oh." Sophy sneezed. "I am sorry to keep sneezing like this. I must have caught cold in the churchyard." Her voice was brittle. "Looking at the graves."

"I was beginning to think you were allergic to me," he said grumpily.

"Not *that*." Her emphasis was inadvertent.

"So you feel something?" he pressed her.

"Terribly hungry. I couldn't eat anything at the wake."

"All right, then, let's go and find some oysters. There must be somewhere we can eat on our way."

"We have no *way*," she cried in pain. "We know nothing about each other. There's an enormous forty-year gap." She turned to look at him again.

"Then start the bloody car and let's see what we can do about filling it," he yelled, losing patience.

Choking with sudden laughter, Sophy switched on the engine, wondering whether what she felt was real or just the whisky.

"We risk making ourselves the object of ridicule," she said as she changed gear.

"It's a risk I am prepared to take." Oliver was content that she had used the plural.

Driving towards Helston Sophy uneasily remembered the old adage: "Be careful what you wish for, for it will surely come true."

HARNESSING
PEACOCKS

for Toby

"Hebe," the old man called.

"Yes."

"Take these letters to the post for me." He had sat in his room writing his letters as if nothing untoward was happening, filling in time usefully while waiting for the arrival of his elder grand-daughters and their husbands. With a flip of his hand he indicated the pile of letters. Hebe took them. He did not look up.

"Close the door."

All her life he had said, "Close the door," driven mad by people who left doors open.

Picking up the letters Hebe viewed his profile, the profile worn by various ancestors hanging in the hall, the dining-room and up the stairs. She wondered whether he would be surprised if she said, "I love you, I am sorry for you, I understand how you feel, could you try just once to understand me?" Or, she thought, gripping the letters between nervous fingers, I could just hit him, hit him as hard as I can.

She left the room, closing the door. Her grandmother, resting on the sofa in the drawing-room with the door open so that she could see what was going on, heard the door close, did not look up.

Hebe ran down the steps into the garden, turned left across the grass burned khaki by the hot summer, walked away from the pink brick house with its kindly windows to the orchard where she would be out of sight. Here she took off her shoes to walk barefoot, pushed her hair back behind her ears and followed the path which led to the churchyard and beyond the church to the post box set in the wall.

In the churchyard she stopped to watch tortoiseshell butterflies clustering on moon daisies growing in the uncut grass and sunning themselves on headstones. Some headstones lurched side-ways. "Your parents would turn in their graves," her grandfather had said several times. He had a habit of repeating himself. Had the people under those stones turned in their graves because they, too, had a troublesome female relation? Troublesome was a mild term compared with whore, liar, disgrace, slut. Hebe stared at the headstones. She felt numb, exhausted by the row which had raged off and on ever since she had come back from the doctor and broken the news which had led to the long interrogation, the painful remarks, the accusations. Hebe wriggled her toes, drew her long hair forward to screen her face. Here in the churchyard, if one sat long enough, it was sometimes possible to see a hedge-hog and quite often toads. In her misery Hebe picked off the heads of daisies, stuck them between her toes and viewed the effect. It gave no comfort. Peering through her glasses at an inscription beside her she traced with her finger, "Died in the course of duty". The poor sod, she thought, making use of one of her brothers-in-law's expressions. She took the daisies from her toes and laid them on the grave. So much for duty. She heaved herself up and began a circuitous return to the house through the stable yard. From the only occupied loose box her grandfather's brood mare whickered. Hebe went to stroke the soft nose, sniff the animal's sweet breath. She blew into the horse's nostrils. "How are you, then?" The horse fidgeted, kicking out with a hind leg. In the corner of the box a goat eyed her with its strange split eyes.

"She'll get used to it. Company for her." The odd job man came up beside her, carrying a pail of fresh water.

"What happened to her foal?"

"It was a little mule. Your grandfather wasn't pleased."

"How did it happen?"

"Ran off, didn't she, broke through the fence. Met one of they Forest donkeys, I'd say." He laughed, putting the pail into the corner of the box. The mare laid her ears back. "Now then," he said, coming smartly out of the box and bolting the door. "She'll soon forget." Hebe watched him walk away, loathing him. "Here," she said to the goat, "post these." The goat snatched at the letters and started to munch. "So he murdered your foal," Hebe said to the horse. "He's arranging an abortion for me."

From the drive Hebe heard the sound of cars. Her brothers-in-law would be arriving, Robert, Delian, Marcus, married to her sisters Ann, Beata, Cara, driving their Jaguar, Range Rover (must buy British) and Alfa Romeo (all right to have a foreign car if you worked in Brussels). Hebe left the stable yard and slipped back into the house to position herself in the hall, to listen to her elders' and betters' discussion, a formality to ratify a conclusion already reached. Drawing her skirt about her knees she sat on the stairs. All her relations articulated clearly – it had never been necessary to tell them not to mumble – and since both grandparents were slightly deaf they made a point of speaking up.

They were having a drink. She heard the clink of glasses, shuffle of feet, the chair creak as her grandfather sat. "Well, then."

Her grandfather's old dog came in from the porch where he had lain all afternoon, crossed the hall and scratched at the drawing-room door. "Let the dog in." The door was opened and the dog went in. Grandfather waited until the door closed and repeated, "Well, then," and Robert, married to the eldest granddaughter, started the proceedings.

Firstly the family name must be protected, he observed. He suggested a private clinic. Though expensive, the cost was an investment as the matter would be dealt with immediately, no messing about.

Secondly, though of course of less importance, the sooner they acted the less chance, Robert cleared his throat, of his constituency getting wind or Marcus's bank (boards of directors were conventional people). Hebe heard Delian chip in. "Shouldn't we consider other ways?" His tenor voice was hesitant. "This situation does occur in families, in the arts, even in politics."

"We've been into that, Delian. If we knew the man, if he were, as it were, all right, we could get a settlement. As it is, we haven't a clue. There is no hope of her getting support. Letting the situation go on as it is is simply not on."

"It's obvious it was some sort of hippy, most probably black. That is why she will not tell us who the man is." Hebe had heard variations of this theme for days.

"Most families have skeletons." Delian tried again. There was a teasing note in his voice. "I mean look at the Bible, look at poor old Joseph."

"He knew who it was!" cried Cara, interrupting.

"Delian, keep blasphemy out of this." Grandfather was crushing. "Please keep to the point. This is no time for bad-taste jokes."

Suddenly, like a pack of hounds finding a fresh scent, the decibels rose. Ann's voice soared above the others. "We have to think of our children, Delian. I don't want some funny sort of cousin for mine, I am sure Cara doesn't and your wife Beata is having her first baby at any moment. You must consider her."

451

Hebe felt a wild desire to laugh. She took off her spectacles and polished them with the hem of her dress. "And who," continued Ann, "who on earth would want to marry Hebe, if she's burdened with this multicoloured child? We really must think what is best for her. We are not selfish, uncaring people. Let Robert decide what is best for the family, best for Hebe."

For a few minutes the assembled relatives voiced their views. Hebe heard yelped half-sentences containing the words careless, selfish, liar, not too late, soon be over, forgotten in no time. Then Robert quelled the chorus, shouting them down, using the knack learned to quell hecklers at political meetings. "Let's stop nattering, shall we? I shall ring Doctor Armitage now. I must get back to London tonight. I am flying to New York tomorrow." The ration of time he was prepared to give was up. The voices stilled. Hebe heard him use the telephone, make the arrangements. A room in the clinic. Operation in the afternoon. Home next day. Splendid.

Listening to Robert's civilised voice buying freedom from embarrassment, eliminating a social nuisance, she thought, I love those people, they are my family, they are not casting me out, they are just making sure I fit into their scheme of things. A puff of wind blew in through the open door. The sky was lurid, long-hoped-for rain on the way. It was growing dark and chilly. On the other side of the door she heard Robert again.

"That's settled, then. Can you drive her up in the morning, Delian?"

"No problem."

"Good, good." Robert's dry hands rustled as he rubbed them together. "Right then, we should be off. Ready, Ann?"

"Time for one more drink?" Her grandmother's voice.

She is afraid of being left alone with me, thought Hebe, but she has not lifted a finger to help me.

"No, no thank you, we should be on our way."

Hebe raced up the stairs, forcing leaden legs to work, reached her room above the porch and shut the door. They would not come near her tonight, they thought she would have gone to bed. Shivering with anguish she pulled on a cardigan, changed her shoes, took from the dressing-table drawer her mother's pearls and rings – Ann, Beata and Cara had the best pieces – stuffed them in her bag, counted her money, seventeen pounds, turned off the light, stood listening by the open window. Rain was beginning to tap on the Virginia creeper. Below, the front door opened, light blazed into the drive. Cheerful voices bidding a goodnight chorus. "Goodbye, then, goodbye." "Glad that's settled." "Very grateful." "Not at all." "See you soon." "Drive carefully." "Lovely night." "If you call rain lovely." "We need it for the crops." "Goodnight, goodnight, God bless."

She watched Robert and Ann kiss the grandparents, get into the Jaguar, drive away.

Next, Marcus with Cara climbed into the Range Rover, then Delian alone in the Alfa Romeo.

"Give our love to Beata," they called. Beata, being pregnant, had not attended the conference; she might have been upset; must not risk a miscarriage.

The cars, their headlights probing through the summer rain, streaked down the drive to the main road.

"Time for bed." Grandfather turned to go in. "It's been a tiring week."

Had the nightmare only lasted a *week*?

"That such a thing should happen to us!"

"Good chap, Robert. Head screwed on. He'll go far, mark my words."

Hebe waited while her grandfather let the dog out for his run, standing in the porch calling to him in tender accents not used for any other creature. The front door slammed. The kitchen door closed on the dog as he went to his basket. Stairs creaked as the old man climbed up to bed, switching off lights as he went. The long-case clock in the hall struck eleven.

"It's late." Grandfather's bedroom door closed. The house grew quiet. Hebe waited.

She felt infinitely tired, sleep an overwhelming temptation. Would a couple of hours matter? But if she failed to wake? The child in her womb kicked out for a swim. She crept down the stairs, felt among the coats slung across the hall table, found her coat, went into the kitchen. The dog in his basket wagged his tail. She bent to stroke his head, feeling the silky ears. The dog mumbled and chop-chopped his jaws. " 'Bye, Smut."

Out in the rain she hesitated. Above the porch her grandfather threw up the sash window.

"Splendid downpour. Just in time to stop those silly buggers on the Water Board banning the use of garden hoses."

Her grandmother answered something inaudible.

"Astute fellow, Robert. Settled that hash in no time. Can't think why the little fool couldn't be like her sisters—"

"The poor—"

"Poor nothing. We have cherished a crocodile."

"My hearing aid is on the blink. I can't hear what—"

"I said we have cherished a crocodile. *Façon de parler.*"

"Crocodiles are wonderful mothers." Faint hint of discord.

"We are not giving this one the chance of showing how wonderful." He slammed down the window.

Hebe put on her shoes, pulled up her coat collar, stepped out into the rain. She hoped never to hear those voices again.

ONE

The young mothers walked abreast, pushing their double buggies. Each buggy held two children. The younger children sucked dummies, the elder sprawled in resignation behind the plastic covers protecting them from the drizzle. The women paused to stare in shop windows, turning to one another to comment on the contents. They filled the width of the pavement. Both were pregnant. People attempting to pass stepped into the gutter or shrank aside in doorways.

Hebe's gorge rose. She felt an almost joyful desire to jostle the young mothers, to shout at them to give way, give them a start, force them to show consideration. That both were heavily pregnant only made Hebe the more furious; she had never, when carrying Silas, taken up so much space; she had never let Silas suck a dummy; come to think of it, Silas had never had a buggy. She had carried him in a sling next her heart.

Cherishing her uncharitable thoughts, Hebe prowled behind the women, disliking their swaying rumps, their mechanically turning heads, their abrupt bursts of inane laughter. As her intolerance grew she felt her face grow hot and her glasses begin to steam over. She let the women draw ahead, took off her glasses and wiped them, enjoying the slippery feel of glass between finger and thumb.

At the street corner, still talking, the women pushed the buggies off the pavement. An approaching car jammed on squealing brakes, missing the children by inches, nearly giving the driver a coronary.

"Can't you look where you're going?"

"Stupid git nearly killed my Kevin."

"Look where you're going, look—"

Hebe swung round the corner, grinning with vengeful delight. Carrying her glasses so that she could see as little as possible of the street she deplored, she wondered whether in her absence of patience and lack of charity she had ill-wished the women. She felt a glow of power, both irrational and delightful as, increasing her pace, she set herself to climb the hill.

Without her glasses she could only see a blur of dark brick, each house as awful as its neighbour, purplish brick with light beige brick round the windows, uncompromising, solidly built, hideous.

Starting the climb, stiff for even the young and healthy, paradisical for the free-wheeling bicycles of reckless children, breathing the damp, salt-tinctured air, she became aware of a smell she could not define, coffee, pepper, smoke, with connotations of the panic nightmare which visited her, catching her as it did now, to bring horror so total that she stood holding her glasses, her hand pressed to her chest, then moving to shield her eyes, in an effort to black out the towering buildings rearing up to blot out the sky, bending inwards to stare from sightless unlit windows with the eyes of deep-sea fish. She heard jeers and laughter, the mindless chatter of an unseen crowd surrounding her with frightful cheer, isolating her in a dreadful cocoon so that she sweated and trembled, unable to move, as the voices began their litany.

"Who is the man? It might be anybody. Who is the man? Don't speak to your grandfather like that. A long-haired layabout. Dirty feet. Beards. You are a whore. Your sisters never— Who was the— Guitars— Don't answer in that tone of voice. Earrings, cannabis, heroin. Probably a Communist. Dirty fingernails. Who was the man? Can't speak the Queen's English. Don't prevaricate. Must have an abortion. What will your brothers-in-law say? Who was it? You must know. Don't be impertinent. Where did it happen? Might be *black*. So many sacrifices, gave you everything. Don't dare to speak like that. Don't lie. If it were not so public you would have it on the National Health. What d'you mean too late? How many months? Of course you know. Think of our friends. I am *not* shouting. Your sisters. You've made your grandmother cry. At least be civil. After all we've done for you. All the right people. Who was it? Might have a police record. Might be diseased, might be a black. This is intolerable. Who – who – who—"

She knew that if she could hang on the terror would dissipate. She would recover as though coming round from an anaesthetic.

"I am not mad." She opened her eyes. She had spoken aloud, looked quickly round to see if she had been noticed, then rushed up the street, forcing her legs to hurry, driving herself. Reaching her door, heart thumping, breath coming in gasps, she fumbled for her key, breathing in the illusive whiff. What was it? Imaginary or not, it brought solace after the horror, even a sensation of happiness which she attributed to relief from the paralysis of fear. It was imaginary. She was safe in the ugly familiar street, safe from the voices mumbling the familiar accusations in weird accents in the strange city, the nightmare background of prying eyes, claustrophobic walls, darkness and that smell mixed with the voices. If only she could control the panic she might recover the shaft of joy which was always out of reach. Finding her key, she felt shame for the envy she had felt of the two women with their children, their buggies, their ordinary lives. Perhaps, she thought, putting on her glasses, it was envy which brought on the panic. She unlocked her door; the telephone was ringing in the house. Her heart slowed its beat. Somewhere behind the dead fish eyes, bullying questions, was gaiety, illusive, poignant, almost blotted out by that other fear. Epileptics must feel like this, she thought, and breathed in the smell of her house: garlic, flowers from the market, herbs. The telephone stopped.

Trip, her tortoiseshell cat, came to greet her, pressing her head against her ankles with sharp little pushes, prickling with her whiskers. She picked up the cat. "Hungry?" Trip purred, pushing a paw against her cheek, flexing her claws, just not drawing blood.

Jim Huxtable, talking to Hannah Somerton further up the street, put the hat he was holding on his head, stopped what he was saying and stared.

"Who is that girl?"

"She's called Hebe. She's a neighbour." Hannah claimed Hebe.

"Hebe, a young virgin crowned with flowers, arrayed in a variegated garment."

"Oxfam shop anorak." Hannah tried to retrieve his attention.

"Hebe, daughter of Jupiter and Juno." She had opened the door, disappeared.

"Who?" What was the man talking about?

"Hebe is the Latin name for Veronica." He looked at Hannah. "She harnessed peacocks. Fell down in a position which—"

"I thought Veronica was a bush. A shrub," Hannah corrected herself, fearing to sound lewd.

"Ah, yes." Jim looked at Hannah, small, fair hair, lovely green eyes, rather like Maudie Littlehampton. He was tempted to get to know her, find out what she was like in bed.

"She's hardly a virgin, she's got a son of twelve." Hannah

laughed, showing her perfect teeth. "She's a cook."

"Really? Well, I must go. If you think of anyone with anything interesting to sell, here's my card. My telephone number's on it." He lost interest in Hannah.

"Thanks, I'll get in touch if I think of anything."

"Thank you." He began to move away.

"Did you see my aunt's paperweights?" She tried to keep him talking; really attractive men were a rarity.

"Yes, she doesn't want to part."

"Pretty, aren't they?" She would like to delay him.

"Very pretty." He moved away. She liked the way he walked, a European lope, an American lope was quite different. His hair under the hat was grey, his eyes dark grey. Wish I knew more about antiques, she thought as she crossed the street, then I could have kept him talking. She looked at the card: "James Huxtable". A London telephone number, Fulham address. She opened Hebe's door and walked into the house.

"You came up the street in a rush." Her statement held a question.

"It's good for the heart, they say." Hebe snapped shut her mind, trapping her fears until the next time.

"What was the hurry?" Hannah pressed her, curious.

"I must get into dry clothes, I am soaked." Why does she walk in on me like this? "There were two idiot girls who pushed their children out into the street and nearly got them killed." She took off her anorak and shook it. Trip moved hastily under a chair to avoid the drops. "They had so many children."

"Not single parents, like us. Shall I put the kettle on?" Hannah moved to pick up the kettle, take it to the sink, turn on the tap. Hebe wished she would not treat her kitchen and her kettle with such familiarity.

"I must change my clothes."

"Where have you been?"

"For a walk." She had no intention of sharing the joy of her walk. The tramp across fields and moorland, the sound of water dripping from trees, the rustle of wind, cries of sheep, shriek of buzzards, the delicious solitude.

"I would have come with you if you'd said."

I dare say you would, thought Hebe, climbing the stairs without answering.

"There's a lot to be said for single parenthood," Hannah called after her.

"Yes." She pulled off her jersey.

"Edward's late with my maintenance," Hannah called up the stairs.

"Always is," Hebe shouted back.

"I've written to my solicitor."

"You always do."

"What?"

She writes every month, thought Hebe, brushing her damp hair. It's amazing the funds don't just dry up. At least I'm spared that hassle. She peered at her face in the mirror. I do not look like them, she thought, examining her face, nor sound much like them. It must be them behind those blind windows chanting their intolerable accusations. She stared at her high forehead, full mouth, dark eyes.

Bernard Quigley had said: "Your face is an asset. You look honest." And he had laughed his creaky old man's laugh.

"I've wet the tea," Hannah called up the stairs.

"Thanks, I'll have coffee," Hebe shouted, then reproached herself for snobbery. Why shouldn't Hannah say "wet the tea" if that came naturally?

"Do you want real coffee, Nescaff or a bag? How was the job? Very boring?"

"A bag will do. It was lucrative."

"When's the next job?"

All these questions. Hebe pulled on a jersey and rejoined Hannah in the kitchen. "I haven't decided." She took the proffered cup, and watched Hannah pour herself tea, resenting the way she made herself at home, sitting behind her teapot. Then, regretting her surly reaction, forced herself to be friendly.

"After the holidays when Silas has gone back to school."

"And when does Master Silas grace us with his presence?" Hannah's lightness of tone failed to conceal the envy she felt of Silas at a fee-paying school, while her own son Giles was state educated.

"Day after tomorrow. When does Giles get back from the Paris trip?"

"Tomorrow."

"I hope he enjoyed it. Silas is longing to see him."

"Not grown too grand?"

"Don't be silly." Hebe spoke sharply.

"Edward Krull could perfectly well afford—"

"Of course he could, but he doesn't want to. You've told me."

Hannah sniffed, scenting a rebuff. "Did you see that fellow I was talking to earlier on?"

"I didn't have my glasses on. I didn't see anybody."

"A dealer. He was calling from house to house. Rather dishy. He visited Aunt Amy."

"People like that are called 'Knockers'. Did she show him her things?"

"He saw the paperweights. She must have liked him or she wouldn't have taken them out of the cupboard. I was talking to him, getting friendly, you know how it is."

"No."

"You are so private. You never stop and chat. You miss a lot. I asked him to come in and see whether I had anything that might interest him. I thought he'd be someone I'd like to know."

"Might be a thief."

"He seemed friendly. Then he caught sight of you and he said, 'Who is that? What's that girl's name?' It was as if he knew you."

"I didn't see him, I told you. I hadn't got my glasses on."

"He went on up the street but he stopped and stared when I came over to you. Pity you didn't meet him, you could have made friends."

"I shouldn't think so."

"He talked with that kind of voice, you know what I mean."

"I don't."

"You do. He talked like the people you go and work for."

"How do you know how they talk?" Hebe was irritated.

"I guess, bet I'm right. You talk like them yourself."

"Did he need a cook?" Hebe mocked.

"I told you, he was looking for antiques but" – narrowed green eyes – "he gave the impression of—"

"Rich?" Hebe was laughing. "Stately homes?"

"Confident." Hannah smiled, not resenting the mockery. "He seemed confident until he clapped eyes on you, then he seemed disturbed, sort of puzzled."

Hebe wondered whether the stranger was a friend of one of her clients. "What was he like?" she asked suspiciously.

"Tall, pepper and salt hair, grey eyes. Until you I thought he was interested in me. Oh, I said that—"

"I expect he was. You are beautiful."

"Do you really think so?" Hannah looked delighted. "Honest?"

"Of course I do," said Hebe warmly.

"Another thing about him, he knew Latin and wore a hat."

"Latin?"

"Said Hebe was the Latin name for Veronica, the shrub. You don't often see men in hats. And something about driving peacocks."

Hebe finished her coffee in a hurried gulp.

"You aren't interested, are you?" Sometimes I wonder whether you are a lesbian." Hannah probed.

Hebe took her mug to the sink, standing with her back to Hannah to hide a broad smile.

"I suppose Silas' father was your one great love."

"Have you been reading Mills and Boon?" Hebe asked coldly. Then – for she did not wish to hurt – she said, "I am busy making a living. Look, love, I have to get the place ready for Silas so—"

"Can I help? D'you want me to leave?"

"It's just that I have rather a lot to do." Difficult to get rid of Hannah, who thought nothing of staying for hours. How much easier life had been before Amy Tremayne's niece had come to live in the street, imposing friendship regardless.

"Okay, I'll leave you to it. Let me know if I can help in any way." Hannah stood up. Hebe reached for the teapot. "No, no, I'll do that." Hannah snatched up the pot, emptied and washed it with meticulous care. "Just give a shout, I've only got Giles and Aunt Amy." Would she never leave?

"Perhaps I should have asked him where he is staying. Invited him for a drink, or something. He seemed to be alone."

"Some people like being alone."

"I could have asked him to meet George Scoop." Hannah ignored the hint.

Hebe refrained from asking after George, not wishing a fresh line of talk.

"I've been out with George while you were away. The only thing is, he spends his days gazing down gullets. Would his being a dentist, dontologist, actually, put you off?"

Hebe remained silent, noting that Hannah was now on Christian name terms with her dentist.

"He is good looking." Hannah was determined to discuss George. "He is in a good practice. I got to know him while he was fixing my teeth. He is about forty, a bit careful with money."

"You told me."

"He takes me out to dinner. I ask him back. We watch telly but he – well, I suppose it's because he is so keen on his work, he keeps making remarks."

"Such as?"

"People's teeth, he notices their fillings when they laugh, whether their dentures fit, whether the teeth are dirty. He doesn't use the word 'dirty', he calls it—"

"Tartar."

"That's right. He admires Mrs Thatcher and Monsieur Mitter-and for having theirs fixed. He never gets away from his work."

"Wedded to it."

Not liking Hebe's ironical tone, Hannah checked. "Well, let me know if I can help." Still she lingered.

"Thank you." Hebe edged Hannah towards the door, closed it after her. Oh, the joy of being alone! The telephone pealed, shattering with its intrusion the welcome quiet. The cat leapt bristling on to the windowsill. Hebe picked up the instrument.

"Hello."

"Allo, allo, vot colour knickers you wear?" A thick French accent.

"Wrong number." Hebe put the telephone back in its cradle.

Higher up the street Jim Huxtable sat on the seat a town councillor had given in memory of aged parents who had lived in the street when it was first built. They had complained of aching legs and breathless struggles up the hill. After their death their son had given the seat, inscribed with his parents' names. Rude boys had carved coarse words and passing dogs did worse. Jim Huxtable waited in case the dark girl should come out of her house, hoping to get another look at her. Pretty name, Hebe, Cup Bearer to the Gods. Not many peacocks to harness in this awful street. What was the indecent posture she had fallen into that got her into trouble, if memory served him right? The mores of the ancients were not so very different from those of the present. He wondered how Bernard had known about the old woman's collection of paperweights.

Down the street a door slammed and the girl with green eyes came out. He didn't want to talk to her again. Tired and hungry, he walked fast up the hill to his car and cursed when the engine stalled.

As Hebe closed her door Hannah crossed the street with a hop and a skip. Between the hop and the skip she decided to remarry.

Thinking of Hannah, Hebe let laughter erupt. A lesbian! What would Hannah dream up next? She thought of Silas, who would be home tomorrow, his brown eyes mercifully not short-sighted, his arc of a nose, hair the colour of a bay horse. Where did the nose and hair come from? Not from me, not from them. She remembered carrying Silas and her love for the unborn child. She had been happy, then, in a precious intimacy which was no longer theirs. Was it envy of those women that brought on her panic? Did they feel for their unborn babies as she had felt for Silas? Perhaps not, since they each had in their buggies the reality babies turned into. I am no baby lover, thought Hebe, yet I loved Silas as a baby with passion.

She considered Hannah's relationship with Giles; a comfortable intimacy. She envied Hannah but Hannah invented for her "a great love". How banal.

Trip sprang up by the sink, making it clear that she was still hungry. Hebe reached into a cupboard for a tin of cat food. She sat watching Trip eat, then wash herself before going out on her night prowl. The cat sat listening to the sounds from neighbouring gardens, making sure there was no danger. Hebe watched the little animal, thinking, Silas loves that cat. Trip rushed to the back fence and vanished over it. Hebe went up to bed, where she lay mentally totting up her income. The total was healthy. If she continued work on the present basis the years of Silas' education were assured, although the very nature of her work was insecure. Old ladies do not live for ever and other work inclined to be impermanent. Fun, though, she thought, luxuriating in the solitude of her large bed, kicking her legs under the duvet; enjoy tonight without some Hercules thrusting himself between her thighs.

TWO

Downstairs the telephone was ringing. Hebe let it ring, pealing its jarring note over and over again until at last it died. She lay looking forward to tomorrow and Silas, planning his holidays.

Trip desecrated the neighbour's garden, making a neat little scrape, and, covering her excrement with tender paw, climbed back over the fence. It was raining. She leapt from the fence on to Hebe's windowsill, dropped into the bedroom, padded across to the bed to insert herself under the duvet. Feeling wet fur against her face, Hebe put on her bedside light.

"I shall never get to sleep." She fetched a towel and wiped the little animal who, purring, burrowed into the warmth. "Silas taught you that. You can snuggle up to him tomorrow."

For the third time the telephone rang. Irritated, she ran downstairs and picked up the receiver.

"Yes?" she said tersely.

"You got big tits?" A strong cockney accent.

"I told you wrong number," she said irritably.

"Vot colour knickers?" pleaded the French voice.

"You don't even get the accent right." She put the instrument back and covered it with a cushion. She went back to bed where the cat made room for her.

Midnight was striking from the town clock when she was disturbed yet again by a scrabbling at her window, a thud as feet hit the floor, the sound of material tearing.

"Sod it! I've torn my skirt."

"God, Terry, I told you wrong number, I told you twice. Twice!"

"Just look at my skirt."

Hebe switched on her bedside light. "Terry, I'm trying to sleep. Silas is coming home tomorrow."

Terry was examining the tear. "D'you think it will mend?" he asked.

Slender with cropped hair, wide shoulders and long legs. His

464

skirt was pleated red cotton, worn with a fuchsia sweatshirt. "D'you think it will mend?" he asked, stroking Hebe's shoulder.

"I shan't mend it for you." She lay back, pulling the duvet up to her chin.

"Listen to why I rang you. I made it with another girl, no trouble at all." Terry spoke excitedly. "It's all due to you."

"Couldn't it have waited?"

"Listen—" He was taking off the skirt and inserting himself into the bed. "What you got in here? Trip, it's only me, don't scratch. Bloody little beast, give over, make room. She's wet."

"Terry," she protested. "I told you—'

"Listen, love." He put his arm round her, settling in the bed, stretching his legs.

Annoyed by the disturbance Trip scrabbled out of the bed and perched on the chair where Hebe had laid her clothes.

Terry snuggled up to Hebe. "I haven't come here to sleep with you." He kissed her neck.

"Sleep is just what one doesn't do."

"It's the crappiest expression for it. Give us a kiss."

"Sleep is what I want at the moment."

"Didn't you hear what I said? I made it with another girl. No problem. You were right. No skirts. No knickers. I did like you taught. I came to thank you, thought you'd be glad to know." Terry was aggrieved.

"I am glad. It's just that I want to sleep. I told you it's all in the mind, now will you—"

"Okay, now listen to this:

She can present joyes meaner than you do;
Convenient and more proportional.
So if I dream I have you, I—"

"That's Donne and the verse ends – 'And sleep which locks up sense, doth lock all out.' That's what I want now."

He laughed. "You are not really angry."

"Are you in love with this girl?"

"She was just a fun girl for an evening. I've got other ideas."

"Someone specific?"

"Maybe." Terry leaned from the bed to pick up a book from the floor. "Could we read a bit? Would you read to me, for the last time?"

"You read." She gave in.

"Okay." Terry began reading. " 'I sing the progresse of a deathlesse soule—' " his young voice rising and falling in gentle cadence. Hebe remembered when she had first met him installing burglar alarms in the Midland Bank, noticed him reading Milton, started talking about poetry, an interest which had evolved into reading aloud to each other after lovemaking. He was taking a course in English at night school. She did not know what connection poetry had with women's clothes. The skirts and knickers were a harmless aberration, the skirt, she suspected, a ploy to rouse her interest. Now it seemed this phase was ending. She had enjoyed the poetry, coming from a boy who looked as though he would be more at home in a disco than reading Donne to the cat, for I am not listening, thought Hebe, and Terry has read himself to sleep. She listened to his breathing, remembering his discovery of "'Tis the Arabian Bird alone lives chaste for 'tis but one, But had kind nature made them two they would as the doves and sparrows do." For a while he had called her his Arabian Bird. Perhaps that's what I am, she thought. The town clock struck the half hour.

"Have a heart, Terry." She shook him. "Wake up."

Terry woke staring at her, puzzled.

"Time to go, Terry."

He was sleepy, his mind far away. Reluctantly he got out of bed. "Don't happen to have any Y-fronts?"

"Silas' would be too small."

"Then I'll go without. Lend us your jeans. I'll see you get them back."

"Are you sure you won't need—"

"Yes. I'll leave my skirt with you as a memento, and the panties now, it's okay without them." He had forgotten Donne.

"I am glad." Hebe watched him struggle into the jeans she had taken off when she went to bed.

"Fit a bit tight, but what the hell. I'm – what am I?" He stood looking down at Hebe, exultant.

"Normal," she suggested, smiling up at him.

"That's about it." He searched in his skirt pocket. "This is for you." He thrust a wad of notes into Hebe's hand. "You earned it. Can't think how you did it. From now on I can be like anyone else." He bent down to kiss her. "'Bye, love."

"Thanks, Terry." Hebe looked at the money. "It's far too much."

"No, it's not. I've got this girl in mind. Don't you want to know who she is?" She could see he wanted to tell her.

"No." He must manage on his own.

"She will be the first to get the straight treatment," he said, zipping up the jeans.

"Without frills." She was amused.

He gave her a friendly hug. "Sending me up."

"Go now. I must sleep." She pressed him to leave.

"But I had to tell you. Analysts try and you did the trick in just two years."

Hebe was counting the money. "This is an awful lot, Terry." She was shocked by the amount.

"I shan't see you again, not like this. I want you to have it."

"Thanks." She did not trust herself to say more.

"I'll take care of Trip when you go away. Keep in touch with you." He bent to kiss her again. "Goodbye now." He moved to the window to climb out. "This is a lot easier in jeans." He gave a snort of laughter.

She heard him land in the flower bed, switched off her light and went to the window to watch him put on his shoes, climb the fence to the alleyway behind the gardens and break into a run, the sound of his feet beating a tattoo.

"There goes a satisfied customer," she said to the cat as she dropped the skirt and the discarded briefs into the wastepaper basket. "God! I must sleep." She got back into bed. She would miss Terry, miss the poetry reading. Buy herself a treat with part of his goodbye money, perhaps; put the rest towards Silas' education. She felt a rush of affection for Terry. Will his new girl make him happy, will they read poetry together as we have? Why should I worry, she thought, as she lay listening to the cat purring. I taught him

> As freely as we met we'll part
> Each one possest of their own heart.

If he has learned that lesson why can't I abide by it? We are friends. Restoration poems are not essential for survival, not essential for Silas. She dozed, thinking of the good times with Terry during the past years – quite a course in Eng. Lit., a profitable spell of work, a success. She remembered thinking him farouche until she had discovered his troubled spirit, grown fond of him for himself not only for the colour of his skin, which in some lights resembled a Mars Bar. So much for you. Briefly she permitted a vision of her grandfather, quickly banishing him from her mind.

Then she reproached herself for not making Terry promise to tell his new girl about his little ways. He would never tolerate Y-fronts, never really change. The girl was on to a good thing if she did but know. Terry was intelligent and caring, which was more than could be said for most fee-paying lovers. The word "fees" brought to mind Silas. Would the term away have changed him?

THREE

Hannah sat in front of her mirror to do her nails. She wore rubber gloves for rough jobs, thought Hebe mad not to bother. Hebe had said, "Making pastry cleans them. The dirt lends zest to the pastry." Hannah wondered what the Cordon Bleu would say to that and remembered Hebe remarking that she had been given the best tips by the French chef when she worked at the hotel on the cliff. Saying this, Hebe had laughed, as though the tips were humorous. Painting her nails, Hannah wondered whether the antique dealer was staying at the hotel. She had dined there with George. It was perhaps too expensive for the dealer. He had climbed the street knocking at doors. Surprisingly, Amy admitted him. Hannah had been watching at her window, hoping to see Hebe return. It had been easy to talk to the man when he left Aunt Amy's. She brushed her hair. Had the stranger noticed it? She lifted her lip like a horse sneering, admired her teeth, straight as a regiment of guards. George had done a good job. Would Jim Huxtable be interested in her year's sessions with George who had gloriously brought to order her set of snaggles? Would he be interested to know she had flogged her only good piece of jewellery, Edward's engagement ring, to pay for her teeth? Annoyance spoiled the joy of her teeth. Edward never sent her alimony on time. His dilatoriness kept alive the tie when she would rather forget him. New teeth, new life, damn you, Edward. But she was pleased with her adoption by deed poll of the name Somerton. Would Giles stop being obstinate and change his too? He hung on to Krull to annoy, to be able to threaten he would run away to his father. She hoped he would soon realise that Somerton sounded better than Krull. Perhaps he would latch on to this through his friendship with Silas and also perhaps get the hang of Silas' and Hebe's vowels. Eyeing her image in the glass Hannah mouthed A-E-I-O-U as taught at the elocution lessons she preferred to call speech therapy. Hebe's vowels came naturally and Silas' were perpetuated at his school. Hannah's thoughts veered to Hebe's odd life working as cook to rich old women. She never discussed the people she worked for. She never talked about Silas' father, had not responded when Hannah told her about Edward, did not, as other women would, tell her own tale. Hannah's mother and Aunt Amy had been sisters. Her mother had married higher socially than Aunt Amy, who had some undiscussed connection with Hebe, who was thick with Amy and like Amy secretive. Hannah realised that she knew as little about her aunt as about Hebe. She had been referred to by her parents as "that poor old maid living alone in that house. You should go and see her, she's your only relative." A year ago, finding herself in the neighbourhood with Giles, she had visited, been welcomed. With no roots after living in America, it had seemed natural to settle here, send Giles to school, keep an eye on her aunt. She had grown very fond of Amy. Hannah's thoughts wandered.

"I must marry again," she told herself. "Have another bash." Though the marriage to Edward had left her bruised and there was much to be said for independence, marriage was what Hannah preferred. Hebe seemed to manage her life extraordinarily well for someone whose income of child benefit and single-parent benefit was only augmented by temporary cooking jobs. What did those old women pay? Hannah blew on the varnish, which was dry at last. What did she do about sex? While enjoying her relationship with George, Hannah had yet to decide whether to make it permanent. George's line in pillow talk was mundane. Dontology does not turn me on, she ruminated. There must be somebody more amusing than George.

Time to see whether Aunt Amy was okay for the night. She looked across at Hebe's house. There was no light.

Up among the hills Jim Huxtable sat with Bernard Quigley outside his house finishing the claret they had drunk with their supper.

"I was wondering how you knew that old woman had that collection of paperweights. They are immensely valuable."

"What?" The old man put his hand to his ear.

"You are not deaf," said Jim patiently and waited for an answer.

"I wanted to know whether, if she still has them, she is prepared to sell," said the old man grudgingly.

"She invited me to come again, she may change her mind." Jim looked at his host, sitting with his cat on his knee, stroking it with gnarled fingers. The cat's purring was loud. The damp air, heavy with the smell of honeysuckle, was counterpointed by Bernard's dog, Feathers, who lay at his feet. "Your dog smells a bit high," he remarked.

"Rolled in a pong. You may bath him tomorrow."

"Thanks," said Jim, ungrateful at the prospect.

"She won't sell," said the old man complacently, reverting to the paperweights. "She's too fond of them."

Jim thought of Bernard's idiotic trick, making him call from house to house. "I don't buy at the door." "Nothing to sell here, not even the balls from a brass monkey." Rebuffs.

"If you knew that, why did you suggest that charade?"

The old man did not answer.

"There was a girl, a few doors up from your friend's house. A talkative girl, gave me an oeillade."

Bernard laughed. "That's her niece."

"Another girl came up the street, reminded me of someone. Who would she be? Lives opposite your Miss Tremayne, seemed short-sighted. She was carrying her spectacles. You know her, by chance?"

"I do not know her." In the old sense to know a girl was to make love, thought Bernard, as he had made love in the old days, tenderness and laughter mixed with passion. How delightful to have such an experience with Hebe. She was born too late, he thought, jealous of the younger man's interest. He remembered his dealings with Hebe, taking advantage of her naïvety by paying her twice the worth of her mother's jewels. He took a snuffbox from his waistcoat pocket, measured, inhaled, sneezed. The cat jumped off his knee.

Watching Bernard, Jim thought the light of dusk, usually so kind, made the old man look like a fossilised bird. "Why did you never marry?" he asked.

Bernard sat thinking. "Impossible to make up my mind. Wasn't prepared to give anything up. *Embarras de choix.* What about you? If you are not careful you will end up a bachelor, not that I can't recommend the state. Got lots of girls, have you?"

"You could say that."

"Don't want any of them to be permanent?"

Jim did not answer.

"If you get a chance to buy those paperweights—"

"Yes?"

"I am off to bed. See you in the morning before you go."

Bernard heaved himself out of his chair. Jim stood up. Bernard snapped his fingers at the dog. "Come boy, bedtime. You could give them to the girl. She probably carried her spectacles because she did not want to see." There was tenderness in the old man's voice.

"So you do know her." Jim expected no answer. He decided to call on the girl called Hebe and ask whether she had any antiques to sell, see why she was worthy of the paperweights. That way he could get a look at her. He could still get to London by evening if he did not dally on the way.

Also thinking of Hebe, Hannah let herself into Amy Tremayne's house.

"It's me, auntie, how are you?"

"Still alive."

"Can I come in?"

"You usually do."

Ignoring this unpromising start, Hannah said, "What did you think of the Knocker?"

"I thought he was rather interesting. Comes from London."

"Did you sell him anything?" Hannah looked round her aunt's cluttered room, absolute hell to dust.

"No." Amy was grumpy. "I saw you talking to him."

"Why shouldn't I? Did you show him your paperweights?"

"They are in the cupboard."

"I know. I put them there. There is such a lot to clean."

"Stopped talking to you when he saw Hebe," Amy chuckled.

"Do you think he knew Hebe?" Hannah quizzed her aunt. "He seemed more interested in her than me."

"Say anything?" The old woman looked up suspiciously.

"He just stared. Perhaps he knew Hebe's husband." Hannah fished.

"She doesn't wear a ring."

"D'you mean she wasn't married?" Hannah seized the chance of discussing Hebe, persuading her aunt to talk.

"Wouldn't be strange these days," said Amy drily.

"Oh, auntie!"

"Oh, auntie," mocked the old woman.

"Perhaps he died before he could marry her, her lover."

"Did she tell you that?" Amy raised an eyebrow.

"She never tells me anything. I imagined she had a great

romance who died soon after they were married or even before they could."

"Perhaps she disposed of him like you did poor Krull."

"Rich Krull." Hannah corrected her aunt, laughing.

"You girls. Chuck a perfectly good husband. Can't stick to anything."

"If she isn't married, perhaps Silas is adopted?" Hannah pressed Amy.

"With those eyes? Perhaps he's her brother." Amy was heavily humorous. "I'm off to bed if that's all you have of interest." She pulled herself up from her chair. The white hair framing her face was thick, her eyes, surrounded by wrinkles, were still beautiful.

"Like a hot drink? Cocoa? Horlicks?" suggested Hannah, still hoping for gossip.

"I'll have a toddy. Make it strong." Amy went up to bed. If Hebe chose to mind her own business, she was not the one to broadcast it. Amy felt contempt for Hannah, who told every Tom and Dick her life story. Stories grew in the telling, it was only sensible not to tell them. Climbing out of her directoire knickers, which were getting difficult to get these days, Amy sighed, wondering whether she had been wise to give Hebe introductions to Lucy Duff, Louisa Fox and at the beginning to that old bastard Bernard. Too late now and the child – she thought of Hebe as a child – had to live. Give him his due, Bernard had not cheated. He had introduced her to the hotel on the cliff and the French chef and she could not approve of that though it had proved useful.

Hannah brought the hot toddy. "I made it strong."

Amy drank, sipping through pleated lips, sitting propped by pillows. Hannah watched with affection.

"She works to pay for Silas' school; it must cost a bomb."

"If you'd stayed married to Krull your Giles could have gone there too. If you marry again you will lose your alimony." Amy grinned over her glass.

"Who said I wanted to?" Hannah was on the defensive.

"It's on your mind. You weigh the pros and cons. Shall I, shan't I?"

"I thought we were talking of Hebe," said Hannah huffily.

"But I was thinking you might marry again. I saw you this afternoon. You can't sit around for ever taking money from Krull, giving nothing. It's not right."

"You can't talk," shouted Hannah, erupting in anger. "You've never been married, you've always been alone, you don't know what it's like."

The old woman was silent. Then, peering at Hannah, she said softly, "None of us should be alone, it's not natural." She looked tiny in her large bed.

"It's better than being stuck with someone you don't want," muttered Hannah, not intending her aunt to hear, annoyed that she must defend herself.

"I heard you. You're as bad as a tart I heard in Paris, she—"

"I didn't know you knew Paris," exclaimed Hannah, surprised.

"This tart" – Amy stressed the word – "this tart said to another tart about a man who had just paid her off, this tart said, '*Et moi, je soulage moi-même.*' Perhaps you don't." The old woman mocked her niece. "How that girl laughed!"

Hannah giggled. "I hope Giles isn't learning that sort of French on his school trip."

Amy raised an eyebrow. "When does he get back?"

"Tomorrow."

"Send him to see me."

"No need. He loves you as much as I do."

"Ho." Amy switched off her light and lay back on her pillows, not waiting for Hannah to reach the landing.

"Old bitch." Hannah fumbled for the light switch. "I might kill myself falling downstairs," she called but Amy did not answer. Searching for the switch Hannah thought of Giles growing up so quickly. He would soon be gone.

Courting sleep, Amy considered her afternoon visitor, questioning whether he had come by chance. He had admired her treasures, talked knowledgeably, known their value. Refusing to sell, she had put a tacit invitation in the manner of her refusal. They had talked about France. He had held the paperweights in his long fingers so that their brilliance caught the light. "Glass flowers last longer than bouquets," he had said.

But are they as sweet? Thinking of her paperweights, she thought of the secret trapped as the flowers were in the glass. Let Hannah pity her as the old spinster aunt who had spent a dreary life. She need never know of the period when she had been *la fille Anglaise.* Later she had had no heart for it, had gone back to work in England, a dully secure secretary.

Amy had watched Hannah waylay Jim Huxtable, watched them talking until, looking down the street, he had seen something which had caught his interest. Maybe, thought Amy, if he comes again I will sell him one. Considering her treasures, her mind went back to the Hotel d'Angleterre fifty years ago. What fun it had been, waking to light filtering through the red plush curtains, the hugging and kissing, the cosiness before coffee and croissants. The warmth, the laughter, the presents. She was unwilling to think of the presents as payment since she had not in that instance wanted payment. It amused her that Hannah, who longed for romantic love, should think of her as "a poor old thing" whereas Hebe, who thought of love with detachment, as an indulgence for others, should long since have correctly assumed her to be a retired lady of pleasure.

Further up the street Hannah restlessly debated whether she should marry George. She had planned to marry a man who pronounced regatta "regattah". George said "regatter".

FOUR

Mungo Duff had difficulty finding a parking space in the multi-storey car park and was infuriated that he had no loose change for the meter. It was a hot day. He was weary of the cathedral crawl Alison had insisted on for her friends the Drews from Santa Barbara, over on a two-week trip. By the time he had found change, tracked back to the ticket machine, stuck the ticket on the windscreen, he was more eager for a drink at the bar of the Clarence than the prospect of trailing round Exeter Cathedral, listening to his knowledgeable wife and her even more knowledgeable guests. However, duty calls, he told himself. Yesterday Winchester, Stonehenge, Salisbury and Sherborne, tomorrow home and put one's feet up. Crossing the street on the way to the Close he caught sight of swirling skirts. There was something familiar in the swinging stride and lift of buttocks. Searching his mind to fit a face to the buttocks, he joined his wife and guests, who stood in the centre aisle gazing up at the minstrels' gallery. By tonight Alison would be complaining of a stiff neck and serve her bloody right. Mungo sat down in a chair, stretched his legs and waited. Let Alison do the work, it was she who had angled for an invitation to Santa Barbara, not he. Mungo sincerely hoped the Drews would keep her for a long visit. Why, he mused, could they not be content with Oxford, Cambridge, Anne Hathaway's cottage and Westminster Abbey, like any other decent Americans? Viewing his wife from behind as she wandered up the aisle, he compared her bottom and her friend Patsy Drew's with the bottom viewed briefly in the street.

"Oh, Mungo."

Damn! Alison had seen him just as memory was about to yield.

"Yes?" He went to join his wife.

"Stay with them, darling. I just want to nip into that shoe-shop on the corner, they've got a sale," murmured Alison.

"They are your visitors, not mine," he hissed.

"Darling, don't be mean."

"Isn't it nearly lunchtime?" he prevaricated.

"Soon, soon. Be an angel. I won't be long."

"Oh, God!"

"If you're not here when I come back I'll meet you in the bar."

"That means you'll be ages."

"No, no." She left him, walking swiftly in her expensive sandals to use her eye for a bargain and buy at reduced price a pair, more likely two, of exquisite shoes to flaunt in California. When, years ago, they had been in love, he had jokingly called her a shoe fetishist. Now he called her a shopaholic. He had loved her jaunty walk, comparing her to a Shetland pony, but now, as he watched her go, he wondered whether her legs were not too short and whether in middle age her body, all right at present, would become barrel-shaped. Sulkily he joined their guests.

"A very lovely cathedral. We were comparing it to Durham and Lincoln."

Patsy Drew never seemed to feel tired. What did Alison see in her?

"This is much cosier." Mungo made an effort.

"Cosy?"

"Friendlier. Smaller. Less far to walk."

"Are we tiring you, Mungo?" Eli was concerned, younger, more spry than Mungo, a lot fitter; all that jogging.

"Lord, no." He rallied his manners.

"It's all new to us. You see it all the time." Patsy was apologetic.

"Actually I've never been to Exeter before."

"You don't expect us to believe that." Must she be arch?

"I've been through it in the train."

"But it's so close to your home."

"Two hundred miles isn't close to an Englishman."

The Drews laughed, appreciating his English wit.

"Why don't we skip the rest and have lunch?" Eli suggested. "Then we can do Bath on our way home, perhaps fit in Wells too."

"Certainly Wells," said Patsy. "Wells is a must."

"So is a drink." Mungo headed towards the cathedral door. "Alison said she'd meet us in the bar."

As they walked across the Close to the Clarence Hotel, Mungo glimpsed the mystery bottom. It vanished through the door but the hall was empty when they reached it.

In the bar Mungo ordered drinks and settled his guests in

comfortable chairs. The bar was full of strangers. "I had better go and reserve a table," he said and made his way to the restaurant. As he went he looked about but saw no familiar face. He peered into the other bars and the buffet but to no avail. Returning to the bar after reserving a table he met Alison.

"Bought anything?"

"Three pairs."

"Oh God!"

"Just what I need for the States."

"Want," said Mungo sourly.

"Want, too, of course. Have you ordered me a drink?"

"Not yet. Didn't know what you'd have."

"I always drink vodka."

"You don't, you often drink sherry and when you are feeling continental you drink Campari."

"Mungo darling, don't be so marital."

When Alison called him marital there was a row in the offing. Mungo apologised. "Sorry, sorry, sorry."

"Patsy, love, wouldn't you like to freshen up?" Alison bent to kiss Patsy as though they hadn't met for a week. Mungo flinched at the Americanism.

"Order me a vodka on the rocks while we are gone," Alison said to Mungo.

Mungo said, "Of course", resisting the urge to say, "Sure". He wondered whether Alison was having it off with Eli, or had it in mind for the future.

The women went in search of what Patsy called the john. Mungo took a swallow of whisky and waited for the feeling of rejuvenation which would get him through lunch and the afternoon. "The wine waiter says they have a good Bordeaux," he said to Eli. This was one of the days he must get a bit drunk if he was to survive.

In the ladies' lavatory Hebe took off her clothes. The only annoying thing about Marks & Spencer was the absence of anywhere to try things on. Over the years, when shopping in Exeter before meeting Silas off his school train, she had formed the habit of taking her purchases to the Clarence, trying them on in the ladies' cloakroom and returning such things as did not fit immediately. The fact that Marks & Spencer now had places where it was possible to try on clothes had escaped her, thanks to her myopia. The cloakroom was empty. Hebe left her clothes and bag on hooks in the lavatory and stepped out into the room to try on bikinis. She had tried on two and was about to try on a third when Alison and Patsy came suddenly into the room.

Alison stared. Patsy's mouth formed an "O". Hebe stepped back into the lavatory and bolted the door. She stood petrified with embarrassment. She listened.

Alison and Patsy went to other lavatories. She heard them go in, bolt the doors, pee, rustle paper, flush water, unbolt the doors, come out, wash their hands, leave the cloakroom and a burst of chatter in the corridor.

Her hands fumbling, Hebe dressed, put the bikinis back in their bag. She could not now remember which fitted her. In the confined space she combed her hair, adjusted her glasses and stood listening. Would they say something to the hall porter, complain at the desk? She had never been to the Clarence for a drink or a meal; she was not known. Assuming nonchalance she strolled into the passage which led to the hall. As she went she adjured herself, look natural, don't hurry. She had not expected to meet Mungo hurrying down the passage on his way to the gents. She dropped her parcels as she put up her hand to shield her face.

"What are you doing here?" Mungo had had two double whiskies and couldn't believe his eyes. He stooped to pick up her parcels. Their faces came close as Hebe too bent down.

"What are *you* doing here?" she said accusingly. "Why aren't you at home?"

"Alison's got these Americans staying. They are into cathedrals – Winchester, Stonehenge, Sherborne yesterday; today Exeter, Wells, Bath and if they notice how close they are to Glastonbury it'll be that, too—"

"You're drunk." She snatched her parcels from him. "Your breath stinks."

"Only a little. Do you live here?"

"No, no, no."

"Near here?" He loomed over her, taller than she remembered.

"Certainly not." She was in retreat.

"Alison's going to America on a long visit. Got her eye on the husband."

"So what?"

"So we can be together, darling," said Mungo loudly.

"Don't call me that," Hebe hissed.

"She won't hear, she's in the bar." He snatched at the hand holding the bikinis and found himself grasping the bag. "Oh," he followed her, "here, this is yours." He caught her arm. "It

479

was your bottom I saw earlier on. I couldn't place it."

"What are you talking about?" She took the bag and hurried on.

"Since when have you worn glasses?"

"Goodbye." Hebe crossed the street in great leaps and jumped on to a passing bus. Looking back she saw Mungo, a head taller than anyone on the pavement, black hair ruffled, staring after her, a wild look in the blue eyes squinting down his highland nose.

Left on the pavement Mungo remembered that he was on his way to the gents. When he rejoined his wife and guests they were laughing as Patsy described her consternation at finding a naked girl in the ladies' rest room.

"She wore nothing except a pair of glasses." Patsy and Alison shook with laughter.

Eli chortled. "Life in a cathedral town. Beats Trollope."

"She's not a trollop," said Mungo, mishearing.

"Who isn't?" Alison took him up quickly.

Mungo sensed danger. "That girl," he said. "You know who I mean, that girl who cooks for mother. Thought I saw her in the street just now. What's her name, can you remember?" he asked Alison. "Does she come from these parts?"

"I think she comes from London. I can't remember what she's called." Alison appeared uninterested. "Don't order more drinks, darling; shouldn't we have lunch?"

"Of course, of course, and we'd better look sharp if we are doing Bath and Wells. We could do Glastonbury too, why not?" cried Mungo, his voice hearty with relief.

Alison, whose intake of alcohol did not match her husband's, took the wheel on the drive to Wells and Bath. They decided they would after all give Glastonbury a miss. Patsy had heard that it was the haunt of hippies and drug addicts. "We have our own in California."

Feigning sleep on the back seat, Mungo wondered what the hell Hebe was doing in Exeter. Secretive girl, he loathed having to communicate via her forwarding address. Did she perhaps live hereabouts? Why had he not hung on to her and forced her to tell him her address? The moment he was sure of Alison's dates for Santa Barbara he would write, get her to join him. It might be possible to take her abroad, she had had a bagful of bikinis. For a while, speeding towards Wells and Bath, he planned a Mediterranean holiday, but as the wine he had drunk at lunch on top of the whiskies began to wear off he ruminated sadly that it was Hebe who called the tune, not him, that it was her who would choose dates and locale as she always did, a service flat off Sloane Avenue.

Alison, in the driving seat, switched the driving mirror to get a glimpse of herself. She was dissatisfied with her appearance. Her hair, naturally the colour of golden-shred marmalade, needed styling. Cornflower-blue eyes were fine but would be better if she had her sandy eyelashes dyed, as Patsy had suggested. Time I bothered more, she thought, sweeping on to the M5 motorway. She twitched the mirror again to look at Mungo on the back seat. She thought with amusement, as she often had before, that he had all the assurance of an old Etonian without having actually been there, whereas she herself felt unfulfilled and insecure in spite of her natural bossiness. I must put that right, she told herself, moving into the fast lane. She wondered how often Mungo had been unfaithful. He had looked shifty at lunch when his mother's cook had been mentioned. Aha! Alison said to herself, sticking out her lower lip. Oho! "I shall get my hair restyled in the States," she said over her shoulder to Patsy, and "We are sending the boys to Eton," she said to Eli, sitting beside.

"Is that so?" said Eli, unimpressed. "Our speed limit in the States is fifty, what's yours?"

"Seventy." Alison increased speed, pushing the speedometer up to eighty.

FIVE

Hebe swept a mile down through Exeter on the bus and walked back up the hill cursing Mungo. She did not think Alison had recognised her; it was years since they had met when she had first gone to work for Mungo's mother. In those days she'd had a fringe, now her glasses were an added disguise. With an effort she dismissed Mungo and his wife from her mind. The day, which she had planned as a peaceful shopping day, had lost its appeal. What mattered was to be in time for the train bearing Silas from school and his other life. She just had time to return the bikinis and get her money back. She forced herself to be patient, not to hurry getting her car from the car park, not to drive too fast to the station, to park tidily, to comb her hair, adjust her skirt, relax, concentrate on Silas.

Always after the separation of term Hebe feared Silas would be changed, no longer hers, that he would not accept her. She was afraid of embarrassing him by too great a show of affection. She paced the platform in painful anticipation.

When the train arrived on time she was surprised. She had persuaded herself it would be late. When Silas hugged her she nearly wept with relief. When they had piled his belongings into the car and he sat beside her as she drove he said, sounding heartfelt, "It's great to be home." She felt overwhelming joy at having so miraculous a child. She loved his chestnut hair, his wide mouth, his nose jutting large, his slightly haughty expression which his eyes belied.

"You have grown," she said.

"What do you expect?" he answered. Her euphoria evaporated.

"What do you want to do these holidays?" she asked. She had been about to ask, "What shall we do these holidays?"

Annoyed with himself but anxious to assert his independence, Silas said, "I thought Giles and I could go exploring. There are places we have not been to."

"I could take you in the car." Involuntarily Hebe included herself in his life.

"We rather like going by bus, if you don't mind." Silas looked at her sidelong.

"Of course I don't mind," Hebe said sharply. "Why should I?"

She thought, my role is to cook, give him pocket money, be there when needed, if needed. For God's sake, she adjured herself, don't cling, don't be possessive.

"One of the boys offered me a lift down. His father's taking him to Cornwall," said Silas. "The Scillies, actually."

"Why didn't you accept?"

"I'd rather come by train. I look forward to seeing you waiting on the platform. I like this long drive home with you."

"Oh, darling." Her heart leapt.

"Of course it would have saved the train fare."

"To hell with the train fare," cried Hebe and they both laughed, mocking the ruinous train fare.

"How are the jobs? When did you get home? Do you mind that sort of work?"

"It's the only work I'm any good at, it pays. Do you mind me doing it?" She feared his criticism.

"Why should I?" Silas was genuinely surprised. "One of the boys has a sister who cooks for shooting parties. He says some of the guns try and lay her."

"Oh." What did Silas know about laying? Academic knowledge, surely.

"I told him you specialised in old ladies because they pay more and he said he'd tell her. Would it spoil your market, Ma?"

"Of course not. There's room for all."

"D'you never get asked to do jobs in the holidays?"

"I wouldn't take one," said Hebe quickly. "Holidays are my only chance of seeing you."

"You could take a quickie, go for a week, I wouldn't mind."

"What do you mean?"

"If you send me away to school I could quite well stay at home while you work."

Oh my God! What a deadly barb.

Silas, who had been meaning to say something of the sort for some time, thought perhaps he had said too much.

Hebe wondered whether she was losing touch, whether she had ever been in touch with Silas.

483

"Are you happy at school?" Ask a silly question.

"It's all right."

"What sort of answer is that?" she cried in distress.

"I'm perfectly happy, Ma," Silas lied, already at twelve adept. "I've lots of friends," he added, knowing that such a statement would assuage her fears. "How is the street?" he asked sweetly, conscious that she thought it ugly.

"As ugly as ever." Hebe glanced at him, wondering where he got that large nose. "But you used to like it."

"I do like it. It's full of secret people."

"Hannah, Giles, Amy Tremayne."

"And other people. You never seem to get to know them. Don't you think you might like some of them?"

"Not really." Hebe spoke truthfully. "I'm not sociable. I'm never at home long enough."

"You think the street's too ugly to have anyone interesting living in it. I heard you say so to Hannah."

"You make me sound snobbish."

"We wouldn't be any different if we lived in another street." Silas felt protective towards the street, which he found fascinating in its dark conformity.

"I would be different in a Georgian square or a country cottage, said Hebe, thinking how different she was while away on her jobs. "As long as it was beautiful."

"It's home, you are there."

Hebe was afraid to speak. One minute he snubs, the next he gives me courage. She wished she knew her mysterious child better.

"I am happy you like it," she said. "And," she joked, "if by some miracle a job turns up in mid-holidays you can see how you get on by yourself."

"I'd get on all right." He was serious.

"They always pay twice as much." She hardly believed it was herself speaking. Would it be good for him to find out what it's like to be alone? "You'd be alone," she said, expecting him to protest.

"I'd get meals off Hannah or Amy if I needed to." Silas mocked her, thinking that being alone would be wonderful, very different from the loneliness of school.

Nearing the steep street, Hebe feared she would never really know Silas. Then she remembered the nightmare of the day before and realised, as she stopped at her door, that she seldom experienced her panic when away working. She thought with amusement of her meeting with Mungo and was laughing as she drew up at her door, enjoying her fondness for Mungo.

"Here we are, my old Miracle," and Silas too laughed, delighted to be back, glad that his mother was apparently unhurt.

"I'll change my clothes," he said as they carried his luggage upstairs, "then find Giles." He was anxious to slot back into his home environment.

"I will get tea." Hebe wished she was not shy with Silas, that he did not keep her at arm's length. He has inherited my secrecy and reticence, she thought. Then, remembering her unfortunate *rencontre* with Mungo, she wished it were possible to share the joke.

Silas came down wearing jeans and a T-shirt. "D'you mind if I go and find Giles now?"

"There's a letter for you on the mantelshelf."

Silas opened the letter. "Oh, great!" he exclaimed. "Magic! Michael Reeves' mother is asking me to stay. How brilliant!"

"Who is Michael Reeves?" Hebe felt a chill.

"A boy at school. They've taken a cottage on the Scilly Isles. They sail. You won't mind, will you? It's only for three weeks."

"Three weeks?" She tried to keep her voice level. "When?"

"That'll be terrific." Silas was overjoyed. "Three weeks' sailing. Just imagine, I've never sailed."

"When?" She felt cold, he was sure he was going.

"She says to say what date suits you. She's quite nice. She came to the sports at half-term."

"I was working and couldn't get away." Hebe avoided school functions.

"You don't mind, do you?" Silas looked anxious. "It's the boy who offered me a lift down."

"I see." She was stunned by disappointment.

"Sure you don't mind?" Silas assumed he would go, did not question.

"Of course I don't. It's very kind of Mrs Reeves." I must not cling, she told herself. "I must write to her. It will be fun for you."

"Can't we telephone?" Silas was in a rush to fix a date, seize the opportunity, pin it down.

"Yes, love, we will telephone tonight." She surrendered.

"Good. I'll be off now and find Giles." Silas left the house, leaving all the doors open as he ran, hungry for life.

For several minutes Hebe was in misery. Then she made her decision. She would work. Not Mungo, that would be too soon, he would think he'd won a point. Mrs Fox would do, no complications there and quite good money. She was smiling when Silas came back, bringing Giles with him.

"And how was Paris?"

"Wonderful." Giles was a masculine version of Hannah.

"Tea?"

"I've had mine." Giles smiled, showing crooked teeth. Would George Scoop fix these for free if Hannah married him?

"Have another."

"Thanks." Giles was fond of his friend's mother, considered him lucky. "I wish my mother was a cook."

"It's a useful trade." Hebe offered Giles cake. "I shall go to Mrs Fox in Wiltshire while you are in the Scillies," she said to Silas.

"Who is Mrs Fox?"

"One of the old ladies who can afford a cook now and then to jolly her up."

"Will you be back when I come back from the Scillies?"

"I will be back," she said. "Of course I will."

SIX

Mungo Duff quarrelled with Alison when Eli and Patsy left, perversely accusing her of selfishness in planning to leave him alone. While he was anxious that she should go to Santa Barbara he did not wish her to enjoy herself, though he hoped she would deceive him with Eli. She must go, feel grateful to him for parting with her, and return to cherish him with a guilty conscience. If he could find Hebe he would welcome Alison home with open arms; if he failed he would be in a strong position to play the injured husband. He hoped Eli would disappoint her in bed. Alistair and Ian were to visit friends, another source of recrimination. Alison had arranged their holiday without consulting him.

"They will grow up without knowing their parents," he had protested. "We might as well be divorced."

"I often think," Alison had answered, "that children of the divorced see more of their parents than those of the undivorced, but is it a good thing? I can't see what benefit they would derive from you in your present mood. It is important," she had added purposefully, aggravating, "that they should make useful friends, then they will meet the right kind of girl. They can't start soon enough."

"All right, go off, enjoy yourself. Leave me on my own."

"You were invited too." She had said this before.

"You know perfectly well I can't leave the office just now."

"I do not. You often leave the office and pop down to London. Your office manages all right then."

"I keep in touch. I am on business, anyway." Mungo thought of how little business he did when he "popped", as Alison called it, down to London: a token telephone call, a business lunch, the rest of the time spent with Hebe. He cursed Hebe's fiendish one-way system, her casual telephone call suggesting a date. Why did he put up with it, he asked himself, not bothering to answer, for if one thing was sure Hebe called the tune. "And I pay," he groaned.

Alison took him up. "You know perfectly well I am paying for myself."

"I didn't mean in money terms. I meant I pay in loneliness."

"Go and see your mother, she's lonely, if anyone is." Alison was unsympathetic. "She'll probably have that woman she gets to cook for her."

"I don't suppose so." Mungo had already checked with his mother that Hebe was not coming until the autumn. "No, dearest," his mother had answered his next question, "I don't know where she lives. Miss Thomson writes to a forwarding address in London. She comes three times a year, as you know, so that Miss Thomson can have time off."

"Miss Thomson," said Mungo to Alison, "isn't due for a holiday."

"Why can't you go when Miss Thomson is there?"

"Visitors are too much for her."

"I don't believe that. She is always very welcoming to me."

"And I don't believe that." Mungo was determined to be disagreeable.

"Believe what you like. I am not going to let you spoil my trip."

In bed Mungo lay thinking of Hebe. What had she been doing in Exeter? Had she not said, the year before, when, after her stint cooking for his mother she had let him take her for a week to Devonshire, that she had never been there? Had she not exclaimed with delight as he drove her through lanes frothy with cow parsley, bright with campion and bluebells? Had she been putting on an act? What had she been doing in the Clarence? Was she staying there with another man? Mungo groaned, remembering Hebe's long arms and legs wrapped round him in her lovely but casual embrace.

"Got a stomach ache?" Alison, half asleep in the next bed, roused herself.

"No, no."

"Let a woman sleep, then. You drank too much at lunch yesterday. It always upsets you."

"I can't wait for you to go to America," Mungo shouted.

"All right, all right—" Feeling herself valued, Alison stretched in her bed, thinking it would do Mungo good to be without her. She was glad he minded her leaving him alone. She was unaware that for years Mungo had spent six weeks a year with Hebe, weeks when he was supposed to be on business in London. She had heard from friends that he was seen about with a girl, but since he came home sweet-tempered she had long since decided that London was good for him. Whoever he saw there presented no threat. She herself, when Mungo was absent, either had a room in the house decorated or went abroad with a friend to look at pictures and cathedrals. It was high time she altered the pattern. If Mungo could step out so could she.

While Alison slept Mungo searched his mind for ways to find Hebe, momentarily considering employing a private detective, deciding against as too embarrassing. Hebe had not wronged him, all that was wrong was her bloody mysterious way of conducting their affair. Unable to sleep, he thought back to his first encounter with her years before. As he savoured the memory, Alison in the next bed snorted, turning away from him. It was thanks to Alison he had met Hebe and, oh God, Mungo groaned, having to be grateful to Alison was hard, for Alison was a good wife, albeit bossy. A wonderful manager, a good mother, a particularly good daughter-in-law, and this, combined with her bossiness, had brought Hebe into his life. His father, long dead, would have been amused, thought Mungo. His father who, satisfied with his own marriage, never strayed, had found the straits his friends got themselves into vastly amusing, recounting unfortunate incidents, illegitimate children to be provided for, abortions arranged, risky ailments – he always referred to venereal disease as a risky ailment – the expensive upkeep of mistresses hilariously funny. Mungo's father had strayed, thought Mungo, into sudden death, leaving his mother rich and lonely in their large house which he would in due course inherit and, the taxman permitting, pass on to his two sons at present at preparatory school, heading for Eton, Alison not considering his old school good enough.

Mungo lay listening to his wife breathing and thought of the time of his father's death, when Alison had taken charge, arranged the funeral, not bothering to make it look as though Mungo had arranged it, had written and answered letters, had comforted and consoled effortlessly, found a cook-housekeeper to run the large house, live-in with colour TV, her own car, regular days out and long holidays, for a modest salary. It was the holidays – a fortnight three times a year – which did the trick of keeping Miss Thomson happy, Alison emphasised, when describing her mother-in-law's arrangements. Then, Alison would explain to incompetent daughters-in-law, then the splendid extravagance of a temporary cook during Miss Thomson's absence, so that Lucy could entertain all the people she wished without annoying Miss Thomson, who liked a quiet routine. "And here," Alison would say, "here I was in for a stroke of luck. I was recommended a woman. She comes when Miss Thomson goes away and everybody's happy."

"Is it expensive?" Alison would be asked.

"Well worth it," Alison would reply, not divulging the cook's salary. "One is sometimes very lucky," Alison would say in a satisfied voice which made Mungo choke, for Alison's good luck was also his. When seven years ago he had visited his mother without warning, she had said, "Darling, how lovely to see you. Go and tell the cook you will be here for dinner. Miss Thomson is on holiday."

Mungo had been bemused. "Do we have cooks in this day and age?"

"Didn't Alison tell you? You will find her in the kitchen; tell her you are here."

And there in the kitchen had been Hebe. The only bloody nuisance, thought Mungo, listening to Alison in the next bed, was that Hebe only appeared when Miss Thomson went away, not when Alison decided to go to Santa Barbara, thus giving him a gorgeous opportunity of seeing her, a golden chance he looked like missing. Mungo wondered whether his mother did, possibly, have an address other than the forwarding address he had himself. He could say he had a friend who had a mother in similar circumstances who needed a temporary cook. He could, perhaps, extract Hebe's address in some other crafty way. It did seem so stupid not to know where she lived. Unable to sleep, he remembered Hebe as he had first seen her.

He had gone into the kitchen expecting a middle-aged frump and found Hebe rolling pastry, intent. She had not heard him. He had time to take in the sight of a tall girl in a pink striped dress and white apron, a parody of a cook. She had glossy dark hair cut shoulder length and a full mouth. She had the largest, darkest eyes he had ever seen. She smiled and he quite simply fell in love and determined to seduce her.

This had not proved immediately easy. To start with, Mungo questioned his mother after dinner – the best dinner he had ever eaten under her roof – as to where she had found so excellent a cook. He had been surprised that she was Alison's discovery, though not surprised that he had not been told about it.

"Dear Alison," said Mungo's mother. "She took so much

trouble. She interviewed at least six people. This girl was the only one who would agree to fit in with Miss Thomson. Miss Thomson plans to go away in spring, summer and autumn. Apparently her plans suit Hebe. Alison took a lot of trouble. Now she does not have to trouble any more."

Mungo noted the repetition of the word "trouble" and wondered if his mother was as fond of Alison as she professed.

"So all Miss Thomson has to do is make her own arrangements."

"I should think she'd do that anyway."

"Yes, dear." Mrs Duff did not rise further than a slight swirl in the conversational pool.

"Where does she come from?"

"I have not asked. I do not believe in prying."

"Did she have references?"

"I believe Alison found she was connected in some way with a woman who worked for your father, all very respectable. She is obviously—"

"Obviously what?" Mungo knew what his mother hesitated to say. He wanted to see whether she would describe Hebe as one of us, a lady, or some similar euphemism such as a nice girl.

"Well, darling, educated."

"Lots of girls are educated."

"You know quite well what I mean."

"Even servants."

"She isn't a servant," Mrs Duff protested.

"Then what is she?"

"Darling, don't be boring." Lucy Duff had changed the subject.

During the two days he spent with his mother Mungo made frequent attempts at conversation with Hebe. She was polite but busy. She did not eat with his mother as Miss Thomson did and when not at work vanished in her car. Mungo ran out of excuses to visit the kitchen and left after two days determined to put the girl out of his mind. She remained in it and a week later he came back to see his mother using the excuse of a hiccup in her income tax. Lucy Duff was not deceived and secretly wished him joy. While taking advantage of Alison's bossiness and capability, she did not like her any the better for it. Let Mungo have some fun.

Finding Hebe preparing dinner, Mungo rushed straight to the point. "I have come back to ask you to sleep with me."

Stirring the sauce she was making, Hebe glanced up and said, "I won't sleep with you here."

"Why not?"

"Not in your mother's house."

"But you will?" Mungo stared at her.

"When I leave here we can go to an hotel."

"You will – oh my God!" Mungo felt exhilarated; couldn't believe his ears.

"I'll see what it's like then—"

"You'll see what what's like?"

"I'll see," Hebe was patient, "whether I like sleeping with you. We can come to an arrangement if I do and you want to go on with it."

"Oh." He was deflated by her calm tone.

"I can't do it for nothing. I have to earn my living. I am very expensive."

"Are you a prostitute, then?" Mungo was puzzled, excited.

"I'm a cook but if you want I'll give you a try."

"Give *me* a try!" Mungo exclaimed.

"It's you who asked me, not me you." She seemed so calm, so detached.

"Please." Mungo put his arm round her and tried to nuzzle her neck.

"Mind my sauce." She pushed him away with her elbow. He saw she was smiling. "We will spend a few days together, see how it goes." She stirred the sauce. "Then, if I'm happy, we will discuss money."

"If *you* are happy."

"You will be happy all right. I have to think of me." Had she been mocking him? "I am a very expensive cook," she said. "The same applies to bed."

Mungo did not grudge her a penny. All he minded was her secrecy. He was no wiser now than when he first met her. He did not know where she came from or where she went when they parted. Meeting her in Exeter was the first clue he had in all the years. Why was she wearing spectacles? What was she doing in Exeter, he asked himself, as futilely he wooed sleep. He knew she did other cooking jobs, that she had other lovers. He groaned with anger and frustration.

"Do stop waking me. If you can't sleep go to the dressing-room," Alison scolded. "Take a digestive pill."

"Your snorting keeps me awake."

"I don't snore."

"I said snort, silly bitch." Mungo got furiously out of bed and made for the dressing-room. Would Eli put up with Alison's snorts? Hebe never snorted or snored. Trying to settle in the dressing-room bed he resolved once more to pump his mother. She must know of something of Hebe's background.

SEVEN

Louisa Fox recognised Hebe's voice when she picked up the receiver. "Hebe, how nice to hear your voice."

"I wondered whether you would like me to come during August. I have a cancellation, so I just—"

"Thought you might come to me?"

"Yes, I—"

Louisa was enthusiastic. "What day will you come? It will be a treat."

"Would the seventh to the twenty-first suit you? Have you got your little book handy?"

"Not necessary. August is a month when I lie low. We shall be on our own."

"Oh good. I'll arrive in the evening and bring a dinner to cook."

"I shall look forward to it. You can tell me your news when you come." Not, thought Louisa Fox, that that girl ever has anything to tell. She switched on the television for the news and wondered whether to ring Lucy Duff. While she thought about this the news reader led her through world disasters to the weather man. She dialled Lucy's number.

"Lucy, that you? Listen, I have the treasure coming in August. Am I not lucky?"

"I thought you never got her in August. I can't. I supposed she had a child for the holidays or another job. I never get her at Christmas or Easter. Miss Thomson has to arrange spring, summer and autumn. She was here in May. Two blissful greedy weeks. Can I come and stay?"

"I don't think so. I will get her to stuff my deep freeze; come later on. Did Mungo visit you while she was with you?"

"No, Alison had him on the lead."

"Really tied?" Both women laughed.

"How do I know?" said Mungo's mother. "Maggie Cook-Popham's Dick swears he saw Mungo with Hebe in London."

"Did he indeed? Where did he see them?"

"Walking in Kew Gardens."

"When was she with Maggie? Don't tell me her boy—"

"I bet he tried, though if he had succeeded the whole world would hear and that wouldn't suit—"

"Wouldn't suit Hebe. Does Mungo ever—"

"Never breathes a word. Wouldn't dare say anything in case I let something slip to Alison, as if I would."

"As if you would." The old women, separated by miles of wire, laughed.

"We are not like Maggie," said Lucy. "Though for news that doesn't matter, telling Maggie certainly saves stamps."

"Wouldn't it be a good thing if you could get Hebe to come in the holidays? Your grandchildren would love her food. If she is coming to me in August it may mean she is not tied in the holidays, as you thought," suggested Louisa.

"I am not having the little beasts to stay," cried Lucy. "Not until they are a lot older."

"Heavens, why not?"

"They picked all the buttons off my Victorian chairs."

Suppressing her inclination to laugh, Louisa said, "How dreadful. What possessed them?" Lucy must have annoyed the little beasts in some way.

"Alison is going away. I gather she is sending them to stay with friends. Mungo is hopeless with them, he shouts and they laugh. She is sending them to people who stand no nonsense."

"They will be better when they grow older," opined Louisa.

"One hopes so." Lucy was doubtful. "We must remember your telephone bill," she said, hinting that Louisa had talked long enough.

"Goodbye," said Louisa, ringing off. It takes the rich to remind one of bills, she thought. Mungo would one day be rich. Louisa considered him fortunate if he was having an affair with Hebe. It was old history now, and it would hurt Lucy to know she had been second choice. Mungo's father had asked her to marry him before he asked Lucy. Mungo might never have existed, since I am barren, and if I am right and Hebe is Christopher's grandchild she might not exist either. Louisa was surprised that Lucy had never noticed Hebe's extraordinary likeness to Christopher Rutter, starchy, pompous, upright, who had long ago proposed marriage and had been surprised and angry when she refused him. He had married a girl as upright as himself. Calculating dates,

495

Lucy decided Hebe was probably a granddaughter, child of the daughter killed in the air crash. Suspecting Hebe's provenance, Louisa forbore telling her friend, since Lucy, who reproached others of gossip, could gossip with the best, and Hebe, for reasons best known to herself, never spoke of her family or friends, not even of Bernard who, by coincidence, knew Hebe since he lived in the same part of the country. Louisa did not think it necessary for Hebe to know of her friendship with Bernard. Bernard was amused by Hebe, she knew, and loved her. Lucy would be fascinated by any connection with Christopher Rutter and gossip. Recommending Hebe as a temporary cook who also worked for Maggie Cook-Popham, Lucy had said, "Not only is she the most marvellous cook, but she's a lady," using the expression which Mungo deplored. Since Hebe never discussed her clients Louisa respected her reticence, believing she travelled from one post to another. While she joked about Mungo with his mother, she would not have credited him as a business transaction. If she considered Hebe's and Mungo's affair, she thought of it as a bit of fun for the girl and for Mungo, married to managing Alison, a well-deserved treat. She would have been astonished to hear the difference in the rates for mistresses compared with cooks.

Looking forward to Hebe's cooking, Louisa welcomed Hebe's visit, blessing the day when Lucy had suggested she should give her a trial. Lucy, thought Louisa with a pang of envy, could afford permanent Miss Thomson whereas she herself could only just manage Hebe's exorbitant fees once or twice a year. She was quite unaware that Hebe, liking her, charged her less than Lucy and charged Maggie Cook-Popham, whom she neither liked nor trusted, very much more.

While Louisa telephoned Lucy Duff and looked forward to Hebe's cooking, Hebe enjoyed the short time there was with Silas before he went to the Scillies, happy to watch him relax from the taut boy back from school, glad that he had a friend in Giles. Though hurt at first by Silas' defection, she found herself looking forward to a fortnight in Wiltshire; better to be busy than sit at home wondering how he was enjoying himself. Meeting Mungo in Exeter had alarmed her. It was possible he might find some lead to her whereabouts. If she was away in Wiltshire it lessened his chances of finding her. She was fond of Louisa Fox, loved her house, enjoyed working for her. But she reckoned without Miss Thomson, who resented hints that the girl who took her place provided imaginative meals and was not opposed to Lucy entertaining her friends, a thing she was not prepared to do, feeling martyred if anyone came for a drink, morning coffee or tea. She feared Hebe, resenting Lucy referring to her as "a treasure" or, worse, "my lady cook". Listening on the extension to Louisa's conversation with Lucy enraged her. The jealousy she already felt of Hebe lit a latent talent for mischief. Preparing the supper she would presently share with her employer, Miss Thomson considered the theory she had hitherto dismissed as absurd of Mungo and Alison divorcing, of Mungo marrying Hebe and of Hebe either superseding her permanently or losing her her job in some sly way. Miss Thomson was saving to retire to a flat on the Spanish Costa. Fearing any interference with her plan, she decided to poke an apparently innocent spoke in Hebe's wheel. She chose a postcard, addressed it to Alison and wrote:

"Dear Mrs Duff: Should you wish to contact H. Rutter, the temporary cook, she will be working for Mrs Fox in Wiltshire from the 7th to 21st. Yrs. Truly, A. Thomson."

Reading this, Miss Thomson hoped that Alison would wonder, What on earth does this postcard from Miss Thomson mean? Is it a warning? She would grow more alert, with luck make trouble for Hebe, leave Miss Thomson in peace to complete her savings. It can do no harm, thought Miss Thomson, opening a can of soup, it doesn't exactly say anything but in Alison's shoes I would have a little think.

The card dropped through the letter-box an hour after Alison's departure for the States. Reading it, Mungo whooped with delight.

497

EIGHT

Hebe let herself in to Amy's house, her spirits lifting with affection.

"Hullo, love." She kissed Amy. "I've sent the boys out for the day. Gave them sandwiches."

"In the rain?"

"Never mind the rain. Have you seen Hannah?"

"Gone to her elocution lesson." Amy grinned. "Teeth, name, now it's her speech has to change."

"If it makes her happy." Hebe sat beside Amy. She looked round, noticing that Amy's paperweights, banished by Hannah, were back on the windowsill where the colours caught the sun.

"Where did you buy those lovelies?" She stroked the old woman's hand.

"Given to me, I did not buy them."

"Ah."

"Valuable now, you know." Amy was complacent. "Where are you going tomorrow?"

"To Mrs Fox. It's better to earn a bob or two than sit around moping while Silas is away."

"Who will mind Trip? Would you like me to feed her?"

"Terry's going to feed her."

"Ho, Terry," Amy mocked. "That one!"

"I've brought the rent." Hebe handed an envelope to the old woman.

Amy counted the money. "You paying a year in advance or something? This is far too much."

"I got a bonus. Please take it."

"Who from?" Amy looked at Hebe, black eyes glinting. "Not that blackamoor?"

"A bonus from *Terry*." Hebe grinned. "A goodbye present."

"Leaving you, is he?" Amy was curious.

"Still friends. He's – er – moving on."

498

"Queer, isn't he?"

"A little fantastic—"

"You're fond of him, aren't you?"

"He makes me laugh. We read poetry."

"So you've told me. Love poems."

"And others, too. He's passed his O-level."

"Failed last time, didn't he?"

"I failed mine!" Hebe looked distressed.

"Took him on to annoy the old man, didn't you? Couldn't resist the combination of a black boy with a failed exam."

"It began that way," Hebe said stiffly. "He's become a good friend."

"What's he do? Still burglar alarms?"

"He is self-employed, goes solo now."

"Like you."

"Like me." Hebe returned Amy's look calmly and added gently, "Like us."

Amy squeezed Hebe's hand. "I never set about it like you. Didn't read poetry and play backgammon. Didn't call the tune. I don't know how you get away with it."

Hebe looked away, not answering.

"Lovely girls like you should get married. Hannah wants to remarry."

"Her dentist."

"But she finds him dull. Edward Krull was dull, she doesn't want to repeat her error."

"Oh, do you know someone who knows him?" Hebe was surprised into gossip, not surprised when Amy did not answer. She sat in the small sitting-room in the house which Amy had made home for her in her time of crisis, sheltering her until after Silas' birth, later renting her the house across the street. "What would I have done without you, Amy?"

"You'd have managed."

"You saved us."

"Don't exaggerate. If not me it would have been somebody else. You had got yourself into a fuss, that's all."

"Fuss." Hebe thought fuss an understatement. She said, "There was nobody else. No, Amy, you saved us all right, then started me on the right track."

"Few people would call it the right track," Amy laughed delightedly.

"You introduced me to Bernard."

"The old bastard. We could have managed without him," Amy sniffed.

"He bought my things, didn't cheat me, introduced me to the job at the hotel."

"Some job. I grant he did not cheat. He had no business to let you meet that Hippolyte. You could have worked for Lucy Duff and Louisa Fox."

"I do work for them."

"Decent people. I worked for them when they needed a secretary before—"

"My grandfather." Hebe spoke stiffly.

"Thought you didn't like him mentioned."

"I don't."

"Well, then. What did that chef teach you that you had not learned at the Cordon Bleu?"

"Soufflés." Hebe remembered Hippolyte. "You laugh, you relax, you enjoy, you rise, light, generous, delicious, ready for a second helping." "He taught me how to make soufflés," she said gravely.

"Ho," said Amy, doubtful still. "Ho."

Changing the subject, Hebe said, "I'm dropping Mrs Cook-Popham, Amy. I don't like her son. I'm okay with Mrs Fox and Mrs Duff and the odd job."

"I distrust the odd jobs."

"I enjoy them," said Hebe, blithely thinking of Mungo and Hippolyte, regretting Terry. "It's the odd jobs that make the money as you—"

"As I should know. Odd jobs don't last," said Amy sadly, remembering in old age the delights of waking up in the double bed in the Hôtel d'Angleterre, the laughter, the rising sun glinting through the red plush curtains, the coffee and croissants. "They don't last," she said in bitter recollection of the lonely journey home to London, the quack doctor in Battersea, the pain and anguish. "They don't last. That's why I became a secretary."

"And worked for the Duffs and Foxes and my grandfather," said Hebe sombrely. She could remember Amy the secretary, but found it hard to visualise Amy in her career in Paris. Who was the man who let her down, she wondered, and heard for a second those other voices asking, "Who was the man?" and "Have an abortion".

"Shall I make us some tea?" She stood up to break the spell.

"Yes, love." Amy watched Hebe put on the kettle, lay out cups. She wondered for the millionth time who Silas' father could be. One would think, if one had not seen the child born, that the man had never existed. She tells me about her lovers, thought Amy. Those grandparents had not found out. Fools, always on at the child, "Don't mumble, don't interrupt," always "Don't". And "Hold yourself up," "Don't stoop."

Hebe, warming the pot, spooning tea, reaching for the kettle, thought, So Amy had an abortion. If she hadn't her child would be older than me, middle-aged. She handed Amy her cup.

"I keep my life narrow. It's better that way." She was defensive. "I stick to business."

"Yes." Amy took the cup. "I suppose it is best."

"I save a lot of money."

"A bank balance is nice," Amy agreed.

"I am getting Silas educated. That's what is important."

"Yes." Amy's thoughts were years away. Why did I panic? she asked herself. Out loud she exclaimed, "The bastard!"

"What?" Hebe was startled.

"I loved a bastard. He was not the marrying kind."

"As you know I think love should be avoided." Hebe's tone made Amy laugh.

"Well," she said, "I have you, I have Silas and now Giles and Hannah. Hannah believes in love; that's why she has changed her name and her teeth and is learning to talk posh. Hannah believes in marriage, but she ain't got *chien*. Perhaps in marriage you don't need *chien*."

"What's *chien*?"

"It's indefinable, sort of smell, what was called sex appeal in my day."

"Smell?" Hebe looked thoughtful. "I bet you had *chien*." She searched Amy's face for the girl concealed by old age.

"Not enough to hold him," said Amy. "He loved somebody else."

"At the same time?" Hebe was shocked.

"You're a fine one to talk, with your collection."

"But I don't love. Love's a disaster. I am an entertainer."

"You certainly entertain me. I live a vicarious life these days. Got Silas' address in the Islands in case of need?"

"I have it for you. The people are called Reeves. They sound all right."

"In what way?"

"Oh, you know." Hebe looked away.

"The right sort?" Amy's tone made Hebe flush.

"Yes, I suppose so." She stood up, hesitating, unwilling to leave Amy's atmosphere of serenity. She bent to kiss the old woman. "You would have made a wonderful wife."

"Not to him. Some men should never marry. I realise that now."

Hebe wondered how much Amy had suffered to acquire wisdom. "Some women, too," she suggested. "Perhaps I am one."

"From the way you are shaping you may well be. Your career—"

"Now, Amy, don't start on 'my career'."

"Certainly not my sort."

"Hannah will marry George Scoop."

"Hannah may not be as sensible as you think," said Amy. "I rather hope not. That dentist does not deserve Hannah."

"Not good enough for her?"

"She is not right for him."

"Gosh! Why?"

"She would treat him as she treated Edward Krull."

"How do you know?"

"You have to be a saint to tolerate bores. She is set on marriage though."

Hebe stood, considering Hannah's relatively simple life. "I must fly." She kissed Amy goodbye.

"Goodbye." Amy was comparing Hannah's intention of marrying with Hebe's mode of life, which to her mind did less damage. She chuckled, thinking, She does enjoy herself. She said out loud, her eyes reflecting the glint of sun on her paperweights: "She entertains, she enjoys variety." She spoke to the paperweights as to a living person. "And she makes people happy." Amy kept these thoughts to herself, having no one to share them with.

NINE

It is against my nature to confide more than the minimum to Amy, thought Hebe, sorting Silas' clothes for him to take on his visit. She wondered whether there was someone somewhere from whom it would not be necessary to guard her tongue. She piled Silas' clothes on the bed and took what was necessary to iron down to the kitchen. Putting up the ironing board, plugging in the iron, she thought of Mungo. Amy approved of Mungo, she was obviously doubtful about Terry. Was it not Terry who had encouraged her to call her clients The Syndicate, finding the joke in dubious taste. But would she approve of Mungo if she knew how foul his language could be, that he boasted ridiculously of the size of his member. Testing the heat of the iron, Hebe thought of Mungo with tolerant affection. Amy likes it when he takes me to Wimbledon, she thought, and the movies and the opera. He is very generous, always pays up without a murmur when I beat him at backgammon. I jolly him along, she thought, ironing Silas' T-shirts. I make him more fun for his family, better for his wife. Go home and practise, I say, you've had a nice change. Hebe folded the T-shirts, reached for some pillowcases, squirted water to damp them. She likes Mungo's class, she thought, smoothing the pillowcases, she knows Hippolyte was born a peasant, refers to him slightingly as Hippo. I call him Hippo to show fondness. He enjoys me, finds me funny. Hebe pressed the iron on the pillowcase. He gives me free lunches in his restaurant on my day off when I'm working for Maggie Cook-Popham, pretends he doesn't know me when I appear in his restaurant. Hebe chortled in recollection of Hippolyte's face when she had come not alone but with a potential client. He succeeded very neatly in putting me off the poor man. I was not planning to do more than tease. I was bored with the man, that was all. Who had it been, what had been his name? Folding the pillowcases Hebe racked her brain. There had been quite a number of potential members tried and found wanting. *"Il y a toujours l'un qui baise et*

503

l'autre qui tend la joue," Grandfather used to say. "Well, old man, it is I who *tend la joue.*" I am making a pretty profit in this career you suggested for me and getting Silas educated. There had been failures, Hebe admitted to herself. There was the man who had taken her to Rome for the weekend, dined her in the Piazza Navona: *prosciutto con figi,* a marvellous risotto, mountain strawberries. But he drank too much Soave, did not know its fatal effect. He had become alarmingly drunk, uncontrollably tiresome back at the hotel. I am not proud of that one, thought Hebe, switching off the iron. It was a dirty trick to throw all his trousers, shoes and pants out of the window, but what else could a girl do? I had to get away. I told Hippolyte about that one, she thought. He was so pleased he invited me to dinner with his partner. I never told Amy. I can't remember what he looked like, she thought, leaning on the ironing board. Some sort of English outdoor type? She shook her head, remembering Edward, head clerk in a solicitor's office, who did his wife's ironing every Saturday, ironing out the clients' marital dramas in imagination. There had been something sinister about him; she had not wanted him to start ironing out her troubles. Hebe folded the board and put it away. "Keep them keen," she said to Trip, who came mewing through the cat-flap. "Limit them to two weeks at most. With Mungo three times a year, four or five trips to Paris with Hippolyte and my cooking we are okay. I shan't really miss Terry. I can still see him. Can't put so much aside for the rainy day or Silas' university, that's all. It's a far cry," she said, picking up the purring cat, "from flogging my mother's pearls and Social Security. Not that I ever intended to depend on that!" The cat jumped out of her arms to lap milk from her saucer. "It's an enjoyable life," Hebe said to the cat, "but I wish Silas wasn't going away."

"Who is this you are taking me to see?" Sitting in the bus beside Silas, Giles wiped the steam from the window with his sleeve.

"An old man in a cottage miles from anywhere. He's got the most fabulous things. He is very old. He is called Bernard Quigley. He has a dog called Feathers and a cat. He's my friend. I found him when I was exploring across country."

"Is he a relation?"

"I have no relations." Silas stared at the passing country.

"You must have. I've got lots of relations in America and

Amy's Mum's aunt. Everybody has relations."

"We don't."

"You must have. Why don't you have relations?" Giles persisted.

"Don't be boring. I don't have any."

"Ask your mum. Doesn't she tell you about them? My mother tells me all about her father and mother, what they did and everything."

"Boring. We get off here." Silas led Giles out of the bus at the stop near a telephone kiosk forlornly posed at a crossroads. Rain was pelting down; the boys pulled up the hoods of their anoraks.

"We go across here." Silas climbed a gate into a field.

"Isn't there a path?"

"No."

Silas led the way through wet grass. Water seeped into their shoes, which squelched. "Should have worn wellies."

Giles persisted. "Surely your father had relations? Hasn't your mum kept up with them?"

"No."

"Why? Hasn't she told you about them? My mother tells me about my father. She wants to put me off him."

"We climb this." Silas leapt at a bank and scrambled over it, dropping down into a field of kale. Giles followed. Silas trudged on, the tall kale brushing against his shoulders.

"Surely," Giles nagged, "she's told you about your father."

"Nothing, I told you." Silas let a kale plant swish back to hit Giles' face.

"But when you ask?" Giles mopped his face.

"I don't. She never brings up the subject, so it's not there." Silas pushed on through the kale.

"Perhaps you were born in a test tube like those kids in Australia."

"They didn't do it twelve years ago."

"Might have done. What else could you be?"

"Son of a murderer? Artificial insemination?"

"Secret agent, titled bloke of some kind, pop star."

"If I were I'd get maintenance, like your mum."

"That's boring, too. Mine goes on and on about my father. One of these days I shall run away, live with him in America."

"You do that. Here's Feathers." Silas squatted down to greet the large wet dog who had appeared out of the mist. "We have ham sandwiches. You like ham." Feathers pranced back a pace then came forward and licked Silas' face. He had large ears with strands of hair round the edges. His tail, long and feathery, waved so that a swirl of drops swished from side to side of his chocolate-brown body. "This is Giles," Silas told the dog.

Giles patted the dog then followed Silas to a clump of trees bent sideways by the prevailing south-wester. From the trees rose a drift of smoke. "He's in." Silas trotted to a wall and began to climb, putting his feet neatly between the stones. Giles followed. Silas called in his high child's voice:

"Mr Quigley, Mr Quigley, are you there?"

Bernard Quigley stood in his porch. "I did not expect visitors on a day like this. Come and get dry by the fire."

"I just thought we would visit. This is Giles Krull. I am going away tomorrow to the Scillies for three weeks."

"What does your mother say to that?" Bernard peered into Silas' face.

"She's pleased for me. I shall be sailing. She's going to do a job for a couple of weeks."

"Where?" The old man moved jerkily about his tiny sitting-room, pushing the boys near the fire, fetching glasses from a cupboard, a bottle of sherry.

"To some old girl called Fox."

"Fox." The old man glanced quickly at the boy. "Get by the fire. Don't let the dog take up too much room. He's wet too. Have a drink, dear boys, a drink won't do you any harm. You're old enough. Eleven, are you?"

"Twelve." Silas held his hands towards the fire.

"Well then, drink up."

The boys tasted the sherry, trying to hide their distaste.

"You'll like it when you are grown up." The old man observed them as he drank, emptying his glass in one gulp, quickly refilling it.

Giles was fascinated by Bernard Quigley. He was small, stooping and old. His face had fallen in in some places and filled out in others so that the original proportions were lost. His nose, once an aristocratic curve, had taken hold and jutted out above a gentle mouth, putting large hooded eyes into shaded misproportion. His hair hung wispily round his collar. He wore brown trousers, a collarless shirt and braces which hung down over shrunken shanks, like the harness of a horse too old to work waiting for the knacker. His straggling moustache was stained with snuff.

"I knew your father," he said to Giles. "Edward Krull."

"Oh, did you?" Giles, beginning to steam, moved away from the fire. "When?"

"When he was at university." The old man took a snuff box from his waistcoat pocket and said: "Edward Krull, so dull, dull, dull. They sent him to America."

"Who did?" Giles was not used to bluntness from the old.

"His friends." Bernard Quigley searched Giles' face for a likeness to his father. "But you don't look like him," he said, adding, after a pause, "fortunately."

"I thought he was supposed to be goodlooking." Giles was defensive.

"I grant you that." Bernard Quigley dismissed good looks. "He was goodlooking all right, but what's the use of that in the dark, ask your mother?"

"In the dark?"

"In bed, dear boy. Perhaps you don't know about bed yet. Have your balls dropped?"

"What?" Giles retreated towards the fire.

"Your voice hasn't broken. Never mind. Think what's ahead of you, all that glorious copulation." He eyed Giles speculatively. Giles grew pink.

"That's a lovely snuff box." Silas, anxious for his friend, tried to distract Bernard's attention.

"George II. Belonged to my grandfather." The old man showed the box to Silas, snatching it back before he could touch it. "I will show you my things when we have had lunch. I have a lot of food in the house."

"Can I help?" Silas offered.

"No, no, get dry and give your sandwiches which your lovely mother gave you to the dog."

Silas laid the sandwiches in front of Feathers, who sniffed cautiously and began to eat, more it seemed from good manners than hunger.

Giles looked round the room. Chippendale chairs elbowed Sheraton, occasional tables overlapped one another, laden with porcelain, silver, jade. Every wall space was hung with paintings and mirrors which reflected the light from the fire. There was barely room for an oil lamp on the table near the old man's chair. Several candelabra stood on the floor, messy with candle grease.

Across the hall they could hear Bernard moving about.

"Do you think he likes snuff or just wants to use his snuff box?" Giles whispered, overawed.

"I should think he made himself like it, just as he likes this."

Silas poured the contents of his glass on to the rug.

"Won't he smell it?" Giles felt uneasy as he copied his friend.

"The smell of the paraffin lamp will drown it." Silas watched Feathers sniff the wet patch then return to his snack.

"I never knew my father was dull." Giles mulled Bernard's insult. "My mother's said a lot of things. She never said he was dull."

"Puts you off America, does it?" Silas asked, cheerfully spiteful.

"Come and have lunch," Bernard called. Silas and Giles joined him in the dining-room which was as crowded as the sitting-room. Giles, counting the chairs, noted there was a set of ten with carvers. Some of the chairs were stacked, giving the room the appearance of a sale-room. Bernard had laid three places. Giles looked at the silver and cut glass. "Is all this very valuable?"

"You don't ask the value of things, you admire their beauty, rarity, workmanship."

"Sorry." Giles was abashed.

"You'll learn. Now eat up, the food's delicious, not like the stuff Hebe put in your sandwiches."

"What a wonderful ham." Silas regarded a ham Bernard stood poised to carve.

"Sent by post." The old man carved rapidly. "Girl friend of mine sends it from Wiltshire, it's specially cured. The pig's right buttock is more tender than the left, it scratches with the left."

"How does the postman get here? There's no road." Giles accepted a plate of ham, wondering meanwhile about the pig's buttocks.

"The man has feet. He walks." The boy is like his father, thought Bernard.

"In all weathers?" Giles persisted.

"Of course he walks. I have my coffee posted, peaches in syrup, Stilton cheese, all the things that matter. Have some salad, make your bowels work."

"They do, thank you." Silas helped himself to lettuce. "My mother's a good cook."

"Get constipated at school?"

"Sometimes," Silas answered gravely.

Giles, disconcerted by the train of talk, asked, "Did you never have a road?"

"Of course there was a road." Bernard Quigley was crushing, shooting a sharp glance at Giles, wondering whether he was going to like this boy sitting there looking so healthy and young opposite himself, so hunched and shrunken, his life behind him.

"What happened to it?" Giles felt impelled to ask.

"I let the grass grow. People might use it. People might visit me."

"We are visiting you," Silas said, grinning.

"But you've taken the trouble to jump a few banks, get yourselves wet. Your mother comes."

"I didn't know." Silas looked surprised. "I thought you only knew me."

"I know lots of people. Keep them separate, that's all. Your mother's like that. Makes life easier."

"How?" Giles' mouth was full of ham, Bernard noticed. A bad mark there. Surely table manners still mattered.

"They do not discuss you behind your back if you keep them separate. Silas' mother may find her life easier to manage that way; other people such as your dull Krull father are gregarious. Have some figs in syrup or cheese. You can have both, of course."

The meal continued in quasi-silence, Giles ill at ease, Silas content. As he ate Giles looked round the room. "You have no electricity," he observed.

"Right. No electricity. Well water. No drains. No road. Any other queries?" Bernard stared at Giles offensively.

"He wasn't exactly querying." Silas felt Bernard Quigley was about to badger his friend. "I like your house as it is," he said.

"Sure?" The old man looked suspicious.

"Quite sure."

"Then I'll show you some of my treasures. Sit by the fire." Bernard led the way into the sitting-room with his braces flapping.

"Your braces are hanging down." Giles was diffident now.

"More convenient," said the old man ambiguously as he opened a drawer in a Sheraton desk. "You can look at these things while I have a snooze." He handed a box to Silas, sat back in a wing chair and fell asleep.

Crouching in front of the fire, the boys inspected rings, watches, early sovereigns, diamond brooches, a large emerald set with diamonds, medals, Battersea boxes wrapped in tissue and jewelled bracelets.

"Must be worth a bomb," whispered Giles. "These medals alone."

Bernard Quigley woke and observed the children.

Giles sat back on his heels and stared at his host. "Where does all this come from?" He waved his hand round the room.

"My work. I live in my bank."

Giles' eyes widened. "A burglar?"

"Certainly not. I am a dealer. You look very pretty." He smiled at Silas, showing beige teeth, amused by the boy who had put the rings on his fingers and the bracelets round his wrists. "Wait a moment," he said, jumping up. "I've got a tiara in the kitchen drawer." He left the room.

"What did he say?" Giles stared at his friend.

"A tiara," said Silas.

"What's a tiara?"

The old man came back carrying a plastic bag from which he took a tiara. He set it on Silas' head. "Keep still or it will fall off."

Silas, cross-legged by the fire, sat looking at the old man. The diamonds and emeralds twinkled in the firelight. Giles gasped. "Beautiful." The old man snatched the tiara off Silas' head and put it back in its wrapping. "Now," he said in a practical tone, "would you chop me some wood before you go? Stack it in the shed."

"Of course." Silas stood up, took off the rings and bracelets, putting them back in their box, which he placed on Bernard Quigley's knee. "Thank you." The boy and the old man looked at each other. Giles felt excluded.

"Trot off home when you've chopped the wood. Come and see me again." Giles felt the invitation was not for him.

"Thank you for lunch," he said. Then, unable to repress his curiosity, he said, "In what way was my father boring?"

"He talked about money, he was respectable, he was conventional." The old man spat out the epithets then, noticing Giles' stricken face, he relented. "A bit of cross-pollination has done you no harm." He edged the boys to the door and pushed them out into the rain, shutting the door behind them.

"Come on, chop, chop." Silas led the way to the wood pile and set about chopping wood, stacking it in a neat pile. Sulkily Giles helped him. When they had finished they set off across the fields towards the bus stop.

"If my father's a bore," said Giles, the cruel description rankling, "what's yours?"

"A mystery," Silas answered shortly.

"You mean you really don't know?"

Silas turned on his friend and hit him on the nose. Taken

unawares, Giles sat down, getting wetter than before. His eyes watered.

"There's the bus." Silas began to run. Giles got up and followed.

"Perhaps you are adopted," he yelled as he ran, the rain mingling with blood from his nose, which had begun to bleed. "I thought you were just a bastard," he shouted as he followed Silas on to the bus. Silas fought his way forward and sat beside a tourist so that there was no room for Giles, who stood miserably in the crowded aisle, jostled by strangers. Seeing his plight, a woman handed him a tissue which he held to his nose.

When they reached the town they walked up the street on opposite sides. As Silas came level with his door Giles called out, "See you when you come back?" in questioning tones.

Silas called back warmly, "Of course," and went into the house.

Giles found he was still clutching the blood-stained tissue and threw it into the gutter.

"Litterbug." Silas had reappeared as though about to say something. He stood in the doorway smiling, then shrugged as though he'd changed his mind and went in again.

Late in the evening the rain stopped. Bernard Quigley, followed by Feathers, picked his way through the fields to the call box.

When Louisa answered the telephone she sounded breathless. "Hullo."

"Are you all right?" Bernard spoke without preliminary. "Having trouble with your heart?"

"I rushed in from the garden. There's so much to do. Why are you ringing up? Has something gone wrong? Are you well?"

"Hebe's boy was here today, told me she is coming up to you—"

"She is. She said she had a cancellation, whatever that means."

"The boy's going on a visit to the Scillies for three weeks. Schoolfriends."

"That explains it. I did wonder."

"Can you afford her?"

"No, not really."

"Want some money?"

"Yes, I suppose so. I had not thought. I had not worked it out. She offered to come and I was so pleased I—"

"I'll arrange it."

"Bernard, should I?"

"Don't be silly. What is the point of keeping things for that nephew? He's never going to marry, from what you tell me. When did you see him last?"

"Weeks ago. He doesn't always come into the house, he's shy. He comes to fish in the evenings."

"I'll send you some cash." Bernard listened to Louisa's small protest. "Wait, I have to put in more money." He inserted the coins. "Are you there, Louisa?"

"Yes, I'm here."

"You must pay her more. Lucy Duff pays a much higher rate."

"Oh dear," Louisa protested. "How shaming."

"The girl likes you so she charges you less than Lucy."

"She cooks wonderfully, helps me in the garden. I don't entertain."

"I will send the money by hand. You will get it in a few days."

"Thank you. Shall I send you more things?"

"No, don't bother."

"Your voice has not changed," cried Louisa in Wiltshire.

"But the rest of me has. Goodnight, darling, get back to your garden."

Bernard rang off. The telephone box smelt of tobacco and urine. How disgusting is the human race, thought Bernard, dialling another number, inserting coins.

Louisa's voice had grown old. Forty years ago it had a lilt. "That you, Jim?" The voice at the other end affirmed that it was. "Listen, I want you to sell some things for me. Shall I send them to you or will you collect?"

"I'm coming your way, I'll collect. There is someone I want to see near you."

"Ah. Meanwhile I want you to get five hundred to Louisa Fox. This is her address." Bernard named house, village and county. "Got it?"

"Yes, okay. See you soon."

"Are you buying or selling from this person you want to see?"

"I don't know yet," said Jim Huxtable. "It's just a hunch I am following."

Bernard walked back to his cottage following Feathers, who trotted, tail aloft. As he walked he considered love in its various aspects. It was probable that he loved Louisa as much as he had forty years before, when they met secretly to love and part; now there was no guilt, no pain. They had not met for thirty years; to do so now would embarrass them. As he reached his door he wondered what Jim Huxtable's hunch could be. He paused in his porch, looking at the fading sunset, remembering Silas in the tiara. Who was it the boy looked like? He cursed his unreliable memory. Indoors, fumbling for matches to light the lamp, he caught sight of his reflection in one of the mirrors. Forty years ago in Louisa's arms, he thought, I wore the mask of youth. This may be the real me. I am still thin, he thought, recollecting the moment when her maid had come in unexpectedly with a message and he had lain flat under the bedclothes until she left the room. Bernard remembered their laughter had led to renewed love-making. Love affairs are much easier nowadays, he thought, applying the match to the wick, steadying the flame, but less exciting. Of all of them now only Lucy Duff had anyone who lived in and she had never had much to hide, seldom lapsing from virtue and not enjoying it overmuch when she did.

Giles, in his bed in the house Hannah had remodelled as George Scoop had remodelled her teeth, knocking rooms together here, making it open plan there, thought of Silas and that Silas would go tomorrow to other friends. The friends had fathers, probably their fathers were with them. Indeed he remembered Silas had said Michael Reeves' father had driven him from school to Cornwall, offering Silas a lift. Giles, puzzling about Silas' fatherless state, was seized by inspiration. He got out of bed and tiptoed down-stairs, and wrote a note to Silas.

"Perhaps your mother is a Hermaphrodite."

Opening the street door with stealth, he darted across the street in his pyjamas and posted the note through Hebe's letter-box.

TEN

Having watched Silas take off in the helicopter Hebe went back to her car to drive to Wiltshire. Silas would slip her from his thoughts until it was time to come home. I will never know what has gone through his mind, she thought. I love him but I seldom know what he is thinking. She wished she possessed the easy relationship some women had with their children. Hannah never bothered about what she said to Giles. Yesterday there had been a row because Giles said he'd been told his father was a bore and Hannah had shouted, "He's all sorts of things I don't like but he's not a bore. Can you imagine me marrying a bore?" making it clear by her denial that it was true. She had taken the suggestion as an insult to her intelligence and Silas, listening and watching, had not asked, as other boys would, "Was my father a bore?" There was no father with whom odiously to compare, for Hannah, when angry with Giles, would often cry, "Giles, you are just like your father."

I should have invented one, Hebe thought, as she drove towards Mrs Fox in her elegant house and lovely garden, but it is now too late. She concentrated her thoughts on Mrs Fox and what meals she would cook during the next two weeks.

In Salisbury she stopped to stretch her legs, parking the car and strolling round the Close to look at the beautiful houses, wondering what sort of people deserved these privileged surroundings. Were they especially virtuous or just very rich? She crossed the grass to the cathedral to sit and rest before the last lap of her journey. She resented having to pay to go in, feeling it made the atmosphere secular. Influenced by the secularity she took biro and paper from her bag and wrote Hippolyte, Mungo, Terry, Louisa, Lucy, Maggie, crossing out Terry and Maggie. The sums represented by the list of clients amply covered the cost of Silas' education. No need these days of help from Amy or to accept the frequently offered help from Bernard. She let her mind dwell on Bernard, grateful that she could love him without payment.

From now on she would be free too of the financial tie to Terry, and Maggie Cook-Popham could be dropped.

On her way back to her car she sighted a hat shop and stopped to stare. Lucy Duff had told her that when young if depressed she would buy a hat to cheer herself up, an infallible cure, advised Mungo's ma, for the mopes. I'll give it a try, thought Hebe, joking with herself, and she went into the shop. If tempted she might spend some of Terry's bonus.

At the sight of her the owner of the shop felt a lift to his despondent heart. What a head to bedeck. Laying down the *New Statesman* he rose from his chair.

"May I look round?" Hebe saw a young man carelessly assembled. Short legs, body leant back from the hips, large hands at the end of long arms, receding hair curling at the back, hazel eyes set in a face which resembled a hare with a long indented upper lip.

"Please look round, yes, do look—" He stepped back, knocking over a wastepaper basket, sweeping the *New Statesman* off his desk. "Do you read this?" He retrieved the magazine, hoping to engage her in talk.

"Not very often. Hebe looked away. He seemed nervous. She studied the hats, at first glance disappointingly Conservative Fête or Conservative Conference, depending on the season they were destined for. A second look revealed rogues in the gallery, a beret, a red hat with a wide brim. She picked it up.

"I'm afraid that's not for—" The shopkeeper moved forward anxiously. "It's just for—" He seemed unable to finish his sentences. "But if you—"

Hebe put on the hat and studied herself in the glass.

"You look marvellous in – of course if you'd like to – I mean it's not for sale because it's—" He spoke like what Lucy Duff would call a gentleman, what "they" would call public school, though public school vowels were not always like "theirs" any more. The mirror reflected people passing in the street. Hebe, hands up to tilt the hat, froze. She should have remembered.

"It's much best worn straight." The young man had got a whole sentence out. "It belonged to my great-aunt, she bought it in 1939 at the outbreak of—"

But Hebe was hearing "long-haired yobbo", "dirty feet", "Communist", "workshy", "whore", "abortion", "black", "who, who?" Her eyes followed them as they walked down the street, that familiar limp his, the bag carried over her left arm hers, a new younger Labrador at their heels. Her legs crumpled and she was sitting on the floor.

"I say, just a minute, I'll—" The owner of the shop sprang to fan her with the *New Statesman*. "Here, let me—" He helped her to feet. "Just sit—" He sat her in a chair. "Half a mo, I've got a—"

Hebe put her head between her knees. The hat fell off. "So sorry. Stupid. No lunch. I—" She could not finish her sentence either.

"Here, have a swallow." She felt a glass knock against her teeth, smelled whisky. She sipped, swallowed.

"So sorry. Have I hurt the hat?"

"Of course not." He fanned with the *New Statesman*. "I'm not really Left—" He was staring at her with his hare's eyes.

"Left what?" She clutched at her composure. They hadn't seen her. They shopped in Salisbury. She felt a fool. It must be Thursday. Their day.

"Wing." He gazed at her; her colour was creeping back. Was she perhaps pregnant, to feel faint? He couldn't very well ask. "Not Left Wing," he assured her. "It's just to counter the hats."

Hebe smiled. "How intelligent of you. I'm all right now," she said. Better not explain, just be casual.

"—so very glad." He did not seem able to begin a sentence either.

"I must be on my way." She stood up.

"But you must take the hat," he urged.

"How much is it?"

"Nothing, it's just it's—" He was putting the hat in a paper bag, striped red, green and white like the Italian flag.

"But how much – I must—" This is infectious, she told herself.

"—part of the decor. It wasn't for sale. I'd like you to—" he handed her the bag, "have it." He smiled triumphantly.

"I can't take it," she said firmly.

"You must. You look super in it. My great-aunt would be so—"

"Is she dead?"

"No, just old. She gave it me for—"

"What?"

"Fun." The hare's eyes lit up. "For encouragement." He gave Hebe the bag. "And now I am—"

"What?" She felt a creeping friendship for this young man.

"Encouraged. You should see what—" Hebe waited "—they buy. Petals, feathers, gauze, but you took the one good hat with unerring eye. Please keep it, it will give me so much—"

"Pleasure." Hebe finished the sentence for him. "Thank you very much." She accepted the hat.

"Are you going—"

"Another ten miles."

"So you don't live—"

"I'm going to a temporary job."

"I see. I hope you enjoy—"

"I shall. I've been there before. Goodbye." She held out her hand.

"Oh." He took her hand in a large dry grasp. She would have expected it to be damp.

"Thank you very much."

He went to the door and watched her go down the street. She turned, laughing, and shouted, "I bet your father was a General."

"He was, he—" She'd gone. He hadn't asked her name. She would read his on the bag, Rory Grant, Hatter. His great-aunt Calypso had said, "Be bold about it, don't let them put you off, always do what you want to do in life."

Hebe put the striped bag on the back seat and drove the last ten miles to Louisa Fox. It had done her good to find the hat, done her good to see them walk by. They had not seen her, no harm was done. Her eyes hurt. She looked forward to an early bed and taking out the contact lenses. She exposed her eyes to the world when working, a counterfeit penance, disguising herself at home with her large glasses.

As she drove she puzzled over her grandparents. Why was she still afraid of them, was it habit? Why had she not smelled the smell which usually accompanied the panic? Trying to assemble her thoughts, to sift fact from fiction, what she already suspected became clear. The smell had nothing to do with the two old people walking down the street in Salisbury. She wondered what the dog was called. The old dog's name had been "Smut".

Hebe drove slowly, feeling safer with every mile. They would have been in Salisbury to have their corns cut, go to the library, prowl in the bookshops without buying, walk back to their car, drive away south to the house on the edge of the New Forest.

They would not go into a hat shop on impulse and allow the hatter to give them a hat. They would walk in the centre of the pavement, unseeing, not noticing their errant grand-daughter. There was no room in their lives for frivolous hats, no room for girls who consorted with long-haired, bearded, bare-foot layabouts. It seemed so very long ago, yet nothing about them had changed. Except, thought Hebe in joyous surprise, catching sight in the driving mirror of the striped bag on the back seat, except that I am no longer afraid. Perhaps that will be the last time I hear their voices, the last time I fear them. Her spirits soared as she turned the car off the main road to drive the last miles to Louisa Fox.

She drew up by the front door. Three mongrel dogs rushed, barking, from the house. The door was open; the hall would be cool and smell of roses.

"Quiet, boys, quiet." Louisa Fox came round the house, a slight woman in a cotton dress, wearing a gardening apron. She held up her face to kiss Hebe.

"I am too dirty to touch you." She showed earthy hands. "Can you manage your bags? Oh my word, you've been to Rory's shop. How comical. What did you buy?" She scanned Hebe, the contents of the car, the paper bag, with bright black eyes. "Rather a brave man to start a hat shop in Salisbury. His father's furious. Show me what you bought. I'm surprised you found anything fit."

Hebe took the red hat from its bag.

"But that's one of his antiques. I know it well. A friend of mine gave it to him."

"He gave it to me."

"I'm glad you accepted. Come in and have a drink and I will tell you about the garden. There's been a disaster or two since you were last here. Bring your stuff in. Down!" she shouted at the dogs who were leaping and wagging round Hebe. "But there are lots of raspberries and the tobacco flowers smell delicious."

"I brought some sauce for pasta which I thought you would like tonight and if you have raspberries—"

"Don't start talking of food straight away, have a drink first. I've put you in your usual room. What would you like to drink, wine?"

"Yes please."

"There's a bottle in the fridge. We will have it on the terrace. Come along."

This is the kind of house I like, thought Hebe, following Louisa through a paved hall where her feet alternately clicked on stone and shuffled on worn rugs. Louisa led her through her drawing-room to the terrace. "Sit down. I will fetch the wine."

"Can't I?"

"No." Louisa left her.

Hebe sat on the white iron seat and looked across the garden to the meadow beyond the fence, where cows swished their tails by the chalk stream, bottle-green water, trailing weeds and the sharp cry of a coot.

"Here we are." Louisa brought a tray with wine and glasses, the bottle beaded. She poured, tasted. "Just right." She handed a glass to Hebe. "There."

The dogs lay down sighing, flicking an occasional ear, glancing up to wag a gentle tail, closed their eyes, slept.

Sipping her wine, Louisa watched Hebe. She looked vulnerable and wary.

"I am glad you have that hat," she said. "Rory needs encouragement. He makes lovely hats."

"I thought they looked rather conservative."

"So they pretend, but did you try one on? No? If you had you would have found that each one has some wicked exaggeration. He uses his hats to mock the Establishment. He guys his customers."

"Rather cruel."

"No, never cruel. His father tried to push him into the Army. He went on strike."

"I wondered." Hebe laughed. "His shop struck me as some sort of protest."

"He comes here sometimes to fish the stream. He's an honorary nephew. I knew his father and grandfather."

"Are they dead?"

"To me." Louisa considered Hebe. Would she ever relax completely? It seemed unlikely. "Rory's grandfather was one of my beaux. Or thought he was," she amended. "It was hard to decide whether he or another man was the most trying. Such a tedious fellow."

Hebe glanced quickly at her employer. "Surely there was no need for you to know bores?"

"Many eligible men were boring. Rory's grandfather was one. His older brother, whose widow gave Rory that hat, by the way, was far from being boring. Alas, not a beau of mine. Once I had a date with Rory's grandfather in the Ritz and at the same time a date with another man in the Berkeley. In those days," Louisa grinned at Hebe, "the Berkeley was across the street from the Ritz."

"I wouldn't know." Hebe was polite.

"Not your line of country?"

"Above my station."

"Mine too, now. Anyway, both these men wanted to marry me. I told the one I would dine with him at the Ritz and the other – he was called Rutter by the way, might be a relation of yours" – Louisa did not look at Hebe – "that I would dine with him at the Berkeley. Then, with both tied down, I rendezvous'd with someone else and spent the night with him."

"Did you marry that one?" She is telling me she knows my family. Hebe grew alert.

"He was not the marrying kind. They were both jealous of the man I did dine with, so I tied them down waiting. Later I married someone else."

"Not a bore," Hebe grinned.

"Not at all. Both these bores live within twenty miles of me. I never see them. I forget they exist. It just happens that I like Rory."

"Because he annoys his father?"

"That is probably why." Louisa put her empty glass on the table, hoping Hebe would feel a little safer if she knew she would not meet her grandparents, would feel liked, as Rory was liked.

"What happened to the man you spent the night with?"

"We talk sometimes on the telephone."

"Doesn't he visit you?"

"No. Now come, let's get some punnets and pick raspberries. It is a treat for me," said Louisa, leading the way to the fruit cage, "not to eat my supper on a tray watching television. Either I can't eat because there is a nature programme with beautiful beasts eating other beautiful beasts, or our Prime Minister is making a speech which upsets me."

"Surely you are a Conservative?" Hebe was surprised. Was Mrs Fox a rebel in these Tory surroundings?

"I was brought up to be one as surely you were." Hebe nodded. "But there are times when I wonder whether the government is not entirely composed of moles from Moscow."

Hebe giggled. "That's why you approve of the hatter?"

"Yes," said Louisa. "I like rebels and I dislike hypocrisy."

"Were the bores hypocrites, then?" Hebe suggested the nail for Louisa's hammer.

"Terrible hypocrites," said Louisa. "Oh, poor bird. Can you help that blackbird out of the cage?"

Hebe gently chivvied the blackbird towards the gate held open by Louisa. She felt grateful for Louisa's ambiguity.

"There!" she exclaimed as the bird flew free. "Thank you."

Hebe unpacked, changed her clothes and cooked a delicious meal. They finished the bottle of wine and Louisa, enjoying herself, opened another. She spoke of her garden and was grateful when Hebe offered to weed. Hebe went to bed early and Louisa read late, hoping the telephone would ring so that she could have a long talk, reverse the charges so that he would not have to search for coins, but the instrument remained silent. She regretted fate had prevented her marrying Bernard, although her marriage had been happy.

As a lover he had been delightful, as a husband he might have failed and, Louisa reminded herself wryly, Bernard had never proposed marriage.

Listening to the night's sounds, an owl hooting, a distant train, a cow cough in the meadow, Hebe thought of her grandparents. They had looked old and proud, impregnable in their prejudices. She cursed her inability to communicate with them. I must communicate with Silas, she told herself. I must stop being afraid of him otherwise it will be a repeat story. Sleepily she considered her family, God-fearing, incomprehensible. How marvellous, she thought, that they had chanced in her childhood to employ Amy who had proved her salvation, defending her when the older sisters had tormented and teased, older sisters who had conformed to the family mores, willingly adapting themselves to the proposed pattern. Six, eight and ten years older than herself, Hebe remembered them as giantesses in riding clothes who demanded service in confident voices, manipulated their grandparents, never lowered their voices when telephoning, thought it a joke when the men they were engaged to and subsequently married arrived back from a party tipsy and shouted, "Let's roger the slave," as they lumbered towards Amy's bedroom. Hebe remembered her terror at the sound of their voices and the charge of heavy feet turning to exuberant delight as Amy delivered adroit kicks and a parting push which sent them tumbling downstairs.

Inexplicably the grandparents had approved of the young men, admiring them for their prowess on the rugby field, the hunting field. Now Robert fielded a Conservative majority in a safe seat; Marcus carved a niche in merchant banking; Delian manufactured microchips in Brussels.

Hebe remembered Amy's refusal to stay another day, her deadly politeness. She had watched her pack, offered her face to be kissed, sad at the pending separation, heard Amy's bright voice, "See you again some day, love!", watched her get into the waiting taxi, seen her burst out laughing as the taxi rounded the bend in the drive.

Amy must have been at least fifty at that time, thought Hebe, which makes her well over seventy now, much the same as Louisa Fox and Lucy Duff. If Amy had been working for either of those it would not have been Amy who left the house but the boy friends. Hebe recollected her arrival years later on Amy's doorstep. Amy had said, "You'll be all right with me," and she had been all right and Silas was all right, really. If only I can be to Silas what Amy was to me, she thought. She remembered her spirits surging up from the depths as Amy drew her into her house, and of how at last she had been able to weep.

As she listened to the night sounds, she was glad that she would have two weeks with Louisa while Silas enjoyed himself sailing. It was good for him to have a wider horizon than the hideous street. She was glad he was having a good time with an ordinary family. Well, not an ordinary family, she thought, wincing at her inbred snobbery, people who were what Lucy Duff called "gentlefolk". "Oh God!" she cried aloud and remembered Hannah saying "Wet the tea" and cringed, reminded of her upbringing by "them" whom she had disowned, the old white ram and his white ewe whose daughter had borne her. She suddenly missed Terry with his knickers. His life is uncomplex compared to mine, she thought, remembering the chocolate skin of silky texture.

ELEVEN

Mungo Duff, a far from patient man, would have liked, the moment he read Miss Thomson's card, to leap into his car and speed across country to Louisa Fox, find Hebe, snatch her up and take her to Venice. The Highlands? To Yugoslavia? But why waste time travelling? There were delightful country hotels in England and Wales. Ireland, too, for that matter. Would she like Ireland? he asked himself, standing irresolute in the hall.

"I say, Dad, have you seen my snorkel? I left it with my goggles. It's disappeared."

"Confound you!" shouted Mungo. "Can't a man even—" He stared at his elder son standing a yard away, his younger brother at his elbow. Both boys looked startled. "What the hell are you doing?" Mungo yelled. Thinking of Hebe, he had forgotten his children.

"Packing, collecting what we need at the Reeves."

"Oh, God!" Mungo's dreams fell about his ears. He cursed Alison for departing so blithely to Santa Barbara. Alistair and Ian had to be packed off to the Scilly Isles. Until they left he was shackled by parental responsibility.

"Got bad news, Dad?" Alistair eyed the postcard in Mungo's hand.

"Of course not. Don't pry," he snarled at Alistair. Why did one burden oneself with children, what lunacy, what a hazard to happiness. He looked again at the postcard. She would not yet be there, not until the 14th. There was time to plan. Then doubt gripped his heart. "What day are you two leaving?"

"Day after tomorrow, Dad. The twelfth. Ma told you."

"Of course." What relief.

"She told us we were old enough to pack for ourselves and that you would put us on the train. It's all right, isn't it, Dad? I mean, if necessary we can go in a taxi."

"Don't be stupid," Mungo snarled.

"We are only trying to remember to pack everything. Ma said

if we left anything behind we were not to bother you to send it on."

"Very sensible of her," Mungo grunted.

"So have you seen my snorkel?"

"No, I have not seen your snorkel. If you are old enough to pack you are old enough to find your fucking snorkel."

The younger boy gave a high giggle. "Fuck" was not a word his mother allowed in the house. ("I will not allow that word in the house.") This applied to most four-letter words. Seeing Mungo's expression he suppressed his giggle. Mungo stared at his sons, fruit of his loins, he supposed, though there was no proof, he thought sourly; they both looked exactly like Alison. "Get on with it," he said, "and don't make a mess."

Ian and Alistair turned and ran. From the back premises Mungo heard an explosion of laughter. Bloody little bastards, they had no respect. Mungo remembered his own father and grinned. He used to give one a clip on the ear and his mother would cry, "Mind Mungo's eardrum." Mungo stooped to pick up the rest of the letters. There was one in his mother's hand. He opened it, tearing pettishly at the envelope.

Darling Mungo. I have to see you on a private matter. When you have got the boys off to the Scilly Isles I would be grateful if you would come and see me so that we can talk. The matter is too delicate to discuss on the telephone. I must ask you to come here. It will not take long. All my love, Mother.

All her love. What about my love? Mungo screamed with inward rage, threw the letter on the ground and stamped on it. Then, glancing round to see whether he had been observed, picked the letter up and put it in his pocket.

That evening, the boys safely in bed, the snorkel found on a shelf in the greenhouse, Mungo telephoned his mother.

"Mother, what's up?"

"I told you, darling, I won't talk about it on the telephone."

"Are you sure?"

"Positive." He knew that tone of voice; there was no budging her.

"Very well. I can't come before the boys go on the twelfth. I'll come on the thirteenth."

"A suitable date." Was she laughing?

"I won't be able to stay." Mungo was defensive.

"I wasn't asking you to, darling. As you know, Miss T. rather hates me having visitors."

Did she think if she referred to Miss Thomson as Miss T. she would not hear?

"Is she listening?"

"She has so few entertainments," said Lucy, amused. "See you, then, on the thirteenth. I'll ring off now, you must mind your bill."

Mungo thought, She is obsessed by bills. Tearing up her letter he noticed she had put a second-class stamp on it.

On August 12th Mungo put Ian and Alistair on the train to Penzance where Jennifer Reeves had arranged for them to be met and taken to the heliport. During the afternoon he arranged with Alison's daily lady to come and feed the cat while he was away, thankful that Alison refused to have a dog. He would not trust a dog to Alison's daily lady. The cat was able to fend for itself if she forgot it. Mungo always thought of the daily lady as Alison's, not his or the boys' adjunct. Her regard, when she bothered to notice him or the boys, was distinctly insubordinate. With Alison she was servile and intimate.

The boys gone, he set off north in his car, stopping to dine on the way at a highly recommended restaurant to fortify himself for any bad news his mother had to impart. As well to stoke up with the good things of life, he told himself, before she broke the news that she had cancer or had lost all her money. As he ate his steak and drank his claret, Mungo let his mind wander. If it was cancer he must get his mother into a hospice, it would be far better than all the hassle of finding a decent nursing home. She belonged though to BUPA so perhaps that side might not be too difficult. On the other hand, if she insisted on dying at home, Alison must come back sharpish and get down to finding private nurses. A terrible bore, but Alison would manage. Mungo ordered another bottle. This really was a good restaurant. If he took Hebe to Scotland they could have a meal here on the way. On the other hand, if his mother had not got cancer but had somehow managed to get into a financial bog, he shuddered to think what to do. One thing he would not do, and here for once Alison would be in complete agreement, would be to have his mother to live with them. No fear, thought Mungo, drinking his claret and ordering Stilton. It was hazardous enough arranging sessions with Hebe without his mother spying on him with those sharp eyes. Mungo sighed, thinking of Hebe's eyes, enormous like a woodmouse, long lashed. He suddenly realised he was intoxicated and broke into a sweat at the thought of the police stopping him as he drove north and using their dreadful new gadget.

"Waiter?" Mungo enunciated with care, even two syllables could betray—

"Yes, sir," falsely obsequious.

"Is there anywhere I can stay the night? I don't feel like driving on."

"Here, sir, why not here? The restaurant is part of an hotel."

"Is it? Thank God." He groaned with relief. "Book me a room."

He spent a sleepless and worrying night and appeared at his mother's house at lunchtime the following day distinctly hungover.

When Mungo saw his mother looking remarkably well, bearing down like a battle cruiser to embrace him, his heart, *malgré lui*, sank. Alison, he decided, would have to find a cottage to suit reduction in circumstances, comfortable of course, or a flat, a flat would do, but not within fifty miles.

"Fifty miles of what?"

He had not realised he was thinking aloud. "I said 'your nifty smile'. Are you growing deaf, mother?"

"Certainly not." She wore a curious expression, amused, sardonic.

"Ill? Are you ill?" He looked at her keenly.

"Why should I be? I am as strong as a horse."

"Is it money, then, have you lost it all?"

"Darling, are you crazy? I am perfectly well and very well off, as you well know, thanks to your father. Come and have lunch. We will talk about your troubles afterwards."

"My troubles?" He stared at his mother.

"What else? Come and have a drink." She headed towards the dining-room.

"Oh, God, no. Well, perhaps yes. A whisky, then."

"Like that, is it? Stiff with lots of soda. Would you like an aspirin, too?" She peered up at him, gimlet-eyed.

"Yes." Mungo was sheepish. His mother had a fondness for weakness which his father had never pandered to. But I oblige her, he thought disconsolately, sipping his whisky while she fetched the aspirin.

During lunch, at which Miss Thomson was present, Mungo

listened to his mother's opinions on the government – not real Tories, no proper background; on the weather – pretty good; her garden as affected by the weather; the iniquities of industrialists polluting the air with the puffs from their chimneys. His mother still talked to him as though he were a child, Mungo thought morosely as he ate his roast chicken. "Puff", indeed.

"What about the rivers?"

"Darling, that's for somebody else to worry about. My plants are not affected by the rivers."

"Your income comes from industry."

"Oh no, Mungo, it does not. Your father would never invest in industry."

"Ask your trustees." Mungo was sulky and nervous.

"I shall leave well alone." Lucy shifted from uncertain ground. "Shall we have our coffee out of doors?"

"I will bring it out on the patio for you, Mrs Duff." Miss Thomson rose from the table and left them.

"Maddening woman, she insists on calling the terrace a patio. It's so common. Come on, let's go into the garden. She also refers to the lawn being manicured."

Following his mother on to the terrace, Mungo reflected that she must be one of the last to dare call somebody "common". He wished he had her ghastly self-assurance.

They sat in the sun, not speaking, looking at the view in the distance of which a factory chimney could be seen, puffs of pollution belching. Miss Thomson brought the coffee tray and retreated. Mungo watched her back, her thick efficient waist, strong plump shoulders, solid legs ending in flat, sensible shoes on inward-turning feet.

"What's your trouble then, Mother?" If it wasn't cancer or money what could it be?

"Not mine, darling, yours, I told you."

"What?"

"Yours."

"Explain." He gulped scalding coffee. What did she mean? What the hell was she up to? "What's up?"

"What's up is that Alison has left you. She asked me to break it to you." Lucy's eyes glinted.

"I don't believe it." Mungo burst out laughing, delighted that his mother neither had cancer nor was going broke. He was really very fond of her.

"She has apparently decided to form a *ménage à trois* with those friends of yours in Santa Barbara." Lucy watched her son's face with curiosity. He could be a bit slow in the uptake.

"Not my friends, they are Alison's." The full impact of his mother's news was slow to sink in. "She met them when she took the boys skiing at Mégeve. They have been staying with us."

"So I gather."

"Do you mean to say she was carrying on with him under my nose?"

"With them, I told you, it's a threesome. I wonder what your father would say." Poor fellow, thought Lucy. It makes him look so ridiculous. To go off with a man understandable, to go off with a woman quite frequently done, but with a pair, unusually esoteric.

Mungo finished his coffee and sat thinking. Lucy pursed her lips, watching him. Who was it who had said, when she was about to marry Mungo's father, "He's a delightful fellow but the kind of man who has stupid children"? That dreadful little friend of Louisa's, Bernard Quigley, who had once made a pass at her, more than a pass if she dared be honest. Lucy blushed in shamed recollection. He'd been rather fun, made one laugh. It had only happened once, in France; she had liked the hotel.

"Well?" She broke the silence lying between her and her only child. "Well?"

Mungo noticed her raised colour. "You may be upset," he said, "but I think it's absolutely marvellous." He let out a shout of laughter. He saw himself speeding down the motorway, snatching Hebe from Louisa Fox, marriage in a register office and happy, happy ever after. Lovely, lovely Hebe. Noticing his mother's expression and unable to fathom it, Mungo stopped laughing and said, "I shall divorce her."

"What for?"

"Adultery, of course."

"With whom?"

"Um, both I suppose. Oh, come on, Mother, why not desertion, incompatibility? There are all sorts of causes for divorce these days."

"Who will care for the boys?" A deadly sentence. Mungo felt a shiver of fear. "You will help me, Mother?"

"No."

"Good God, Mother, you are their grandmother, you—"

"I know I am."

"So you will—"

"Won't."

"Mother!" Mungo was aghast, his joy dissipated, alarm rushing into the vacuum. There was a long pause while mother and son confronted each other. Mungo was the first to look away.

"Alison is your wife," said Lucy. "We may neither of us be particularly fond of her—"

"Mother!" He was shocked by her honesty. It was all right for him to be disloyal, not for her.

"After your reaction to my news just now, I think you had better listen. As I was saying, we may not be fond, but my word, dear boy, she is useful. She looks after you and the boys faultlessly. You are fed, exercised, have your holidays arranged, your bills paid. She arranges the servicing of your cars, she plans your social life and that of the boys, she sees that they go to the right schools, spend their holidays with the right people."

"She's a dreadful snob."

"So am I, so are you. If that pretty girl who comes to cook for me were not a lady do you suppose you would pursue her so briskly?"

"How do you know?" Mungo shouted furiously.

"Don't be silly, Mungo. You may think it secret, so perhaps does she. There is such a thing as the grapevine. Maggie Cook-Popham's boy saw you with her twice."

"Does Alison know?"

"Probably. Anyway it wouldn't bother her, she would not care."

"Oh." Mungo felt his mother had kicked him in the teeth. "When did all this happen?" he asked weakly.

"Quite suddenly. Alison telephoned me. She has also written. She had never been unfaithful to you before, by the way. This is an arrangement arrived at in the 'plane going over. Alison telephoned me on arrival. Her letter came yesterday, dotting the 'i's. She used the word 'finalised'." Lucy sniffed.

"She must have been drunk or drugged."

"I gather neither. She has been contemplating some such move for a long time and it happens this American couple are offering her exactly the life she has always longed for."

"What utter rubbish."

"Read her letter." Lucy handed Alison's letter to her son. A practical, lucid deposition. Alistair and Ian's holidays over, Mungo was to assume responsibility. Alison would, if necessary, advise from Santa Barbara, otherwise it was up to Mungo. Her lawyer, who was also Eli and Patsy's lawyer, would be in touch shortly. Lawyer's address attached.

"My God, my God!" Mungo felt like weeping. "She cannot know what she is doing. She cannot have made up her mind so quickly."

"She went snap when she clapped eyes on you," said Lucy drily. "Your father said he'd never seen such a fast worker. She saw you and, as I say, went snap."

"I thought it was me."

"You were supposed to, darling."

Some people love their mothers, thought Mungo.

"Are these people, Eli and Patsy, rich?" asked Lucy.

"Seem to be rolling."

"There you are, then."

"I shall have to make the best of it." Mungo did a rapid rethink. He would get Jennifer Reeves to help with the boys. She was an able woman with a boy of her own; two more wouldn't matter one way or the other. He could still marry Hebe, still live happy ever after. His mother was talking. "What did you say?"

"I said we had better get to work at once."

"Doing what?"

"Getting her back of course."

"Why, for God's sake?"

"For mine if not for yours and the boys. I cannot possibly do without her."

Mungo stared at his mother. When she spoke in the deadly tone she had just used resistance was sheer waste of breath.

Noticing her son's alarm, Lucy explained. "Dearest, some day I shall get cancer or some such nuisance and need looking after." Mungo winced. "Who other than Alison do we know capable of coping? Not you, dear boy. Some day I may have a financial worry or two, need to move house, be too old to manage. Who do we know other than Alison capable of taking charge of me?"

Mungo buried his face in his hands. His mother was a horrible old bitch, he loathed her. How could people be so utterly selfish? It was damnable.

"So what?" he muttered through clenched teeth. "So what or just so." That was what Alistair and Ian said when they wished to be annoying. "So?" Never, of course, to Alison; they wouldn't dare.

"So we get to work," said Lucy calmly. "You grovel, I blackmail. We use the telephone and spare no expense. We begin, let's see—" she looked at her watch, "in half an hour. Catch her asleep. You will talk to Alison and I will talk to this Eli and Patsy."

"I thought they were just rather boring Americans who were into intensive sightseeing."

"My poor innocent." Lucy laughed at Mungo as though he were ten years old. "Come now, let us try and enjoy this. Grovel, grovel, grovel, tongue in cheek." She was enjoying the situation.

Mungo made a last desperate appeal. "Mother, please, there must be some other way."

"I am not changing at my age and nor are you at yours. Do you imagine I would ever have had a child if it had not been certain I would have a nanny who would take charge of you, if you had not been certain to go away to boarding school when you left the nursery?"

"I was miserable at my prep school," Mungo muttered sulkily.

"I notice you send your boys to the same one. People like us did not put up with the horrors of having children at home, which even quite nice people do these days."

People like us, nice people, must she? Mungo writhed.

"And you," Lucy fixed Mungo with her clear eyes, "are just like me. If you had not had Alison to manage, direct and bring up your boys you would not have embarked on having a family."

Mungo made a choking sound of protest.

"I do not mean, darling, that I do not love you. I do very much. I might not if I had had to change your nappies and nurse you through mumps. In principle I also love my grandsons."

"I am not sure I do."

"Nonsense, of course you do. They have not had mumps yet, have they?"

"I don't know. I can't remember. Alison—"

"There you are, you don't know. Measles? Chickenpox? Athlete's foot? Those little mites that burrow into your – er your, your, you know what I mean."

"Crabs. Mother, must you?"

"Are you prepared to tackle all that on your own?"

Mungo was silent, thinking of Hebe. He did not want Hebe tackling the care of Alistair and Ian, dealing with their crabs. He wanted Hebe to himself, her undiluted attention. Tears came to his eyes. He gulped.

Perhaps he loves Alison, thought Lucy. No, he can't, it's the shock.

"When do we start? What do we do?" Mungo gave in.

TWELVE

Silas, catching a foreshortened glimpse of his mother from the helicopter as it swung away towards the Scillies, wondered what a Hermaphrodite could be; whether Giles, who liked useless bits of information, had discovered some new religious sect – whether Hermaphrodite was an esoteric dish like Moussaka, or an autonomous republic of the USSR. Giles particularly treasured gems such as "It takes three years to digest black pepper", and had eagerly taken note of Bernard's information about the pig scratching. Silas promised himself a trip to the Public Library to rummage among the dictionaries.

He settled in his seat to watch Land's End disappear and peered ahead to catch a glimpse of the islands. He looked forward to meeting Michael and wearing the denim shorts Hebe had bought him. They had never seen one another in anything other than their school uniforms. He wondered what his friend would be wearing. Looking down at the choppy sea, he hoped the weather would clear and that the sun would show more enthusiasm than it had during the last fortnight. His fellow travellers in the helicopter seemed to be prepared for the worst, carrying yellow oilies and rubber boots. Arrived, Silas shook his head to free his ears of the din of the helicopter, followed the other passengers on to the tarmac and looked around for Michael. A female voice hailed him. Mrs Reeves waved. Silas waved back and went to meet her carrying his duffle bag.

"Hello, Silas." She had large teeth and showed her gums when she smiled, which she was doing now. She was tall, with thick fair hair pulled back in a bun, which made the sou'wester she wore look peculiar. Her face was red from the wind, her eyes blue. She wore a yellow oilskin with a velvet collar, an old Guernsey jersey, a denim skirt. Her legs were bare. She wore blue ankle socks and trainers. Her handshake was firm.

"Nice to see you, Silas." She was not as he remembered at the

533

school sports, he must have confused her with some other boy's mother.

"How do you do, er, hullo." Silas looked around for Michael.

"They are all sailing. I had some shopping to do in St Mary's so I said I'd meet you." Her voice had carrying quality.

"Oh, thank you."

"They will be back for supper. Come and help me load my stuff in the boat. Alistair and Ian only arrived yesterday and were keen to get cracking. They knew you wouldn't want them to wait."

"Oh, oh no." Bugger Michael, thought Silas. It's not lunch time yet, what am I supposed to do stuck with his mother till supper? "Of course not."

"D'you know Alistair and Ian, Silas?"

"No, no, I don't. Who are—"

"You wouldn't, I suppose. They are at a different school. But you might have met them in the holidays." She looked brightly enquiring.

"I don't think so." Where was he supposed to have met them? Silas followed his hostess. Who were they, anyway?

"Hadn't you better put on a mac?"

"Yes, of course." He unzipped his duffel bag and found his anorak.

"Does nothing but rain here," she said.

She seemed frighteningly competent, guiding him to a mountain of shopping, getting him to stow it in large baskets. "There's a fantastic basket-maker in Totnes who makes these. I can't stand plastic bags, can you?"

"Er, no I can't." Silas had never thought about it.

"D'you know Totnes? Delightful place. These baskets come from there. He makes every conceivable European shape. No Eastern rubbish."

"Rather heavy," Silas ventured.

"But last for ever. Their being heavy shouldn't worry a strong boy like you."

"Of course not." They had reached the quay.

"That's right, stow them. Not like that, not all on the same side, the boat will sink. Here, like this." She rearranged the baskets, grouping them in the middle of the boat.

"Sorry." Silas felt foolish.

"Done a lot of sailing, Silas?"

"Er, no." Ask a silly question.

"Alistair and Ian make a useful crew, Julian says. Julian is my husband."

"Oh."

"My name is Jennifer. Call me Jennifer, everybody does."

"Thanks." I shall call her "You", he mutinied.

She had the boat stowed to her satisfaction. "Sit on that thwart."

What's a thwart? he asked himself.

"Cast off, can you?"

Silas managed that.

Jennifer Reeves started the engine and steered the boat into the rain, phut-phutting over the waves. "Soon be there."

Silas kept silent. They were apparently going to another island.

"When you've helped me get all this to the cottage I expect you'd like lunch and then you can explore the island."

"Thanks, yes."

"Know the islands well?"

"I've never been here."

"Goodness, and you live so near."

"Well." He felt put down.

"Lots to do on the mainland, of course. Didn't Michael say you live in the town?" She sounded unconvinced.

"Yes."

"Oh." She savoured this. "Like it?"

"Yes. We live in a street."

"Really?" It sounded "reahly".

"It was built by a crazy old man who hated Cornish granite so he imported these dark red bricks from Devon and built a street of brick houses, dark brick with yellow bricks round the windows."

"Yuk!"

"That's what my mother thinks, but it's so ugly I love it. It's hideous and frowning and secret and built up a very steep hill."

"Reahly." He could see her uvula.

"All the houses have nylon curtains and gardens at the back, and there's an alleyway between the gardens and the backs of the houses in the next street, which is built of granite like the rest of town. Ours is called Wilson Street."

"Reahly," said Mrs Reeves, sitting at the tiller, steering the boat across the water to Trescoe.

Silas sat quiet after his outburst, listening to the snap and crunch of the boat on the water, rather enjoying the bouncy movement but disliking the smell of stale fish. He wondered whether the oily, smelly bilge would slop up as it threatened to and wet his hostess's feet. It did not.

"Here we are," she said, quelling the engine.

Silas helped carry the baskets to the cottage which the Reeves had rented for the holidays. Jennifer Reeves moored the boat and carried her share of baskets without showing any strain. Silas followed her into the cottage, deciding she was a good ten years older than Hebe.

"If you unpack the baskets I will put everything away." Gosh, what efficiency. Not that Hebe wasn't efficient, Silas told himself, she just didn't make it so obvious.

"Put the baskets in the porch. I shall have a drink and get us some lunch. That be nice?"

"Thank you very much." He stacked the baskets in the porch.

"Not there, silly, everybody will trip over them. Up on the shelf."

"Sorry." He stacked them on the shelf. Why hadn't she said "shelf" in the first place.

Jennifer dripped drops of angostura and poured herself a generous gin.

"My father was in the Navy," she said.

Silas looked blank.

"Pink gin, Silas, pink gin."

He watched her take a swallow, wondering what she was talking about.

"That's better. Now for lunch. There's a stew – baked pots and fruit. Do you?"

"Lovely."

"Shocking of me. Didn't offer you. Would you like a Coke?"

"No, thank you."

"The boys always help themselves. Want to go to the loo? Like to see your room?"

"Thank you. Yes please."

"I'll show you." She led the way. "You're all in this big room together, you won't mind that, will you?"

"Of course not." Just like school, he thought. Hope I like them. He looked doubtfully at the four beds.

"When you're ready come and eat. Here's the bathroom. Mercifully there's another loo downstairs. I'm not keen on people peeing in the garden, one might sit – kills the grass, too."

Silas rejoined her. In silence they ate a very good stew, baked potatoes and fresh fruit. He helped her clear the table, stack the dirty plates in the dishwasher.

"All mod cons in these cottages."

"Yes," he said, putting in the last plate.

"Right, then. You unpack and explore. I'm going to have my rest. They will be home for supper, if not before. You'll be all right?"

"Yes, thank you."

Jennifer Reeves went upstairs. He heard her drop her shoes, gentle thuds on the floor and her voice saying "Aah" in relieved tones. She turned on a radio for Woman's Hour. Silas crept upstairs into the assigned bedroom. Three beds were rumpled. He put his duffel bag on the fourth, searched for a jersey and trainers, put them on. He looked out of the window. It was still raining and he debated whether to keep on his jeans or change into shorts. He changed.

He followed a path uphill from the shore to find some sort of view. The path was bordered with tamarisk and fuchsia, the air soft and salty. He began to enjoy himself.

He explored, finding Trescoe Abbey Gardens, wandering dazed by the exotica, loving the surprises, avoiding other people. Presently he left the gardens and, after a long tramp, found a sickle-shaped beach empty except for birds. He sat on a rock and watched the water, a blue-green he had not seen in Cornwall. A boat rowed by a girl came slowly into view. A man sat in the stern with a fishing rod, casting a fly. Silas watched as the man caught and played mackerel as though he were on a lake fishing for trout. The man and the girl talked in low voices. Silas was not the only watcher, for seals' heads bobbed inquisitively quite close to the boat. Silas had never seen seals. The boat went slowly out of sight, the man and the girl still talking in quiet voices. Silas watched the seals watch them go. The rain had stopped. He undressed and walked down to the water and waded in. He did not want to splash and alarm the seals, who might still be close. He swam out from the beach, then turned to look back at the white sand, grey rocks and the low cliffs ornate with purple heather. Near the shore there were overhanging clumps of thrift, their grey seed heads like the woolly heads of pantomime footmen. The water was cold; he swam for the shore. He had no towel and liked the way his clothes clung stickily to his body. Carrying his shoes he walked inland. Presently the sun came out.

He lay in the heather listening to the gulls, watching a kestrel hover. Lulled by the sound of gulls and breakers thudding on rocks round the headland, he fell asleep. When he woke the sun was hot on his face and the salt from his bathe drew the skin tight. He rubbed his hands on his cheeks, making a small dry noise, echoed close by; beside him on a flat rock was an adder. Silas lay watching the beautiful creature as it moved away into the heather, making a thin papery sound. He closed his eyes. The ecstasy of the adder on top of the sighting of seals was almost too much. Feeling hungry, he got up to walk back to the cottage. He had come further than he thought; the sun was slanting from the horizon and gulls flew towards their evening haunts.

Coming up from the jetty he met Michael Reeves with his father and two boys of about his and Michael's age. They were talking in loud voices, carrying bits of impedimenta from the boat and their day's sailing. Michael hailed Silas loudly.

Michael's father said, "Hullo, how are you? Nice to see you. Got here all right, I see. Hope my wife looked after you, fed you and that sort of thing. Been exploring, have you? Sorry to leave you, we couldn't miss a good day's sailing, knew you wouldn't mind," in a louder, deeper voice than Michael's.

Nobody introduced him to the two other boys, whom he later knew as Ian and Alistair.

Michael and his father wore crushed and dirty linen hats which had once been white. Ian and Alistair wore blue denim hats which were too small for them, having borne several seasons. Michael's father wore red Breton fisherman's trousers with patched knees and all the boys wore very tight denim shorts like Silas, but old and dirty so that he felt awkward. The whole party wore Guernsey jerseys like Mrs Reeves and smelt of boats and sweat. Silas wished Hebe had not said, "Your jerseys will do but take my old white thing if you want to." The old white thing was a Guernsey. Silas felt vaguely resentful towards Hebe. His own jerseys were serviceable but not Guernseys.

Michael and his friends jostled in the porch, talking loudly, shouting about the day's sailing to Jennifer in the kitchen, who shouted back, and above the cacophony Julian Reeves boomed that what he needed before anything else was a stiff whisky.

"Help yourself, then, I'm getting the nosh." Jennifer clattered pans, ran water into the sink. "Boys, boys, put your filthy boots in the porch, the floor was washed this morning."

Michael and his friends kicked off yellow rubber boots and threw them down in the porch. A reek of hot feet drifted into the cottage.

"Take your boots off, darling." Jennifer addressed her husband. "Mrs Thing did the floor."

"Okay, okay." Julian Reeves stepped out of his boots and stood pouring whisky into his glass. Silas silently took the boots and put them with the others.

"Brought boots, did you?" Michael addressed him.

"No, I didn't know I'd need them."

"We can lend you some, I expect."

"Go and change your filthy shorts before supper and for God's sake wash," Jennifer shouted at Michael who was standing close beside her. Michael muttered. Silas followed him and the other boys upstairs. They started rummaging in the chest of drawers.

"Quite glad to change," the boy Silas would subsequently know as Ian said, stepping out of his shorts. "These things squeeze my parts."

Alistair and Michael laughed.

"Large parts run in the family," said Ian, encouraged. "Father says his are much admired."

"Who by?" enquired Silas, feeling left out.

"Our father has a mistress, thinks we don't know. Haven't heard mother's opinion, suppose she takes them as they come."

"As they come." Alistair, younger than Ian, laughed lewdly.

"My mother continually expects Pa to have a mistress. It's her constant dread," said Michael, intent on keeping his end up. "Actually he wouldn't dare. He gets slapped down if he so much as looks at a girl."

"Supper's ready," Julian Reeves shouted up the stairs in a foghorn voice. The boys pattered downstairs in bare feet. Silas slipped off his shoes and followed them.

Jennifer doled out large helpings of a stew similar to the one they had eaten at lunch on to Habitat plates and everybody started eating.

Julian Reeves opened a bottle of wine and helped his wife and himself, then offered the bottle to Silas.

"Thank you." Silas held out his glass. Julian filled it three quarters full. The other boys helped themselves to Coke. Silas felt he had made a *faux pas* and shyly gulped his wine.

Julian and the boys regaled Jennifer with their day's sailing, constantly interrupting and contradicting one another.

"We thought we'd sail round the Bishop's Rock tomorrow if the weather holds. Like that, Silas, eh?"

"Oh yes, lovely."

"Silas tells me he lives in a very interesting street." Jennifer was refilling her glass. "Apparently he lives in the town. I hadn't realised." She fitted an aitch into the word, "reahlised".

"What's the street called?" Julian asked in an expansive voice.

"Wilson Street. It was Lord Kitchener Street but they changed it to Harold Wilson Street a few years ago."

"Golly! Under the Labour government?"

"He's got a bungalow at St Mary's, you know." Jennifer was deprecating.

"What a funny thing to do." Ian's mouth was full of stew.

"I wonder why." Passing cheese and Bath Oliver biscuits, Jennifer eyed Silas speculatively, as though he were responsible for the renaming.

"He did something for the town. It was a way the Council had of saying thank you." In the ensuing silence Silas refused a Bath Oliver and helped himself to bread.

"Takes all sorts, I suppose." Jennifer buttered a biscuit, munched, caught her husband's eye. "Early to bed tonight if you are Bishop's Rocking tomorrow. Clear the table, will you, boys."

"Okay," said Michael, Ian and Alistair. "Okay."

Silas opened his mouth and shut it again.

Jennifer stood up. "Pub?" she signalled her husband.

"Of course."

Silas watched his host and hostess stroll out into the dusk.

"Let's get this done." Michael started clearing the table. Silas helped. Ian and Alistair made vague movements without contributing.

"Your family Labour, then?" Ian enquired.

"Labour?" Silas was puzzled.

"Ya, Labour not Tory. You know, Wilson Street, I ask you. Goes to show."

"What?"

"Reds under the bed and so on."

"Don't be stupid, Ian." Michael hedged his bets, remembering he was host.

"I have a pot under mine." Alistair was gleeful. "Used to wet my bed." He sounded almost proud.

"Kiddo." Ian was dismissive.

"What's on the box?"

They moved into the next room to sprawl and watch a Western on ITV. Ian turned up the sound but carried on a desultory conversation with Michael. To the accompaniment of saloon doors swinging, guns firing, the rattle of the stagecoach and galloping hooves, Silas learned that Michael's family often joined forces with Alistair and Ians' in the holidays, that they regularly ski'd at Megève, that they had spent last summer holidays in the Canadian Rockies and that there were plans afoot for a trek in Ladakh the following year, although it was possible that Alistair would be considered too young to go.

"You can always go to Uncle H in the Highlands," Ian consoled his younger brother.

"Piss the Highlands," shouted Alistair above the background music of the film, voicing the anger and frustration of younger brothers. It all sounded very glamorous beside holidays spent in the dark brick Harold Wilson Street and expeditions to see Mr Quigley with Giles.

"Why the hell are you not all in bed?" Jennifer Reeves shouted when she came back from the pub.

"It's their holidays," Julian was alcoholically amiable.

"Up, up you all go," cried Jennifer, as though addressing recalcitrant dogs.

Silas took a long time going to sleep. He would have liked another blanket. He would have liked his duvet and Trip nestling furry and purring against his stomach in his own bed in his mother's house in the absolutely hideous street called Wilson Street. He wondered whether the rumour that the street had not been renamed out of gratitude but out of spite might not be true. He woke twice from his uneasy sleep to listen to the wind buffeting the cottage and to the sea growling.

THIRTEEN

Availing himself of Louisa's open invitation to fish, Rory Grant, having eaten a solitary supper, took his rod and drove the ten miles to the point where Louisa's stretch of water began. He parked his car, tucking it into the side of the road, pulled on his gumboots and, standing in the quiet of the August evening, put up his rod. Choosing a fly from his flybox, he listened to the gurgle of water flowing under the bridge and the evening sounds, the imagined rustle of bats hunting over the water, the rhythmic chewing from a group of recumbent cows who watched him benignly as he climbed a stile and began his slow progress along the river, casting his line over the water with the flick of wrist and movement of arm of inborn talent. As he cast his line he cast his cares. The mesmeric flow of the water brought solace and comfort to his insecure soul. When a trout rose to the fly and he struck, excitement took over until he had landed it, killed it with a sharp knock on the head and put it in his bag. He almost resented the interruption to his peace. By the time he had fished up the river it was nearly dark. He had caught four good fish. He stood looking up at Louisa's house, debating whether to go home without calling on her or whether to visit. He decided on the latter.

He cleaned the fish by what light was left, wrapped them in leaves and, walking through the garden, went round to the back entrance. He found the key Louisa kept hidden near the back door and let himself into the kitchen. Feeling for the light switch in the dark, he was aware of a delectable smell of cooking lingering in the warmth of the Aga and of tails thumping a greeting from the heap of mongrels lolling against the stove. He switched on the light.

"You're a fat lot of good as watchdogs." He crouched down to stroke friendly heads and pat silky flanks. "Suppose I'd come to mug Aunt Louisa? What about that, then?" The dogs seemed mildly amused. The largest got up and went to sniff the fish Rory had put on the table.

Rory stepped out of his boots and padded to the dresser for a dish. He laid the fish neatly head to tail and took them to the refrigerator.

"She in the drawing-room watching TV?" The dogs looked at him brightly. "Or has she gone to bed?" They wagged their tails, mouths slightly open. "I'll go and see, you stay here." But as he opened the door into the hall one of the dogs, Rufus, pushed past him and ran ahead. Perforce he had to follow.

The hall was in darkness, a grandfather clock tic-tocked in the silence. Rory went to the drawing-room and found that dark also.

"Hell, she must have gone to bed. Where's that dog?" He stood listening, not wishing to disturb the sleeping house. He could leave a note or ring up in the morning, but the dog had gone upstairs, presently it would scratch at Louisa's door. The animal would wake her if she were asleep. Rory snapped his fingers, whistled softly. The dog did not wish to hear. Rory switched on a light at the foot of the stairs and made his way to his aunt's bedroom. To his surprise the dog was not standing outside Louisa's room or anywhere to be seen.

"Curse it." Rory tiptoed past Louisa's door and set off in search. No dog on the first floor. He climbed the next flight.

Outside a bedroom he considered his own, since he had spent many happy holidays in it, the dog sat, head raised in expectation. Rory snapped his fingers. Rufus wagged more briskly. Rory, seeing light under the door, knocked, opened, walked in behind Rufus.

In front of the cheval glass he had known all his life, a glass before which he had pranced, draped in his bathtowel pretending to be a Roman Emperor when he was eight, stood the girl he had given his great-aunt Calypso's hat. The girl was trying on the hat, posing in front of the mirror. She hadn't a stitch on.

"Oh, hullo," said Hebe, surprised.

"I was trying to—" Rory gasped. Gosh, what a girl! – "to catch the – he ran ahead up—" Wasn't she going to cover herself? "I was afraid Aunt Louisa might have—"

"What?" Hebe removed the hat, reached for a slip which she slung round her waist.

"A headache." Rory gazed, fascinated.

"No, she hasn't. She went to bed early. She's been gardening all day." Hebe was putting the hat back into its striped bag. "She was tired. Do you want the hat back?"

"Oh no!"

"What are you doing here then?"

"I'm only – I was fishing – I put some trout—" Rory still stared in stupefaction.

"Where?"

"In the refrigerator." She was stroking that bloody Rufus. He watched her hands fondling the animal's head.

"Good." She watched him. Was he aware he was getting an erection?

"Could you put that hat on again?"

"Of course." She took the hat out of its bag and put it on. Rory watched her back, her raised arms putting on the hat, her reflection in the mirror. She turned round.

"Why don't we?" With a gentle gesture she indicated the bed. Rory had no recollection later of taking off his trousers or Hebe taking off the hat. Rufus sniffed round the room then, finding an armchair, settled in it to sleep.

Waking with the sun shining through partly drawn curtains, Rory was aware of eyes watching an inch from his face.

"I'm very short-sighted," said Hebe.

"Oh, ahh, I've never ever been able to do—" He tried to speak. "Not properly so that I – er – not like—"

"Well, it's lovely, isn't it? And you can, can't you?"

"Yes, oh yes, it was simply—"

"Once more then before I get up? How would that be?" She was not laughing at him, not mocking him as others had.

"Wonderful. Wonderful. Wonderful," he sang.

She gentled him. "Take it slow."

"I've never been able – then suddenly seeing you in the hat I—"

"Did your great-aunt wear it in bed?"

Rory laughed, holding Hebe in his arms. "My great-aunt didn't need hats to get her going."

"Nor will you now."

Presently Rory asked, "Who are you? What are you doing here?"

"I'm a temporary cook, one of your aunt's indulgences. Has she never told you?"

544

"No, well yes. I've heard she sometimes—"

"I'm also—" Hebe paused.

"What? Tell me. Also what?" Sudden gloom seized him.

"I'm also a prostitute. I do this for money." He would now leap out of bed, causing a draught, and flee. Hebe sighed, turning away, but Rory said, "I like the word courtesan better."

"Oh." She was surprised by his tone.

"I can pay you. I'm quite well off."

"Let's discuss that later if you want to. I have to get up and get breakfast. We could have trout. Does your aunt like trout?"

"She says so, when I bring them."

"Come and talk to me while I bath." Hebe slid out of bed and disappeared into the adjoining bathroom, an old-fashioned room, once a dressing-room converted at some pre-Great War period. The bath had a mahogany surround; the lavatory also. The walls were papered with an exuberant pattern of roses. There was a small fireplace in a corner, an ottoman and an armchair covered in cretonne to match the walls; a marvellous background for Hebe, filling the bath, feeling the temperature, stepping in, lying back.

"Why don't you sit down?" She indicated the armchair. Rory, a bathtowel round his loins, sat.

The dog Rufus came and leaned on the mahogany surround and stared at Hebe's face through the steam, his intention to lick, if possible, taste soap. Hebe stroked his nose with soapy fingers.

"You spoil him." Rory felt a pang of envy for the dog's proximity, his casual acceptance of Hebe's kindness.

"He's a dear good dog, I like him."

Rory sat, watching her soap her neck, sponge her face, lift feet from the water, soap her toes.

"How did you get in?" she asked.

"I'm Louisa's nephew, I know where she hides the key."

"I see."

"She lets me fish her water whenever I feel low. My name is Rory Grant."

"I know, it's on the bag the hat was in."

"Of course, how silly of—"

"Why do you never finish your sentences?"

"I suppose they are not worth finishing."

"It could become a very irritating habit."

"I hadn't—"

"Thought. Say 'thought'. Say it."

"You are mocking me. Thought."

"Good. My name is Hebe."

"Hebe, a pretty bush, I mean—" Rory floundered.

"What?"

"Shrub, I meant shrub."

"You didn't." Hebe stood up in the bath. "Could you pass me my towel. You've got it wrapped round you." She held out her hand.

"Oh, sorry." He divested himself. "I'd better dress." He backed towards the door.

"Okay. See you downstairs. I'll give you breakfast."

In the doorway Rory looked back at Hebe vigorously towelling. "So beautiful."

"Take Rufus down, he must be pining to pee."

Rory pulled on his clothes, snapped his fingers at the dog and hurried downstairs. The dogs in the kitchen greeted him and Rufus with much wagging, yawns, chortling whines and growls. Rory let them out into the garden where they disappeared in the mist rising from the river, a bank of cotton wool with the sun's shafts angling through. He stood staring, unseeing, exhilarated.

In the house Louisa switched on the seven o'clock news, quickly dousing the volume.

The dogs came back full of jollity, jostling each other, prepared for another happy day. Rory groaned in disbelief. Was this event true? Behind him in the kitchen Hebe switched on the coffee grinder, a discordant screech.

"Ghastly noise." She wore a pink cotton dress and a white apron, her hair demurely brushed in its shoulder-length bob. She wore no make-up.

"Sit down, Rory, don't get in my way."

"Can't I help?"

"No. Just sit while I get us breakfast." She was terrifyingly efficient, setting the coffee to percolate, choosing a fish to cook, spreading a tablecloth, laying three places, forks, knives, spoons, cups, saucers, salt, pepper, butter, marmalade, all placed swiftly on the table, loading the toaster.

"When you said that—" Rory's sentence was strangled by his nervous throat.

"What?"

"That you are – that you – er – that—"

"That I'm a tart?"

"Er, yes."

"I sleep with people for money. Got that? I have to earn my living. I have certain commitments like gas bills to pay." And, she thought, school bills. "The only things I'm good at, Rory, are cooking, so I take temporary cooking jobs and, as you've found out, fucking."

Rory muttered in protest, "Lovemaking."

"No, Rory, not lovemaking. It's not lovemaking, it's—" Hebe paused, searching for a word which would suit him.

"What is it, if it's not lovemaking? You've made me love you."

"This is not nineteen thirty." Hebe poured him coffee. "Milk, sugar?"

"Both, please. What was last night, then?"

"A free sample. If you enjoyed it and want repeats you'll have to pay." Much better, thought Hebe, to get the financial bit over fast, then one could relax and enjoy. "Them's my terms," she said lightly. "No money, no fuck."

"Don't call it that!" He winced.

"Precious." Hebe laughed, but her mockery was not hurtful. "I feel very friendly," she said, observing Rory's long upper lip and hare's eyes over the rim of her cup.

"Are there other – er – other men?"

"Yes."

"Many?"

"That's my business. You are not likely to meet them and what you and I do has nothing to do with them, right?"

"Right," said Rory bravely. "So what – er – what happens?"

"I fit you in when I can."

"Like a dentist's appointment."

"More or less."

They both were laughing when Louisa came into the kitchen. "Hullo, Rory." She kissed him as he stood up. "You're up early. Any luck on the river? Oh, I see you've had a good morning." She eyed the fish Hebe had ready in the pan. "How delicious, trout for breakfast. I see you've met Hebe. Am I not lucky to have Hebe for a couple of weeks? All the glorious food without the bother of travelling to France." Her quick eyes skimmed Rory's unshaven face. "What time did you get here? The dogs didn't bark."

"No, they didn't." He looked embarrassed.

"Coffee?" Hebe held the pot aloft.

"Yes, please," Louisa accepted. "Someone at the door, I think." Rufus growled and the other dogs set up a loud cacophony.

"Quiet!" shouted Louisa. "Quiet, you beasts."

Hebe went to the back door. A uniformed constable stood outside.

"Anybody here got a Volvo registration, er—" He consulted his notebook.

"Yes, it's mine," said Rory, standing up.

"Parked in a rather dodgy place, if I may say so. Morning, Mrs Fox." He saluted Louisa.

"Good morning, Constable. Like a cup of coffee?"

"No, thank you all the same."

"I'll move it." Rory pushed past the policeman.

"Quite a lot of traffic along that road, people going to work. You left the window down; the night dew won't have done it any good."

"Or harm, either," Rory shouted over his shoulder.

"Come back for your breakfast when you've moved it," Louisa called after him. "Goodbye, Constable." She watched his retreating back then turned back into the kitchen. "Well, now we can have breakfast in peace." She smiled at Hebe, cooking the trout. She did not expect Hebe to answer and Hebe was obligingly silent, thereby rising several notches in Louisa's esteem, one of her beloved husband's maxims having been "Never explain, never apologise".

FOURTEEN

"I was wondering" – Louisa put down her napkin – "whether I could ask you to do my shopping, Hebe. I do so hate Salisbury when it is full of tourists. Would it be very selfish to ask you to do it?"

"Of course not." Hebe, who had been silent through breakfast, wondering whether her new acquaintance with Louisa's nephew would endanger her job, met Louisa's eyes. "Have you much to be done?"

"One or two things I have ordered and my library books changed."

"Could I do that? I hardly know your taste in reading."

"I read thrillers," Louisa answered. "Crimies – the more complex the better. I never understand the plots but find them excellent soporifics, better than Mogadon. You will be more than able to choose for me. Not American, though."

"And not bacon and egg." Rory, who had reached the erroneous conclusion that his aunt believed he had got up early, spoke with the knowledge of years. "Louisa objects to traces of other people's breakfasts in library books, bits of egg, tea stains, crumbs." His eyes swivelled from Hebe to Louisa.

"I also object to the prudes who cross out four-letter words like 'shit' and 'fuck'," said Louisa primly, "and those who correct grammatical errors and write in the margins."

"Tell you what," exclaimed Rory, "I could—"

"What could you?" Louisa watched Rory's surprise at his own temerity. He is going to offer to drive her.

"I could drive – er – Hebe in and – er – give her a lift back when I come back to fish."

"Shall you be fishing this evening?" Louisa affected surprise.

"Yes," said Rory. "The weather's – er – propitious."

"Splendid. How glad I am that I have a deep freeze. Would that arrangement suit you, Hebe?"

Hebe nodded. "I might find something special for dinner," she said.

"So you might." Louisa stood up. "I shall spend an uninterrupted day in the garden. Have a good time. No need to hurry back." She left the kitchen followed by her dogs.

"I could give you—"

"What?"

"Lunch." Rory forced the word out as though it were dangerous.

"Then say 'lunch'. Don't leave it in the air. I bet your father the General finished his sentences. If he hadn't, wars would have been worse."

"Or better." Rory thought of his father. "He's still alive. Do you have a father?"

"I'll clear up the kitchen and get ready." Hebe ignored Rory's question. They were not likely to be in Salisbury, she thought. They only go there once a month and I, she thought, have altered so much they would not recognise me. "While I get ready, will you find Mrs Fox's books and get a list of what she wants? Make yourself useful," she finished, rather cruelly, for she felt irritated that she was still rather uncertain about Rory. If only he were not Louisa's nephew he would fit perfectly into the gap left by Terry.

Having watched Rory drive off with Hebe, Louisa settled to enjoy a potter round her garden, her dogs strolling behind her, pausing to scratch, snap at flies, indulge in a little larking about, enjoy in their middle age the security felt by animals aware of their own worth, generous in their love for their owner, prepared when necessary to bark their heads off at strangers but rarely bite. Dead-heading her roses, Louisa anticipated her next conversation with Bernard, when she would regale him with the getting together of his one-time rivals Christopher Rutter and Algy Grant's descendants. Her peace was interrupted by the dogs' wild barking at a man coming round the house. He paid no attention to the dogs, who reared and rushed round his legs. Louisa watched his lips move. "Quiet!" she yelled and the dogs subsided. The man came up to Louisa.

"Mrs Fox? I've brought you a packet from old Bernard Quigley. My name is Jim Huxtable."

Louisa shook hands. "Is he so very old?"

"*Façon de parler*. I thought as I was driving past I might be quicker than the post." He took from his pocket a thick envelope and gave it to Louisa. "Will you count it?"

"I don't think I need." Louisa liked the look of Bernard's messenger. "Shall we go into the kitchen and I will give you a drink."

"Thank you." He fell into step beside her.

"Or a snack. We could have a snack before you go on your way. Have you far to go?"

"Cornwall."

"To Bernard?" Her face lit up.

"Yes."

"You must tell me how he is. It is ages since I saw him, ages."

"I think he is well." Jim Huxtable paced beside Louisa. "Have you known him long?"

"More than fifty years."

"That's quite a long time."

"It depends how you look at it." Louisa looked back along the telescoping years to see herself and Bernard young, she twenty, he rather older. "How is he keeping? Do you see much of him?"

"When I am in Cornwall I stay with him. Do you know his house?"

"No. Tell me about it."

"It's very isolated. He lives in it with his cat and his dog."

"Feathers."

"Yes, his dog is called Feathers." Jim looked with interest at Bernard's old friend. "He has a great collection in his house. He sometimes buys from me, occasionally sells." She was beautiful once, he thought.

"So he's still an active dealer?"

"You could say that. Sometimes he asks me to sell things for him."

"Then he trusts you." Louisa looked at Jim with interest.

"I hope so." Jim suffered her glance.

They went into the house.

"Let's see what we can find to eat. Is it too early for you to have lunch? My cook is in Salisbury." She did not wait for Jim to answer but flitted about the kitchen emitting little cries of pleasure: "Ah, bread. She makes bread – delicious. Ah, pâté, here we are, she makes this too. And wine, here is a bottle, and salad, she makes the most gorgeous dressing, here it is, and if we have any room left we can eat fruit and cake. How would that be? Are you hungry?"

"I am beginning to be," said Jim, appreciating Louisa.

"Sit down, then." Louisa found plates and glasses, poured Jim a glass of wine. "We can finish with coffee, though I cannot make coffee like my cook."

"Perhaps you'd let me. I learned how to make coffee in a bar in Italy," Jim offered.

"Certainly, that would round off our snack. Tell me more about Bernard. How is age treating him?"

"He keeps it at bay; he has some trick."

"He walks across country to the telephone. That keeps him fit."

"It's a long walk, very long in rough weather. I have begged him to have the telephone put in."

"He won't," said Louisa, spreading pâté on crusty bread. "From Bernard originated the expression 'Don't call me, I'll call you.' He is fierce in the preservation of his privacy, always was."

"It's inconvenient." Jim remembered with irritation times when to get hold of Bernard had been impossible and necessitated the long trip to Penzance. "He does not answer letters. Does he ever write to you?" Jim asked, then wished he had not, sensing her pain.

"No." Louisa was expressionless. "Have some more pâté? No? Fruit, then."

"Lovely pâté. It was excellent. Your cook has talent."

"I'll tell her. She is only here for a fortnight. I treat myself to a cook once or twice a year. At my age travel is an effort and to be honest I don't care for it any more, so I have this splendid girl. She cooks divinely and when she is here she fills my deep freeze so that for a long time I have treats. Do you not think this a good idea?"

"Brilliant." He tried to imagine this woman and Bernard in their prime.

"There are other considerations," said Louisa. "I don't have to leave my garden or my dogs." She looked at the dogs lying by the Aga. "And if the telephone rings I am here to answer it."

She is still in love with Bernard, thought Jim, fascinated. How does it work in old age? Is it purely cerebral? "Shall I make coffee?" he asked. "I'm sure I can't compete with your cook but I'll try."

"Thank you. She's gone to Salisbury with my nephew. He

was here fishing. We had trout for breakfast." Louisa smiled, remembering Rory's unshaven appearance. "He must have got up very early. He is fishing again tonight." She laughed, thinking of Rory. "I am sorry you missed them," she said, watching Jim make coffee. Then, "Perhaps you can stay. Would you like to stay the night? It would be no trouble since I have my cook. She is bringing back some delight from Salisbury for dinner."

"Alas, I can't, I must push on."

"Would you take one or two things to Bernard for me, since you are going his way?" I can trust this man, thought Louisa, and he's jolly attractive.

"Of course."

"Bernard sells things for me. When we have had our coffee let me see what I can bear to part with. It is a question of balance; cook versus things."

"I see." Jim felt distress.

"Cooks are expensive," said Louisa. This man would be much better for Hebe than Rory, she thought, and I wonder whether he is married.

"Yes."

"But she gives me so much pleasure." She watched him make coffee, pronounced it delicious, "Even better than Cook's." She amused herself referring to Hebe as "Cook". Then she led him through the house and, while he envied her furniture, she opened a drawer and exclaimed, "Ah, this," and again, "Ah, this and this," producing pieces of jewellery, a snuff box, a watch, putting them into his hand. "Put them into your pocket so that I do not see them," and seeing his surprise she explained, "If I hide things I may sell and forget them then I feel less wrench at parting. I think that should do for the present."

"I'll give you a receipt," Jim said.

"No, no. Bernard trusts you, that's enough." But Jim wrote a receipt while she watched him.

When she stood by Jim's car to say goodbye she said, "I enjoyed seeing you. Tell him to telephone me."

"I will do that." It is important; Bernard is not a stale old man to her.

"I wish you could have stayed and met my cook."

"Thank her for my lunch. I will tell him to telephone."

A lonely old thing, Jim thought, driving away. What would I want to meet her cook for? He switched on his car radio and settled himself for the long drive to Cornwall, calculating, as he listened to the afternoon concert, the value of Louisa's "things". However much the cook cost Louisa could afford to pay her quite a few more times.

Weeding her herbaceous border with the sun on her back and the sound of bees among the flowers, Louisa thought Bernard's friend a handsome man; tall – she liked tall men – nice hair, must have been that rare colour she liked before it went grey – good eyes, a humorous mouth. He was the type she admired, the type she had married. Why then the tug at her heart when he spoke of Bernard, why after nearly fifty years was Bernard, who was small and had never been good looking, so special. "Ah," said Louisa, sitting back on her heels and pushing her hair back from her forehead, "he made me laugh." The dogs wagged their tails, glad that she was happy. Remembering the big bed in the Hôtel d'Angleterre in Paris so many years ago, with the light shining through the chinks of the red plush curtains and the breakfasts of croissants and coffee, Louisa grinned. "He was a rascal," she said to the dog Rufus who was her favourite, "a rascal but he still makes me laugh." Rufus bowed down, inviting her to play, waving his plumy tail. "But I couldn't be part of a team, could I?" she said to Rufus, voicing the suspicion she had taken care never to verify, that she was by no means the first girl Bernard had taken to stay in that hotel room in those long ago days which in old age seemed clearer than yesterday, infinitely more real than the present.

FIFTEEN

Jennifer Reeves believed in her menfolk, as she thought of her husband, her son and his friends, starting the day with a good breakfast. Silas ate what was put in front of him, a bowl of porridge followed by bacon and eggs, washed down with tea, and listened to Michael arguing with Julian about the merits of a boat they had had the previous year compared with the boat they were to sail that day. As they talked it dawned on him that his hosts thought nothing of sailing to France or Holland and that Julian and Jennifer had sailed down the coast from Sussex during the summer term, taking several weekends to bring the boat to the Scillies, returning to London after each trip. He was impressed by so much effort. It became clear as he listened that Mrs Reeves was giving him her place in the boat on the day's expedition. When he politely protested, Jennifer cried, "No, no, Silas, I don't mind at all. I have lots to do here and you have never been to Bishop's Rock. You must go, you will love it. I have been often, haven't I?" She appealed to her husband and son, showing her fine teeth and healthy gums.

"Ma's a great sailor," said Michael with his mouth full.

"Pass the marm, Pa." Julian pushed the marmalade towards his son. "Are we taking our lunch?"

"Mrs Thing has made pasties. Super for sailing."

Silas wondered what Mrs Thing's name could be.

"Mind you all take lots of sweaters, it can be cold out there. Has someone lent Silas boots?" asked Jennifer.

Michael said, "He can wear mine, I've got two pairs."

"When's the off?" enquired Ian.

"Half an hour." Julian's voice grew louder at the prospect. "If you're not all ready by then I'll go without you."

"Time to empty our bowels." Alistair, the younger brother, left the table. "Bags I the upstairs loo." Nobody commented.

Presently, wearing Michael's spare boots, which, too large, made walking difficult, wearing his favourite sweater and carrying Hebe's Guernsey for spare, Silas stood waiting for the others. He noticed that the wind had not dropped during the night and that the sea between Trescoe and St Mary's was choppy. When the boys and Julian were assembled they proceeded down to the landing stage, carrying lunch baskets and a variety of objects strange to Silas which would be needed on the boat. Julian handed him a lifejacket and Alistair officiously showed him how to put it on. At the landing stage they clambered into an inflatable dinghy and set off across the water to St Mary's where the Reeves' boat was moored.

Silas had never been in an inflatable boat and enjoyed the crossing; the wind made his eyes water. When they reached the boat in which they were to sail he clambered in after Michael and sat down where Julian told him, out of harm's way. Michael, Alistair and Ian busied themselves about the boat, obeying Julian's orders. Silas surreptitiously put on Hebe's sweater over his own and flexed his toes in the too large boots to keep warm while he readjusted his lifejacket.

Julian and the boys exchanged shouted greetings with people on shore. Silas sat hoping his ignorance of sailing would not show, wondering if he would ever learn which rope did what. He wondered belatedly whether he had the guts to say he would rather stay on shore and watch birds and as he wondered Michael cast off and they moved out into open water.

From time to time Julian shouted at Silas, pointing out to him St Agnes. "That's St Agnes. Splits in two at low tide," and "Shags, d'you know the difference between a cormorant and a shag?"

"Yes."

"Interested in birds, are you?"

"Quite."

"Like to take the tiller?"

"Oh, thank you." Silas felt tremulous pleasure. Was he now responsible for all their lives?

Pleasure was succeeded by anxiety. Suppose somebody shouted "Port" or "Starboard", what was he supposed to do? "Port on the right is never left," he remembered. Julian had gone below. He could see him putting on another sweater, balancing with his legs apart. Alistair and Michael were further up the boat near the mast, Ian right in the bows. The boat was crashing along on her side. Ian shouted something and pointed. Silas looked up. Coming in from Penzance was the *Scillonian*, a familiar friend moored in Penzance harbour but out here doing a chopping roll, sending up a steep wave at her bow, menacing. Silas watched with interest as she drew nearer. "Watch out, you shitty idiot!" Julian snatched the tiller, tipping Silas off balance so that he sprawled backwards. Julian, white and furious, altered course, ignoring angry shouts from the *Scillonian*.

"What d'you want to give him the tiller for? He's never sailed in his life," Michael yelled. "Ma would have a fit," he raged at his father. Julian shouted, "Shut up!" and chopped at his son. Michael dodged. It began to rain viciously, coldly, cruelly. Silas, on his feet again, wondered where he could go to be out of the way. He felt futile, ashamed, small.

"Why don't you go below?" Michael suggested, but Silas shook his head. He was supposed to be enjoying this. He would not ask how far to the Bishop's Rock, how long before we get there. He stared at the sea and braced himself against the movement of the boat, wishing his feet in the two big boots were not so terribly cold.

When they reached it the Bishop's Rock was scary in its defiant loneliness. Julian, who had been silent after his spat with his son, laughed as he steered. Silas, watching Michael, guessed that they were far too close for safety and that Julian was punishing Michael as he drove the boat close in where the sea surged and sucked at the black rocks.

It was Ian who suggested lunch and fetched up the basket of pasties. They were now tacking for home. Silas had seen boats tack in Mounts Bay but had never realised how much work it entailed. It seemed crazy for Julian, Michael, Alistair and Ian to be trying to eat pasties as they worked the boat, dodging and ducking the boom. The wind had increased and Julian yelled that they must shorten sail. Silas caught snatches of incomprehensible jargon and admired the boys as they nimbly obeyed. They looked serious now and Silas saw Julian look up at the sky, frowning.

Clouds bulging with rain were surging in from the west. A black mass suddenly sheeted rods of water, as he remembered seeing in a Rembrandt print in a book of Hebe's. The squall hit the boat, drenching them in the few minutes it took to pass. In his fear, Silas gulped and gobbled his pasty, noticing with one cell of his brain that the pasty was greasy, had been made with fat meat, was in no way comparable to the pasties made for him by his mother when he went picnicking with Giles, nor had Mrs Thing put in any turnip.

The sensation that he had a stone in his stomach, that he would never be warm again, that he was going deaf, assailed Silas so suddenly that he barely had time to reach the side to be sick. To compound his misery the wind blew the vomit back on to his chest, splattering Hebe's jersey, and down into Michael's boots. Pasty, porridge, bacon, egg and tea in a greasy agonising rush. Oh God! I wish I could die.

"He's thrown up into my boots," yelled Michael, and Ian, who never became a friend, laughed.

SIXTEEN

With the courage many timid men acquire behind the driving wheel, Rory found himself able to speak to Hebe sitting beside him in a butcher-blue cotton dress, her shoulder-length hair tousled by the air from the open window. Her legs were long and bare. He noted with relief that she had not painted her toenails and that her rather large feet were beautifully shaped.

"When last night I came into your room," he began.

"Yes?" She looked at the road ahead.

"When I came into your room, were you surprised?"

"Of course."

"What puzzles me is that you didn't scream."

"What good would that have done?"

"You didn't cover yourself up."

"I had nothing to hide." Hebe looked at the road. Soon they would see the spire of Salisbury Cathedral, the tallest in England.

"You – er – the words you used – I—"

"Would you rather have me say I saw something stirring in the undergrowth of your trousers? That it?"

"No, it's just—"

"Too well brought up? What about your aunt and her library books? She isn't afraid to use four-letter words."

"She shocks my father and mother."

"You needn't." Hebe turned to look at him. "You needn't, if I shock you, have anything more to do with me. It's no skin off my nose."

"Hebe, you know I—"

"What?"

"I want to. I – er – want – I—"

"Do you *never* finish a sentence?"

"Only short ones."

"Tell me what you want, then?"

"You. That short enough?" Rory said with a burst of spirit.

"You want to join the Syndicate?"

"Is that what you call it?"

"For want of a better word."

Rory was silent. He was both excited and horrified. Presently he said, "It sounds so cold."

Hebe sniffed and said, "Businesslike."

"How can you?" Rory protested in anguish.

"Look," she was growing impatient. "My body is my business. Business is buying and selling – right? You sell hats."

"Not many," he sighed.

"Don't interrupt. I sell. If you want to buy, you buy. There's no obligation."

"Oh – I—"

"I enjoy my business. Surely you noticed that last night?"

"Oh, I did." Rory's cry was heartfelt.

"Well, then." She was smiling now.

"How do I set about it? How do I join?" Rory capitulated, looking sideways at Hebe, trying to see the eyes he had woken to find watching him at close range.

"Keep your eye on the road, love, you nearly had us in the ditch."

"Oh." His eyes swivelled back to the road. "Sorry."

"This is how it works." Her voice was dry. Inwardly she cringed, loathing this part of the transaction. "I tell you when I am free. We decide a place to meet and I meet you there for a weekend or a week."

"Not longer?"

"Not longer. We decide in advance how much you will pay, you give me a cheque or cash if you'd rather, and it's up to me to tell you when I will come."

"You decide that, why can't I?"

"I should think that's pretty obvious."

"Fitting me in with the rest of the Syndicate." Rory bristled with jealousy.

"Yes."

"Why don't you sack them and marry me?"

"Marriage is not on the menu, that's one thing you must get into your head."

"Are you married already?" Rory was appalled by the thought. Hebe married to some brute, forced to make pin money as a cook, as a, ah me, he groaned inwardly, a tart.

"No."

Rory felt the conversation coming to an end, that Hebe sitting beside him was some sort of female oyster clammed shut. He mixed metaphors in his muddled mind.

"Do I have a choice of venue?" he asked.

"Yes, you can have that," she conceded.

Driving the last three miles into the city, Rory wondered whether to have Hebe to stay in his house behind the shop; he was happy there and had a garden which was pretty and not overlooked. Or whether he dared take her to a cottage his great-aunt Calypso occasionally lent him in the middle of her wood famous for its flowering cherries, daffodils and bluebells. He steered the car thoughtfully through the maze of streets, with their infuriating one-way system, to the place he parked his car. Beside him he noticed with baffled rage Hebe was calmly checking her shopping list.

Rory had never before found shopping fun. They went first to the fishmonger, where Hebe discovered grouse flown from Scotland. "Why not buy grouse?" She felt the breasts of the dead birds, murmuring, "These had pitifully short lives." Rory volunteered to pay, since he felt this might repay Louisa's hospitality. They stood discussing the matter, annoying the fishmonger, holding up a queue of people. Hebe explained that she always bought extra for Louisa's deep freeze, which she filled with pâtés and preserves. The birds were piled into the shopping basket. They went to the delicatessen, argued over cheeses and bought German mustard and a bottle of Greek olive oil. They carried their shopping back to Rory's shop before returning to the market to buy vegetables and fruit. Rory watched Hebe choose, setting aside the unripe or slightly off, regardless of the fury of the stallholders. "In France they don't respect you if you just take what you're given. Look at that peach, a Saturday night bruise, and that banana's lame." Her shopping done, she turned to Rory. "Shall we do the library before lunch?" They fetched Louisa's books from the car.

In the library Rory took over, collecting armfuls of crime from the shelves, sitting on a bench to look them through. "You help," he said to Hebe. "She used to get home and find she'd taken out a book she'd already read. She puts a little sign, look, here's one, a dot in a circle. Discard that, check for the purely American, she can't read the language, and lastly for other people's breakfasts."

"What about the rude words crossed out?"

"That, too." Rory laughed.

The librarian from her desk pointed to the sign which said

"Silence". Hebe whispered to Rory, "I am enjoying my day," filling him with joy.

They chose four books and added them to their pile of shopping.

"Why don't we have lunch here? What have you got in your fridge?" Hebe peered into the refrigerator.

"Don't you want to go to a restaurant?"

"Not particularly. Here's a nice wine." She held up a bottle of Muscadet. "Why don't you run to the fishmonger and buy prawns or something. There's brown bread and butter here."

Rory came back with a lobster and a lettuce. Watching Hebe make mayonnaise, he knew he had never been happier.

During lunch he told Hebe of his life, his parents, his schools, his stand against going, as his father wished, into the Army, his sudden declaration that all he had ever wanted was a hat shop, an inspiration based on his resemblance to the March Hare, about which his family teased him.

"I bet that floored them."

"It did. Then I had to have one. That's how I started. I had never really considered such a thing."

"And your Aunt Louisa backed you up?"

"Yes. She doesn't like my father, and my great-aunt Calypso helped me too."

"The aunt who gave you my hat? That aunt?"

"Yes. Her husband planted the wood where I want to take you when – er – when it's my turn. There's a cottage."

"What a long sentence, Rory. You finished it and several others."

"You are mocking."

"Only a little. Let's go to bed and you tell me about your great-aunt's wood."

"Oh, I will." Rory got up from the table. As they went upstairs he said, "I hope you'll find – er – find the bed—"

"Comfortable?"

"Yes and er—"

"And you can tell me about your other girls."

"I'm not much good with girls. They – er—"

"Don't know what they're missing." Hebe caught her dress by the skirt and whooshed it up and over her head in what seemed to Rory one waving movement. "Come on," she said, climbing into his bed, "let's enjoy ourselves."

Should he enjoy himself? Should he not feel the puritan shame his parents had instilled?

"Work up an appetite for dinner," urged Hebe cheerfully.

"You are so prosaic," he cried. "So—"

"Practical."

"Perfect." He was delighted.

"Not that." Suddenly she held him. He sensed fear in her and feeling her vulnerable held her close. When she slept he watched her until she woke. "We should be getting back if I am to cook dinner. This has been quite a long day off and a lovely siesta."

Rory wanted to ask how it came about that she was a tart, guessed she would not tell him. Standing under the shower, watching her dress through the open door of the bathroom, he realised she had told him nothing about herself.

"Rory," Hebe called, "you still haven't shaved. What will your aunt think?"

"My aunt," said Rory thoughtfully, "may not—er—may not—"

"What may she not?" Hebe came to sit on the edge of the bath to watch him shave.

"May not expect me to stay."

"You mustn't stay."

"But last night – er—"

"Last night was exceptional. Really, Rory, it was. I never mix my cooking commitments with my tarting."

"Don't say—"

"All right, but it's true I never mix the two. Today's a day off."

"You mean I've got to wait?" Rory, with his face covered in lather, looked slightly mad.

"I shall have to see when I can fit you in."

"When do you leave Louisa?"

"On the twenty-first."

"So then we can—"

"I have other commitments." In Hebe's mind a vision of Silas coming to greet her off the train. Only this time he would be getting off the helicopter, his wonderful visit over. "I'm sorry," she said gently. "I really do have other things to do."

Disappointed, Rory shaved, his anxious eyes trying to catch sight of Hebe in the glass.

"I could drive you."

"I have my own car."

"Where do you live?"

"I never tell anyone where I live."

"Blast!" shouted Rory. "Blast you!"

"That's the way it is. That's the only way I can manage. You must put up with it."

"You give, then take it all away," he wailed.

"If it's any comfort to you, none of my clients knows where I live. Your aunt doesn't."

"Even she?"

"Even she. I ring her and suggest dates. You will just have to trust me and if you find someone better, well and good."

"But I want to be able to telephone – er – talk to you, write to you."

"Sorry, Rory, you can't. I have an address in London which forwards my mail. I'll give you that. I don't mind if you write."

"I can't bear it!" Rory shouted through the lather. "I really don't—" Clumsily he mopped his face.

"Then stop now. No need to go on. Forget the whole idea." Stupid of me, thought Hebe, to think this man could take Terry's place. This is a clinger.

"But I – I – want—" Rory cried like a deprived child. "I do so want."

"Think about it. No need to hurry. There's no rush. I don't blame you if you don't want to go on. I see your point of view. It's just that I pay more attention to mine."

In silence they collected the parcels, in silence they drove back to Louisa's house. He grew sulky, almost surly. Hebe felt oppressed, her cheerfulness left her. She reproached herself for encouraging him, for enjoying herself, for accepting the hat, for inviting him into her bed. She felt sad.

Louisa's dogs greeted them with barks and yelps, leaping up on Hebe as she stood with her arms full of parcels, Rufus jumping up to her face, bumping her with his wet nose.

"Down!" shouted Louisa, coming out of the house. "Down, you beasts." She took one of the baskets from Hebe. "You clever girl, grouse. Shall we have a grouse for dinner? Quiet!" she shouted at the dogs. She followed Hebe into the kitchen where she was putting her parcels on to the table.

"What's the—" Hebe sniffed the air. "There's a—"

Louisa looked at Hebe; she seemed odd. Rory, catching sight of her face, saw her as he had first seen her in his shop and wondered whether she was about to faint.

"Here." He pushed her into a chair. "I'll get a glass of – put your head between —"

"It's all right." Hebe took his hand. "I'm not going to faint, just for a moment I imagined I smelt something that," she buried her face in his sleeve, "reminded me."

"Of what?" whispered Rory.

Oh dear, he's fallen in love with her, thought Louisa, watching them. Poor dear Rory.

"I don't know. I don't know what it reminds me of, that's what worries me." She tried to laugh. "I'm just being silly. It's like coffee or wood smoke, something of that sort." She let go of Rory. "I feel a fool, like when you can't remember a word which you know really well."

"I'm often at a loss for a word," Rory comforted.

"I had a visitor today. He made coffee after lunch, perhaps that is it," Louisa volunteered. "A friend of a friend of mine brought me a packet I was expecting. He made the coffee. It was even better than yours, Hebe."

"That must be it." Hebe looked relieved, though still puzzled.

"Smells are very evocative." Louisa watched Hebe anxiously. "And it's a tease when you can't remember what they remind you of," she gabbled on, while Hebe collected herself.

Although the grouse were delicious, conversation at dinner was strained. Louisa was not surprised when Rory decided that it was not after all a good evening for fishing, a lie which he took little trouble to hide. They watched the news on television and Louisa thought of Bernard in his tiny isolated house when the weathermen forecast gales coming in from the Atlantic, knowing that when the wind blew and rain pelted down Bernard was loath to adventure across country to the telephone. She would have to wait to question him about Jim Huxtable; wait to tell him about Hebe's meeting with Rory. He was always interested in Hebe's visits, a subject which almost superseded their gardens. Her thoughts took her away from the young people who presently took the dogs for a run. She tried to visualise Bernard, old and pottering in his garden, and failed, only seeing him young with no interest in flowers other than to order in quantity at a florist and send with a card: "Louisa, my love, Bernard".

They had walked by the river and back to Rory's car. "Goodbye." Hebe held out her hand.

Rory bent to kiss her. "When shall I —?"

"I have written down my forwarding address; here it is. I will get in touch, I promise. Are you sure you want me to?"

"Of course I—"

"I don't want to make you unhappy."

"I will take the risk." He got into his car and Hebe watched him drive away. She looked up at the threatening sky, hoping that Silas' pleasure would not be spoiled by storms, and forgot Rory as she tried to visualise Silas in the company of strangers. As she sniffed the scent of jasmine and tobacco plants and watched moths fluttering round the flowers, she wished herself away from Rory, so easily hurt, bruised, as she herself was by the world they had both been born into, had both escaped. And yet, she thought, part of me wishes it for Silas. Why else do I send him to that school, encourage him to stay with those people? Do I still believe he should have that chance? Do I believe in that mould which I fought to escape? Am I not as hypocritical as they were? They brought me up to be like them, to marry a man with money as my sisters did. Am I not tarting with Mungo and Rory to pay for Silas to have what I rejected? Am I misusing the Syndicate money?

In bed she lay reading Rory's copy of the *New Statesman*, finding cheer in the Heartsearch column. "Attractive Intellectual – Well worn – Unconventional colour-blind male/female – passionate – scrawny – happy – myopic – Nigerian – nonsexist – tallish – working class background – jazz media orientated – educated – divorced – academic." None of these paying propositions. She had once answered an appeal from a lonely Hampsteader in a bedsitter. He had needed to have a girl walking beside him across the Heath. I must look him up some time, she thought, when I am doing a stint with Mungo. It had been an agreeable sexless interlude. After the walks they had eaten chocolate eclairs and drunk camomile tea. He had given her ten pounds a time. She turned the page. Ah, here goes! She took note of an advertisement. "Love Lingerie, Ultimate in Undies, slinkiest pure silk, cut to dazzling American minimum." The illustration showed a lady with her pussy slung in the sort of bag Leni Riefenstahl had made for the Nazi athletes when filming them for the Olympic Games. Must send for one for Terry, a parting gift; his neat little apparatus would fit into that pure silk job nicely.

Consoled by cheerful memories of Terry, she turned off the light.

SEVENTEEN

The storm, which in infancy had made Silas sick, grew that night to monster proportions unusual even in the South–west. The gale gusted in from the Atlantic, bringing rain which lashed the streets, racing down the gutters. At high tide waves leapt across the sea wall, scattering stones and kelp over the promenade. Ships made for the shelter of Mounts Bay. Lifeboats from St Ives and Sennen battled to the rescue of a French trawler. Rogue water, gaining speed as it travelled, swept cigarette butts, lolly sticks, cellophane wrapping towards drains which, already blocked, refused entry. Gathering force in the alleyway behind the houses, the water found a weakness in a wall, sucked until it discovered a chink then, crawling through, gained entry into Amy Tremayne's garden, travelled to the back door, spread through the house, souping wet the rugs in her sitting-room until they could hold no more, re-formed and found the way out to the street.

Disturbed by the ferocity of the gale, Amy got out of bed to close her window. Reaching up to pull down the sash, a fierce pain in her chest assailed her. She collapsed in a chair, sick and dizzy. Her pills, out of reach, mocked her from the table by the bed. The telephone was on the ground floor. How often Hebe had begged her to have an extension. She tried to breathe, willing the pain to go, willing time to pass so that daylight would bring help. Rain driving in at the window drenched her knees. If Hebe finds me dead she will be upset. I can't die yet. She willed herself to live, sitting huddled in the chair by the window. As time passed she dozed, forgetting that Hebe was away working for Louisa Fox.

Terry, on his way to feed Trip, hurried up the street in the dawn, his chin tucked into his upturned collar, looking about him fascinated by the violence of the weather. Level with Hebe's door he noticed muddy water across the street, investigated, looked up at Amy's window, saw that it was open, looked more closely, saw the huddled figure in a chair. He tried the front door, found it locked, water seeping through.

He called up, "Hi, Miss Tremayne, you're flooded."

The old woman jerked awake. Terry saw her face. "Christ, she's dying."

He leapt on to the low wall which separated a strip of flowers from the street, gathered all his strength, sprang, catching the window ledge, hauling himself up to fall head first into the room at Amy's feet.

"Don't be afraid." He picked himself up. "Let me get you back to bed." He gathered the old woman in his arms. "You are cold." He laid her on the bed, propped her with pillows, pulled up the bedclothes. "Have you got pills? Is it your heart?"

"Yes," she whispered.

"These the pills?"

"Yes."

He tipped out the pills. "One? Two?"

"One," she whispered.

He put the pill in her mouth, held a glass so that she could drink. She gripped his hand.

"You are Hebe's black revenge." He could hardly hear her.

"What?"

"Hebe's black—"

"You need something hot. Don't move, I'll see what I can do. Okay if I leave you a moment?"

He ran downstairs, splashed into the flood. "Christ!" Hurried into the kitchen, put a kettle on the gas, rummaged for brandy, found a half bottle of whisky, saw a hot water bottle hanging on the back of the door, filled it, made tea, poured in a dollop of whisky, carried them upstairs.

"Don't try and talk." He tucked the hot bottle in by her feet. "Soon get you warm. Drink this." He sat beside her spooning hot tea into her obedient mouth. "That better?" He willed her to live.

"Yes." She felt better for the tea, the hot bottle was warming her feet. Terry put the empty cup aside and started rubbing her hands between his.

"I must telephone your doctor."

"No."

"Surely—"

"I don't want a doctor."

"Okay." He went on rubbing her hands. Should he tell her the downstairs was awash? Would it set her heart off again?

"Did you say flood?" Her voice was stronger.

"Yes. It's coming in at the back. I should—"

"Stay with me." She held his hands. "Hebe's black revenge."

She stared at his anxious face, liking his fine high-bridged nose and sculptured mouth.

"I'm not with you." He was puzzled.

"Hebe's black joke." What a spit in the eye for Christopher. She had never seen Terry close up, only catching an occasional glimpse from a distance. "Hebe never told me you were so beautiful."

Terry looked embarrassed. "We're still friends. The other's over."

"I know."

"I was on my way to feed her cat. What d'you mean, black revenge? Black joke?"

Amy began to laugh.

"Don't laugh, mind your heart," Terry exclaimed, but she looked better, a lot better.

Amy grinned, thinking of Christopher Rutter, how furious he would be, his worst accusations come true. Why had she never had the enterprise that Hebe showed? Where had Hebe found him?

"Where d'you come from? What's your job?"

"I met Hebe up country. I make burglar traps. I'm self-employed. I was adopted by liberal whites. I dropped out of a posh school they sent me to. It's my own invention." If he went on talking she might go to sleep, then he could get the doctor. "I make a contraption like an abacus with marbles. It's set under a strip of carpet to match what's in the room. When the burglar treads on it he feels insecure, scarpers."

"Do you sell many?" Keep him with me for a bit longer, she thought.

"Quite a lot. A friend of Hebe's gave me introductions, lists of names, old fellow called Quigley."

"Oh, him."

"Do you know him? He made this list of people all over the country. Some bought."

"Tell me who he sent you to."

Terry recited a litany of names, his pleasing voice lulling her until suddenly she grew alert. Among the names were Robert, Delian, Marcus. Did Hebe know this?

"Did he send you to anyone called Rutter?" she asked sharply.

"Yes, an old bloke called Christopher Rutter, same name as Hebe's. Mr Quigley says everyone is interconnected. It's a common name, he says."

"Did you tell Hebe?"

"I don't think so."

"How did you get on with him, old Christopher? Did he buy?"

"He did, said my quotation was cheaper than most."

Amy began to laugh.

"Hey, don't laugh, this isn't the time."

"*Ce n'est pas le moment.*" Her mind wandered.

"What?"

"In the Hôtel d'Angleterre he said" – Amy remembered the tone of voice – "he didn't want to know, thought it would sound easier in French. He left and I left soon after. Bloody Bernard."

Terry frowned. What was Amy on about? He was trapped. She was hanging on to his hand. He should have got the doctor straight away, or the niece, the blonde across the street. Hebe had not said Amy was gone in the head. His eyes, roving round the room in search of escape, hit on Amy's clothes.

"Hey! Do you wear those things?" Amy followed his glance.

"They keep the draught out." She eyed her directoire knickers. "They are to my taste." She turned to look at him. "And yours is different."

So Hebe had told her. "Yes," he said, looking Amy in the eye. "Yes," he repeated. "Knickers for comfort, skirts for a lark."

"Good lad," she said unexpectedly. "And you and she read poetry."

"She talks to you a lot." He grew suspicious.

"She must talk to someone. Recite me something before you go."

"I'll try. What do you like?"

"The one about the chestnut tree, know it? Great rooted something?"

"Blossomer. Chestnut tree. Yeats?"

"That's the one. Then fetch Hannah. Do you know her?"

"I'd like to."

"Chestnut poem first," Amy insisted.

Terry cleared his throat and began. As he recited he saw the rain had stopped and the sun was shining. "O chestnut tree great rooted blossomer." Amy held his hand and closed her eyes. When he reached, "How can we tell the dancer from the dance," Amy lay quiet, her hand in his. Terry looked at her face, no longer twisted with pain. Sitting beside her, examining her face, he thought he understood why Hebe loved this old woman. It was peaceful in the room. Soon he must get help, but he was loath to break the peace between himself and Amy. She opened her eyes.

"Better now."

Terry stood up. "Will you be okay if I leave you and wake your niece?"

"Yes."

"I should get the doctor."

"No. I hate fuss. I'll be all right." Her voice suddenly peevish, she said, "You want to get away. Thank you for coming. Just fetch Hannah." She was annoyed with herself. She had betrayed Hebe. "I'm very grateful," she said stiffly.

Puzzled and hurt, Terry let go her hand, stood up awkwardly. "I'll go." He left Amy's room and ran down the stairs, splashing into the flood. He had forgotten the flood water, had concentrated on Amy. Now, ankle-deep in water, he forgot her. The flood was urgent. He pulled open the front door and water surged into the street. He ran to Hannah's house and hammered on the door.

Opening the door in her dressing-gown, Hannah stared at Terry, her mind foggy with sleep, filled with an unexpected and strange exhilaration. Wow! Terry was talking, his voice eager; he too was excited. She heard, "Your auntie's flooded, muddy water is coming in from the back." But his eyes conveyed another message. He pushed past her into the house, towering above her so that for a moment all she saw was his neck and throat.

Hannah yelped, backing away. "Who are you? What do you want?" She stared at the ebony youth.

"Name's Terry, friend of Hebe's. Get some clothes on, for Chrissake, you silly female. The old girl's awash." His excitement was infectious.

"What's the matter, Ma?" Giles, in pyjamas, called from upstairs.

Terry shouted the situation to Giles. In minutes they were in Amy's house. Giles dialled 999 on Amy's telephone. Terry went to the back of the house to find the source of the flood. Hannah arrived wearing yellow boots, jeans and a green jersey.

"What's it like out there?" she asked.

"Job for the Council. We telephoned. Got a spade so we can divert the water?"

"No, we haven't."

"I'll get one from Hebe's. Got to feed the cat, anyway." He darted out into the rain.

"Who is that? He sure is bossy," said Hannah to Giles.

"Friend of Hebe's. Lucky he found the flood. Hurry up, Mum, stop staring."

"That you, Hannah?" Amy's voice from upstairs.

"I'm coming up." Hannah went up, expecting Amy to make a fuss.

"You all right, Auntie?" She stood by Amy's bed.

Feeling ill but unwilling to show it, Amy said, "Just a bit tired," unconvincingly.

"You don't look well," Hannah was anxious.

"I shall stay here until the mess is gone. That boy can help you. He's been reciting poetry to me."

Hannah glanced out of the back window at Terry, stripped to the waist, digging a ditch to divert the water. "Doesn't Hebe know him?" she asked.

"Lovely, isn't he?"

"Lovely?" Hannah stared at Amy. "How did he get in?" she asked suspiciously.

"Jumped. He's a jumper."

"You're joking—"

Amy closed her eyes. Hannah looked more closely at Terry. He was lovely. He was also making Giles laugh. Hannah's spirits soared. Mm, she thought, why not? "I'd better go and direct operations if you are comfortable," she said.

"I'm comfortable." As Hannah left the room Amy chuckled, pleased at the prospect of vicarious entertainment. Time Hannah loosened up, she thought, and who better than Hebe's joker to do the loosening. She knew Hebe's standard to be high, but this one was superb. She quite understood Hebe breaking her unwritten rule never to have a local involvement.

By the end of the morning Terry and Giles had stemmed the water, the ground floor of the house was ready to be scrubbed, Council workmen had unblocked the drain. Hannah, filling the kettle to make tea, was almost sorry the crisis was over. As she handed Terry his tea she looked at him appraisingly. Waking her in the morning and grubbing at the back of Amy's house with Giles, she had thought him not much older than Giles. The look he was giving her now was in another league. Her eyes widened when he advanced on her, catching her round the waist so that the cups in her hands joggled.

"Watch out, you'll spill the tea." She showed her toothy regiment as he pushed his face close to hers.

"How about a quick little screw before din-dins?" he suggested.

She pulled away from him, laughing. "I must look after my

aunt." She tried to look disapproving.

"After, then," he pressed.

"And look after Giles. Let go, Terry."

"I'll wait." He let go. "I'll show you a thing you'll enjoy."

"Cheeky." She could not help laughing. Then, "That's enough," slightly nervous. She tried to snub him.

"It will be," he leered, looking lascivious.

"Will somebody bring me my treasures?" Amy's voice came in quavery descant from upstairs.

"I'd forgotten her. What treasures she got? Nothing like yours, I bet." He put his hands over her breasts.

"Hey, hands off."

"Treasures," came Amy's voice. "My treasures," on a higher note.

"Coming," shouted Hannah, backing away from Terry. "Terry can bring them up." She thrust a tray into Terry's hands. "Stand there." She opened the cupboard and started arranging its contents on the tray.

"They real?" Terry looked in wonder.

"She thinks they are."

"Baccarat, Clichy, St Louis, my, my!" He stared in surprise.

"Don't drop them. Take them up to her. Give you something to do with your hands."

"Worth a fortune these, they're the real McCoy."

"What?"

"Your boobs, luvvy." He was irrepressible.

"I'm going to ring George and tell him what's happened."

"Who's he?" Terry's eyes, reflecting the multicolours of the paperweights, were jealous.

"George Scoop, he's a dentist, a dontologist," she corrected herself.

"Scoops the tartar off your gnashers? Scoops you into bed, does he?" Terry, his face close to Hannah, mocked. "What a name for a dentist!" He leant across the tray which he held between them to kiss Hannah, his tongue flicking across her teeth.

"Keep off." Hannah pushed. The tray slanted and the paperweights began to slide. "Watch it!" she cried. "They'll smash."

Terry righted the tray. "I'll take 'em to her, you telephone your fella."

Hannah watched him leave. He had a beautiful back. As she dialled George's number she compared it with George's whitish lardy version.

"Can I speak to Mr Scoop?" she asked the receptionist called Jean.

"Do you want an appointment?" Jean recognised Hannah's voice.

"It's Mrs Somerton. I want to talk to him."

"He's busy, Mrs Somerton, can I take a message?" Jean giggled.

"Just see if he's free."

"Well, Mrs Somerton—" Jean's impertinent voice set Hannah's teeth on edge.

"Just try, girl." She used asperity. "It's important."

"Just a minute, Mrs Somerton." Hannah listened, heard the receptionist say, "Tell Mr Scoop, Evie, Hannah Somerton wants to speak to him, says it's important – to her."

"Hallo?" George came on the line, suspicious. "Who is it?"

"George, my aunt's flooded, oh, George, water all over the ground floor."

"Have you rung the Council?"

"Yes, but I—"

"Did they come?"

"Yes, but it—"

"They'll take care of things. Look, I'm busy, Hannah."

"I thought you'd help, I thought you'd like to know."

"But you've got help, love, what could I do?"

"I thought," Hannah cried, "that you—"

"I'm a dentist, Hannah, not a labourer. Can't the neighbours help? Your street's full of idlers."

"Only because they can't find work."

"But I can. Hannah, I have a difficult extraction to do. I can't waste time rabbiting to you."

"I'm not rabbiting," Hannah shouted.

"Yes, you are. I'm busy. I don't like being interrupted when I'm in my surgery. I'll ring you some time."

"Some time!" Hannah yelled.

"Look, love, I'm sorry, it's a compacted wisdom tooth, it's—" but Hannah had replaced the receiver.

"Not rushing to your aid, Scoop?" Terry was back in the room. "Your auntie says she'd like a sandwich. Hey, you're crying." He put his arms round her. Hannah laid her head against his shoulder. He smelt of warm flesh and fresh perspiration. Suddenly she hated George's deodorants, his aseptic body. Terry tipped her head back and licked her tears away.

EIGHTEEN

Jim Huxtable left his car in the pub car park and went into the bar, ordered a pint of bitter and stood drinking it, glad to stretch his legs after the long drive. "Got any sandwiches?" he asked the landlord.

"Brown bread with crab, brown bread with beef, brown bread with turkey."

As he ate he listened to the talk of the storm, the street up the hill flooded. He pricked his ears. So, Bernard's friend of the paperweights was in trouble. As he finished his sandwich he watched a black youth and a white boy arguing with the barman.

"Ya, ya, he's under age. Beer's not for him, it's for the helpers," the youth was expostulating to the barman. "Council blokes who helped at Miss Tremayne's. His ma wants to give them a beer."

"So long as you know under eighteens can't be served."

The youth burst out laughing. He nodded towards Jim. "He's a dealer, not a copper. Come on, Giles." He loaded Giles with beer cans. "See you."

"Have to be careful," said the barman to no one in particular.

Jim walked up the street. The wind was drying the surface of the road. A magpie from a nearby park hopped beside the gutter, searching for titbits, flew off sideways. Jim stopped outside Hebe's house, hesitated, rang the bell. If she came to the door he would get the pang of disappointment he had grown to expect. He pressed his thumb on the bell, saw a curtain move. Was she nervous? What was she afraid of? He turned his head. The curtain moved again. A tortoiseshell cat peered out, fixing him with a green stare. Jim gave up.

Across the street the door of the owner of the paperweights was propped open. Jim knocked. A weak voice from upstairs called. "Who is it?"

"Jim Huxtable. I came to see you a while ago. Friend of Bernard's."

"Come up."

She was in bed, the paperweights on a table beside her. She looked frail.

"I see you've had a flood."

"The boys and Hannah mopped up. I'm waiting for something to eat. Sit down."

Jim sat by the bed. "Still not for sale." He eyed the paperweights.

"Not for sale." She smiled, observing him.

"Know me the next time," he said. "Are you ill?" It seemed strange that with her ground floor in a mess she should lie so calmly in bed.

"Just a bit. Better now. The chocolate boy climbed in and saved me. A little bit of heart trouble, that's all."

"Is the doctor coming?"

"Don't want him, my niece—"

"The dark girl?"

"No, Hannah, the fair girl. Do you know Hebe, then?" Amy's voice was suddenly sharp.

"No, I don't. I just wondered whether she had any antiques to sell. I called at all the other houses. I thought I'd—"

"Hebe has no antiques. She wouldn't sell antiques, not now." Amy was weakly aggressive.

"Did she once?"

"Sandwich coming up, Auntie." Feet on the stairs, Giles hurrying into the room. "Mum says would you like anything else." Giles caught sight of Jim. "Hullo, saw you in the pub." He put the plate of sandwiches beside Amy. "She'll be over soon. This enough?"

"So she's called Hebe," Jim reminded Amy, ignoring Giles.

Amy answered Giles. "Yes, love, that's plenty, tell her, and thank her."

Giles stood poised to leave. "You okay, then?" He watched Jim with suspicion.

"Yes, love." Amy reassured him.

"Some of us are going to the beach for driftwood, it's low tide."

"Have fun."

"Bye, then." Giles sprang away, his trainers going thud thud thud on the stairs.

"So Hebe was selling things at one time." Jim tried to place her. Camden Passage? Some antique shop in the provinces? Portobello Road?

Amy munched her sandwich. "She sold some things to an old scoundrel, that's all." Why was she telling him this, she wondered, champing on her sandwich. Because I like the looks of him, that's why. "Give him his due, he gave her a good price."

"Bernard?" Jim hazarded. "D'you know him?"

"Hebe's a cook." Amy ignored Jim's question. "Cordon Bleu. Hannah, who made this sandwich, isn't Cordon Bleu but she's a good cook too. I saw you talking to her."

"Yes, very pretty. Green eyes."

"That's right, Hannah Somerton. Her name was Krull but she changed it. Changed her teeth, too." Amy snorted.

"Beautiful teeth, I remember." Jim was polite. How did one get her back to the dark girl?

"They were," Amy leant forward staring at Jim, "snaggle every which way."

"Oh."

"Didn't prevent her catching Krull. He's rich. She wants someone else now, though."

"I'm not rich." Jim drew back from the old woman blowing crumbs.

"You're safe, then. Take this tray down when you go, there's a dear. I'm now going to have a nap." She looked old, ill, wanted him to leave.

Jim took the tray. "Put it in the back kitchen. Nice of you to call. Goodbye." She drew the sheet up, pursing her lips, the movement matching the folds of the sheet, dismissing him, slipping away into old age.

Jim took the tray down. He could report the safety of the paperweights and, if Bernard was interested, come again. In the street he wondered whether to renew acquaintance with Hannah, glanced at her door, decided against and went back to his car. The old woman had choked him off. Why?

"Now then." Terry drew the curtains of Hannah's bedroom. Let's get down to business." He cleared his throat, pushing Hannah gently back on to the bed. "D'you like it under the duvet or on top of the duvet?" His voice was husky. He cleared his throat again. "Suppose you take off your panties and I'll take off mine."

"Panties!" Hannah gasped. "Do you wear—"

"Nice, ain't they, and this," he was on top of her, "is nice too."

"I didn't know men wore them." She was interested.

"Real silk. I'll buy you a pair. Now pay attention."

She was half amused, feeling the silk. "Are they satin?" This was unusual, exciting.

"I am."

"You are." She touched him. There was something about a very young man. Now George, she forgot what she had been about to think of George. "I don't usually—" she began.

"Shush. Come on, get cracking, it takes two."

Presently Hannah, watching Terry asleep, breathing silently through his nose, remembered George who had been known to snore. George had money. She shook Terry gently.

"What do you do?" she asked.

"I'm self-employed."

"Doing what?" But Terry wanted sleep. She remembered she must scrub Amy's filthy floor. She lay for a few more minutes considering George. Would he or would he not come and help her? Like hell he would. He would say that his hands were precious. Rubbish, she thought resentfully, he could wear gloves. The expression "rabbiting" rankled. She turned to reach for Terry's hand, smooth, firm, nice nails. George, under stress, bit his.

"Terry?"

"Yes?" Terry woke, glinting a dark eye at her. "Hullo, goosegogs."

"Say 'regatta'."

"Regattah." He was smiling. "Received pronunciation suit you? I regattah, you regattah, she begat her. You on the pill?" A flick of anxiety.

"Yes." She blushed at the admission. George had insisted.

"Ah— Ah—" He stroked her face gently.

"I have to scrub auntie's floor."

"I'll help you." He sprang up. "Where's me knicks, then?"

"On the floor."

She watched him put them on. They really suited him. Much nicer than George's baggy boxers.

NINETEEN

Walking Louisa's dogs along the river after dinner, Hebe felt pleased with life. She was enjoying her work for Louisa, revelling in the countryside so different from the dark brick street in which she lived. If Silas were with her it would be perfect, she thought, but if he were it would not be possible to arrange the addition of Rory to her troupe. She considered Rory. He was endearing but against this he was Louisa's nephew, a potentially embarrassing connection. She liked to keep her cooking and tarting separate. It might be difficult, with Rory living so close to Louisa, to manage this. But why not, she encouraged herself. My old home is not far away and they, my grandparents with their new dog, don't know I am here. Amy would approve of Rory. Hebe smiled to herself. Rory was unmarried, belonged to the strata of society Amy envisaged as Hebe's. Amy, a romantic, would see Rory as the Mr Right she secretly hoped for her. Thinking of Amy, she felt a surge of love and gratitude. It was ungrateful to hate the hideous street. Amy had provided a loving home in it. In the street she had found refuge when filled with apprehension, waiting for Silas, experienced exuberant joy when he was born, reshaped her life, destroying the person she had been brought up to be, plotted her survival, planned her cooking career, found friendship with Bernard and through him discovered Hippolyte and the formula for survival she had carefully planned. Strolling by the river, pausing to throw sticks for the dogs, hearing a water vole plop, watching it swim close to the bank then vanish, seeing the swirl and rise of secret trout in the bottle-green water, Hebe counted herself fortunate, congratulated herself on the profitable career which with balanced planning was so enjoyable a way of keeping herself amused while educating Silas. She dismissed a tiny cloud of whingeing doubt which occasionally assailed her as to whether she had truly chosen the right education for her child.

Hebe peered at her reflection and that of Rufus in the darkly waving water. Hippolyte, founder member of the Syndicate, had urged her to put a high price on herself, had taught her about bed. It was after learning "The Soufflé System" that she had enlarged her horizon when occasion arose and became a tart as well as a cook. Mungo was the most profitable of her lovers, Hippolyte both friend and lover, constant. Latterly there had been Terry, a delightful novelty, and now Rory. She stroked Rufus' wet head. "Everything's fine," she said to the dog, whose reflection in the water wagged its tail. "I like my work. I am giving Silas the chance to be whatever he likes. A few more pleasurable working years, Rufus, old dog, and I can retire." She leant forward to watch a trout sliding under the weed, its movement so beautiful she held her breath. "It's a wonderful evening," she said to the dogs. "Run, run, you must get dry, run." Hebe ran with the dogs along the river, fleet and happy, for she would soon be home with Silas for the rest of the holidays.

The sun had set. From the French windows of Louisa's drawing-room yellow light streamed into the garden, alive with moths, the sound of the news on the television, jasmine and tobacco plants scenting the air.

"What a perfect evening," said Hebe, coming into the drawing-room from the garden, carrying flowers, accompanied by the dogs.

Louisa, sitting on her sofa opposite the fire, where a log glowed even though it was August, looked up, smiling.

"We are just listening to the news," she said.

In armchairs on either side of the fire sat Mungo on Louisa's left and Rory on Louisa's right. Both looked at Hebe expectantly.

The news announcer was saying, "—to be unveiled by Her Majesty – happily the rain – informality mixed with pomp – the umbrellas have come down – generations represented here today – now the Queen – one might almost say – pulse of history – roll of Gotha – inspiration – pride – the Queen's walkabout – adversity – hope – affection – great man – Prince and Princess of Wales – great—"

"Great philanderer, had a lot of affairs, they say. I don't call that much of a likeness." On the screen Her Majesty had pulled the string and the statesman was revealed in bronze. Louisa went on talking. "You've met Rory, of course, and I believe you know Mungo." She was enjoying the situation.

"Yes, of course. How do you do. Hi!" said Hebe, who never said "Hi". "Is there anything you'd like?" she asked Louisa. "I am on my way to bed."

"No, thank you, my dear."

Mungo and Rory had risen to their feet.

"I thought I'd take Rufus to sleep in my room tonight," said Hebe, looking her employer in the eye. "He was very noisy last night."

Rory gasped.

"So he was. A good idea. Goodnight, my dear." Louisa exaggerated cheerfulness.

"Goodnight, then. Come along, dogs." Hebe left the room, followed by the dogs.

"Switch off the television, Mungo. Would you draw the curtains, Rory, as you are on your feet?" Louisa turned to Mungo. "Now tell me how dear Lucy is. Your mother, Mungo. Do pay attention."

Mungo stopped staring at the door which had closed behind Hebe. "My mother's all right," he muttered.

"And Alison, how is dear Alison, hasn't she gone to America or something?"

"Or something," said Mungo heavily. "She eloped to form a troika."

"Goodness!" exclaimed Louisa. "But you will get her back?" she teased.

"Unfortunately *yes*," cried Mungo. "My mother—" He stared at the door. Why the hell had Hebe gone off like that, taking a pack of dogs with her as though she needed protection? He knew the dog Rufus, it had once bitten him. Did she imagine he would rush up and rape her in front of this crowd of people? Of course he wanted to rape her, wasn't that what he'd come for? What the hell was that fool Rory doing here, anyway? Why was Louisa acting so funny?

"Your mother, you were saying?" Louisa pried.

"She's said something, implied something. Oh, I don't know but Alison is coming back." In his fury and pain Mungo was almost shouting. "Coming back on the first flight she can get."

"What did your mother say to her?"

"I don't know," Mungo moaned weakly.

"I expect she told her the man had AIDS. Alison wouldn't like that."

"Christ! Do you think he has?" Mungo was shocked.

"I should be surprised if he has, but I cannot see your mother managing without Alison. She depends on her." Louisa grinned. She did not add, "And so do you."

Rory, who had arrived at the house simultaneously with Mungo, and was a-bubble with suppressed rage at the advent of his cousin, let out a loud guffaw. He had never liked Mungo, who was ten years older, had the advantage of a richer background than his own and had been held up to him as an example by his father. "Your cousin Mungo fits into the family business, follows in his father's footsteps. Why cannot you join the Army? You would be made welcome in the old regiment." Rory's hesitation over joining the Army had been welded into determination by Mungo's willingness to join his father's firm. If he had not been in such a rage with Mungo he would have felt grateful for this negative influence. As it was, watching Mungo's behaviour since arriving in Louisa's house, the way his eyes wandered in obvious search, a feeble excuse to fetch water from the kitchen, his restless inattention to Louisa's small talk, he had guessed that Mungo was a member of Hebe's Syndicate. When Hebe came in through the French windows, surrounded by dogs, carrying flowers, looking in her light cotton dress like some latterday Diana, Rory's heart had leapt, and so, quite obviously, had Mungo's. Hebe had barely glanced at either of them but with a barefaced lie about feeling tired had swept out of sight to lock herself no doubt into the bedroom he considered his, where so lately he had lain in her arms and she brown, soft, warm had— Rory closed his eyes in an effort to blot out the intruding vision of Hebe in Mungo's arms. Oh, God, Oh, God! Rory cried to his maker, I cannot bear it. His fury switched from Mungo to Louisa. She was tormenting Mungo about Alison, his mother and his schoolboy sons Ian and Alistair. Rory overheard odd words which did not make much sense but, forcing himself to pay attention, became alert.

"Not really, Mungo, none of the beds are made up."

Mungo, it appeared, was inviting himself to stay. "I can't ask Hebe to do housework. She comes here to cook, nothing else. She is tired, as you no doubt saw." Looking the picture of bounce and energy, thought Rory. "I suggest" – Louisa was swinging into her stride – "that you ask Rory to put you up for the night. You will gladly do that, Rory, won't you?"

"What?" Could one really choke with emotion, Rory wondered.

"You will have your cousin Mungo for the night. He has to leave early so that he can be home when Alison telephones the time of her arrival from California. The west coast of America," Louisa added, as though Rory were some idiot child, who knew no geography.

"I don't think—" began Rory.

"A good opportunity to see something of each other. You are, after all, cousins, even though perhaps you may not have very much in common."

"I – er—"

"Perhaps you have more in common than you think." Was she being purposely malicious? "You are of the same generation. I am sure you will find mutual interests."

"I had hoped—" began Mungo querulously.

Louisa stood up. No need for Mungo to voice his hopes. "It was lovely of you to visit me on your way, and you, too, Rory. Come and fish whenever you like. Now you must forgive me, I am feeling my age – rather overdoing it in my garden while Hebe is here. Such a cook, such food! I am sorry I cannot ask you – but of course Alison is a wonderful cook, too, and such a good manager. Next time you come" – Louisa was moving towards the door so that Mungo and Rory had perforce to follow – "next time, ring me up and give me notice. It will be so nice." It was possible, thought Rory admiringly, to gather that it was not nice now.

"I always enjoy seeing the young." Louisa had the drawing-room door open, was leading them across the hall. "You must bring your boys to see me, Mungo. So lovely for Lucy to have grandsons." Was that malice in her voice? She had hold of Mungo's arm. Does she think he is going to sprint upstairs after Hebe? Rory wondered. "Did you bring anything with you?" Louisa asked. "No?"

"No," said Mungo, who had his suitcase in his car. I used to love Aunt Louisa, he thought bitterly. The old viper.

"Then goodnight. God bless." Louisa put up her face to be kissed. "And goodnight, Rory. Lovely to see you, lovely."

Mungo and Rory walked to their cars.

"I'll put you up for the night," said Rory, with unexpected pity for his cousin.

"Oh, go to hell." Mungo got into his Jaguar and slammed the door.

Rory got into his Volvo and shut the door quietly before switching on the engine.

Louisa watched the cars drive to the main road. "What a pantomime!" She burst out laughing.

Leaning from her open window with the dog Rufus beside her, Hebe grinned. Louisa stood on the steps until the sound of the cars died away then went in, closing the front door. Hebe saw the light in the hall turned off. She listened to the soft sounds of the August night, a roosting bird in the creeper resettling itself, distant traffic, the cow with a cough in the meadow. "Come, Rufus." She got into bed, followed by the dog. "Your mistress is a lovely lady." She put an arm round Rufus, who groaned with pleasure. "I am not going to worry about it tonight," she said to the dog and lay hoping for sleep, without dreams or voices chanting dirty fingernails – Communists – earrings – abortion – bare feet. She switched her mind to other moments when things had not gone exactly right: the embarrassing episode in the Clarence at Exeter; Rory walking in when she was trying on the hat; Hippolyte, surprised by the sound of his wife's return from shopping, leaping from the bed to pull on his trousers, exclaiming, *"Il faut sauver les convenances,"* before glissading out of the window. "You don't worry about *'les convenances',"* Hebe said to the dog lying beside her. Rufus braced his feet against the wall and heaved his back against Hebe. "You take up more room than any lover," she said.

Refusing to review the tangle her carefully ordered existence was faced with, she slept surprisingly well.

TWENTY

"Don't be such an oaf, Michael, wash them out, there's a tap by the back door – yes there *is*, use your eyes, you nitwit – I will give you some Jeyes, that will get rid of the smell – yes, it *will*. The sooner you do it the better – don't be so *wet*. How dare you talk to me like that?" The sound of a slap, a cry of indignant pain from Michael. "I have never known anyone make so much fuss, everybody's seasick some time—"

"Not into my boots." A whimper.

"Shut up about your fucking boots, stop beefing." Another blow sounded.

"That hurt!" Michael yelped.

"It was meant to." Jennifer Reeves' voice spitting venom. "He is your visitor, you insisted on inviting him." There was the sound of another blow and Jennifer saying something Silas couldn't catch.

Changing his wet clothes, Silas peered out of the window as Michael, holding the boots into which he had been sick, approached the tap under the window, dribbled Jeyes fluid into each boot and turned on the water. Silas saw that Michael's cheek flamed red and that he was crying. Pulling on dry socks he felt pity for Michael, even though he had been foul and unsympathetic on the boat. Ian and Alistair had laughed high shrieking laughs until, looking at Julian to see whether he too was amused, they had abruptly sobered, realising something more than Silas' seasickness was afoot. Julian was angry at his own temerity. The weather, far rougher than he had bargained for when they set out from St Mary's, punished the boat. He would need all his expertise on the run home without being bothered with a seasick child. "Get below," he had shouted at Silas, "out of the way."

Silas had crept unsteadily below, crawling into a corner of the cabin. It had seemed for ever before the bumping, crashing, heaving and jolting had stopped. Listening to Julian shouting orders at Michael, Alistair and Ian, he was glad, if this was what fathers were like, that he had none, and now Mrs Reeves (less than ever could he think of her as Jennifer) was steamed up.

Silas reached for a dry shirt and put it on. Standing in socks and shirt, he looked down at Michael. The boots were full of blue-white water. Michael stirred with a stick and emptied them down the drain. Silas craned out to see if there were any identifiable bits of pasty, then began to search for dry pants and jeans and his one dry jersey.

"Bring your wet clothes down with you when you have changed, Silas. I will wash them," Jennifer called.

Silas called back, "Thank you very much," and went back to the window, one arm in the sleeve of his jersey, pulling the rest over his head. "Are the boots spoilt for good?" He leant out of the window.

Michael looked up. "Only unusually wet." He was grudging.

"I will stuff them with newspaper," suggested Silas. "That's what my mother does."

"Good idea."

"I am awfully sorry."

"Forget it." Michael's cheek was fading.

"Your mother's—"

"Got a filthy temper," muttered Michael. "They both have."

"Hot tea," shouted Jennifer up the stairs, falsely cheerful. "Hot tea, Silas." Then, changing tone, "For heaven's sake go and change, Michael, don't hang about, you'll be catching cold. Tell Alistair and Ian to change too. You are too old to need a nanny."

"Nanny never hit me." Michael came up the stairs at a run, looking as though he had dodged another blow. "Take your wet clothes down to her," he snapped at Silas. "Give her something to do. She can put them in the machine."

"Thanks." Silas collected his clothes. Hebe's white Guernsey smelled of vomit. "I didn't mean—"

"Nobody means to be sick." Michael was pulling his jersey over his head. "Does your mother create?"

"No." Hebe seemed very distant from the Scilly Isles. "No, she doesn't." He tried to imagine Hebe shouting like Mrs Reeves. The idea was ludicrous.

"Ours does." Ian and Alistair, who had joined them, were also pulling jerseys over tousled heads. "Our mother makes fury, our father makes sound."

"They all do." Alistair was philosophical.

"Today was all my father's fault," Michael said, searching for dry clothes. "He knew sailing round the Bishop's Rock would frighten him, he was showing off."

"Oh." Silas stood in the doorway holding his wet clothes.

"Tea," Jennifer Reeves called up the stairs. Silas ran down to the kitchen. Jennifer took his bundle from him. "Ugh!" She held it at arm's length as she crossed the room to the outer kitchen. Silas heard her open the washing machine and say "Ugh!" again.

Julian, already changed, sat at the kitchen table. "Tea?" he offered Silas.

"Thank you." Silas watched Julian pour tea into a large cup. He had a heavy jowly face; he was scowling.

"Milk? Sugar?"

"Yes, please."

Julian poured in milk and added lumps of sugar. Taking a flask out of his pocket he added a dollop of whisky. "That will settle your stomach." He winked at Silas. "Drink it up and you will feel better."

Silas drank, thinking the mixture disgusting. He hated being winked at and wondered morosely whether he would throw up again. Julian clearly hoped he would. Instead he felt a revivifying glow. The cup empty, he held it out and asked for more.

"Oliver Twisting?" Julian stopped scowling. Jennifer came back into the room, shutting out the sound of the washing machine as she closed the door. She said, "Really, Julian," in mock reproach, then sat at the table to drink tea and eat buns. Julian switched on the radio, muttering, "I want to hear the weather forecast."

"You should have listened last night," said Jennifer sarcastically. Her husband raised his eyebrows in mock resignation. Somebody was interviewing a politician.

"Mumble, mumble."

"That's a very good question," said the politician.

"Fuck. Bloody watch has stopped. Missed it." Julian switched off the radio, wound his watch, stood up. His stomach sagged over his trousers. "What time's supper?"

"Same time as usual?" Jennifer did not look up.

"Same old stew?" asked Julian nastily.

"Mrs Thing doesn't have a large repertoire," said Jennifer snappily.

"Time for a drink. I'll ask them whether they heard the forecast at the pub. You coming?"

"Get me some cigs, I am running out. No, I'm not coming. If

you'd listened to the forecast last night instead of trying to pull that girl in the pub, you wouldn't have—"

"Oh, Christ!" shouted Julian.

"Here we go," muttered Michael *sotto voce*.

"She was hardly likely to look at you, she's on her honeymoon." Jennifer's voice rose.

"You stupid cow, shut up." Julian left the cottage, banging the door. Jennifer began clearing the table. "Put on mackintoshes if you are going out," she said. It was an order.

"I will help you hang the clothes on the line." Silas had noted the cessation of sound from the washing machine.

"Thank you, Silas," said Jennifer.

Michael, Ian and Alistair put on boots and oilies in the porch and went out, leaving Silas with Jennifer.

"Come on, then." She sounded martyred.

The rain had almost stopped. Silas piled the damp clothes into a basket and took them to the line. Jennifer shook each garment and pegged it up. Silas helped, observing as she stretched up that her heavy breasts wobbled and that where her jersey parted from her skirt there was a roll of white skin. He compared it with his mother's taut brown body. Jennifer's blonde bun came loose and lopsided on to her neck. Silas thought of Hebe's brown bob.

"I am going to rest before supper. Shall you go for a walk?"

"Yes." Silas took off his shoes and set off up the hill barefoot, hoping to retrace the way he had walked on his first day. Perhaps he would see the seals again, find the little beach.

He climbed until he could look across the water to Bryher. The wind had dropped, the sea was subsiding. Between the islands the water was pewter-coloured in the evening light, smoothing itself calm. He watched the sunset begin its spectacular. Yellow light seeping under storm clouds gave the impression that golden treacle had been spread over the sea between the islands. As he watched the colours changed from gold to pink. The heather at his feet was spun with spiders' webs, raindrops reflecting the reddish-purple of the heather and occasional blue of Devil's Bit. There was no sound other than the soughing of the wind, gulls and the sea pounding on the rocks. Away from the voices of his hosts Silas felt comforted. Then the raising of his spirits begun by the whisky in his tea ceased. It had been an awful day. He hated sailing. He loathed the Reeves family. Ian and Alistair were awful too, but he promised himself he would buy a postcard and post it to Hebe: "Having a wonderful time. Wish you were here."

Below him two people walked along the path talking in quiet voices. He recognised the couple who had been in the boat on his first day. Silas felt a pang of envy at their happiness, quiet voices, gentle pace, so different from the strident aggressive Reeves. He watched them move out of sight, then looked back at the sunset. He had missed the beach off which he had seen the seals, where he had swum and later seen the adder, but here was the sunset. He watched the clouds roll away and the sky blaze; tomorrow would be fine. His feet were cold. He stood up. Would he be late for supper?

Silas ran, arriving back at the cottage panting and out of breath. "I'm sorry I'm late."

"It doesn't matter, we started without you."

"Have a glass of vino." Julian poured Silas a glass of wine and pushed it towards him. Jennifer compressed her lips and handed Silas a plate of stew. Michael glanced anxiously at his mother. Ian and Alistair smirked. The stew was the same as the stew of the night before.

"This food's bloody monotonous," Julian said aggressively. He ate with a spoon, shovelling the stew into his mouth, crouched over his plate, heavy shoulders bulging in his jersey, green quilted waistcoat hanging open.

"It's a very good stew," Silas ventured.

Julian looked up and stared at Silas. Silas shyly gulped some wine and looked at his plate.

"I didn't say it was bad, I said it was monotonous," said Julian.

"Yes." Silas swallowed more wine.

"Monotonous. Comes from the Greek. Means lack of variety, sameness. Don't they teach you Greek at your establishment?"

"No." Silas felt confused.

"Not taught Greek? What sort of school is it, then?"

"We don't learn Greek," said Michael.

"We don't learn Latin, either." Ian joined the conversation.

"You know they do not take Latin," said Jennifer. "They take modern languages."

Julian ignored his wife.

"We opted for German," said Alistair.

"What's that to do with the stew? Why can't you ask Mrs Thing to give us a bit of variety?" Julian glared at Jennifer.

"I have. It doesn't make the slightest difference." Jennifer helped herself to bread. Julian looked away from his wife and glared round the table at the boys, who studied their plates. Silas decided not to ask for a second helping. He crumbled his bread and drank more wine.

"Do you get stew at home?" Julian was glaring at Silas, masticating with open mouth.

"Sometimes."

"Not as good as Mrs Thing's, I don't suppose. Mrs Thing's a stew artist. Have some more. You need a refill after today." Julian laughed abruptly.

"No thank you, sir." The "sir" slipped out. The atmosphere was so like school.

"The boy calls me 'Sir' now. Have some more stew, I say. Give the boy some more, Jennifer, give us all some more." Julian held out his plate. Jennifer spooned stew on to it. "Don't suppose you get stew like this at home. Make the most of it while you can. Mrs Thing's excellent stew. Hah!"

"Silas' mother is a cook," said Michael.

There was a pause while Silas drank wine, Julian masticated and Ian and Alistair passed their plates for second helpings, exchanging covert glances.

Jennifer Reeves, spooning stew on to the plates extended towards her, said lightly, "One of my uncles married his cook."

"Blotted the old copybook there, didn't he? Wasn't even pregnant, was she? Still, think what it must have saved in wages. Quite a good idea, when you think on it. Marry a cook, good idea, good idea." Julian ate.

"Must you use a spoon?" Jennifer exclaimed.

"Yes, I must. Knife and fork are okay, but for Mrs Thing's stew a spoon's the thing." Julian's truculence was almost tangible.

"You are drunk." Jennifer spoke through clenched teeth.

"Not very. Mrs Thing's stew will soak up the surplus alcohol. So Silas' mother is a cook, is she? Well, I never. How, ah, did that come about? I mean in these days it's pretty rare to find a cook. Endangered species. Clever of your father to find her." Julian stared at Silas. Silas drank his wine, emptying the glass, reaching out his hand towards the bottle to help himself to more.

"Let me." Julian took the bottle and poured wine into Silas' glass. Jennifer sighed. Michael, Ian and Alistair sat watchful. "So this endangered species married your father. What does your father do?"

"Julian."

"All I ask is what his father does. No need to say 'Julian' in that tone of voice."

"Silas' mother is very beautiful." Michael's voice gave its first pubertal crack.

"Beautiful, is she? Hah! A beautiful endangered species. She must have been something before she was a cook." With the doggedness of intoxication Julian worried his prey.

"My mother is a Hermaphrodite," said Silas proudly, "and you are disgusting." He flung his wine in Julian's face, stood up, threw down his napkin and left the cottage.

TWENTY-ONE

Looking at the clock on the dashboard, Mungo noted the lateness of the hour. Too late now to find a bed for the night. He had been driving at random, angry and frustrated since leaving Louisa's house. My dreams have fallen about my ears, he thought morosely. Where the hell am I? He had been travelling fast along unknown roads; the petrol gauge was dangerously low. "That's all I need," Mungo muttered, driving slowly now, on the lookout for a signpost.

Presently he came to one which said "Salisbury 5 miles". There would surely be an all-night garage. He nursed the car, glancing at the gauge which arrowed the red line. It seemed an age before he was on the outskirts of the city, passing one closed petrol station after another. Soon he was in the one-way system designed by clever councillors to entrap tourists. Close to the centre the engine sighed to a halt. Mungo drew into the kerb. He was tired, fed up and far from home. He got out of the car, locked it and started to walk. Rounding a corner he sighted a bay window in a small Georgian house, a white front door with a fanlight above it, a highly polished dolphin knocker. Light shone through the fanlight. Above the bay window the words "Rory Grant, Hatter." If only I had a brick to hurl through the bloody window. Mungo used the knocker – bang, bang, bang.

"Hang on, I'm coming. What's the—" Rory opened the door. "Oh, it's you." He recoiled.

Mungo shouldered past his cousin. "I've run out of petrol."

"Come in, then." Rory looked at Mungo anxiously. "I may have – a—"

"Have you got anything to drink? I'm done in."

"—can in the garage. Yes, of course. Coffee? Whisky? Come into the—" but Mungo was already in the kitchen and slumped at the table.

"You are up early," he said in a surly voice.

"I haven't been to bed, I was too—"

592

"Upset. Me too. I've been driving in circles."

"Here's some—" Rory produced a bottle of whisky, poured half a glass and pushed it across the table towards Mungo, then helped himself. Mungo drank, eyeing his cousin, who looked rather ahead of him in the drinking stakes.

"You drunk?" he asked.

"Not yet. Would you like some soup?"

"Oh, God," said Mungo. "Soup."

"You look hungry." Rory busied himself finding bread, butter, heating soup.

"I haven't come to stay." Mungo put down his glass with an aggressive clunk.

"Of course not." Rory pushed a bowl of soup towards his cousin, handed him a spoon. "We can hate each other better when we've eaten."

Mungo ate his soup, buttered his bread. "Got any cheese?"

"Yes, I, yes I have." Rory got up, lurched to the larder, came back with Stilton in a jar. Mungo dug with his knife with vicious jabs, disgusting Rory at the combination of soup and cheese.

"She is an absolute bloody bitch. I was going to marry her. I am going to marry her. This come from Fortnum's?"

"So am I," said Rory, pushing his soup plate from him with a jerk. "Yes, it does."

"I was first, I have first go," Mungo growled.

"You are married to Alison." Rory peered sagely at Mungo. "While you get, while – er – start again. While you get shot of horrible Alison I will marry Hebe. Me first."

"Don't call my wife horrible," Mungo roared.

"There we go," Rory let out a crow of laughter. "Horrible Alison and," he shot a glittering look at Mungo, "you have two horrible little boys."

"True." Mungo spooned soup. It was delicious, revivifying, probably also Fortnum's. Bachelors could afford such luxuries.

"Got to think of them." Rory was uplifted by whisky.

"Can't bear to. Never have children," Mungo advised Rory. "Millstones, total millstones." He stared at Rory. "What she see in you? You are such a funny shape."

"Okay in bed," Rory answered cockily, "and she, oh Mungo, she is so, so, so—" Tears began to gather.

"So marvellous," said Mungo, moved too. "So soft, so warm. Not a bit flabby. So tender, just the right weight. I could eat her."

"You talk as though she was a prime steak," cried Rory, indignant, lachrymose.

"I shall if I want to, she's my mistress." Mungo tried to whip his rage into fresh life.

"We are just members of her Syndicate."

"Her *what*?" He glared at Rory.

"Syndicate. That's what she calls it."

"Oh, holy Jesus Christ, oh, the cow, what an absolute cow!" Mungo yelled.

Rory, leaning across the table, slapped his cousin. "I have wanted to do that for years, ever since—"

"When?" Mungo stared at his young relation with interest.

"You said I looked like the White Rabbit."

"Only your expression. I don't think it's going to bleed, is it?" He fingered his nose.

"I fear not. More whisky?"

"Why not? We'd better finish the bottle or it will feel lonely." Mungo pushed his glass towards the bottle. Rory poured, squinting.

Mungo felt an improbable stirring of friendship.

"What shall we do?" Rory cried, sensing an ally.

"If you knew that girl as well as I do you would say what will Hebe do," said Mungo gloomily. "Any more soup? It's good, what is it?"

"Game. She made it. We found grouse at the fishmonger's. Aunt Louisa gave me a thermosful to bring home." Rory poured the remains of the soup into Mungo's plate.

"We should not be drinking whisky with this. Haven't you any claret?" asked Mungo aggressively.

"Oh, God." Rory got up and disappeared through a doorway. Mungo listened to his uncertain steps on stone stairs and vague mutterings in the cellar below. He reappeared carrying a bottle. "I was saving it for, saving it for—"

"Hebe." Mungo took the bottle, rummaged in a drawer and found a corkscrew, uncorked the bottle. "I would like to strangle her." He set the bottle on the table between them.

Rory looked appalled. "What has she done to deserve that?"

"Cheated."

"No, no, she is absolutely—"

"Fair," Mungo grunted. "Why don't you finish your bloody sentences?" He snatched at the bottle and sloshed the wine into his empty whisky glass.

594

"That's what Hebe says. Oh Hebe, oh hell." Rory helped himself to wine. "It hasn't had time to—"

"Breathe." Mungo was morose. They sat in gloom, sharing something akin to comradeship.

"How long?" asked Rory.

"Six years," said Mungo. "Six years. Six weeks a year for six years. Three lots of two weeks, always when it suited *her*. I've a service flat in London she comes to. I take her to the theatre, to bloody highbrow films, to exhibitions. I let her shop. *She* sends me to my office or my club when *she* gets bored, we play backgammon."

"You make her sound like a feminist virago."

"She's a pimpless tart, a soloist. I tried to install her in a flat of her own, but no, she wouldn't hear of it, too bloody independent. For six years I've been trying to find out where she lives. D'you know, if I want to get in touch with her I have to write to a fucking little shop in Earls Court which forward her letters."

"Won't they—"

"Clam up. It's a Pakistani family, they just laugh."

"Where did you – er where—"

"Meet her? In my mother's kitchen. She goes and cooks when the housekeeper is on holiday. Alison's arrangement, can you beat it?"

"Your mother, Aunt Lucy – great chum of Aunt—"

"Louisa's. Yes."

"Does your mother, does Aunt—"

"Neither of them know," Mungo was perversely proud, "where she lives."

"It can't be true."

"It bloody is true," said Mungo, adding, "I hope."

The cousins sat drinking the chilly claret, their soup plates pushed aside. Mungo dug his knife into the jar of Stilton, fishing out crumbs of cheese which he conveyed thoughtfully to his mouth. Rory, too depressed to protest, decided to put the remains of the cheese on his bird table. He did not fancy Mungo's spittle.

"What arrangement have you got?" Mungo asked in a threatening tone.

"I shall take her to Aunt Calypso's cottage in the wood when the cherries are in flower." Rory was not prepared to admit there was as yet no arrangement. "Of course she's very happy – er – happy—"

"Happy?" Knife loaded with Stilton halfway to his mouth, Mungo repeated, "Happy?"

"Happy here." Bravely Rory spoke. He watched his cousin, ready to spring out of reach should he attack.

"She's expensive." Mungo put the cheese into his mouth. "She costs."

"I can afford her—"

"Rich bachelor." Mungo was contemptuous, also envious. "I suspected you of poofery."

"Must be a drain on your resources what with Alison and the boys," said Rory nastily, "quite a—"

"I dress some of it up as expenses."

"What a good idea. I could say she—"

"What?" Mungo was instantly alert.

"Models my hats." Both men began to laugh. Rory refilled the glasses.

"Do you know who the other members of the Syndicate are?" Mungo enunciated carefully.

Rory said, "No, I can't bear—"

"Nor can I. Doesn't bear thinking of." Mungo dropped his knife on the table with a clatter. "What say we keep her in the family?"

"Share her?" Rory was startled.

"Yes. Let's go and put it to her. You half, me half, fair do's, eh?" Suddenly he felt friendly towards this young cousin with his hare's eyes. "And when the boys grow up they can join the Syndicate. Put their names down now as you do for Eton. Brilliant. That's what we'll do."

"Disgusting!" shouted Rory.

"Do you think so?" Mungo was still amiable. "I thought family Syndicate – er – like Rothschilds or something, junior partners, Marks and Sparks."

"Certainly not," said Rory, shocked.

"Okay, just you and me then."

"I am going to marry her," said Rory, enunciating carefully.

"Not that again. Listen, if there is one thing I know about Hebe it is that she won't marry us."

"Not you, perhaps."

"Nor you."

"Then why did you say—"

"What one wants and what one gets are totally different things," said Mungo philosophically.

"Ah me." Rory picked up the bottle. "Empty."

"Tell you what." Mungo stood up and began lurching round the kitchen. "Tell you what, we had better go back and have a confrontation."

"At Aunt Louisa's? What for?"

"Clear the air," said Mungo. "What's the time?"

"Five o'clock."

"Better shave first." Mungo started towards the stairs. "Have a bath." He seized the banisters. "This your bedroom?" He had reached the landing, rocking up the stairs.

"Yes – er—"

"Your bed? Where you and Hebe?"

"Yes, we—" Rory followed his cousin.

"What say we have a nap first?" Mungo caught Rory's arm and they fell together on to the bed.

"I say—" Rory felt he did not know what he wanted to say. He felt dizzy.

"Just a nap, then bath, shave, go together to fix the bloody Syndicate, fix Hebe. Lie still, can't you." Mungo kicked off his shoes.

"I don't like being in bed with you." Rory sniffed, hoping for a faint reminder of Hebe on the pillow then, remembering he had changed the sheets, felt desolate. It was horrible having his great lump of a cousin sprawling on his bed. It was also impossible to sit up, get off the bed, stand up. Rory surrendered to exhaustion, alcohol and Mungo's bullying.

As Mungo began to snore Rory reviewed his dreams. He had seen himself wandering with Hebe through the wood, the cherries in flower, at their feet bluebells and late primroses, early pink campion, birds singing their spring chorus, the sun would slant through tender leaves of oak, beech, ash, in the depth of the wood the cuckoo – Oh God, the cuckoo! He turned away from Mungo, away from the light now streaming in from the world outside. How could he defeat Mungo, what arguments could be used? Alison, Ian, Alistair, seemed to carry no weight. Would the sentence so often used by his parents to thwart him – "What would the family say?" – be of the slightest use?

TWENTY-TWO

On the way from the heliport Silas rehearsed what he would say to his mother. He carried Hebe's Guernsey sweater. He pulled up the hood of his parka, shielding his face from cars passing along the road who might recognise him, stop, offer him a lift, ask with kindly curiosity whether he had a good time sailing. On the beach the high-tide mark was a line of weed wrenched from the seabed by the storm. Along this children ran shouting to each other as they gathered driftwood into a pyre, building a bonfire which would burn with blue flames from the lumps of coagulated oil. To the debris they would add refuse – plastic containers which would explode in the heat, adding a tinge of risk to their pleasure. People would complain about the smoke which would drift inland to sully their nylon curtains. Silas watched. Many times he had collected driftwood, taking armfuls home to burn in the sitting-room fire. He felt a sharp desire to join the girls and boys. Then he saw Giles was with them. He did not at all want to see Giles.

His thoughts reverting to Hebe, Silas recited to himself: "It was marvellous. They have asked me to come again. I am home early because Mrs Reeves' father is ill. They are all going back. They sent you all sorts of messages – the food was very good – my clothes were just right – I'm afraid I spilled something on your Guernsey. We sailed round Bishop's Rock lighthouse – no, not dangerous at all, it was thrilling – I liked the other boys – a terrific family – it was brilliant." A load of cock, he told himself. Cock was an expression fancied by Alistair. She will know it's cock when she smells the sick on her jersey. What am I to say? he asked himself for the hundredth time. Perhaps she will take it for granted the visit was okay, just as she believes what I tell her about school. About the only thing I've got from the Scillies is to use the word "cock" and the seals and the adder and the colour of the sea. Should he "lose" Hebe's jersey, drop it over the sea wall? Then she would not smell the vomit. No good. He remembered that she had paid a lot for the jersey and justified herself by saying, "You will be able to wear it, it will come in useful when you've grown a bit." God, how he hated the thing. And what was he to say about his duffel bag, how to explain its loss? Silas urged himself on. She would be so pleased to see him she would forget to ask questions. She never questioned him much, that was one of the marvellous things about her. Silas broke into a run.

Swinging round the corner, starting the stiff climb up the dark brick street, he forced his pace, his spirits rising. Soon he would be with Hebe. She would look as she looked on the station platform when he arrived back from school, eyes large, wearing a rather mad expression. She would hug him, he would put his arms round her, lay his head against her chest, they would laugh with relief at being together. It would be all right, Silas told himself, nearly there. He ran, arriving on the doorstep in a rush of joy.

The door was locked.

Silas was stunned. Peering from the window Trip, opening her mouth in a silent mew, showed her needle teeth and pink palate. Silas ran round to the back of the house. The back door was also locked. He rattled the handle. Trip came out through the cat-flap and wound herself purring round his legs, nudging him, turning in and out so that her whole body, including her tail, was part of the caress. Silas picked her up and held her close to his face. He remembered. He was to have been three weeks in the islands. She had said she would do a job in Wiltshire for a fortnight while he was gone. Silas sat down on the wet doorstep. He had guessed when Hebe told him about the job that she was only going because he was robbing her of a chunk of his holidays. He had blocked the knowledge. He had wanted to go to the Scillies. He had not cared. He had known perfectly well she was only filling in the time because he would not be there. Holding the cat against his face Silas wept; the addition of guilt to the shame and mortification he was suffering was too much. His eyes streamed, his nose trickled, he disgusted the cat, who jumped away, going back into the house through the cat-flap. Silas put his head between his knees and sobbed. He decided to throw himself over the cliff and have done with it.

"Can I be of any help?"

Silas saw feet, legs in jeans, tweed jacket over a dark sweater, above that a face he had not seen before. He struggled to his feet. He was cold and stiff from squatting on the doorstep. The man wore an old felt hat, rain dripped from its brim. "Who are you?" he asked and was ashamed of his tearful voice.

"Name is Jim Huxtable," said the stranger. "Rather wanted to see the girl who lives here."

"She's not here." Silas started to cry again. He was cold, tired, hungry, wet. He wished the man would go away. He wanted to die. Failing that, he wanted his mother.

"And you are shut out?"

"She's away."

"Who has the key?"

"Terry or Hannah or Amy but I—"

"Don't want to ask them."

"I *can't.*"

"Who feeds the cat?"

"Terry or Hannah."

"When will she be back, your mother?" What a bedraggled child.

"Not for days and days." Silas' voice rose in lamentation.

Jim took stock of the situation. If the child knew people who had the key it was their business to help. The sensible thing would be to take him to one of them, let them take over.

"Do you happen to know somebody called Bernard Quigley?" he asked vaguely, thinking Bernard might help were he here.

"Yes!" Something about the boy's eyes, the way they lit up, touched him. "My mother does and I do too but it's a separate friendship, it's nice to—" How to express, how to explain that it was nice to see old Quigley by himself without Hebe being there?

Jim thought, Really, these latchkey children, how irresponsible people are. "I am staying with Bernard Quigley," he said, watching the boy's face. "Been doing his shopping. Would you like to come and see him? Perhaps you could tell him your trouble."

"Yes, please," said Silas adding, "there's nothing to tell."

"Come on, then." Jim led the way to his car. Silas followed. Jim wondered why he was angry, why he was behaving in this mad way. This boy was no business of his. But as he drove out of the town with Silas beside him Jim thought, This will help me to meet that woman. Knowing her boy I can call later to ask whether he is all right. To see her would get rid of the niggling idea he had had since he had first seen her. Just one more who isn't, this one is obviously a bitch of the first order.

They did not speak on the drive. Jim thought small talk

unnecessary. Silas was sunk in nervous gloom. When they reached the lonely call box Jim asked Silas to open a gate into a field. "The farmer lets me leave my car here." He locked the car.

They walked across the fields in Indian file, Jim leading the way, carrying the shopping. Silas followed. If I run, thought Silas, it's only a half mile to the cliff. I could jump, there would be no need for explanations. He mulled this dramatic vision. Common sense told him the man walking ahead would run faster than he, would catch him and he would look even more idiotic, an even greater fool. He followed Jim sulkily through the wet field. Halfway to the house Feathers met them, bouncing and bounding, wagging his tail, yelping with joy.

"I have brought a friend of yours to lunch." Jim greeted Bernard who stood in his porch, watching them walk towards him through the rain. "Got himself locked out."

"Come in and get dry." Bernard expressed no surprise. He put his hand on Silas' shoulder and guided him into the sitting-room. He was moved by Silas' appearance. Someone had hurt the boy.

"We must find you dry clothes," he said. "You had better change. But have a drink first. Just a spoonful of brandy. You hate sherry, you won't like this either but it will warm your guts." Bernard poured a small measure of brandy and handed the glass to Silas. "Don't pour that on to the rug. Drink it."

Silas blushed and swallowed the brandy obediently. Bernard kept his hand on his shoulder. Silas stopped feeling he must throw himself off the cliff. Bernard waited until Silas' shoulder muscles stopped feeling like a wound spring. In the kitchen Jim was moving about unpacking the shopping, talking to Feathers, who, being a vocal sort of dog, rumbled and groaned in response. Bernard said, "Now go upstairs, first door on the left, take off your wet things. Jim," he called, "find clothes for Silas to wear until his are dry."

Jim brought a towel. "These will keep you warm." He handed Silas a T-shirt and a heavy sweater. "Put them on. Socks." He handed Silas socks. "Can't do anything about trousers. Try this, wrap it round you." He took a shawl off the bed.

"Thank you." Silas stripped off his clammy clothes and pulled on the T-shirt and sweater, which reached his knees. It was warm and smelt delicious. He wrapped the shawl round his waist like a sarong, pulled on the socks.

Bernard called up the stairs. "You had better stay here until your mother comes back."

"Can I?" Silas was amazed.

"Of course. Come down and sit by the fire with Feathers when you're ready."

Jim beckoned from the kitchen. Bernard joined him.

"There's something badly wrong," Jim whispered to the old man. "What sort of people are they? I've heard about children being locked out and what it leads to." His voice rose. "What does the child's father do? He should be prosecuted—" He was blazing with righteousness.

"There is no father. Keep your voice down."

"And the mother's a prostitute I suppose," Jim sneered.

"Yes, she is."

"Then *she* should be prosecuted. It's criminal leaving a child alone. I found him shivering and crying, shut out, afraid to go near the neighbours. What sort of bitch is she?"

Bernard was wheezing in an effort to stifle his normal cackle.

"What the hell's funny?" Jim snarled.

"Silas is supposed to be staying with some rich school friend in the Scillies. His mother is consoling herself for his absence by working as a cook for my friend Louisa."

"Mrs Fox, who you sent me to? That one?"

"Yes." Bernard used his snuff-stained handkerchief. "The boy has an adoring mother who slaves to—"

"Prostitutes, you mean," said Jim nastily.

"If you like. To educate him at a lamentably expensive prep school. When not, as you put it, prostituting, she takes jobs as a cook with old ladies. I assure you whatever happened to Silas happened in the Scillies and more than likely he has brought it on himself. Since when have you been so puritanical?"

Jim was deflated. "He will tell you what happened?"

"I doubt it, knowing his mother. She makes an oyster look like an open safe. Silas takes after her."

"What shall you do?"

"Keep him here. Telephone Louisa presently."

"Here he comes." Jim listened to Silas coming down the stairs.

"It was unforgivable of me to tell you what I have just told you." Jim saw that Bernard was distressed by his indiscretion.

"I too can oyster," he said, listening to Silas approaching.

As Silas reached the bottom step Feathers, a dog with a sense of occasion, jumped up, putting his paws on his shoulders, knocking him back into a sitting position, licking his face. Silas laughed.

The old man and the younger man exchanged relieved smiles.

Eyeing Silas' feet, Bernard said, "You'll break your neck in those socks. See what you can do about them, Jim. Sit down, Silas."

Silas sat by the fire and Jim showed him how to tuck the socks back so that he would not trip. Feathers huffled and snuffled round him, noting that Jim's smell was now joined with Silas'.

"Lunch," cried Bernard. They followed him into the next room. "Sit here by me." Silas sat beside Bernard. He was furiously hungry. Jim put a bowl of soup in front of him. "Start eating," said Bernard. Silas obeyed.

"Wait a minute," Jim said to him. "It's out of a tin, let me add a drop of sherry."

"I—"

"It improves it no end." Jim poured a little sherry into Silas' soup. "Try it." Silas sipped.

"Like it?"

"Yes, thank you." Silas had never met a friend of Bernard's, imagining him forever solitary. He drank his soup, feeling safe with Feathers' chin pressed on his knee, wriggling his toes in Jim's socks.

Then they ate fish baked with fennel. "Tonight," said Bernard, "we are eating grouse which clever Jim found in Salisbury. Ever eaten grouse?" he asked Silas.

"Never."

"I would have bought more. There was only a brace left, some greedy woman had bought nearly the whole stock. She was filling a deep freeze, the fishmonger said. I shall make soup from the carcasses."

"Fancy yourself as a cook." Bernard was mocking. "Silas' mother is a paragon, you can't surprise him."

Silas looked down his nose. There was a drop in the temperature. Jim caught Bernard's eye. Bernard, using his great age as armour, asked, "Were you proposing to kill yourself when Jim found you?" Not waiting for Silas to answer, he turned to Jim. "When did you last wish to do away with yourself, Jim? I can't remember when I last had the impulse. It's something which dims with age. It must be thirty years since I seriously considered it. Come now," he was looking directly at Jim, "tell us."

Sensing the appeal (did Bernard hope to cauterise Silas' wounds?) Jim rose to the occasion.

"Quite some time ago I imagined myself in love."

"You!" mocked the old man, encouraging Jim. "In love?" he scoffed.

"In Italy," said Jim. "I was taken to a party. It was a feast day, you know the sort of thing, a procession, statues of saints carried wobbling, priests, altar boys swinging censers, people singing and chanting, smell of garlic, wine, incense, children shouting, getting over-excited, their mothers slapping them."

"Italians don't slap their children," interrupted Bernard. "But go on."

"I was watching the procession. It was at night, did I tell you? There were brass bands, tumpity-tump."

"Carry on." Bernard watched Silas' interested face.

"The dark town lit by candles, candles stuck in all the windows of the town, lined along ledges. It was Lucca. Ever been to Lucca?"

"No."

"I was watching from a balcony. The procession wound through narrow streets which make the houses seem tall when they are not really tall. By the light of all those candles they did seem tall—"

"Where was the girl?"

"What girl?"

"The one you fell in love with."

"She was down in the street with a group of hippies. There were stalls selling necklaces of hazelnuts. I saw she wanted one. I ran down and caught up with her. We walked together. I bought her necklaces and put them round her neck."

"What did she look like?"

"Very long brown hair, long dress, could hardly see her face. You know how it was at that time, one didn't see people's faces, there was so much hair. I had a beard."

"I remember you, a sad sight."

"It was the long hair and beard era." Jim was defensive. "Flower Power and so on, tremendous crops of hair on both sexes."

"Go on."

"We spent the evening together. She was lovely."

Silas was absorbed. He was with Jim in Lucca walking with the candlelit procession, he could hear the people singing, the bands. It was wonderful.

"She had brown eyes, a wonderful walk. We were happy. Then

she went wild, it was quite hard to keep up with her at times, she moved so fast."

"And then?"

"Then" – Jim spoke fiercely – "the night went sour. There was a fight of some sort. I lost her. Everyone was running to get out of trouble."

"So you didn't make love to her—"

"I had, before the confusion, the fight, the running away. She vanished. It was as though she'd never been. Can you understand? Perhaps," Jim said, "she was an illusion."

"Yes," Bernard sighed, "perhaps she was."

"When I could not find her I felt like killing myself."

"Ah," Bernard sighed. "You had not known her before that night?"

"No, I told you."

"So you have been seeking her ever since."

"Sometimes I think I see her," said Jim, "catch a glimpse."

"And it's never the girl." Bernard snapped his fingers. "I would not have believed you capable of such flights of fancy. Shall we have coffee by the fire?"

"All very well to mock." Jim got up to make the coffee. "Some of us, not you of course, are romantics."

"I have had my moments." Bernard was dignified.

Silas burst out laughing. The idea of Bernard in a romantic situation was hilarious.

Bernard looked satisfied. "I was never so stupid as to mislay them," he said, stooping to put logs on the fire. "When I was no longer in love with a girl I arranged matters so that love turned into friendship. In that way I have kept up relationships with nearly all my amours."

"And how do you manage that?"

"When you are – er – on the wane, you work it so that it is she who thinks she is cooling. She keeps her *amour propre*, you keep yours and you remain friends. It works," said Bernard smugly. "In every case except one it has worked with me and even that one – well, we were talking about you. What was your girl called?"

"I don't know. I asked the people she had been with. They said she wasn't of their party. I was not surprised, they were not her kind of people – into drugs, I'd say."

"So she had no name. What nationality?"

"We spoke French. Her Italian was poor. She said, 'Do you

speak French?' I remember that. She may have been French."

Bernard was laughing. "A girl without name or nationality. You are inventing her."

"I would not wish to kill myself for a myth," said Jim stiffly.

"You have not even described her appearance."

"I told you, she had long hair, brown eyes, brown skin. If I saw her now as she was then I might know her, but by now I might not recognise her. We met at night, by torchlight. I made love to her in darkness. It was quiet, near the church, the noise of the procession muted. There is a black Christ in the church." Jim was back in Lucca.

Silas looked at Jim's face lit by a sudden blaze from the fresh logs. "What happened?" he whispered.

"I searched for days. I was working in a bar to earn money. Nobody admitted seeing her. I described her as a girl running. They said a lot of people were running that night. It was a disgrace to have a fight on the Saint's day. It was the fault of foreign hippies. I suppose she left the town."

Jim poured coffee into cups, handed it to Bernard, offered it to Silas.

"Silas?" It was the first time Jim had called him by name. Silas accepted coffee, helped himself to milk and sugar. Bernard sneezed. "It is quite refreshing to find that people still fall in love. What happened?"

"I decided against suicide, had an affair with an American blonde, became a philanderer." Jim spoke flatly.

"But you still look for her," Silas suggested.

"Exactly." Jim looked at the boy. He is recovering, he thought, feels safer now, not safe enough for us to ask what happened, probably won't even tell his tarting mother. Perhaps he won't tell anybody until some occasion arises like today, when I have told him about my love in Lucca to distract him. "Sometimes I see a woman who reminds me of the girl. It never is her."

"That must be tantalising." Bernard was almost sympathetic.

"It keeps me young." And single, Jim thought, surprised.

"Perhaps she is still looking for you," Silas suggested, liking the idea.

"I doubt it. Last seen in full flight," said Jim. "She was a fast mover."

They sat drinking their coffee, Bernard by the fire in his wing chair, Jim opposite him, Silas, Feathers and the cat at their feet. Outside the rain poured pitilessly, soaking the peninsula from the

Atlantic rain clouds. Feathers licked his chops in a dream. Bernard put his cup into its saucer with a clink.

"I have never before told anyone about that girl." Jim caught the old man's eye.

I am supposed to believe it never happened, thought Bernard. He is as vulnerable as the boy. "It was generous of you to tell us," he said. Presently, he thought, I shall stumble across the fields to the telephone and alert Louisa about Silas. She will tell Hebe. I must wait as late as possible; I have not the strength to stump across the fields twice. We must see that Hebe does not take fright and drive recklessly on her way home.

TWENTY-THREE

From the call box by the bus stop Bernard dialled Louisa's number and listened to the ringing tone which would rouse her in Wiltshire.

Many years before, knowing that she was in London with her husband, he had visited the house, prowled round, explored the garden, posing as the man who was calling about fire insurance. He had asked the maid to accompany him round the house so that no suspicion would be aroused. Thus when he talked to Louisa he could picture her in her surroundings, enduring grief when her husband dropped dead (quite a shock) and the change to widowhood, pushed for money but enjoying her garden, her dogs and latterly the joyful treat of Hebe's cooking visits. He could visualise her in the drawing-room with the view of the garden through the French windows. When he rang up at night he saw her in bed, library books, clock, pills, spectacles on the bedside table. Sometimes he forgot that she had grown old and imagined the girl who had shared bed and breakfast in the Hôtel d'Angleterre with such zest.

"Hullo?" Louisa's voice was clear. "Bernard?"

"Yes." She always guessed right.

"Darling Bernard, I have so much to tell you that will make you laugh." She bubbled with delight.

"You have Hebe with you?" He cut her short.

"Of course I have. What's the matter?"

"Her boy. You know she has a boy?"

"She doesn't know I know. You know I am discreet."

"Louisa, I have the boy here with me."

"With you? Why? How strange."

"Hebe let him go and stay with smart schoolfriends in the Scillies."

"I know. You told me that was why she has come to me. What's happened?"

"Jim Huxtable, our go-between—"

"Yes? I liked him. I liked his looks. Nice manners, too." She would have liked to discuss Jim.

"He found the boy sitting on the doorstep, his mother's you understand, locked out, blubbing. The man doesn't know what to do, the boy won't tell him what's the trouble, so Jim brings him out to me. He is here in my house."

"But what happened? What—?"

"Child doesn't say. Just like his mother, a clam. I have not asked."

"Was it something terrible? Was he raped? One reads such awful things in the papers."

"No, no, nothing physical. He's run away, that's all I know, and needs his mother."

"Of course he does," she cried.

"Will you then, darling, tell Hebe to hurry home but to drive carefully."

"Of course I will. No need to use that tone of voice."

"Can't think why people have children, they are nothing but grief," Bernard grumbled.

"Come now, Bernard, just because we—"

"Let's stick to the point."

"Very well." Louisa was quiet.

I have hurt her, thought Bernard. She always wanted children. Supposing we had married— "Are you still there?" he asked.

"Yes. I was thinking that although it's worrying for Hebe, she will be glad of an excuse to leave me."

"Why? She enjoys going to you enormously."

Louisa told him – the tale growing with the telling – of Mungo and Rory calling at the same time. "If you had telephoned before I would have told you about Rory. She wandered into his hat shop on the way here. He is *épris*, everything going very nicely and then Mungo appears and, oh Bernard, she was splendid, such aplomb, an example to any girl in her situation, such nerve."

"That's one way of looking at it."

"I will tell her in the morning. She must get some sleep."

"If what you tell me is true she will not be sleeping, she will be worrying."

"I did my best, I turned them out."

"They will come back, Louisa, they won't stay away. One might but two together won't. Neither will trust the other not to steal a march."

"Do you think so? Is that what you would do?" She was amused.

"Go and wake her, Louisa. She must come back, the child

needs her. Make haste."

"I will, I will."

"I can't keep him indefinitely."

"How selfish you are. What about Amy Tremayne and that Hannah girl?"

"Jim says he refused to go near them. Probably afraid of being laughed at."

"Very well, I will rouse her. Bernard, darling?"

"Yes, Louisa."

"Keep in touch, tell me—"

"That I love you?" Bernard laughed. "You know I do. I love you," he said.

"Yes, that, but tell me what happens, what upset the boy."

"I will if I ever find out. Goodnight, Louisa."

"Goodnight, my love." She rang off. Bernard laid the receiver back in its cradle. Time was, he thought, we said, "Goodnight, my love," and meant it. Has time robbed me of feeling? How this call box smells. Bernard stood with the door of the box open, breathed in the wet night air, took a pinch of snuff and set off across the fields sneezing luxuriously.

As he walked he saw Louisa spring out of bed, put on the lace dressing-gown with satin lining which they had chosen together, run along the passage and up those stairs (hung, he remembered, with quite interesting prints) to knock on Hebe's door, wake her. What would she say, how would she put it? Bernard laughed grimly. She was old, the dressing-gown would be of wool, Louisa had changed. In the old days she had not liked other women; she had feared potential rivals. She was right, he conceded, when once meeting unexpectedly he had been with another woman. She had been right to be jealous. But I always loved her best, he thought, trudging through the wet grass, or almost best. She need not have made such a fuss about that girl; I only slept with her once, can't even remember her name. Now, he thought, as he caught sight of his house in the moonlight, she likes other women, she is friends with Hebe's lover, Mungo's mother – she never knew about my caper with her – and she loves Hebe. As he scrambled through the gap in his garden wall he was pleased that, while he could visualise Louisa in her house, she had never seen his. He was one up on her there. Time was, he thought, letting himself in, stroking Feathers' soft head, time was we talked of love all night, now we discuss our beloved prostitute. I hope she drives carefully. It is a long way, she will worry. Should I have sent Jim to fetch her? I may not have wanted children, he thought, pushing his cat aside with his foot so that he could put a log on the dying fire, but I love Hebe as a father might or a grandfather. I am not, thank God, a dirty old man who pinches bottoms, fumbles up skirts. I did pretty well in my prime. I have memories enough to carry me to my grave. "You still awake?" he called softly to Jim in the next room.

"Yes. The boy is asleep. Is his mother coming?"

"Yes, Louisa is telling her."

"Shall you tell the boy she is coming?"

"No. He may fret if she is delayed."

"I am going to bed. Goodnight." Jim went upstairs.

Bernard sat in his wing chair, Feathers at his feet staring into the fire, twitching his ears when the fresh log caught and sparkled. Bernard listened to the prickle of burning wood, watched the flames. He thought of Louisa. Had she been happy? Would she have been happier if he had insisted that their love was large enough to flout convention? The opposition had not been insuperable; he had used it as an excuse to save the single status he enjoyed. She had married conventionally. He knew she had loved her husband. But not as she loves me, he thought jealously. Bernard stroked the cat as she leapt on to his lap. "She still loves me best," he murmured to the uninterested animal. "Things are best as they are. We are old, I am rich, I help her." Bernard liked his role. He thought, I send her money. She does not know that the things she has parted with when really short are here, that I kept them for her, pretended I had sold them. Some day when I die she shall have them back, the rings, the ridiculous but valuable tiara. I have left them to her; a farewell surprise. Thinking of Louisa, Bernard cursed old age, its tricks of memory, words, people growing illusive and ephemeral. Who, for instance, was the girl Louisa heard he had been dining with the time he told her he had 'flu – he had spent the night with her in an hotel afterwards. She had not been up to much, he remembered that, but not her name, nor could he put a face to her. Louisa had made a scene. It had not been the first girl.

"One often had 'flu," Bernard said to Feathers, who laid his head on his master's knee. "Alas, one never gets it now."

Feathers groaned sympathetically.

"I loved her so much." Bernard stroked the dog's muzzle. "But I could not stop having 'flu. It wouldn't amuse her, even now."

TWENTY-FOUR

Not a nice thing to leave them in their party clothes, stuck there until somebody takes pity. Not nice at all. Holding the steering wheel tightly, Hebe drove west to get back to Silas. She cursed herself for working at Louisa's when she should have waited at home in case he needed her. She had been apolaustic. Absorbed by self-reproach, she missed the turning which led to the faster, less winding road to Exeter. She had driven several miles before she realised this calamity. More time would be wasted going back, better to go on, praying that the holiday traffic would not be too diabolical. She told herself, He will be with Amy or Hannah and Giles. They will look after him until I arrive. Try not to fuss, she adjured herself. She was sitting upright, the safety belt cutting into her shoulder, tense. She made an effort to relax, to drive less fast. It would not be nice to have an accident.

Nice – now there was a word which didn't apply. She drove feeling jolted and shocked by the meeting she had just experienced.

They have not changed; they are no nicer than they were. What a terrible hat she was wearing, and he all dressed up for some function. They are still my grandparents, she thought, with the mixture of love and hurt she had long suppressed. Have I not watched the obits in *The Times*, hoping they would die? She was amazed by the strength of her feelings. What a ludicrous coincidence that they should also use the short cut. If I had not I should be well on my way to Silas. This is the last thing I need. She stopped her car by a telephone box and leaned on the steering wheel, reliving the scene which had just taken place.

The old people's Rover interlocked with a Land Rover. The farmer abusive, her grandfather furious. She had asked if she could help. They had not recognised her. He had said, "We could ask this young woman to telephone a garage for us." How pompous his voice sounded; it had changed. Did he have new teeth which fitted better than the old? And the new dog. It had come wagging. She had asked its name, seen the old man's head jerk up, known that he recognised her, heard him call the dog back in the tone he used when the dog was about to roll in a smell. It was as if he thought I would contaminate it, she thought, horrified. She had said, "I will ring the AA for you." She had been polite. "I like your dog," she had said, and, "Goodbye." Why, she thought angrily, did I not say, "I will find a black layabout, drug addict with dirty nails to fix your car." She looked at the call box, turned the key in the ignition, started the engine. Let someone else find them. I am wasting time, I must get back to Silas. The telephone is probably vandalised, she excused herself, treading on the accelerator, speeding away.

They brought me up to be nice, she thought. I was not nice leaving them sitting there. I bet they trusted me to phone the AA. Someone else will come along and be nicer. An involuntary gust of laughter seized her. Louisa Fox had been nice waking her when she had just got to sleep. Really nice. Hebe smiled, remembering Louisa.

"Sorry to wake you, Hebe. There is a message that your boy has come back on his own from the Scilly Islands. He is all right. Naturally he wants you. No, of course you must go to him." She had been seized by manic anxiety.

As she scrambled out of bed to dress and pack, Louisa had given her money, far more than she was owed, waved aside protests, said something about it being perhaps a blessing in disguise that she had to cut her stay short; a hint, of course, to the Mungo-Rory duet, the disarray of the Syndicate. She had seemed amused, murmured something about having had less cooking but greater entertainment.

Yes, Louisa had been very nice. Not nice as "they" would be, but nice from the bone. She had made her eat breakfast, stood in her dressing-gown on the front steps holding Rufus, who had indicated that he would like to come too. He had got into the car and had to be dragged out. Louisa had held him by the collar and waved with her free hand, calling, "Let me know how he is. Come again. Drive carefully in the holiday traffic. Take the short cut to the main road."

"Damn the short cut. If I had not used it I would not have met them. They probably also thought themselves clever using it." Hebe talked to herself. "It was not nice meeting them. Nice, not nice. Nice people. The right sort of people." She could hear their voices.

Louisa was nice and the right sort. She does not like my grand-father. Hebe remembered the dropped hint; she had casually accepted Silas' existence, asked no nosey questions.

Should she have telephoned Amy or Hannah? Why had she not done so? It would have been so simple to telephone one of them. This is what being crazed with anxiety means, thought Hebe. All I want is to be on the road on my way back to him. I shall not stop fussing until I see him. Why did he send me that postcard, "Having a wonderful time, wish you were here." What does it mean? Try and think of something else.

What else? What would block out her need to see Silas' brown eyes, arched nose, russet hair, to hold him close, to hug him. I shall have a crash if I don't think of something else. She was near tears.

Deliberately she set herself to think of her grandparents – her childhood, her upbringing. Forcing herself she recollected the intolerable boredom of long meals, wondering what to talk about, what subject would be neutral and not cause an argument. No politics other than Tory; literature tricky, too many writers were Left Wing or not nice in their private lives or wrote about people who were not nice; gardening safe but might lead to one being asked to weed or plant out the Canterbury bells, so boringly tedious. She had not been horsey. Horses. Her sisters, before they married, had talked almost exclusively of horses, hunting, eventing, racing or point to points through those meals. Dogs, tennis, golf, bridge, all safe but wrapped in a pall of platitudes. Parties? Okay if they were nice people's parties where one met the right sort, the euphemism for a marriageable man, the benefit acquired from a nice upbringing. So I suggested the Cordon Bleu cookery school when I failed my O-levels, suggested I would meet nice girls. It never occurred to them that I saw cooking as an escape. It was good of them to send me; I should be grateful. Why did someone not tell him he had got cabbage stuck in his teeth? Hebe, driving as fast as was safe, perhaps too fast, mut-tered, And the relations! Who was related to who, through whom, by whom, and always they were potentially nice, or related to the right sort. Failing the gentry bit, titled. Hebe grin-ned, pressing her foot on the accelerator. So why the surprise when they exploded about dirty nails, beards, guitars, bare feet, blacks, earrings, Communists, long hair? Why the surprise, Hebe wondered as she drove. Were they not terrified by the Permissive Society? How naive she had been at sixteen and what a prig,

Hebe mocked herself. I thought they were fond of me. Not as fond as of my sisters, but fond enough to stand by when I became pregnant. I had thought I would be original, I would keep my virginity. Oh, the irony. Talking to herself she fretted, caught in a long line of cars, held up behind three lorries all impossible to pass, just as many cars travelling east as west, the traffic crawling to a halt. She drummed her fingers on the driving wheel chanting, "Virginity, Virginity, when, where, how did I lose it?" The traffic going east had halted also. Hebe sang, "Virginity, where did I lose you? You don't lose it like dropping a purse, for God's sake."

"Did it hurt?" a man driving a Ford Cortina towards London asked across the gap between their cars.

Hebe wound up her window. That's all I need, a pick-up. I shall get myself arrested. The traffic moved on. He called me a whore, she thought, he called me that. Perhaps he remembers, sitting by the roadside in his morning coat and top hat, perhaps he remembers what he said, perhaps she in her flowered dress remembers too. They were not nice that day. Remembering her grandparents, Hebe's tears coursed down salt as she caught them with her tongue. The traffic increased speed, it was possible to overtake the lorries. There was the respite of a dual carriageway. She hurried on; it was imperative to reach home and Silas.

As she sped down the A30 Hebe was glad she had made herself think of her grandparents. She had bottled them away too long. I should have had the guts to tell them they have a beautiful bastard great-grandson. Then later she thought I am a fool, I am educating him in the way they educated me. I too am a snob. I despise Hannah's vowels; I didn't want Silas to talk like Giles. I sent him to a school where he makes friends with the right sort of people, who invite him to stay in the Scillies and something has happened to him, something not nice. During the long drive she experienced the catharsis which left her weak but with a clear mind. She even recovered enough to think wryly of Mungo and Rory as the right sort of nice men to have in her Syndicate, and of Lucy Duff's and Louisa Fox's houses as the right sort of houses in which to work.

Tired and anxious, impatience overwhelmed her on the last stretch into Penzance, but she felt relief as she left the traffic to swing uphill into the steep and hideous dark brick street, roar up to her house, jam on the brakes and jump out. She let herself in, calling, "Silas, I am back, darling."

Trip looked up from an armchair, showing displeasure at being disturbed. No sign of Silas. The house was slightly dusty, everything exactly as she had left it, in her bedroom an indentation on the bed where Trip had slept. Silas' room was neat, empty. She opened windows, letting in the August air. He would be with Amy. She filled the cat's bowl with fresh water, bent to stroke her. Trip moved into the garden with a preoccupied air. Hebe ran across the street to Amy's house and walked in.

"Hullo, Amy." Amy was resting in her armchair.

"You are back early." Amy kissed her, reaching up to hold her.

"Is Silas not with you?" Hebe drew back.

"Silas?"

"Staying with Hannah, is he?"

"He is in the Scilly Isles, not due back. Why have you left Louisa so soon?" Amy got up from her chair. "I expect you'd like a cuppa." Then, looking closely at Hebe, "Something wrong?"

"You telephoned. I rushed back. Is he with Hannah and Giles?"

"I never telephoned."

"Then it must have been Hannah, he must be there. I will go round to her."

Amy caught Hebe's hand. "What am I supposed to have telephoned about? What was the message? What's wrong?"

"The message was that Silas had come back and wanted me. Naturally I thought it was you. He must be with Hannah." Hebe was filled with incipient panic.

"Hannah doesn't know where you were. Unless she has second sight."

"I will go and ask her." Hebe ran out of the house leaving Amy's door open, raced up the street to Hannah, anxiety treacherously transforming itself into blind fear. She let herself into Hannah's house. Empty sitting-room, kitchen and garden. She took the stairs two at a time, sounds of Bach from Hannah's bedroom. "Hannah!" Hebe burst into the room. Curtains drawn across open windows, the joyous sound of Bach, Hannah and Terry lying contentedly in bed listening to the radio.

"Is he with Giles?"

"Is who with Giles?" Hannah switched off the radio.

"Hi, Hebe." Terry, lying with his head cushioned on pillows, an arm round Hannah's shoulders, smiled up at Hebe. She scarcely noticed their happy faces, their nakedness, the clothes scattered on the floor. "You are standing on me best knickers." Hebe kicked away the knickers and in so doing caught her heel and tore the garment. "There now, you've torn 'em."

"Where is Silas?" Hebe stood over them. "You sent me a message. I've come back. He needs me."

"Sit down." Terry reached out and pulled Hebe down on to the bed. "You look as though you'd lost your marbles."

"I've got to find him. You sent a message," she pleaded with Hannah.

"No, love," said Hannah, sitting up, beginning to worry.

"Then who?" Hebe's voice rose.

Terry held her wrist. "Why not tell us what this is in aid of?"

Hebe told them of the message and her drive.

"Somebody being funny?" suggested Hannah.

"Couldn't be. I thought it was Amy but she says not. She's the only person who had my number."

"Didn't Silas have it?"

"Of course he did, but the message wasn't from him, it was about him." Hebe's voice wobbled.

"We had better get dressed." Hannah got out of bed. "Look sharp, Terry."

Hebe sat on the bed watching them.

"You don't mind, do you, Hebe?" Hannah zipped up her skirt.

"Mind what?"

"Terry and me."

"Why should I? Oh, sorry. I hadn't taken it in. I'm glad for you."

"Told you she wouldn't mind." Terry spoke across Hebe to Hannah. "She hoped you would be jealous," he said to Hebe.

Hebe smiled wanly.

"You both up there? I've made a pot of tea," Amy called up the stairs.

"Tea!" Hebe almost screamed. *"Tea!"*

"Yes, tea." Terry took her arm. "Come to Amy's while we think what to do next. Amy's not been well, her ticker." Hebe appeared not to take in what he said. Amy gestured to him to shut up.

As they reached Amy's house Giles appeared at the bottom of the street, his arms full of driftwood.

"Giles may know something," said Hebe.

They waited for Giles walking slowly up the street. Terry ran to meet him, taking some of the driftwood. The women saw Terry question Giles, Giles shake his head.

"Come and sit down, you look done in." Amy led Hebe into her house. "Sit down." She poured tea and gave it to Hebe. "Drink that."

They watched her drink.

"That better?"

Hebe shook her head. "Not much."

"Why don't you ring up Mrs Whatsit in the Scillies?" suggested Giles. "She would know why he has left, if he has."

"What a fool I am." Hebe sprang up. "I will telephone from home, it's easier." She ran out of the house.

"Hadn't we better—" Hannah stood up, ready to follow.

"No, leave her." Amy was firm. "It's a private conversation."

"Jennifer Reeves speaking." The line to the islands was clear. Invisible Jennifer Reeves sounded as though she stood next to Hebe.

"This is Hebe Rutter," said Hebe.

"I see." The voice was chill. "About time," it said mysteriously.

"I got a message about Silas that—"

"Does he want to apologise?" Sharp, chill.

"I don't understand." She was mystified.

"So he has not told you? I am not surprised. What excuse does he give? We do not usually put ourselves out to have strange boys to stay."

"Strange boys?" Hebe felt blood rushing to her face.

"Very strange, and that's putting it mildly. Poor Michael asked to have him as we were also having two very nice—"

"Nice?" Hebe felt anger and suspicion.

"Very nice boys. The right sort, not at the same school as Michael and your boy, of course, though how—"

"Right sort?" Was this woman really speaking like this?

"Of course they will all be at the same school soon. I am talking of Ian and Alistair, not your son. I don't know what school will take him – not Eton, naturally."

"I—"

"I would suggest you teach him some manners, make him write and apologise for—"

"For what?" Hebe restrained a shout.

"For his behaviour, his language, the inconvenience to say the least. His rudeness to myself and my husband—"

"What are you trying—"

"I am trying to tell you that we were quite worried until the

Harbour Master at St Mary's told us he had been seen getting off a boat from Trescoe and going up to the airport to the helicopter. We thought something unpleasant might have happened to him."

"It obviously had," said Hebe grimly.

"What did you say?" Jennifer tripped in mid-stride.

"I said it obviously had. Something very unpleasant."

"Mrs Rutter—"

"Did you send me a message?"

"Of course not. The boy is message in himself." Jennifer Reeves laughed, pleased with her witticism. "By the way, he left most of his luggage behind. Not a very good packer, either."

Hebe felt fury at the word "either", cast brutally into the murk.

"If you would like to be at the heliport on Thursday we are cutting the holiday short, you can collect it. I take it you will be there."

Hebe put the receiver back in its cradle. She was shivering.

"So who sent the message?" Terry put his arms round her.

"You were listening?"

"No need for a loud hailer, has she?" He kissed the top of her head.

"Oh, God!" Hebe leant against him. "What can have happened? Where can he be?"

"We had better go back to square one, telephone the old lady you were working for, ask her to tell you again."

Louisa did not answer when the telephone rang. She was at the bottom of the garden, feet up on her garden seat, surrounded by adoring dogs enjoying the afternoon sun, listening to the Bach concert on her transistor radio.

TWENTY-FIVE

Mungo surfaced to the sound of cathedral bells, light filtering through closed curtains, an unfamiliar room. He closed his mouth, parched from snoring. An attempt to breathe through his nose was partially successful. The scent of hair roused his curiosity and a response in his half-waking state of sensual arousal. The smell was not Alison's, which he had been used to before they slept in separate beds, nor was it Hebe's. With shock he remembered he was in Rory's house, in Rory's bed. And here lay Rory, asleep with his head on Mungo's shoulder, breathing sweetly, relaxed and peaceful. As though aware of Mungo's gaze he snuggled closer, turning trustfully towards him, nuzzling close.

Recollecting the evening and night before, listening to the bells, Mungo remembered. It must be quite late. There was action to be taken, plans to make, but what action, what plans? He remembered his mother, her appalling direct approach to what she called Alison's elopement. Sending him out of the room while she telephoned to Santa Barbara, she had said, "Leave it to me. You cramp my style if you listen. I will call you if I want you." He had gone downstairs to listen on the extension but Miss Thomson had been sitting by the telephone. His only consolation had been that while in the room with Miss Thomson she had not been able to eavesdrop either. Mungo envied his mother's lack of hypocrisy. She is right, he thought, she cannot manage without Alison and neither can I. Fourteen years of Alison's competent bossiness had unmanned him. The drive across country to sweep Hebe off her feet into Happy Ever After was poppycock. He would be fortunate if he could keep the arrangement with Hebe which had worked so well up to date.

Rory stirred, mumbling in his sleep. Mungo began a manoeuvre to extricate himself from Rory without waking him. If he could get to Louisa's without Rory he could see Hebe and arrange to spend time with her soon. But before that, thanks to his mother, he had to meet Alison, see that she was settled back at home in her role of wife, mother and daughter-in-law. He would have to spend a little time with her. Mungo tried to calculate how long. Since Alison had never defected before the question was academic. He squinted at his watch. Eleven thirty-five. He reared away from Rory whose hair was tickling his nose. Rory woke.

"Hullo." Rory smiled cheerfully. "Good morning."

There was nothing good about it. Mungo swung his legs off the bed and tottered to the bathroom. His head was throbbing, his mouth felt like a grouted roof, he felt dizzy. Rory joined him. "I'll get some tea." They urinated together. Rory flushed the lavatory. Rory looked bright-eyed, alert, healthy. He said, "You look revolting." He appeared concerned.

"I feel it," Mungo grunted.

"Go back to bed while I dress, then I will get breakfast." Rory guided Mungo back to bed. "I'll get you an aspirin." Mungo lay back with a groan. Rory brought a glass of water and aspirin. "Take two, come on, swallow." He had taken charge.

Mungo lay hoping the aspirin would work, listening in disgust to his cousin shave, shower, whistle, sing, clean his teeth, gargle. Rory had hit him the night before and now this. Mungo felt middle-aged, resentful, jealous. Rory brought strong Indian tea, sat beside the bed and persuaded him to drink two large cups. "You are dehydrated, you must—"

"I must go to Louisa's," Mungo muttered.

"We will go together," said Rory firmly.

Mungo was too weak to protest.

"There's no hurry." Rory still looked concerned. "We will have something to eat and go to – er – gether. I won't – er – I won't sneak off without—"

"Me?"

"No."

Mungo felt a vicious desire to do something unpleasant to Rory for playing so fair. Had he not had the intention of doing just that, reaching Hebe first? Drinking his tea he sneaked a look at Rory, who looked young and, oh God, spry in clean jeans and white T-shirt which flattered his hazel eyes. His freshly washed hair, though thinning in front, curled jauntily at the back. He looked what he was, young.

"Take your time," said Rory, in the voice of one talking to an invalid. "Have a bath, borrow anything you want."

"My bag is in my car," said Mungo grumpily.

"Give me your keys; I will get it for you. When you have had a bath and changed you will feel better."

"There's nothing wrong with me," Mungo shouted.

"No, no." Rory took the car keys and disappeared with the tea tray, presently returning with Mungo's bag. "It's a beautiful day. We will eat in the garden when you are ready. There is no hurry."

How dare he be so nice? Mungo was consumed with self-pity. Trying to whip up his hatred he only succeeded in breaking into an alcoholic sweat. One way and another he had overdone the booze during the last few days. I am not a real drinker, he told himself.

When Mungo came downstairs Rory had laid a table under a tree in the garden. "Brunch," he said to Mungo heartily.

They sat down to orange juice, kidneys and bacon, fresh rolls, butter, bitter marmalade and strong coffee. They ate in silence, watched by a robin which ventured on to the table, helping itself to crumbs. Mungo felt a pang of envy for his cousin's mode of life.

"You live very comfortably," he said grudgingly. Rory looked at him, nervously cleared his throat and said:

"Alone."

"But you do what you want."

"Within reason."

They had finished their meal. Mungo felt almost human. They sat watching the robin hop among the plates, flash back into the tree, return when Rory crumbled a piece of toast.

"Tell me," began Rory, "um, tell me about—"

"Hebe?"

"Yes." Rory blushed. Sure of himself with Mungo hungover, he was unsure with Mungo recovered. "Six years?" He shied away from the thought.

"Alison," began Mungo, "was looking for someone to cook for my ma when the dragon housekeeper has her hols. She found Hebe, recommended by an old girl who had worked for Aunt Louisa at one time. I met Hebe in her capacity of cook. I fell in love with her."

"Love." Could one in charity imagine Mungo in love? It seemed doubtful to Rory.

Mungo helped himself to more coffee. Rory waited.

"I found," Mungo went on, "that she was willing to sleep with me if I paid, that her conditions were like any other tart."

"She isn't a tart."

"She *is*. Conditions, money in advance. Fair enough, I said, to that, but the other conditions make her different. I don't call her as I would any other call girl—"

"I wouldn't know," said Rory primly.

"Actually I don't either," Mungo admitted. "*She* would arrange dates. *She* found the flat we go to. *She* tells me when and for how long we may be together. I haven't the foggiest idea where she lives, there's only this Pakistani shop which forwards—"

"She sounds as bossy as—" Rory hesitated.

"Alison. I know, but not the way she sets about it. It took me three years before I realised she had suggested, planted the seed if you like, of anything she wanted to do. When she wanted to go to Greece I found I wanted to take her there. My firm has connections so it's easy. Same with Venice and Rome. She never suggests Paris for some reason. I have suggested Paris but no, she won't." Mungo sighed. "I go to Paris alone or take Alison."

"Nice for Alison." Rory's voice was downbeat.

"Alison doesn't really go for French food. Now Hebe, you can't fault her on food."

"She is a cook, she—"

"I know, I know, but she *knows*, she talks about food like a restaurateur."

"Perhaps she comes from a—"

"No, no, Hebe's what my ma calls a lady. One of us, you know what a snob she is."

"Almost as bad as mine."

Rory, momentarily distracted, thought of their mothers. Mungo thought of the joys of Hebe in London, Rome, Venice, that island in Greece. He sighed. "I love the girl," he said heavily.

"So do I." Rory stated his feelings obstinately.

"We read aloud to each other," said Mungo. "We play backgammon."

This piece of information disturbed Rory dreadfully, revealing a depth of intimacy infinitely more alarming than sex.

Mungo shifted his chair, disturbing the robin. "One doesn't like to link money with love," he said, "but if one does I warn you, Rory, keeping Hebe is like having a third son at school. Six weeks a year. For that I could have another son."

"Do you want another son?"

"God forbid."

"I have no sons. I'm not bothered. Besides, you say you charge her to expenses. That's pretty sordid and morally wrong." Rory was on the attack.

"Last night you were all for it."

"Last night I had a few drinks and last night you were suggesting your sons, your well-educated sons, should join—"

"The Syndicate? Does she really call it a Syndicate?" Had Rory been pulling his leg?

"Yes," Rory admitted sadly.

"I wonder who the other members are?"

"We may know them." Rory was not pleased with this thought.

"Aren't we wasting time? Are we not going to see the girl, was not that the idea last night?"

"Last night we were both going to marry her, today you seem to be content to keep her as your mistress. I still want to marry her." Rory began clearing the breakfast table. "Help me with this," he said sharply to his cousin.

Mungo helped stack the remains of their meal on to a tray which Rory carried into the house.

"Suppose I make you an offer, buy you out?" Rory brought out the sentence in a rush. Could he borrow from the Bank perhaps, a sexual mortgage?

"You must be joking," said Mungo haughtily.

"She might be – er – she might be—"

"What?" Mungo snarled.

"Pleased," Rory stacked the plates in the dishwasher, "to get rid of you."

Mungo tried a sarcastic laugh. This was an awful thought not to be voiced.

"What about the forty-six weeks a year she is not with you?" Rory mustered courage. If only he could undermine Mungo's self-confidence.

"She cooks."

"Only occasionally for your ma and Aunt Louisa, Louisa told me. Six weeks with your ma, that leaves forty, and about three to four with Aunt Louisa, that leaves thirty-six for the rest of them."

"Who?"

"The Syndicate, you fool," Rory shouted in exasperation. "Just think, she—"

"She must be a millionaire," said Mungo in admiration.

"All you think of is money." Rory, outraged, stared at his cousin.

"All I think of," Mungo stared back at Rory, "all I think," he said quietly, "is what I may lose."

The two men looked at one another, full of unvoiced thoughts of Hebe's skin, eyes, mouth, hair, thighs, her laughter, her manner of giving, her voice, her talent for making them feel supermen.

"Come on," said Mungo.

"Right," said Rory.

They drove out of Salisbury in silence. To Mungo the unspeakable thought of his clumsy young cousin fucking Hebe was distracting. Never allowed to swear or use four-letter words by Alison, he habitually used them to himself and outside her ambience. To Rory the vision of Mungo lying on top of Hebe with his, with his, oh God, with his thing up her was an obscene vision which would not go away. As he drove he wondered vaguely whether it would be first-degree murder if he killed Mungo, if he had the guts to do so, how to set about it.

"There's a hell of a lot of traffic on this road," said Mungo, remarking on what was obvious, a heavily congested road.

"The races. Salisbury races."

"More like an air-show. Anyway, can't we get off this bloody road? You live here, you ought to know."

"No short cuts, only very—"

"Very what?" How can Hebe consider this ass? It's crazy, I must tell her it's madness, he can't churn out a single sentence.

"Only very long cuts. You know, narrow and – er – winding."

"Are they full of traffic?"

"No – nothing because you can't—"

"Can we get to Louisa that way?"

"Yes, but—"

"Then get us off this road. Can't you see, it's jammed for miles. We will never get cracking along here."

"You can't pass anything on the narrow—"

"You said there was no traffic on them. There will be nothing to pass."

"Oh, all right." Rory swung the car into a narrow lane which wound charmingly along a flattish valley. The lane ran back and forth, crossing and re-crossing a graceful chalk stream. Cows looked up in ruminative surprise, Rory slowed to let a pheasant pass. It was a lane unchanged since the era of the horse and cart.

"What shall we say to Aunt Louisa? I usually only turn up in the – er—"

"What?"

"Evening, to fish."

"No good fishing in full sunlight, any fool knows that. Old Louisa's no fool."

"She'll – er – smell—"

"She's already smelt it," snarled Mungo. "Don't be an oaf. She sided with Hebe last night, practically saw us off, treated us as though we'd come to rape the girl."

"Wasn't that what you, what you—" Rory who was driving swivelled hare's eyes to look at Mungo.

"Watch where you're going," yelled Mungo. Rory braked and stopped the car. The lane was blocked by a shiny Rover, its wings jammed into the mudguards of a Land Rover, the machines interlocked like fighting dogs.

"Accident," said Mungo, stating the obvious. He opened the door of the car and got out. Rory followed.

The Land Rover contained some bales of hay, bags of fertiliser and a pitchfork. There was no sign of a driver. By the side of the road, sitting on the grass, an ancient couple and a Labrador dog. The Labrador wore the customary expression of such dogs – just say what you want and I will try to oblige if it is within my humble capacity. The couple stood up, expunging from their faces exasperation, anger and impatience, to greet Mungo and Rory with the reserved half-smiles of country gentry. They were dressed for a function. The woman wore a longish dress of flowered silk, over it a thick silk coat of navy blue, white shoes, white gloves and a hat which made Rory flinch. If there was one thing which upset his sensibilities it was plastic cherries. She wore a double row of pearls, a diamond brooch and good rings. Her husband wore morning dress of dated cut.

"See you have had a bit of a smash," Mungo suggested, moving towards them.

On hearing Mungo's impeccable vowels the elderly couple smiled with less reserve.

"Driving too fast, always in a hurry these fellows," said the elderly man.

"I see. Anybody gone for help?"

"A – er – a young woman went for help," said the man. His hands trembled as he pulled a handkerchief out of his pocket, then smoothed his trousers which had grown uncomfortable as he sat. Mungo wondered whether the old-fashioned expression "adjusting his dress", which was what the man was doing, was still used. He noted with interest that the old fellow's trousers had fly buttons, not a zip.

"Where's the driver of this?" Rory slapped the Land Rover with a comradely hand.

"We have waited hours." The elderly lady looked at her watch. "We have been here since dawn."

"They won't want to know how long we've been here," snapped her husband, putting her in her place.

"The driver of that thing got tired of waiting," said his wife, her voice tremulous.

"She said she would tell the AA to come," said the husband. "They are usually reliable."

"But *she* never was," said his wife bitterly.

"So a friend went for help?" Rory brightened.

"She said she would tell the AA."

"Well, someone will be along soon." Mungo was impatient to get on.

"I told you nothing can pass along this lane," Rory shouted at Mungo in exasperation.

"So only locals use it. I suppose the Land Rover's local?" Realisation was dawning.

"Yes," they spoke in unison. "Yes, he is."

"I shall have to back all the way to the main road." Rory was furious. Then, remembering his manners, he said, "We will tell the AA to rescue you."

"We'd better write down the car numbers," said Mungo, making an attempt to be practical, "although your friend will have told them already." He found a pencil and walked round the car and the Land Rover, writing their numbers on the back of an envelope.

"I expect your dog wants his dinner." Rory made a feeble try at amiability.

"She drove away and left us on purpose." The woman spoke through clenched teeth. Rory was startled to see tears in her eyes. "She will not have told the AA." Then, recovering, she said, "He has his dinner at night." Her smile was socially pure. "I have it for him in the car. It is we who shall miss our luncheon. My husband was to have made a speech."

"Where are you going?" Rory made conversation.

"Ledbury. That is why we made an early start. A wedding."

"I have friends near Ledbury. They are – er – called—" Rory blurted out the name of a titled uncle and aunt. "He's – er – my godfather."

"That is near where we are going. I shall tell him you rescued us. My husband was at school with him."

"Don't worry." Rory was not liked by his uncle who, he had heard, referred to him as the poofter hatter. "We will back away now and telephone the AA for you."

Rory and Mungo got into the car and Rory, putting the car into reverse, began the drive back to the main road. "This will rick my neck."

"What d'you want to suck up to those people for?" asked Mungo. "Boasting about your bloody godfather."

"It was you who let us in for ringing the AA. I was just being normally polite. You wrote down their car numbers – pretty officious."

"Who do you suppose they were? They looked like something out of a pantomime."

"Poor old things, they were going to a wedding." Rory felt a spasm of tenderheartedness. "The dog was rather nice."

"You can't judge people by their dogs," said Mungo aggressively. "Cats, now, are another matter."

"I shan't invite you to my wedding," cried Rory spitefully, twisting his neck as he reversed the car, "to – er – to Hebe."

Mungo refrained from hitting Rory, possibly causing another car crash and further delay.

TWENTY-SIX

Eileen Rutter walked away. She was afraid Christopher would lose his temper. She tried not to listen to the sound of tearing metal as the surly owner of the Land Rover wrenched the vehicles apart with scant respect for the Rover. All he had said, arriving with a mechanic and a breakdown truck, had been, "Must get these apart before milking time." The mechanic had got on with the job.

Her shoes pinched. She was conscious of looking ridiculous in these surroundings and that Christopher looked an old buffoon. She was glad of the dog's company. "She recognized us," Eileen said to the dog. "That is the only chance we've ever been given. We missed it." Thirteen years ago Christopher had refused to look for Hebe. For thirteen years she had been taboo. "She looks lovely," Eileen said to the dog. "I wonder what her child is like." She talked to herself these days, Christopher having grown as deaf as herself. "He didn't hear the beastly thing blow its horn. He shouldn't really drive." The dog walked beside her companionably. "She's so different from the other girls," Eileen cried. "She always was." The dog glanced up. One could have asked whether the rumours one had heard were true. Seen at Wimbledon by Beata with a male companion; in a restaurant by Marcus, also with a man; walking along Knightsbridge, again by Beata; at the theatre with a man he said he knew quite well by Robert; glimpsed briefly in the West Country with a black youth too old to be her child, by Delian. Did that prove anything? One met black people, like it or not. Christopher had liked the enterprising young man who installed those devilish burglar traps. None of the sightings added credence to Christopher's conviction that Hebe lived in Brixton in the black community. "At least we know she is alive," Eileen said to the dog. "She was wearing good clothes, driving a decent car. Perhaps she is all right. Small thanks to us," said Eileen bitterly to the dog. Her hat was pressing on her forehead. "She lied, she deceived, she betrayed, she went her own way." Eileen faltered. "Was that so terrible?" she said to the dog. "Might I have not done something to help her—" She felt as she had felt before in the sad watches of the night, a hesitant doubt. She looked at the hat in her hand. "I could see she didn't think much of this," Eileen said to the dog, and with all her strength she threw the hat towards the hedge. The hat sailed in the light summer air over the low hedge then, weighted by the cherries, fell. With a joyous bark the dog bounded to retrieve it.

"What on earth are you doing?" Christopher drove up in the battered Rover. "You will teach him bad habits. Get in, get in," he said irritably, opening the car door. "That young chap keeps a hat shop in Salisbury. You had better try his wares." He was sarcastic.

Eileen got in beside her husband. "You might at least have told her the dog's name," she said loudly so that he would hear, "not called him away."

Christopher Rutter drove forward with a jerk so that the dog slid off the back seat on to the floor. "Careful, we shall have another accident."

"Shut up, woman!" yelled Christopher in his cracked old voice. "Shut up!" Eileen began to weep, tears smearing her sunken cheeks.

"If you had told her his name—"

"Shut up!" cried her husband.

Eileen stopped crying. From nowhere came an ancient memory. Who was it she had deceived Christopher with, on that one dubious delightful occasion? Some friend of that girl Louisa. What was she called now? One forgot names. He had been small but very attractive. He had made her laugh. Eileen searched her mind for his name. She realised with pleasurable surprise that she no longer felt guilty.

"She never meant to tell the AA about us." Eileen Rutter experienced a fleeting admiration for her granddaughter. "You should have let her pat the dog," she goaded her husband. "Look out, you'll have us in the ditch."

"Shut up!"

"Then if those young men have not also forgotten us the AA can get us out of that."

"Shut up!"

"You should have let her touch him, told her his name—"

"God!"

He had been a delightful little stoat. Eileen sat back, remembering the name. Bernard Quigley, that was it. She wondered whether he was still alive. She looked at her husband's profile. Good looks aren't everything. She leant back in her seat and fastened the seat belt.

TWENTY-SEVEN

In Amy's house they gathered to question Giles. Had Silas sent him a message? No. Had Silas said anything before he left to suggest that he was worried? No. Had Silas—

"Look, Mum, I'm hungry. Can I have some tea?" Giles felt oppressed by the torrent of questions. Should he protect Silas? Was there something Silas would not want told?

"I'll get the boy some tea." Amy busied herself producing a meal, trying hard not to look anxious. She felt unwell, had felt wretched since the morning of the flood. There was no time for that now. It had been nothing, she told herself she'd taken fright being alone. It had been all right when Terry appeared; the pain had eased off when she took her pill.

"He was looking forward to going. Sounded okay to me." Giles filled his mouth with bread and butter, spread jam lavishly.

Hannah stood over him, hoping to extract some crumb of information. Terry, leaning against the wall, watched her appreciatively. Some girl. Lovely rhythm. Quite different to Hebe. Couldn't compare them, really. He liked the way her eyes grew dark when she came. Poor old Hebe was looking blotched with worry.

"You were with him the day before he went away, did anything happen?" Hannah stood over her son.

"We got wet." Giles, munching, recollected the field of kale and Silas hitting him so that he fell back in the mud and got wetter. One couldn't tell her that, not in front of this crowd. "No, Mum."

"Did you have a row?"

"No." Giles shook his head. His conception of a row was plates flying as Hannah hurled them at his father. He remembered sheltering under tables and behind chairs until the storm spent itself.

"No row? You sure?"

Giles remembered Silas last seen waving across the street. "He called me a litterbug." Can't do any harm to tell them that.

"You were having a row." Hannah pounced.

"It was a joke." Giles helped himself to cake. "He was laughing when I last saw him."

"Nothing to do with the Scillies, anyway," said Terry, hoping to get back to the point.

"I am going to try to telephone again." Hebe went out. "She may be back by now."

As Hebe left the house she brushed past George Scoop in search of Hannah.

"Anyone home?" he sang. "Hullo, Amy." He walked in uninvited.

"Hullo, Mr Scoop," said Amy, not wishing to call him George. "Sit down. Cup of tea?"

"Thank you, I'd love a cup. Thought you might be here." George addressed Hannah who, answering without her usual gusto, merely said, "Yes."

"Hebe's son Silas is missing." Terry looked George up and down. So this was George. "I am Terry." He held out his hand, smiling. George shook hands, took note of Terry's lovely teeth, regular, not a single stopping. Often the case with blacks.

"Are the police informed?" George looked round the room. He had not been to Amy's house before. He noticed that it showed few signs of the flood. Hannah must have exaggerated the damage. It had been a ploy to get him involved.

"It's hardly a police matter—" said Hannah.

"Let's listen to the local news." Without asking Amy's permission George switched on her television. "Might hear something on the news." He sat down opposite the set. Amy drew in her breath.

"You want the football results," said Giles, guessing correctly, feeling hostile.

George registered a sensation he had had before. It would be dicey to be Giles' stepfather. He watched the announcer. "I know that man's dentist," he said. "He has a practice in Wimpole Street."

Amy watched George, sizing him up to his disadvantage. Terry smiled broadly.

The national news finished, the local announcer took over. "Now he is a patient of mine. Gets troublesome plaque. I stopped three of his teeth last month," said George. "Saved a molar."

Terry caught Hannah's eye. She grinned. Amy said, "Well,"

non-committally, then again "Well", on a downbeat.

"If I get it right and Silas sent the message, then it's not a police—" began Terry.

"No, no, Hebe got a message. We don't know that it was Silas that sent it," said Hannah.

"My God, I wish I could get at him." George leant forward to stare at a man being interviewed on a fishing boat. "One could do a lot for that chap."

Hannah burst out laughing. "You don't watch telly, you watch their teeth. What did the man say, George, bet you didn't hear." She crowed with laughter, catching Terry's eye, turning to Amy, who suppressed a smile. One should not make fun of visitors even when self-invited in one's own house. George looked discomfited, began seriously to doubt any future with Hannah, though in bed she was terrific. Who was this bloke Terry? A bit young for Hannah, and coloured, black, not to put too fine a point on it. A friend of Giles? Not exactly suitable. There were other things in marriage besides bed. He turned to look at Hannah. No, dammit, from the way she was grinning at Terry she and Terry had a thing going. Tricky bitch, how could she?

Giles, passing his cup for a refill, thought, None of them are concentrating on Silas. George is bothered by Terry. Mum is teasing George. Terry feels pleased with himself for some reason. Oh, high oop, Mum's switched to Terry, that's it, and Amy's just watching. They didn't notice when Giles left the room and crossed the street to Hebe's house. Hebe, sitting by the telephone, looked up. "Giles."

"Any luck?" He sat beside her.

"She must be out. I am ringing every five minutes. I know what she is doing, she is gardening. She will come in when she is tired. I must be patient."

Trip peered round the door and walked in, pressing her flank sensuously against its edge. She strolled across to Hebe, leapt on to her lap, pressing her head up under Hebe's chin with hard little jerks, purring.

"She wouldn't talk to me when I got home." Hebe stroked Trip.

"Cats get affronted. We had one in the States. Very unforgiving." Giles looked at the clock. "When is the five minutes up?"

Hebe watched the second hand. "About now." She dialled. "Try, try and try again." She listened to the telephone pealing in Louisa's drawing-room in Wiltshire. "Still out." She put the receiver down. "Oh, Giles." She began to weep. "What on earth can have happened to him?"

"Shall I get Mum?" Giles was near tears himself.

"No, I must just keep on trying until Louisa answers. Then, when she tells me who sent the message, I may get some idea of where he can be."

Giles fetched a roll of paper towel from the kitchen and handed a strip to Hebe. Hebe mopped her eyes, loving Giles for his action, thinking, Small wonder Silas is such friends with him. Giles blew his nose, while outside on the rooftops the sea gulls shrieked and quarrelled.

"I must pull myself together," she said, and remembered that when she was a small child she had heard her grandfather tell a man who had lost both legs to pull his socks up.

"It's pretty difficult," she said, taking another piece of paper towel from Giles. "I feel I am going mad."

"Oh, no," said Giles, catching his breath.

"Do you think he is dead?"

"Of course not," said Giles stoutly. "He may be anywhere. He has no idea of time."

"You know that's untrue."

"What do you think of Mum and Terry?" Could he distract her?

"What do you think? It's you that matters."

"I'm pleased." Giles grinned, thinking, Nobody can call Terry boring. "Try that number again," he suggested.

"I must not be hysterical." She started dialling.

Louisa, sitting on her garden seat, watched Mungo and Rory snipping dead heads off her roses. She was amused by their visit, their transparent show of solicitude and affection. Enjoying the late afternoon sun she laid bets with herself as to how long the two would stay.

They had arrived in Rory's car. They had been clearly disconcerted at not finding Hebe. Bound to secrecy by Bernard, Louisa was unable to tell them that Hebe had hurried to care for her child. Neither Mungo nor Rory knew she had a child. It had become obvious that they both thought Hebe had either gone out to avoid them or that Louisa, in spite of her denial when asked by Rory, knew where Hebe lived and could be tricked into giving her address. Since she only knew by accident through Bernard,

Louisa would only say, "She has a forwarding address in London, but it is she who telephones when she is free and might like to come. I can give you the address." From the way they hedged and hesitated, Louisa guessed that Mungo at least knew of this address and knew it to be a dead end.

Since they showed no inclination to leave, Louisa set them to work in the garden. Rory had done some ineffective weeding and Mungo had tied back some prickly ramblers. Now she watched them snipping away with secateurs. Lying with her feet up, her dogs lolling around her, Louisa enjoyed the spectacle of them spinning out the day as their hopes faded, unwilling to give up, suspiciously watching each other. She rehearsed what she would tell Bernard when next he telephoned. "Neither dared let the other out of his sight," she would say, hoping to amuse him. Rory came and sat on the grass beside her.

"I thought Mungo had to go and meet Alison," he grumbled. "What can Hebe see in him? He is far too old for her, nearly fifty."

"Forty-five, nice-looking, rich," Louisa murmured.

Rory muttered under his breath, watching Mungo. Then, looking up, he hissed in a whisper, "He says she's a – well, she says so, too, but I can't – it's not possible, it's—"

"What isn't possible?" Poor fellow, he looks so distressed. Louisa felt pity for Rory.

"What he says – what she – that she's a tart," Rory whispered.

Louisa raised her eyebrows. "I only know her in her cooking capacity," she said delicately. "That's what she does here." Louisa hesitated, recollecting that Hebe had done other than cook with Rory.

"Could it possibly be—"

"True?"

"Yes."

"What did she tell you?"

"That she is, but I – I can't—"

"You had better believe it." Louisa raised her head, watching Mungo approach. "What are you doing about Alison?" she asked him.

"I am going to telephone. I said I would meet her at Heathrow but she may have arrived by now. All this made me forget."

"All this being Hebe?" Louisa pried.

"All this being Hebe, yes," Mungo shouted in exasperation. "Oh, bugger it!"

"Temper, temp—" Rory crowed.

"Shut up, you little jerk," shouted Mungo.

Louisa's dogs began to bark, the barking started as usual by Rufus, seconded by the higher yapping of the smaller dogs. Louisa shouted, "Quiet!" Dogs and men fell silent. When the cacophony died down Louisa said, "I think, dears, you had better give up. Hebe has gone and you, Mungo, must sort yourself out with Alison."

"Oh my God!" Mungo's reluctance was tangible.

"Go on, Mungo, get it done. You have your boys to consider. Stop chasing shadows."

"Hebe's no shadow," Mungo blurted in protest.

"Go on, telephone. Take Rory with you as moral support."

"God forbid!" Outraged by this frivolous suggestion, Mungo shambled away into the house.

Dialling Louisa's number Hebe listened to the engaged signal.

"Perhaps it's out of order," Giles suggested. "Ask the operator." The operator checked and said, "The line is engaged. Do you want me to break in? Is it urgent?"

"I will wait." She felt despair. She had often known Louisa, regardless of her telephone bill, gossip for hours with Lucy Duff, Maggie Cook-Popham, whom she professed not to like or other old ladies referred to as girl friends.

When Hebe's doorbell rang it was Giles who answered the door to Jim Huxtable, but Hannah arriving at a run brushed him aside.

"Quick, Hebe, come. Aunt Amy's collapsed, I think it's her heart. Terry's ringing the doctor."

Jim watched the two women race to Amy Tremayne's house. Soon a doctor's car braked to a stop. The doctor, met by George, hurried into the house. The boy who had opened Hebe's door came out to stand on the pavement looking irresolute. Ill at ease in this hideous street, Jim walked up to the seat erected in memory of aged parents too puffed to climb the hill in one go. He sat leaning back against a lovingly carved obscene inscription. He wished he had the dog Feathers with him. He waited, watching the houses.

The doctor came out after twenty minutes, pausing for a last word with the girl with green eyes before driving off. Almost immediately George got into his car and drove away. The boy on the pavement made a two-finger gesture. George did not look back. Still Jim waited. A black and tan dog with curling tail came busily down the street, paused, sniffed the seat, lifted its leg, caught Jim's eye, looked doubtful.

"Hullo." Jim held out a hand. The dog dropped its ears, allowed itself to be patted, looked up with a conniving expression, went its way with jaunty step. Feathers, had he been there, would have started a fight. Jim watched the street, taking in its remarkable ugliness, snatching at what he saw to steady his mind, attempting to come to terms with what he had seen. Should he go down the hundred yards which separated him from Amy's house, go in, introduce himself to Hebe? Did he want to? What should he say? Would she recognise him, would she think him mad?

"Her name is Hebe," he said out loud in the horrible street. It made the situation no better. Could he say, "I am the man you met in Lucca. I made love to you." By candlelight in Lucca he had been able to talk to her. He tried to remember what they had talked about. They hadn't said much, there had been too much noise, too much doing. He shivered, sitting on the hard bench, its slats cutting into his thighs. Suppose it was not the girl? Suppose he was wrong, after all? She had not lived with a dream for – how long? Thirteen years. "Sod it, bugger it, what am I to do?" Jim muttered. The suspicion that he was opposed to reality, wanted to keep his search unresolved, niggled at him. He had lived with it for so long he feared its ending. It was a part of his life; to end it was a terrible risk.

From Amy Tremayne's house came the fair girl, a slim black youth holding her hand, then Hebe. The boy who belonged to the group joined them. They walked along the pavement to Hannah's house. Jim stood up. The black and tan dog was coming back up the hill. Jim walked towards it. They met outside Amy Tremayne's door. Would she be able to help? "I wish I knew what to do," Jim said to the dog, who looked sure of himself. The dog wagged its curled tail, flattened its ears. On impulse Jim tried the door, telling himself she had invited him to come again. The door opened, he went in. He listened in the narrow hall with the dog beside him, walked slowly to the back kitchen where not so long ago they had talked. There were remains of tea on the table, chairs pushed back. With the dog Jim climbed the stairs and went into Amy's bedroom. She lay stretched on the bed, eyes closed in a waxen face.

The dog went close to the bed lifting its inquisitive nose. Jim noted the paperweights on the windowsill, twinkling and glinting in the afternoon sun, delightfully alive. He was overcome with embarrassment. He crossed himself. "It's just a gesture," he said to the dog, fighting the panic and surprise. I cross myself when I see a magpie. He remembered a woman with whom he had had an affair mocking him in Normandy, where there are many magpies. The dog farted. The noisome smell reached Jim's nostrils. "Come on," he said to the dog, "we have no business here. She's dead." The dog followed him down the stairs and went up the street without à backward glance.

Jim ran down the dark red brick street to the car park. He felt dazed. It was not until he was back in Bernard's house and saw Silas that he realised he had not fulfilled his mission.

TWENTY-EIGHT

Alison, on arrival at Heathrow, telephoned her mother-in-law, who greeted her with "I hope you had an enjoyable holiday. You are back sooner than I expected," as though there had been no crisis.

Alison understood that her elopement was to be ignored. "I wondered whether Mungo was staying with you. He is not at home." She tried the casual unconcerned approach.

"He is visiting Louisa. I was talking to her earlier. He seems to have taken up with Rory. I would not have imagined they had anything in common, would you?"

"No. Not that I don't rather like him," Alison amended, since she was in no position to cast aspersions. "What is Mungo doing there?"

"Fishing?" Lucy suggested, thinking fishing for Hebe.

"I doubt it. He has better fishing at home."

"Neglecting his work," said Lucy sardonically.

"He's by way of having a holiday, which reminds me we should fetch the boys soon. They are in the Scillies." Give the impression of united parents, thought Alison.

"They have had dreadful weather." Lucy was undeceived.

"I must telephone Jennifer—"

"Why don't you join Mungo at Louisa's," suggested Lucy. "It would be a neutral situation." Which was as far, Alison realised, as her mother-in-law would venture on to the tricky ground she presently occupied. "Take a taxi and surprise the dear fellow, it will save him the drive to the airport."

"I might do just that," said Alison gratefully. "It should not take me long to get there."

Lucy Duff went out to her terrace wet from recent rain. Miss Thomson brought the tray of tea things and sat beside her. "Shall I be mother?" she asked in her fat voice.

"No," said Lucy. "No, thank you." She looked at Miss Thomson with ill-concealed dislike. First "patio", now "Shall I be mother?" Irreplaceable Alison must be set to work replacing Miss Thomson. She poured tea. "Mrs Mungo is back from the United States," she said, well aware that Miss Thomson called Alison "Alison" and would be affronted by the expression "Mrs Mungo". "Mrs Mungo is joining Mr Mungo at Mrs Fox's in Wiltshire. I believe Mrs Fox has the lady cook there at the moment. Oh, must you go?" Lucy watched Miss Thomson retreat into the house to compose a letter of resignation. ("I know when I'm not wanted.") Lucy drank her tea, visualising life without Miss Thomson and the shortly to take place arrival of Alison at Louisa's. Surprise for her when she finds what Rory and Mungo have in common is Hebe, Lucy thought pleasurably. "How I miss you," she murmured to the ghost of her dead husband, who would also have been amused. She rose stiffly and went to apologise to Miss Thomson, to whom she had behaved despicably, pausing en route to look at her husband's photograph, so like Mungo and yet sure of himself. He had a theory, she remembered as she looked at the long-dead face, that only his insecure friends got themselves into pickles with women. If that were true Mungo must be insecure, and from what Louisa said his cousin Rory also. On her way to be nice to Miss Thomson Lucy decided not to apprise Louisa of Alison's imminent arrival. It would give Alison a sporting chance to find Mungo making a fool of himself over Hebe. Lucy did not know that for equally suspect reasons her friend had not informed her Hebe had left in the morning.

Alison, paying the taxi in Louisa's drive, was surrounded by baying dogs. The driver drove away leaving her to fend off Rufus who leapt and bounced, scratching her legs, hoping to lick her face. Alison beat off Rufus' unsolicited attentions by whirling her bag and shouting "Down, down, down" in a voice which rose higher and higher as she became infected by fear. Such a lot of dogs, brute of a taxi man to leave her to cope alone. Mungo, coming out of the house, came down the steps in a rush, kicked Rufus, grabbed Alison round the waist and kissed her. Alison flung her arms round his neck and kissed him back, then leant back, holding his arms to look up into his face in surprise.

"Oh Mungo" – her carefully prepared speech lost. "Darling," said Alison, "darling."

"Darling," said Mungo, kissing her again. "How wonderful

to have you back." He was astonished to find himself acting pleased to see her. He was amazed. "Heavens," he said, "you are looking pretty." He looked at his wife with delight. Her pale marmalade hair caught the afternoon sun, her blue eyes were striking. What had she done to her eyelashes? "What have you done to your hair?" He kissed her again. "Have you had a good time?"

"No, I have not. Oh, Mungo darling." She gripped his arms.

"You look like a Botticelli angel," he said. "Why have I never noticed?"

Alison said, "You have forgotten what I look like. Let me look at you." She looked up at him, her remarkable eyes admiring his thick hair, his dark looks. He seemed to have grown more lined since she last looked at him. "I had my hair done in Santa Barbara."

"It's lovely." Will she admit she's had her eyelashes dyed? he wondered.

"And my eyelashes treated." Her gaze did not falter.

"Treated," murmured Mungo, smiling. "Treated."

"We have to meet the boys when they come back from the Scillies." Alison looked up at Mungo. "I talked to Jennifer from Heathrow. They are all coming back on Thursday because the weather has been so vile."

"Day after tomorrow." He examined her face. What else had she changed?

"I spoke to your mother. She told me you were here."

"Good." Mungo began to laugh.

"What are you laughing at?" She laughed with him. She looked even prettier laughing.

"We can cut all these prepared speeches. Come and see Louisa. Rory is here. Remember him? Rory Grant, my cousin."

"Of course I do." They were moving into the house, Mungo carrying her luggage.

"What speeches were you going to make?" she asked courageously.

"We can discuss our speeches on the way to meet the boys, if we have to meet them. It's a bit of a bore. Shall we take Rory along, if we go?"

"As an umpire? Why not." Alison felt like a swimmer who, having swum too far, struggles weakly back towards the beach. With a bit of luck she would reach *terra firma*, retrieve her breath (for breath read marriage).

"Alison, dear." Louisa was advancing from the garden, accompanied by the dogs wagging good-naturedly, no longer threatening. "How lovely. You will stay the night, won't you? We were coming to see about tea. This is Rory, do you remember him? Put it all on a tray and take it out under the tree. There are scones in the kitchen, Rory. Hebe left a supply."

"Hebe?" Alison felt a threatening whiff.

"The darling girl who cooks for Lucy. You were the clever one who found her. She comes to me, too. Unfortunately she had to leave today. Now come on, Rory, make yourself useful."

Smirking, Rory went to the kitchen followed by Louisa's voice. "There is Devonshire cream for the scones and strawberry jam."

"Bought by me and darling Hebe in Salisbury," Rory said to Rufus, "as well she knows and she is making sure Alison does too, my old beauty. Everybody knows somethink but nobody says nuffink, not in so many words."

Rory stacked cups and saucers on the tray, put the kettle on, found the scones, dropped one, found cream and strawberry jam. "Alison won't let Mungo go," he said to Rufus who, thin streams of greedy saliva swinging from the corners of his mouth, ate gratefully. "What's more," Rory told the dog as he made the tea and carried the tray out to the garden, "if I smell right, something has happened to Alison to make her value Mungo."

Rory put the tray on the garden table by Louisa, who looked up at him with an amused expression. She was savouring the undeclared peace between Mungo and Alison and looking forward to her next conversation with Bernard. She would describe the unlikely development of comradeship between her nephews. She would suggest that Mungo, much as he loved Hebe, was also attached to his wife, and lay odds on Hebe losing a customer. As she poured tea and passed cups she assessed Alison's appearance, new hair-do, make-up, clothes. She saluted Alison's nerve. Summoned back from an elopement by her mother-in-law Alison should by rights be embarrassed, apprehensive, apologetic, uncertain. She was none of these things. She was eating her tea and describing her visit to Santa Barbara with animation, entrancing both her husband and Rory. She was not, Louisa noted, giving many details of her hosts while she described the house, its setting, its furnishing, its pool. Watching Mungo, Louisa counted several occasions when pertinent questions came close to expression but each time Alison, dolloping cream and jam on to her scones, switched the talk to topics nearer home, rounding off bravely with the question, "Shall we drive down and meet the boys, darling, as I suggested? It would be nice to see Jennifer and Julian. And it will save the boys that dreary journey they so hate."

"I never heard them object to it." Briefly Mungo reverted to the argumentative mood he used to counter Alison's bossiness.

"Love! They have to change trains at Exeter. It would be fun to meet them. Why don't you come with us, Rory?" She doubted whether Mungo had been serious in suggesting Rory.

Rory, meeting her eyes, recognised an appeal. She was really much prettier than he remembered. He said, "I should love to."

"You can make an early start," Louisa chipped in. "Come and help me make up a bed, Alison. You must have an early night to get over your jet lag."

Alison sprang to her feet.

"Mungo stayed last night with Rory," said Louisa, looking at Mungo. "Would it be all right if you stayed one more night with him? It would save me the bother of making up another bed." Without waiting for an answer Louisa led Alison into the house. "You can tell him anything you may want to when you are less tired," she said.

"Thank you," said Alison, sensing an ally.

"What is she separating us for?" Mungo turned angrily to Rory.

"I imagine the idea is to get you – er – get you reunited." Rory began to laugh. "They don't know how we – er – how—"

"We spent last night." Mungo finished Rory's sentence for him. "I don't particularly want you on this drive to Cornwall," he said with chill.

"But I am coming," said Rory with unusual determination. "I – er – want to—" He did not say that, remembering the number of Hebe's car, he had realised that her number plate was Cornish. "I want to have a snoop round Penzance. Nice antique shops," he added by way of excuse.

"If Louisa is mean about beds I shall stay in an hotel," said Mungo, who was growing suspicious. "There's a plot of some kind between these women."

"Then stay with me and we can – er – can – er—"

"Stick together." Mungo finished the sentence automatically. "Alison is full of bounce," he said thoughtfully, "very full of bounce."

"Perhaps she found you – er – found you bouncy when you came back from the – er – Syndicate."

"Oh God!" said Mungo. "Do you think Alison knows?"

"It's probable." Rory handed the last of the scones to Rufus.
"Do you – er – want to sleep with her tonight?"

"I had not planned to," said Mungo stuffily.

"Gosh." Rory began stacking the tea things on to the tray.
"You had better plan something of the sort. Better be – er –
spontaneous," he advised.

Mungo restrained his longing to kick Rory, to thump Louisa,
to assault Alison, all spontaneous reactions. He even refrained
from ringing up and insulting his mother. Hebe, he thought,
never brought out the worst in him.

Back in Rory's house Mungo felt exasperation. He looked
at Rory's possessions with loathing. The absence of vulgarity
maddened him. Good silver, lovely glass, enviable pictures, a
collection of good books. The whole set-up would appeal to
Hebe. Rory was watching as he glared round.

"What's – er – wrong?"

"Nothing," said Mungo sulkily. "That's your trouble."

"I put my evil spirit into the hats," Rory said. "You wouldn't
find anything in the shop that would suit – er – Alison. Have a
look." Hebe had the only suitable hat for a beautiful woman, he
thought. "I made a good one for Louisa," he said.

"Louisa." Mungo stood undecided. Rory watched him.
"Louisa is manipulating me."

"Yes – er – she is." Rory tried not to laugh.

"She is keeping me apart from Alison."

"Yes – er—"

"Why?"

Rory shrugged. "To let her rest?" he suggested.

"I am going back." Mungo turned on his heel and left the
house. Rory listened to Mungo's car drive away, then went to
bed and lay plotting how to find Hebe's car and Hebe in
Cornwall, quite a large county.

Mungo let himself into Louisa's house and stilled the dogs. He
went upstairs. A light showed under the spare room door. He
walked in. Alison lay in the bed, her pale marmalade hair framing
her face, dark blue eyes startled.

"Mungo," she chirped.

"Shut up." Mungo was undressing. He felt domineering, masculine, randy.

"Mungo!" Alison exclaimed again in a whisper.

Mungo got into the narrow bed. "Move over."

"I can't, I'll fall out. What do you want?"

"To fuck you."

"Don't use that word. You know I cannot bear—"

"Oh, shut up," Mungo grunted. "Let's get on with it."

Presently Mungo, holding Alison, said, "We don't do this enough." And Alison began to laugh in a way she had not laughed for a long time, so that he said, "That's right, my love, one should laugh. Now I shall make love to you."

Alison bit back the question "Who else have you laughed with?" and whispered "I'm glad I came back." Mungo fell asleep taking up more than his fair share of the single bed. So far, so good, thought Alison, enduring the discomfort. Perhaps I can wean him away from whoever it is who laughs. Could it be that cook? She tried to remember what the girl looked like.

Sitting between Mungo and Rory as they drove the next day, Alison felt a sense of levity usually alien to her nature. When Rory, sensing her high spirits, ventured to suggest, "Tell us — um—er—tell us about your hosts, these—er—friends of yours—"

"Yes, do," said Mungo, driving the car. "What do Eli and Patsy do when they are at home? Come on, tell."

"What time does the helicopter arrive?" Alison feebly tried to deflect the attack.

"Alison!" Rory protested. "Come on."

"What was this *ménage à trois* like?" Mungo met Alison's eyes in the driving mirror. "This troika."

"All right." Alison took a deep breath. She tensed her shoulders, gritted her teeth.

"Go on," said Rory and put his hand over hers which were clenched in her lap.

"Bed," said Alison in a rather high voice, "with him first. Then Patsy came and watched. I did not like that. Then she got in on the other side of me. I think it was what's called an orgy."

"Go on," said Mungo, scowling at the road ahead. "Go on."

"Well," Alison's voice rose higher, "I enjoyed it with him, it was different, a change—"

"A nice change," said Rory in an unwarrantably plump voice.

"Well, it was. If it had been only Eli I might still be there."

"Oh," said Mungo, his face clouding, but Alison was back in Santa Barbara. "He was far worse than you, Mungo." She did not notice her husband's eyebrows rise. "He used words I have never heard. Your language pales. That put me off a little."

"Only a little." Rory's voice betrayed no feeling.

"But Patsy did not like it. She did not like the Eli and me combination."

"Fancy that," said Rory under his breath. "So what happened?" he asked, for he could see, glancing at Mungo's profile, that Mungo could not or would not ask.

"What happened," said Alison, the words coming in a rush, "what happened was that Eli suggested he and I should take a trip to New Mexico without Patsy. I said, 'Fine, I'd like that.' Patsy was getting on my nerves, alternately pawing me and being nasty to Eli. I got packed and as I was coming down to the car I heard a scuffle on the stairs. She had torn all the buttons off his shirt and was tearing at his trousers. Then," Alison gasped, "then she went down and bit him in the leg."

"Oh," said Mungo. "Gosh! How shocking."

"Ah," said Rory. "Then what – er – what—"

"I got into Eli's car and drove myself to the airport. I had talked to your mother, as you know. I had lied, of course. I had no intention then of coming home."

"You lied to us," said Mungo.

Alison's voice was tired. "Of course I lied. Your mother was so obvious. Eli has not got AIDS but your mother can't manage without me."

"Nor can I," Mungo blurted, red in the face.

Rory noticed that both Mungo and Alison were close to tears. "I have never seen man bitten by woman," he said. Then they were laughing with the unstoppable hilarity usually confined to adolescents.

TWENTY-NINE

Cramming her spectacles on to her nose, Hebe ran to her car, started the engine and roared down the street, swinging dangerously into the traffic as she joined the main road. The agony since Louisa had given her the message, the anxiety she felt for Amy, the resentment engendered by her grandparents, the cumulative distress waiting for news of Silas combined to feed the panic which had begun in Amy's house. She forced the maximum speed from the engine, nipping perilously through the traffic, so tense she almost forgot to breathe. Jim, following, flinched at the risks she took, hoped she would not lunatically crash, that he would not have to carry a corpse to the hospital, be harbinger of woe to Silas.

Hebe travelled into the country out of sight. Jim caught up with the car by the telephone kiosk, its door swinging open, engine running, saw Hebe racing across the fields towards Bernard's house.

He parked his car and ran back to Hebe's car, shut the door, pocketed the keys and started running after her. Twice he saw her leap at a bank and scramble over. Once she fell, but was quickly up and running. As he ran Jim muttered to himself, "This time, this time, this time." Hurdling the last bank into Bernard's garden he collided with Feathers, stumbled, fell, swore. Feathers made haste to greet, snuffling at Jim's face, delighted to find it within reach.

"Bugger off." Jim pushed the dog away. "Out of the way, damn you." He was on all fours in the wet grass.

Bernard stood over him. "Hurt yourself?"

"No." Jim staggered to his feet. "Out of the way," he said to Feathers.

"Stop," said Bernard, as Jim turned towards the cottage. He caught Jim's arm and Jim swung round nearly knocking the old man down.

"Why?" Jim cried furiously. "Why?"

"They have to be alone." Bernard held Jim by the sleeve. "We are going out."

"I have to see her," panted Jim. "I've got to."

"Presently," said Bernard. "You and I are going to the cinema. Go home," he said to Feathers. "It doesn't matter you being here. Come along," he said, "we must go out so that Silas can talk to his mother."

"I have to see that girl," Jim shouted.

"Not now. She has to be alone with him, it's important."

"It's important that I see her," Jim insisted.

"Only to you."

Jim stared at the old man, deflated. "I had not thought of that."

Bernard, old and shrunken, looked up at Jim. He said, "She won't run away."

"I have her car keys."

"We will put them back in her car." He led Jim towards the road. "Did she recognise you?"

"I don't think so. When I went to her house she was talking on the telephone. I told her Silas was with you and she rushed off. I don't think she noticed me, just registered the message."

They walked slowly. Jim helped Bernard over the banks. "This is not a suitable progress for a man of my age," Bernard remarked, "but we shall sit in the cinema and be warm and dry."

"Why the cinema?" Jim was rebellious.

"It is dark." Bernard spoke stoically. They had nearly reached Jim's car. "I can sit and mourn."

"Mourn what?" Jim was ill-tempered.

"You seem to forget," Bernard got into Jim's car and began tying himself in with the safety belt, "that you went twice to the town. First you saw Amy dead and forgot to tell Hebe her boy is safe. I sent you back. Going to the cinema does not mean I am not shaken by Amy's death."

"Are you? Why?" Unwillingly Jim started the car.

"Once we were in love. Very agreeable it was, too."

Jim found nothing to say, his mind on Hebe.

"If we find a movie which is a weepy I can pretend I am moved by that."

"Yes." Jim began to pay attention.

"We were in the Hôtel d'Angleterre. It ended badly," said Bernard. "Long ago in Paris."

"Why?" asked Jim.

"She discovered I was sleeping with Louisa. Why do women

always expect this one-at-a-time business? It makes no sense. That is what upset her most." In old age Bernard refused the memory of Amy's pregnancy.

"All these years," said Jim, momentarily forgetting his own troubles. "All these years I have never known you visit her."

"We were not on speaking terms," said Bernard. "Latterly, since she befriended Hebe and I got to know the girl, I tried to make it up. Louisa and I have remained close. Amy was bitter. There was nothing doing."

"Perhaps she had reason to be bitter." Jim had never considered his old friend a particularly nice character.

"Hebe has no need of you," said Bernard nastily, confirming Jim in his view. "She is even more capable than Amy of managing on her own." Then, as Jim did not respond, he said, "It's the mode for women to live alone these days. You must have noticed, even you."

"Why even me?" Jim asked, but Bernard was pretending not to hear, leaving Jim feeling he had in some way made himself ridiculous.

THIRTY

Silas clung to Hebe and Hebe clung to Silas. Too breathless from
running, she felt, in the joy of relief, that it was enough to hold
him. He was alive, in one piece. She feared if she spoke she might
say the wrong thing. Silas, holding his mother, felt her heart
thumping. They huddled together in Bernard's wing chair in the
dark little room. The fire flickered and Feathers sank down at
their feet with a grunt.

Silas, his face pressed against her chest, said, "I was seasick. I
had no boots. They all know each other well. Mrs Reeves is a
sort of horsey woman. I felt stupid because they all knew how
to sail. I went off alone. I saw seals and an adder and people in
a boat. There were two other boys. They boasted about their
father's mistress. Well, the younger one did and the size of his—
Then he said he wet his bed as if it was clever. There was stew
at every meal and Mr Reeves – he's called Julian – picked on Mrs
Reeves. She said to call her Jennifer. I couldn't. He picked on her
about the stew and they called the woman who came to clean
and cook Mrs Thing. He niggled on at me about school. Why
don't we learn Latin and he and Mrs Reeves quarrelled without
saying anything – they are snobs about everything – it was like
that all the time. He gave me wine before I noticed the others
only drank Coke. I felt so stupid. I've been sick on your jersey.
We had to share a room, the four of us. It was a lovely cottage,
very pretty but I wished— I sent you a postcard, I didn't want
you to know I wasn't enjoying— Now when I go back to school
it will be awful – I was sick into Michael's boots and all over the
front of your jersey. They talk in loud voices – he niggled me
about you and what did my father do. Mrs Reeves jumped in
and said— And they looked down their noses because we live in
a street. It's okay to live in a street in London but otherwise you
have to live in the country – and Michael said you were a cook
and Mrs Reeves said she had an uncle who married his – Mr
Reeves said cooks are an endangered species – he was drunk – he

651

kept giving me wine and there was a thick feeling in the room then he asked what my father does and I hated him and said my mother is a Hermaphrodite and I threw my wine in his face." Hebe's arms tightened. Silas drew breath. "I looked up 'hermaphrodite' in Mr Quigley's dictionary so now I feel stupider than ever. When I'd thrown my wine at his head I rushed out – I grabbed your jersey off the line where Mrs Reeves had hung it, she washed it but it still smells – I didn't know what to do, but I was lucky because the people I had seen fishing were going across to St Mary's. They gave me a lift – I am sorry I left everything behind I just brought the jersey – the people didn't ask anything – next day I managed to get back on the helicopter, the crew remembered I had a return ticket. When I got home you weren't there and I cried – I'm sorry. Amy or Hannah would have asked questions – Jim found me and brought me here – he and Mr Quigley have been kind. It's been great to be with Feathers and the cat – it hasn't got a name, he says cats don't need names, he doesn't even call it 'Thing' like the Reeves call the cleaning lady. They said – no, they didn't say, but I felt they wanted to say I've got no bottle. Well, they haven't got all that much. Michael cried when she hit him and I felt – I felt Hermaphrodites don't hit their children – Giles started it, he asked if I was a test tube baby and I said I couldn't be because they didn't do it when I was born – we had a row – I hit him – he fell into the kale and his nose bled. Mr Quigley had said his father was dull which was awful for Giles – he pushed a note through the door which said 'perhaps your mother is a Hermaphrodite' – I felt proud of that until the dictionary – it's all been so awful – have I got a father?"

"No." Hebe felt terribly cold.

"Don't you know him?" Silas tightened his grip.

"No."

Silas, sitting with his arms round Hebe, looked up at her face, put up a hand and gently removed her glasses.

"They are misted up." He put the glasses on the table beside the chair, ran his hand through his hair. "It's wet from your tears." He looked at his hand. Then he said, "Not even a Hismaphrodite?"

"Silas." Now is the time for burning boats, she thought.

"Never mind," said Silas. He felt the pleasurable relief at being with her, the contentment at having poured out his troubles. He wrapped his arms round her. She began to speak, now or never.

"I have never been able to talk to you because I didn't know how to begin. I was in Italy and after I came back I felt peculiar, so they sent me to the doctor and he said I was pregnant. They – I have never told you that I was brought up by my grandparents. When they found out they were furious – horrible. I still get nightmares. I hear their voices say, 'Who was the man?' and things like 'Long-haired layabout, yobbo or black or bare feet and dirty nails.' They kept asking 'Who was the man?' – I couldn't answer because I didn't know. They wouldn't believe me. I wanted you. They wanted me to have an abortion. Do you know what that means?"

"Of course I do. But you didn't have one."

"I came to Amy who looked after me. I sold things I had to Bernard Quigley, we became friends. I learned to earn money. I have tried to think who your father could be, but I don't know. All I get is this panic, I hear voices going on and on about an abortion and calling me a whore and asking who the man was." Hebe drew a shaky breath. Silas tightened his grip. A log shifted on the fire; Feathers groaned. "When I get these panics I hear their voices and it's mixed up with running in dark streets, I run and run and the buildings all round me are taller than skyscrapers and people look out of blind windows. I hear that repetition, "Who was the man?" Hebe hurried on. "I must tell you, otherwise someone else will. As well as cooking jobs I am a part-time tart to make money to pay for us." There, she thought, it's out.

"Don't you realise," Silas shifted in her arms and looked up, "don't you realise that what happened was a bad trip, probably LSD." He sounded older than twelve. "Rather fascinating."

"I have never taken drugs in my life." She was horrified. "What do you know about them?" She sat up and stared at him.

"You can be given LSD in your drink. People think it's funny."

"Funny!"

"You don't know and you go on a 'trip'. A master at school gave us a lecture on drugs. Who were you with? It happens at parties. Was it Hismaphrodite?"

Hebe began to laugh.

"Then," said Silas, laughing too, "he seduced you."

"Oh Silas, I don't know, I honestly don't."

"Just this nightmare thing?"

"No, one other thing. There's a smell." Hebe sat up. "My God, Silas, you smell of it now, how weird, and I haven't told you. I quite forgot. Amy is ill. How could I forget?"

Silas gave a shuddering sigh. "Will she die?"

"She had a heart attack. She is in bed resting."

"I can hear yours. Amy won't leave us."

Hebe kissed the top of the head laid against her chest. Time later to worry about Amy but for this moment she felt lighthearted, overjoyed by Silas.

"It's this jersey that smells, Jim lent it to me," he said.

Hebe was not listening. Her relief at finding Silas, telling Silas, blocked all other thought. She filled her lungs with the smell of Bernard's cottage – woodsmoke, garlic, paraffin, herbs, coffee, wet salty air coming across the fields from the sea. She breathed it all in and let out an exhausted sigh. Silas could be right about LSD. She simply couldn't remember.

"What's the difference," Silas was speaking, "anyway?"

"What difference?"

"Between marrying for money and being," he hesitated, then, "being a tart? I don't think there is any difference except—"

"Except what?"

"Except that you seem happier than a lot of people at school's mothers."

"Oh."

"We are happier, Giles and I, than people at school. Mr and Mrs Reeves don't seem happy. Do I have to go back to that school?"

"I—"

"You know Giles talks like us when he wants and when I am with him I talk like him."

Hebe said nothing.

"Giles only talks as he does to tease Hannah and it's easier to be like other people. It's a waste of money, Hannah having elocution lessons. Who wants to sound like Mrs Thatcher?" Silas laughed. "What is your nightmare about, do you think?"

"My grandparents trying to find out who your father was."

"What did they say? Tell me again."

Hebe whispered, "Who was the man? Long-haired layabout, dirty feet, might be a foreigner, who was the man, abortion, might be black, earrings, cannabis, dirty fingernails, may have a police record, who was the man—"

"I'm not bothered," said Silas.

THIRTY-ONE

"Take me to Wilson Street." Bernard, who had sat hunched in silence during the drive, now spoke.

"I thought you wanted to go to a movie." Jim, too, had been silent, prey to feelings of anger, anxiety and exhilaration, an uneasy mix which made him so inattentive of his driving that several times along the road there had been a near miss with another car.

"I've changed my mind. Stop at the corner, I want to buy flowers for Amy."

Jim drew into the kerb. "Wouldn't it be sensible to wait for the funeral?"

"Sensible!" Bernard snorted as he opened the car door. "Shan't be long." He darted across the pavement into the flower shop.

"We're on a double yellow line," Jim yelled after him. He watched the inexorable advance of a traffic warden. "This is all I need." He drummed impatient fingers on the steering wheel, cursing Bernard. The traffic warden sauntered down the street slipping tickets behind windscreen wipers. "Come *on*, Bernard." Why am I in such a rage, what does it matter? Jim asked himself. "Hurry up!" he shouted to the old man. Bernard, arms full of roses, emerged from the shop.

"Hullo." Bernard and the warden met beside the car. "Karen, isn't it?" Bernard bared his ancient teeth. "You are looking very beautiful. How's your mother? I don't think I've seen you since you left school. You have your mother's looks."

"I am married now, Mr Quigley," Karen chirped.

"Goodness, how time— I say, were you going to put one of your *billets doux* on our windscreen?"

The warden laughed and held the car door open for Bernard. "Courting, Mr Quigley?" she queried, eyeing the roses. Bernard showed his teeth again. The warden snapped shut the car door. "Don't forget your seat belt, Mr Quigley." Bernard leant back in his seat. "I love women, can't do without them."

Jim drove on, wondering why Bernard had not long ago got himself murdered.

At Amy's house he stopped the car, deciding he would play no part in whatever obscene pantomime Bernard planned.

"Come on." Bernard extricated himself from the seat belt. "Idiotic infringement of personal liberty, these things. Look sharp. Follow me."

Reluctantly Jim followed.

Bernard crossed the pavement, pushed open Amy's door. "Never locks her door. Get raped one of these days, the old fool." He mounted the stairs, opened Amy's bedroom door. Jim heard a faint exclamation and Bernard said, "Stupid ass told me you were dead, brought you roses. Don't tell me you've had a heart attack."

Jim heard Amy's crisp reply, "It's not only Louisa who has a weak heart."

"Still jealous after all these years," Bernard crowed. Then, "Let's look at you. You don't look too bad, give us a kiss." Then, raising his voice, "Jim, come in here."

Jim went in. Amy lay with an arm round the bouquet of roses. Her free hand held Bernard's old claw. She smiled at Jim.

"Thought I was dead, didn't you? Where's the dog?"

"He wasn't my dog." Jim felt acute embarrassment. "I must apologise for coming into your house like that. I wanted—"

"Sit down, both of you." Amy indicated chairs. Bernard sat holding Amy's hand. Jim sat uneasily by the window. "You came to see my paperweights," Amy said to Jim. "I've got real flowers, now." The hand holding the sheaf of roses tightened its grip round the cellophane wrapping.

"Just because I thought you might be dead doesn't alter anything," said Bernard loudly.

"I'm not deaf any more than I am dead," said Amy angrily. "It never occurred to me you would change."

It seemed to Jim that here was confirmation of an old quarrel.

Amy went on, "You are not getting the paperweights. I have left them to Hebe."

"I don't want your paperweights," Bernard shouted, his voice cracking.

"Then why are you here?" Amy's eyes watched Bernard. Jim felt her hostility.

"Can your heart stand a bit of news?" Bernard peered into Amy's face.

"Of course. Spit it out." Amy had the upper hand in this subterranean feud.

"A surprise?" questioned Bernard on a rising note.

"Go on," she said.

"This friend of mine, Jim, has reason to believe he is Silas' father." Bernard stared at Amy, his mouth slightly open, as though sharing in the surprise he was causing.

"He looks very like him," said Amy unsurprised. "Same nose. Your hair was chestnut before you went grey, I take it." She was talking now to Jim. "Silas has Hebe's eyes, though."

"Dammit it, Amy, must you be so calm?" Bernard yelped.

"Doctor told me to keep calm."

"He's been looking for her for *years*."

"Does he want to marry her? Do you want to marry her?" Amy tried to see Jim's face, sitting with his back to the light.

"I'm," began Jim, "I've—"

"He's in love with her," Bernard volunteered.

"Ho," said Amy. "Love! You are in love with me." Bernard made a clucking noise. "And with Louisa. There was talk of love with Lucy and even Eileen. That's Hebe's grandmother," Amy spoke towards Jim, "and a lot of others. Used to take us all to the same hotel in Paris. Talked of love. It didn't mean a thing."

"Rubbish," yelled Bernard. "Am I not here with roses?"

"You came to make sure I was dead and pinch my paperweights."

"Unfair," yelled Bernard. "I came because I love you."

Amy said, "Fancy that."

In the silence that followed Jim stood up, disturbed by these grotesque old people.

Amy said in accusation, "You keep in touch with Louisa."

"I telephone," admitted Bernard, "sometimes."

"And why not?" Amy was magnanimous. "But you don't let her see you, poor shrivelled old manikin."

"No." Bernard closed his eyes. "I don't."

"He didn't want to marry any of us." Amy switched her attention to Jim. "Not that it matters now. Do you want to marry Hebe?"

"I—" Jim felt distraught. What business was it of this old crone to question him?

"It's up to Hebe, isn't it?" said Amy.

Bernard opened his eyes. "Only Hebe?"

"As far as I am concerned only Hebe matters," said Amy, her

eyes flicking from Jim to Bernard. "And for Hebe read Silas, for Silas is what matters to Hebe. Wherever he is, he seems to be lost."

"Silas," said Bernard smugly, "is at my house and Hebe is with him. That is why Jim is here. I tactfully removed him so that Silas could explain why he ran away from the Scillies without a problematical father getting underfoot."

"I thought you came to visit the dead. Is Silas all right?"

"Perfectly," said Bernard. "We cherished him as I" – he squeezed Amy's hand – "cherish you."

Amy heaved with laughter.

"Mind your heart."

"Actually," murmured Amy, "my heart is better."

"All the better for seeing me?" asked Bernard slyly.

These outrageous old people are flirting, thought Jim. He wondered whether they would notice if he slipped away. They did not, he thought, need an audience for their reunion.

"Actually," the word seemed to amuse Amy, "actually yes."

Hannah chose this moment to come into the room, followed by Terry and Giles, her green eyes sparkling, teeth aflash.

"Goodness! Is this a party?" She looked from Bernard to Jim. "We came to impart our good news."

"Impart?" questioned Amy, holding Bernard's hand.

"One of Terry's words. We wondered whether your heart was up to it."

"My heart is fine."

As he left the room Jim thought the good news is the white girl and the black boy are, for want of a better word, in love. As he ran down the stairs and out to his car he resented the almost tangible glow of happiness surrounding the ill-assorted couples. He had yet to confront Hebe.

Jim parked his car beside Hebe's. He walked fast across the fields, fighting the inclination to go back to London, recapture the shield which had effectively protected him from serious relationships for thirteen years. Skirting the kale field and climbing the banks he reviewed the girls of past years. Fun girls, pretty girls, clever girls and stupid, he had shielded himself from any depth of feeling, with the memory of the perfect girl in Lucca, the girl who had left him, running fleet of foot, disappearing into the crowd. Remembering Hebe racing across the fields earlier in the day, he thought, She still runs pretty fast. He gritted his teeth, forcing himself on. She is there in Bernard's house. I have to put an end to this one way or another, he thought, as he climbed the last bank into Bernard's garden. Put an end to my dream, he thought resentfully, face up to some sort of reality. It is destruction, he thought, opening the door and walking into the house. He felt desolation and regret for his loss, now that it was too late to run away. If I had had any sense I would have stopped looking years ago. Not finding her I would have had something to keep.

Hebe was sitting in Bernard's chair, her arms round Silas curled beside her, asleep.

Jim sat on a chair by the door. Feathers came wagging and grumbling to greet Jim, pressing his head on his knee, inviting attention. Jim stroked the dog's head and looked at Hebe, who peered at him over Silas' head.

"Is he all right now?" indicating Silas.

"Yes," she said evenly.

Feathers wandered back to sit at Hebe's feet. Jim felt exposed. Hebe had Silas as protection and now the dog also. He cleared his throat, unable to think of anything to say. Minutes passed. Hebe and Jim looked at one another. Hebe said something in a low voice.

Jim said, "What?"

She said, "It's the smell. I think I recognise the smell, it's – this jersey you lent him."

"You mean *me*? I smell?"

"Yes."

"I smell of coffee. I keep a coffee shop, my clothes are impregnated with it. Why?"

"I get panics, nightmares. Then there's this smell which is nice."

"I'm glad of that." He studied her. She had cut off most of the long hair, the eyes were the same, the face thinner. "It's a coffee shop on one side and antiques on the other." Must keep talking, he thought.

"Oh." She was not giving him much help.

"I was working in a coffee bar in Lucca; do you remember me? Do you remember the fiesta, the nut necklaces, the candles along the window-ledges, the narrow streets? You ran away—"

Hebe watched him. What were her thoughts?

She said, "My nightmare panic."

"It's been a marvellous haunting memory for me," said Jim.

"I'm sorry if it was a nightmare for you." He was stupefied. After all these years all she remembers is a bloody nightmare.

"The smell is mixed up with something else. I see now it was you. It's the other, the result, the – the – I—" She looked at him, distressed. "I tried to tell Silas and do you know what he said?"

"What?"

"He suggested I'd been on a 'trip', that someone had given me LSD."

"That would explain a lot," said Jim. "You were with a bunch of hippies, people said, when I tried to find you."

"I'd just met them. I was living with a family as an au pair learning Italian. I didn't know them."

"In Lucca?"

"I was going home next day. I remember now. I must have blotted it out when the horror came later. I am sorry."

"I am Silas' father," said Jim, making the effort. There is no retreat now, he thought. For years my dream has been her nightmare. "I think, I mean it's obvious, look at his nose and hair, he's my son." Hebe said nothing. "He has got your eyes," said Jim. "Perhaps we could get to know each other." Still she said nothing. "We seem to have put the cart before the horse," he said. "I don't want to bother you but Silas seems to be the result of our encounter. Perhaps if we—"

"The result." Hebe looked down at Silas. "I see I—" She tightened her hold. She is afraid I may hurt Silas, Jim thought. I must stop her being frightened. She makes no attempt to deny my fatherhood.

Hebe said, "If you are—" defensively.

"I am sure I am." Idiot, there is still time to back out.

"Yes." She was not in doubt.

"Look," said Jim, "when I met Silas yesterday he was pretty upset. Perhaps we could start from there. Perhaps I could help if he is in trouble. How would that be?"

"Put the cart before the horse again?"

She's intelligent. Thank God. "Put Silas first and possibly we will get to know each other."

"I don't mind you getting to know Silas," said Hebe, keeping herself out of it, reminding herself not to be possessive.

Jim, who had been sitting grim and strained, smiled for the first time. "You don't know me," he said. "You can keep yourself as private as you like." I don't mean that, he thought. I want to know her but it may take the rest of our lives to break down this privacy.

Hebe reached for her glasses and put them on to see Jim clearly. He is already assuming possession, she thought. He thinks he can barge into my life, Silas' father. I can't deny it, they are alike, he even talks like Silas. What about my Syndicate? My cooking? How does he think he will fit in with Mungo, Rory, Louisa, Lucy, with Silas who I live and work for, and Hippolyte? Does he think he can just appear like this? Do I want this man barging in? Thoughtfully she regarded Jim through her glasses.

She is not a bit my dream girl, thought Jim. She looks a fighter. The dream girl was so vulnerable. What is this woman holding my son in her arms going to do with my life? How will she fit in with my coffee trade, my antiques? And the boy, my son, what of him? Oh God, he thought, do I want all this? Resentfully he regarded Hebe, blaming her.

"If we were writing a book," Jim said, "this would be a joyful occasion."

"In real life it's a positive quicksand," said Hebe.

They succumbed to laughter and Silas woke.

THIRTY-TWO

Silas, looking from his mother to Jim, remembered where he was. The humiliations of his visit to the Reeves came crowding blackly back.

"What am I to do about my bag? I left it behind." His duffel bag seemed of paramount importance.

"Mrs Reeves is bringing it tomorrow. We can collect it at the heliport," said Hebe.

"And have to talk to her?" Silas was aghast. "Meet them all?"

"We'll be with you." Jim stood up and stretched. "It's rather claustrophobic in this small room," he said. "What about a cream tea somewhere?"

"Brilliant. There's a farm which does teas over the hill. We could walk along the cliff." Silas was delighted at the prospect. "I'm starving."

"Come on, then," said Jim. "It stopped raining long ago."

"All right." Hebe felt violently hungry, tried to remember when she had last eaten. Breakfast in Louisa's house in the early hours. Was it the same day? "I'm quite hungry, too," she said carefully.

Feathers ran ahead across the fields, carrying his tail high, signalling them to follow as might a tourist guide in St Mark's Square. They crossed the road to the cliff path winding above the sea. We look like any ordinary family, thought Jim, as they walked in single file. Family dog, child, mother, father, but the dog is not our dog, the father has not spoken to the mother for thirteen years, he only met his child for the first time yesterday. Bringing up the rear of the procession he studied Hebe's back, observing her long stride, the dark hair falling against her shoulders. She walked ahead above the sea which, calm now in the afternoon sun, was cobalt blue, the rocks shading lighter and paler over sandy patches. What is she thinking, Jim wondered. If we were what we appear to be, an ordinary family, would I know?

Silas led the way up a valley which clove the cliffs running down to a sheltered cove. Halfway up there was a farm with tables on the grass, chairs and benches. They sat at an empty table. Jim ordered tea, Hebe sat slumped, white faced. She put her glasses on the table, a curiously secretive act. She doesn't want to see too clearly. Jim observed her surreptitiously. "When did you last eat?" he asked.

"Louisa made me eat breakfast."

"Fool." Jim got up and went into the farm. "Would it be possible," he asked the woman serving teas, "to give the lady a boiled egg? She hasn't eaten since breakfast."

"Poor thing. She had better have two and bread and butter."

"Thank you." Jim went back to the table and sat in silence until the tea was brought.

Silas watched teapot, milk, sugar, scones, cream and jam placed on the table. Two brown eggs arrived next.

"Salt," said the waitress. "Okay?" She caught Jim's eye.

"Most okay," he thanked her.

"Who are the eggs for?" Silas asked.

"Your mother. Eat them," he said to Hebe, pushing the eggs towards her.

"Oh." She looked at him quickly. "Thank you."

"You will need your spectacles."

"Yes." She put them on obediently.

They ate in silence. Jim watched colour return to her cheeks. Silas ate and drank, feeding snippets to Feathers. If I bought a house in the country we could live like an ordinary family, thought Jim, watching Hebe and Silas. We could have a dog of our own. I don't somehow see her in Fulham. I could run my business just as well in a country town. I can't believe she likes living in that hideous street. That cat of hers would like the country. We could find a house in Dorset, perhaps. He visualised Hebe against a backdrop of downland within reach of the sea. Other families who had been having tea left, wandering up a path which led to the road and their cars. From the farmhouse came sounds of washing up, an occasional laugh or burst of music from the radio.

"Did you see Amy?" Hebe turned to look at Jim. "I have been too afraid to ask."

"Much better," said Jim. "Last seen flirting with Bernard. Almost as though they were having an affair." He failed to keep surprise out of his voice.

"Old people still have feelings," said Hebe.

"Bernard seems to have distributed his feelings rather widely," said Jim.

Hebe smiled, thinking, What about my feelings distributed among the Syndicate? What about them?

"Will they marry?" Silas was curious. "They could. Amy could look after Mr Quigley."

"I don't somehow think a sunset home for Bernard fits into Amy's calculations," Hebe murmured.

"He is too independent to marry," said Jim, defending the male sex.

"But he likes romance," said Hebe, amused.

"Even so, he will go on living alone in that isolated house. And some day the postman will arrive with his letters and find him dead," Jim suggested.

"That is what he would like," agreed Hebe.

"Amy accused him of being in love with a lot of women."

"Probably true." Hebe did not wish to pursue the subject. "Did you see Hannah?" she asked. "Isn't she looking after Amy?"

"She did appear. Brought with her a handsome black chap."

"Ah yes, Terry." Hebe was thoughtful. "M'm yes."

"They seemed bursting with the joys of life, a romance there, would you say?"

"Hannah would call it a conjunction of vibes."

"What about George?" enquired Silas. "He's her dentist," he explained for Jim's benefit.

"Too dull. Hannah wants marriage and romance."

"Will she get it with Terry?" asked Jim.

"I think she will."

"Where does he come from?" Jim was interested. If I can find out about her friends I may discover Hebe, he thought.

"He comes from London. He is self-employed, he makes quite a lot of money. He loves poetry, fantasy—"

"Ah—" What was that in her voice? Affection?

"He has lots of interests: music, antiques, poetry – yes, he will make Hannah happy. Gorgeous contrast, don't you think? Very fair Hannah with bitter-chocolate Terry?" Hebe was enthusiastic for Hannah's future.

"Milk chocolate babies," said Silas, munching.

"Great," said Hebe. "All those in favour—"

"In favour." Jim and Silas agreed lightheartedly.

"And those against?" asked Jim seriously.

"Hannah will enjoy the challenge. You see, with Terry," said Hebe seriously, "she will never be bored."

"Mr Quigley said Giles' father was boring," volunteered Silas. "It hurt his feelings."

"There you are, then." Hebe took off her glasses and looked myopically out to sea.

Watching her Jim thought, She cannot have seen me clearly when we met in Lucca, no wonder she had nightmares. Jim was not without vanity. We are no nearer what matters, he thought, disgruntled. Discussing Amy's, Bernard's, and Hannah's affairs does not help me.

"Shall we go down to the sea?" Silas suggested.

Jim paid for the tea and they walked back to the cliff path and scrambled down towards the cove. This time Jim led and Hebe brought up the rear. On a ledge of grass Hebe sat. "You go on," she said. "I'll wait here." She watched the man and boy climb down the cliff, heard their feet crunch when they reached the pebbles at the bottom. Feathers sat beside her, mouth open, panting. Hebe lay back. She could hear Silas' voice call and Jim answer. Giving way to exhaustion, she was grateful for the lulling warmth of the sun and the sound of the sea grinding the pebbles.

On the beach Jim and Silas played ducks and drakes then undressed and swam, letting the sea welcome them. They raced to the ledge of rock which flanked the cove, pulled themselves out of the water and lay on rocks warm from the afternoon sun. Silas shaded his eyes and looked up at his mother. "Is my mother the girl you met in Italy, the girl you told us you were looking for?"

"Yes." Jim looked at the sea, furious that he could not look Silas in the eye. This is all wrong, he told himself, the boy should not be involved until we have sorted ourselves out. This is putting the cart before the horse again.

"I thought so." Silas lay back and closed his eyes.

My God, thought Jim, why doesn't he say something? Is he glad, is he sorry, is he even interested? Lying there so calmly he's exactly like his mother.

Silas felt the blood drumming in his ears. So I've got a father, this man, this Jim. What do I do now? What does Ma do? What did they do in Italy? Silas kept his eyes tightly shut, sparks from the sun on his eyelids. Did they kiss as people do on TV, as though they were eating a banana? What happens now? Do I go back to school as usual? What will Ma do, will she go on being a cook, a prostitute, will she be there to meet me when I get off the train? "I'm cold," he cried out in fear, and dived off the rock into the sea. Jim watched the boy swim back to the beach, scramble out of the water to his pile of clothes. When, twenty minutes later, he rejoined them Silas sat on guard by his sleeping mother and eyed Jim watchfully as he climbed up to them. Feathers barked and Hebe woke.

"Time to go home," she said. "We have a tough day tomorrow meeting Mr Reeves, Mrs Reeves, Master Reeves and the duffel bag." She set off up the cliff. The man and the boy followed. When they reached the cars Hebe said, "Thank you for the lovely cream tea and the eggs. I am quite restored." She held out her hand as to an acquaintance.

"Perhaps," began Jim, taking it, "perhaps we can talk—"

Hebe let go his hand. "There is altogether too much to talk about," she said despairingly, "or nothing." She got into her car. "What seems to matter most at the moment is the bloody duffel bag." She drove off with Silas beside her. Jim followed Feathers through the fields to Bernard's house. He had never before felt so lonely.

THIRTY-THREE

It had been an interminable day. Crawling into bed after reassuring herself that Amy was on the mend and Hannah and Terry as happy as it was possible for lovers to be, Hebe prayed for sleep, but she was too tired. Her head buzzed with sounds. Traffic on the motorway, dogs barking, a jumble of voices from which she could pick Louisa's or Bernard's, the stranger in the traffic jam, the waitress at the farm, Jennifer Reeves' offensive intonation, Amy. Resolutely she excluded Jim, muttering to herself, "I'm in no fit state," repeating, "No fit state." She tried to relax her fingers and toes, tried not to flinch when a late motorcycle roared up the street, tried to recover the murmur of the sea on the cobbles of the cove as she heard it that afternoon when all too briefly she had slept.

Trip nudged the duvet and crawled in beside her to settle, her gentle heaving flank pressed into the small of Hebe's back.

"Now I can't turn over." It was ridiculous to consider the cat's comfort before her own, yet she did. Two motorcycles in rapid succession raced up the street, drunken voices shouting harshly.

"I can't sleep, Ma." Silas, standing by the bed in his pyjamas. "Can we talk?"

"Of course." She sat up.

"Have you got Trip? She left me."

"Yes."

"I think I'll just get my duvet to wrap round me."

"Do."

She heard his bare feet on the landing, the rustle as he came back trailing the duvet. She resisted the impulse to switch on the light.

"I suppose it would be cowardly not to meet my duffel bag. Not to meet the Reeves tomorrow." He settled himself at the end of her bed, a hunched figure wrapped in the duvet.

"I'm afraid so."

"Thought you would say that." Silas said no more for a while.

MARY WESLEY

She could not see his face in the dark. Another motorcycle roared up the street.

"They do make a filthy noise, don't they?"

"Terrible," she agreed.

"What are you going to do about Jim?"

"He's my father, isn't he?"

"I think so. Yes."

"Funny, isn't it? He's been looking for you for years. He told Mr Quigley and me about it yesterday evening."

Yesterday evening she had walked by the river with Rufus and the other dogs, been happy, gone in to find Mungo and Rory with Louisa. Another life. "How did that come about?" she asked.

"Mr Quigley wanted to cheer me up, he was joking. He asked Jim whether he had ever been in love. Jim told us about this girl he had met at a fiesta in Italy. There was a procession, people, crowds, incense and a band played tumpity-tump. He was really there, Ma, at the fiesta. Bought you a nut necklace. Then he lost you. He said he'd been looking for you ever since. What happened to the necklace, Ma?"

"I left it behind when I ran away from home." Surprised, she remembered the necklace. A lone motorcycle sputtered up the street, not as fast as its predecessors. "They take the baffles off the silencers to make more noise. It's 'machismo'."

"Yes. I don't want a motorbike."

"I'm glad."

"Shall you marry Jim, Ma?"

"I don't know."

"Oh."

"I don't know much about marriage. What do you think?" she asked.

Silas sat thinking. Then, "I don't know much, either." He laughed.

"You should hear Giles about Hannah and his father and you should see Mr and Mrs Reeves. Oh, God, you will tomorrow." He stopped laughing.

"Yes, I shall."

The town clock struck one, the sound reverberating in the exhausted afterstorm atmosphere.

"Married people *can* be happy." He was speaking again. "I think Terry and Hannah will be a riot. Super for Giles." He sounded envious.

"Yes."

"What do you know about marriage, Ma?"

"My sisters —"

"Sisters? Do I have *aunts?*" Silas jerked upright in surprise.

"Yes."

"Could you tell me, or are they a big secret? It's embarrassing at school not to have relations. The boys boast about theirs. Are they tarts or what?"

"I'm the only tart in the family."

"Oh, Ma." Silas moved up the bed to crouch beside her. "I nearly sat on Trip. What happened to them?"

"They married." Hebe thought of Ann, Beata and Cara. "Ann married a man called Robert. They had a Jaguar. Beata married Delian. They had an Alfa Romeo. And Cara married Marcus and they had a Range Rover."

"Rich." He was surprised.

"That was it."

"What do you mean?" Silas was made anxious by her tone. There was a tightness in her throat.

"Well." She found herself speaking more freely. "They were a lot older than me. I used to watch and listen to them. They talked a lot about men and marriage. Whenever one of them met a new man they discussed him. They'd say, 'I've met a new man,' and the others always asked, 'Is he rich?' It didn't seem to matter whether he was talented or good looking. It was always, 'Is he rich?'"

"Rich?" Silas repeated the word. "Rich?"

"Of course they were all suitable," said Hebe.

"What's suitable?"

"Suitable meant – oh, suitable meant public school, related to nice people, the right sort. They'd ask, 'Is he rich? Then they'd ask, 'Are his people nice, are they our sort?' "

Christ, just like school, thought Silas.

"Then they would telephone copiously, giggle and shriek down the telephone. They never minded being overheard. It was a sort of ritual."

"Charming."

"I never felt I fitted."

"I don't want to be suitable," said Silas, who had been mulling the word.

"I don't think there is any danger of that."

"I'm awfully hungry, Ma, shall we raid the larder?"

Wrapped in their duvets they trailed downstairs. Robbed of her warm covering Trip furiously burrowed under the pillows. Hebe made bacon sandwiches and they returned to her bed carrying plates and glasses of milk. Trip went out of the window into the night.

"What were your father and mother like?" Silas asked with his mouth full, munching.

"I never knew them. They were killed in an air crash when I was a baby. My grandparents brought us up."

"Were they 'suitable'?" He adopted the word.

"I saw them this morning."

"*What?*" Silas put his glass down with a thump. "Where?"

"On my way home. I met them in a lane, a short cut I was taking, they'd had a collision with a Land Rover." Hebe described the scene as she remembered it. "They had a sweet dog. He called it away when I was going to stroke it and I said, 'I'll find a long-haired yobbo, a black layabout to mend your car.' What are you laughing at? I didn't really say that."

"It's so funny. What does it mean? Why should you say that?" Silas went off into a fit of laughter.

Hebe found herself describing the inquisition, the family meeting, the planned abortion, the grandparents, the sisters, the brothers-in-law, the running away, the journey down to Cornwall hitching lifts, the final arrival on Amy's doorstep, her recurrent nightmares. She did not mind that at moments Silas bubbled off into near hysteria. She guessed his laughter was as necessary for him as her tale-telling was for her. Now that she had begun she could not stop. She poured out the life that she had kept secret from him. The town clock struck twice and at last three times. Far away in the country a cock crowed, and on the town roofs the seagulls started screaming. Hebe trailed to a stop. Silas rolled into a ball in his duvet, managed to reach up and kiss her and say: "I don't think Jim is suitable," before falling asleep, and Hebe pulling her duvet to her ears relaxed at last, feeling as close to her child as she had been when he was still in her womb.

While Silas slept she reviewed the day ahead.

First the duffel bag must be collected from the Reeves, an ordeal for Silas, who dreaded the embarrassment. Was it only the duffel bag and the Reeves, she mused, or something else? Her mind clear now after the disgorgement to Silas, she reviewed Silas' situation. Did not the Reeves represent the sort of people, the nice sort of friends he was meant to be happy with at school?

"But he isn't happy," she whispered to the cat coming in from her patrol, creeping up on to the bed. "He isn't happy at all." With the clarity that extreme fatigue occasionally engenders she reviewed her plans for Silas, the opportunities he was to have of friends and education. It began all right, she thought. Before boarding school she had left him for short periods with Amy while she cooked for Lucy, Maggie Cook-Popham or Louisa. And once the Syndicate got going she again left him with Amy, latterly only working in term time so that holidays would be free for Silas.

"And now?" she whispered to the cat, lying warm against her neck. "Now Amy is not well enough to help, Silas is not happy and I," she whispered, "must decide what to do." Listening to the gulls' angry shrieking she faced the question, Did she send Silas away for his good, so that he would get the best education, or did she send him away so that she could enjoy her Syndicate? "Is he at school for his sake or mine?" she whispered to the purring cat. But she was not really in doubt. She thought of the weekends in Paris with Hippolyte, the high spirits and delicious food, of the weeks with Mungo whom she was fond of. "He has improved so," she whispered to the cat, "we've been on such lovely trips," and of Rory not yet tried, Rory of whom she felt she could grow very fond. Oh God, she thought in tense alarm, there's this Jim, Silas' father. What of him? She felt threatened.

We have no memories in common, she thought, feeling recalcitrant. I do not even know whether he likes cats. "It's altogether too much," she said aloud. "First things first. Concentrate on the duffel bag."

THIRTY-FOUR

Mungo drove with verve and dash. They had spent the night in an hotel by the Helford river. He had feared, when Alison insisted on stopping at a chemist in Truro, that she was planning one of her fucking headaches (to be exact a non-fucking headache) but this fear had been groundless. After dinner with Rory, who entertained them during the meal with a description of his life as a milliner, he had, elevated by circumspect consumption of wine, gone up to their room to find that she had bought not, as he supposed, soluble aspirin, but a choice of contraceptives.

"Which do you prefer?" Alison presented her offerings. "Arousal? Elite? Fiesta?"

Mungo cried, "Fiesta every time. Or should we," he suggested, recollecting the night in Louisa's house, "rename it, 'Stable Door'?"

"Face that fence when we come to it." Alison had drawn him into bed. "*I* wouldn't say no to another baby."

"There's a lot to be said for you girls from the Shires," said Mungo, hugging her.

Driving towards Penzance, Mungo considered Alison's trip to Santa Barbara had done her a power of good. I am a fair man, he thought, as he drove. I owe that bastard Eli a vote of thanks. That there had been times when Alison should have been similarly grateful to Hebe did not occur to him.

Rory, silent as they drove through Cornwall, listened to Mungo and Alison talk. They seemed to look forward to the reunion with their children, the horrible little boys. Had not Mungo cursed them as positive millstones when in his cups?

"We should have Michael to stay next holidays," said Mungo. "We owe it to the Reeves."

"Why not the family Reeves for Christmas?" suggested Alison. "Invite the lot."

"A tallish order. Jennifer's heavy going, bit of a drag."

"I'll take care of her. You can take Julian out shooting or play golf."

"Okay," said Mungo good-humouredly.

"I believe they have a boy from Michael's school with them. If Ian and Alistair have taken to him we could invite him too. They can't have enough friends. He's bound to be all right if Jennifer has passed him."

"Is this Jennifer – a – er – an—" asked Rory.

"Expert," said Mungo. "A powerful sort of lady, knows who's who, goes in for influence and the right sort of chums for her boy. Any boy she has to stay must be er – um – you know what I mean."

"The right sort," Alison suggested.

"Socially oke – oke?" Rory teased. "Okay? One of us?"

"Yes, of course."

Rory thoughtfully compared Mungo reunited with Alison, doing his loving husband, father of the family bit with the Mungo wailing for his mistress who had shared his bed three nights before. Leaves the field a bit clearer for me, he thought, as he plotted a tour of garages who might know Hebe's car. Possibly, he thought hopefully, the AA might help or even, if really stuck, the police.

"Car park's bloody full," said Mungo, swinging off the road into the heliport entrance. "Where can I fucking park?"

Alison compressed her lips.

Mungo cast her an affectionate glance. "Not allowed that word. Won't happen again except in the right place."

How does Hebe put up with him, for crying out loud? Rory asked himself.

"I think that must be their helicopter." Alison craned her neck as Mungo squeezed the car into a gap. "Jennifer said they'd be on the twelve-thirty."

Standing beside Hebe in the heliport lounge Silas, already nervous at the prospect of meeting the Reeves, was seized by a fresh horror. "Oh, God, Ma, Mr Reeves will have to pay excess on my bag. It says here," he pointed to a notice, "that 'excess baggage costs thirty pence a kilogram'."

"If it's excess I'll pay. Don't worry so." He is working himself into a stew and it's making me jumpy, thought Hebe, feeling sorrow and sympathy for her child. "Here comes a helicopter. It's probably theirs."

"Oh, God," muttered Silas, "what am I to say?"

"Just be normal."

"What's normal?" cried Silas, anguished.

They watched the helicopter clattering down, standing close together, braced for the confrontation.

Jim, arriving late, having been delayed by Bernard's obsessive need to buy flowers for Amy (I am making up for fifty years of gross neglect), approached the heliport as the helicopter shut off its engine. He ran to the arrival lounge, pushing in behind two men and a woman who were apparently also meeting friends. A party from the helicopter came surging into the heliport hall. A trickle of confident vowels swelling to a stream as their voices bounced off the formica tables, tinkled round the fruit machines, rose high in greeting as they sighted the people ahead of Jim.

"Alison, darling!"

"Jennifer, love, Julian!"

"Dear Mungo, how are you, how well you look."

"This is my cousin Rory Grant, Jennifer Reeves."

"How do you do and you know Alistair, Ian and Michael, of course. Do look round, dear, that tiresome woman is supposed to be here to collect her wretched boy's bag."

Jim watched Hebe and Silas as they faced the crowd of people, sunburned, healthy, laden with baggage, overladen with self-confidence. Silas had drawn himself up to stand by his mother, hair ruffled, brown eyes so like Hebe's, glaring down his nose. He experienced a thrill of pride. Hebe, recognising Alison, Mungo and Rory, struggled to keep her heart from her boots. This was the appalling sort of coincidence she had blithely felt could never happen.

Passengers from the helicopter milled through to the car park to stow their luggage, pack themselves into their cars, fasten seat belts, drive away to London, Bristol, Birmingham, Stevenage and Harlow new town.

Jennifer Reeves cried again in her carrying voice, "Look round, Julian, and see whether you can see that woman."

"No need to look far," said Hebe, stepping forward.

The group of the confident vowels was stilled, frozen into what Silas in later years described as social glue.

"Thank you very much." Hebe took the duffel bag from Michael. "Do I owe you for excess weight? Silas has been worrying." She turned towards Julian. "Oh, hullo."

With his back to the light Julian resembled momentarily the

man with whom there had been the fiasco long ago in Rome. Hebe's heart took another lurch downwards. Julian, recognising in Hebe the sort of woman for whom one could almost risk alienating Jennifer for ever, responded with a hearty "Hullo", and a delighted grin. Jennifer, sniffing danger and fast off the mark in defence of her own, brushed aside Julian's hand extended towards Hebe as he said, "It's been super having Silas." He was about to add that he hoped Silas would come again and Hebe must come too. This must be stopped.

But Hebe was smiling with relief, which had nothing to do with Jennifer, at the realisation that what she had recognised in Julian was a potential applicant to join the Syndicate. She had taken off her glasses and while staring at them with her myopic gaze was fully occupied choking back unsuitable mirth. This charge of feeling between Hebe and the Reeves by its very variety created a spark which was near tangible. Watching them Jim felt a sensation of mad elation.

Alison, coming up to Hebe, taking the hand which Julian had hoped to shake, said, "How *nice*. It's you who saves my mother-in-law's life with your wonderful cooking, isn't it? All that exquisite food." She kept hold of Hebe's hand.

"That's right." Hebe fought to recapture her cool. "I love working for her, she's so appreciative."

"And so is Mungo," said Alison, smiling up at Hebe, almost a head taller.

"And are these your boys, the little millstones?" asked Hebe, laughing affectedly to hide incipient hysteria.

"Yes," said Alison, squeezing Hebe's hand before letting it go. "He doesn't hate them all the time. We may even have another." She lowered her voice confidentially, distancing herself from Jennifer as she stood beside Hebe, smiling up as friendly as you please.

"Women!" gasped Mungo admiringly to Rory. "Old Julian damn near put his great foot in it there, nearly made a bid."

"How dare he?" whispered Rory, disgusted.

But Julian, undeterred by his wife, was persevering. "Why don't we make a date? We could – perhaps next holidays—"

Jennifer, interrupting again, said, "We never see you at the School Sports or on Founder's Day." She struggled to regain the superiority she considered her right.

"I fear now it's unlikely that you shall," Hebe replied coolly. "There's a good comprehensive school here full of nice people of the right sort." Beside her Silas flushed and glowed with joy. "Ah, there you are," she said to Jim who had ranged up beside her.

"Shall I take the bag?" asked Jim. "You can't keep this up much longer," he said in an aside.

"I don't think you have met Silas' father," said Hebe, raising her voice, looking round at the ring of faces blurred as much by her emotion as her nearsightedness. "Yes, do take the bag, darling." She surrendered the bag to Jim.

Rory came up to Hebe. "I had hoped, I was going to look for – to look—"

"Me?"

"Yes. Your – er – car number is – er – is—"

"Cornish?"

"Oh, Hebe." He stood before her.

Whereas Hannah had decided between a hop and a skip to remarry and almost immediately found Terry, Hebe was faced by temptation. How easy to take Rory, unhesitatingly loving. How tempting to settle in his Georgian house with the fanlight and the dolphin knocker. How agreeable to spend weekends in his great-aunt Calypso's bluebell wood. There would be no hassle. There would be peace. Perhaps too much peace. It would be unfair. Short-sightedly she met his anxious eyes.

"Goodbye, Rory, dear. Give my love to your Aunt Louisa." She did not touch him. "I have liked working for her more than anybody. One of these days I will come and buy one of your hats."

"Will that be all?" Rory's usually swivelling eyes looked directly at Hebe.

"I'm afraid so," she said sadly.

"I will design – a – er – an especially marvellous one." Rory was valiant.

"I shall wear it on celebration days," she said.

"I wish – er – oh, I wish I could celebrate."

Reluctantly Rory followed the others, who were now drifting awkwardly away, saying, "Well, I suppose we'd better be going."

"See you soon, I hope."

"Have we got everything?"

"What about lunch one day?" and things of that sort.

Alison did not, Mungo took note, invite Jennifer to bring her lot to stay for Christmas.

Michael, Ian and Alistair did not speak but exchanged looks, raised eyebrows and tried to catch Silas' eye to seal a non-existent friendship.

Julian, striving to regain ground grown slippery, was speaking to Jennifer.

"I promise you I never clapped eyes on the girl before." His intonation guilty.

"I don't believe you for one moment. She recognised you, she said 'Hullo'."

"She said hullo to us all." Desperately Julian tried to distract his wife. "She's a perfectly ordinary girl."

"I think she's a perfectly ordinary tart. You *shall* tell me how and where you—" Striding towards their car Jennifer began the inquisition. If anything united the group which had been so confident it was a general feeling of commiseration for Julian who, it was felt, was in for a tough time, undeserved for once.

"I always suspected old Jennifer of a mean streak, of being a bit bogus." Mungo headed the car towards home.

"Of course she is bogus." Alison assimilated the fresh view of the family friend. "And it's silly to be publicly jealous." A few miles on she said: "I've always thought we should consider state education as an alternative to Eton."

Mungo drove in surprised silence for several miles before responding, "We shall have to consider it if we are adding to the family."

"My goodness, what a bill and coo." Rory began what was to be a long process of cheering up.

Ian and Alistair had exchanged sly looks, reassessing their parents, as Mungo manoeuvred the car out into the holiday traffic. They had seen Silas running and jumping across the heliport garden, his every movement as he threw up his arms and leapt the flower beds an expression of unadulterated delight as he ran to find Giles. Ian later suggested to Alistair that Silas had been shouting, "I'm not out of a bottle," which Alistair said was nonsense.

Slumped on the back seat behind his warring parents, Michael continued the sulky drift into adolescent revolt which had started at the supper table during Silas' visit.

THIRTY-FIVE

The people in the helicopter office were indifferent to Hebe and
Jim. They had telephones to answer, bookings to make, cups of
coffee to consume. The next helicopter would leave in an hour
and a half. Until then they could exchange pleasantries, flirt, catch
up on gossip.

"I must apologise for calling you darling," said Hebe stiffly.

"That's quite all right," said Jim.

"It was a temptation," said Hebe.

"I quite understand," he said.

"Thank you."

"There's a seat outside, shall we sit on it?"

Has he noticed my knees are knocking together? I must not
give way now. I wish Silas had not rushed off and left us. I wish
I felt something. I wish I knew what I feel.

"There, sit there," he said. "It's nice in the sun. No need to
say anything."

How does he know? she asked herself, sitting on the seat.

There's a hell of a lot to say. How ghastly this is. Why doesn't
he say something?

Jim said nothing.

Hebe said, "Did you hear me? I told that woman Silas wouldn't
be going to that school any more."

"Yes, I did."

"He isn't happy there," Hebe cried. "He's miserable."

"You are doing the right thing, then."

"Do you think so? Do you really think so?"

"Yes, I do."

"I do so want him to be happy," she exclaimed.

"Yes."

"Oh," Hebe cried. "*Bang* goes my Syndicate!"

Jim did not know what she was talking about.

What can I say without putting my foot in it, he thought. I
don't know this woman. What the hell does she mean – Syndicate?

If I ask she may bite my head off. I wish I was home in Fulham with my coffee shop and antiques, without all this bloody bother. "Oh, Christ!" he exclaimed. "You are crying." She was racked by sobs. He fished out a handkerchief. What a messy crier. He gave her the handkerchief. (What have I let myself in for?) She blew her nose. (If she were a man I'd say she trumpeted.) She stopped crying. She looked a mess. He waited for her to say, "I look a mess." She did not. She gave her nose a final blow, crushed up the handkerchief and put it in her bag.

"Thanks," she said.

The handkerchief was one of my best, he thought, admiring her action. I doubt whether I'll see it again.

"You'll get it back when it's clean," she said.

It must be her knowledge of men which enables her to read my thoughts. He felt rather pleased with his percipience.

"You got the duffel bag back all right," he said, to get the conversation flowing.

"Yes."

"And decided Silas' future."

"Yes."

"Are you always so impulsive?"

"I've been thinking about it for quite a while." Several days, she thought.

"He looked awfully pleased, radiant."

"Did he? I had taken off my glasses."

"That chap Julian Reeves—"

Hebe began to laugh. I may tell him, she thought, if I ever get to know him, about that fiasco in Rome.

"I felt rather sorry for the one who looks like a rabbit."

"Hare. He's a hatter."

"But the one with the wife who allied herself with you found it all rather funny. Is she a friend of yours?"

"She may become so."

"But he seemed to know you very well, her husband."

Hebe, eyes and nose puffed by crying, looked at him pityingly.

"Oh, I see," said Jim, latching on, "he's one of—"

"Yes."

"I get it. They were all—"

Hebe nodded. "Nearly all." She looked away.

He tried to guess what she was thinking, watching her face, trying to read her thoughts.

They sat on in the sun.

Jim thought, We ought to be talking. She should tell me what the hell she's been up to all these years. She should tell me about her lovers. She should explain her life, tell me how she manages. She could tell me about her cooking jobs and then we could get on to the men. She obviously can't carry on with that lot, but are there others? She should tell me about her friends, about our child.

Hebe sat beside him apparently relaxed, sleepy.

I should tell her how I've chased after every girl who looked remotely like her. I should tell her that I've never got her out of my system, that I've always hoped to find her, that I'm in love with her. But am I? He watched her as she sat, face held up to the sun, eyes closed, her glasses held loosely in her lap. He shivered. I am a coward, he thought.

"In Lucca." He cleared his throat. "I—"

Hebe turned towards him, put on her spectacles, measured her words.

"It is just an idea," she said, "an idea you had. I am not that girl you remember. I am not silly and naïve any more. You remember her, I remember a smell. I didn't know the smell was you until yesterday. I am grateful for your help with Silas. I am grateful for your help today, I—"

"Oh, shut up," said Jim, furious.

"That's what my grandfather always said to my grandmother."

"He was probably right," Jim snapped.

"No, he wasn't," Hebe shouted in fury.

"How old are you?" Jim asked.

"Thirty. Why?"

"I wanted to calculate how many years we have to talk and fight."

"Oh."

"Shall we start with a row? Then you can tell me about your bloody grandfather," cried Jim, his patience gone. "I can tell you about myself. You can tell me what you know of Silas, our son. We have years and years. Come on—" He no longer wished himself back in Fulham, he wondered what would happen if he hit her, she would probably hit him back. "Come on," he said, "let's begin. Talk."

"All right," she said, and wondered whether the half of it would get said and knew it did not matter. "Where shall we start?"

"Was that the lot?" Jim asked.

"What lot?" she prevaricated.

"The entire Syndicate." He tried to be patient.

"M'm." She took off her glasses. "No."

"Don't take them off. You must see me clearly."

Hebe pushed the glasses up her nose defiantly, turning towards him, meeting his eyes.

"How many more?" asked Jim bravely.

"One."

What will she do about that one, he asked himself, and found his heart was beginning to beat rather fast.

"I had better telephone. Have you got any change? It's long distance," she said.

Jim emptied his pockets, gave her change, watched her walk to the telephone booth, dial, insert coins, push the button, begin to talk. He felt horror. What a fool I am, he thought. Why did I let her telephone? The bloody man will tell her to look sharp and come at once. No, he will say, Stay where you are. I am coming to fetch you. How can I have been so idiotic, so moronic, I've positively handed her over. He watched her talking, trying to read her lips, shuddered when she laughed, winced when she said something so sweetly, so confidingly he could have killed who-ever she was talking to. At last she came back and sat beside him.

"So," she said. "So." She was weary.

Jim said, "What did he say?"

"He said, '*Quelle garce*.'"

"Oh?"

"That was Hippolyte," said Hebe, "the founder of—"

"Your Syndicate?" Jim felt a rush of fury.

"I told him what has happened," she said gently. "I – um – explained. He now has a restaurant in London. He has offered us free meals in perpetuity." Her mouth twitched into a smile. She did not look at him. Just as he had admired her over the handker-chief he respected her for not saying "You will like him." Like hell he would. She had again taken off her glasses.

They sat on in the sun while Jim's heart resumed its usual tempo. Presently revived, he said, "All peacocks gone."

"Peacocks?"

"Surely you know the story of your namesake, Hebe, or must I tell you?"

"I do know it," she admitted.

"Suppose I volunteer to be harnessed. What would you say to that? I must stipulate that I run solo." He took her hands. It was the first time he had touched her since Lucca.

Letting her hands rest in his, Hebe watched his face. She longed to say something witty and original which they could remember in years to come, but all she said was, "You're on."

George Scoop, who had been alerted by his receptionist Jean of rumours of happenings in Wilson Street, thought he would drive past the heliport in his lunch hour. Having a horror of scenes and a great fear of getting involved in matters which might turn nasty, he was yet sufficiently curious, keeping a safe distance, to drive that way. He was disgusted to observe Hannah, wearing an outrageous purple dress strolling with her black beau who sauntered, dressed entirely in white so that his damson-coloured skin vividly contrasted with Hannah's fairness. They laughed their heads off at some joke shared with the boys Giles and Silas as they walked along the prom eating ice creams. Blackamoor, Coon, thought George with rage. What perfect teeth. To hell with Giles. He had thought, when he had it in mind to marry Hannah, that he would accept the challenge of Giles' teeth, straighten them as a wedding present to his bride. I am well out of that, he congratulated himself. I was right to get shot of her. (Already he persuaded himself that he had denied Hannah, not she him.) Let her boy go through life with his teeth as they are, he thought sourly, refusing to acknowledge Hannah's merry wave or Terry's cheerful shout. There are other fish, he told himself.

Driving past the heliport he espied Hebe sitting on a bench with a strange man. He peered through his windscreen, trying to get a better view. Was she laughing or crying? He slowed the car, thinking, I could offer her a lift home. It's time I got to know her better, find out what she's all about. But from the way Hebe and the stranger sat sideways on the bench, turning towards each other, there did not seem room for a third party. A car behind George tooted its horn. George accelerated and drove on.